HATH NO FURY

— AN OUTLAND ENTERTAINMENT ANTHOLOGY —

HATH NO FURY

EDITED BY
MELANIE R. MEADORS

HATH NO FURY

Outland Entertainment | www.outlandentertainment.com

Publisher & Creative Director: Jeremy Mohler | Editor-in-Chief: Alana Joli Abbott

All stories within are copyright © their respective authors. All rights reserved.

Published by Outland Entertainment
5601 NW 25th Street
Topeka KS, 66618

ISBN-13: 9781945528057
Worldwide Rights
Created in the United States of America | Printed in Taiwan

Editor: Melanie R. Meadors
Editorial Assists by: Alana Joli Abbott, Gwendolyn Nix, Richard Shealy
Cover Illustration: Manuel Castañón
Interior Illustrations: Nicolás R. Giacondino, Keri Hayes, M. Wayne Miller, Oksana Dmitrienko
Cover/Interior Design: STK·Kreations

Though we come and go, and pass into the shadows, where we leave behind us stories told—on paper, on the wings of butterflies, on the wind, on the hearts of others—there we are remembered, there we work magic and great change—passing on the fire like a torch—forever and forever. Till the sky falls, and all things are flawless and need no words at all.

—TANITH LEE (September 19, 1947 - May 24, 2015)

CONTENTS

FOREWORD

ROBIN HOBB

"HELL HATH NO FURY LIKE a woman scorned."

Um, no. Take away those quotation marks! This writer has been hacked! He never said that!

"Hell hath no fury like a woman scorned" and "Music has charms to sooth a savage beast" are possibly among our most familiar incorrect quotes in the English language.

(Right up there with "Peace on Earth; goodwill toward men." No. That should be translated, "Peace on earth to men of goodwill." Rather a different sentiment. But here I am, in only paragraph four and already wandering off topic. Melanie can't say I didn't warn you here. Essays are not my forte!

But let's go back to the focus of this piece.

In 1627, William Congreve wrote a play entitled *The Mourning Bride*. A playwright who became known for writing comedy of manners, this five act play is his only tragedy. And here we are, hundreds of years later, still misquoting the poor fellow.

The Mourning Bride is among his lesser works. Congreve is better known for *The Way of the World*. Here I will admit that I've only read portions of *The Mourning Bride*. I am by no means a scholar of this work! But as a reader, any play that features a kidnapped bride, a shipwreck, a vengeful Queen Zara, a man who is mistakenly executed by his own orders...well, this William Congreve definitely was stirring up some of my favorite ingredients for a tale.

But what were the actual lines he penned that have come down to us in mangled form?

In Act III, it is Perez who declaims:

Heaven has no rage, like love to hatred turned,
Nor hell a fury, like a woman scorned.

(Another aside. Wikipedia, in its quaint way, insists that Queen Zara is the one who speaks these lines, and references Act III, Scene VIII. Unfortunately, Act III does not have eight scenes. And the error is now widely repeated across the internet, on many "quotation source" boards. Poor William Congreve. Not only misquoted, but those transcendent lines ascribed to the wrong character in a scene that doesn't exist!)

As in Romeo and Juliet, the princess Almeria has fallen in love with the son of her father's enemy, King Manuel. She is separated from her husband Alphonso during a shipwreck. Then, both he and King Manuel are captured and held as slaves, along with Queen Zara! Manuel is the fellow whose own orders get him executed, and Queen Zara exits via suicide. Alphonso and Almeria survive for a joyous reunion and an overthrow of the government!

I can see why this play was so popular in its time!

As for the other quote, "Music has charms to soothe the savage beast." Well, as long as I'm setting the record straight, let's look at that one, too. In its correct form, it is actually the opening line of the play, spoken by Almeria who is full of grief and apparently seeking solace in music.

"Music has charms to soothe the savage breast,
To soften rocks, or bend a knotted oak."

Sad to say, not even the music can cheer her from Aphonso's loss!

As I so often do when I sit down to write something, the research has distracted me from my original intent!

Is there a lesson to be learned from all of this meandering? Besides, of course, "Never trust Wikipedia" and "Double check all quotations?" Perhaps.

The fury of women, scorned and otherwise, is scarcely a new concept. But within this anthology you will find a collection of tales that present that fury in new lights.

Enjoy!

INTRODUCTION
MARGARET WEIS

I WAS AN AVID READER when I was young, growing up in the fifties. My family did not go to movies on Saturdays. We went to the library. One of my proudest moments was when I was old enough to have my own library card!

My mother and grandmother introduced me to books featuring strong women characters written by women authors, both sharing their own favorite books with me.

These books were published in the late 1800s and early 1900s, when women were struggling to obtain the right to vote and asserting themselves in other fields. My favorites included *Little Women* by Louisa May Alcott, *Freckles* and *Girl of the Limberlost* by Gene Stratton-Porter, and the *Anne of Green Gables* series by Lucy Maud Montgomery.

I learned not only from the characters in the novels, but also from the authors. Alcott made her own way in the world, writing novels, poems, magazine articles, and thrillers. Stratton-Porter was a naturalist and photographer who used to go into the Limberlost Swamp carrying her camera and a gun to deal with poisonous snakes. She was one of the first women to start her own movie production studio. Her heroine in *Freckles* saves the hero from the bad guys instead of the other way around!

The other types of books I enjoyed growing up were those that drew me into worlds of exciting adventure such as *The Three Musketeers* by Alexandre Dumas, *Sherlock Holmes* by Sir Arthur Conan Doyle, *Captain Blood* by Rafael Sabatini, and *Kidnapped* by Robert Louis Stevenson. Sadly, there are few women characters in these books. The two strongest, Milady and Irene Adler, are both villains!

This lack of strong female characters was never a problem for me, however. I simply devised my own plots for my heroes and added myself in as the heroine. I rode in hansom cabs with Holmes and Watson. I was the first female musketeer, a member of Captain Blood's pirate crew, and I roamed the moors of Scotland in company with Alan Breck and David Balfour.

I spent hours in my mind, creating these plots, refining them, having fun interacting with my heroes. I suppose, in a way, the lack of strong female characters in adventure novels led me to become a writer.

These days, girls growing up have a wide range of books featuring strong women characters with whom they can identify, just as they have strong women role models in all walks of life. We still have a ways to go, however, and it is therefore with great pleasure that I introduce you to the stories in *Hath No Fury*.

I hope you enjoy them!

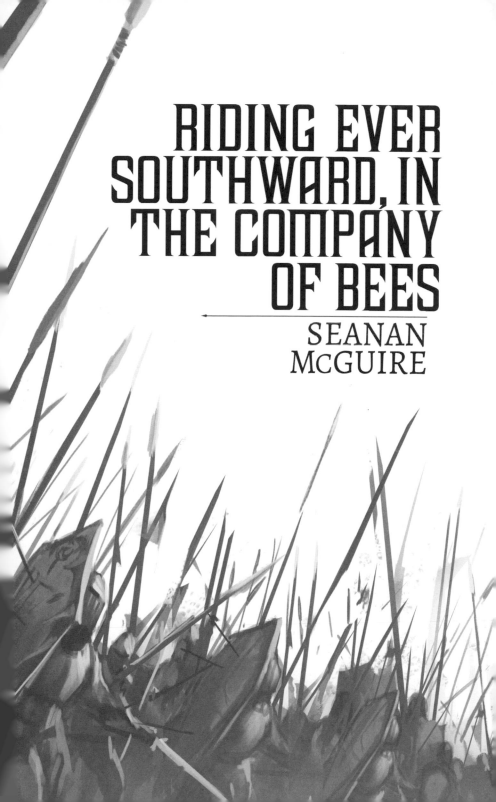

RIDING EVER SOUTHWARD, IN THE COMPANY OF BEES

SEANAN
McGUIRE

Honey for the baker, sweet and gentle on the tongue;
Honey for the teacher, for the virtue of the young.
Honey for the doctor, for the kindness of the bees,
Honey for the lovers. May they do just as they please.

SUNLIGHT LIKE HONEY ON I-5 southbound, dribbling in thick streams, pooling at the center of the road, where it casts blacktop phantoms against the blistering sky. It lacks honey's sweetness, honey's forgiving nature, but the comparison is a natural one, especially in this season, especially on this road. Sunlight like honey, the rolling tires like the buzzing wings of bees, turning distance into dreams, turning the long haul into something that tastes a little bit like hope when it's balanced on the tongue. A little bit like freedom.

A little bit like loss.

The gas rations don't apply to us, not during pollination season: we roll in full glory, taking up the entire road. It's a parade rich in pomp and circumstance, and I hate it, because it paints a target on our backs the size of the central valley. When the roar of engines is audible from a mile away, people know what's coming. They know what we *have*. And yeah, there have been problems. There are always

Illustration by KERI HAYES

going to be problems when something familiar goes scarce, turns from common coal into dearest gold. Hell, we saw it happen with coal and gold themselves, when Kentucky burned, when all the gold in the world stopped being enough to buy an extra drink of water.

They use gold in bee-shrines these days, decorate their plaster honeycomb with chains and coins and pray that somehow, their schoolyard alchemy will undo what man has done. Will turn the honey in the air into honey on the tongue; will bring back the bees. Oh, how they yearn for the bees. What once they swatted without thought has become a symbol of a better time, a better world, a better life for them and everyone that they care about. So we roll down the road like a traveling fortress, ever watching the hills around us, ever waiting for the attack.

This is the honeycomb structure of our hive:

At the front, the bikes, four of them, two riding point and two hanging back just enough to form a blunted V-shape. They clear the road for us, keeping things rolling smooth. Any one of them can call off the ride if they feel like things are going sour, and any one of them would die to keep that from happening. They know how important what we do is to the survival of the state, to the souls of the people who watch us from the hills as we roll by, gold chains in their hands and honey in their hearts.

Behind the bikes, the three advance cars, all pre-Burn, all kitted to run on whatever we grind and stuff into their tanks, all tough enough to take a direct missile hit and keep on racing the horizon. When we get closer to the fields the bikes will fall back and the cars will move forward, trading places in a dance that we have long since choreographed to perfection. While each bike has a single rider, each car carries two: one to hold the wheel and one to hold the gun. The lead car's gunner, Poppy, has been making this run for fifteen years. She wasn't in the first convoy, but she was in the second, and she has a bee tattooed on her left arm for every person she's killed in the process of getting the bees to the fields. When she takes her shirt off, it looks like a swarm taking flight, swirling endless toward the sky. When she puts her arms around me, it's like being in the heart of the hive.

The ink on her latest tattoo was still fresh and weeping when we loaded up for this trip. She's running short on skin that hasn't been striped black and gold and bitter with another life lost; she's said, several times, that she hopes she can make it just one run without adding to her arm. So do the rest of us. We've always been hoping for that sort of peace.

Behind the advance cars, the truck, ghost of a shipping company's label still visible through the gaudy paint that decorates its sides, wheels armored with makeshift shields that weigh the vehicle down but have done almost as much to keep it moving through badland routes as the bikes, as the guns, as the whole damned human orchestra of violence and hope and hopelessness. Six people ride atop the vehicle, strapped into bolted-down chairs, guns at the ready, drenched in sun like honey and praying, just this once, to make a life-giving run without taking it at the same time.

Behind the truck, three more cars; behind them, two more bikes, riding single-file, the stingers on the bottom of the bee. Unlike the advance bikes, these have passengers, sharpshooters trained in the strange and delicate art of picking off a target from a distance. All told, we ride thirty strong, from the drivers to the alternates to the ones who hold the guns. It's not enough. It's never enough. We could ride with fifty, with a hundred, and it still wouldn't be enough, because there would always be someone so desperate or so foolish that they would look at our convoy, rolling down the line, and think that we were a target worth taking.

Desperate times. Desperate measures. And sunlight like honey, bleeding over the horizon, drowning us all.

Honey for the liar, help him spin a sweeter tale;
Honey for the sailor, help her set a swifter sail.
Honey for the student, help the pen write swift and true,
Honey for the farmers. May they plant the world anew.

When it's not pollination season, the last bees on the west coast are kept in a secure facility in Muir Woods, surrounded by fences and snipers and everything a tiny pollinator could want to ensure that they don't wind up trapped in a jar and sold on the black market to someone who doesn't know the first thing about bees, or beekeeping, or why the hive is so important. They just know that once, bees were everywhere, and food was plentiful and cheap, and paintbrushes were something you bought for your kids to paint with, not tools that narrowed the gap between your hand and the end of the world.

"Hope."

I grunt, eyes still on the honey-soaked road. We left the Bay Area this morning, when the sky was still pink and the heat of the day was still an unfulfilled rumor that might yet be proven untrue. It hadn't been, of course; there hasn't been a cool day any lower than Portland since before I was born. Every day, the sky burns, and the sun bleeds honey, and we struggle with cooling units and ever-moving convoys to keep the world alive for a little bit longer, while clever scientists in secret bunkers work to heal the world.

Nijmi rides with the point bikes, following Lou, who says the bunkers are a lie. Lou likes to claim she rode all the way to Ames, Iowa, once to bang on the bunker door and ask to be let in, only to find a rusted-out hole in the side of a mountain, leading down to nowhere. She likes to tell the newbies that we're the only true salvation of the world. Us, and the bees, who don't understand that things have changed. They only understand the age-old dance of field and flower, and the slow manufacture of honeycomb and hive. It must be nice, to be a bee.

Alan sighs. "We have to stop soon," he says. "The engines don't like going this hard in the heat. We need to give them a chance to cool down."

"We're still six hours from the first farm on this route." Six hours from an armed militia standing ready to receive us, to guide us and our precious cargo to the fields where the bees will be allowed, at last, to dance. There used to be more farms, but most of them have dried up and blown away, consigned to memory and dust. Others are still struggling for survival, paintbrushes in hand and children flooding the fields to do the work of insects. They've dropped off our route for other reasons: failure to pay, failure to protect, failure to follow the rules. We can't afford repeat offenders. Not with the resources already stretched so thin. Not with the hives so few, and so precious.

"Doesn't matter." Alan shrugs, expansive as a mountain range. He's a skink of a man, all long torso and quick-moving limbs, but he still somehow manages to take up twice his share of space. "The engines don't care how far we are from farmland."

I grunt, wishing I had a better objection, knowing that Alan will overrule me if I try. He's the lead mechanic for this convoy: without him, we'd be hauling our bees on foot down the curve of the coast. We all know how long *that* would last. The lesson of the Oregon hives is not one any beekeeper will forget any time soon.

Alan looks at me expectantly. Finally, I sigh and hit the horn, two long bursts, signaling the bikes to fall back, because a stop is coming, and they're going to need to follow my lead.

"There's a small settlement about twenty miles up," I say. "We dropped them off the list because they weren't big enough to be worth taxing the hives, not because they did anything aggressive or against the rules. They hand-pollinate their fruit trees. We can swap them a few hours pollination for water and a chance to rest the engines."

"There we go," says Alan, content in his victory.

I wrinkle my face into a scowl and blow the horn again. I hate unscheduled stops almost as much as I hate smug mechanics, and the loss of the open road.

Honey for the children, let them know what we have done;
Honey for the mothers, for their trials have just begun.
Honey for the fathers, let them keep what any can.
Honey for the drivers. May they find a better plan.

There are children in the trees when we pull off the road, the whole convoy rolling in noisy tandem, like the hand of God reaching out to touch these people's lives for no good reason. I can see their faces speckled through the leaves, eyes wide and staring in awe at the vehicles, which must seem like something from a fairy story of the before-time. People who work a farmstead like this, they're not thinking about hitting the road and heading for the horizon; not when there's a paintbrush in their hand and work still to be done. And there is *always* work to be done.

Poppy and I got Nijmi on a farmstead a lot like this one, payment offered for a turn with the hives and a chance at a better growing season. We wouldn't have done it—we don't trade in slaves—but we could see the way she was looking at the bikes, and the way the boys in my age group were looking at her. She needed out. We needed someone with young reflexes and sharp eyes who was ready to be indoctrinated into the way of the honey and the hive. A deal was struck, a price was paid, and if her parents slept poorly for the loss of her, good. They deserved to understand what they'd done. Maybe they kept a better eye on their girls these days. Maybe they were better about making sure that they were *safe*.

Nijmi is the youngest of us. She doesn't remember clean water from every faucet, electric hair dryers, air conditioning in every room. For her, the world has always been the black and broken road, the honey on the tongue, the eager eyes of everyone who sees us and knows what we carry, cargo more precious than bread, more irreplaceable than shade. It's almost refreshing, watching her interact with the world. For her, there is nothing left to lose.

The orchard is a stunted crescent of pink and green. Peach trees, from the looks of them, water-intensive and hard to hand-pollinate. Both qualities that make them rare in this world, and hence valuable. Even a small crop will be enough to trade for almost everything they need to keep body and soul together. Not much more. There's never much more.

Some of the children must have run ahead when they saw the trucks coming, or maybe the engines are even louder than I thought: a group of adults is already waiting for us when we come around the curve of the orchard and pull into the open space at the center of the settlement. The bikes circle as the cars settle into position around the truck, making sure that I am never undefended. When I kill the engine they stop, rear wheels inward, headlights and weapons pointed at the locals. It's unfriendly. It's untrusting. It's the only way to even approach safety, and all of us know that if these people were better-fed or better-armed, it wouldn't be nearly enough. We are the greatest treasure in this part of the world, and the temptation we represent has turned the heads of better men than these.

No one moves toward us. They wait, and so I unhook my belt, open my door, and swing my whole body out of the truck with a single practiced motion, jumping down rather than taking a single, vulnerable step to the ground. The shotgun in my hands bounces a little with the impact, metal socking against the skin of my palms with a small but audible slap. All around me I can hear the clicks of safeties being released—the weapons that have safeties, anyway. About half of us ride with weapons that can't be rendered useless without removing the bullets, because sometimes that split second is too much to spend. We've lost a few drivers to friendly fire, over the years. It's always been worth it.

A woman steps forward. She's older than I am by at least twenty years, or looks it, anyway; it can be hard to estimate the age of the people who still farm out here, purifying their own water and pollinating their own trees. That kind of labor ages a body long before its time.

"To what do we owe the honor of this visit, Beekeeper?" she asks. There's a quaver in her voice. She's trying so hard not to allow herself to hope that they have somehow been put on this year's list. Not an impossible dream: every year, the curators select a few farms that were dropped for inability to pay and put them on the route. It's important for us to have stops, and for the people to continue thinking that the system is fair.

It's not fair. How could it ever be? When you compare the number of farms we can service with the number of starving people left in this state alone, fairness doesn't even enter the equation. Only survival matters, now that the sun is honey and the road is the closest thing to equality any of us will ever have.

"Our engines need to cool," I say, and watch the light go out in her eyes. We can stop here for as long as we like, we can demand whatever we want from their supplies, and they can't ask anything in return; not if they want any chance at the list.

There are some Keepers who would take advantage of this, strip the place of clean water and whatever fresh fruit they've managed to hold back for themselves, tell the people they leave hopeless and hungry that this will guarantee them a better spot on next year's list. Those Keepers maybe outnumber the rest of us, at this point.

But I am not among them.

"We have honey," I say. Every person within the range of my voice goes still, even the ones who ride with me, who knew that this offer would be coming. Their stillness is warier than the stillness of the settlers: they know that my announcement, which seems so generous and good, could very easily be the thing that tips us over into anarchy. Some treasures are too great to be spoken of in open spaces such as this.

"Honey?" asks the woman. She makes no effort to hide the longing in her voice. She's honest, this one: she knows that I would know her for a liar if she tried to keep her hope at bay.

"Honey," I say. I do a quick count of the faces I can see, and compare it to the children who peeked at us through the trees, the ones who still aren't here. I know what I have. I know what we can spare. "Three jars, in exchange for water for our engines and a sample of whatever it is you grow here. I'd like to taste your land."

A low, disbelieving murmur breaks out among the crowd, not unlike the gentle buzz of bees. Finally, the woman asks, "What else do you want?"

"Nothing," I say. "Time for our engines to cool. Your assurance that no hands will be raised against us. Perhaps a tour of your orchards, if you're feeling generous."

Her laughter is as dried out and enduring as her land. "You've just offered my people honey. For that, we're more than generous. Whatever you like."

I smile a little, turning to Poppy and offering her the nod. She presses her rifle into Nijmi's hands and heads for the truck, moving so that her body is shielded by the great metal beast. It wouldn't do to have anyone see the combination on our safe, the way the keys are meant to be turned, any of the things that keep our treasures locked away.

For the safety of the bees we haul—the most precious cargo in the world—the truck is a labyrinth of keyholes and secret compartments, no two of them alike. Only I have all the keys, all the codes. Poppy has access to the honey, as do half our gunners; it's the trade good that lubricates our passage down the coast. Supposedly, we're meant to use it to pay off brigands and remind farmers of all the things they do not know about beekeeping, all the secret tricks of our trade that would be lost if they shot us where we stood and claimed our cargo for their own. Maybe some of the drivers use it for its intended purpose. Maybe some of them are paying off warlords from Vancouver to Baja. Me…

Honey should be sacred. The taste of a whole growing season, of a world where life is rich and sweet and free for anyone who wants it. Honey should be shared with the people who need it most. People like these, who have probably gone years without a trace of luxury on the tongue, without the hope of a full and vibrant harvest.

Poppy returns with three jars, selected from different places in our store. I can tell from the way the liquid shimmers, dark as bruised peach-flesh in one jar, pale as spring sunrise in another. I couldn't tell you what the bees sipped to make each one, not by looking, but I could tell with a single taste, and my tongue aches for the challenge. Honey is an addiction. No matter how much we have, we always want more.

Maybe that's the nature of mankind. No matter how much we have, of anything, we will always, always want for more.

Poppy hands me two of the jars, keeping the third for her own hands. The people of this farmstead line up without needing to be told. Poppy produces a spoon from inside her vest and walks down the line, offering them each a taste of the darkest honey. No one refuses. Some of the people weep. Others sigh and close their eyes. The children—those who have come back in time for this first, sweetest treat—become all wide-eyed wonder and delight, fading swiftly into dismay as they realize that they have just tasted a thing they have never had before and may never have again. Knowledge can be its own kind of torment.

I walk to the headwoman, who stands at the back of the queue, waiting until all others have had their sweetness before she reaches for her own. "These are for you," I say, handing her the two full jars of honey. "Spread them as you will."

She takes the jars as reverently as she would take a newborn child. "This is too much," she says—but she does not offer to return them, and I know that were I to try to snatch them from her hands, she would fight me. She wouldn't even mean to. Some things, once given, were never intended to be taken back. "All we can offer is water, and space."

"And a tour of your orchards, remember that," I say, earning myself a sliver of a smile. "I saw peach trees. How is your harvest?"

The smile dies, taking some of the light from her eyes with it. She looks past me to the line of her people, where Poppy still walks with her jar of her honey and her glistening spoon. The jar is more than half full, and she's nearing the end of the line. Maybe the headwoman is right. Maybe I have been too generous. But if we can no longer afford generosity in this world, what's the point of continuing on?

Some things must remain good. Some things must grow.

"We teach the children to pollinate," she says softly. "They can climb the high branches; we can't. We do what we can. Every season, the trees bear a little less. I'm not sure how much longer we can endure."

"Perhaps we can help."

She frowns at me, unwilling to have hope. I can't blame her for that. "How? You know as well as I do that the bees are gone."

I know better than she does that the bees are gone. I know why they left, each pesticide and climate alteration and foolish piece of legislation that knocked out one more wall of nature's delicate honeycomb structure, until there was nowhere left for the swarms to fly—nowhere but the safety of our gardens, and the hives under armed guard, never to be free again.

I also know that the loss of the honeybee, while devastating, is not the end of the world that most people take it for. That's another place where I differ from many of the convoy drivers: I don't think we should lie to people just so they'll see how necessary we are. Anyone who works the land can see how necessary we are, at least for now, at least until the world finds a new equilibrium. Recovery isn't the goal: if recovery is coming, it won't be in my lifetime, or the lifetimes of the children now licking their lips and swallowing hard, searching for one last trace of honey. Recovery is a fairy tale meant to be told until people are ready to face reality. The world has changed. The world will not be changing back.

"Come," I say, signaling to Nijmi that I am going with the head-woman. She nods. She will relay my location to Alan and Poppy, and they will relay it to the rest of the convoy, closing ranks around the cooling bulk of the truck, the sheltered secret of the bees, until we're ready to roll again.

> *Honey for the lonely, give them something sweet to know;*
> *Honey for the dying, let them let their troubles go.*
> *Honey for the outcast, give them just a moment's peace.*
> *Honey for the scholars. May they make our troubles cease.*

The orchards are not thriving. That would be too much to ask. The orchards are surviving, alive against a landscape gone dead. The flowers are bright and hopeful, as flowers always are. The headwoman peers into them as we walk, nodding approval when she sees the paintbrush skirls of pollen, frowning when the work is shoddy, or worse yet, absent.

"How do you water?" I ask.

"Reclamation. We set dew traps, rain barrels, all the tricks we were taught before the world burned," she says. "We have a working firetruck, and a hand desalination pump. We trade preserves for fuel about three times a year, and brew our own biodiesel. The ocean's a three-hour haul if we've contacted our allies, let them know that we're coming. We go down, fill our tanks, and desalinate right here on the property. Best part is, we can even sell the salt, after we've baked it and purified it and picked the dead fish out of it." She smirks, just a little. "There's a market for everything if you look hard enough."

"There is," I agree. I wonder what the people who don't have a convenient ocean are doing for salt these days. The pre-collapse stores will be wearing thin before much longer, if they haven't already. Salt, water, honey: the currencies of a new and bitter world. I start walking again, and the headwoman moves to keep up with me, matching her steps to my own.

Finally, halfway through the orchard, I see what I was hoping for: a splash of vivid orange growing on a sunlit strip of earth, where the trees are widely set enough that the sun will filter through consistently, creating the perfect growing conditions. Poppies. California poppies, bright and blooming and perfect, the same as they've always been in this brilliant, brutal desert land. I walk over to them and crouch down, studying the pistils and stamens as best I can without actually sticking a finger inside the flower and possibly damaging it. There are no paintbrush swirls in the pollen, no tell-tale signs of human intervention.

"They're wasting time on flowers again." The headwoman has come to a stop behind me. She sounds ashamed, like the children of her encampment have betrayed her on some deep and essential level. "I am so sorry you've had to see this, Keeper. I assure you, we're not frivolous here. We work for everything we have."

"And the children deny pollinating the flowers, don't they?" I look over my shoulder at her. "They swear they didn't do it, that the flowers just grew on their own."

She nods. "I know it's not possible. We root out the offending plants whenever they appear. Nothing that doesn't contribute is allowed to waste our water, Keeper, I swear."

I sit back on my haunches, trying to level out my breathing. This isn't her fault. She's been lectured, no doubt, threatened and yelled at ever since the Great Drought began, presaging the changes that turned California into the wasteland it is today. She's been told that anything "frivolous" doesn't deserve to live—and "frivolous" is a label that people have always applied to flowers. They wring their hands about the disappearance of the bees and grind the poppies under their heels at the same time, and then they don't understand why the bees won't come back.

Finally, I say, "The children are telling you the truth. These flowers were naturally pollinated."

"What?" Her voice is a small, biting thing, pinned beneath its own weight. "That isn't possible. The bees—"

"There are no honeybees here," I say. "I know. If you were hiding them, I'd know that too, and I'd confiscate them and burn your houses to the ground, to make sure you understood your crime." I wouldn't. I think she knows that, too. If the bees are ever going to come back, we will have to remember that they were wild things once, before we learned to box them up. But the law is the law, and I must at least pretend that I would obey it. "Honeybees are the focus. They're the most efficient pollinators for most cultivated crops, and we need the honey for a lot of reasons. That doesn't mean that they're the only bees in the world. California had native pollinators before the Europeans brought their bees over. Most of them are solitary, which means you don't need a hive. You don't get honey, either, but that's not as much of a concern when it means you've got *bees*." I lean forward, touch a poppy with one careful fingertip.

"This is the work of the blue orchard bee," I say softly. "They like flowers. They like fruit trees, too. It would take years to build up the kind of population you'd need to handle an orchard this size, but if you were willing to invest the time, plant flowers, make sure you have a certain amount of soft mud for their burrows…they'd come. They're already trying, as much as they can. You wouldn't have honey, but you would have bees." They would have hope. Their children would have their childhoods back.

They would have bees.

She opens her mouth, about to say something—about to thank me, or to apologize for her foolishness at not knowing there were other pollinators in the world, when that's never been a thing that people just *knew*. Especially not now, when we roll in sunlight like honey, past altars draped in gold, hoping to summon back the fat, splendid bees of the world we killed, and not conjure the hardy, swift-winged bees of the world we stole.

The sound of gunfire from the encampment stops her. Her eyes go wide, mirroring my own. I take off running, heading for my people.

I will give her this much: for the first twenty yards, she almost kept up.

> *Honey for the poets, to remember in their rhyme;*
> *Honey for the dreamers, to bring back a better time.*
> *Honey for the hopeless, to remind them what's been lost.*
> *Honey for the gunners. May they never face the cost.*

Smoke rises from the encampment like a flag to call the raiders home. I see it long before I hit the hill and see what they have done.

My drivers—my brave and brilliant girls, my bright and bonny boys—have managed to pull back the bikes, forming a tight circle around the truck. They're braced behind the cover of their vehicles, shooting at the ring of unfamiliar bikes that now surrounds them. There are bodies in the no-man's land between them, some of them shapes I recognize even without being able to see their faces. Poppy's tattoo will never have time to heal. Daniel will never tell his girl he loves her again, or see his son grow up. Crystal's husbands will mourn for her a thousand nights, taking what comfort they can from one another's arms.

Others are unfamiliar, residents of this encampment, brought into danger by our presence.

Nijmi is not among the fallen. I take the time for a short and private prayer of thanks before turning my eyes to the attackers. There are only ten of them. They shouldn't have been able to hit so hard, so fast, especially not with Poppy standing guard—

But there is Alan, standing among their number like he belongs there, and everything makes sense, and nothing will ever make sense again.

I should be careful. I should be cunning. I should retake what's mine through stealth and treachery, even as it was taken from me.

I am Hope, of the California Beekeepers, riding southward through sun like honey, and my lover is dead in the dirt, and the daughter we took between us is in danger. This is not the time for care. This is the time to show them why I hold the position I do.

The headwoman reaches me, panting from the run. Her gasp is all I need to hear. I whirl, hand raised to shush her.

"Be still and be silent and know that I am sorry," I hiss. "Now stay here."

And I am away, I am running, moving with the tree line, keeping low, where I won't be seen by the attackers, whose attention is all on the convoy. I pull the guns from my belt, and when I am close enough, I open fire, bullets like bees buzzing through the open air, and I am still moving, *I am still moving*, they cannot touch me, they cannot reach me, they will not hurt me. They cannot have my people. They cannot have my bees.

Three of them are down before they realize the game has changed. My surviving drivers cheer, and the gunfire intensifies. The attackers are fighting on two fronts now. They no longer know what to do, or where to aim. Alan is shouting. The noise obscures his words, but I hope he's afraid; I hope he's terrified.

No one aims for him, not even me. All my people know the punishment that waits for those who would endanger the hives.

It is over in minutes. The last of Alan's backup falls, and he is alone, gun in shaking hands, surrounded by people who would be thrilled to pull the final trigger. I do not walk toward him. I *saunter*, allowing my hips to roll, allowing my hands to dangle. He is no threat to me now. I know that, and so should he.

He does. "Please, Hope," he says. "It isn't what it looks like, it isn't—"

"He called them as soon as you were gone," says Nijmi. "On his walkie, he called them."

"They said he promised them the honey, and the survivors of the raid, and one of the hives," says Michael. There's a bleeding gash on his arm, a sign of a bullet that passed too close and barely missed its mark. His lip twists in a snarl. "One of the *hives*," he repeats, in case I missed it the first time.

I did not miss it. I turn to Alan. "Well?" I ask.

He knows he's lost. He stands a little straighter, and spits in my face.

I do not wipe it away.

"We could be *kings*," he says. "We could rule this state. We could have *anything*, and you won't even let us demand our fair share of the harvest."

"Your idea of 'fair share' is everything," I say, mildly.

"Why shouldn't it be? There wouldn't *be* a harvest without us!"

"That's the thinking of the world before the drought," I say, and raise my pistol, aiming between his eyes. "You are no longer a Keeper. You are no longer welcome in the company of our bees."

The gun speaks once. Alan does not speak again.

He only falls.

Honey for the table, that we all be safe, and fed;
Honey for the sleepless, let them sink into their bed.
Honey for the Keepers, for the price they all must pay,
Honey for the bees, my love. They'll fly again someday.

We pull out of the encampment two days later, after we have buried our dead in the soil beyond their orchard, where the ground yields easily to the shovel. We have left the dead with honey on their lips and we have left the living with a promise: we will be back next year, and we will let our bees fly free, to pollinate their crops. They fought with us, not against us, and the memory of those who tend the hives is long. We will remember our friends.

Two of their adolescents ride with us of their own free will, one to learn a gunner's trade, one to learn the engines. Sometimes the only way out is forward, into the unknown.

Sunlight like honey on the I-5, and Nijmi riding shotgun, her eyes on the horizon, scanning for trouble. We are rolling again, rolling into the desert and the patchy green, rolling into the future, riding ever southward, in the company of bees.

SHE TORE

NISI SHAWL

WENDY DROVE FAST. SHE TORE through the spring night like the howl of a wolf. Damp, misty air blew in through the Invicta S-Type's open windows, making a mess of her normally tidy crown of braids.

In the passenger seat, Tink scowled and rubbed her bare shoulders. "Are you sure we shouldn't stop and take the top down?" she asked sarcastically. "I can still feel my wings."

"No time." The crossroad loomed ahead. Wendy signaled her turn even though there was no one in sight. She wasn't going to get stopped, ticketed for an avoidable infraction. Fast and legal—that was how she handled motors on or off the racetrack. She slowed as little as possible and spun the steering wheel. Tires screeched as she sped up again coming around the corner. "Lily's note said dawn."

"Do you even know where we are? How long will it take to get—"

"Shut up." Peter had been always been rude to Tink, and Wendy was, too. Politeness never made any difference in the fairy's own manners.

"Well fuck me with a pry bar. I was only asking. And if you're in such a rush, why poke along on the ground like this when we could fly?"

Illustration by NICOLÁS R. GIACONDINO

For answer, Wendy removed one gauntleted hand from the wheel to lift the submachine gun tucked between her and the door, tilting its elegant muzzle to the windscreen. "Weighs something," she said. "Plus we'll want plenty of ammo." She lowered the gun back down, point made.

Never mind that flying terrified her.

At a bend in the road Wendy turned the car's nose northeastward. The fading lights of the British city of Boston disappeared from the rearview. She twisted the knob, brightening the Invicta's headlamps. One more jog to navigate. She took it at cruising speed: 40 miles per hour. Then the way ahead stretched flat and straight, a Roman rule dividing black fenlands on either side. Gradually the faint glow of the lights of Skegness climbed up from what must be the horizon. She checked the dash's chronometer. Two hours till sunrise. They were just on time.

Tink had been suspiciously quiet for far too long. Wendy spared a glance from the road and saw by the instrument panel that the fairy's blond head drooped to the passenger seat's far side. A low snore confirmed that she slept. Effectively immortal, Tink fought off aging with the magic of dreams. When she wasn't busy stirring up trouble, she tended to drowse away like a human-sized cat.

Not Wendy. She looked every bit of her thirty-five years. Wendy was one of those who enjoyed growing up.

Now she steered the Invicta through Skegness's streets, avoiding as well as she could the traffic caused by the market at its center. But the car's interior was nonetheless flooded with the cries of vendors, the sweet scent of milk from grass-fed cows, the soft clop of horses hauling wagons filled with the last of the winter's root vegetables, the chatter of ice poured into tubs and barrels, the blood-and-salt-and-iodine smell of the morning's catch. A Londoner born and bred, Wendy found the village market's atmosphere strangely familiar. For how many centuries had these folk gone about their bucolic business, striking bargains in tongues rooted in the ancient shifts of tides and time? Telling stories immemorial—

"What a stench!" Tink had wakened.

"We'll soon be away from it." And indeed they'd come at last to the village's outskirts. Soon the road reduced in size. One lane only. For fear of crashing into a vehicle headed the opposite direction, Wendy couldn't urge the Invicta on with the quickness she'd anticipated. They were going to be late.

"Throw us a map up, Tink."

The fairy gave an ill-natured sigh. "I *asked* if you knew where we were."

"I do. But there may be better routes to the spot Lily's expecting us to show at."

"May not."

The windscreen stayed stubbornly dark. A greenish glimmer in the corner of Wendy's eye proved to be nothing more than Tink's wings half unfurling, only to settle back again into the semblance of a fashionably spangled wrap.

"There's a thimble in it for you." Wendy said this as carelessly as she could. Her reward spread across the screen's glass like colored dew sparkling in an unseen sun. On one side, the map's sea shone a transparent, purplish blue; the road beneath their tires was represented by a thin stream of crimson slanting right. A miniature mango-yellow Invicta crept upwards along it. A clear brown reminiscent of ginger beer filled the rest of the display.

"Thank you. Any footpaths?" Scrawls of white appeared; several of these tangles ended at an undeviatingly straight section of the red line along which they proceeded, further up. Another remnant of the Romans, that would be: a stretch of road laid out as if drawn on the Earth with a protractor.

Lily's note said they should meet precisely at that stretch's midpoint.

"We won't be able to drive on any of those," Wendy said.

"Then why'd you ask me to put them on?" The paths began to vanish.

"No! Tink, don't, please—" The road relaxed its kinks, and she accelerated a touch. "We'll have to walk at the last anyway—to keep from scaring the kidnappers off with too much noise."

"Walk—not fly? You want me to walk in *these*?" Tink pointed one limber leg toward the Invicta's roof. A delicate slipper dangled from her small pink foot. "Silly girl!" But the promise of a thimble had sweetened her normally acid tone of voice.

"Take them off, then." Wendy focused on matching the map up with what she saw of the road. The straightaway's exact midpoint should be roughly a hundred meters on—but the shortest of the footpaths they needed to take started—*here*. Wendy swung the Invicta to the shoulder, cursing softly as the sandy soil dragged them askew.

An unwelcome beam of newly-risen sun bounced off the chromed radiator cap. Dawn.

Why couldn't it still be dark?

She switched off the ignition, opened her door, grabbed the gun, and climbed free of the car seat. Scraggly, starkly backlit wild plants scratched her shins. Golden light stabbed out of the clouds in the east, dazzling her. She lifted one gloved hand to shade her eyes and could barely see back to where the plants thinned to nothing. She'd overshot her mark—only by a bit, though.

She peered in through the Invicta's open window at the fairy feigning sleep. "Up and at 'em, Tink."

Black eyes snapped open accusingly. "You were supposed to thimble me awake!"

"Sorry. Other fish to fry." Wendy winced inwardly at confessing her distraction. Tink's jealousy of Lily might easily have kept her from going with Wendy on this rescue mission—if she'd been willing to admit to it. To placate her, Wendy offered the fairy a helping hand out. Which Tink stubbornly ignored, spreading her shining, shawl-like wings and flying ostentatiously through the cranked-down window. A neat trick, Wendy had to admit, unfurling the whole of that yardage inside the car. She smiled, then pursed her lips and leaned forward to plant a thorough thimble with them on the sensitive crown of the fairy's head.

Not that you needed wings to fly. Tiger Lily had no doubt assumed they'd make an aerial entrance. In the darkness. If only—

Heavy grey overcast obscured the rising sun. Too much visibility for flying regardless of whether or not she had the courage. Wendy released her hold on the fairy's naked upper arm to sling on a couple of belts of ammo. Then, hefting her weapon, she trudged resolutely toward Lily's rendezvous.

THREE OF THEM. BLUE IN the dimness, Lily's captors stood on the edge of a shallow depression in half-grassed sand. Give them credit for facing the right direction at least: the one they'd expect her come from.

Down in the depression's center, Tiger Lily did their best to lure the three into looking their way. "Heyyyy, you wanna find out how good my pussy feels? My mouth and my ass too? I got a special hole for each and every one of ya." Lily's normally husky voice—the only thing about them that never shifted with their shape or gender—trembled with what probably sounded to the men surrounding them like longing. More like laughter to Wendy's ears. No change in tone or register as Wendy lifted her arm and waved a signal from the surf-wet sands at the thugs' backs.

Didn't these men know Lily wouldn't be here unless they wanted to be? The chains linking the shapeshifter's hands together behind their back were useless. Lily could turn to a snake and slither arm-lessly out of them. Could be anything, become anyone, including who they appeared to be now: an "exotic" "Red Indian" woman—a favorite manifestation—waiting hopelessly to be ransomed by her rich white friends.

Chilly seawater lapped against Wendy's knees. She rose to a crouch, hoping her silhouette resembled a rock's. Green glittered in the air to her left where Tink flew in circles, speeding faster than the human eye could follow. Motioning with the gun for Lily to flatten themself on the scrubby sand, Wendy took aim at the furthest man's back and fired.

Her darling SK kicked at her heart once, twice, then settled into an even purr as her bullets ripped into the unsuspecting kidnappers. Waiting only a moment for their screams and groans to subside, Wendy ran to Lily's side.

Already the "Indian" had slipped their bonds. "Ta for coming. I was gettin' right bored."

Quick hugs and thimbles to each other's cheeks were all the greeting circumstances allowed. The two headed inland. "Why'd you wait for me then?" Wendy asked.

"Seemed best to get you onsite. These fellows have been thinking they're going to wreck the coastline, build a great big, sewage-spewing holiday camp here."

"And?" Wendy gave the dead bodies a brief glance as they passed between them. "Not much of a threat if you ask me. Not this adventure." Maybe next time they'd have a bit more success.

"Ah. But how'd they know I was spying on 'em, like? How'd they come to try kidnapping me? Someone smart's behind this one."

"Someone like—" Suddenly Wendy realized there was an important absence in the air.

"Lookit the business card they gave me when they thought I was an investor." Lily pulled a white pasteboard rectangle from an obscure pocket and thrust it at Wendy—but Wendy barely noticed it. She whirled on her heels, searching wildly for even the faintest gleam of Tink's green glow.

"What?"

"Where'd she go?" Guilt at robbing Peter of the fairy's fidelity—such as it was—pricked at Wendy's mind like midge bites. "Where's Tink?" A question no sooner asked than answered. A patch of jade-colored light shimmered above the water's edge—which was nearer now than before, with the tide coming in. Wendy reversed course.

Lily followed. Wendy wondered if the shapeshifter's presence would exacerbate Tink's moodiness—if moodiness was the problem. She slowed to consider that. The fairy had a way of becoming scarce when trouble threatened.

"See?" The pasteboard rectangle reappeared. Wendy took it and peered at it, but the early gloom defeated her attempt at reading the card's tiny type on the go. "It's for 'Smee & Assoc.'" Lily explained.

"Hook!"

"Right! And if *he's* involved, no telling what this story is *really* about. Don't you want to know?"

But they'd reached the first curling breakers. Wendy waded out—Tink's shining had drifted further away—or perhaps stayed stationary while the tide rose? So swiftly, though? Sand and salt water dragged at her custom cordovans. She should have shed them. She hesitated and her feet sank deeper. The swirl of the sea on her calves felt like cold hands.

Because it *was* cold hands. Hands pale as foam emerged from the wine-dark combers to wrap around her legs and tug at her twill skirt; muscular arms embraced her hips and waist and clasped her to broad and pearl-like bosoms. Wendy fought, but the mermaids were too many. Waves filled her mouth when she opened it to cry for Lily's help. The scene was all too reminiscent, though the pain a great deal less. As Wendy was forced beneath the surging surface of the icy April ocean she pressed her lips tight again but kept her eyes angrily open, glaring into the mermaids' mad grins. She breathed out, then in, choking. Black defeat swallowed her.

WENDY WOKE PUKING AND SHIVERING. A puddle of bile tilted and ran back and forth as the smooth boards beneath her face rocked. So it wasn't just nausea making everything move about. She must be aboard a ship. The flame in the lantern on the table where her head lay burned upright, though the candlestick itself heaved about under it mercilessly—

"Ah. Awake enough to vomit, I see. Very good." That rich, dark baritone, like licorice soaked in honey, belonged, she was sure, to only one man: the captain of the *Jolly Roger*. Wendy attempted to push herself upright so she could see him and verify that. Her arms wouldn't obey. She shoved with her neck and shoulders.

"Shall I help you?" A velveted steel grip closed on her collarbone and hauled her torso up against a knobbly wooden chair back. "Nicer, don't you think?" A metallic "click" and the grip released her.

Wendy's head swam with that small change in altitude. Her vision blurred, then cleared, and she was looking at the long, once-handsome countenance of Captain James Hook. Olive skin—now sadly etched with time—provided piquant contrast to the delicate cornflower blue of his eyes. Glossy corkscrews of an impossible sootiness spilled from beneath a many-feathered cavalier's hat.

"Do you dye your moustaches as well?"

Hook tittered. "Splendid! I knew I could count on you to recover quickly!" He smiled a sickeningly insincere smile. "Smee! Attend us!"

Wendy heard the rattle and bang of an opening and shutting door. Again she tried to move, attempting to twist toward the sound. Now she saw the problem: thick ropes, dirty with tar, had been wound around her tightly. At least, unlike her clothing, they were dry.

Her bandoliers of ammunition were gone. Her SK likewise.

"Cap'n?" A woman's voice? A child's? The Smee Wendy knew was neither. But there was no way to turn around, no telling who spoke behind her.

"Swab the table clean. Then prepare and serve a light luncheon: champagne, lobster, asparagus, and creampuffs."

"For how many?"

"Two, of course—can the presence of our guest have escaped your notice?"

"No, Cap'n."

"No. And yet? And still? You hesitate? Go!" Scampering steps sounded, then, once more, the noises of the door's operation. Had Hook left the cabin as well as this new Smee? Was Wendy alone? Alone, she might plot her escape—

The touch of velvet on the back of her neck snuffed out that hope.

"My pretty dear. I apologize for the lack of ebullient warmth in your welcome here. Though you've saved me the trouble of executing my least competent underlings, I neglected to thank you as perhaps I should have. Gossip has informed me of your quarrel with Pan—but I'm hesitant to put credence in mere rumor. Will you forgive me?"

"We've split up. It's true."

The chair was gimbaled. Hook spun her around to face him. "You swear so?"

"Solemnly." Pirates put great faith in pledges and oaths, much like the little boys who pretended to be them. "Are you going to untie me, then?"

That slimy smile. The flash of a long sword drawn and lifted to the cabin's low ceiling. "This will be faster."

She shut her eyes. She couldn't help it. A breeze stirred the loosened tendrils of her brown braids. Another. A third.

"There. Raise your arms."

The rope's tight coils fell away—except where they stuck stubbornly to Wendy's wet skirt and tunic. "Thank you."

"Of course. I'd advise you to immediately remove those damp things but for the danger of misconstruction...."

She shuddered or shivered. Or did both. "Yes. That would be bad." Hook was nothing like her type.

"Most distressing," the pirate replied calmly. "Instead, I offer you this nice, warm dressing robe." Reaching to his right with his velvet-covered prosthetic, Hook removed a heavy garment of quilted maroon silk from a wooden peg. Standing creakily, she slipped it on and tied its sash.

"And as we have a while to wait, perhaps, before the refreshments I've ordered arrive—for Smee is new to the crew, and not yet as efficient as one could wish—perhaps you'll allow me to explain to you a bit of what I'm about?

"Your father is a banker, is he not?"

CHAMPAGNE WAS PERHAPS NOT THE most sovereign remedy for nausea provoked by near drowning. Sipping from her never-empty glass, however, Wendy allowed its charms. Like angel hair or some ethereal form of excelsior it cradled her muzzy thoughts, protecting them from damaging each other without crowding them out of her head.

"For a modest sum I can guarantee you'll be recognized in our initial round of construction—and for ages to come. A street name, the name of a building—or for a higher contribution, we'll give you a more substantial form of commemoration such as a statue," Hook said. "Later, when we get around to hiring strolling entertainers and booking acts into the theater—"

"Theater?"

"Certainly! Some days it will rain—this is England, after all—and our holiday-goers must be amused or they'll leave. We should have a cinema as well—though not, I think, a library. Too bookish. Perhaps some sort of indoor games center…" Dipping a quill pulled out of his hatband into a dish of chocolate sauce, the pirate marked a square on the map pinned to the cabin wall. "…about *there*." He nodded. "Yes.

"But as I was saying, when all that's under way we'll naturally expect you, as one of the principals, to exercise a bit of discretion as to who fills your part. Actually collaborating on the show itself would require further financial involvement, but I'm sure you'll want to take the opportunity. Won't you?"

There was a long pause; the first, really, since Hook's disquisition had begun. Unless Smee's silent interruptions when bearing in trays of food counted.

Evidently it was time in the program for Wendy to assent to helping Hook with his scheme. Instead, she asked, "What's in it for the mermaids?"

"More bathers," Hook answered promptly. "They are particularly partial to adolescent boys. I've promised them plenty."

"But don't they know..." Wendy was at a loss to describe the ruination she felt sure Hook's unnecessary plans would result in. They'd affect not only the seaside, but all the country for miles beyond—the ancient markets would fail for lack of custom. Farmers and goose girls and their ilk would disappear; in their stead thousands of strangers would descend on Skegness's environs, bringing with them their loud motors; their stinking tons of refuse; their demands for fresh water, food, petrol, and who knew what else. All this was to transpire under her aegis? Watched over by her distorted likenesses?

This was nothing like true immortality.

Hook mistook her speechlessness for disbelief. "Mermaids are notoriously bubble-headed," he said. "Fairies with tails rather than wings."

At this Wendy kept her council, though inwardly she shook her head. Creatures born to magic could be called venal perhaps, but never stupid. Look how Tink disappeared when the action was about to start. And where was she now? And Lily—what had happened to them?

The door opened a crack, then a little wider—wide enough for Smee to squeeze in. Without a word he began gathering their used crockery and the remnants of their feast.

Hook protested the removal of the shell-shaped serving dish of pastries. "Leave that. No—no—I've not finished—and bring us some port. And suitable glasses. No, the champagne stays! Do you understand me? Don't mumble!"

No longer high and piping but hoarse and low, the servant's assent came clear enough to gladden Wendy's quailing heart. It was Lily's voice.

No surprise, then, when on "Smee's" return the cabin's door remained open behind him. Though the faint green tinting the shadow it threw was another matter.

Tink had returned. A happy ending must be in sight.

"Put the glasses there. You may pour," Hook instructed. With seeming clumsiness the shapeshifter spilled a gout of deeply crimson wine, creating an enormous stain on the table's white cloth. "Fool! I warrant you'd foul up so simple a task as walking the plank. Shall we discover if tis so?"

"Smee" cowered back toward the doorway, shaking his dirty-looking hair, lips and beardless jaw moving wordlessly in apparent terror.

"Well? Take care of this mess you've made first! Then we shall see!"

The shapeshifter left and returned again—too soon?—carrying a basin of steaming, soapy water. They promptly tripped over absolutely nothing and dropped it. More swearing from Hook. Exeunt Lily. With their next entrance, they introduced a wooden pail from which a pair of long rods protruded: a mop handle and a familiar length of gunmetal. Would her captor notice it? Hook's eyes narrowed. "Smee" slipped in the water and fell, spattering suds on the pirate's satin brocade breeches. While rising and fending off

Hook's fists, they placed the pail near enough for Wendy to retrieve her lovely KP from it. She raised and aimed it.

Hook froze in the midst of a roundhouse swing. His olive complexion paled to a yellowish ecru. "No! Please!"

Was it possible Peter had neglected to inform the pirate captain of the life cycles natural to Neverland's inhabitants? It would be very like him to forget.

"'To die will be an awfully big adventure,'" sneered a glint of emeralds from the corner by the door. Tink grew to full size and spat a gob of foaming saliva at the pirate's polished boots. It landed accurately.

"You wrong me!" Hook cried. "I'm as brave as any—"

Lily—still being Smee—thrust one grimy hand over Hook's mouth. "Enough yammerin'. Crew's sleepin' sound and won't be comin' to investigate anyways." They puffed up into a semblance of the pirate captain himself—wickedly exaggerating the leanness of his vulpine face, the dramatic slant of his brows. "'Break out the rum! Triple rations for every man jack of you!'" The roaring growl of the shapeshifter's delivery served as excuse for their un-Hooklike sound.

"All hands accounted for?" Wendy asked. "We can just leave?" No wonder Tink was back.

"What about them plans? After I brung you all the way here to ruin 'em—don't you wanna?"

Wendy looked over at Tink. No sign of jealousy. "Was that why? I have a hard time imagining you couldn't have handled this on your own, Lily."

"Whoa there! Stop that squirmin' about, you!" Lily clamped their arm around the throat of the original Hook. He continued to struggle. Freeing one befrilled hand he tugged at its copy.

"Let him talk. No harm in that."

"So you say." But Lily dropped their hand from the pirate's mouth and wiped it on the satin pantaloons he wore—not on their own.

"Papers," Hook gasped. He bent forward as far as Lily's throttling arm let him, gulping for breath. "Before you leave—sign what I've drawn up—I'll not bother you—further. No pursuit—"

"What you've drawn up?" Wendy frowned. "Your notes?"

"Not those—agreements. Dressing gown—lower left pocket—"

Shifting her submachine so it nestled in her crooked right arm, Wendy felt for and found a folded square of stiff foolscap sheets. She opened it one-handed, read the first page, and snorted in derision. "When did you expect to trick me into going along with this?"

"Show me!" Tink demanded, moving to hover at her shoulder. Of course the fairy couldn't read. Wendy pretended not to know that. "Poor penmanship, and it's a very legalistic document. Shall I summarize? Basically this assigns all rights to reproducing my likeness—Ha!—or 'any reminiscent renderings or associated memorabilia'—that's vague enough!—to 'Smee & Assoc.' You, I take it?" She scowled at Hook, who left off his pitiful wheezing.

"For 'a consideration'—the amount's left blank! And I've framed similar contracts for you pair as well. You could each of you name a tidy sum if you chose. And you'd be immortal to boot!"

"Hunh. So you say—a tidy sum of what?" asked Lily. "Tell us why we shouldn't simply slit yer gizzard here and now and have done with you?"

"Two words," simpered the captain with a flirt of his preternaturally long eyelashes. "Peter. And Pan."

The *Jolly Roger* rocked. The empty bucket slid a small distance on the cabin's floor. The scraping sound it made filled a minute's silence.

"You must understand." Hook stepped away from Lily. Who let him. "I've inquired most minutely into the cause of your disagreement with your former beau, Miss Darling."

"You are going to die."

"The point being, I gather, at whose hands?" Strutting over to the table he lifted the black-labeled bottle and poured himself a generous amount of the remaining wine. "Having bargained away the right to kill me yourself in exchange for Pan's acquiescence to the presence at your side of your lovely companions—and they having made like treaties—I believe you have no option left at this point except to join forces with me. Or sign."

"Here." Wendy held the SK out to the shapeshifter.

"What?" But they took the gun.

"Just for a moment." Wendy gripped the unsigned contracts with both hands and tore them in half. Tore the halves again. Again. Opened her fingers and let the pieces flutter down to add to the sad mess of suds and red stains.

"The pleasure of killing you will be Peter's, ultimately, yes. But some lesser sweets we are entitled to claim for ourselves."

"Tink." Wendy undid the dressing gown and removed the sash. "Take this and tie him." Lily gave the SK back to her and helped as well.

WENDY DROVE FAST. SHE TORE through the new night like the screams of the man tied up in the *Invicta's* rear driver-side seat. Once they passed Skegness Lily had gotten rid of Hook's gag. Who was there to hear him? At first Tink and Lily added their delighted cries to his wordless yowling.

But now they neared Boston. Too much noise would attract unwanted attention. Nor was Boston to be the only population center on their way to the Peaks. Wendy's companions would have to subdue their prisoner anew. She told them to do what was needed.

A meaty slap resounded behind her, followed by loud snivels. "Will you hush!" Tink scolded. "We've hardly done anything to you yet!" The pirate subsided into low whimpers. "Only a few cuts—no worse than you'd expect from shaving!"

Lily chuckled hoarsely, turning in the passenger seat to comment. "It's his blood. He don't like to see how the stuff's so yellow."

The shapeshifter had abandoned their sly parody of Hook's looks for the appearance of his nemesis, Peter. A little taller, a little heavier, a little swarthier about the cheeks—though he wasn't exactly a grown-up, any more than the original. Who would probably laugh heartily when he caught sight of Lily's impersonation.

For that to happen, though, they had to reach him by take-off. No being pulled aside by police officers for investigations of screaming passengers.

And Hook's wails had once again resumed, rising in volume. Reluctantly, Wendy slowed the Invicta to an idling standstill on the A52's bleak emptiness. Setting the brake, she swiveled in her seat to assess the situation by fairy light.

Snot smeared the pirate's bare upper lip, which quivered unbecomingly. But at least he wept more quietly now they'd stopped.

"Mayhap he's grievin' for his moustaches," Lily opined. They had been fine, decorative specimens of hirsute masculinity, to be sure.

"Here—give him a hankie," the shapeshifter added, offering their own.

The pirate's hands were bound by the dressing gown's sash. Tink took the used-looking wad of blue cambric with no sign of disgust and swiped it across Hook's face several times, sopping up most of the tears and mucous.

Wendy smiled—encouragingly, she hoped. Perhaps gagging him again would be unnecessary. "That's better, isn't it? Anything else before we get going again to find Peter?"

"Before we—" Hook's red lips hung apart wordlessly. A whine issued between them, building dangerously toward a shriek.

"What's got you so scared? This can't be the first time you've died." Lily's matter-of-fact tone of voice halted the pirate's screeching mid-crescendo.

"You don't like seeing your blood spilled?" Tink asked scornfully. "Ask for a blindfold—Peter won't mind."

"Maybe it *is* his first time." Wendy bit her lip, recalling her fall from the empty sky to the hard surface of the ocean. Her aerial powers had vanished with the fairy dust blown off in the wind of her passage between Britain and Neverland. She well remembered the fear, the bone-breaking pain, the frigid depths opening below, the shrinking circle of her conscious self—all the self she'd ever known. "It's always the hardest."

"I suppose." Lily sounded doubtful. They died whenever they changed.

"Look here, Hook." Wendy took her hands off the steering wheel to grasp his shoulders. "You lost. But you know we're nothing but stories, right? 'Our little life is rounded with a sleep—' and then we wake up to be told again.

"When Peter kills you, you'll die, strictly speaking. You won't stay dead, though. 'As long as children are innocent and heartless' they'll play at being you. You'll die. But you'll never be dead for long. Trust me.

"Now let's finish up this adventure right. You two take care of him if he gives so much as a peep!"

Wendy turned to face forward again, checked the fit of her leather racing gauntlets, and gripped the wheel one-handed. Ignoring Hook's quickly smothered protests she slipped the Invicta back in gear and headed straight on till morning.

THE SCION

S.R.
CAMBRIDGE

THE WOMEN IN OUR FAMILY *die young.*

That's what Nana liked to say.

Not that I ever heard it from Nana; Mam would often say it. Nana herself died when I was eight days old. She had eight days to cluck over me and stroke my hair—Aunt P once said to me she knew right then I'd be bold, born screaming like I was, my head of hair like a black bear's—before she left the world pistols blazing on the road west to Georgian City. Nana had been forty-five, longer than a Zawisza woman had made it in years, longer than her four sisters. She'd taken out nine faithful with her.

Nana was buried in the wild, outside the gates of New Creemore. We had a cemetery, but Mam hadn't wanted Nana put there. *Nana liked being out better than being in*, Mam explained to me. *Like you, Nika.* So I patted Nana's grave for good luck every time I left New Creemore.

Nana's nine faithful wasn't even the record for a Zawisza woman. Before Kaja, that belonged to Aunt P. Three months before Aunt P died, a gang of thirty-two faithful strayed near New Creemore's battlements, when Aunt P was on patrol. In fewer than ten minutes, she picked off every last one of them with her rifle like they was the old beer bottles she and I liked to use for target practice.

Illustration by NICOLÁS R. GIACONDINO

banged up bad—or once, had half my ear bit off—it was a comfort to be able to tell myself I was fine, I was fortunate, I'd cheated my fate a while longer.

And when I found Aunt P dead out in the wild, I lit her body on fire and let it burn down to nothing as the sun set red around me. I didn't cry. I figured she'd met her natural end. I swept her ashes into a canteen and buried them beside Nana. Through it all, I whispered Nana's words again and again.

The women in our family die young.

NOT A YEAR AFTER AUNT P died, I turned twenty—older than three of Nana's six daughters ever got to—and I found out I was pregnant.

I didn't know the name of the man. I still don't. He came from Sixteenth Line along with three others; New Creemore had sent four men in exchange. With little settlements, you have to change people up, elsewise the babies might turn out funny. When I was waiting for my turn with one of the men, I heard a girl behind me laugh and whisper to her sister—both of them Pollocks, and working in the underground factory because they couldn't be rangers; Pollocks can't shoot for shit—*oh, we're outta luck; Nika Zawisza's going to scare them soft for* days.

But it wasn't like that. I liked the man that made me pregnant better than any of the men I'd been assigned to before. He wasn't handsome like the unformed boys in Kaja's magazine. He was around my age but his hair was already going. He had large hands, and his clothes smelled of smoke, and he kissed my poor ruined ear.

At the time, it made me think it wouldn't be bad to have what anyone could have before, when people—sane, healthy people, I mean—were plentiful and you could be in love with someone all your own and not have to share.

I think Kaja felt the same, and that's why she'd traded for stupid pictures of boys who'd died long before she was born.

Although I'd liked the man who'd got me pregnant, I didn't like *being* pregnant. It seemed like something that couldn't happen to me, not *Nika Zawisza*, who frightened other people, even other rangers.

So—and it was stupid as all hell, I know—I didn't tell Mam or Kaja. I would have had to stay in New Creemore. At that time, with Aunt P dead, I was its best ranger. Mam was thirty-eight, and her years of ranging in the wild had made her knees achy, and I didn't want her to worry. (Mam never did live as long as Nana. She died suddenly at forty-two, not on the road but in our house, from a heart problem nobody knew about.)

And Kaja—well, I just couldn't tell Kaja.

There's this thing about families. I suppose some families are generous when it comes to one another, but that's not the Zawiszas. Families like ours remember your vulnerable moments like they're a light shining on some deep truth about you. When they see you, they see you when you were hurting. That's what they measure you by.

Like Aunt C once up and had a breakdown. I never knew how apt that word was until I saw Aunt C in the clinic: it *was* like she'd broken down, like a rusted car coming apart, its frame bent and its wheels flat. Aunt C got meds and started ranging again, but after that she was always, always *Aunt C, who had a breakdown*, even if she was just coming round for dinner.

When Aunt P and Mam first brought me outside New Creemore to teach me how to handle a rifle, I shot four of five targets and turned around and asked when could I start practicing on real faithful.

A year later, when Mam did the same for Kaja—Aunt P didn't even bother to go; she knew how Kaja was—Kaja couldn't do it. She hated it. She *cried*. *Fine*, Mam said, Kaja didn't have to be a ranger like the rest of our family if she didn't have the guts, but she had to be useful.

Kaja first got pregnant at fifteen. She made it three months with that one. I was home then. That was when Kaja still lived with Mam

and me; we shared a bed. I woke up to her sobbing and bleeding through her skivvies. I took her to the clinic and told her it'd be all right, which turned out to be the wrong thing to have said.

I wasn't there—I was out ranging—for the second, third, *fourth* ones, and after that Kaja was ordered not to line up again when men from other settlements came around.

Kaja did find her place. She apprenticed with New Creemore's biochemist. She learned hundreds of things, like how to brew up the shots everyone had to take. I got injections from her four times a year. She was smart and quiet and read more books than the rest of the Zawiszas put together. Yet, in our family, Kaja was forever *Kaja, who hasn't a use.*

IT WAS A JULY MORNING, heavy and humid, when I returned to New Creemore from a four-day range. The power went out that evening.

The range had been a good one, though I'd thrown up each morning and I'd steadfastly ignored that my khakis had begun to feel uncomfortably tight. I'd killed three faithful. Two of them were furious things, shouting at me about how I was damned before I shot them down. Nothing good from either of them, but the third, him a got I haul from. He'd been old. He'd had on him a handgun; a backpack with three books; a packet of still-good plantain chips; and a knit scarf, blue and orange and coming apart. Worthless, but I took it for Kaja, since she liked to collect fabrics and yarns.

He also carried a big sheaf of drawings I couldn't make head or tail of and had a crumpled photograph in his shirt pocket. Three smiling children. I took the drawings but left the picture on him when I burned him.

When I got home, Kaja was there for dinner. She lived in an apartment underground, and most of the time she didn't see Mam or me, but that night she'd come for her token once-a-month ap-

pearance. I gave her the scarf. She unfurled it in her hands and said, "I don't use things like this anymore."

"I didn't know."

I expected her to give it back, but instead she sighed and folded it carefully and set it by the door to take with her when she left.

I told her about the faithful I'd got it from. "Strange that he managed to get that old," I said. "He might've been around, you know, *before*. Like Nana was."

"So you killed him," Kaja said.

"He was a *faithful*," I said. Mam plunked down three plates of bean paste, and I took out the papers I'd retrieved. "Got these, too. Reckon the library can figure them out."

"No need for that," Kaja said, taking them from me. "They're blueprints, Nika." At my blank expression, she added, "Like a map, but for a building or a piece of equipment." She paged through them, her brow furrowing. "Blueprints of Feversham Station."

Feversham was a research and power station to the north of us. I knew it, but Kaja hadn't ever been there. "How would you know?"

"There's nothing else they could be. Nothing around here, at least." She showed me a page. "This one's of the interior of a power station. See, here's a combustion engine."

She might as well have been showing me something writ in a foreign language. Through a mouthful of bean paste, I started to tell her so, but the dim light that hung over the kitchen table flickered and died.

It was the whole house out. I went to the window. New Creemore's battlements had gone dark, though I could still see the shadows of the turrets, the razor wires, the rangers on the walls. "It's hot," I guessed. "Power's out because it's hot, but it'll be up and running in no time."

"Could be," Kaja said. She headed for the door, the blueprints rolled under one arm. "But the power's generated at Feversham. It's

a remarkable coincidence, a faithful carrying these the same time the power goes out."

I didn't like it, either. I followed Kaja outside. A little crowd had gathered; flashlights bobbed in New Creemore's square. (*Square* makes it sound fancier than what it was, which was the well-trod junction where the clinic and the school and the radio station and the armory met.) Kaja's boss, the old biochemist—Alvaro, that was his name—motioned Kaja over to him.

There were murmurs about what could be going on. Aunt C was there, and I went to say hello to her. Before we got past our pleasantries, though, someone grabbed my shoulder: Ranja, who ran the radio station. With her were Kaja, Alvaro, and the mayor. "Nika Zawisza," Ranja said. "Come with us."

We went down the road past the radio station. In darkness, the rest of New Creemore looked like one of the hundreds of ghost towns I'd passed through on my travels. When we were far from the square, the mayor said, "I don't want there to be a panic, Zawisza, but—well, Ranja can explain."

"Before the power went out," Ranja said, "I received a message from Feversham. It was in code. There must be something what stopped them from using their audio channel. Two words: *SOS*, then *faithful*, again and again."

"Shit," I said.

"Eloquent, as ever," Kaja muttered.

"With no power," the mayor said, "we can't communicate with Georgian City or elsewhere. I'm sending out messengers, but we've got to find out what's happened to Feversham. Zawisza, I understand you killed a faithful who had on him blueprints for Feversham Station?"

"If that's what Kaja says they are. I couldn't tell you different."

"Anything else stick out about him?"

"He was old," I said. I strained to remember more. The details

of his face had disappeared. I've heard some rangers say that they're haunted by the faces of all the faithful they've killed. Never been a problem for me. I came up with, "He had books."

"What kind of books?"

"Don't know," I said. "I was going to drop them at the library tomorrow." I didn't read the books I collected out in the wild. That was more Kaja's thing.

We went back to the house to check them. There wasn't much to them: an old course guide for an engineering class at a long-dead college; a battered paperback of *Hamlet*, which I'd once been assigned to study in school but had neglected; a loose-bound copy of *The Parson's Prayer*.

This last was the scripture of the faithful. Like many of the copies I'd seen, it was a photocopy of the original handwritten version. I'd never read it, but Kaja had; the only thing I ever heard her say about it was that it was full of spelling errors.

"Was the man you killed going to Feversham? Or coming from it?" Ranja asked.

"West of it, heading east," I said. "So he might've been on his way. You'll appreciate that I didn't quite sit him down for a nice chat about his intended destination before I put a bullet in him."

"If the faithful have done something to Feversham," the mayor said, "we've got to understand what's happened. *Before* there's a panic. Zawisza, how long would it take you to get there?"

"Day and a half if I hoof it," I said. "I've been there before." Feversham had rangers, too, and I'd helped them a time or two. "Give me fifteen minutes to get my things. I'll be on my way."

"Good," he said. "You and your sister will scope it out—*don't* do anything foolish, not before we can get help from Georgian—and report back."

"Kaja?" I asked, and at the same time Kaja spluttered, "Me?"

"Alvaro can't keep up," said Ranja.

Neither can Kaja, I thought, but it was true about Alvaro. He was in his sixties and had bad knees. He hadn't a year of life left in him, though of course I didn't know that then. "No need for Kaja to come with," I said.

"Sure there's a need, Nika," Ranja said. "Feversham's full of scientists. Biochemists. If there's a threat as regards the work being done there, well, Kaja's the one who can comprehend it."

I could tell Kaja was balking at the idea; her small face shone, bright and anxious, in the starlight. She'd never gone far into the wild. "She'll slow me down," I said.

But Kaja bit her lip and straightened herself up and said, "I will not. We ought to get going."

IT WASN'T UNTIL AFTER WE'D crept outside the walls, after I'd patted Nana's grave, after we'd put New Creemore half a click behind us, that I spoke to Kaja further. "You sure you're all right with this?" I asked.

"It's not like I have a choice," she replied. "Unless you're going to tell me you've secretly studied engineering and biochemistry and apprenticed with Alvaro yourself."

I was tempted to give her the finger. Kaja could be a bitch about the fact that she was smart. But she was afraid. Her eyes were darting around every which-way, like she expected a dozen faithful to pop out from behind a bush and start shooting. "It's safer than you think," I said. "Faithful got to sleep at night, just like us."

She let out a *hmmph*.

"And I got your back, Kaja," I added.

Kaja didn't say anything to that. Lips pursed and shoulders squared, she looked everywhere but at me. With a big backpack on, she seemed tiny. We had different fathers, of course, and she was darker and shorter than me, and knobbly, and near swallowed by her swathe of curly black hair. She was the prettier of us, was Kaja, but

I didn't mind that. That wasn't the sort of thing people got jealous about, not anymore. Watching her, I felt a protectiveness I hadn't felt about her in a long time.

Outside New Creemore used to be farms, but it had turned to dead land, rendered barren and scarred with trenches from the last desperate days of the fighting that had gone on before I was born. There weren't many buildings in the wild. Just the hollowed shells of them. I knew every half-gone fence, every collapsed silo, every slab of burnt barn board; I could use them for hiding places if I needed to. I checked them off in my mind as we went. I was surer by them than by the north star that Kaja and I were heading the right way.

When the first morning light began to crest over the horizon, Kaja broke the silence between us. We'd just climbed the hill that looked over the first big ghost town on the way to Feversham, a row of rotting buildings I had nicknamed *Rubber*. (I thought of it as that because the first faithful I'd ever killed in it had on her a pair of black rubber rain boots that fit me nice.) And Kaja asked, "How can you *like* this?"

"How can I like what?"

"This," she said, swooping her arm to indicate Rubber and the land around it. "Here. Being out here, in the wild. It's so quiet, and, well, *sad*."

"It isn't sad," I said. "Not to me. Gives me space to clear my head. Out here, I don't have to worry about anything."

"Except being killed by faithful."

"That's what makes it interesting." I waggled my eyebrows. "See, there's a real good way to fix that worry. You got to shoot *them* first."

"Very funny," she said.

"Shush," I told her, not to piss her off, but because I'd spotted two men down in Rubber, coming out from behind one of the abandoned storefronts. "Get down. Now. Flat in the grass."

Kaja obeyed, unstrapping her backpack to lay it beside her. I

crouched beside her, pulling out my rifle as I did.

Kaja was breathing very hard. I blocked her out. There is a calm that descends on me when I'm concentrating on shooting, like the rest of the world fades. I fired and fired again, and in the space of a few seconds both faithful were down on the ground.

I got up and jogged to where they lay. One I'd shot in the chest; he was dead. The other I'd got the shoulder, and he was holding his wound and keening. He rolled to look up and me, and I put him out of his misery with another shot. I knelt down to check them; that was when Kaja caught up with me. She stood a few paces away, looking a bit stunned as I retrieved a small knife from one and a box of rounds and a canteen from the other.

When I took out my little pack with matches and lighter fluid from my satchel and began dousing the bodies, Kaja asked, "What are you doing?"

"Burning them."

"What? Why?"

I shrugged. "Just something I do. You're the one that's read *The Parson's Prayer*. You know what they believe. You've got to be burnt if you're going to have an afterlife. I figure I ain't going to deny them that."

"Unexpected," Kaja said.

"Come again?"

"I'm surprised. I wouldn't have thought you'd care."

"I don't *care*," I said. "It seems disrespectful not to, that's all. You know I burnt Aunt P. Can't hurt to hedge your bets, in case the faithful are right about this one thing."

Kaja watched solemnly as I lit a match and tossed it on the corpses. She looked away when the fire caught in earnest, and said, "What you do, Nika? It's not bravery. It's butchery."

If she expected that would hurt my feelings, she expected wrong. "The world needs people to be butchers, too," I said. "Elsewise we'd

all be eating beans for Sunday dinner. If the faithful weren't handled, you better believe they'd be at our doors, raring to kill us."

Any kind of bravado I'd put on with my words was undercut by the fact that just then, a horrible nausea seized me. I bent down and retched. It was the baby doing it to me, but Kaja didn't know that. She looked confused as she strode over to me to pat me on the back.

After a moment, with her hand still rubbing circles between my shoulder blades, she said, "Guess the sight of them bodies got to you, after all."

"Guess so," I said.

We picked our way through Rubber. I counted familiar landmarks as we went: the ruins of a stone church; a busted van with *Denny's Discount Moving* in yellow letters on the side, tangles of weeds growing from its open windows; a coffee shop with shattered windows and a sign out front saying cupcakes were on sale for a dollar each.

It was shaping up to be another hot day. I shucked off my jacket, leaving a T-shirt that I'd torn the sleeves off of. Kaja stared at me. My left arm had a gash from when a faithful had slashed me with a knife, my right arm had a healed-up bullet wound, and of course, there was my ear. It was this that Kaja pointed at. "How did that ever happen?"

"I never told you? It was a day or so outside Georgian City. I found a nice place to sleep, a turned-over train car. A pack of faithful jumped me. One of them got my earlobe right in his teeth."

"Goddamn."

"Exactly. The asshole swallowed it, too. Hope it tasted like shit on the way down. Anyway, I got away."

"You know," Kaja said, "those two back there? They're the first faithful I ever saw."

Now that was something. Faithful were a big part of me. It hadn't ever occurred to me that my sister could live her life not ever

seeing them. "Obvious ones, they was. They twitched more than they walked. Sometimes it's hard to tell. Some of them look near normal. You have to stalk them for a bit before you strike."

Faithful lived aboveground, and they didn't get the treatments people who lived in a proper settlement got. Being exposed to and unprotected from all the biochem shit still left in the atmosphere made them—*sick*, although that's a word that hardly explains it. Not right in the head. *Batshit crazy*, if you want to be technical about it.

Kaja knew the science of it better than I did. But I'd paid some attention in school, particularly in history, where things sometimes got interestingly gory. New Creemore's school had a library of old newspapers, yellow and crumbly and covered in plastic so they wouldn't be smudged, the front pages loud with images almost boring in their sameness: bodies, covered and uncovered, in shopping malls, in football stadiums, in bus stations, in houses of Parliament. Once we'd watched a video: people spitting, screaming, convulsing in the seconds before their deaths. I don't remember who started the fighting but soon enough every nation on Earth had a biochem agent stockpile.

The first faithful were people who *didn't* die in biochem attacks. I reckon that when you survive something like that, you're so shook up that you look for the why of it. So survivors banded together, and along the line they decided that they were special, they were holy, they were *chosen*. Their prophets—parsons—preached that everyone else, everyone who'd had the gall to protect themselves by hiding in a settlement, had to go.

That was in Nana's time, but hatred's something what gets passed on through generations like it's genetic, like it's brown eyes or black hair or the ability to curl your tongue.

"I do feel a little sorry for them," Kaja said. "It's not their fault."

"It ain't the fault of dogs when they get rabies, but when they do, you don't pet them."

"The faithful aren't dogs."

"No, but they're not us, neither." Kaja still looked troubled, so I added, softly, "It's best not to consider the faithful, once they're gone."

She favored me with a small smile and nodded, and we moved on.

WHEN WE STOPPED TO EAT—soy bars and handfuls of black-berries from New Creemore's underground greenhouse—I had to force myself to. The baby had made food seem urgently necessary and unappealing all at once. Kaja seemed surprised, since I've always had a healthy appetite, but she didn't comment.

Nor did she comment when I said no to her offer of a swig of whiskey from a flask she'd brought with her. Or when we stopped to sleep in an abandoned motel on the edge of a crumbling road, and I spent the night up and wandering. Or when, in the morning, I promptly threw up the dregs of dinner. But her eyes remained on me, always assessing.

The harsh shape of Feversham appeared, far on the horizon and shimmering in the heat. It always was strange-looking. It wasn't a real settlement, just a facility. Its sparse buildings were high enough to peek out from above its battlements, so from afar it looked like great sentinels were rising from its walls. "That's it, then?" Kaja asked. "Alvaro says I could work there, if I wanted. *Do something better with your brain*, he says."

"Why don't you?"

She shrugged. "Could be I will. Once I've got a look at it."

I couldn't picture her packing up and leaving New Creemore, but I didn't say that. As we approached, I began to hear a thrum of noise, like there were hundreds of people shouting at once. I'd never heard such a thing from Feversham, populated as it was with untalkative scientists.

Then, when Kaja and I came to where the north road split and led to Feversham's gates, we were met with four bodies hanging from a tree.

Two men, two women. I recognized them all. Rangers from Feversham. One of the women I'd once got a bottle of homemade gin from; I'd happened on her injured and helped her home, and she'd paid me with the fruits of her still. Beneath them, there was a wooden sign on which a single word—*MURDERERS*—was painted.

"Fucking hell," I said. I got out one of my knives to cut them down, but Kaja grabbed my arm.

"Don't," she said.

"Why not?"

"This is a warning. We're at a crossroads. There are going to be travelers. Whoever's done this has to know it'll be seen. It'll do us no good to give them the message that we've been here."

She sounded shaken, but she was right. "Fair enough," I said. "It's a shame to just *leave* them here to rot in the sun. They were good rangers."

"And they died like they lived. That one has a relatively new wound on her face, and that one's arm's broken. They went down fighting. I reckon, Nika, there's no better death for rangers. You might even think of *this*—" Kaja motioned at the corpses, at the sign, "as the proper sort of grave for them."

Kaja's words did make me feel better about leaving, but still their bodies, bloated by the heat, surrounding by buzzing flies, made me uneasy. I looked at them again, let out a couple curses beneath my breath, then said, "We ought to get away from the road."

We continued to Feversham obscured by a low hill, close enough to the road for me to check things out every few minutes. With my battered binoculars, I spied more trees, more bodies hanging from them. I couldn't see the fine details of them, but I could tell not all of them were rangers. Some had on scrubs or long white jackets.

"What are you looking at?" Kaja asked.

"Nothing."

But she plucked the binoculars from my hands and peered

through them herself. When she trained them on a cluster of dangling corpses, she sucked in a breath. "Nika, is something like this— well, out of the ordinary, out here in the wild?"

"Very," I said. Truly, I'd never seen anything like it. Faithful were never so *organized*. The most I'd ever seen together were the ones who banded into loose gangs, but even the largest gang hadn't ever killed so many, and never in so showy a way. A sick feeling, one that had nothing to do with the baby, had begun to knot itself up in my belly. "Listen, Kaja, you can hide around here if you like. I'll go check on Feversham and come back for you."

"That's what you believe I'd do, isn't it?" she asked, her lower lip curling. "Cower here? We have to report on what's happened to Feversham Station. We're not there yet. Someone's killing Feversham's people. We have to find out more."

"All right," I said. "We're not far."

I led Kaja higher, approaching Feversham downhill from the back. The sounds from it grew louder. And raucous. *Cheering*, I realized. Feversham's battlements were well in sight; no rangers patrolled them.

We got closer and closer until we hit Feversham's back fortification. Something was clearly happening out front; the noise of it was painful in my bad ear. Leaning, I turned around to survey the scene behind us. Nothing but sun, sky, dirt. "Nice day," I murmured.

"Now what?" Kaja whispered.

I nodded to the left. "That way. We'll have to sneak around."

I went first. We moved slowly, our backs pressed against the wall. We rounded one corner, then another, enough to give a partial view of what was going on.

A huge crowd was clustered around a haphazard platform set up in front of Feversham's gates. Two men stood atop it: one grizzled, wearing a patched brown cloak around a faded jean-jacket; the other a younger man, clean-cut, obviously from Feversham, with his arms

bound behind his back.

There were people behind the platform, lined up two by two. Half of them had their heads covered with burlap sacks, the other half—faithful—holding them at gunpoint. In front of the platform was a neat pile of bodies, stacked like bricks.

"Norman Johansson, botanist," the cloaked man announced. Then, without another word, he drew out a knife and cut the younger man's throat. As the man's blood spewed and his legs crumpled, the crowd howled, I felt a dreadful rage rise up in me, and Kaja threw up on the ground.

I caught a glimpse of the cloaked man hurling Norman Johansson into the pile before I turned to attend to Kaja. "Hey, hey, easy," I said.

"We've got to go home *now*," she whispered. "Holy shit, Nika. That man's a parson. He has to be. The faithful might've taken over Feversham entire."

"I know."

I guided Kaja back around a corner. I couldn't put what I'd seen out of my head, in particular the people who'd been waiting, up next after poor Norman Johansson. I glanced back, and though I didn't realize it, my hands fell upon my pistols.

Kaja saw. "There's nothing you can do, Nika," she said. "Not unless you're keen to die. We need help from home and Georgian City and everywhere else it can come from."

"I know," I said, but still I didn't move.

"*Nika.*"

It hurt to turn around, but I did it. But not a minute later, I rounded a corner, Kaja behind me, and collided with a small knot of faithful.

Quickly, in the second of confusion that afforded me an advantage, I counted. Four of them. One of them—an older woman—screamed and came at me. I lunged at her, connecting my elbow

hard against her ribs, and heard a satisfying *crack*.

Then they rushed me. I managed to draw my left pistol and fire; I hit one in the chest, another in the groin. That one grabbed me around the middle, and I caught him in a hold around the neck, slamming my fingers hard into his windpipe. I growled as he gasped, and when his hands on me grew slack I threw him to the ground.

Another pulled at my arm, hauling me backward. I clawed at her, but managed only to scrape her face. She and I toppled to the ground, and my chin hit the earth so violently I knew it had split. The faithful rolled atop me, pinning me with strong legs. I twisted my head around; she had a hammer raised. I struggled, but before she could hit me, she let out a grunt of pain and rolled to the side.

I sprang up to see Kaja hitting her with her huge backpack, swinging it by one strap. She clenched her teeth and hit the faithful again. In the sunlight, for a swift second, she looked ferocious, but then she dropped the backpack and staggered, her mouth open with horror.

I saw to the faithful—only one was actually dead; as fast as I could, I shot the other three—while Kaja pried my rifle from me.

I rounded on her. "The hell are you doing?"

"Drop your pistols."

"What?"

"*Now,*" she said. Her hands were trembling; the barrel of the rifle shook. "There's no way we weren't heard. I—I think I can help. Otherwise they'll kill us the second they catch up to us. *Please.*"

I'd never seen her look so grave. I opened my hands and let my pistols fall to the ground. Kaja edged the rifle against my stomach. I lifted my arms in surrender, and, absurdly, though I knew Kaja didn't intend to hurt me, I felt a brief surge of panic for the baby. Then a swarm of faithful rounded the corner. In the moment before they were on us, I whispered, "Hold it straighter, Kaja."

The parson who'd been on the platform was in the lead. Up

close, he had a white, windburnt face. His eyes were pale blue. His forearms were spattered with blood. Most of his teeth were gone, and the ones that remained were brown. "What's the meaning of this?" he demanded.

Kaja hitched her chin up. "I found her in the midst of this," she said, nodding at the dead faithful at her feet. "I couldn't stop her in her madness, damned ranger what she is. But I surprised her. She's our prisoner now."

"*Our* prisoner," the parson repeated. "But we haven't met, little sister."

"Nay," Kaja said. Her voice sounded altogether different: confident, colored with a gentle twang. And somehow she was managing to make her eye twitch. "I like to keep to my own self. Simpler that way. But I've heard tell of what you've planned here at Feversham, and it's like nothing else I've ever heard of chosen doing. I had to see it."

Chosen. That's how faithful referred to themselves. I was grateful that Kaja had spent so much of her life reading. I would never have remembered that.

"And who was it told you?" the parson asked, looking amused.

I saw a flicker of nervousness in Kaja's eyes, but it appeared only I noticed. "I didn't get his name," Kaja said. "Old man. Blue and orange scarf. Had the plans for this place on him. This ranger here shot him. Been hunting her ever since."

There were whispers. "Charlie," a man behind the parson muttered.

The parson regarded Kaja for a long moment, then grinned. He seemed quite with it for a faithful; nonetheless, a stream of spittle escaped the corner of his mouth. "Seems we're in your debt, little sister. I'm Parson Prince."

"Kaja."

"As for the prisoner here, there's a place set up for her right around the corner. Nothing gets the troops riled up like a dead

ranger." He prodded my arm. "I got a beauty of a knife for you, darling."

"No!" Kaja said.

"No?"

"I—I mean—" Kaja stammered. "She ain't just a regular ranger. This is *Nika Zawisza*. She's the best ranger what New Creemore has. She's killed hundreds. Don't you think, ah, there ought to be a bit more *spectacle* here?"

"New Creemore, is it? We'll be there soon enough." Prince's smile widened. "Right you are, Sister Kaja. There's a better use for her. In fact, I believe I recognize the bitch." He reached out and turned my cheek with a blood-stained knuckle. When he saw my ear, he made a *tsk*. "Thought so."

We'll be there soon enough? I didn't like the sound of that. "I thought your face looked familiar, too," I said. "But it's just that I've seen the ass-end of a shitting dog."

Kaja shot me a look I could read well enough—*shut up, Nika*—but Parson Prince just laughed, delighted, and ordered me locked up.

FEVERSHAM DIDN'T HAVE CELLS, BUT it did have facilities that were used for experiments. I was stripped of all weapons and marched through the open gates and into a gleaming building. The room I was in couldn't have been more than six by four, white, with nothing in it but a blanketless cot and a pot to piss in. The lights were out, but I had a square window up high. All through the day, I heard faint cheering.

I realized Parson Prince *was* familiar to me. I placed him after a few hours. He'd been there when my ear had been bit. A scumbag in a gang then; now, a parson with followers. An unlikely ascent, but sometimes shit rises up and floats.

The door of my little prison opened when it was full dark. The door rattled for a few minutes first, and I got to my feet, fists

clenched, ready to pummel the person coming for me, but it was just Kaja.

I say *just* Kaja, but then, in shadow, she looked different. Her hair was pulled tight into a bun. She'd shed the excess layers of her clothes. My satchel was slung across her, and the stock of my rifle peeked out from above her shoulder, as though she were dressing up as me.

"Kaja?" I whispered. "How'd you get in?"

In response, she clicked on a flashlight and shone it at me. "Nika," she said, sounding relieved. She held up a bent hairpin, then pulled me into a short hug. "Are you all right?"

"Starved, but fine. You?"

"I'm good." She rummaged through my satchel and turned up a protein bar for me. I bit into it, but once I did I didn't feel like eating.

"Feversham's done for," Kaja said. "The faithful have occupied it. They've killed nearly everyone, and more of them are coming. Word of what the parson's done has got around. If you thought that demonstration we witnessed in front of the gates was bad—" She grimaced. Even in the dark, I could tell from her eyes that she'd seen things she couldn't erase.

"Still feel sorry for them?"

Kaja huffed. "Don't be smug. There's a lot you need to know, but first, they're intending to execute you."

"I figured."

"There are *particular* plans for you, Nika. Parson Prince plans to lead his followers to New Creemore, it being the closest settlement to Feversham. They'll kill you, then they're going to use your body for a standard. The parson's already got a pike picked out. The body of New Creemore's best ranger is going to be the first thing they throw over New Creemore's walls."

"Guess it was too hard for them to come up with a flag."

Kaja sighed. "Can you refrain from being flip for once in your

fucking life? We're talking about *our home*. Mam, Aunt C—everyone."

"Kaja, the faithful might've managed to take over Feversham, but New Creemore has ten times the people. It has more rangers. I didn't see *that* many faithful here. A couple hundred, perhaps? We can hightail it out of here, warn everyone, and our rangers'll send out a nice hail of bullets for the faithful for a *hello*." Briefly, I entertained the sweet thought of Parson Prince at the business end of my rifle. "Simple."

Slowly, Kaja shook her head. "No, Nika. Not simple."

"Why not?"

"There's a *second* thing they're aiming to throw over New Creemore's battlements. We can't just escape. Come on. You should see."

KAJA LED ME OUTSIDE. I had never before been in Feversham Station proper. It was dead quiet, and it felt small and sterile, composed as it was of steel and aluminum. It didn't feel like a place where people lived. Kaja and I passed several pits dug for the remains of Feversham's residents. I glanced into one and didn't dare glance into another.

There were faithful circling around, but we avoided them as Kaja brought me to the central research station, a squat building in the center of Feversham. The front doors had been torn open, ugly, like a wound in a carcass; clearly, the faithful had gone at it with bullets and hammers.

A guard was posted, but I slipped behind him and punched him in the back of the neck before he saw us.

Inside, we went underground. Rows of rooms lined the corridors. Kaja shepherded me into a small, cool chamber lined with locked cabinets. Its security door, too, had recently been pried open with rough instruments; I could tell by the scratches around the steel frame.

Kaja used the flashlight to illuminate the cabinets. Within them,

protected by a layer of reinforced glass, were all manner of containers, ordered and labelled: bottles, gas canisters, sleeves of slender tubes. "Unbelievable," Kaja said, to herself rather than to me. "What the fuck were they thinking?"

"Not sure I follow, Kaja."

"Poisons," she said, pointing out labels. "Sulphur mustard. Lewisite. Fucking *nerve agents.* The researchers at Feversham were storing—or *making*—the things that ruined the world." Her fingers brushed the glass, indicating a particular canister. She glanced up at me. "This one—you'd die if you got a drop of it on your skin. There's enough here to kill everyone in New Creemore a thousand times over."

"Enough to kill a thousand New Creemores," I said.

"Exactly," Kaja said. "In bad hands—"

There wasn't a need for her to finish her sentence. The cabinets were beat-up like the door, but it looked like the faithful hadn't yet raided them. The larder was full, so to speak. It was unimaginable, that the cabinets' contents could be more lethal than the combined power of New Creemore's rangers, but Kaja knew what she was talking about.

"Here's the prize," I said, a chill running through me. "Here's why Parson Prince came to Feversham. This is why the faithful started—whatever it is they're starting—here. Not to cut our power, not to kill everyone—though I reckon that's a nice benefit for them—but for this."

"The parson's not shy about it. He's making speeches, Nika. I heard them. About how we're at last going to understand what it's like to suffer like they've suffered."

"We have to get rid of this shit," I said. "*Now.* There's not going to be time to get home to tell of it." I saw in Kaja's expression that she agreed. "Can it be done?"

Kaja hesitated. "There's no chance we can safely dispose of

substances like these," she said, sounding a bit choked up. "Do you remember how, in history, we were taught about treaties on chemical weapons? Back then, when governments agreed to destroy them— well, they needed the right people, the right equipment, the right *everything*. We've got us and what's on our persons."

"What do we do?"

Kaja fidgeted with the strap of my satchel. "That's why I wanted you to see, Nika," she said slowly. "To understand how big this is. You always say Nana's words, you know. As regards the women in our family. If you—I mean, one of us—"

Whatever Kaja had been about to say was interrupted by the lights coming on, sudden and blinding. My vision went momentarily white. Large arms pinned Kaja. My rifle was ripped from her back; my satchel from her middle. And, for the second time, I felt the barrel of a gun against my skin. This time, a pistol against my forehead.

Parson Prince stood at the door. A gang of armed faithful surrounded him. He smiled, his mouth wet and jittery, as one of his followers handed him my rifle.

"The sisters Zawisza," the parson said. At Kaja's startled expression, he continued, "You believed I'd be stupid enough to let you wander unwatched around Feversham? I wouldn't suspect a little girl who claimed she'd taken down Nika Zawisza?" He took a step forward. "I wouldn't recognize your bitch sister the second I saw her?"

"Fuck you," I said pleasantly.

The parson's gaze shifted to me. He was still smiling. I wanted nothing more in the world than to bash his filthy teeth in. "You've found the stash, I see. I imagine Kaja's filled you in on what's going to happen to the shithole of a settlement you come from."

He snapped a finger, prompting his followers to seize Kaja and me.

We were dragged several corridors down and thrown into a room even tinier than the one we'd been in, bare except for a few rotting

wooden crates. I scrambled up, but Kaja sat where she'd been flung, her head bent and her knees drawn up to her chest.

"Now, Sister Kaja," Parson Prince said, "you might find that *this* room won't be broke out of with a hairpin."

Kaja stared at the floor.

"Not feeling up to a chat, eh? All right. I bet you told your sister she's scheduled to die in the morning. I'm willing to reconsider that, if that's what you'd like. One of you'll be executed tomorrow, and one of you can hang on until the day after." He turned around. Over his shoulder, he said, "Ladies' choice."

AFTER THE PARSON LEFT, KAJA remained curled up and silent, her forehead resting on her knees. Her hair had come undone, falling like a veil around her. But she didn't look upset. She looked like she was *thinking*.

I spent a good hour checking the reinforced door and banging around the corners of the room. There was indeed no escape. Parson Prince had put a stone-faced guard out front; he opened the door once to show me he had a gun.

Finally, I slumped next to Kaja. I was good at getting out of tough situations, but this was different. This was *bad. The women in our family die young*, I told myself, and the time had come for Kaja and me.

I'd forever held in my heart the notion that I'd meet my death at the hands of the faithful. Just like Aunt P, just like Nana, both of whom had left the world alone, and in violence. I'd once thought there was an elegance to that: better to bow out with howl rather than a whisper. But now, with death nigh, it didn't seem elegant. It seemed small and meaningless.

Exhausted, I leaned against a crate, nestling my head on the crook of my arm. That was when I felt the faintest of sparrow flutters, deep within me. I wouldn't have noticed it if I hadn't been still.

The baby was something I constantly forgot about—or, if I'm to be honest, something I'd decided not to remember—but there, in that cramped and fearful place, it had decided to remind me.

I must have made a surprised sound, because Kaja's head perked up. "Nika? What's wrong?"

"Nothing."

Kaja's eyes narrowed. "Nika."

"It's not important."

She exhaled. "You're pregnant, aren't you?"

I sat up straight. "How'd you know?"

"Goddamn." Kaja pinched the bridge of her nose, as though she'd got a sudden headache. "You would be, of course. I was telling myself you weren't, that I was imagining things. You fucking *would* be." She sounded resigned. "How do I know? The throwing up, the not eating. The fact that you've sprouted a gut."

"I didn't want to tell you."

"You haven't told *anyone*," Kaja said. "I can't believe you. Going on like nothing's changed. You shouldn't be ranging. You shouldn't be *here*. You should be getting proper care in New Creemore. God, you got in that fight—"

"I'm pregnant, not feeble."

For an aching moment, she just stared at me. Then, her voice cracking, she said, "Oh, fuck you, Nika. That's not the point and you know it."

"Kaja—"

"Do you even know that my last baby was born alive? She was too tiny, but she breathed, my last one. Little nothing breaths like death rattling around in her, and then *nothing* at all. She didn't open her eyes. And here you are—out here—not even *caring* when I had my poor baby what never got to open her eyes."

"Kaja—"

"And, Nika, you weren't there when it happened. You weren't

there. You got back from ranging. I was walking with a cane; you didn't even ask about it."

"Oh, Kaja—" I reached for her, but she pushed my fingers away so furiously I was surprised none of them snapped.

"Don't you dare," Kaja said. She was crying now, but not noisily. Her tears were so under control that I wondered how often she'd cried them. "Sometimes I can't stand you. You're Mam's favorite. You're *everyone's* favorite. You're the goddamn scion, and I'm the just the little sister. The afterthought."

"That's not right."

She dropped her forehead back on her knees. "Don't pretend it's not."

Though I itched to hug her, I let her be for a long time. I couldn't recall ever having felt so guilty. As kids, we'd been close, Kaja and me. I couldn't say when things had broken apart between us. It hadn't been sudden; it was more like the listless way land changes over time, and you don't notice until one day you pay attention and it looks altogether like unfamiliar terrain. I yearned to pull time back, to restitch it, to pull Kaja through her grief. I pictured her at eight, ten, twelve: cheerful, relentless, full to the brim. Then I'd become a ranger; then I'd left her behind.

"Kaja," I said finally. "I'm sorry. I should have been there. For your baby—and for a thousand other times. I'm so, so sorry. I didn't *think*."

"I know you didn't," Kaja said.

"Sometimes I'm envious of you," I added. I knew my words, though true, would ring hollow to her, but I had to tell her something. "How bright you are. How you can just read something and remember it and *use* it. That's nothing I could ever do."

Another silence stretched between us, then, in a tired tone, Kaja said, "You're going first."

"Hm?"

"Tomorrow," she clarified. "When the parson comes back."

Oh. She meant I was going to die first. I should have been suspicious, then, but so keen was my regret that whatever few precious hours of life we had left to divvy up between us, I wanted Kaja to have them. "If that's what you want," I said.

She didn't respond. I draped an arm around her shoulders—this time, she didn't push me away—and guided the both of us to lay down on the ground. Her eyes shining with tears, she turned around and snuggled against me. It reminded me of when we were kids, when we shared a pile of threadbare blankets between us.

"Kaja," I whispered. "I know we haven't talked proper, not in a long time. If I'm going to leave the world tomorrow, I'd prefer to leave it without you hating me."

I felt her smile against my collarbone. "I don't hate you, Nika," she said. "You're a pain in my ass, but I don't hate you. I couldn't ever."

EVEN THOUGH I WAS BONE-TIRED, I figured that if I was going to die, I was going to use my last hours. Kaja and I talked through the night. She told me things like how when she'd first started apprenticing with Alvaro she'd screwed up a solution and turned her hands orange for a month; he'd nearly fired her then, but now it was a joke between them. Or how she had to go to the library at night because the librarian who worked mornings forever hated her for accidentally tearing a page in a schoolbook. Or how she missed Aunt P, too, but for different reasons; in quiet moments away from me and Mam, unknown to me, Aunt P had taught Kaja to draw and sew and make jam. A hundred tiny things, the sum of which made up the Kaja I hadn't bothered to learn.

As promised, Parson Prince arrived in the morning. By then both of us were falling asleep. The door clanged open against the wall, and, startled, I disentangled myself from Kaja and sat up, while Kaja groaned and opened her eyes.

"Morning!" the parson greeted. He held up a pair of manacles. Behind him were, again, his armed followers. "Well, sisters, have we decided?"

I rose and stood between him and Kaja. Immediately, a dozen guns were pointed at me. The faint hope I'd had that I'd be able to punch my way through disappeared. I'd have been riddled with bullets in seconds if I'd tried.

"Call off your hounds," I said to Parson Prince. "We *have* decided." I held out my hands, wrists up. "Go ahead, you unhinged shit. Restrain me."

For the first time, the parson's mouth formed into a pout. He'd obviously expected Kaja and I to fight. He glanced at Kaja, who had got up, too, and said, "Say your farewells, then."

I turned around and embraced Kaja.

"Love you, Nika," she said.

"Love you." The words were heavy in my throat.

Then Kaja tilted her head back and smiled up at me. Her smile was so sad and so *knowing* that I got confused. In the second before the parson's followers ripped me away from her, she shifted my hand from beneath her shoulders to just above her belt. I felt something there: small and hard and familiar.

"When you can, Nika, *run*," Kaja murmured, softly, so only I could hear.

My lighter fluid, I realized. *My matches.* She had to have retrieved the little pack from my satchel before the faithful confiscated it. She'd kept it on her the entire night and she hadn't said a thing about it.

No, I mouthed, but by then it was too late. "No," I said out loud, as I was manacled, as the door slammed closed. "No!" I shouted. "No! Kaja! Goddamn it, no!"

Parson Prince got the spectacle he wanted. He laughed as his followers crowded me and marching me up the stairs of the central research station. I became a wild thing. I flailed against the faithful.

But a hand clamped over my collarbone, a pair of arms encircled my ankles, a blindfold was forced over my eyes. Something that tasted like cotton dipped in mud was jammed into my mouth.

Kaja'd had a plan. She had to have known I wouldn't have gone along with it, if I'd known. A helpless anger surged within me. She hadn't given me a choice. *I wouldn't have let her*, I thought. *I wouldn't have let her.*

She'd taken my fate from me, and I couldn't stop it, I couldn't demand to go back, I couldn't give her up. I could only try to buy her time.

So I struggled so hard that the faithful had to carry me outside and to the gates like they were hauling an enraged log. I was dropped four times, and each time I fell I managed to kick several of them. I even spit out the wad in my mouth to bite a leg. But there was only one of me, and so I was forced up on Parson Prince's platform. My blindfold was torn away, leaving me shackled and standing. The pile of bodies hadn't been cleaned up. There were more faithful than there had been yesterday, or perhaps they looked different because I was facing them: a sea of mad and hungry faces raring for my blood.

Parson Prince climbed up beside me. He put on a show, giving a sweeping bow as he brought out his knife. He opened his mouth to announce my name, but he got out only "Ni—" before an alarm sounded, loud like a scream, from within Feversham's walls.

The parson looked back. So did most of faithful guarding the platform. I took my chance. *Kaja*, I thought, as I rammed my body full-force into the parson's. *Kaja*, I thought, as I drove a knee into his back. *Kaja*, I thought, as I brought the chain between my hands around his throat and pulled up as hard as I could. "Kaja!" I screamed, as his head turned and clunked against platform and the life vanished from his eyes.

Everything went to shit. Some faithful did come after me, but I was possessed of such a rage that none of them managed to keep hold

of me, and they were distracted by Feversham fast growing engulfed in smoke. I was shot at, but I couldn't be sure from where: all I felt was a bullet entering my thigh and another grazing my shoulder.

I ran toward the gates, toward Kaja, for a few frantic seconds. The smoke assaulted me. It smelled sour, not like smoke from a normal fire, and the memory of the neat cabinets of biochem agents Kaja had shown me flared up. Within the gates, people had fallen to the ground, their limbs spasming.

Kaja hadn't a chance. She was gone. The fire spread, black columns of smoke spiraled high into the sky, and I did what hundreds of faithful were doing. I did as Kaja told.

I *ran*.

I HAVEN'T GOT MUCH MEMORY of how I got back to New Creemore. It's a wonder I didn't die. Driven more by instinct than intent, I stumbled home in forty-eight hours, still manacled, coughing and bleeding and sleepless and starving. I got to Nana's and Aunt P's graves and collapsed before them.

That was where Mam found me.

I didn't cry over Kaja then. Nor did I cry when I was carried home and fed and put to bed. Or, hours later, when I woke to find Mam and the mayor and, while the medic extracted a festering bullet from my leg, had to explain to them that Kaja had burned down Feversham Station, that Kaja had saved everyone.

I didn't cry in the days that followed. Numbness had a chokehold on me. I thought again and again of how Kaja's last moments might've gone. Had her kind heart grieved what she'd been about to do to the faithful? Had she been afraid? Had the parson's guard found her; had he tried to stop her; had he hurt her before the fire consumed them? Hundreds of possibilities, none of them peaceful.

I didn't cry when I confessed to Mam about the baby, though Mam cried. I wanted to go back to Feversham, to see if I could find

anything of Kaja, and I swore at Mam and Aunt C when they told me I wasn't in any condition to. Aunt C went instead, and reported back that Feversham was rubble.

Aunt C brought back a fragile bundle of ashes. They couldn't have been Kaja—it was probable they were a mix of Feversham and dead faithful—yet we buried it next to Nana and Aunt P. Mam asked me did I want to say anything. I shook my head, and stayed stony, and afterwards I felt more like a coward than I ever had.

The power was out for three months before New Creemore got connected to another facility to the south. Lining up for hot water, I heard one of the Pollock girls complain that the power being out was the fault of *that Kaja Zawisza*, and though I was seven months pregnant, I clocked her in the jaw so hard her teeth rattled.

Shortly after that, Mam and I had to go to Kaja's rooms to clear them out. Mam did most of it, since I was more waddling than walking then, but I packed up Kaja's books and swept her floor and folded her clothes. In her closets, I found dozens of items she'd sewn. A few were in Kaja's size, but most were tiny, warm, sturdy. Clothes for children. Many I recognized as having been made from things I'd brought to Kaja: a pair of trousers made from a red denim jacket I'd taken from a faithful, a collared dress made from a dusty ream of green velvet I'd found in the ruins of a store.

I didn't cry over Kaja, not until I imagined her lonely hands making all those things.

My baby was born in the winter. A girl, like me, born red-faced, black-haired and squalling. Mam and Aunt C proclaimed her a true Zawisza.

Of course, I named her *Kaja*.

I hope she grows old.

HARRIET TUBMAN

SCAPING FROM SLAVERY IN THE 1800s southern United
States was considered nothing short of miraculous. Slavery
was considered a business investment; the livelihoods
of plantation owners—and some would argue the very way of
antebellum Southern life—depended on it. Slaves were guarded
closely to protect against their loss. If a slave escaped, but then was
captured, they were often used as examples to show other slaves
what would happen to them should they try to escape. They were
subjected to horrific punishments and deaths.

Harriet Tubman was born into slavery in Maryland around
1820. When she was a teenager, her master threw a heavy object
and hit Tubman in the head. She suffered a traumatic head injury
as a result, which gave her spells of hallucinations, dizziness, and
vivid dreams throughout her life. Nevertheless, in 1849, Tubman
managed the all but impossible task of escaping from her master in
Maryland and fled to Philadelphia.

Most slaves who ran considered themselves supremely lucky
to survive and stayed in the safety of the North. And who could
blame them? They were fortunate enough to survive a first escape.

To return South for any reason would have been equal to a suicide mission. Yet that is exactly what Harriet Tubman did.

She returned to Maryland to help free her family. Then she went back to free other slaves, one small group at a time, over about thirteen missions. Every time she returned South, she carried the same risk as she did escaping for the first time. Yet every time, she escaped again, leading more and more slaves to their freedom, and even helping them find work once they reached their destinations.

During the Civil War, Tubman joined the Union Army as a scout and spy, and was the first woman to lead an armed expedition in the war. She guided a raid that freed more than seven hundred slaves.

Even after the war, into old age, Tubman never stopped fighting for freedom and equality, and was a strong voice for the women's suffrage movement.

Further Reading:

http://www.harriet-tubman.org

Harriet Tubman: The Road to Freedom by Catherine Clinton

CASTING ON

PHILIPPA BALLANTINE

ELLEN FOUND THE BODY.

Or, rather, it was her toe that found his leg sprawled out between the bookshelves. She windmilled her arms, trying to keep from tumbling over. At her age, an unexpected fall came with its own set of risks that she'd rather not encounter. Still, she looked better than he did.

The other women of the Doumount knitting circle quickly rushed to her aid. Catelyn and Sophie heard her gasp, and both being younger, got there first. Rose and Molly followed at a slower pace, clutching each other as they peered down the aisle with startled eyes.

Ellen was hardly surprised to see Rose's glasses were in danger of slipping off her nose, and Molly's wig off her head. It didn't take much to undo them these days—not that she was much of an improvement.

Still, the young man was worth getting in a fluster about, even in Ellen's jaded opinion. His dark hair was wildly tousled, but as he was face down, it was hard to judge much else about him. He was sprawled under one of the poorly patched sections of the library roof where the bombardment last summer had struck. Sometimes water would leak in, but so far, no young men had.

She heard Rose draw her breath in over her teeth. They all had

Illustration by M. WAYNE MILLER

lost men in the war, but she was the only one who still had two sons who had not been listed as Missing or Killed in Action. The dead man was not Tommy or Jeremy though; they both had bright blonde heads.

"Who is it?" Molly said, being so short she had to push to see past her friends.

"A young man, but a stranger," Rose whispered in a tone that might be used when finding a bomb, even though she was stating the obvious.

The women all shared a glance that combined equal measures of hope and terror. Ellen, despite her aching bones, was the first to reach down and check if he was alive. As a young woman, she'd been a nurse in the last war, and she tried to recall her training while searching for a pulse. It fluttered against her fingertips, but she couldn't decide if she should be happy about that or not.

"He's alive," she pronounced, "but he is most definitely shot." Pulling up his jacket and shirt, she found a bullet had punctured his belly.

Catelyn pressed a hand to her lips, as her words came bubbling out. "That's not our side's uniform."

In the flickering light of the single oil lamp suspended above them, that much was apparent. The Glorious Commander's troops wore a smart tan uniform with dark brown belts and epaulets—or at least they had in the early days of the war. The man currently laid out in their little library wore what had once been pale blue cloak but was now tattered and covered in soot. That could only mean one thing.

"A magician, then," Molly said, leaning on one of the shelves and adjusting her wig. Back in the days before the war, her friend had many fine wigs, but the one currently nesting on her head was almost as threadbare as the rug their circle set their chairs on.

"Well we can't just leave him lying here," Rose said, and she

had to be thinking of her own boys, even if this man was from the other side. The women stared at each other. Ellen didn't have to say it. They all knew the price for harboring an enemy combatant, let alone a magician.

Despite his injuries, the man might overhear them, so Ellen jerked her head and led them back to the circle of chairs and their abandoned work. The windows were covered with newspaper, but one had peeled away at the corner so that the night sky twinkled at them. Though there was no moon tonight, they had dared three small oil lamps to light their covert knitting.

"What do we do?" Sophie pushed her curly dark hair out of her eyes, and looked around to the other women. The young woman said little, but concern was etched in her face. For a brief second, Ellen wished she was a hugger. Yet if she did it now all her friends would know how truly awful the situation was.

Already Catelyn was rubbing the purple scarf she was working on between her fingers. They all shared who their secret projects were for, and Catelyn's was for her daughter Joanne who had been taken by soldiers in the spring.

All of the knitters had stolen tiny scraps of wool from the Doumount mill they worked in during the day. They all knew the price of stealing from the war effort was flogging, but they still did it. Ellen was proud of all of them, for keeping the secret and the circle together.

Most of them were making scarves, but Sophie made socks. Her husband might have been gobbled up by the war, but she had two young children to feed and keep warm.

Rose adjusted her glasses and glanced over her shoulder. "Well… what would they do…if they found him here?"

Ellen took a ragged breath and glanced around at the tiny library. Once it had been the center of Doumount, but now its roof was near to falling in, and its books out of order, damaged or lost. Molly had

been the village librarian back in its heyday, but those times seemed as far away as a myth. She'd been stronger back then, healthier too. However, as it stood a little apart from the main square, it had been spared the majority of the deadly bombing raids.

Now, it was a tiny pool of relative normalcy for the five of them, since no one else really came into the library anymore. People had far graver things to deal with. No one wanted to read about things they could not have. Instead of reading, the women knitted, and talked in low voices, and tried to pretend none of the horrors of the recent war had happened.

Catelyn cleared her throat. "We all know what they would do: burn the place down with him and us in it."

It would have felt like a threat only a year ago, Ellen realized, but at this point in the war it didn't seem too terrible of a thing. Each of the five of them had seen worse.

Ellen's throat tightened. Perhaps she presumed too much. Sophie had her two young children, Catelyn still had hope of seeing her daughter again, and even Rose and Molly had each other. Maybe she was the only one without anything to care about.

Rose gave a shrug of her narrow shoulders. "I never understood why we had to have another war with Mensognes. You know, when I was a little girl, they never bothered with us. Sometimes I would climb the oak in the village square and I could see—"

"Don't get lost in the past," Molly said, her eyes darting to Rose with a hint of sharpness. "We have the here and now to deal with and that is plenty!"

As if on cue, from back in the shelves the young man let out a groan. Ellen and all the other knitters sat taller in their chairs, and all conversation ceased for a long moment.

"That's it then," Molly said, her fingers tightening on the back of her chair, "we can't just leave him there all by himself, magician or not."

Molly, as per usual, had a point. The young man was not going to go away, either as a patient or a corpse. They had to deal with him.

That was indeed it. Ellen let out a sigh, hustled back to the shelves, and got down on her knees—some feat for a woman of her age. She could feel more of her old nursing habits kicking back in as she examined him more thoroughly. "Yes, there we are, a bullet to the abdomen." She felt around some more, and found the exit wound. When she withdrew her hands, they were covered in his blood, but these women had ceased to be shocked by anything. "I won't know how bad it is until we get him to my house," she told them.

"Your house..." Sophie spoke, her gaze leaping up from the floor where it usually resided to collide with Ellen's. "Isn't that... dangerous?"

She had the good grace to blush as she said those words, and then she waved her hands in front of her face. "Forget I said it—of course it is. Everything is."

"I'm too old to care," Ellen said standing up, and rubbing the blood off her hands and onto her once fine skirt, "but I shouldn't speak for you, Sophie...Catelyn..."

The younger women glanced at each other, but Ellen knew it was Sophie who had the most to lose. Catelyn's Joanna was not in the house, her husband was in the army somewhere, but Sophie was an entirely different story. She had two young children to protect.

Her chin tilted up, and her green eyes regained—even if it was for just an instant—a portion of their old sparkle. In reply, she strode over to one of the collapsed shelves. It was covered in a few bricks and torn up books, but she soon shook the shelf loose.

"He's thin. We can carry him on this," she said. "Give me a hand, Catelyn."

The two younger women maneuvered the make-shift stretcher over to the young man, and with some awkward shuffling managed to lie it just above his head.

Ellen pressed Rose into holding the bandages tight over his wound, as the other four pulled him as gently as they could manage onto the stretcher. Despite all that, he let out a strangled scream and jerked in their hold. They might not know his name, but Ellen was sure all of them had the same reaction; he could have been one of their loved ones.

The women and their village had suffered a great deal—little food, military stationed down the road, long hours at the mill, and a series of bombardments from the airships of the resistance—but they had never seen the full extent of the war. Ellen had lost her whole family, sons and grandsons, and while the rest of the circle had suffered the same, they had never seen the direct results of it on a young man before.

However, one thing still remained close to their minds. Before they set off, Rose tidied up their knitting bags, stuffing them under a loose board beneath the window. It would not do to save the magician only to be caught for wool theft.

They hoisted the patient carefully up between them and set off.

Luckily, it was windy outside, so the noise covered their scuttle from the library to Ellen's home. The residents of the village were under blackout conditions, but it wasn't as if they had much oil to burn in the lamps anyway. Most people had given up taking any notice of their neighbors' activities.

Catelyn and Sophie took front and back. Rose and Ellen trotted as best they could on each side of the patient, while Molly went ahead to open the door to Ellen's home.

Fortunately, it was the closest home to the library. Once it had been a beautiful white stone building, bursting with flowers in the front garden, but the war had taken a toll on it, too. The time for flowers had long passed, leaving only the time for weeds.

The white stone was reduced to a smeared gray color that was a result of the clouds of soot that emanated from the machines of

war. Ellen, despite herself, always flinched when she approached her own home. She'd once been so house-proud; even her own sons had been afraid to come in with muddy boots. Now, she would have gladly let them enter, in whatever state they were.

She flinched. That wound was too fresh—she had to concentrate on the one in front of her.

Finally, they managed to get the man into the house, and Molly closed the door tightly before pulling the thin curtains shut. Sophia and Catelyn laid the patient on the table. Though the outside was wrecked by the war, the inside of Ellen's house was immaculate. She scrubbed the table, now marked by blood, with sand every morning, but it mattered little today.

"Help me cut his shirt off," she demanded of no one in particular.

Sophie found the fabric shears and quickly did as demanded. All of the women—except seasoned Ellen—let out a gasp.

It was not the amount of blood that shocked them—there had been plenty of that around over the years, but the faint green glow emanating from his body. It had the appearance of mist.

"What is *that?*" Catelyn asked, leaning forward.

It was Molly that pushed her back. "Aether," she replied, her face folding in disgust. "They use it in all the weapons meant for the magicians these days."

"Terrible stuff," Ellen said. She had already pulled out her nursing bag from under the sink. "I have a tin of activated charcoal that should fix that. Stole it last year from the factory for Molly's stomach problems. Now let me have some room, please."

They took the hint. Pulling their knitting from its hiding spot, Catelyn, Molly, and Rose settled around the hearth. Sophie stoked the fire against the wintery chill, but stayed nearby Ellen to offer help. The normalcy of the click of their needles and their low conversation steadied the former-nurse's hand. Something she was honestly worried about.

The firelight and a lone tiny oil lamp was all she had to work by. All the while she mumbled under her breath. It was a remarkably clean wound that seemed to have, by some miracle, missed his organs.

Ellen cleaned the wound, stitched him back up, and then eased herself upright. Letting out a long, pained sigh, she went to scrub her hands in the sink. When she turned around, wiping her palms on her apron, she couldn't help the tiny smile on her lips.

"I think we've stolen one back from the god of death, ladies."

Though there were no great cheers, the women of the circle looked up from their work and smiled. For a moment, Ellen felt a tiny glimmer of hope—an odd sensation that hadn't touched her in years.

Then, Molly spoke up. "Well, that's all well and fine...but what now? The constabulary will know they brought one down, and sure as eggs, they'll be looking for him."

It wasn't that they were afraid of death—they had all been in dangerous situations before—it was just there were more terrible things than that.

"It's the whole village that is in danger too," Rose said, carefully taking off her glasses and cleaning them on her sleeve. "If they knew we had concealed him, it would be one thing, but now we've healed him..."

Sophie pushed the young man's hair back from his eyes. "Are you saying we should hand him over?"

Rose sat up taller and glared at her young friend. "Most certainly not! I am just making sure we are all well aware of what we are risking."

They nodded at each other, slowly, thoughtfully.

"Well then we shall have to make sure we don't get caught." Molly got up from her chair and went over to examine the man. "He's got youth on his side. How long before he's fit to walk, Ellen?"

She considered the question. "A few days at the very least, but where is he supposed to walk *to* exactly?"

"One problem at a time," Molly snapped. "Now, how about we share the hiding of him?"

"All except Sophie," Catelyn broke in. "She can't possibly..."

"I can and I will." Sophie's voice cracked like a whip in the confines of the room. "There is no point pretending that if one of us is caught the rest won't be as well. Everyone knows we are friends."

She glared around her, locking eyes with each of the others. "Besides," she went on, "my house has a nice false floor. Remember my Da was a sly grogger back in the day."

They all blinked that, but it was Rose who laughed first. "That I do, best damn gin in the county." Behind her glasses her eyes grew a little damp with the remembrance, too.

"Not yet though," Ellen warned, "I want to keep an eye on him for the next day or two. I might not have a false floor, but I do have a root cellar."

Morning was breaking over the village, its sly fingers working their way through the threadbare curtain to remind them all this whole situation was a reality.

Ellen could see that they were all transfixed with the revelation, so she got to her feet. "Well, I don't think I can move him myself."

They got the hint. Together they managed to maneuver the young man on his makeshift stretcher down the stairs and into Ellen's root cellar. She had some old potato crates in there—even if they only held the memory of potatoes—and they moved those to conceal him at least from the casual gaze from the top of the stairs.

Then the women dispersed to their houses. Ellen watched them from her window. Catelyn entered her place directly opposite, Sophie disappeared next door, and Rose and Molly ambled arm-in-arm down the street. They were careful not to do anything to expose the nature of their relationship, but Ellen had seen it when they were teenagers. Through Rose's marriage, and Molly's sickness, it had not gone away. Their houses further down the road actually leaned

against each other now, mirroring their love for each other.

It was none of Ellen's business, she had decided long ago, and if two lonely, old women could find a little happiness in this broken world, then that was somehow cheering.

Usually all of the women would have been working at the mill, but with the wool shortage, their days had been cut. It wasn't as if The Glorious Commander paid them much anyway, or that there was much to buy. Still, it had given them structure to the day.

Now, Ellen was glad of it. She levered herself upstairs to her tiny bedroom, and pulling a blanket over herself, tried to get some sleep.

Only a few hours passed before she awoke again, and though Ellen tried to get back to sleep, it eluded her. Then, the banging on the door brought her fully alert.

That was also something else new; she had barred it. Throughout the war, she had defiantly left it unlocked, perhaps hoping some desperate villager might finish her off, but last night had been different. Last night had reminded her she was still alive.

And now someone was banging on it.

It took two tries for her to get up, but once she was moving she felt a little better. Her hip was sore, but she ignored it as she stumbled down the stairs.

A quick peek out her window ascertained that her fears were real. She caught a glimpse of a tan uniform.

Taking a deep breath, she almost opened the door, but then realized there was blood on the table she had not cleared from the night before. She took a moment to wipe it down, even as the banging persisted.

When she was done, Ellen opened the door with her back bent at an angle it was not used to. It didn't hurt to look even more decrepit than usual after all.

Easing the door open, she peered out and saw Mercier, Commandant of Doumount, standing on her top step. Ellen's heart sunk

a little. She'd been hoping for one of his minions, but obviously a downed magician warranted more seniority. Mercier cut a striking figure, his gleaming black hair slicked back, his square jaw clenched, and every one of the brass buttons on his tan uniform polished to high sheen.

Everything Commandant Mercier did and said was designed to show how important he was. Ellen's lips twisted. He was not fooling her. She'd chased him down the street when he was only five years old for stealing flowers from her garden. Now, she wished she'd caught him and given him a sound thrashing. At this moment, he looked ready to do much worse to her.

"*Jai* Vinceni," he said spinning around on his heel. The honorific came out forced and twisted from his lips, and Ellen's heart began to race. Formality from him was not a good thing.

She bobbed her head in response. "*Jar* Commandant, a pleasure to see you." She hoped he remembered the incident with the flowers, but either way she would not give him any information, as innocent as it might seem. Who knew who he had been talking to.

Behind him, two of his soldiers kept their rifles at their sides, but that could change at any moment. The commandant gestured up the road with his leather clad hand. "Last night there were reports of a possible enemy spy in the area. Did you see anything from your vantage point here?"

A spy—so that was how they were going to play it. Ellen gave a slight shrug and adjusted the shawl around her shoulders. "I don't see much at all these days." It was hard to keep the anger out of her voice.

He had been a mean child, and he had grown into a cruel man. He'd strung up two boys in the village square only a month ago for the crime of selling their own wool to support their families. Supposedly, the owners were allowed to sell some in order to make a living, but in reality, the country wanted it all. Mercier had trumped up charges against the lads, executed them, and driven their fami-

lies off their farms. The flocks of sheep had been absorbed into the patriotic effort. That happened to a lot of things.

If he knew that the women were knitting for their families, they would be lucky to be flogged. It was a good thing her needles and work were hidden in the library.

"Well, we are searching all the houses." The commandant stepped back and the soldiers pushed Ellen aside without any warning at all. She nearly fell but managed to catch herself against the doorframe. She felt lightheaded and positive this was it. This was how her life was going to end.

They were going to find the magician, and Mercier would think up some truly dreadful thing to do to the circle. It was not for herself Ellen felt the cold clamp of fear on her throat, but rather for Catelyn and Sophie who still had living to do.

To calm herself while the soldiers tramped around her cottage, Ellen took out her embroidering which she kept near the window. Fabric was also hard to come by, but not illegal. She had washed and beaten and scrubbed one her old flour sacks until it was quite soft. It was only a little thing, but it would make a nice dress for Sophie's youngest—if she was alive to finish it.

The cottage creaked and groaned as the men turned over her bedroom upstairs. Ellen tried to block it out by sitting on her stool by the door and working on the dress. She had already stitched a series of wild roses in pink around the collar, but she set to picking out some bluebells to go with them. The fine needlework was a challenge with her eyesight, but if she kept the fabric right near her nose she could manage. While she drew the thread, the thumping and gruff comments intruding into her house died away. A small hum grew in her throat. It was a song her mother had sung to her as a child, and even if she could no longer remember the words, the rhythm gave her comfort.

For a long while there was only the fabric and the moving needle.

Soon enough, they would find the magician in her root cellar and then such small delights would be snatched away.

Except they weren't.

"*Jai* Vinceni," Mercier broke her concentration by standing directly in her light. "You be sure and tell us if you see anything. We'll be checking on your neighbors now."

And with that they trumped out, slamming the door behind them. Perhaps they were as disappointed as she was surprised.

Ellen carefully finished the flower she had been working on, and then put down the fabric. The breath she drew in after that felt as sweet as any from her youth.

"But how..." She shook her head, mystified by what had happened. Getting to her feet, Ellen went to the root cellar. It took her far too long to get down there, but a tumble would serve no one. She hated being cautious as well as puzzled, but she made it to the bottom and lit the oil lamp.

There he was. The young magician was visible even to one with poor eyesight like herself. The boxes did a poor job of hiding him, so how had two perfectly healthy soldiers missed him?

A frown added to the creases on her face as Ellen checked on her houseguest. His color had improved, and his breathing had a good pace. A peek under the bandages showed no sign of inflammation.

She patted his hand. "You are a lucky young man, and I am a lucky old lady...somehow."

Her elation eventually died down, and she was able to sleep through the day, because that night the circle met in the library. Even the fear of discovery did not put them off their regular schedule.

"They turned over my house and didn't find him," Ellen explained to them. "I didn't think at my age I could be surprised by anything, but there you are."

The women kept knitting, the sound of their needles curiously comforting in the half light.

"My house is next," Sophie said quietly. "The soldiers already turned it over, so it should be safe. The children will be asleep, if we want to take him up to the attic tonight."

Rose grunted a little. "Damn, dropped a stitch."

They all tutted comfortingly at her, and nodded at Sophie's suggestion. Ellen didn't like it, but all of them wanted to share in the danger, and it wasn't like she could berate them into doing what she wanted. She had tried that with her own children, and all it had done was get them out of the door and into the war faster.

Once her fingers tired, she got to her feet. "Let's do it then."

They all packed up their needles and projects, hid them under the floorboards once again, and trouped back to her cottage. Sophie and Catelyn went with her down into the root cellar to see the young man.

"No sign of aether contamination," Ellen told them, and a surprised smile formed on her lips. "The joy of being young and healthy. Enjoy it while you can, ladies."

"I miss bouncing back like that," Rose muttered from the top of the stairs.

"We all do," Molly said with a snort. "I might not have lost my hair if the sickness had hit me then."

The two youngest managed to get him back upstairs, and Ellen climbed up after. Barely had they put the stretcher down when the wail of the air-raid siren went off. It had been a while since any of them had heard it, but they moved quickly into action. Sophie darted out the door. "I'll bring the children," she shouted over the howl of the siren.

"Back into the root cellar then," Ellen barked, though she immediately realized, with only Catelyn left, they'd have no hope of moving him back.

If only the damn thing had sounded a fraction earlier, she thought, as the four remaining women stood stock still in her kitchen.

Just when the young man lurched upright was hard to say. Ellen glanced down and locked gazes with her tousled-haired patient. He was handsome she realized, in a long, lanky way, but he looked so confused she wondered if his head was muddled.

"Wonderful timing," Rose yelled, and with a jerk of her head to Catelyn, she slipped her arm under his.

Thus, with Catelyn on one side, the elder woman on the other, and the man keeping his feet under him, they struggled down the steps. Perhaps the howls of the sirens were mere precautions, perhaps it was another of the commandant's damn tests.

When the screams of the munitions rose above the klaxon though, it seemed she was going to be disappointed in this world once again.

The detonations shook the cellar, and the women all crowded together for protection and comfort. They didn't leave the young man out either. He was stuck in the middle of them, wide-eyed and confused. Ellen hoped he wouldn't end up dying in ignorance.

At first, the impacts sounded a long way off, somewhere in the hills outside of Doumount. Sophie burst into the cellar just as they began to shake their way closer. She had her baby on her hip, and a terrified Julia clutching her hand.

Ellen opened her arms, and the child ran to her. Only five years old, she had never known a world outside of the war, and that thought haunted the old woman most of all. Her babies might be dead—daughter, sons, and grandsons—but at least they'd had that.

Julia buried her head against Ellen's side, while Sophie crowded in with her son, Corwin, clutched to her breast.

The explosions were now so loud and so close that her little cottage seemed ready to shake apart. Surely, there was only so much thatch and stone could take. The air filled with the taste of dust and charcoal, and that was when Ellen found that she didn't want to die. Odd, since she had cared so little about it that very morning.

She mulled it over as pebbles dropped on their heads, and the tiny lamp-flame flickered backwards and forwards.

Perhaps it was the pointlessness of being killed in a barrage, as compared to standing up to the commandant. Perhaps it was because she had found a new purpose. Or maybe it was because she hated that damn klaxon.

If it wasn't so loud, she might have enjoyed the sensation of being hugged tight, of feeling Julia's solid little body pressed against her side, of having everyone she still cared for in one room.

If she had kept her faith in the gods, she might have prayed, but that had died with the last of her children. Instead, she held on tight, and hoped it would be quick.

The barrage stopped as suddenly as it had begun. The last explosion echoed through the valley like a sullen giant forced to go home. And then all was quiet.

Julia looked up at her, her eyes wide, but a slight smile forming on her lips. What a world it was where the end of a military bombardment could make a child smile. She should smile for much better things than that.

Slowly, the women untangled themselves, but Ellen felt the sense of regret each of them had in doing so. Rose and Molly might have each other, but for the rest of them, hugs were in short supply.

"What was that?" the young man's voice abruptly reminded them that they were not completely safe.

"What do you mean," Ellen snapped. "Those were Mensognes's bombs."

He raked his hair back from his face, and winced in pain as he stepped from their embrace. "Begging your pardon, ma'am, but Ulluran does not use machines at all." At their blank expressions, he cleared his throat. "I know you call my country Mensognes, but that is not what we call ourselves."

Catelyn leaned down and peered into his face.

He looked around at all of them, obviously confused and also a little frightened. "I mean we do not make bombs. We only have magic to protect us from the Corrupt Commander's guns. We have been fighting for years to keep the invasion from happening..."

"Invasion," Molly straightened herself upright, and gave voice to the general confusion. "You have been trying to invade us..."

Their patient only shook his head mutely. Ellen could feel the understanding rising around her. Maybe the bombardment had shaken something loose, or maybe she'd suspected something all along. They had all been part of a war machine against an enemy none of them really knew. A machine of deception to keep the population under the thumb of someone far worse than Pareiz's neighboring country.

Ellen let out a long sigh, seeing the same understanding dawn on the other women's faces. They had lost so much, and it had all been a lie. Sophie looked on the verge of tears. Rose and Molly held hands. Catelyn stared at the floor, her hair obscuring her expression.

TOUCHING HIS SHOULDER, ELLEN FOUND herself the only one capable of words. "It seems we have been living a lie all this time, but nothing can surprise us these days—except you. What is your name, young man?"

"Nico," he replied in a quiet voice as if it would get him into more trouble.

"Well then, Nico, you will be spending tomorrow in Sophie's attic, and then after in Molly's priest hole."

Her friend recovered enough to state, "It's a priest*ess* hole, from two hundred years ago when the they were being hunted and..."

"Perhaps no history lesson tonight," Rose ground out, patting Molly on the shoulder. "We all have had a bit too much excitement and a lot to digest."

They had indeed. Ellen squeezed them all as they left, one by

one returning to their homes. Nico remained in the root cellar. She heard him moving around, getting as comfortable as possible.

What he had said made sense, as awful as it was. The State had easily fooled the populace, fed them lies about the evil others which lay beyond their borders, and they had fallen for it.

Ellen leaned against her front door and tried to breathe, but it was hard. Memories of her father, her husband, and sons all going off to war filled her head. Sometimes they had seemed happy about it, serving their country, but her sons—now she looked back on it, recalled their faces—she wondered if they had not somehow known.

She felt foolish to have swallowed the lies, and she felt foolish that she had fed the war machine—not only with her labor at the mill, but also with her family. Tears filled her eyes, her hands clenched against the door, but it didn't matter. She didn't matter.

Ellen slept on the floor that night, huddled in a ball. The next morning, her muscles and bones ached so badly she might as well have been beaten.

When Sophie turned up at the back door to usher Nico through the garden to her house, she did not say anything. She kept her eyes on the ground, and hurried their patient away. Ellen knew how she felt. Lost.

Still habit took her to her needlework. She had only a little to go, so Ellen took her dress to the window, sat on her stool, and began. The morning was nearly done when a commotion out on the street got her to her feet. The village seldom had much shouting these days, but there it was: the sounds of a man's voice barking orders, swearing.

Without thinking, Ellen got to her feet and went out to see what was happening. Her throat tightened when she saw Rose surrounded by the soldiers. The commandant had her by the arm and was shaking her like a rag doll. Rose didn't cry out, but her glasses flew off her nose and bounced across the cobblestones. Ellen approaching the

group, her hands out. "*Jar* Commandant, what is happening? Why do you have this poor old lady?"

The commandant's eyes narrowed on her, and she suddenly felt the emptiness of the street pressing in on her. He had a platoon of soldiers at his back, while she had nothing.

"This poor old lady," he said giving Rose another shake as if to prove his point, "has been reported as a wool thief. She has been stealing from the glorious war effort."

Ellen and Rose's eyes met, and the captured woman gave a tiny shake of her head. Ellen knew it meant, back off, go away, don't get involved. However, after last night Ellen had found out what not getting involved led to.

She straightened as much as her back would allow. "Rose has been a faithful worker for the cause for more years than you have been alive, *Jar* Commandant. She has given her two sons, and her health. I hardly think she would take wool from their backs."

The soldiers behind the commandant shifted, just a little. They were somebody's sons too, and a flicker of emotion on one or two of their faces said they weren't comfortable with this. Ellen hoped she read them right.

The commandant frowned, but his grip tightened on Rose, making her flinch. Old flesh hurt as much as young.

"*Jai* Ambrose is an honest sister of the State." Sophie was out on her front steps, babe in her arms, speaking to the armed men as boldly as Ellen remembered her grandmother doing.

"Look at her fingers." Now it was Catelyn who spoke, leaning against the door of her house. "See how she has worked them for the Glorious Cause."

The commandant glanced down at Rose's bent and crooked hands, and he let go of her arm.

"Her life is nearly spent, *Jar* Commandant. Let her work her remaining days." Molly stood at the bend of the road. She was

huffing and puffing, so she must have run as fast as she could to follow the soldiers.

Ellen realized that the rest of the knitters had formed up around the men, with Rose in the middle. The air felt odd, warm, with a faint hint of spring in it. She wondered why she had not noticed that before.

She also wondered if the entire circle was about to be killed.

The commandant shook his head, and let out a short laugh. "Rumors, stupid rumors. Go on, you old biddy, back to work." And with that he turned on his heel to leave, but then spun around. "Besides, I have more important things to do." As soon as the words were out of his mouth, he looked as though he didn't quite know why he had said them, but it was too late. He and his soldiers turned and marched back towards the village square.

In a brief moment, it was only the five women of the knitting circle standing on the empty street. They drew together. Sophie picked up Rose's glasses, which had miraculously survived, and handed them back to her.

"What just happened?" Catelyn gave voice to the jumble of thoughts crowding all their minds. "Did you...did you feel that?"

Ellen glanced down, and realized she still had her needlework in one hand. It was even prettier outside in the sunlight.

"I think we need to ask Nico a few questions," she said.

All of them hustled over to Sophie's house, whispering amongst themselves. Yes, indeed, they had all felt it, but what exactly it was remained to be seen.

Nico was looking positively charming sitting in the garret among the boxes of Sophie's former family life. He looked up as the women climbed the stairs, and his initial smile faded. "Ladies?"

They all settled around him, sitting on the boxes.

"Here's the thing," Molly began as she had a wont to do, "we have never met anyone from Mensognes—let alone a magician."

He frowned again. Sitting up straighter, he replied, "Never met a magician...but I thought you were a circle of witches?"

They all burst out laughing as if he had delivered the best joke in Doumount. Molly dissolved into a hacking cough.

Rose carefully cleaned her glasses on her sleeve. "What would make you think that?"

His frown was almost adorable. "Well, you found me, you healed me, you have protected this village even though it is right on the border with my country...and well...your country was known for its powerful witches. At least that is what our school children learn."

Ellen wondered if perhaps she was dead and dreaming all this. She went to tell Nico he was completely wrong, and then stopped in her tracks. A memory, dusty but beloved, scrambled up in her mind. Her grandmother with her curly gray hair standing in the sunshine holding Ellen's little cat. It had been hit by a cart, and all of Ellen's sisters had told her it would be dead soon. She had known to bring it to Nona. Sitting in the sun, her grandmother had laid it on her lap as she began to knit. Its blood stained her apron, but she worked on stitching and singing in the sun. After an hour or so, the cat had sat up, purring with its whole ginger body as if nothing had happened.

Nona had told her to tell no one, and kissed her granddaughter on the forehead. After that, the memory went strangely fuzzy and distant.

Ellen grabbed one of Sophie's hands and one of Rose's. "He is right, dearest friends. He is right."

They all looked around at each other, slow smiles dawning on their faces.

"I never thought to see anything worth smiling about," Molly grumbled, as if she couldn't help herself.

"Oh, tosh," Rose said with a grin, "You say that every night."

"But how does it work?" Catelyn asked. "Is it the knitting, the sewing?"

Nico shrugged. "I do not know. Each magic is different. Mine... mine is like a breeze in my face. I must sing." He raised his hands, a smile spreading over his bruised face. "And then it comes to me. I am as free as a bird."

"The commandant will keep looking for you though," Rose said, her shoulders slumping. "How will we protect you?"

"We just shall," Ellen said, her hands tightening on the sleeves of her cardigan, "and in return you shall teach us." Out of her pocket she fished the sewing she'd been doing when they had come looking for Nico. "This was how they couldn't find you. This is our weapon."

"It's only women's work," Catelyn said, the sunlight gleaming off the gray in her hair.

"But it can be powerful." Ellen leaned forward. "Imagine if we knitted the commandant a scarf. Imagine if we knitted a set of socks for all the boys out there fighting. Imagine if we made something, just a little line of somethings to change The Glorious Cause. Stop it even."

Nico beamed up at them, and she knew he could also imagine the possibilities.

But it was Sophie that spoke, jiggling Corwin on her knee. "Maybe the time for perseverance is over. Maybe the time for safety is done. I think it is time to get *angry*."

The woman shared glances, which became broader and wickeder by the moment. It was heady, this taste of power and hope combined.

Rose planted her glasses on her nose and looked about. "Well then, let's get back to the library. I'm heartily sick of the machines of war and the lies, so let's make something new, shall we?"

Ellen thought of all those men and boys gone. She thought of their broken lives, and she decided that getting angry was entirely appropriate.

"I rather think it is time to cast on and do something different."

AN ESSAY BY
SHANNA GERMAIN

FOR THE LOVE OF ETTA CANDY:
ON THE IMPORTANCE OF THE FEMALE FRIEND

"Fight? We use our principles. Although, I am not opposed to engaging in a bit of fisticuffs should the occasion arise."
—Etta Candy

T HIS WAS THE BEGINNING OF my downfall: a pair of red glasses and hot pink stirrup pants and a note in my locker. The scene: middle school. Mid '80s. Me, the geek when geek wasn't a good word. The girl who didn't get it. The girl whose mother had dumped her so many years ago and who'd been raised by her father and who did not understand women. Or girls. Or boys. Or, really, anything at all. The not-quite-bisexual because she-didn't-have-those-terms-yet girl. The girl in red glasses that she hated and the cheap-but-new hot pink stirrup pants that she realized in zero-point-zero seconds of getting on the bus that morning were a giant, giant mistake.

In my memory, the glasses, the giant, giant mistake of pink stretch pants, and the note in my locker are woven together in the seamless tapestry of story. Consequential, or at least correlational.

But perhaps it was a different day. A different year. A parallel universe.

In my memory, I am wearing the glasses and the pants when I open my locker. I am about to go to the lunchroom and sit with my friends.

Friends.

It's such a beautiful word, such a pure word. My whole life, I've wanted friends so badly. Particularly friends who were girls. I am a reader, a quiet scared girl who looks like a haunted ghost-child in photos, so pale, so sad. Those big eyes. The girls in my books all have girl friends. Nancy has Bess. Laura has Mary. Even Harriet the Spy has Janie.

And now I too have friends, half a dozen girls who seem to like me, who spend time at my house and who invite me to theirs. Who tell me their secrets. One has an alcoholic mother. The other believes she must match her socks to her underwear before she can leave the house or else something bad will happen. Another has a story about her brother that she hints at via Duran Duran lyrics, but has not yet spoken aloud. I believe in the power of these friendships, in what will blossom if given enough of my time, attention, and yearning.

The day of the pink pants, I open my locker. Inside is a piece of paper, tucked into the metal slats. It hangs there, poised with possibilities. Boys sometimes put notes in girl's lockers. *Do you like me?* Y/N *Can we hold hands between classes?* I've never had a boy give me a note, except my father to miss class for an orthodontist appointment (did I also mention the braces?). I am not a note-getting girl. I am not the hero of anyone's story, and I am definitely not the hero's love interest.

But today? Maybe that is changing. Because there is a note. In my locker. Hanging. I am already imagining what I will tell me friends at the lunch table. How S. will flatten it out on the table with

her perfect hands so we can see it better. How A. will say, "Who do you think it's from?" and I will say, "I have no idea!" And together, we will dream.

I open it, this untold possibility, this secret promise.

The handwriting is not from a boy. It is, based on the curves of the letters, from my friend S.

WE DO NOT WANT TO BE YOUR FRIENDS ANY-MORE. DO NOT SIT WITH US AT LUNCH.

A pair of red glasses and hot pink stirrup pants and a note in my locker. My feet poised on the edge of a rocky descent that I can't yet see. When I get home, tear-smeared, devastated, destroyed, my new step-mother says, "Girls are just mean. Why don't you play with boys instead?"

I took her advice. For the next ten or so years of my life, I had few female friends. They were, I believed, untrustworthy, likely to stab me in the back, dump me at a moment's notice, break my heart with words. My male friends were fun, exciting. They taught me to play soccer and D&D. They didn't talk about diets or shoes. They let me ride their motorcycles. But most of all, they didn't dump me. They were loyal, at least until they got girlfriends, and then our friendship succumbed to a slow fading away, a ghostly afterimage of what we'd once had. Sad, but not painful.

Who, after all that, needed female friends?

It turned out that I did. I just didn't know how to find them, or even what a healthy female friendship might look like. And so, I did what I always do when I am lost and uncertain, when I need information or a role model: I turned to books.

In the pages of my favorite science fiction and fantasy novels and comic books, I searched for what I then thought of as the confusing and elusive female friend. But it turned out she wasn't confusing and elusive at all. She was right there, in novels and short stories and particularly in my favorite old *Wonder Woman* comics.

There, in the faded and yellowed pages, I rediscovered Wonder Woman's female friend *extraordinaire*, Etta Candy. Etta traveled to another planet to rescue the hero. She stormed a Nazi concentration camp with candy and her wits as her only weapon. She jumped in front of a bullet to save Wonder Woman from being shot. She was smart, sexy, unashamed, and unafraid. Etta Candy, it turns out, was the perfect role model for the woman—and the friend—that I wanted to be.

After that, I started seeing the friend everywhere. She was the one answering the door in her pajamas to a late-night knock, seeing her friend-turned-werewolf, saying, "Oh my gosh, what happened?" She was up late in the library, looking up the method for getting rid of demons so that her best friend could kick their asses. There she was, crawling through the air ducts of the spaceship, so that she could overhear the evil overseer's plans and relay them back to the hero.

In reading about Etta and the others, I discovered a lot about myself, about my own prejudices and perceptions, about the way that my uncertainty about my sexuality colored my understanding of friendships, and about my own role in the world. In the beginning, I'd thought I was the hero of this story, looking for a friend. Instead, I was the friend of this story, looking for a hero.

Stepping back, we can look at the female friend from a more analytical perspective. When it comes to common story archetypes, we see a number of characters that typically work alongside the hero: sidekick, mentor, love interest, caretaker…the list is extensive, but rarely do we see the word "friend" on there. Granted, sometimes the friend also fits into one or more of the archetypes listed above, but that is not their main role. Their main role is to be a friend—a true friend—to the hero.

Why isn't friend on there? Some might argue that it's not important enough or that it doesn't play a big enough role in and of itself to merit recognition. That a friend is essentially a sidekick

with a little mentorship (or love interest or family ties) rolled in.

But I would argue otherwise. I would argue that the role of the friend in fiction is a vital—if oft overlooked—one, with the opportunity to teach us a number of important life skills. Such as:

It's Okay Not to Be the Hero of Every Story

"Woo-@&#%ing-Woo" —Etta Candy

I WAS LUCKY ENOUGH TO grow up in a time and place where people said things like, "Everyone can be a hero!" and "You can be whatever you want to be!" and "It doesn't matter that you're a girl!" But even then, I understood that sometimes grownups tell lies to make shy, bespectacled, bookwormish girls feel better.

Except that it didn't make me feel better. Instead it made me feel awful because I knew I wasn't a hero. I even made a list of all the heroes I wasn't: I wasn't the plucky hero (too shy). I wasn't the ass-kicking hero (too nice and the only weapon I had was made by a toy company). Or the sassy hero (I never thought of the right thing to say until the day after). I wasn't the daredevil hero (near in sight, short in stature, and afraid of almost everything). I wasn't even the sneak-around-looking-for-clues hero (too clumsy and impatient, and also not very observant).

As an adult, I understand that I am sometimes the hero after all, and sometimes I am the friend. And that both of these roles matter. That I am greater, not lesser, for choosing the role that best suits me and the situation at any given time.

I've run into a fair number of people who believe they're the hero (or at the very least, the main subject) of every story, even if they're not the ones who are best equipped to do the job. If it seems like someone else might be the hero, they're not quite sure what to do with themselves, because they never learned vital lesson number two:

How to Act When You Aren't the Hero

"Sweetie, just go. You were given all that power for a reason, weren't you?" —Etta Candy

FICTIONAL FRIENDS TEACH YOU WHAT you can do when you're not the one in the limelight. In short, they teach you how to support other people in order for the entire story to have a better ending. Sometimes that support is kicking the asses of the enemy alongside the hero. Sometimes it's listening, doing research, cracking jokes, or serving up candy when candy is required. Sometimes it's just shutting up and being there—always.

Being the friend isn't about lurking in the shadows, taking a back seat, or being lesser than. It's a vital role, one upon which outcome of the story hinges. While everyone's looking at the hero, the friend is the one who's setting plans in motion behind the scenes. But perhaps the friend's most important role isn't what she does, but who she does it for: the hero. It's the relationship between the friend and the hero that creates the catalyst for beautiful, world-saving things to happen.

And that brings me to the final lesson that friends in fiction teach us:

How to Change the World

"Here's the enemy. Let every girl get her man!" ~Etta Candy

I HAVE NEVER FELT MORE alone than the moment I stood in that school hallway in my pink stretch pants and read that note. That moment stretched into something so much larger than itself. It changed me, it defined me, and it haunted me. I knew that I didn't want to ever make someone else feel the things that I was feeling, but I didn't know how to prevent it.

And then I found myself in the reflection of fictional friends,

and I understood. I could change the world simply by helping others, by being their friend. It wasn't a cop-out. It wasn't weak. It was necessary and important, and it was mine.

Our world is in a time of great uncertainly and crisis. We are going to need heroes now more than ever—and those heroes are going to need great friends at their sides.

If you're a hero, come and find us. If you're a friend, come and join us. You'll know us by our red glasses and pink stretch pants. By our smarts and our sass. You'll know us by our shoulders, which have been leaned on, cried on, and probably bitten or shot or held tight by a pair of scrabbling claws. You'll know us by our library cards, our trick of showing up at just the right moment, and our Nazi-punching skills.

Mostly you'll know us by our unfailing, unwavering loyalty to our heroes, and to everything that is right and good in the world.

There's a little wonder in all of us. So often, it shines the brightest when we're in that quiet, all-important role called friend.

SOME ENCHANTED EVENING

ANTON STROUT

OUT OF THE WAY, TOURIST."

Aurora "Rory" Torres's dance bag slammed into the idiot dumb enough to stand directly outside the doors of Lincoln Center's Beaumont Theatre. All she craved was her couch and the sweet oblivion of junk TV. No thoughts of dance rehearsals or the leg numbing ache of complex repetition. Resting and going full on lady-sloth was blissful agenda enough for tonight.

But no. There had to be this jerk blocking her way. After her day of trying to master a hardcore mashup of hip-hop and Bhaṅgṛā, this guy should count himself lucky she didn't clear her path by pulling out her collapsible polearm hidden in the art tube strapped across her back. She hated feeling even a hint of stereotypical Latina fieriness about it, but checked herself and instead shouldered past him in a huff.

"Is that any way to treat your former roomie?" the figure called out. "Or should I say current boyfriend...?"

Rory spun and pushed her long blue bangs away from her glasses, a mix of excitement and confusion washing over her. "Marsh?"

Marshall Blackmoore's blue eyes met hers from under his shaggy mop of dark hair. Just seeing his nerdy cool self helped kill some of the fatigue she felt.

Illustration by M. WAYNE MILLER

"I mean, I guess I'm still technically your roomie." he said. "More of a roomie with benefits now, really." His mile-a-minute pace barraged her as it so often did, catching her off guard. Marshall fussed nervously with the straps of the overstuffed shoulder satchel he always carried with him.

Rory checked the time on her phone. "What are you doing here?" she asked. "I thought you had secret gargoyle liaison business to attend to."

"That was actually a cover," Marshall said with the most sheepish of grins. "More of a lie, really. But one of those good relationship sort of lies. I mean, without those, how else am I supposed to surprise you, right?"

Rory eyed him warily, then wrinkled her nose.

"You know I hate surprises," she said. "Surprises in my line of derring-do can get me killed."

Marshall pointed to the posters on the side of the theater. "You're not going to die *dancing*," he reminded her. He eyed the Lincoln Center crowd drifting past them in the plaza and lowered his voice. "Kicking supernatural ass is only a part-time profession for you. When you're not playing guardian to our master Spellmason."

"Leave Alexandra out of this," Rory said. She fought to shake off her post-rehearsal gruffness and craned her head around the courtyard outside the dance school. "My point still stands. So what's the surprise?"

Marshall smiled, his eyes lit with excitement.

"If I told you it would ruin the fun. Come with me."

Marshall held his hand out to her, and she took it in hers, warming at his grip as he led her off east across the plaza towards the intersection of Broadway and Columbus Avenue.

Despite her weariness, Rory submitted to the tug of his hand. Learning to be with Marshall as more than a friend felt like a constant exercise in practicing patience with herself. Whether that

was just a couples thing overall or a warning sign of impending relationship failure, she wasn't sure.

"At least give me a clue," she pleaded.

Marshall pondered it for a moment before speaking.

"You've seen *Lord of the Rings*," he said.

Rory nodded with a heavy sigh. "After you threatened to double my half of the rent if I didn't, remember?"

"Well, in it, they've got swords that magically glow when orcs are near and rings that make people invisible. Don't you ever wonder who made all that stuff in the first place?"

"Elves or some such crap like that?" she asked as she followed him down the plaza steps to street level. "They're the same ones that make cookies in a tree, right?"

Marshall rolled his eyes. "There's a world of difference between Keebler elves and Tolkien ones, hon."

"Sorry," she said and stopped in her tracks on the sidewalk. "But how is any of that a clue?"

Marshall raised his arms and spread them wide. "Happy six-month-iversary!" he shouted.

Rory couldn't help but stare as a sinking sensation hit her stomach. "Is… that a thing? For reals?"

Marshall crinkled up his face, but his arms remained raised. "I hope so, otherwise this was a huge waste."

Rory simply stared at him as he stood there, statuesque. "*What is?*"

"This," he said and gestured to a boxy vehicle parked at the curb directly behind him. Painted on its side was a giant taco shell stuffed with what looked like pierogis and kielbasa.

"Who in their right mind would want Pole-Mex food truck?" Rory asked.

"Exactly the point," Marshall said. "Step right up."

Rory sighed as her fatigue creeped back into her. "Marsh, you're

not making sense, and you know how I get when things don't make sense to me."

Marshall's eyes went to the art tube strapped across Rory's back, no doubt imagining her assembling the three collapsible parts of her polearm within. "You get all slashy slashy?"

Rory gave a slow, purposeful nod.

"Fine, fine," he said with what Rory took as a mock pout. "Some six-month-iversary this is!"

A chuckle came from the truck where an older Rosie the Riveter looking blond leaned against the rail of the pick-up window. She looked down at the two of them then nodded in Rory's direction.

"This the one?" she asked in a voice with more Brooklyn in it than Manhattan.

Judging by the thick smokiness in the woman's tone, Rory guessed her to be in her late forties or possibly early fifties.

Marshall nodded. "This is the six-month-iversary girl!"

Rory squeezed his hand. Hard. "You have got to stop saying that."

"Sorry," he said, then turned his attention back to the woman in the truck. "Yes, this is the one."

The woman looked Rory up and down before giving her a smirk.

"Come around to the back," the woman said and shuttered the service window.

"Come on," Marshall said, his voice practically vibrating.

With an excited jerk on Rory's arm, he led her to the rear of the truck and into the back.

Once he escorted her inside, one thing became immediately clear to Rory.

"This isn't a food truck," she said, stating what was now obvious to her own eyes.

The cramped space looked far more like a workshop on wheels. Vices, clamps, and an anvil built into one of the counters filled

the space, along with bins of assorted metal bars and other bits of unidentifiable mechanisms that Rory couldn't begin to guess the purposes of.

"This is Freya," Marshall said. "My gift to you. I thought your polearm might need an upgrade, and well, she's a maker. You know, like those Tolkien elves."

The woman cocked her head at Marshall quizzically.

"You could have just got me a piece of jewelry from the mall," Rory said to him.

"Think of me as a traveling mall," Freya said. "Except what I create helps augments weapons by enchanting them."

Rory's hands moved defensively to the strap of her polearm carrying case. "And you work out of a food truck…?"

Freya nodded. "In my line of arcane work, it pays to be mobile," she said. "If you're on the go, it's harder for anyone to track you down or rip you off. Some of my more demanding militaristic clientele tends to be a bit more…aggressive."

"I'll bet," Rory said. "Weapons freaks, no doubt. Insecure, looking to compensate for what they lack downstairs, right? Effing men."

Freya shrugged. "Actually, the women are the worst. Sick of the status quo, I think." She stepped to one of the workbenches and leaned against it with one muscled arm, gesturing towards Rory with the other. "You have your weapon on you, yes?"

Rory stiffened at the mention of it, even under what appeared to be friendly circumstances.

Marshall stepped behind her, reassurance in his voice. "Let me help you with that."

Reluctantly, Rory undid the quick release of the art tube and Marshall slid it off her back.

"Freya and I met because I carry some of her wares at Roll for Initiative," he said. "I told her about you when I was trying to come up with six-monthi—umm, anniversary ideas, and well, it turns out

she asked to meet you first."

Freya nodded. "I prefer to know who I'm dealing with. This city is crazy, what with gargoyles and the like being the norm these days. Can't be too careful with whom I'm equipping."

Marshall handed the tube to Freya, who undid the end and slid the three pieces of the polearm free. The maker ignored the two shaft pieces and set straight about examining the bladed section.

"Ah, the glaive-guisarme," she said, then gave Rory a look. "A bold choice for the streets of New York City."

Rory shrugged. "What can I say? I tried my first one out of necessity in a museum and the thing just danced in my hands. After that, I needed one of my own."

Freya gave a wicked smile. "I bet you make a nasty dance partner."

Rory looked to Marshall, feeling some of the tension run out of her. "I'm beginning to like her," she said.

"I'm glad," he said, "because my deposit's nonrefundable."

Freya opened one of the cabinets on the wall of the truck. She sorted through a pile of long bundles of cloth, then pulled one free to lay out on the workbench.

"Here it is," she said, unfolding the material. "Fresh from my forging yesterday."

A long thin blade similar to the action end of Rory's polearm lay against the cloth, the precision metalwork pristine with swirls of delicate symbols set into the steel itself. An empty circular slot sat just above where the blade's socket attachment was, and Freya took no time in twisting the new piece onto one of the wooden shafts Rory still held in her hand.

Rory's eyes lit up. "This…is for me?! It's gorgeous. It's magic?"

Freya shook her head. "No," she said. "Not yet, anyway." She tapped her forefinger against the empty slot on the base of the blade itself. "I can augment the blade for you, no problem. It's the

enchantment that's still needs doing, and that's going to cost you more than just money. I'm going to need you to help me obtain the right components for it."

"Can't just head to Home Depot for them, eh?" Rory asked.

Freya shook her head. "Not for something like this," she said. "We need to recover something very unique to enchant this blade, and there might be a little bit of a fight in getting it."

Rory looked at the abundance of weapons in various states of finish that lined the walls of the truck. "You're an arsenal on wheels. Why not just get it yourself?"

"I'm a craftswoman, not a fighter," Freya said. "That's where you come in. You help me get what we need, and I'll help you with your weapon." She looked to Marshall. "Who knows? If it goes well, I might even knock a few bucks off the traditional payment method."

Rory turned to Marshall, unable to hide a newfound excitement that had all but pushed away her earlier fatigue. "You got me a weapon *and* a fight?"

Marshall nodded.

"I don't know what to say," she said. "They don't really make a Hallmark card to reciprocate that."

Words failing her, Rory flew into a hug, which Marshall returned with equal vigor. They stood in their embrace for a long moment before Freya cleared her throat.

"Enough of that, you two," she said and headed off to an opening that led to the cabin of the truck. "Better buckle up."

"Wait…we're doing this now?!" Rory asked. "What? Where?"

Freya looked back over her shoulder through the edge of her gray-blond hair. "You ever watch *The Luxury Ladies of New York City*?" she asked.

Rory's eyes lit up. "I love that show! That's what I was going to catch up with on my DVR tonight before this surprise abduction!"

"Oh," Freya said with a disappointed tone in her voice, then settled down at the wheel. "Too bad then."

RORY AND MARSHALL RODE IN forced silence, simply because there wasn't a choice. Talking wasn't an option, given Freya's breakneck pace through the night streets of Manhattan. The back of the truck clanged and jangled with the sound of various weapons and raw materials clashing together as the food-truck-turned-battlewagon tore up Central Park West. Silence finally fell when Freya laid on the brakes at one of the stop lights, and only then did Rory get a chance to peek her head into the cabin.

"So what's this got to do with the *Luxury Ladies of New York City* again?" she asked.

"You'll see, soon enough."

Rory slipped into the passenger seat beside the older maker as traffic started moving once again.

"I mean, I love the *Luxury Ladies of New York City*," Rory said. "I used to watch all the versions of the show—Beverly Hills, Chicago, Texas—but I had to cut back on them severely. Between my dance stuff, being the guardian of our fair city, plus keeping Clan Belarus alive since Alexandra turned all master Spellmason... well, those take up pretty much most of my time, so now I only have New York as my guilty viewing pleasure."

"Well then consider today your lucky day," Freya said. She jerked the wheel with her muscular arms and pulled the truck to the curb before slipping it into park and killing the engine. Freya pointed out the passenger side. "See for yourself."

Rory took in the sight, one she had seen thousands of times in television credits. The ornate Gothic structure of a towering apartment building rose high above her, and she nostalgically recalled the time she had paid pilgrimage to it in the most fangirlish phase of her life.

"Oh Sweet Christmas," she said. "We're going to see The Baroness?!"

"Well, hopefully not, if all goes well," Freya said. "We just need to secure something she has in her possession: a luckstone. I caught a glimpse of it in one of the background shots on the show. We need to liberate it from her possession. Without notice, if possible."

Marshall popped his head in from the back of the truck and craned his neck toward the building. "I don't think we can just waltz right in there," he said. "The Baroness probably has security, more so thanks to the being a celebrity and all."

"I know of a discreet way in," Freya said as she undid her seat belt. "Gather your things."

"Even my polearm?"

Freya nodded, giving a dark and serious look.

"*Especially* your polearm."

With some careful maneuvering, Freya managed to sneak the three of them away from the view of the building's doormen and down through a back alley to a service elevator of the high rise. Once inside, Freya pulled a hairpin from her graying blond curl of hair, bent it, then slotted it under the button marked "PH." Freya gave it a sharp twist, then reached up and pressed the button.

Rory fought to center herself. She removed the sections of her polearm from the art tube as the elevator rose and set about reassembling them, all the while hoping she wouldn't have to use it.

"So how exactly did The Baroness come by this luckstone we need to retrieve?"

Freya's eyes stayed on the numbers that lit as the elevator ascended. She shrugged.

"How does any rising society woman like these reality show monstrosities get anything in life? Probably from an ex-lover. The rich and powerful get ahead somehow. Sometimes they get lucky,

sometimes they buy their luck—or maybe they do it through ruth-less practices."

Rory gave an uncertain look at the newly fashioned section of her glaive-guisarme. "And this luckstone will improve my weapon how exactly?"

Freya tapped the dull side of the blade. "Right now, you can cut through most mundane things just fine with that blade as is. What you *really* need is something with a bit more kick, that slices and dices through even the creepiest of crawlies."

"And you can do that just off the top of your head, on the fly?" Marshall asked as he inventoried the contents of his satchel, pulling out a pair of black leather gloves. "Too bad we didn't have to scale the building. I'm dying to test these Spider-Man gloves I've been crafting for the store."

Rory gave him a smile. "Always prepared. You're such a Boy Scout."

"Hey!" Freya scolded. "Focus, you two."

Marshall nodded, blushed, and shoved the gloves back into his satchel, pulling a Moleskine notebook free instead.

"Enchanting comes from imbuing an object with power," Freya said. The elevator slowed as it approached its destination. "Giving something up to it. You have to give it importance, transferring a little piece of yourself over to it. Ask any artist. Don't they give a little bit of themselves up in their work? Such is the price of creation."

"Giving up a part of yourself?" Rory said with a shudder. "Sounds dreadful."

"Yeah," Freya said, with a shrug. "It stings. I'm not gonna lie, but as a maker, well, the money helps soften the blow so…"

The elevator stopped.

"So what *are* you giving up to the blade then, to enchant Rory's polearm?" Marshall asked.

The doors slid open, and Freya walked out of the elevator with-

out a glance backward. "Oh, honey, nothing. I gave my piece of me to this long ago. To that luckstone. Stay sharp."

Rory readied her weapon and followed the craftswoman, Marshall close behind.

Rory's head roiled with a mix of emotions. It was both surreal and exciting to her reality-show junkie mind to be entering so familiar a location as The Baroness's luxury apartment, but the fact that they were there with hostile intent clouded those happy feelings. Still, something about what Freya had said bothered Rory.

"What did you mean back in the elevator, that you 'gave yourself to the luckstone'?" she whispered.

Freya only shushed her, calling for further silence as they continued to sneak their way through the eerily quiet apartment. Despite the fact that there were no signs of anyone there, she led them along with caution until their path entered a massive master bedroom and then into an equally massive walk-in closet. Down the center of the room-sized space were waist-high shelves with drawers covered in every variety of purse imaginable. Along every wall a technicolor rainbow of clothing hung from hangers.

"It's like being in a store," Rory said.

Marshall laughed. "So… we came here to trash a closet?"

Freya shook her head and pointed to the center unit of the closet. At the end of the clutter of purses stood a hideous twist of carved rock. A lone blue gem shone brightly from its setting at the top of the man-made crag.

"The luckstone," Rory said.

"We just need to pry it free," Freya said. "Then I can slot it into your blade."

"What's this?" a woman's voice spoke up from behind them.

Rory jumped, her heart racing.

"Another group of zealous autograph seekers, I see," the voice said with a hint of bemusement to the words.

Rory turned. Despite her game face, it was hard to contain her surge of excitement.

It was The Baroness herself! The high profile semi-celebrity was quite different from her HD television persona: her hair too unnaturally black, her smooth skin pulled far too tightly over her near-skeletal frame. Her over-the-top makeup twisted her into a plastic faced doll that looked uncannily in her thirties, despite her wrinkled hands betraying an age nearly at least twice that number.

Rory swung her polearm into position in front of her, assuming a defensive stance despite the strange struggle between fangirling and preparing for a fight.

"We're not here for your signature, Isabella," Freya said, the last to turn around.

One of The Baroness's over-manicured eyebrows rose. The rest of her Botoxed face remained motionless.

"Hello, Freya." The Baroness looked Freya up and down before then shifting her dark-circled eyes to Rory. "And who is this little blue-haired moppet? Your new lover?"

Marshall scoffed. "She wishes," he said as his face reddened.

The woman's eyes switched to him. "Well, surely this scruffy little *man* isn't your type now, is he?"

Rory glanced at Freya. "'New lover?'" she repeated. "Implying that *you're* her old one?"

"Oh sweet little pet," The Baroness said. "She didn't tell you…?"

Freya gave a sheepish grin then turned back to The Baroness. "I'm afraid that I haven't been entirely straight with you two: this is more than just an object recovery mission for me."

Rory shot Marshall a withering look. "This anniversary of ours keeps getting better and better," she said.

Marshall managed a half smile. "Happy six-month-iversary…?" he said in an unsure whisper.

"Don't worry about all this, anniversary girl," Freya assured her.

"I'll keep my part of the bargain. Believe me, this won't take long."

A low impatient growl rose from The Baroness. "What won't take long?" she demanded.

Freya pointed to the luckstone mounted in the hideous piece of art, raising her voice. "You didn't think I'd catch seeing that on TV? A constant reminder of *us*? You think I'd just ignore that and let you keep it after flaunting it like that?"

The Baroness gave a chuckle that dripped with the Devil in it. "Aren't you being a little dramatic, darling?"

"Not by half," Freya said. To Rory's eye, the craftswoman was getting good and worked up with no signs of relenting. "That thing symbolized what you meant to me. That thing meant *us*. You broke my heart, and for what? To marry some old British billionaire for a chance at fame? You know how much it sucked turning on the TV to see a constant reminder of that? On national television for all to see? And how the hell do you still look thirty, and since when were you into men, anyway?"

The Baroness waved Freya's words away. "Don't be so judgmental. We love who we love."

Rory felt Marshall's hand slip into hers, pulling her back towards him. "Maybe we should wait by the elevator," he suggested.

Freya remained focused only on The Baroness. "The only thing you love is yourself, Isabella, and fame. I gave you the luckstone to better *our* fortune. You used it to secure all this from that poor old man you married."

The Baroness folded her bony arms across her chest and smirked, the smooth skin of her face unmoving. "Is that what this intrusion is about? You're upset that perhaps I preferred him to you?"

"Well?" Freya asked. "Was he worth it? This man who made you The Baroness?"

The Baroness shrugged, but a crooked smile crept across her face. "Well, he's dead these past two years or so, and I got to keep

all the trappings, so you tell me."

"Yeah, we should probably definitely go," Marshall whispered to Rory. "I'll get you earrings or a nice glaive-guisarme cozy..."

"Nobody is going anywhere," The Baroness shouted. "Not until you meet my husband, anyway."

Rory cocked her head. "Excuse me, Baroness, but didn't you just say he was dead?"

"Correct," The Baroness said. "Feeble as he was in life, you'll find him far more formidable in death. Oh Reggie...."

A great rumbling arose in the walk-in closet. The collection of purses tumbled off the long shelving unit in the center of the room, a great stone slab revealing itself as it slid to one side.

"Oh crap," Marshall said.

Rory fell in beside him. "What is it?"

"This isn't just a closet... it's a barrow."

Rory cocked her head at him. "A barrow...?"

Marshal sighed. "Like in *The Lord of the Rings*. Right after Frodo and Sam flee the Shire?"

The great slab of stone reached its tipping point, and one end slid with a thunderous thud to the floor.

"I might have been asleep," she admitted.

"Really?" Marshall looked genuinely hurt, and Rory's heart twinged.

"Do you really want to get into this now?" Rory asked.

"Fine," he said, the pointed at the center of the room. "But I think we're about to meet The Baroness's Reggie. This is a crypt."

Leathery skin stretched taut over the bony hands that rose from the tomb at the center of the room. The lengthy yellowed nails on the fingers that now gripped the edge of the coffin reminded Rory of corn chips as it pulled itself up into sight. The creature's silver hair had grown long since the creature's death, cascading over its shoulders in wispy tendrils, followed by the rest of the creature's

withered figure, its suit hanging off its skeletal frame.

Its dead sunken eyes glowed with an eldritch fire as it looked past them to the one who had summoned him.

A hollow British voice moaned softly from its sunken-in chest. "What is it, dearie?" the Reggie creature asked.

"Dispatch these intruders, won't you?" There was casual dismissal in The Baroness's voice. "That's a good chap."

"Now we're talking," Rory said, whirling her polearm in an arc around her to face the creature. "Just give me something unnatural to fight and we're all good. This I can handle!"

"Coming, my love," the Reggie creature said as it started to climb from its not-so-final resting place.

Marshall leaned into her. "Careful," he said. Already he had shoved his hand into his satchel and was thumbing through one of his notebooks. "I think that thing might be a wight."

"Great," Rory said. "So basically I'm fighting 'The Real House Wights of New York City'...?"

Marshall gave a groan that was not unlike that of the shambling creature. "I'm going to pretend I didn't hear that." He tapped at a page in his notebook. "Um, Ror? You might want to watch your step. These undead mofos can be nasty."

Rory looked over to Marshall as she stepped back. "Nasty? Nasty how?"

"Like it might try to suck the life out of you by touch nasty."

"Awesome," Rory said, deflating a little. "Good thing I'm using a polearm then." As the creature attempted to step out of its coffin, she lunged forward with the polearm, dragging the blade across its chest.

The tie of the Reggie creature's suit fell away. The cloth of both its shirt and coat tore open but the blade itself left not a mark on the skin beneath it.

Rory swore under her breath. "I can't cut it."

"Don't worry about that. Focus," Freya shouted. "Just get the

luckstone out of that 'headstone.' If I can slot it into your weapon, you should be able to take that abomination down."

"Don't talk about my Reginald like that!" The Baroness snarled.

Marshall stepped to Rory's side. "I'll work on removing the gemstone," he said. Already he was rifling through his messenger bag again. "You just keep that thing at bay."

Rory nodded. "I might not be able to kill it outright, but I can definitely keep it occupied."

Without another word, Rory strode toward the creature, keeping the length of her polearm between her and it.

The creature looked down at its suit, its bony fingers reaching for what remained of its tie. "Cor, that was my favorite," it said. "You didn't have to do that, you know."

"Yeah, well, maybe if you weren't trying to kill us..."

The Reggie creature let out a loud rattle of breath that terrified Rory until she realized it was a sigh.

"But killing you is my duty now, innit?" he said. The wight stepped free of the coffin and shuffled toward her. "The mistress calls, and I do what she says, don't I? Don't really get a choice in it, do I? I mean, sorry I have to kill you and your friends. Hearing your voices has been rather refreshing from having to listen to what comes out of my ex-wife's mouth most of the time."

The Reggie creature's attitude brought a smile to Rory's face.

"I almost hate to have to kill you," she said.

"Please don't take offense, miss," the creature said, the glare in its dead eyes becoming far more sinister as it snarled at her. A bony finger pointed to her polearm. "But I don't think that pointed stick of yours is going to do the job."

"We'll see about that," Rory said. She spun the polearm away from the wight itself and instead swung the dull end of it low against the back of the creature's legs. It struck right behind its knees, unbalancing the Reggie creature and causing it to fall in a swirl of

long gray hair and flailing limbs.

Rory chanced a glance over at Marshall, who stood by the hideous statue. "Any luck with that luckstone, Marsh?"

Marshall held up the Leatherman's tool he always carried, its plier grips extended. "Not yet," he said. "The gem is in there pretty damned solidly."

"Then try something else, Boy Scout," she shouted as she continued to keep the Reggie creature at bay. "You're the one who's always prepared!"

"Usually," he said. Marshall flipped the tool shut and dropped it back into his messenger bag. "I just didn't think I'd be reenacting the cover of the original *Player's Handbook* tonight."

"Leave that gem alone!" The Baroness screeched and charged from the doorway into the walk-in closet.

Freya grabbed for her, but the plastic-faced woman was far more agile than she first appeared. The Baroness darted back from Freya while her hands quickly flew through a series of intricate arcane gestures. With one final rush of motion, The Baroness extended her hands and a sharp gust of wind caught Freya, flinging her up against one of the walls of the closet.

The Baroness sneered and closed in on her pinned ex-lover. "You poor deluded thing. For all you can craft, for all you can make, you really don't understand true power, do you?"

"I knew the power of what we had," Freya said. "I loved you with everything that I had to give!"

"No, apparently, you didn't," The Baroness said. "Don't act like yours was a selfless love, and don't act like you're surprised when I threw you to the curb for greener pastures. Your attention and fawning over me... you know how quickly that became unbearable?"

"Because I gave attention to the woman I loved?" Freya laughed out in disbelief. "I did what I did because—and this is a crazy thought, Isabella—I genuinely *cared* for you."

"That selfless routine was old when we were together, Freya," The Baroness said with a shake of her head. "And let's be honest—everything you did was simply to make yourself feel good."

"That's what healthy couples do!" Freya said. "They make each other feel amazing about each other, and get it back in turn. It's not a foreign concept."

Given the look of open disdain on The Baroness' face, Rory couldn't help but feel a twinge of pain for the old maker.

"Why don't you back off, Baroness?" Rory said, shouting past the Reggie creature between her and them. "Forgive Freya for being a bit of a romantic optimist there. Geesh."

The Baroness ignored her, but leaned in closer to Freya. "Here's a hard truth for you," she said, lowering her voice. "You were, in fact, nothing but a stepping stone to me. Foolish Freya."

Between the Reggie creature and the couple's drama playing out before her, Rory grew more and more exasperated. She chanced a look over at Marshall.

Option after option flew out of his satchel as he struggled to find something, anything, that would help remove the luckstone from the hideous statue.

"Any time now, Boy Scout," she said, turning her attention back to the threatening creature.

"I'm less a Boy Scout," Marshall said as he continued rummaging through his messenger bag. "More of a Batman, really."

"How does that remotely help us now?" Rory asked, honestly perplexed.

Marshall sighed but spoke with patience as he continued his search. "Look, I know I maybe over prepped this whole six-month-iversary thing, but you know I'm a planner. Like Batman. He caught grief for it too, only from the Justice League. Sure, they're super friends and all, but the League discovered he was keeping dossiers on all of them, on their weaknesses. You know, just in case he ever

had to take them down, which he *has* had to do on several occasions."

Confused, Rory shouted across the closet. "Marsh, I love you, and I promise you we can discuss all this relationship nonsense later so we don't become all this crazy like these two, but I kind of need you to get to a point here, okay?"

"That *was* my point," he said. "Preparation. Batman prepped to deal with the Justice League, and well, that's sort of how I am will the gargoyles we work with." Marshall held up a tube he pulled from within his satchel. "I whipped this up to be used on them if they go rogue, but you know what? It should also help with getting this damn luckstone free from this carving here. Stone is stone, after all."

With a flick of his wrist, Marshall unstoppered the tube and poured its contents over the gem. The stone surrounding it popped and sizzled like butter hitting a hot pan. The crystal's glow faded as the stone around it crumbled away, before the gem tumbled free into Marshall's waiting hand, unharmed.

The Baroness let out such a scream that Marshall almost reflexively dropped the stone, but managed to wrap his hand around it before he could. He turned to throw the gem to the still pinned against the wall Freya, but froze at the sight of the transformation happening in front of him.

The youth and beauty of The Baroness was melting away by the second. Wrinkles rose around her eyes like cracks in the desert, her cheeks sinking in, and her chin all but disappeared into the ever-growing creases and folds of her thickening neck. Gray streaks washed through her once-black hair like cascading waterfalls until the color drained from it completely.

Whatever spell The Baroness held over Freya broke, and the maker dropped back to the floor of the closet.

"I may be a fool," Freya said as she composed herself, looking The Baroness dead in the deep, hollow sockets of her eyes, "but at least I haven't been living this vain lie that you've become. Had I seen

the darkness of your true self, maybe I could have spared myself the hurt. Or better yet, let you get together with this Reggie of yours sooner by leaving. So was I a fool? Absolutely. Love is a wager at best. Its lasting is unlikely, but its potential is so vast, my rational, optimistic mind would rather risk loving than not, even if it fell on so deaf an ear. I'd take that chance. Every time."

Whether The Baroness heard Freya, Rory wasn't sure. The former beauty's eyes stared down at her own body, still transfixed on her own true form.

Freya turned from her to face the back of the closet.

"Mister Blackmoore!" she shouted, raising an open palm.

Marshall snapped out of watching the horror show that The Baroness had become, and threw the stone Freya's way. The Reggie creature lunged for it, darting past Rory, but his bony form only managed to stumble forward without actually catching it.

Freya, however, caught it deftly in one hand. A smile rose on her face, one that faded moments later as the Reggie creature charged at her. Freya's hair grayed at the creature's touch as it managed to ensnare it in one of his claw-like hands.

"Sorry about this," Reggie said, and drew back his other hand to strike.

"Save it," Rory said, leaping toward the two of them. "You're the one about to be sorry."

The blade of her polearm sliced down where the Reggie creature held Freya's hair. Rory couldn't cut the wight itself, but Freya? That was another story.

Or her hair, at least.

Rory's blade sliced cleanly through the woman's hair, breaking the creature's grip on her and unbalancing him at the same time.

As the creature stumbled back, Rory slid behind it and pressed the bladed end of her polearm against its throat, subduing him.

Freya brushed the ends of her freshly shorn hair, then opened her other hand to examine the luckstone. She stepped closer to where Rory held the blade of the polearm against the struggling Reggie creature's throat.

"Hold still," Freya said as she looked over the empty socket for the stone.

"Trying," Rory said. "He's pretty lively for a dead guy."

Marshall ran across the room to her, grabbed the shaft of the polearm and fought to keep the creature restrained, but not before handing his Leatherman tool to Freya.

Using its needle-nosed pliers, the craftswoman set about slotting the gem. When she was done placing it in the socket and clamping its prongs into place, she clasped her hand over the setting itself, and arcane words flew from her lips as a burst of azure light shot straight out of the craftswoman's closed fist around it. When Freya pulled her hand away, the shining gemstone faded until it settled into a low but still hypnotic glow.

"Try it now," she said with a dark smile to Rory.

Rory jerked her polearm away from the struggling wight, using the dull end of it to jab the Reggie creature square in its sunken chest.

Power coursed through Rory's hands and she was surprised that her blow drove the creature with an unnatural force back into the closet. When the back of its knees hit the edge of the open tomb in the center of the space, the Reggie creature simply toppled over the edge into the tomb itself.

Confident in the newfound power of the weapon, Rory leapt up onto the edge of the tomb and stared down at the creature.

"Sorry, Reg," Rory said. "You seemed nice enough."

"I was, I suppose. Despite my flawed taste in women."

Freya laughed from across the room, but Rory could hear the bitterness behind it. "You and me both, brother."

Rory couldn't help but hesitate with the weapon in her hands.

"No worries, love," the Reggie creature said. "I'll consider this a gift. My soul has toiled on this earth for far too long enough under her control."

Without another moment of hesitation, Rory took her weapon up in both hands and plunged the blade down into the center of the creature's chest. Clean, simple, efficient, without cruelty.

The Reggie creature gave a final gasp before it withered into itself as its lifeless form fell silent.

Freya turned away from the spectacle and crossed to the now sobbing form of the still rapidly aging Baroness. As the craftswoman approached her, The Baroness crawled back from her until her back hit a wall. With nowhere to go, The Baroness cowered with her hands held up protectively in front of her.

Freya knelt down in front of the cowering crone. "Do you really think I'm going to kill you?" she said.

The Baroness nodded. "You let her kill Reggie," she spat out.

Freya shook her head. "No. She put that thing to rest. She did it a fucking favor."

The craftswoman raised her hands, and The Baroness flinched. She closed her eyes as if expecting Freya to strike, but when nothing happened, The Baroness opened a wary sunken eye.

Freya stood with a groan. "Relax," she said. "I'm not going to kill you. I want you to have to live with yourself. The real you, not that sideshow reality television version of you."

The Baroness whimpered, shaking her head.

That sound alone was too much to bear, which Freya seemed to sense, and swiftly guided Rory and Marshall back through the penthouse to the elevator they had arrived in.

"You two shouldn't have to deal with the fallout of this," Freya said. She pressed the call button. "I'll handle dealing with the rest of this mess. *My* mess. Sorry you had to catch all the baggage of our relationship. I'm afraid I wasn't thinking straight. Love makes

people a little crazy sometimes."

Rory hesitated. "You okay?" she asked.

"Honestly, no," Freya said. "But I will be."

"You really loved her, didn't you?" Rory asked with a bit of marvel in her voice.

"You know what?" Freya said with a hearty and refreshing laugh. "I'm not even sure anymore. Love plays tricks with you, messes with your mind, talks you into things. Sure, it was nice to date someone with money, but in the end there was just loneliness in a room with two people in it. It's then that you really get to know who that person truly is. Truth is, I wanted to be in love, and maybe I projected things on her that were simply what I hoped she would turn out to be. Would I have put money on her turning out to be an ancient soul sucking monster, though? No, but even before tonight that's what our relationship felt like at times."

Rory laid her polearm across one of her own arms and moved the blade low enough so it was at eye level. "You sure you don't want the luckstone back? I mean, with everything you sacrificed for it."

Freya smiled, but shook her head. "Thanks, but I'm good. It was never really about the stone, anyway, only what it symbolized. It has no power over me any longer." Freya looked back over her shoulder into the apartment, then gestured toward the elevator. "You two get out of here... enjoy your anniversary."

"Oh, right," Rory said with a short laugh. "I almost forgot." She raised the polearm and gave a nod to the maker. "Thanks again, for the gift."

"Don't thank me," Freya said. She raised her hand and pressed the door close button before withdrawing her hand from the elevator. "That's a good guy you've got there."

Freya smiled, but Rory saw it disappearing from the woman's face as the elevator doors closed, leaving her and Marshall to ride in silence down through the high-rise. Only after Rory finished

breaking down her polearm and stashing it back in her art tube did Marshall speak.

"So… that was a thing, huh?" he said. "Sorry about our anniversary. Sorry about tonight."

"Don't be," she said. Rory leaned against him, pressing her cheek against his chest, taking a calm comfort in it. "In its own twisted way, it was… fun."

Marshall laughed. "You have a strange idea of what's fun."

"And you have strange ideas about what gifts are," she said. "Next time, flowers will suffice."

"Noted," he said and wrapped his arms around her. "And I promise I'll stop making up strange, arbitrary half-year anniversaries to celebrate."

The warmth of his embrace felt like a heavy blanket against the cold winter of the past few hours, and Rory gave herself over to it gladly, completely.

"Don't you dare," she said. "Don't you dare stop being you, being who you truly are. We can celebrate every damned six-month-iversary you want. Just promise me one thing."

The elevator slowed as it approached the lobby. "Name it."

"Let's never get to like those two, okay?"

"Oh hell no," Marshall said. "Don't worry. I've already got a plan in place for just such a contingency."

The doors opened, and Rory took his hand in hers as they set off across the high rise's lobby and whatever awaited them out in the bustling New York City beyond it.

"Thanks, Batman."

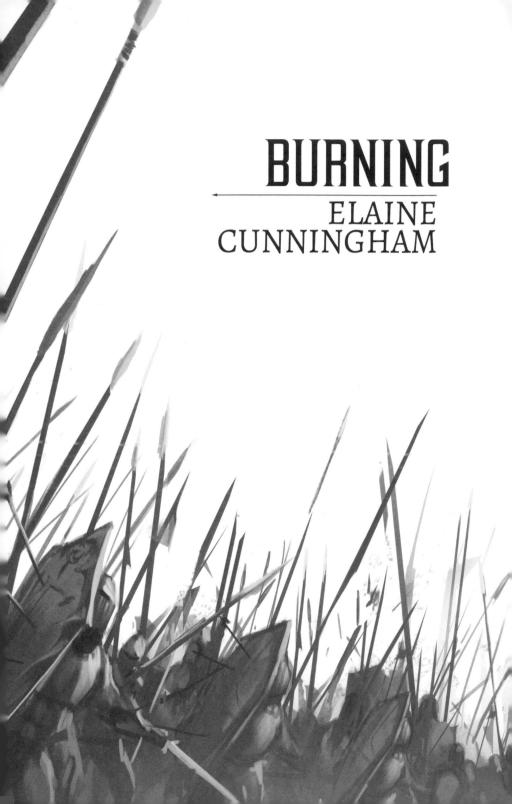

BURNING

ELAINE CUNNINGHAM

DRAGON—A SOLITARY DRAGON—CAN fly faster than rumors, but when the dragons' inner fires kindle and they gather to mate and burn and rampage their way across the Vast, a team of pack mules can outpace them. Never in human history has this proven untrue. When the first refugees from the sunrise kingdoms staggered into Dinistari, the lore keepers told us we'd have five years, perhaps as many as seven, before everything we knew burned to ash.

That was six years ago.

It had taken me nearly that long to reach the outskirts of Bluestone Castle. Never mind why. The dragons were coming, and I was finally going to take my place among the women who would stop them.

I hurried through the maze of narrow streets, only dimly aware of the dark looks and the gestures of warding the town folk threw my way. The seabirds' complaints grew louder as I neared the cliffs, and the jumble of marketplace scents yielded to the tang of the sea. Finally, I caught sight of the seawall, and the gatehouse guarding the entrance to the castle causeway. I brushed aside my upper veil so I might get an unclouded look at my new home.

The castle stood on a tall, rocky island just off the coast, con-

Illustration by NICOLÁS R. GIACONDINO

nected to the mainland by a narrow strip of rock. Bluestone walls soared into the sky, crowned with tall, flat-topped towers that defied the winds blowing in from the sea. Above the highest of these towers, I glimpsed the silhouettes of battle-beasts Dinistari necromancers had created from ancient fragments of dragons' eggs.

One of those beasts would be mine to command.

I dropped the veil back over my eyes and strode toward the gatehouse. The three guards fell silent at my approach, their eyes wary as they took in my sand-colored robes and the veils that hid my face. One of them drew his cutlass with a slow, menacing flourish and tested the edge on the pad of his thumb.

It was a fine performance. Very intimidating. Fortunately, my veils hid my smirk.

I presented my papers to the gatekeeper. He ignored them. He was also careful to avoid meeting my gaze, which told me his knowledge of far-seers was based more on rumor than truth. This was disappointing; I'd expected better of the castle guard.

He dismissed me with a flick of his fingers. "Turn around and follow your nose to the fishmonger. The Jade Jug stands two doors down. Only place in town that'll have the likes of you."

"Got a weakness for your kind, the innkeeper does," said the guard with the cutlass. "His daughter burned out, too."

His words stung, as they were meant to. I pulled his name from his mind—not the name on his commission, or the lineage he'd invented for himself, but the name his lowborn mother used to scream at him.

"Things are seldom what they seem, Dajeeb," I said pleasantly. "Don't you find it so?"

The gatekeeper reached over to cuff the guard's head. "Keep your eyes on your boots and your thoughts in your own damned head. And you," he said, rounding back to me. "It's the Jade Jug or it's the sea-tide dungeon. Choose."

I held up my commission, which bestowed upon me the title of Torch, a commander among the elite warriors these men were pledged to serve.

"Since Lord Narkahesh summoned me for duty, why don't we let him decide?"

Perhaps they could read and perhaps they could not, but judging from the sudden pallor of their faces, they knew the necromancer's seal well enough.

DAJEEB ESCORTED ME INTO THE castle and into the tallest tower. In a narrow stairwell, hundreds of stairs spiraled skyward. The climb was nothing to me, but the guard was blowing like a hard-ridden horse long before we reached the threshold of the necromancer's lair.

There could be no mistaking the nature and purpose of this chamber. Who but a necromancer would fill his workplace with furnishings fashioned from bone?

The mounted heads of various monsters and men decorated the walls, staring into eternity with eyes of glass. A long table held jars and pots and vials filled with substances that glowed or bubbled, whispered or hummed. In the center of the hall stood a raised scrying bowl, a shallow vessel that resembled an oversized birdbath. Narkahesh, lord of this castle and one of the most feared and powerful men in the realm, stood beside the vessel, watching as servants emptied bowls of fresh blood into it.

The necromancer was much as expected: rich robes, black hair woven into a multitude of tiny braids, a beak of a nose, and cold, intelligent eyes. My gaze skimmed over him and settled on the trio of women near the hearth.

They stood at ease, sipping from goblets and chatting softly. All wore the Torch uniform, multi-colored dragonscale tunics that seemed to glow with inner fire. Their forearms were bandaged from the bloodletting, which had dimmed their fire-hued eyes to the color

of warm coals. None of them wore veils.

Not that I expected veils—only far-seers went about veiled—but after ten years among the farsighted I was more comfortable gazing into an unsuspecting mind than a naked face.

It was easier to look upon the suits of armor that ringed the room. Lord Narkahesh had amassed quite a collection: the head-to-foot plate of the northern knights, leather armor crafted by the forest elves, even the intricately woven rushes from the sunrise kingdoms.

More fascinating still were the three dragon hatchlings, two green and one red, chained to iron loops bolted onto the floor. Each was no bigger than a raven, and they lapped at a single saucer containing a few spoonfuls of the Torches' blood.

I understood the reason for this. Necromancy was the art of binding and shaping, and blood supplied both the chains and the clay. It bound the battle-beasts to the Torches, and the Torches to the necromancer's will. This method was time-tested, proven. I was certain I could do better.

Gently, carefully, I reached out to the red hatchling. When I touched its mind, the creature leaped back from the saucer like a startled cat and spun toward me. Its head turned this way and that, seeking despite the hood that covered its eyes.

Hoods! These were battle-beasts, not mewed hawks! These Torches couldn't handle a hatchling without first chaining and blinding it?

I forced my gaze back to my new sisters. As I'd feared, one of them was familiar—a woman from my village, the only other girl of our generation born with eyes the color of flame. Laurel, her name was. In our village, girls were usually named after flowers and herbs. She'd have a different name now, of course. All Torches took a new name along with their first battle-beast command.

The Torch glanced toward me. She leaned toward one of her comrades and said something in a low voice. Laughter rippled

through the group.

My cheeks flamed. I reminded myself that she would have burned, but for me, along with everyone in our village.

Yet here she was, and her dragonscale tunic proclaimed that she had succeeded where I had failed.

Dajeeb, who had been clinging to the doorpost and wheezing like a leaky bellows while I made my study of the chamber, finally gathered enough breath to announce me. The necromancer turned toward us and tipped back his head, the better to stare at me down the length of his nose. He strode to the throne-like chair at his writing table and waved me toward the lesser seat across. Dajeeb hastened to pull out the necromancer's chair, then he took up position behind his lord.

Narkahesh picked up a sheet of paper bearing Lord Oksari's sigil and scowled at the precise runes.

"Your name is Rue? Just that, and nothing more?"

I resisted the urge to recite a long string of invented names and titles, each more ridiculous than the last.

"It suffices. My lord."

His eyes narrowed at my tone. "And you're a far-seer."

"Yes."

"A dabbler in the magical arts, a mind too weak for anything but peering at the world through other people's eyes."

I brushed back my upper veil so that I could meet his gaze directly with my flame-colored eyes. "If that is what you believe, why did you summon me?"

Narkahesh put down the paper, folded his hands on the table, and leaned toward me. "Oksari is an old friend. Honest, as wizards go. Secretive, of course, but more plainspoken than you'd expect a spymaster to be. I've never known him to exaggerate."

"Nor have I."

"Yet the abilities he describes are unprecedented, and his claims

hard to credit. Convince me."

I'm no orator, but I've always found that actions make a fine substitute for words. A thought, a mere nudge, and suddenly Dajeeb drew that dagger of which he was so proud and held it against the necromancer's throat.

Three swords hissed free of their scabbards. Narkahesh raised one hand, halting the sudden rush of the Torches.

"I have no need of guards. You may go. All of you."

I released Dajeeb so that he could do his master's bidding. He all but ran from the chamber, closely followed by two of the women. Laurel remained, her sword still held in guard position. "Are you certain, my lord?"

Judging from the raw, incredulous fury on the necromancer's face, he was unaccustomed to disobedience. Apparently, Laurel had found her courage since we'd last met.

"Have you ever known me to be uncertain, Mirianda?"

Laurel—no, she was Mirianda now—sheathed her sword and gave me a warning glare. "No, my lord."

Nakarhesh watched her leave the chamber and close the door behind her. His expression, when he turned his attention back to me, was decidedly unfriendly.

"According to Oksari, you were not tested as a child, but went directly to the far-seer's tower."

"That is correct."

"Is it?" he said coldly. "I have heard a different tale."

Not surprising. Mirianda was with me the day a salamander lay in wait near the pond where the village girls went to swim after a day's work. I wonder if she'd also told him that she'd run like a scalded cat.

"You were tested," Nakarhesh repeated, "if not in the proscribed manner. A fire lizard attacked, and you could not hold it."

"I did hold it. For nearly an hour I held it, while the other

children ran for help and the men came to hack it to pieces with scythes and hoes."

"But not quite long enough."

This I could not deny. "No. Not long enough."

He let silence frame my admission for several long moments. "So," he said briskly, "you trained as a far-seer, you spied for Oksari. You exceeded your mandate. Brilliantly so, he claims."

"I would not presume to contradict Lord Oksari."

A spark of amusement lit the necromancer's eyes, then disappeared. "He says you took control of a man whose eyes you were using. You killed him to protect Sultana Zuly."

"Strictly speaking, the Sultana's guard, the man whose eyes I was using, fell to an assassin's blade."

"And you have no qualms about pushing him onto that blade?"

"He should have seen the dagger. He did not. I merely ensured that he did his duty to the Sultana."

Narkahesh nodded, his face thoughtful. I'd seen that look before. The first time I seized control of another human, I'd expected Lord Oksari to be appalled. Instead, he encouraged me to take on harder jobs, using people as weapons as well as windows to distant places.

"Oksari claims you can influence minds as well as control bodies. Powerful minds. You induced either Cardish or Omani to start a spell battle that killed them both. Which one, I wonder?"

"You are assuming, my lord, that I can control only one man at a time."

The necromancer lifted one eyebrow. "Show me."

I turned to the alcove that displayed two matching suits of plate armor and seized the minds of the elite warriors hidden in them.

In unison, they stepped off the platform and clanked toward the balcony. I raised my hand, and they stopped.

"What demonstration would you prefer, my lord? Should they fight each other, or shall I have them leap to their deaths?"

"Either option seems excessive." He reached for a bell and gave it a shake. Almost immediately, the door opened and a portly man draped in a seneschal's green robes stepped into the room.

"Farook will take you to the aerie to meet your crew. You will spend the day in flight and report back at nightfall." He reached for another parchment and began to read.

Astonishment rooted me to the chair, despite the obvious dismissal.

My crew? *Flying?* Torches commanded from the tower, bound to their dragons with bonds of blood and magic.

I gestured toward the scrying bowl. "Wouldn't I be better able to command the battle-beast from here?"

The necromancer glanced up. "You're not taking control of a beast. You'll be controlling a castledrake crew."

I stared at him, too stunned for speech.

"Will that be a problem?"

"Not for me," I said slowly. "But extended periods of mind control carry great risk. The crew could go insane."

His lips twisted into an unpleasant smile. "Should that occur, I doubt anyone would notice the difference."

THE DOOR TO THE AERIE creaked open, and I climbed onto the flat rooftop, shielding my eyes with one hand against the sudden brightness.

Wind whipped at my skirts and veils. I steadied myself against one of the enormous iron perches that ringed the roof and took stock of my new command.

On opposite sides of the aerie perched two dragons—castledrakes, to be precise—one with scales of pale silver and the other as blue as rain-washed slate. They glared at each other with hate-filled golden eyes, hissing like giant cats.

Fearsome beasts, certainly, but much smaller than I'd expected.

I couldn't imagine how four people could fit into the scaly dome that rose like a burl between the wings—the "castle" that gave these magically cultivated beasts their name.

Six women—the castledrakes' crews, I assumed—gathered around supply tables, filling flasks from an assortment of small kegs or packing food and sundries into travel bags. All the women were small in stature and lightly clad, which made sense, given the close quarters they were forced to share. With a jolt of something like panic, I realized that I'd have to shed my veils and robes.

A long shadow fell over the aerie. I looked up to see a black castledrake swooping into a descending spiral.

Someone shouted an alarm. The women dropped everything where they stood and scrambled into their respective castles.

The blue and silver dragons swept their leathery wings into high, taut curves. The downbeat lifted them into the sky with a sound like a thunderclap. They winged off together, their earlier differences apparently forgotten in the face of this new foe.

The newcomer dropped onto one of the vacated perches with a loud *whuff*, a sound that, adjusted for size, brought to mind my grandmother's groan as she sank into her chair after a day's work. The black dragon settled back on its haunches and raised one massive clawed fist, tossing an obscene gesture in the direction of the departing castledrakes.

That, too, was familiar.

The castle's hatch—a massive domed scale the approximate size and shape of a giant's battle shield—creaked slowly open...

And then fell off.

The scale clattered onto the aerie's stone floor and traced a rumbling arc as it rolled toward me. I leaped aside before it teetered and fell, rocking like an upended turtle.

A small, gray-haired woman nimbly climbed out of the castle and down the dragon's side. She moved like a woman half her age,

and her sleeveless vest bared arms that were lean and muscled. She strode over to the still-rocking hatch and regarded it for a moment, hands on narrow hips.

"That's not ideal," she observed.

"*Not ideal?*" demanded an incredulous voice from the castle. "Captain, we're *buggered sideways!* One good rainstorm, and we'll be floating tits-up like fish in a bowl."

Lilting bubbles of laughter, also from the castle, greeted this observation. "Fish don't *have* tits. Honestly, Gelanna, that's the sort of thing I'd expect a druid to know."

I looked up, and my jaw dropped. Two women peered over the edge of the open castle. One was a matronly woman with gray-streaked hair plaited into druid's braids. The other was a creature of legend.

I knew elves still existed, of course, but an actual encounter had never entered my realm of possibility.

The druid scowled at her fey crewmate. "Mermaids, then. You like mermaids better?"

"They're lovely," the elf said wistfully. "Especially with butter and lemon."

"She couldn't mean that literally," I murmured.

The captain glanced up. "If it makes you feel better to think that, go right ahead. Who the hell are you?"

"Your new Torch."

One eyebrow rose. "Shouldn't you be somewhere out of the wind, eating dates and sipping sugared wine?"

"Probably, but I'll be flying with you today."

"Why?"

"I'd like to get to know the crew and the dragon."

By now, the other women had scrambled down from the castle. At close quarters, the elf's appearance was decidedly feline. Green and brown stripes swirled across her angular face. Golden eyes

slashed with vertical pupils regarded me with curiosity. Her pointed ears rose nearly to the top of her close-cropped head. I found myself wishing she'd turn around so I could see if she had—

"No tail," the elf said. The druid elbowed her sharply. "What? Everyone asks."

The captain looked me up and down. "Why aren't you wearing dragonscale?"

"I haven't earned it yet."

Elf and druid exchanged a glance. "She hasn't *earned* it," the older woman said. She turned a cold gaze my way. "No offense, Torch, but we'd just as soon you didn't start 'earning it' here."

"Nevertheless."

"You're no use to us," she continued. "This dragon's the oldest in the fleet. Her fires burned out a few years back, and no Torch has ever been able to kindle her magic."

"After today's flight, feel free to take the matter up with Lord Narkahesh."

The captain huffed. "*That'd* go well. All right, let's get this over with. I'm Zim. That's Gelanna. No one can pronoun the elf's name, but we call her Anook. And the dragon's name is her own damn business."

I let that pass. "Rue."

"You'll need to shed the draperies, Rue. We'll be tripping over each other enough without all that."

This was the moment I'd been dreading. I reached under my veils, fingers sliding over ridges of ruined skin, and released the clasps that held the various straps in place. The wind did the rest. I unclasped my belt and shrugged off the robes. My shift bared my arms and legs, revealing deep whorls where flame had melted flesh. By the end of the day, my scalp would be burned anew, this time by the sun's fire. My hair, which once had been as black and glossy as raven's wing, had never grown back.

Zim's eyes narrowed. "You're a survivor, I'll say that much for you. Salamander?"

I nodded.

"Nasty buggers. Happened a while back, looks like."

"Nearly fifteen years."

"Fifteen—" She shook her head in amazement. "You were… what? Ten years old?"

"Almost twelve. Even so, I held it for nearly an hour."

"Huh." Zim looked to her crew, one eyebrow raised in silent inquiry.

I left the crew to make up their minds about me and walked over to the dragon. I'd come to Bluestone Castle to command a battle-beast, and that was what I intended to do. Narkahesh, as far as I was concerned, was welcome to befriend an amorous camel.

I pulled a dagger from my boot and slid the blade across my forearm. When the blood began to flow, I offered it to the dragon.

The crew's collective shock hit me like a sudden gust. No Torch fed a dragon directly, not even a hatchling, but the accepted method of blood-bonding took time. I didn't have that luxury. Either I would die, or I would command.

A low rumble of sound came from the dragon. After a moment, I recognized it as laughter.

The dragon bared fangs that shamed my dagger and raised a paw to its jaws. It hooked one tooth under a loose scale and tugged. The scale lifted, and a drop of blood fell to hiss and bubble on the stone floor. The dragon leaned down from its perch and presented its massive wrist, mirroring my own offering.

Or perhaps calling my bluff.

For a long moment, I held the dragon's gaze, which was an act of insanity rivaling the blood offering. Slowly, carefully, I slid into the creature's mind. It perceived me, not as an intruder but an intriguing guest. She welcomed me with a tapestry of emotions:

delight, curiosity, understanding, amusement. Our minds opened to each other, sharing and discovering in something very much like a swiftly unfolding friendship.

This, I had not expected.

The dragon's forked tongue flicked out and lightly touched my wrist. Before I could decide how to respond to Ysindre—for that was her name—Zim's slap spun me around and knocked me to my knees.

"Don't even think about reciprocating. Dragon blood would burn right through you and then melt the chamber pot. And it's a new chamber pot."

"Reckless," muttered Gelanna as she helped me to my feet. "Crazy as a shithouse rat."

The elf nodded happily. "She'll fit right in. Let's fly!"

I FOUND DRAGONFLIGHT BOTH TERRIFYING and exhilarating. Each downbeat of Ysindre's wings sent us lurching into the sky, followed but an equally sudden drop as her wings lifted for another stroke. Flight no longer came easily to the dragon. I could feel her bone-deep weariness.

But Ysindre's flight-joy remained undimmed, and so did her vast curiosity. Her gaze roved the landscape below, and through her eyes I saw details that redefined realism, heat patterns expressed as colors my human eyes had never perceived.

The castle was as crowded as I'd expected, but some sort of magic kept the noise level low enough to permit conversation. Zim stood at the front, peering through a small opening in the dragonscale wall. She directed orders to Gelanna who, I assumed, communicated them to Ysindre. The elf busied herself with arranging the bags and vials hanging from a net fastened top and bottom to a section of the castle wall.

"Food and weapons," she said, noticing my scrutiny. "Pretty much the same thing, really. Our dragon's fire might have gone out,

but it's amazing how much damage we can do with elven alchemy and good case of indigestion."

"Funeral feast ahead," Zim called. "Fifteen degrees north of moonrise."

Ysindra banked and adjusted her course in response to the druid's silent command. Through the dragon's eyes, I saw in the distance a circle of stones around a raised platform. The man lying upon it was as only as warm as the stone beneath him. Sunlight glinted off the tool or weapon at his side, and also on the silvery scales of another dragon winging in from the south.

"Got some competition," Zim said. "That's Mirianda's dragon. It'll be close race."

"No, it won't," the druid grumbled. "Sylvani is the fastest castle-drake in the fleet. The deceased will be dragonshit before we even clear the circle."

Her words puzzled me, but at the moment the stone circle claimed my full attention. Through Ysindre's eyes, the huge, rounded stones were no difference in color, shape, or heat than other boulders littering the rough terrain, but something about them bothered me. I reached out with my thoughts and slammed into a wall of malevolent cunning.

I lunged forward to grab the captain's arm. "Those are rockwains! They must have scattered the stone circle. They're laying ambush."

Zim darted a quick look back at me. "You're sure?"

"Very. I saw a dozen of them run down and rip apart a battalion of armored knights and horses in about as much time as this telling just took. A dragon the size of that silver hasn't a chance."

"Bugger. Can you warn off the crew?"

I reached out to the women in the silver castle, but a solid wall of magic held me back. No wonder Narkahesh had wanted me to fly with my crew—the castles were warded against intrusions of mind and magic.

"No," I admitted, "but I think Ysindre can."

The crew turned and stared. Judging from their stunned expressions, I gathered that dragons weren't quick to share their names.

One corner of Gelanna's mouth lifted. "Sylvani might see moonrise, after all."

I formed a mental image and sent it to Ysindre. Not control, not command, not even permission, but a vision of what we might do together. My domain encompassed the minds and will of the living, but she was a creature of necromancy. I saw no choice but to unlock her will, and trust her to do the rest.

Ysindre's surprise jolted through me, followed by a flood of grim joy and the sudden release of cold, dark magic—more power than I'd ever glimpsed in the mind of any human necromancer.

On the distant platform, the corpse jerked up into sitting position, then lurched to its feet, weapon in hand. I'd never seen a more awkward throw, but the dead man's aim was true. Sparks darted skyward when metal stuck living rock.

No metal weapon can hurt a rockwain, but the creatures are as skittish as sand squirrels. The startled monster leaped to its feet, revealing the "boulder" as the massive homunculus it was.

Even from this distance, we could hear the silver dragon's scream of fear and outrage. Her pale wings spread wide as she pulled out of her descent and skimmed over the funeral platform, then beat steadily as she winged back toward the castle.

Zim whooped in triumph and punched one fist into the air. "Message received! Light 'em up, Nook."

Anook cut the cord holding a large glass. She pulled the cork with her teeth, spat it out, and looked to me.

"Hold tight, sister."

With one swift movement, she surged to her feet and lobbed the vial high and hard.

I seized a handful of net as Ysindre rolled sharply. Through

the connection we shared, I felt her snap the bottle out of the air and swallow.

The "indigestion" took less than a heartbeat to catch fire. Roiling, grumbling pain rolled through the dragon and thrust me out of our connection.

"The buggers are back in formation," Zim called. "Probably haven't seen us yet. We're going in."

As Ysindre labored steadily toward ambush, Gelanna leaned toward me. "Was that puppet show down there really Ysindre's doing?"

"It was."

"Necromancy?"

"Yes."

The druid let out a long, low whistle. "Ysindre and I are bonded. How could I not know?"

"For the same reason that Torches focus all their magic on controlling battle-beasts. Ysindre and her kind are more powerful than the necromancers who created them. The blood-bond turns our dragons into locked crossbows, unable to release an attack unless someone pulls the trigger."

"Which keeps the necromancers in control."

"Exactly. If dragons could use their fire and their magic as they wished, who knows what they might do?"

A slow, grim smile spread across the druid's face. "Looks like we're about to find out."

Anook thrust a handful of small vials at us. "Get these ready to throw. Don't spill anything on a body part you'd like to keep."

By now I could see the funeral platform with my own eyes. The dead man was back in position, and so were the rockwains.

"Get ready," Gelanna said. "Deep breath and hold it in three, two...."

Loud, rumbling thunder rolled behind the dragon. I slid into Ysindre's mind and felt her sudden relief. As she banked hard to the

west, I saw the dense, gray-green cloud in our wake, sinking toward the stone circle like morning fog.

Ysindre began a swift climb.

"Now!" shouted Anook.

We hurled vials over the side.

"Brace!"

The explosion shook the sky. I felt Ysindre's satisfaction, as well as her mental wince as rock bounced off her belly armor.

Gelanna rose to her feet and gestured for me to join her. We peered over the edge of the castle to the shattered landscape below.

The stone platform was gone, and so were the rockwains. All that remained was smoking rubble and a circle of blackened sand.

"Behold the power," the druid said with mock solemnity, "of elven alchemy and dragon farts."

It felt good to laugh together. Our shared mirth was brief, though, and Zim gave voice to the fear that gnawed at me.

"Let's see what got the rockwains this far south."

The color drained from Gelanna's face. "Salt mines."

That seemed likely. Rockwains fed on metal and crystal. The only place that offered both in sufficient quantities would be the salt mine.

We flew northward in silence. I'd never seen the famed Dinistari mines and had never tasted the piquant blue salt miners harvested from the warrens of tunnels and deep caves. The blue salt commanded fabulous prices and accounted for a significant portion of Dinistari's wealth, so the mine was as heavily guarded as any castle. I've seen rockwains at work, and I didn't think the herd we'd just destroyed were sufficient to overcome the mine's defenses.

The sun was passing its zenith as Ysindre spiraled down to the blackened courtyard.

We climbed out of the castle and walked down the wing Ysindre extended into a landscape of nightmares. What had been a thriving town was now silent, smoking ruins. A few scorched bodies—far

fewer than I would have expected—lay here and there.

Gelanna walked among the ruins, stooping now and then to peer closely at a still, blackened face. Only a few moments passed before she fell to her knees beside a dead guard. A single, keening cry burst from her.

Zim and Anook bowed their heads in respect and shared sorrow.

I reached out into the town, and then the tunnels, searching for another living mind. When Zim sent me an inquiring look, I shook my head.

Ysindre lumbered over to the ruined barracks and nosed aside a smoking timber. I felt her hunger and her intent.

Horror filled me, and I wrenched free of our connection. Suddenly Zim's reference to a "funeral feast" made perfect, terrible sense.

The captain noted my expression. "Dragons need to eat."

"The aerie farms raise livestock."

"True, but we range for hundreds of miles. Flight requires food. Where else should they get it? Cattle? Farming folk don't much like that. Deer? How, exactly, would the dragon hunt them without burning down the forest? Perhaps they should dig for rabbit warrens?"

I took a long, shuddering breath. "This is common practice?"

"I'm surprised you didn't know. Our dragons clean up battlefields and pick up after bandits. We have funereal arrangements with certain towns and villages. But every now and then, a dragon gets hungry and the crew goes rogue. Self-defense, sometimes, or maybe Narkahesh" —she paused long enough to lean to one side and spit— "gives the order for reasons of his own. Either way, we'll find and kill whoever did this."

Today had been a day for revelations, so I shouldn't have been surprised when a great Presence edged into my farsight's perimeters.

"It wasn't a castledrake that did this," I said.

Gelanna looked up sharply, and I saw understanding kindle in her tearless eyes. "You're sure?"

I opened my mind to the druid, a sharing like the one I'd forged with Ysindre. Her eyes widened at the sudden connection to my thoughts, and through them, the first faint tendrils of the wild-wyrm's mind.

She rose to her feet, her face grim. "The first wild dragon is here. Let's go kill it."

WE RACED THE WILD DRAGON to Bluestone Castle, and lost.

The destruction was terrible, especially for a battle so young. A green castledrake lay sprawled and broken on the castle causeway. Another battle-beast plunged, wreathed in flame, into the burning town. The tallest tower, the lair of Narkahesh, stood in smoking half-ruin.

The creature circling Bluestone Castle was red as blood, as large as a battleship. When a young castledrake darted in, fires blazing, the dragon simply bit it in half. Flying on unperturbed, it tossed back its head and swallowed the hindquarters.

All my life, I'd prepared myself to fight dragons. Nothing had prepared me for this.

"I have no idea how to kill that thing."

Anook held up a vial. "With this."

Gelanna's thoughts were still open to me. Two things rose above the tumble of grief and vengeance: a deep sense of resignation, and the word *dragonsbane*.

I knew that word, but only from legends of a deadly elven potion, lethal to any dragon that would be persuaded to swallow it.

Or to eat the flesh of another dragon that had swallowed it.

"It's time, sisters," Zim said. "Let's go out well."

Ysindre climbed toward the clouds, readying herself for the attack that would kill us all, and, if the fates were kind, the red dragon as well.

Anook drew back her arm to throw the vial to Ysindre. Suddenly, Gelanna seized her arm and ripped the vial from her hand.

"There's a surer way," she said, and tossed back the poison in a single gulp. Tremors seized her immediately.

"Hold tight!" howled Anook.

I seized the net as our dragon folded her wings in close to her body and went into a roll.

Earth and sky changed places. When order was restored, I shared the castle with only two women.

The red swooped under us, so close that I could smell the brimstone stench of its breath, and snapped Gelanna from the sky.

Ysindre's grief and rage burned through me. Or perhaps it was my own. Overwhelmed by the force of emotion, I responded in a manner that, before today, would have been too insane to contemplate.

I seized a passing tendril of the dragon's thoughts and pulled myself into its mind. As I had with the salamander, I commanded it to hold.

There was a moment of surprise, comically human, then the all-consuming blaze of the dragon's mind filled me until I was certain I would explode.

The agony of my battle against the salamander's mind, the fire it breathed when I lost control? That was only a pale, weak flicker. Now I understood real pain.

Every instinct screamed at me to retreat. Instead, I moved deeper into the maelstrom of fire and fangs, rejoicing as the dragon's pain flared into a blaze to match my own. The poison was taking hold.

But not soon enough.

Surprise had given me a moment's advantage over the monster, but my hold on it faded swiftly. The massive red chest expanded as it drew breath to fuel a killing blast of fire.

That, we could not permit. Inner flame would burn off the poison.

Ysindre darted in, clinging and savaging the red dragon's throat like a weasel attaching a wolf. Massive claws tore at her again and again, but still she held.

We rode the dragon down, and through Ysindre's eyes, I saw the grassy plain beyond the town rise up to receive us. Just before impact, my sister released her hold and spread her shredded wings. I felt the jolt of a collision, and then nothing at all.

I AWOKE LYING IN A goat cart that was trundling along the plain behind a pair of mules. The sun was sinking toward the horizon, which meant we were headed for Bluestone. Several Torches walked on either side of the cart, like an honor guard. Or perhaps a funeral procession.

"She's awake," someone said.

Gentle hands raised my head and held a waterskin to my lips. I tasted healing herbs and forced myself to swallow a few sips. When I could no longer bear the pain of not knowing, I pushed the skin away.

My gaze fell on Mirianda. "My crew? My dragon?"

"The elf survived."

Her tone told the rest of the tale. I nodded and lay back, dimly aware that the cart was turning around and heading eastward, but not caring enough to wonder why.

We pulled to a stop, and two of the Torches helped me from the cart. A soft cry broke free from me as I beheld the still, broken thing that had been Ysindre. Some hundred paces beyond, the red dragon's corpse rose like a small hill. Red and black scales scattered across the plain like fallen petals.

Mirianda pointed to a small, shining scale. "That's a good one. Shall I pick it up for you?"

Her meaning came to me suddenly. They had brought me here to harvest scales for my armor.

"Would you have me skin my human sisters for boot leather, as well?" I snarled.

Mirianda jerked back as if she'd been slapped. "What would

you have us do instead?"

"Call your dragons."

Her brow furrowed in puzzlement. "*Call* them?"

I hissed in exasperation and reached for the mind of the silver castledrake circling overhead. Sylvani swooped down and landed with a few running steps. When I relayed my request, she turned to look expectantly at Mirianda, who in turn looked to me.

"Let her breathe fire," I said. "The red dragon will provide food for the castledrake fleet, but Ysindre was our sister. Give her the dignity she deserves."

The Torch nodded. Gouts of flame poured from her dragon's jaws, and we stood in silence as Ysindre burned.

After a moment, Mirianda reached for the shoulder clasps of her dragonscale tunic and let it fall into a shimmering puddle. She stepped out of it, picked it up, and tossed it into the funeral pyre.

One after another, the other Torches—my sisters—did the same.

When nothing remained of our fallen dragons but ash, the Torches gathered around me.

"What you did to call Mirianda's castledrake," one of them ventured. "Can it be learned?"

"Lord Narkahesh would not approve," another said.

"Narkahesh is dead," Mirianda said harshly. "We need new ways."

"And a new commander."

Murmurs of agreement rippled through the group, and all eyes looked to me.

A command of my own, not just of a battle-beast, but an entire aerie!

For several moments, the desire to seize control raged through me like dragonfire. I fought it back until it was banked coals.

"Do you know your dragon's name?"

Mirianda's brow furrowed in puzzlement. "Its name?"

"*Her* name." I took Mirianda's arm and led her over to the

Sylvani. "It's time you were properly introduced. And tomorrow, all of you will be flying with your crews. The dragons are coming. Let's find out exactly how they're going to die when they arrive."

AN ESSAY BY
SARAH KUHN

IT AIN'T BAD TO GET MAD:
THE ANGRY HEROINES OF SF/F

WHEN I WAS LITTLE, ONE of my favorite *Sesame Street* bits involved a cartoon goat who was always getting epically pissed off. The message—set to a catchy song, of course— was that it was *okay* to get epically pissed off. "It ain't bad to get mad!" went the chorus. Have your feelings, goat! Emotions are cool, even when they aren't necessarily positive!

(I would just like to note here that as an adult, I've come to the realization that the goat's other animal friends are *total dicks*. They pull his beard, scare him with fireworks, won't share their ice cream. Um, *of course* he keeps getting mad.)

I learned a lot of useful lessons from *Sesame Street*, but while the cartoon goat was one of my favorite *dramatis personae*, I never quite internalized what he was trying to teach me. Because as a young girl, everything and everyone else constantly conveyed to me that it most definitely *was* bad to get mad.

Adults told me—via reactions, subtext, and/or actual words— that two of the most prized qualities in young girls were 1) being nice and 2) calming down. I can still remember my mother chanting, "I need you to calm down—callllmmmmmm," and then repeating

that single word over and over again like a mantra. I was like that fucking goat, always mad about something. And I knew that was definitely not okay, even if I didn't always know why.

I saw how getting mad affected everything: how it caused you to get in trouble, punished, dismissed, talked down to, made fun of, ostracized. How it was even seen as something dangerous, an uncontrollable blaze that needed to be contained, tamped down, extinguished. And because of all this, I was definitely on the path toward stamping out any and all vestiges of rage forever, toward residing permanently in Being Niceville, toward learning the exact opposite of what my wise cartoon goat friend was trying to teach me.

I am forever thankful that I discovered the Angry Heroines of Sci-Fi/Fantasy at exactly the right time.

First there was Princess Leia (Carrie Fisher) in *Star Wars*: all bold, commanding swagger, never afraid to raise her voice (because that was another thing young girls weren't supposed to do, right?) in order to get her point across to walking carpets or scruffy-looking nerf herders. And—very important for my hopelessly romantic, young 'shipper's soul—the angry blaze didn't dim when she fell in love. Nope, her anger was an essential piece of what her partner loved about her, a key element that made her the galactic badass she still is today.

Then there was Major Kira Nerys (Nana Visitor) on *Star Trek: Deep Space Nine*, a combat booted powerhouse who stomped around the space station like she owned the place, regularly butting heads with everyone and always ready to go into battle with all possible guns blazing (I read somewhere that Visitor went out and bought a pair of Doc Martens in order to get into Kira's stompy-footed mindset, and that solidified my adolescent Docs obsession that still lives on today). As with Leia, I loved that Kira very decisively got shit done, and that rather than being positioned as a repellant personality trait, her anger drew others to her—friends and lovers

and fellow officers admired the passion and verve housed in that rage and didn't try to shame her for it (This is probably for the best as I can't even begin to imagine Kira's reaction to being told to "be nice."). Yes, she had some things to work through as far as honing, channeling, and nuancing out that anger, but the complexity of her journey just made me love it even more.

On the animated side of things, I thrilled in the literally fiery rage of Sailor Mars, aka Rei Hino. I loved Usagi, Sailor Moon, for her klutzy, imperfect, can-do attitude, but I *related* more to Rei's determination, impatience, and near constant annoyance with the world around her. And I deeply appreciated the fact that even though she and Usagi bickered non-stop, that Rei yelled at Usagi for crying too much, and Usagi whined about Rei being "mean" to her, there was always a deep undercurrent of sisterly Sailor Senshi love between them, perhaps best expressed when Rei notes—right as the pair are about to be plunged into deadly danger—"We always fought, but it was fun."

I've been thinking about these Angry Heroines of SF/F a lot lately, as every week on the Internet where we all reside seems to bring another round of "what are you so angry about/why are you always outraged/calm down/be nice." Sometimes, all it takes to prompt that is existing as a woman—particularly a woman of color—who dares to take up space at all. If all I'd had growing up was that lone pissed-off cartoon goat, I might be tempted to listen to those voices. But as someone who discovered the Angry Heroines of SF/F at various crucial moments in her life, I know that I've finally internalized what my little goat friend wanted me to know in the first place: it ain't bad to get mad. Feeling your anger, showing your anger, taking power in your anger is a thing you can do and still be a heroine. Hell, it's a crucial part of what *makes* you a heroine.

I am thankful to have these characters to look up to, to admire, to embody. I am thankful to have discovered even more examples

in both fiction and real life. I am thankful that I have been able to incorporate Angry Heroines into my own work and to show their anger as something to be validated and celebrated.

You know that meme that went around recently? The one where you had to pick three fictional characters to represent you? As I was assembling mine, I noticed something: two of my three (Mars and my beloved Jessica Huang, played by Constance Wu, from *Fresh Off the Boat*) had photos where they were legit angry: eyes rageful, mouths open to yell. It made me pause for a moment as my finger hovered over the "upload" button: how did I feel about that?

Fucking proud, I realized. And I hit "upload" with the confident swagger that would make my Angry Heroines of SF/F proud, too.

A DANCE WITH DEATH

MARC TURNER

TEREN SAT ON A BENCH, staring out across Speaker's Park as the shadow of the White Lady's Temple crept towards him. He scratched the remains of his left ear. The top of it had been bitten away long ago, and the teeth marks of the person responsible were still evident in his flesh. There was no tension in his bearing that might have alerted Jenna to trouble. As she advanced to stand behind him, he did not look around. Usually turning your back on an assassin was an unhealthy mistake to make, but Teren would know it was the only thing keeping him alive at that moment. For eight months he had worked as Jenna's agent, and not once had he seen her face.

"You took your time," he said brightly. "I was beginning to think you hadn't got my message."

Jenna pulled a flask of juripa spirits from her pocket and took a swig. "There are lots of people about this evening," she said. "I had to make sure none of them followed you here."

"And did they?"

"No."

"Too bad. There was a brunette a few streets back I was certain had her eye on me."

Enough with the pleasantries. Another time Jenna might have

Illustration by NICOLAS R. GIACONDINO

enquired as to the well-being of Teren's sister and nephew, but oddly people tended to get nervous when an assassin asked after their family. "You've got a job for me?" she said.

"Indeed. Senator Erekus Rayne."

"My target's a politician? It'll make a nice change to be on the good side for once."

Teren passed her a scroll over his shoulder, and Jenna tucked it away to read later.

"Everything you need to know is in there," Teren said. "Erekus Rayne is quite the rising star. Recently he married into the Storn family, giving him the ear of Tyrin Lindin Tar herself. He has also just been promoted to the Third Tier of the Senate, and is said to own half the property in the Wharf District."

"A powerful man, clearly. But is he *happy*?"

Teren chuckled. "He must be, considering the number of enemies he has made lately. There's his new wife, obviously. Then there's the greater half of the Fourth Tier of the Senate, along with the lesser half too. Unfortunately that makes it more difficult for us to work out who wants him dead."

A pity. Jenna always liked to know who was paying her bill in case that person decided later that she was a loose end that needed tying off. "What about the go-between you spoke to?"

"A Maru, judging by his white hair." Teren grimaced. "Sour fellow. He was probably brought in just to place this contract, and if he's going to be returning to Marul now, he can't get there fast enough."

Jenna eyed him skeptically. If making new friends was so important to Teren, he'd chosen a strange line of work.

The sun set behind the dome of the White Lady's Temple, framing the roof in fire. The stones had that familiar shine to them that always made Jenna wonder if the building would retain its glow even after night came. But it never did. In the end, even the brightest light must succumb to the dark.

Teren said, "There's one condition to the contract you should know about. Our client wants Erekus killed outside the auditorium on the night of Fool's Grace. Apparently that date is significant to our patron. As to the relevance of the auditorium, the Maru would not say."

Most likely, Jenna mused, it was not the place itself that was important, but rather who would be with Erekus when he was there. Sometimes her clients wanted to be present when the mortal blow was struck so that they could confirm the kill. Or for the dubious pleasure of watching the life fade from their enemy's eyes.

Teren said, "You haven't asked about the fee they're offering."

"Is it fair?"

"More than fair."

"Then what's the problem?"

Teren hesitated over his next words. "You *never* ask about the fee," he said. "That tells me one of two things. Either you trust me implicitly to represent your interests—which sounds very flattering, until I remember you won't let me see your face. Or it shows you're not interested in the money."

Jenna did not respond.

"Why do you do this if not for the coin?" he asked. "There has to be a reason."

The assassin sighed. It appeared the time was fast approaching when she would have to dispense with Teren's services. Since arriving in Arkarbour, she had been represented by three different agents, and each of them had eventually strayed over the line that divided professionalism from familiarity. It was always the same: spend enough time in an associate's company and sooner or later their wariness gave way to respect. Then before you knew it, you were on the path to camaraderie and even attachment. It was a slippery slope, for sure. Jenna had never understood the progression. Teren knew almost nothing about her except for her voice and her

vocation. And a shared interest in killing people was hardly a strong foundation upon which to build a friendship.

If Jenna did have to part ways with him, it would be with regret. The man was efficient. He was also surprisingly good natured for someone in the trade. Last month Jenna had seen him at the Feast of Hands, where he had passed within an armspan of her without realizing it. He had spent the night dancing with every woman who would humor him—including the Beloved of the White Lady. Afterwards, the Beloved had sensed Jenna watching her and looked across. The priestess's subsequent smile had left the assassin feeling like an intruder. The Feast of Hands marked the longest day of the year, and the revelers who had come to celebrate it had been eager to shake Jenna's hand or toast her health with brim-full tankards. Just as if she belonged in their company, and wasn't a cold-blooded killer at all.

Teren shifted on the bench. Jenna had still not answered his earlier question, and the silence stretched out.

"Apologies," he said at last. "I didn't mean to pry."

"Of course not," Jenna replied. "That's why you started asking personal questions." But she made her voice light to take the edge off her words. She took a final drink from her flask, then replaced the cap and put the flask back in her pocket. "Let me read the papers you've given me on Erekus. Tell the client they will have my answer within the week."

JENNA LISTENED TO THE SWELL of voices from the auditorium across the street. The troupe of singers giving tonight's concert was testing the boundaries of what constituted song, and whenever the racket died down, Jenna could make out a strained silence as their audience struggled to find some redeeming feature to the performance. A handful of people had already abandoned the effort and departed. Jenna suspected it was just a matter of time before Erekus

too remembered important business elsewhere.

It had been a simple matter for Jenna to choose a vantage point from which to shoot the senator. Opposite the auditorium was an abandoned house that had recently been damaged in a sorcerous quarrel between a fire-mage and an earth-mage. Jenna was stationed at a broken window in an upstairs bedroom. The chamber had a stink of charred wood and an even stronger whiff of privilege about it. The paneled walls were covered in brass fittings and blackened tapestries showing hunting scenes. At one end of the room was a hole in the floor through which the bed had fallen, while at the other end was a fireplace. Around the fireplace was an area of roughly ten square paces where the floorboards had been burned away or ripped up. The crossbeams beneath remained intact, and between them Jenna could see the shadows of ruined furniture in the room below. Every breath of wind outside drew a creak from the exposed timbers, as if the house were stirring in its sleep.

Jenna's breath was warm against her skin, trapped by the scarf that covered the lower half of her face. This was the part of the job she disliked most: the waiting. With too much time to think, her mind could travel down all sorts of treacherous paths. None of those paths led to places that Jenna cared to revisit, but as a friend of hers had once said, if you didn't feel regret as an assassin, you weren't doing your job properly. To pass the time, Jenna considered again the various scenarios she might encounter tonight. What happened if her view of Erekus was obstructed as he left the auditorium? What if her preferred route of escape was blocked? She couldn't anticipate every eventuality, of course, but at least if one of these things transpired, she would be able to react without hesitation.

Earlier, she had walked every step of the house, opened every door, committed every exit to memory. An abandoned building immediately outside the auditorium was too convenient a boon to be regarded with anything but suspicion. Yet Jenna had watched the

place for two days prior to this one, and she had seen no one enter or leave. Upon arriving tonight, she had searched it and searched it again, only to find the house empty save for an echo that had dogged her steps. The back door had been ripped off its hinges, while most of the furniture had been smashed into firewood. The only piece that remained intact was a high-backed chair that Jenna had carried up from the drawing room and positioned to her right.

She shifted her grip on her crossbow. Three women emerged from the auditorium before setting off along Harbour Street at a pace that suggested they were keen to put the singing out of earshot. Then behind them appeared . . .

Jenna went still. Erekus Rayne.

If she hadn't seen him previously, she might have wondered if the senator had swapped clothes with one of his bodyguards. Erekus's haircut looked like shaving stubble, and he had the crooked nose of a brawler. If the rumors were to be believed, he was a man who, in the conduct of his affairs, was not only willing to get his hands dirty, but positively enjoyed doing so. Last month, one of his servants had been fished from the sea off Baker's Point, his face smashed almost beyond identification. By a quirk of fate, Jenna had been there to see the man dragged ashore. And pure coincidence, obviously, that the servant had apparently been overheard a day earlier questioning his master's virility to a friend who has also gone missing.

Jenna always demanded from Teren a detailed report into her targets' backgrounds. She had taken to watching them before accepting a job too, seeing their lives in action, developing a sense of their character. It was the height of foolishness, she knew. Who was she to weigh another's life in her hands? She was granting herself the role not just of executioner, but of magistrate and jury too, as if her targets—and not herself—were the true villains in this business. The reality, of course, was quite different. And she never let herself lose sight of that fact, however uncomfortable it might be.

The truth must always be confronted, not dressed up in frills so it looked more palatable.

Yet she was turning down more and more commissions of late. Where once the world had seemed black and white, now all was shades of gray.

Erekus halted outside the auditorium. With him were six body-guards. Three carriages were situated a short distance away, but Jenna knew a man of the senator's self-importance wouldn't demean himself by walking to them. Instead he hailed a driver and waited for the coach to come to him.

Jenna lined him up in the crossbow's sights, picturing the shot she would make.

The breeze picked up, eliciting another chorus of creaks from the house.

Sudden movement through the doorway to Jenna's right. In the hall outside the bedroom, shadows gathered.

Crossbow strings twanged.

Jenna had already reached for the armrest of the chair beside her. Earlier, she had positioned it just *so*, and a tug now was sufficient to turn it so that its back piece screened her from the doorway. Two missiles crunched into the wood, throwing up splinters.

Jenna peered over it.

A Maru entered the room, his white hair seeming to glow in the gloom. Was this the same Maru who had placed the contract with Teren last week? *It has to be.* He walked with a strut that said he knew his worth and held it considerable. Judging by his sneer, his opinion of Jenna was less lofty, but the assassin no longer troubled herself with the views of others. She was perfectly capable of per-ceiving her own faults, thank you very much.

The pieces of the picture were falling into place for her—a picture that she had glimpsed just enough of previously to warrant positioning the chair where she had. Her contract was a sham; *she*

was her client's real target in this, not Erekus. And how do you eliminate an assassin whose identity you do not know? An assassin who hasn't shown her face even to her agent? You give her a false job, of course, and lure her to a location of your choosing. But the luring has to be done with care. If Jenna had been instructed simply to kill her victim from this house, she would have known something was wrong. So instead, her client had told her that Erekus must be killed as he left the auditorium—an auditorium that just happened to be situated opposite an abandoned house that offered unrivaled views of the street. It was obvious that Jenna would choose this window to shoot from. And thus easy for her employer to set a trap.

In the hall, more figures assembled. Jenna's skin prickled. *Half a dozen at least.* Too many for her to fight alone.

Fortunate, then, that she had helpers standing by—albeit helpers of the unwitting kind.

Looking down into the street, Jenna saw Erekus still waiting for his carriage. She took aim and pulled the trigger.

Her crossbow bolt hit the senator square in the chest, and he was knocked back into the arms of his bodyguards. In case those guards weren't sure where the shot had come from, Jenna waved to them through the window.

A man shouted a challenge.

Jenna looked back at the Maru and cocked her head. It was clear from his expression that he hadn't anticipated this development. It was equally clear he understood the gravity of his predicament, for Erekus's bodyguards would soon be breaking down the front door, and the Maru would have a hard time explaining his presence in the same building as Jenna. What were his options? The assassin knew he couldn't retreat. If he fled, he and his troops might be mistaken for the killers, allowing Jenna to slip away. His only choice would be to split his force and send some warriors to slow down the bodyguards while he himself engaged Jenna—then hope to overpower Erekus's

men after she was dead.

The Maru barked an order to his companions before entering the room. He wore a blackened breastplate sculpted to resemble a muscled torso, and he carried a shield and a longsword. Only one other person came with him—a woman with a face as round as her shield. Neither of them had crossbows.

Jenna liked her odds better all of a sudden.

There wasn't time for her to reload her own crossbow, so she left it on the window seat and scampered towards the fireplace. The floorboards here had been destroyed, and the exposed crossbeams groaned as they took her weight. She drew two throwing knives.

From downstairs came the first thuds as Erekus's bodyguards pounded on the front door. The Maru's female partner, Round Face, looked back towards her colleagues in the hall. Missing the safety of their company already? Jenna's face twisted. As if such safety existed. True strength came not from numbers but from standing alone. Lean on others and one day all your power would be shown for naught when their support was taken away.

The Maru stepped confidently onto the first beam and advanced. Round Face, when she followed, was less sure-footed. The timbers were aligned at right angles to her progress, meaning Round Face had to step from one to the next, and she tottered forward as if she were crossing the deck of a pitching ship. When the woman next lifted a foot, Jenna sent a throwing knife spinning towards her. Round Face raised her shield, and the blade ricocheted away. But with her attention on Jenna's knife, it couldn't also be on her feet. Her boot slipped off a beam, and she fell forward onto the other timbers, her shield trapped beneath her.

Jenna's second throwing knife took her in the eye. Round Face collapsed, and her body slithered between the beams and toppled into darkness. With a thump she hit the floor of the room below.

Jenna unsheathed her longknives.

If the Maru was concerned at the loss of his friend, he gave no indication. He stepped onto the next beam, and it creaked beneath him.

Jenna glanced at the Maru's breastplate. "Nice armor," she said. "Looks heavy."

The man did not respond. Setting his feet on adjacent beams, he stabbed out at the assassin with his sword. Jenna parried the blow, then countered with a backhand cut that her opponent blocked with his shield.

So far, so simple.

Voices came from the hall. It seemed the Maru's companions meant to make their defense at the top of the stairs, for a woman ordered her fellows to look for something to use as a barricade.

Jenna circled right, staying on the Maru's shield side so he would be forced to attack her across his body. For an instant they stood on the same two beams, and the left timber groaned. Jenna stamped on it, making it judder.

The Maru wobbled but stayed upright. "Surrender," he said. "No assassin is a match for a trained warrior. That's why you must strike from the shadows like the cowards you are."

"This from the man who tried to ambush me just now."

"We are nothing alike," the Maru snapped. "I serve a man of vision. A man of breeding. I kill for a cause, not for coin."

A distinction that was unlikely to bring much comfort to the souls he sent through Shroud's Gate.

Jenna continued her circuit of her opponent, watching his feet all the while. As he twisted to keep her in view, his legs became briefly crossed, and Jenna surged forward, feinting high with one of her longknives. When the Maru lifted his shield to block, the assassin checked her attack and planted a kick on his shield.

He staggered back, only for his boot to land safely on the beam behind him.

Lucky bastard.

Downstairs, the banging on the front door continued. Jenna could also hear running steps in the atrium, meaning someone must have thought to try the back door. Clicks sounded as the bolts to the front door were drawn back. Voices spilled into the house.

Jenna went back to circling her opponent. The Maru tried to surprise her mid-step with a bash from his shield, but a tensing of his posture had betrayed his intent, and the assassin was able to dance back out of range. They came to stand on the same two beams again. When the right one voiced its complaint, Jenna stomped on it and was rewarded with a crack. The wood shifted, and the Maru hurriedly lifted his boot from the beam.

That gave the assassin an idea.

From the direction of the hall came pounding steps as Erekus's bodyguards stormed up the staircase. The crossbows of the Maru's troops strummed in answer. A man screamed. There was a clang of metal as two swords met.

"Surrender," the Maru said to Jenna again. "You are only delaying the inevitable. Prolong this, and when I am finished with you, I will track down your family and make them suffer."

Jenna's voice was flat. "You can't do anything worse to them than I have already done myself." Another regret, another memory best left undisturbed. It mattered not that what had happened all those years ago had been an accident. Some mistakes were too grave to ever be forgiven—at least by Jenna herself.

She jabbed at her opponent's groin with her longknife, testing his low guard. The Maru parried, yet did not counter. He was trying to encourage her to attack again, but the assassin wouldn't let herself be drawn into a longer engagement. She recommenced her circling. The Maru clucked his frustration. He would have to start taking more risks soon, for Erekus's bodyguards might fight through to the chamber at any moment. If that happened, Jenna would risk

a drop into the room below and seek to slip away in the confusion. But the Maru? Encumbered by his armor, he was less likely to be able to walk away from a plunge through the beams.

He unleashed a decapitating cut at the assassin, and Jenna ducked beneath it. The damaged beam was now in front of her. She made a point of stepping over it, then quickly retreated from the Maru, forcing him to come to her.

Her opponent followed her lead, stepping over the damaged beam.

Except it *wasn't* the damaged beam that he had stepped over; Jenna had stepped *onto* that one in the hope of tricking the Maru, and he had fallen for the ruse admirably. It had been a gamble, of course. Jenna weighed less than her foe, but that hadn't guaranteed that the beam would support her. The assassin's steps, though, were as light as they were sure, allowing her to skip over the timber and onto the one beyond.

The Maru was not so fortunate. When he trod on the damaged beam it snapped with a noise like a breaking bone. His lower half disappeared through the floor. He released his shield and curled his arms over the next beam to halt his descent.

Oh no you don't.

Jenna stepped forward to kick him in the face.

The Maru surrendered his hold and dropped into the room below. There was a crash of furniture, a screech of metal. The Maru turned the air blue with a string of curses.

No time for Jenna to toast her victory. If the shrieks in the hall were any indication, the battle between the Maru's warriors and Erekus's bodyguards was nearing its end. She scurried to a broken window on the east-facing wall of the room. Her pack lay on the floor beside it, and from the pack Jenna withdrew a grappling hook to which a length of rope had been tied. The need for haste put a tremble in her hands. She leaned out of the window, taking care not

to cut herself on the glass shards protruding from the frame. The roof was several armspans above. Drawing back her arm, she cast the hook into the air. It caught on the eaves, and Jenna tugged on the rope to ensure it was secure.

Then she left the rope hanging there and darted back to the fireplace. Her enemies, after all, would now expect her to escape to the roof, and the thing someone expected her to do was always her last consideration.

The flue of the chimney was large enough to accommodate a person. There were no convenient handholds Jenna could use to climb, so she put a foot against one wall and slid her back up the opposite one. A push up with one leg, a shuffle, then she was high enough that someone arriving in the chamber wouldn't be able to see her. She braced her legs to stop herself slipping down. A stone dug into her back, but she could put up with a little discomfort. *Better a stone than a sword.*

From the hall came a final scream, then a figure clomped into the room and over to the window. One of the Maru's warriors or one of Erekus's? It hardly mattered, since neither would have come to enquire after Jenna's health.

She held her breath.

Twenty of the most disagreeable heartbeats of Jenna's life followed—and there had been some pretty stiff competition on that score. The soot in the chimney tickled her throat. She felt a cough coming but held it in.

Then a man's voice yelled, "She's on the roof!" There was a grunt and a scratch of boots on the wall outside.

Jenna allowed herself a smile. The man was climbing the rope.

She lowered herself into the fireplace. It was tempting to stay put in the chimney until the dust settled on tonight's events, but she suspected it wouldn't be long would before someone realized they'd been duped. She crossed to the window and looked out. Above, the

climber had vanished. Below was a flower bed, and beyond that a lawn bounded by a low wall. The auditorium was to her right. In the street a crowd had gathered, but no one appeared to be looking her way. Jenna climbed through the window and sat on the sill. Twisting around, she took her weight on her elbows before dropping to the ground. She landed in the flower bed, her boots sinking into mud. There were no shouts of alarm, no orders to halt.

She dashed to the southeast corner of the garden and vaulted over the wall.

JENNA WAITED IN THE DOORWAY of the Tasian Countinghouse. The breeze had picked up off the Sullen Sea, and on it the assassin heard the fretting of waves against the coast. Overhead, tattered clouds ghosted through the blackness. The commotion outside the auditorium had finally died away. Something about an assassination, she had heard. What was the city coming to? Jenna still had no idea whether the Maru's troops or Erekus's bodyguards had triumphed in the abandoned house, or if the Maru himself had escaped. If he *was* still alive, though, Jenna vowed that the next time they met, it would be she who did the surprising.

Over this part of the city—the Market District— an unnatural stillness hung. No lights showed in the buildings about the assassin, for the shopkeepers had long since fled with the coming of night. The silence weighed heavily on Jenna. The adrenaline from her exertions had worn off, and her thoughts were spiraling downwards. It was always the same after a mission. At times like this she would usually find a table in a tavern and watch the world continue to spin on its crooked axis. She needed people close—strangers, inevitably, since she wasn't going to inflict her mood on people she knew. The burden she carried was one of her own making; it was only fair she bore it alone.

Ahead, the road opened out onto a deserted marketplace with

a statue of the Matron in the centre, while behind her—

Jenna stiffened.

Footsteps, approaching swiftly.

Jenna leaned farther back into darkness.

Teren passed her position. This was the route he always took to get home. When Jenna first hired him, she had made it her business to find this out in case a contingency such as tonight's ever arose. A hitch in the agent's stride suggested he had sensed her presence. She stepped into the street behind him.

He stopped and turned.

Jenna's face remained concealed behind her scarf, but Teren must have recognized her all the same. His look changed from curiosity to concern to confusion. Never before had she sought him out after a contract; never before had there been the need. In her right hand she held a small crossbow, pointing at the ground. Teren glanced at it before meeting her gaze. He looked nervous. Too nervous, perhaps? Then again, was there such a thing as too nervous when you were accosted by an assassin in the street?

Jenna looked at his half ear. Not for the first time, she found herself wondering how he had sustained the bite. She knew as little about him as he did her, and yet he was the closest thing she had to a friend in Arkarbour. She was like the shadows she dwelled in—always drifting across the surface of things, never leaving a mark. But that was what she needed to be to survive in this game.

"What's wrong?" Teren said.

"The job went bad," Jenna replied. "It was a trap. I'm guessing the Maru works for someone who knew one of my old victims. That someone came looking for revenge." Jenna couldn't blame him, either. In his position, she would have done exactly the same—though with greater success, she liked to think.

"Who?"

Jenna shrugged. The Maru had given her a few clues to follow

up on. He said he served a man, so at least she knew she wasn't up against a female. The rest would have to wait.

"So you came to warn me?" Teren asked.

"Naturally." Most people didn't hold an assassin responsible for a victim's death. Most people knew the difference between a weapon and the person wielding it. But not the Maru's employer, evidently. "If someone is after me, they'll probably come for you, too." Jenna paused, then pointed her crossbow at him. "Unless, of course, you were in on this from the start."

The muscles of Teren's neck stood out as he swallowed. "I knew nothing about this."

"Didn't you? *Someone* has to have told the Maru's employer that I was the one who killed his friend."

"Then it must have been our client from that job."

"Perhaps," Jenna conceded. "Unfortunately it is difficult to confirm that when we don't even know who that client was."

Teren did not respond.

Jenna watched the agent, trying to get a read on him. She studied his expression, the involuntary movements of his eyes. If this was an act, it was a good one. But then the man would be an accomplished liar; he lived a lie every day, since he wouldn't have told his family or friends about his work. If he was capable of deceiving them, wouldn't he be capable of deceiving Jenna, too? She didn't know. But what she *did* know was that Teren had become her one point of weakness in Arkarbour. The events of tonight had proved what a threat he was. It was time to end that.

Teren apparently disagreed. "You haven't thought this through," he said. "There was no reason for the Maru's employer to approach me, and every reason for him not to. If he'd told me what he was planning, I might have warned you."

"But think of what he stood to gain. For all he knew, you might have been able to lead him straight to me. And even if you couldn't,

you could still have given him information about my other jobs. He could have studied my routines, my methods."

"If I'd betrayed you, do you really think I'd be walking home alone like this? Unarmed?" Teren shook his head. "I'd have gone to ground until I knew you were dead. Better still, I'd have left town by the fastest road possible."

"Maybe I tracked you down before you could. Maybe you underestimated my chances of surviving tonight's trap."

Teren's voice showed irritation. "Maybe, maybe. You can't kill me on a suspicion."

Jenna's smile was rueful. "I've killed people for a lot less, I'm afraid."

To that, Teren had no good answer. He opened his mouth to speak, but shut it again when he realized his cause was hopeless. Jenna's mind was made up. It had been, she realized, from the moment she'd started speaking to him. True, she couldn't be *sure* whether he had betrayed her, but sometimes you had to trust your instincts. Plus if she didn't act now, she wouldn't get another chance later.

Teren held her gaze without flinching. Jenna couldn't deny she was impressed at his composure. There was no greater test of a person's character than being forced to look the Lord of the Dead in the eye. Most of Jenna's targets begged, or sobbed, or attempted to run, but her agent was forged from a superior metal. This probably wasn't the first time he had been threatened with death. For all his good humor, he was still an assassin's associate, and that meant she couldn't afford to take him lightly. What could he do, though? He was too far from Jenna to close with her, and there was no way he could outrun a crossbow bolt.

No more putting this off. A witness might come this way at any time.

Jenna pulled her crossbow's trigger. The quarrel took Teren in the chest and punched him from his feet. He sprawled to the ground.

The assassin crouched beside him. He lay on his back, staring up at the sky. His skin was pale, his eyes glassy with shock, as if he hadn't really expected her to shoot him. Jenna's quarrel had sunk into his flesh to the feathers. Around it his shirt was dark with blood, the cloth sticking to his skin. His breath came quickly. He tried to shift position, only to grunt with pain.

"Quit whining," Jenna murmured. "You'll live." One of the benefits to being a practiced killer was that you knew where to strike if you didn't want your target to die. Her bolt had taken Teren high in the shoulder, safely away from his internal organs.

"You shot me," he said, somewhat unnecessarily.

"Better me than one of the Maru's thugs watching us right now."

Teren blinked. "What? Where?"

"Two in the doorway to the Petty Court—no, don't look!—another two behind the statue in the marketplace." Jenna had spotted them when she arrived earlier to wait for Teren. Rough types they were, with tattoos for armor, and not a crossbow between them. But then it made sense that the Maru would have saved his best troops for ambushing Jenna at the house. At the distance they were from the assassin, they would have caught snatches of her conversation with Teren, but they wouldn't be able to hear their whispers now.

"Then shouldn't you be shooting them instead?" Teren grumbled. "Just thinking aloud here."

"Shooting you is more fun," Jenna said. "Besides, when I send the thugs running now, they will report to their boss that you're dead. You'll have a chance to leave Arkarbour before this gets any messier." Which it would do, Jenna knew. The Maru's employer was sure to have devised a plan B in case Jenna escaped the trap at the house. A plan B that might involve Teren.

She felt the eyes of the Maru's men upon her. She needed some excuse to continue crouching over Teren, so she ran her left hand over his body as if she were searching for something.

Teren said, "If this was just about you getting your hands on me, there were simpler ways."

Jenna sighed, then gestured to the quarrel sticking out of him. "Careful," she said. "I have plenty more bolts where that came from."

She took one from a pocket now and placed it in her crossbow's slot.

Teren caught her gaze and held it. "Why?" he asked. "Why are you doing this?"

Jenna ignored the question. She made to rise, but Teren grabbed her wrist, and she couldn't pull free without drawing her watchers' attention. She silently cursed. This was madness! The success of her scheme depended on the enemy thinking Teren was dead or at least dying. The fool was going to ruin everything.

"Why?" Teren said again. "You didn't have to come here. You could have left me for the Maru's thugs."

"If I'd done that, they might have captured you and found out what you know about me. Or used you to try to lure me into the open."

"Then you could have played safe and aimed your bolt at somewhere more sensitive. I wouldn't be any use to the Maru's employer dead."

Jenna did not reply. She wasn't certain if she knew the answer herself. Maybe she liked the idea of saving someone for once. Maybe she wanted to know how that felt. And she had to say it made a . . . not unpleasant change. She only hoped she didn't come to regret her decision. Killing Teren would have been the more prudent course. It was still possible, after all, that he *had* betrayed her. Just because the thugs were waiting for him didn't mean he was innocent. The Maru's employer might have chosen to eliminate him because he had outlived his usefulness.

Jenna *wanted* to believe he was innocent, though. And perhaps this once that was enough.

She wasn't going to explain that to Teren, though. There were times when a woman simply shouldn't have to account for her actions.

She freed her hand from his grasp and rose. "Wait here," she said.

Teren grimaced. "I'll try not to go anywhere. What about you, though? What are you going to do?"

"I'm going to introduce myself to the Maru's friends." Odds of four to one shouldn't trouble Jenna against cut-throats like these. The hardest part would not be defeating them, but leaving one alive to report to their master.

"And afterwards?" Teren asked. Then, "You should come with me. Put Arkarbour behind you."

Jenna didn't even have to think about it. "That's what the enemy will expect me to do," she said. And the assassin always chose her own path rather than letting someone else dictate it to her. She would stay and fight. It was what she did best. And if life had taught her anything, it was that the faster she ran away from one problem, the sooner she ran into the next.

A last look at Teren, then she rose and started along the street. Ahead, the shadows came to life and rushed at her.

ADA LOVELACE

I T MIGHT SEEM ODD TO include someone like Ada Lovelace in this anthology. The only daughter of poet Lord Byron, born into British nobility…what could she have had to rise above? What could she possibly have had to fight for?

Well, Ada was Lord Byron's only legitimate child. He did, however, have a reputation for having many affairs on his travels abroad and sowed some wild oats along the way. Lady Byron separated from her husband only weeks after Ada was born, and when Byron left to go abroad a few months later, it marked the last time he would be in her life—physically, anyway.

Lord Byron's behavior, however, left its mark on Ada's life all the same. Convinced Byron was a bit insane, Lady Byron was determined her daughter would not follow in his footsteps. She engaged tutors for her daughter from an early age to instruct her in mathematics and science, subjects not in the standard curriculum for women of the early nineteenth century. Lady Byron also insisted her daughter lie completely still for long stretches at a time, believing this would instill a sense of self-control in the girl and surpass any tendency the girl might have toward her father's unpredictable nature and

moodiness. Thankfully, rather than being oppressed by this seemingly overbearing treatment, Ada Lovelace seemed to thrive under it. Gifted in the subjects of math and languages, she learned from some of the top people in England, and at age seventeen befriended inventor Charles Babbage, who became her mentor.

Ada was fascinated by Babbage's work, and when asked to translate an article about his analytical engine from French into English, she added her own notes to the piece, which were three times the length of the article itself. These notes outlined how codes could make it possible for Babbage's machine to handle letters and symbols along with numbers, and suggested ways the engine could repeat a series of instructions, something we know today as looping. Sadly, Ada Lovelace's work didn't become well known until the 1950s, but since then, she has become recognized as a pioneer in the field of computer science.

How ironic it is that the tool so many people now use as a vehicle to harass women and put them down was actually made possible via the work of this progressive and ingenious woman.

Further Reading:

Ada's Algorithm: How Lord Byron's Daughter Ada Lovelace Launched the Digital Age by James Essinger
The Bride of Science: Romance, Reason, and Byron's Daughter by Benjamin Woolley

PAX EGYPTICA

DANA CAMERON

L IGHT DANCED ACROSS THE WATERS of the Middle Sea, producing a blinding glare against the pale stone of the lighthouse and government buildings. The princess ran along the quay, her sandals slapping against the sun-heated stones. Lesson in navigation over, her destination now was the great Library. Egypt was the center of the world, and this sliver of bustling, cosmopolitan Alexandria was the beating heart of Egypt, creating the world's history and wealth. As fascinating as she found her royal father's court, to the princess, the Library was the key, the source of all knowledge and learning.

Clouds darkened the sky so abruptly the princess stopped short. A terrible roaring noise filled her ears, and fire rained from the sky, as arrows, trailing flames like comet tails, found their targets. The rigging of the ships caught, and sailors and merchants ran screaming, only to be caught by the fiery bolts themselves.

Burning ships and carts hedged in the princess, preventing her from escaping into the sea. At the far end of the quay, the magnificent lighthouse exploded when its entire fuel supply ignited. Ahead of her...

Ahead of her, the Library blazed, its thousand scrolls feeding the inferno that consumed the building from the inside out. The princess cried out, running toward it.

Illustration by KERI HAYES

Keri H.

The ferocious heat stole the breath from her lungs, driving her to her knees, and finally, the princess felt her linen robes burning, her flesh searing then bursting...

Cleopatra Auletes, Philopater, Queen of Two Lands, the New Isis, woke, gasping, from a nightmare of fire and loss. Her ships were gone, the Library, her Egypt—

She clutched at her heart, trying to still its pounding through her ribs. It was only the sound of the hard rain outside, and the biting cold of the salt air that roused her from one misery to another. As far as she knew, Alexandria still stood. The more immediate wretchedness was the weather of Germania, a hell the likes of which she never imagined.

A slave hesitated by the doorway, shifting from foot to foot in anxiety. The slave smelled like sheep and resembled one, with her bland, pale features and lumpy, wool-cloaked figure. Still, she didn't seem to feel the cold as keenly as Cleopatra, so perhaps there was truth in the notion that every country's inhabitants were bred to survive its particular hardships.

"It is the day, Queen. Our spies have reported that Caesar's legions in Gaul prepare to invade. It is the day we win or die."

"Never call him Caesar," the queen said. "I took one Caesar as consort and another as ally. Marcus Junius Brutus is an upstart puppy with an unbalanced mind poisoned against me."

The slave prostrated herself. "Forgive me, Queen!"

"Get up, and fetch me hot water. It is not your fault, but not every Roman who leads an army this way is called Caesar."

The slave nodded obediently, rose, and scurried away.

Cleopatra shivered against the bite of the cold, but her warrior's heart sang. Trusting one Roman was not the same as trusting them all, and she'd always known this day might come. The slave was correct: Today meant only victory or death.

JUST THREE YEARS BEFORE, WHEN the old woman appeared so suddenly in the desert, the refugee queen had wondered if the crone was some trick of the brutal sun. Cleopatra knew her own death was likely near, either from starvation, or by military defeat followed by execution, so a hallucination was not out of the question. The utter barrenness of the desert eradicated even the memory of Alexandria's beautiful streets and brilliant society, so there was no place from which the old woman could have appeared so suddenly. Her garments were of a material and color no longer identifiable; perhaps they had once been blue. Her face was as weather-worn as the markings on the ancient monuments, blurred and unreadable after many years of exposure.

"Hail, Cleopatra, Holy Vessel, Imperatrix, Empress of the lands from Britannia to Parthia. Why do you tarry here?" The cryptic use of nonsense titles and the heavily accented Greek—with a hint of the Medic dialect?—by the old woman confirmed it: A delirium consumed Cleopatra.

And yet...sometimes gods appeared in visions or dreams. In any case, it would be impolite not to answer.

"No queen, I," Cleopatra said. "If you haven't heard, I'm an exile. My little brother-husband, the co-king Ptolemy, and his scheming priests hunt me like an animal. My sister Arsinoe has fled, waiting to see which of us will win, so she may side with the victorious one. To call me queen of anything at the moment is cruel mockery."

The crone laughed. "No mockery; we must discuss how you will tear the world apart and restitch it anew. Your realms will far exceed those of your ancestor, Alexander."

The exhausted queen, though well trained in politics and composure, could not restrain a hopeless laugh. "Another time, I would be delighted to help you, sage. But my kingdom hangs by a thread and my people suffer from this uncivil war my brother wages against me." Though restoring peace to her people was paramount, this last

saddened her. Her young brother had always been a favorite of hers, until they ascended the throne, and he fell prey to the poisonous whisperings of his priests. "I have more pressing matters at hand."

"Give me a drink of water, and I will explain how that can be changed."

The waft of onions and incense filled the queen's nose and she could hear the wind flapping the woman's loose garments around her bony frame: The old one was real. Cleopatra shrugged. As beggars went, it wasn't a bad line; it would be less trouble to hear her than to summon the guards to give the wretch a beating.

She handed the crone a cup and poured the last from of her jug of water. The old woman nodded her thanks, took a sip, then gazed into the cup. "You will be banished to the edge of the world, triumphant, having had all power in your hands. You will return from that death to reign again. Your realm will exceed that of Alexander himself."

"As you've said." The queen's fatigue threatened to over-topple her. "Enough."

"You have powers. Let me show you. If I disappoint, you may take my head."

She spoke like a queen herself, to suggest that the younger woman wouldn't take her life anyway. Cleopatra inclined her head. "You have the space of fifty heartbeats."

The hairs on the back of the queen's neck went up, as if lightning had struck nearby. She watched as the crone's face became unrecognizable, bones shifting and features blurring and skin thickening.

The old woman turned into a massive serpent.

Cleopatra stifled a scream. No fever dream, but a miracle.

The giant serpent curled up, enjoying the warmth, and then darted, with inhuman speed, at a lizard. The lizard squirmed violently, its tail caught in the great serpent's mouth. The serpent then returned the lizard to the ground so it could scuttle away.

A shimmer in the air, then the crone returned to her human form, struggling into her robe. The young queen helped her. "Thank you. I can teach you to do the same. In exchange, you must do three things."

"Oh yes?"

"Make an ally of Rome. Preserve the great Library. Refuse the rituals of the priests."

Cleopatra laughed harshly. "If it were so easy to do those first two things, I should have done them already. And why the last?"

"I have seen that a united kingdom around the Middle Sea is closer to your hand than anyone's in several centuries. Do one task and the rest will follow. And if we are very lucky?"

"Yes?"

"We will see a return of the gods."

Cleopatra was not certain seeing any god was a good thing, and the idea of seeing all of them returning was downright terrifying. But yes, she was intrigued. "Very well."

"Give me your hand."

Without a second thought, Cleopatra extended her hand. The old woman grasped it, and suddenly, the queen's mind filled with images. She saw

A race of powerful half-human creatures, some with the features of a snake or a wolf, who walked on two legs. She saw them as actors in a series of quick dramas, working to protect ordinary mortals and slay evil-doers.

The first, the walking snakes, had bright eyes and sharp fangs, but they healed with their venom, bringing the dead back to life, like Asclepius. They had killing venom, too, like boiling water, that ate the skin.

The second, the walking wolves, using their long snouts and keen ears to seek out and destroy villainy.

And there was a third, who took on no animal aspect, but possessed myriad powers. Not drugged girls in caves, but true oracles—those who could communicate with thought—and those with tremendous luck. These

guided the others in their fight against evil.

She saw the rise of Alexander; he could transform into a hunting wolf. She saw his mother Olympias in the aspect of a snake. Then, too young, Alexander struck down before the world could be united, by some Persian magic, in retaliation for the destruction of Persepolis. A great plague followed, destroying many of the Fanged and the Talented.

The priests, who saw the Talented as an affront to the gods, kept those who survived ignorant of their powers by drugging them. Behind their obsequiousness, the priests smirked, knowing that their rituals and potions controlled beings of great power.

The crone suddenly collapsed.

Cleopatra, reeling from all she saw, eased the older woman and wet her lips from the dregs in the cup.

The old woman pushed the water away. "Show me you can do as I did. Show me that you can change your form."

The queen had always been a quick and clever student, capable of learning languages, mathematics, military tactics, as well as many kinds of physical activities—sailing, hunting, dancing. The idea that she might now have the power to truly protect Egypt and regain her rightful place inflamed her, so she did not hesitate. Recalling the images she saw and the sensations she experienced watching the other woman change, she found that making the metamorphosis was as easy and agreeable as slipping into her favorite shift. She assumed the walking serpent aspect, then the full serpent form, readily.

Cleopatra Changed back to her human form. When she looked down, giddy from her success, the crone was dead.

BY THE TIME SHE RETURNED to camp, Cleopatra had formed a plan. She summoned her generals: A small force would escort her to within a day's march of Alexandria, and then a smaller group would smuggle her into the city, for General Julius Caesar had seized the palace. She hated the notion of having to sneak into her own palace,

but she could not enter with the pomp she deserved and expect to live. She had to see Caesar—while avoiding her siblings, their generals and priests—and convince the Roman to take her part.

In disguise, she listened to the merchants outside the Alexandrine walls to see which of them had an audience with Caesar the next day. Picking the most likely one, she found the tent with his wares, found a place to hide, curled up, and fell asleep.

The next morning, a gargantuan snake surprised General Gaius Julius Caesar as he inspected the pottery merchant's wares. As the creature—all glittering black and gold and blue scales—uncoiled from inside the pot in which she had spent the night, he was struck temporarily speechless. Although she knew that he had an abhorrence of snakes that he strove to conceal, Cleopatra hoped the general would believe the appearance of such a creature could only be an omen. With an explosion of dazzling light, the large snake turned into a small naked woman. She glanced up at the general regally, and began to speak in perfect, courtly Greek.

When he did not answer, she repeated the speech in Egyptian. And then in Syrian, in Hebrew, then the Medic language.

"You may speak," she said finally, in decent, if accented, Latin. Truth be told, Cleopatra rather enjoyed the look of amazement the general could not conceal. His strong features and aquiline nose built authority into his face. She suspected it didn't happen often that confusion shone in his black eyes.

"Ahem—ah, thank you, er, Queen Cleopatra, for that lovely welcome, and for your condolences on the death of my friend Pompey. I would certainly entertain a discussion of alliance with you—"

Of course he would consider it. When a god shows up in the form of a serpent and a queen, you pay strict attention.

And when that imperious queen-god tells you she has a plan to create an empire for you to share, one that will exceed that of Alexander, you do exactly what she says.

First, however, once the courtesies had been extended, there were details to attend.

"Your brother? Husband? He's just a boy," Caesar said.

"If ten is old enough to overthrow a co-ruler, it is old enough to die," Cleopatra replied.

Caesar nodded. "And your sister?"

"We shall see," came the cool answer. She could see him evaluating her as a realist and a strategist. Patient. Cleopatra realized that, since she'd stopped taking the priests' potions, her insights had grown more acute than ever. She asked, "What is your intent for Egypt?"

"Nothing but peace and prosperity, a continuation of our long and happy friendship."

She held him in a commanding stare.

"With you as its rightful queen," he finished.

It was still not enough. "If we are to be allies, you must fully understand what Egypt is. It is not only grain to feed hungry Roman bellies," she said, filling her words with all the conviction she could muster, willing him to take her words to heart. "It is not merely a port or a piece of land for you and your enemies to squabble over. It is a kingdom with a pedigree going back to the sun-god, recently rediscovering its ancient powers, as you've just seen."

Her stare deepened; she could see Caesar was fascinated, unable and unwilling to break it. She knew it was ridiculous for her to lecture him or demand anything of a general at the head of an invading army, and yet...

"If we ally, you must swear that Egypt shall be mine, and descend to my heirs forever. A friend, as you said, not just a vassal state feeding you tribute. You must swear to protect Egypt and her people. I will no longer have them be pawns in political squabbles. In return, we shall gladly share our bounty of grain and power with you."

"Agreed," was all he could say, and he meant it with all his soul.

She nodded once, and kissed him on the mouth, an agreement

between princes. Inside she trembled: She had now succeeded in two of the crone's three commands.

She was also trembling because Caesar was. Their formal kiss had evolved into something much more passionate.

AFTER THE MATTER OF HER siblings' defeat and deaths had been settled, the queen received her brother's priests in the great hall of her palace, with all the courtiers, as well as Caesar and his advisors.

The priests bowed deeply. "Majesty, it has been far too long since you've undergone the purification ritual—"

"No," she said in a carrying voice. "I have been given special insight directly from the gods themselves, and new powers, too. I will no longer be following your 'purification' rituals. No more potions. No more prayers. I am quite pure enough."

"I must warn you, my queen, that—"

Without warning, the queen hissed as if with the voice of a thousand serpents. Cleopatra began to shake, and she assumed the aspect of a snake-headed creature, covered in the sleek scales of a reptile. And yet she was still garbed in the white linen, golden collar, and the double crown she'd donned that morning, having first made certain the two rearing cobras in the pschent had been polished until their gold shone.

She had practiced speaking clearly around her fangs. "Do not dare to disobey me."

"But my queen—!"

Hissing again, she struck the priest with a mighty blow. Claw marks appeared in lines of blood down his torso. Two more slashes, and the priest's body collapsed in two ragged pieces. She gestured to the priest's remains.

"You, priests—Achillas and Manetho! Take those with you as proof that I no longer require any priest's rituals," she ordered. "Either obey me in this, or pay the ultimate price for disobeying the gods.

Any of you who feel I did wrong may leave. No harm will come to—"

As one, the crowd of attendant nobles and slaves prostrated themselves.

"Well, that's that," the queen murmured. She took Julius Caesar's arm, and slowly returning to her fully-human form, left the audience chamber.

IT TOOK QUITE SOME TIME before the retainers dared to raise their heads. They all left without speaking, each deep in their own thoughts. That is what happens when one is in the presence of the miraculous.

The two priests carried the remains of their colleague out of the palace, and dumped the body as quickly as they could. "I'm taking her part," Achillas said. "Blasphemy or no."

The other, Manetho, was still quivering from anger and fear; the blasphemy of his colleague's murder was so terrible, it was hard to imagine the consequences. "Maybe...I will go back with you."

But before they had gone halfway back, Manetho vanished into the crowds.

Revolution of a kind had begun. He swore to undo it.

EVEN BEFORE LEARNING OF THE existence of those born to the Talents, Cleopatra had collected gods the way other monarchs collected jewels. It wasn't piety, or no more than that of the average Egyptian, but a thirst for knowledge. As a descendant of the gods, it behooved her to understand them. But now, with her new knowledge, she had her private scholars fill a secret annex of the Library with references to her Talented kin. Knowing the source of her powers would help protect her people, Talented and mortal alike. Histories of other cultures mentioned shape-shifters. Her scholars studied each of these descriptions and copied them into a set of scrolls known as the Book of Talents.

But as diligent and clever as the scholars were, they were no closer to determining where the Talented came from. "Gods are unknowable, queen," they'd say, with as close to a shrug as one dared in the presence of a royal personage.

Even Julius Caesar, with all his erudition and knowledge of the classics, could provide little help. She took him to the Library, where he was stunned by the extent of the shelves of scrolls, room after room, the greatest repository of knowledge in the world. They expanded their search, sending couriers with instructions to search other libraries and private collections for anything that would tell them about the Talented Ones. They agreed that harnessing the abilities of the Talented, like understanding the rhythms of the Nile, was the clearest path to peace and power.

All through her first pregnancy—of course there was sex; nothing was more erotic than brains, friendship, and shared ambition—the queen and general worked. All was calculation and study before they could return to Rome, together. Oracles were scrutinized to see if they truly had the Talent. Philosophers were consulted, their studies of nature examined to find the origins of the Fanged and the Talented.

By the time their second sons—twins—were born, the civil war in Egypt was won and Caesar declared they would make no further progress learning about the Talented Ones. "It's time. We must leave."

Cleopatra nodded. "But our news must precede us. Such an upheaval of everything they know—men and women with the powers of gods—is dangerous. We must start slowly, and the news must appear to arise from the people themselves."

Caesar frowned. "I agree, but how?"

"Let our agents speak to potters and painters about a new style said to be favored by the great General Caesar himself, and all the rage in foreign parts. Graffiti might appear, made by unseen hands in the night, with wolf- or snake-headed men and women, with some

of the happier classical references to the gods and their servants. From Ovid, perhaps."

Caesar's brow cleared, and he nodded. "I have had good success using poets. Let us hire a few to compose on the theme of heroic shape-shifting."

She took his hand, smiling. "The surest way to a welcome reception is to create the fashion before it is announced. We will secure the foundation of Rome, and heal her after this civil war."

As they traveled from Alexandria, they continued the search for other Talented within the army. Caesar proposed the idea of finding a convicted rapist and walking him through the ranks. Those who responded, compelled to attack the murderer, were chosen to form the new vanguard of each legion, and these were called "Victorious Janus."

In every city they passed through, they stopped first at the temples. They offered up sacrifices and prayers, and then conducted a brief meeting with the priests and priestesses who guarded the treasure. In key cities, one or two of the newly discovered Fanged ones were left behind, and the priests and priestesses given strict instructions to obey them as if they were Caesar himself. The serpent-headed Ones' special trick of persuasion and delusion proved especially helpful.

The gates of Rome were thrown open with wild adulation. After a decent interval, Cleopatra met with Calpurnia, Caesar's wife, at a reception. After the two exchanged formal greetings, they moved to a quiet room and got to business.

"My husband has appointed Octavian his heir," Calpurnia said briskly, arranging her veil around her.

"My sons are very young and will inherit Egypt," Cleopatra said. "I have no designs on either Rome or Caesar."

"Excellent. Then we have no quarrel." She paused. "I have foreseen Caesar's murder; you must help me prevent it. I hear no one

can resist your arguments."

It was then Cleopatra realized the first lady of Rome was born with the Talent of prognostication. She had kept her abilities quiet, a secret protection for her husband.

The Egyptian queen nodded. "I shall prevent it."

Thus, encouraged by his wife's "dream," Cleopatra's skill at politics, and their joint efforts at bringing the senators and their wives to their side, Caesar assumed the role of dictator for life. He gave the volatile Brutus the governorship of Asia and dispatched him at once. Octavian commenced a campaign against Parthia. While Parthian chariots were nigh-on invincible over the open ground, the Victorious Janus units, with their fleet wolves and the terrible venom attacks of the serpents, helped ensure a Roman victory.

Two months later, disaster struck. Caesar was struck down, not by assassins, but by the illnesses that had plagued him all through life. Falling insensible, he hit his head upon a marble table and died. Cleopatra was distraught, not only for the loss of her love and her children's father. If she had been there when it happened, she might have used her healing powers to save him. But now...

Almost overnight, Brutus turned on Cleopatra. Those legions loyal to Brutus seized and held Rome, claiming this was a chance to rid Rome of the Egyptian witch and her heresies.

Cleopatra, devastated by Caesar's death, now found their plan for peace threatened by Brutus on one side and the vanquished Pompey's sons on the other. She dispatched the bulk of her household with her two young sons, and sent for Octavian, now Caesar. After, she fled to the small temple housing copies of the Book of Talent. She would not allow Brutus to destroy such valuable work.

She raced ahead of her guard detail, her own Talent alerting her that there was someone nearby, waiting to ambush her. Cleopatra, tired of diplomacy and politics, thrilled to the idea of battle.

She gasped. The runaway priest, Manetho, crouched there,

clutching a basket of her scrolls.

The queen felt the ecstatic rush of righteousness filling her as she transformed. Her mouth grew sharp, sharp fangs, her fingers grew into claws, and her reactions became quick as lightning. She spat and lunged at him.

Manetho was powerful, and much larger than her. When the venom hit the flesh of his neck, she could smell the burning flesh. He roared and slammed his fist against the side of her head. The queen was knocked from her feet, but instinct, rather than training, informed her speed and power. She rolled out of the way, and leaped up.

He did the unthinkable. He thrust a torch down into the basket of scrolls, then threw it at one of the walls of shelves.

With a cry to her guards, who were now arriving, the queen began to pull at the flaming baskets in an attempt to curtail the conflagration. "Find the priest, the one called Manetho! He's been wounded, but we need him alive! He is in league with Brutus, and I would interrogate him!"

In her half-Changed form, the queen suffered little injury, but many of the scrolls were lost.

The guard came back with the body of the priest. Rather than be captured, he had killed himself, but not before he had spoken a terrible curse against the queen and her kind. Cleopatra he took the hand of one of the seers among the guard, and she saw a vision of a fire devouring everything from Gaul to Parthia, the flames reflected in bloody streets.

"And now? What do we do?" the captain asked, shaken.

"We go north," Cleopatra said. "I need an army. I'll find it among the German and Gaulish legions loyal to Caesar."

AND SO IT WAS THAT, a month later, Erminia, queen of the Chatti tribe, entered Cleopatra's tent.

"Does it ever stop raining in this pestilential country of yours?" Cleopatra asked.

"Do you weak-shouldered Asians ever stop whining about the weather?" Erminia retorted.

They both smiled and embraced warmly, as much for reassurance as for formality. Today would be a test of them both. The fate of the world depended on the outcome.

"I've heard from my spies; the pro-Julian legions are holding well along the Rhine, but the Parisii are threatened from Brutus's legions in Hispania."

"I've heard from mine. Brutus's generals are building up his forces along the Black Sea and Rome is swaying dangerously in his favor." Cleopatra paced. "Octavian is holding Egypt, but we need to break the lines."

"So you think Brutus will take Byzantium, before returning to Rome?"

"I would." Cleopatra took out a map. "I think we have to go to Byzantium and stop him there."

Erminia shook her head. "I cannot go so far. My time is too close." She spread her hands over her swelling belly. "I will not leave the safety of my people nor my family; I will go only as far as the borders of Pannonia."

Cleopatra nodded. "If the worst comes, I'll try to bring the survivors to aid you at the Rhine. We must protect the copies of the Alexandrian records of the Talented, especially if Egypt falls."

"That must not happen," Erminia said. "And what about our plan to preserve the Book of Talents? It's far too dangerous to attempt it now."

"It's the danger that makes it necessary to go ahead with the plan now," Cleopatra said. "No matter what the outcome, we must preserve our lore."

"It is risky to act, or to stay." Erminia shrugged. "Very well. I

shall send word to Anglesey—the farthest outpost of our kind from Rome—and to our kin in the other tribes between here and there."

"Thank you. If I fall, I shall hold out as long as I can to ensure you have as much time as possible."

"We'll pray that doesn't happen." She paused, an idea suddenly blossoming. "Our priests have long spoken of a secret. A weapon, a warrior, I know not what, but something to be called in desperate times. I do not guarantee success—it may be naught but a legend—but your arrival put it in my mind. I will speak to them and see what can be done."

"These are the most desperate times. I thank you, sister."

They embraced again, and went to prepare the baggage trains.

THE INTERVENING DAYS EN ROUTE from Germania to Byzantium blurred together in a nightmare of fire, iron, and blood. The renegade priest's dying curse seem to follow them everywhere, and Cleopatra worried her view toward the gods, the priests, and the revelation, was terribly wrong.

The battle at Athens was particularly brutal. The citizens were pro-Julian allies but the nearby legions were rabid followers of Brutus. At the last, Cleopatra's tribal allies and the faithful legions had to abandon hope, as the priests at the vaults of the Acropolis refused to turn over their history scrolls to either army. Blood flowed down the marble steps, as the Talented forces tore at other Roman soldiers, now their enemies. The ability to heal quickly that Cleopatra and her Talented family enjoyed was a double-edged sword. Though she was always ready to fight again—having insisted on training as a soldier—the toll on her mortal soldiers and citizens was disastrous.

But the defeat at Athens helped Cleopatra's cause a little, even as her army retreated. Her ranks were swelled by sympathizers and more of the Talented deserted the opposing troops. It was only these successes that kept spirits up, and by excruciatingly small

increments, Cleopatra's army made their way to the far coast of the Aegean, where it was by great good luck that a wealthy merchant league pledged them ships to carry their troops to Byzantium. They had beaten Brutus's forces by just a day.

The queen made her headquarters at the acropolis on the near side of the river and sea harbor. The hill gave an excellent view all around, and a shout soon came from the lookout, echoing against the stone walls. "Ships! Ships coming from the northern sea!"

The enemy fleet soon covered the river so completely that they obscured the water itself. The hilly terrain made it possible to hold their position for a while, but the enemy's great numbers made defeat inevitable. Indeed, Brutus was so sure of his victory that he himself had arrived, his flagship and standard visible at the back line of vessels.

"Will you retreat, my queen?" an African general, Rebilius, asked. "Best to escape and choose another battle."

"I will not."

"It is a miracle we have survived this long. This attack will be the end of us. Better to get you to safety; we have no more tricks left."

"I do."

Taking her bow, Cleopatra climbed to the roof of the acropolis, followed by other archers, and soldiers who were instructed to carry as many bundles of arrows as possible. Assuming her half-serpent form, she nocked an arrow, selected a target, and invoked her many gods. Each time it was the same prayer.

"Isis and Anubis, Athena and Hermes, Visucius and Sulis and Ahura Mazda, may all the gods, any god, hear me! Brutus and his army kill my people, undoing a peace I hoped to make eternal. They destroy learning, and other of your gifts, out of fear. Aid me now. My people built the foundations of this upstart empire; I will tear it down, if need be! Help me now! I call on you directly, o gods!"

She pulled and shot until her arms shook with fatigue, even in

that powerful, holy state of the Change. With each pronunciation, the other archers also drew, until bows splintered and bowstrings snapped. Those around her, even those who understood the nature of her transformation and power, marveled at her persistence and courage, and took heart, redoubling their efforts. Her voice grew hoarse and still the names flowed from her serpentine tongue.

But good will and stout hearts could not match an onslaught from sea and land by a well-rested force. When the last arrow flew, and found a mark, it was still not enough. Brutus's troops had landed and now advanced up the hill of the acropolis.

There were no more gods to call on.

"Bring every one of our people into the fortress," Cleopatra ordered. Her hand still clutched the heavy bow, though she'd never been so exhausted. Her eyes were distant, her words almost rote, as if she was still in the thrall of her prayers. "If we are to fall, it will be here, fighting as Caesar and I planned, as one nation."

Screams from below. She could smell the edge of the city burning. The queen turned away, her eyes closing for a moment against the knowledge that her doom had come.

A terrible roar enveloped them like a flood. Cleopatra looked up, and saw what had until this day only been the stuff of poets' songs and cartographic warnings.

A beast like the giant serpent Ladon who guarded the Hesperides, or Python, the enemy of Apollo, appeared in the sky. Brilliant bronze and golden eyed, teeth like spears, a neck as long and sinuous as a river, and iron-boned wings that were like those of the Erinyes, the monster stooped like an eagle. It landed on the largest ship at the beachhead, and the weight of the beast tipped the galley over, blocking the next ship's way to the beach.

The great, thick dragon roared again, vanishing only to reappear at the next largest ship. Claws like swords raked the decks and rent the sails, scattering rowers and archers alike, some jumping overboard

to escape the dreadful beast. The dragon picked up a smaller ship and hurled it at two others.

By this time, some of the ships were fleeing, breaking ranks, and the assault had largely ceased against the city. The dragon amused itself by slowing their attempted escape, dropping wreckage of one ship upon another. The more clever rowers unshipped their oars and used them to float away from the wreckage before the dragon seized it.

Suddenly the queen's rapture at this unexpected ally was shattered. A booming voice, speaking in an ancient and unintelligible language, erupted in her head. She looked around, but none of her soldiers or advisors seemed to be affected. She sank to her knees, screaming, "Speak more quietly, or else you shall kill me!"

An image of Brutus, on the beach and fleeing, filled her mind, along with the irresistible urge to chase him down and kill him. She signaled her generals, but could not wait for them to join her. She would hunt him herself.

Seizing a discarded sword—her arrows had all been spent in answered prayer—she all but flew up the stairs to the highest tower. Indeed, it seemed as if Hermes, Iris, Isimud, and Pappsukal aided her flight. The power of Sekmet, the lioness, and Inanna the Warrior suffused her being.

"To me! To me! Help me slay this traitorous pretender!" she cried to the dragon.

She hoped the dragon would pick her up and carry her down to the shore, but suddenly, she experienced an overwhelming sense of being...nowhere. She found herself alone in the streets along the river. She heard her guards shout with amazement, far above her.

As the fires raged through the streets, the queen felt the heat rising, heard the thunder-claps of great stones cracking. Past the temples, and down alleys into the heart of the city, she found Brutus's trail. The sound of his passing footsteps seemed to loiter, hanging

in the air for her to follow.

She could smell his desperation as easily as she could follow his tracks, and a part of her delighted in that. And then she saw him.

Brutus ran in a panic, discarding his armor as he fled. The fire cut him off, and he was forced to choose between the dragon circling overhead and the strong current of the river below. Brutus dove from the quay.

Cleopatra followed him in. Of course she could swim; Alexandria's wealth came from water, Egypt's life came from water. Her half-reptile form lent speed and strength to her strokes, as if the crocodile god Sobek himself had blessed her and Father Poseidon aided her against the strong current. The cold, dark water smelled of stone and decay, but she could see easily enough.

When she broke the surface, gasping for air, the queen felt a sharp biting pain above her left breast: Brutus's dagger had found her heart. Locking eyes with him, she pulled the dagger from her chest. His jaw dropped as he watched the wound close instantly, and the blood washing away. She threw the dagger back at him, and he ducked away terrified.

Cleopatra dove back under the waves and swam as quickly as she could, until she saw the bottom of the wrecked ship Brutus had climbed upon. Summoning the full Change, she became a serpent and slithered up the side as silently as the crocodile god himself. She darted, looping strong coils of her body around Brutus's arms, and rearing back, sank her fangs into his neck. Not to kill—no, the crone in the desert had taught her well. She had to bring Brutus back to Rome in chains.

The beneficence of every god from every pantheon seemed to flow through her for a moment. Cleopatra finally felt him cease to struggle. She Changed to her half-serpent form, then threw Brutus into the water and dove in after him, pulling him to the shore. She hoisted herself to the quay, dripping and exhausted, but exhilarated.

The guards had arrived and swarmed around her. She accepted a cloak from one of them, and pointed. "Fetch *that* out of the water. I have subdued the man who roused the people against the lawful empire and would have killed me. He will live, and return to Rome, but not as he imagined."

The guards regarded their slight queen with reverence and awe. "It's true! The gods came upon her and aided our cause!"

"How goes the rest of the battle?" she demanded.

"The dragon...it is hungry," one of the guards replied, tremulously.

"I shall deal with it," Cleopatra said, not knowing how she would do so. One of the officers quickly turned into a giant wolf, and she rode on his back through the burning streets of Byzantium to the acropolis. She found the dragon sunning itself on the rampart, idly gnawing the bones of a freshly slaughtered cow sticky with drying blood.

"Where did it get the cow?" she whispered to another officer.

"The marketplace," the guard whispered back, not taking his eyes off the sated beast. "The merchant...made no protest."

"Very well. Reimburse the merchant, and purchase another cow, or two or three, for our...ally. And deploy the troops to accept surrender; use the captured legions to help put out the fires."

By now, Cleopatra understood the dragon could hear her thoughts; she watched as the dragon inclined its head in thanks for her hospitality. The dragon cracked open the cow's skull, its eyes half closed with contentment as it gnawed.

"How did you know to come? What god sent you?" she called.

A feeling like laughter bubbled up inside the queen's mind. This time, there was no deafening voice in her head, but the sure knowledge of the dragon's thoughts filled her.

No god, but your sister-queen Erminia summoned me from long slumbers. Your song of arrows guided me to you.

"What is your name?"

I was once called Saris. You may call me that.

"And what I can give you, my friend? What reward? For you have served me beyond reckoning today."

There is no reward but satisfaction for kin rendering duty to kin. But if I may, now that I am here, awake again after many long years, I would stay and view the world. Where best to do that?

"With me," Cleopatra said. "I am expanding the heart of the world from Alexandria. Stay with me, and watch."

A FEW WEEKS LATER, BRUTUS'S generals surrendered formally and Queen Cleopatra entered the city of Rome. It was not a triumph, of course, but looked rather like one: piles of treasure confiscated from Brutus and his allies were scattered to the populace, Brutus and his generals marched in chains, and the queen wore armor made from the melted gold of the armor once worn by her traitorous brother.

If anyone thought about raising a protest at the unseemliness of a foreign queen inside the walls of Rome, or the spectacle with which she entered with the large number of soldiers, they were put off by her surrounding Janus guards, their banners bright with silver and gold embroidery of fierce wolves and fanged serpents. The sight of the dragon, Saris, well-fed and dozing, pulled into the city by elephants, also led potential naysayers to decide they were better off silent.

A note arrived from Octavian by the swiftest wolf-man couriers. The letter, though polite and politic, did not conceal the fact that he was uneasy about a foreign monarch—even an ally—living in Rome. Discussing matters of state with the Senate. Entertaining on...an imperial scale. Perhaps it was time for her to depart for Alexandria, he wrote, with thanks for defeating the traitorous Brutus and securing the city.

Cleopatra wrote back: "I am delighted to be of service to Rome,

the second city of my heart, and I will not rest easy until you've returned to Rome to prosecute Brutus. While Brutus is alive, there is always the chance of another uprising. After such a narrow victory, the dragon Saris—an ancient relative of mine, it turns out—has advised me to stay until your safe return. After that, we will certainly depart, for Saris has determined to visit Parthia and farther east, both to secure the new peace treaty and introduce me to more of my dragon kin. But rest assured, Saris has become just as attached to Rome as I have, and has chosen a part of the Tiber Island to dwell as a permanent guardian of the city."

"Perhaps some sort of more permanent alliance between us?" wrote Octavian. "It will be the joining of powerful families, Rome and Egypt, Fanged and Mortal. Perhaps we should discuss marriage."

"Perhaps," wrote Cleopatra. "Come to Rome and we shall see."

QUEEN ERMINIA WATCHED AS THE children of the Chatti tribe studied reading and writing with one scribe, while another led older youths in a copying exercise. A cohort of her priests joined the queen as the Roman ship approached with its precious cargo. She shushed her baby, then handed him to a waiting attendant before going to greet the ship's captain. The captain bowed, a little unsteadily, for he had spent a great deal of time at sea. He handed a scroll to another attendant.

"Your voyage was uneventful, I hope?" Erminia took the scroll, and broke the seal.

"Pirates, majesty, but our Fanged warriors dispatched them easily." He stood a little straighter, pride lending steadiness to his joints. "I heard that the ship to Britannia has also arrived safely."

"This tells me that the other two reach their destinations, at Charax and Seleucia, but two others were lost to storms or enemies."

"Fewer and fewer every day, majesty. The empire is reinforced by the Empress's wisdom and our new found brethren."

"Good. The Library at Anglesey has started sending copies through Britannia and the northlands, and in the south, the Library of Hispania Baetica has almost completed another copy for Volubius."

"First Citizen Octavian Augustus is making great inroads in Parthia."

"And from there, even farther east. There will be no civilized country on earth without its own Library."

She gave orders for the captain and his crew to be made welcome and comfortable while the cargo was transferred to the nearby stronghold. She traded the scroll for her son again, who promptly spat up. The queen wiped her son's mouth and proceeded up the hill to her home passing a group of adults sitting by a fire, being taught the new writing style. It was now the law of the land that every citizen be literate and numerate; rhetoric and logic were also obligatory. Students who showed the most aptitude were hired away to work as scholars in the new Libraries, to further the availability of the texts to the world.

If it had been destroyed, the Library of Alexandria could never have been replaced. Indeed, as the new capital of the Empire, Alexandria was now even more important as a source of learning—but neither would it ever be endangered as it had been. It was a fortunate series of events indeed that ushered in the glorious Pax Egyptica.

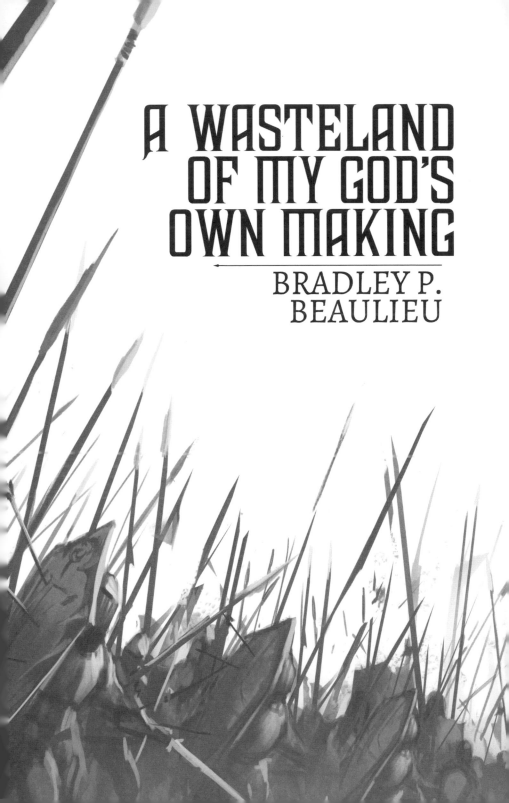

A WASTELAND OF MY GOD'S OWN MAKING

BRADLEY P. BEAULIEU

S THE SUN BROKE ABOVE the horizon, Djaga Akoyo rushed from the heavily shadowed streets into the entrance hall of the *collegium medicum*. The streets were cool from the chill desert night, but this place was frigid, a feeling that seeped deep below Djaga's skin, making her quicken her pace all the more.

"May I help?" An attendant—from the looks of him a scholar fresh from receiving his laurel crown—strode toward her, calm as a wading heron. When he saw the dried blood caked along the front of her beaten leather armor, however, his eyes went wide as the moons. "Oh!" was all he said.

"Calm yourself," Djaga told him. "It isn't mine." *Not all of it, in any case.* "A woman named Nadín was taken here yesterday. A stab wound to the gut. Where is she?"

The young man opened his mouth, but nothing came out. "I've only just arrived."

"Well, go find her!" Djaga shouted.

"I'll take her, Ari." A tall, black-skinned woman had exited the hallway ahead of them, a high physic named Malanga. She had striking eyes and a pretty smile. The wheat-colored robes she wore was the preferred uniform in the *collegium medicum*, yet it seemed chosen to match her lustrous black hair, which was braided into a beehive

coil. She'd treated Djaga several times, courtesy of Djaga's more vigorous battles in the pits; she even hailed from Djaga's homeland of Kundhun, yet they'd traded no more than a bit of idle chitchat over the years. Djaga felt poor about it now.

After waving the young scholar away, Malanga motioned for Djaga to follow. To Djaga's relief, Malanga seemed to have a sense of urgency about her.

"You should be prepared," she said to Djaga as they strode swiftly along the halls, "we've done all we could, but—"

"Just tell me how much time she has left."

Djaga had known Nadín's fate from the moment she'd seen the extent of the wound to her stomach. She'd prayed that Nadín would still be alive upon her return from the desert.

"She won't see the sunset," Malanga said. From the occupied rooms to either side of the hall issued the sounds of low conversation, coughing, moaning, or the shuffle of sandaled feet. "She's refused milk of the poppy in hopes that you'd return, but she is in deep pain. The longer you wait—"

"Djaga?" The voice had come from the room ahead but it sounded frail, ghostlike. "Djaga, is that you?"

Djaga swallowed before speaking softly to Malanga. "I would spare her pain, but I must speak with her first."

"The longer you wait—" Malanga tried again.

"She must know this before she departs for the farther fields."

After a pause, Malanga nodded and left.

Djaga used tentative steps to enter the room. She turned toward the bed, and the world seemed to spin. Nadín lay there, but she looked like a completely different woman. Her copper skin was pale, almost yellow. Her lips were bloodless. She seemed to have fallen in on herself, a beautiful cavern collapsed after an earthquake. Swallowing the hard knot in her throat, Djaga stepped to the bedside. She'd known this was going to happen, but to now be faced with it…

Nadín grimaced, reached one hand out. "Did you find her?"

Djaga pulled a chair close to the bedside and took Nadín's quivering hand, swathed it in her own. "Yes, I found her."

Nadín swallowed once. Twice. She licked her lips before saying, "Will you tell me?"

"Could we not speak about other things? About our days sailing your ship? Or your family we met?"

"I would know what happened." Before Djaga could say anything more, her fingers gave a squeeze, a weak gesture surprisingly strong for a woman in her state. "You can't deny a dying woman her last wish. Do, and you'll be cursed. You don't wish to be cursed, do you, Djaga?"

Despite all the worry roiling inside her, Djaga laughed. "No, I don't wish to be cursed." Djaga paused, her eyes brimming with tears. "Very well, my sweet. I'll tell you my tale. " She took a moment to regain her composure. "I brought you here. You remember? After, I returned to the harbor with Osman, and we took your ship to the desert…"

Nadín was shaking her head. "No. All of it. I deserve that much."

Djaga nodded, resigned. "As you say…"

But where to begin? How could she tell this tale to her one true love when she'd hidden so much? *One word at a time,* her father used to say.

"It was high sun the day Afua came to Sharakhai."

ON A DAY AS HOT as anyone in the city could remember, thousands gathered to watch a bout in Sharakhai's storied fighting pits. They had waited a long while already, the seat sellers charging triple the already-dear rate for bouts in the central pit. They drank lemonade and wine. They placed money with the bet takers wandering up and down the aisles, receiving special chits for the money and the bet taken. They argued about which opponent, Djaga or Talashem,

would win. All the while, their eyes drifted to the two darkened mouths of the tunnels where the combatants would soon emerge. When Pelam, the lanky master of the game, strode calmly from one of them, they rushed to their feet, threw their arms in the air, and began shouting to the oven-hot air.

Pelam, who wore long, purple robes, a bejeweled vest, and an embroidered ivory cap stained with sweat, waited for the cheer to crescendo. Only then did he raise his hands and make a tamping motion. Like a flock of skylarks landing on the banks of the Haddah, the crowd went still, but they sat with ill-contained exuberance, ready to burst into motion once more.

Pelam spread his arms wide, as if welcoming them all to his home. "You are wise, my good people." He said these words quietly, yet such was the timbre of his voice that it carried to every corner of the yawning pit. "Either that or you are gifted with the keenest foresight." He turned suddenly, sweeping his attention to another section of the choked seats. "And if not that, then surely the desert gods have shined on you this day, for you will soon bear witness to one of only two final bouts that Djaga, the Lion of Kundhun, will ever fight!"

As one, the crowd roared their appreciation. Pelam would normally go on for a time, recounting her exploits, but Djaga needed no introduction to the spectators of Sharakhai. As the sound began to die, Djaga emerged from the tunnel. Knowing when it was his time to be the center of attention and when it wasn't, Pelam merely flourished an arm toward her and backed away. With the sun's heat washing over her, Djaga took to the center of the pit and slowly turned, allowing the crowd to take her in.

It was a thing she did to build excitement, a slow teasing of the battle about to begin. It felt familiar as heat in the desert, and yet she hardly knew what to feel, seeing so many gathered, eager to see her trade blows, eager to see blood. Since coming to Sharakhai,

she'd practically lived within these walls. If it were only a matter of her body, she'd stand within them and fight a while longer. She was young, yet. Her nagging wounds hadn't accumulated so badly that she couldn't still scrap in the dirt with the dogs. But during the bouts, the things she rummaged up within her mind to wage these battles so effectively, and for so many years, had become like a canker, painful to the touch. They'd grown worse over the years, until each felt as if it would consume her.

"Take him!" A young man in the crowd rent the air before him as if opening up some imaginary enemy before him. "Open him up!"

Many spurred the young man on, but Djaga ignored him, turning her attention elsewhere to a strikingly beautiful woman sitting at the very edge of the pit's walls. Nadínamira. Nadín. A woman who'd long ago captured Djaga's heart. She sat in a seat Djaga had arranged for her long ago, to take if she so chose. She rarely did, though. She was too worried over the wounds Djaga received, the danger she was in, but she'd come today, and for that, Djaga was glad.

Like a perfect marble statue in the midst of a riot, the crowd raged around Nadín. She held Djaga's eye, smiling her worried smile. Djaga nearly broke, then, nearly allowed the worry that emanated from Nadín like rays from the sun to enter her consciousness. She regained herself a moment later, choosing instead to see only Nadín's beauty, her dark lips, her curly hair lifting every so often in the meager wind. Look any deeper and she would become lost, and that was a thing Djaga couldn't allow. Not now, so close to the end. If she were going to start a new life with Nadín, she needed the money these last two bouts would bring. They both did.

The crowd had become an undulating beast now that Pelam was announcing her opponent. "Talashem," Pelam was saying, "may be a man born of the desert tribes, but he is fresh from the killing pits of Ganahil at the edges of the Thousand Territories of Kundhun." Djaga's ears perked at this—she had been born and raised in

Kundhun, after all—but the rest was lost, for the bout was near.

She paced back and forth over the dusty floor of the pit she knew so well. The shouting of the gathered crowd faded. The desert's hot wind became like to a dream. She focused on Talashem. Only on Talashem. The way his battle-kissed armor hung on his spare frame. The way he favored his right hip. The way he stared at her as if he hadn't a care in the world.

I will wipe that look from your face. I will grind it against the dirt until it's gone. You will remember this fight until your dying days.

He matched her in weight. His muscles were lithe. It made her wonder just how quick he was. Osman wouldn't have pitted her against him if he weren't a good fighter. Her opponents had always been skilled, but since the public announcement of her retirement, they had featured fighters as good as the desert had to offer.

The crowd burst into a renewed flurry as pit boys ran out in a train carrying an assortment of weapons. Talashem chose a spiked shield and a shamshir while Djaga chose one of the tall leather shields from her homeland and a heavy, curving club, its end round like a fist, studded with nails.

All the while Djaga whispered under her breath. *I ask not for your favor, Sjado. I ask not for your favor. I only give what you require, Sjado. I only give what you require.*

As she returned to her starting point, images of the dead returned to her. Her cousin, lying on green grass, his blood bright beneath the summer sun. Her uncle not so far from him. Her brother as well. Seven others. Her family, by the gods. All of them her family.

She heard no murmur of reply. Felt no sense of favor from the god she'd invoked. But she felt Sjado's hunger. It was growing inside Djaga, as it always did when she called upon it. An old friend, it sat within her chest, crouched like a lion. It enlivened her frame, making her club feel as light as air, her shield invincible.

Nearby, Pelam struck his gong, signaling the start of the bout. Djaga strode forward.

I ask not for your favor.

Talashem moved to meet her, wary, ready.

I only give what you require.

Perhaps Talashem saw it within her. Perhaps he was simply being wary. But he backed away as Djaga charged, bringing her club down on him as Sjado's light filled her from within. That was when she felt it, a familiar sensation coming from somewhere in the crowd. It was something she hadn't felt since leaving her homeland: another who could touch Sjado. Another spurned by the two-faced god.

Afua…

MANY YEARS BEFORE THAT BOUT in the pits, far, far away from the heat of Sharakhai, a younger Djaga stood on a hill as the ceaseless winds of Kundhun swept over the grasslands.

Like standing on the shore of an emerald sea, Djaga thought.

"Come now," Afua called from the base of the hill. "Always mooning."

Afua wore a leather dress with wooden beads sewn into the shape of an orange dahlia, the sign of their tribe. She shouldered a leather bag, within which were the tools they would need to commit their crime.

"I'm not *mooning,*" Djaga replied, taking to the downward slope. "I'm admiring the beauty before me. You should try it one day."

Afua replied with a jaunty air as she headed off between two of the hills. "No time. We've *work* to do."

"Work to do…" Djaga spoke softly, the wind stealing her words. "Conspiracies to commit, more like."

Even so, she followed Afua willingly.

They soon came to a hill that was shaped differently than the rest. It looked like a spearhead, and into its narrowest slope, the

place from which the spear's haft would extend, a stone door was set. Green moss and white lichen grew along the threshold and the door's surface. Now that they were here, the worry that had seemed so far away felt close, a crow flying above her, cawing and judging, like a servant of Sjado herself.

When Afua reached into her bag and pulled a length of stout iron from it, Djaga said, "Are you sure we should do this?"

Afua shrugged, handed the iron bar to Djaga, and pulled out a second from the bag. "Is all not fair in war?"

"We are not at war." The pry bar's weight felt obscene.

"Did your father not tell you?" Afua used the tapered end of her bar to prize at the tomb's seal. "The grasslands are *always* at war."

Djaga waited, watching the way behind them though she was certain they hadn't been followed. They'd come to a place that had been hidden for a hundred years. Only a handful knew anything more than the stories told around the fires, stories of warrior women who'd led the Great Reclamation of the central hills, bringing two generations of peace. *And here we are, come to steal their glory.*

No, Djaga told herself. It wasn't glory they were after, but a way to touch Sjado and Jonsu both. It wasn't for *themselves* that they had come. It was for the good of the king and queen. For the good of the tribe. War stood on the horizon. It was their duty to do all they could to prepare. Wasn't that what Djaga's father had told her growing up?

Well, here I am, Djaga spoke to his memory. *This is needed.*

"Well, put your shoulders into it," Djaga said, sick of watching Afua struggle with the seal. She took her own bar and drove it into the gap with a sharp, full-bodied thrust. When she leaned against it, powering her weight into the bar, she felt the door shift. A sigh of air was released from the tomb. It smelled of loam and decay and long-forgotten days.

They descended into darkness. Well below the surface of the

barrow, lit only by the sunlight filtering in from behind them, was a stone-lined space reaching out into the darkness, until it was swallowed by the gloom. On either side of a central aisle were dozens of sarcophagi. Wreaths of withered grass and flowers lay centered on their dusty lids.

"Which one?" Djaga asked.

"To the far end," Afua replied. "The spear's tip. The place of honor."

They counted as they went, a dozen, then two, then fifty, until at last they came to the end of the great, subterranean hall. The stories had told of five score buried here, but Djaga could see now that there was one last sarcophagus standing apart from the rest—the hundred and first.

Djaga was suddenly fearful of approaching it. "What does it mean?"

"It means that her story was lost to the passage of time, nothing more. Now quit acting like a scared little grass maiden and help me open it." She motioned to the place beside her. "Unless you wish to weave baskets and paint gourds for the rest of your life."

Djaga moved to stand beside the last of the sarcophagi. *Their leader, surely.* Together, they pried the lid up. When they pushed it aside, the harsh scraping echoed eerily. It felt like an affront to the gods. Inside the sarcophagus, barely visible, were a pair of desiccated legs held loosely together with a cord woven from stalks of grass. Upon the toes were golden rings. Around the right ankle were three bands of gold.

"Those," Afua said, pointing to the anklets.

Djaga swallowed. "You're sure?"

As Afua reached in and slipped one of the anklets around the foot, the cord of grass crumbled as if it were made of ash. "Stop asking me that." She held the anklet up, admiring it, then took off the rope sandal on her right foot and slipped it on. When she noticed

Djaga hadn't moved to do the same, she snapped her fingers. "Hurry up, you moon-eyed girl!"

Djaga took one deep breath. *I do this for you, Sjado.* She reached in and slipped the second anklet from around the frail foot but, unlike Afua, slipped it around her own ankle while hardly looking at it. That done, they quickly moved to the opposite side of the sarcophagus and shouldered the stone lid home. Djaga shivered as it boomed shut.

"Let's go," Djaga said. "The air is pressing down on me." She refused to run—the two-faced god would not be pleased if she did—but neither did she dawdle. Soon they had made it out and had done their best to close the crypt door. It was too heavy, though, and they had no leverage. They managed to scrape it only a little before they gave up and began heading back toward the village.

Only then did Djaga realize she felt no different. No different at all. The anklet did not make her feel closer to Sjado, as Afua had promised. It only filled her with shame.

IN THE FIGHTING PITS OF Sharakhai, Djaga's battle with Talashem continued. In the tempest of her swings, her awareness of Afua was nearly, though not completely, lost. Why she'd come to Sharakhai, and why *now*, were mysteries Djaga had yet to solve, but of this much she could be sure: it was a tale that could only end in misery.

Talashem was no fool. He saw Djaga's preoccupation and knew enough to press the advantage. His shamshir spun, dealing blow after blow. Djaga was barely able to fend him off. When he followed a block with a furious charge that knocked her off balance and drove the spike at the center of his shield into her shoulder, the pain and the blood brought her back to this place, to the dirt, to the warrior before her, to the satisfying heft of the club in her hand.

For you, Sjado. All is for you.

After blocking Talashem's low sword swipe, she spun around

his shield and the head of her spiked club into his back. His armor blunted the blow, but he reeled from the pain and backed away, trying to regain his center. But Djaga advanced too quickly. She ducked a hasty swipe of his sword, kicked his knee, causing him to buckle, and drove her club against the side of his shield when he raised it. She put the whole of her body, the whole of her years of rage, into that blow. The release felt sweet. The club landed so hard it dented the shield's edge and sent Talashem reeling.

That one small opening gave her all the time she needed. She raised the club and drove it against the top of his helm. The blow rang sharply against the metal, but beneath it was the satisfying sound of a meaty strike. Talashem collapsed, his body spasming several times before he came to a rest, arms splayed against the pit's dirt floor.

The crowd raised their hands to the desert sky, cheering as one. Djaga's breath came in great huffs, her rage still wrapped around her like a flaming cloak. She turned, examining the crowd, forgetting who or what she'd been looking for. The crowd thought it was for them, and their full-throated roar rose to new heights.

Then her purpose returned. Afua. She was looking for Afua.

But she was gone. Just as Djaga had been able to sense Afua's presence earlier, she sensed her absence now. Afua was no longer in or near the pits.

Djaga's eyes swung to gaze at Nadín. None of the worry she'd shown earlier had ebbed. She'd seen Djaga's frantic search for Afua for what it was, and was as worried for Djaga as she'd been before the bout had begun.

How can I explain it to you? Djaga thought.

She couldn't—she'd hidden too much from Nadín—so instead she turned and headed down the cold, darkened tunnel.

AFUA CAME TWO DAYS LATER. Djaga was working on Nadín's ship, *Yerinde's Needle*, repairing the sails as Nadín had taught her.

It was calming work, sandships. Always something to do. Always something to take Djaga's mind away from Sjado's hunger, which some days felt as if it were gnawing at her from the inside. The feeling never truly left her, but simple, hard, physical labor, was one of the most effective remedies. As was fighting. The days after a bout were always the most peaceful for her, Sjado's appetite having been fed to some degree.

The harbor's kaleidoscope of sounds mingled with the hot breeze. The dull pounding of a hammer. The sad call of an amberlark hiding in the shade beneath a pier. Old Ibrahim telling a story, coins clinking as patrons tossed them onto the carpet he'd laid out for that purpose. From the harbor's opposite side came the shrill voice of a woman hawking her wares. "Elixirs, my lords," she called to those walking by. "Elixirs made from the fabled dune drake, known across the desert for bringing a twinkle to your eye, a thing your lady love will thank you for." The western harbor was a ragtag assemblage, to be sure, but they were Djaga's adopted family as well. She'd accepted them early, and they, with Nadín's help, had accepted her in return. It was this, as much as the work on the sandships, that Djaga loved.

Finishing a line of stitches in the canvas, Djaga arched her back, working out the kinks. Nadín stood not far away on the deck, waving with a smile to someone along the quay. She looked beautiful standing there, as much a part of the ship as the lateen sails or the skimwood runners.

Nadín, catching Djaga's gaze, stared down at her. "And what do *you* find so interesting?"

"You."

Her stern look turned to a smile. "I am nothing."

"You are the brightness of the sun as it shines through the rain."

She looked as if she were going to brush the compliment aside, a thing she always did when Djaga showered her with praise, but the words seemed to die on her lips as she stared out to the end

of the pier. Footsteps approached, thumping along the pier's heavy planks. Djaga knew without turning who it would be. She had the same feeling as she'd had in the pits.

As Djaga stood and turned, she was back in the grasslands, stealing the artifacts of the dead, ready to use them so that the gods might witness her. *And they had,* Djaga thought, a flash of dead bodies swimming before her eyes. She blinked and shook her head, focusing on the approaching woman once more.

The Afua heading down the pier walked with a bit of a limp, and of course she appeared older than Djaga's memories—she was now on the lean side of thirty summers, just like Djaga—but otherwise she looked remarkably similar to the years they'd spent together in the grasslands, especially the smile on her face, the demon's glint in her eyes.

That was how her grandfather had always described her: *that little demon.* He'd been joking, of course—the sort of thing a grandfather said to get a mother riled—but it had stuck. It was as much a part of Afua as her broad cheeks, her rounded chin.

"Good day to you, Djaga," Afua said in Kundhunese.

"What are you doing here?" Djaga replied.

"I've been in Sharakhai for some time." Afua looked over the ship with a pinched expression, as if she'd come to buy it but now found it wanting. "I've been meaning to seek you out."

"And only now found the courage?"

"Who is this, my sweet?" Nadín asked in Sharakhan.

Afua turned to face Nadín, but continued to speak to Djaga in their tribal language. "I'm surprised you haven't told your little pet about me. I'm sure you sensed me in the pits. Are you *embarrassed* of me, Djaga?"

Pet, Afua had called her, which meant she knew about the two of them. "You've been watching me..."

"In *Sharakhan,* if you please." Nadín took a step toward Afua

with a look that could wither stone. She was not a tall woman, Nadín, but in that moment, she looked every bit Afua's equal. "Tell her to stop staring at me with that smug smile of hers before I smash it off her face."

Djaga moved quickly to Nadín and took her hand, easing her away from Afua. "Forgive me. Afua is my cousin, raised in the same village as I. We haven't seen one another in some time. Afua, this is Nadín."

Though clearly annoyed, Nadín gave Afua a bow of her head. Afua returned the gesture crisply, almost coldly, then considered Djaga anew. "The news I have is for you alone," she said, thankfully in Sharakhan.

Djaga squeezed Nadín's hand. "I need but a moment."

Nadín was wary, and tight as a bowstring, but she trusted Djaga. After a pause in which she regained her composure, she nodded and went below decks as if there were more important things that needed tending to. Djaga motioned Afua to sit along the gunwales, but Afua jutted her chin toward the end of the pier. "Let's take to the sand."

Djaga shrugged and followed her. They took the ladder down and strode away from the ship, making for the center of the harbor's expanse. "What is it you want?"

"Want?" Afua laughed, a bark that rose above the wash of sounds around them. "I'm here to *help* you, cousin."

"Help me? My life was *ruined* because of you."

"If I recall it rightly, you were right by my side when we entered the barrow. You took the pry bar from my hands willingly!"

Djaga had never forgotten the shame of what she and Afua had done, but it hadn't felt so deep as this, not in a long time, not since coming to Sharakhai. Djaga stopped walking. "You've come to help, you say, but first you wish to rub my nose in my failures?"

Afua stopped and turned, the skirt of her purple dress flaring as she did so. "Forgive me." She took a deep breath and pinched the

bridge of her nose. "It feels like yesterday. I'm sure it does for you as well. But I *have* come to help you. I've come to release you from the torture you've endured."

There was always a gnawing feeling within Djaga. With the rage she'd expended in the pits the other day, it was little more than a simmer, but when Afua had said those words, the feeling began to roil once more. "Release me from what?"

"Don't be thick. I know what's plagued you. You know the same of me. The two-faced god, Djaga. Sjado's rage lives inside me, Jonsu's peace ever out of reach. Can you say it isn't the same for you?"

Though it felt strange to admit it, Djaga felt exactly the same. She'd never told anyone. Not the people of her village when they'd held her for trial. Not Osman, the owner of the pits. Not Nadín. Even here, standing before a woman who knew her tale, who knew her shame, Djaga couldn't say it aloud. It felt too much like blasphemy.

"What of it?" Djaga finally asked.

"You can be free of it. I've found a way!"

A STORM THREATENED THE HORIZON as Djaga and Afua jogged over the grasslands. Over the stand of low trees that marked the northern edge of their village, a twisting column of smoke rose into an overcast sky. The scent of woodsmoke came to them, and roasting gazelle, one small portion of the feast that would be consumed when the rites of passage had been completed.

As they reached the dirt road and passed through the stone archway, people began waving to them from the doorways of their huts. "Be stout," old Elu called to them, her gray hair wild, her smile even wilder. "Be stout and you'll win the heart of the goddess."

Afua and Djaga shared a look. Afua smiled, but it was forced. She'd said over and over that there was no harm in touching the artifacts of the fabled warriors—*that we would risk so much will prove our passion*—but even *she* must be having doubts by now.

Soon they'd arrived at the village center. Hundreds moved about, readying all for the ritual and the feast to follow. Tall wooden posts had been freshly painted in red and white and yellow. Hanging from each was a horsetail dyed indigo and blue. The wind played with them, made them flutter in alternating rhythms as the southern storm pressed closer. The mock battlefield—little more than a shallow depression—held a number of the other aspirants already. Djaga's uncle and brother talked with one another at the edge, along with others from the temple.

"And there she is," her uncle said, arms spread wide. They hugged. His tall headdress, made of bright beads and painted quills, rustled and clicked as he moved. He introduced her to others from nearby villages, who had come to witness her in her attempt to join the temple of the two-faced god. Her brother brought her fermented horse milk and bade her drink it quickly. It would make her shine more brightly to the gods, he said. She took it, not because she believed him, but because she thought it might quell her nerves.

Her ankle burned from the weight of the gold wrapped around it. She and Afua had stopped on the run back home and covered them with mud, but to Djaga it looked like a child had done it. How could they not see what it truly was? How could they not point and name them blasphemers?

Djaga nearly went to her uncle to confess it all, but just then Afua strode up to her and gripped her by the elbow, holding her in place. "Will you calm yourself?"

"I want to take it *off*, Afua. The shame of it burns my skin."

"We did it for a reason. Find your nerve, girl. Sjado rewards the *bold*."

Time and again, the old tales spoke of Sjado winning at any cost—against mighty Hiwe, against swift Pemaru, against even Onondu, using his own tricks against him—before the aspect of the warrior faded and peaceful Jonsu rose to prominence once more.

"It still feels shameful."

Afua's face grew angry. She gripped Djaga's arm to the point of pain. "Bury your shame, girl, and find your heart. You'll not deny me this day." She softened a moment later, and nodded to Djaga's uncle. "This is as much for him as it is for you. You know as well as I how his heart will swell with pride when the mark of the warrior is cut into your skin."

She watched her uncle, who had become like a father to her and Idé after their true father died five years earlier in their tribe's ceaseless border skirmishes with the neighboring Halawari. Just then he was smiling as the King of a nearby tribe told a story, motioning to his daughter, who had been a member of Sjado's temple for years now. Djaga could tell her uncle smiled not for the King, who was a blowhard if Djaga had ever heard one, but for how proud he would be should Djaga be accepted as well.

"I just want this day to be done."

"It will all be over soon." Afua smiled. "In the flit of a hummingbird's wings."

The next hour passed like a dream. Greeting the dozens who'd traveled from leagues all around. Taking the sacrament of goat's blood. Being painted with yellow clay by the high priestess herself, a woman with green eyes that seemed to pierce Djaga's heart.

Soon Djaga, Afua, and five others were ready to take their final test. Rattling circlets were tied around their wrists and ankles. They were granted spears and tall, wickerwork shields. They stood in a tight circle in the center of the ritual's arena. Then, seven full initiates of Sjado's temple were arrayed around them with spears and shields of their own.

The task was simple: draw blood before submitting or being forced to withdraw. Not so easy considering how well the initiates to Sjado's temple were trained, but something that young aspirants were often able to do on their first or second ritual day. Afua hadn't

been convinced it would be enough. She'd wanted to impress. So had Djaga. But now all she could think about was the stolen anklet and how it weighed on her.

"Through war we find peace," the high priestess said.

"Through war we find peace," Djaga and the others intoned.

The high priestess swung a whip over her head and sent it cracking over the aspirant's heads. Immediately, the initiates closed in. Djaga lowered her stance, ready to defend herself, but the woman across from her was so swift she got in a strike against Djaga's shin before Djaga was even set. Djaga winced and backed away, lowering her shield. But when she did, her opponent thrust the spear lightning quick and scored another strike against her leading shoulder.

Djaga tried to counterattack, but her thrust was met by the orange shield. Her heart pounded in her chest. The sounds around her—the battle cries of the warriors, the shouts of the crowd, the screaming of the children—all became a wash, a numbing rattle akin to the monsoons of the wet season as rain drove hard against the grasses. That was when Djaga first felt it. A presence. Like the one she'd felt as a child when she went out alone to the grasslands at night. It was an indescribable fear, surely the presence of Odokōn, the god of death who came for all. Djaga had run back to the village to her home. She'd buried her face in her mother's breast and cried, and her mother had consoled her until she'd fallen asleep at last.

There would be no running now, and Odokōn had already come for her mother. This was a thing undeniable. A demand from Sjado herself for Djaga to fulfill her desires. *Battle leads to salvation. War is how we survive.* Djaga felt the goddess move within her. Felt her take up her shield, felt her heft her spear. Sjado moved, sinuous as a mamba, spear darting, sinking deep into flesh.

She heard grunts of pain, heard shouts of surprise. She became the kingfisher, flitting between dull thrusts of weapons held in deadened hands. She became the acacia, stout against the blows brought

against her. She became the midnight finch, drinking the blood of her enemies. One fell, a spear cutting her throat. Another dropped, holding her stomach where the spear had pierced her through. Others came. Tried to swarm her. But she was the wind. She was the storm. She was the strike of lightning and the bellow of thunder.

One by one, all that stood against her fell to the ground, until none remained in the arena but the dead. She held her spear to the sky and released the almighty rage that still burned in her veins. She shouted for any to come near. But none would. They'd seen the goddess in her, and they feared.

She nearly went to them, nearly charged to take more with her spear. Among them, however, she spied a woman, staring at her from outside the circle, her spear, still to hand, pointing at Djaga as if she feared she would be the next victim. It was Afua.

The storm winds blew, tossing the horsetails while all else was still.

You left the arena.

The wind blew, cool against her burning skin.

You left, and this was all your idea.

The wind blew, and the rain began to fall.

I'VE FOUND A WAY!

The words hung between Afua and Djaga like a mirage. This was trickery, Djaga knew, nothing more. She already knew the way to release, and it was through atonement, through giving Sjado what she wanted. One day, the two-faced god would judge her worthy of becoming her own woman once more. Not before. Yet the possibility of release, of Afua knowing some secret Djaga had overlooked, was so tantalizing that Djaga found herself saying, "How?"

"Do you see the man standing at the end of that pier?"

Djaga turned to look. On the pier stood a stout Malasani man. His hair was cut straight over his brow, an echo of sorts to his simple

black tunic. He had a rough-and-tumble look about him—an ever-hungry wolf, sated for the moment. She'd never met the man but she recognized him immediately. She'd seen him twice, in the killing pits.

"That's Hathahn," Djaga said, already starting to understand what Afua wanted of her.

"Very good."

"You wish me to fight him. In the killing pits."

Afua bowed her head, the sly nod of a merchant toward a particularly wealthy patron. "Your final bout flies ever nearer, does it not?"

"I refuse to kill, Afua. You've been here in Sharakhai long enough. You must know that by now."

"Yes, I've been watching you. I've asked around the pits as well. But I know the girl you *were*." Afua's face turned sour. "You hope to appease *Sjado* by toying with your food and never eating it? You should have known even before your first bout, but surely you know it by now—it will *never* work, Djaga. Sjado demands her due."

"You've found your own peace, then?"

Afua smiled, an expression as sad as a thunderstorm over the grasslands. "I've done my killing. But I cannot be free until you are. We are bound. How could it be any other way?"

It made sense. They had entered the arena together. Afua might have left before it was done, but what would that mean to the two-faced god? Sjado would have punished her as well, and why not bind them together like Sjado was bound to Jonsu?

"Is that it, then? You wish to find release if I kill Hathahn and appease Sjado?"

"You are a warrior, Djaga, a thing you deny despite playing at war in the pits. Sjado's wrath will be quenched only when you kill, not before. When that is done, I will lead us both to Jonsu's peace."

Djaga looked to where the brute, Hathahn, stood at the end of the pier. He was watching them as if he were curious, nothing more, though this had as much to do with him as it did Djaga and Afua.

"Just like that? He'll lie down and let me kill him?"

"Of course not. He's long heard of you, and when I told him I might convince you to join him in the killing pits for your final bout, he quickly agreed. To his own god would go the glory."

Djaga crossed her arms, turning away from the wind and the biting sand until it died down. "I took a vow."

Afua's face screwed up in anger. "Wake up, girl! Who do you think was it that took those lives? Was it you? Me? No, it was Sjado herself. She was angry with us, true, but she was showing us her very nature. I have been haunted by her and Jonsu ever since. Neither of us will find peace until we atone for our sins."

"I took a vow."

Afua stared at her for a time, but then she huffed like one of the desert's bone crushers. "You would deny yourself *peace*?"

"I haven't seen you in a dozen years. After all this time, after abandoning me in Kundhun, after leaving me to wonder what had happened to you, you darken my doorway, reciting honeyed tales of how *I* might be freed from the chains of the gods, and you would have me believe that it's for *my* benefit?"

Afua raised her hands to the sky, shook them as if she were calling for rain. "I want to set things *right*, Djaga! I want to right at least *one* of the wrongs I've committed." When Djaga continued to stare coldly, a crack formed in Afua's composed face. "Do I not deserve *some* peace in this life?"

"I won't do it."

"You *must*."

"You may not believe that vows have meaning, Afua, but I do." She began heading back toward Nadín's ship, the supple sand grasping at the soles of her boots. "Go. Return to Hathahn and tell him you'll need to find another, for I'll not fight him, no matter how much you plead."

NADÍN STOOD AT THE SHIP'S small stove, stirring a pot of soup. "So she left you there to face the tribunal alone?"

It was well past sundown, but it had taken a long while to explain it all to Nadín. Djaga had never told her the truth. Not all of it, anyway. When she'd learned more, she'd wanted the rest, and Djaga finally relented. It was the lowest moment of Djaga's life, a thing she was shamed to speak of, but if she were going to start a new life with Nadín, she needed to share it or she'd be living a lie.

"Yes, she left me, though I don't blame her for it. Not anymore. The tribunal would have ordered her death. I'm sure of it."

"Maybe she *deserved* to die."

Djaga shrugged. "I don't decide who lives and who dies."

Nadín frowned at that, but said nothing in return. After ripping two hunks of bread so dark it was nearly black and dropping it into the waiting bowls, she turned and leaned against the hull. Her arms were crossed and she gave Djaga that stare of hers, the one that said she wouldn't be satisfied until she knew everything. "Why didn't they kill you?"

"They were scared." Djaga could still remember it, the look of fear in their eyes as they stared at her, blood coating her spear, dead bodies all around. "Every single one of them."

"Scared you would fight them?"

"The *goddess* was in me, Nadín. They'd seen it, and they were afraid she'd come for everyone else. They didn't know yet what Afua and I had done, and even after I'd confessed they still wondered at Sjado's intentions. No one had witnessed her like that in generations. Kill me, and they risked Sjado's wrath."

Nadín ladled soup into bowls, dousing the hunks of day-old bread, then topped it with a sprinkling of chopped parsley. She set one before Djaga, then took the chair across from her at the small galley table. She blew on the soup, then slurped a spoonful noisily.

This is what I want, Djaga thought. *Me and Nadín on a ship, far*

away from the violence of Osman's pits.

In the days ahead, she planned to sail with Nadín and trade with the people of her tribe far to the west of Sharakhai. They'd sail to other tribes and trade with them as well. Then, they'd return to Sharakhai and sell the goods and use a portion of the proceeds to buy more to fill their hold, enough for another voyage out to the baking sands. It would be a simple life, but a life Djaga would treasure. If only she could enjoy it. Nadín had been after her for months to leave the pits once and for all.

Djaga had scoffed at first. "I know nothing else," she'd told Nadín one night as they lay in bed.

"I'll teach you," Nadín had said, leaning in to kiss her.

"I'm an old lion, with teeth and claws and little else."

"Are you saying you *can't* learn"—she ran her fingers along the riddle of scars that marked Djaga's arm—"or that you don't wish to?"

Djaga grabbed a fistful of Nadín's hair, pulled her near, and kissed her soft lips more deeply than Nadín had done a moment ago. "I'm saying I am a beast trapped in a Kundhuni's skin. I'm saying no amount of hoping will change that."

"It will only take *time*, my sweet."

Time, Djaga thought. It sounded so reasonable. More and more, though, as the day of her retirement approached, she worried it was only a foolish wish and nothing more. She hadn't been able to find the peace she'd hoped would come with the knowledge that she would soon leave the pits. Now, she worried that it would *never* come. Already, the itch to fight was in her. Already, it made her want to push Nadín away. Soon, it would become a need, and then, if it wasn't quenched, the goddess would come to occupy her form as she had in Kundhun.

I must find a way. I will die before I let anything happen to Nadín.

"You're looking at me like that again."

"Like what?"

"Like you're lost."

I am *lost. In a wasteland of my god's own making.*

Nadín motioned to Djaga's bowl. "Eat."

Djaga picked up the spoon and used its edge to hack off a piece of bread. It was good, the two together, the silky, saffron-laced broth with the earthy bread.

"You never saw Afua again?" Nadín asked.

"Not until today."

"The way she strutted up to my ship," Nadín said under her breath, "acting as if she's some queen from the grasslands."

As if her words had summoned it, there came the sound of footsteps on the pier outside their ship. But the tread was heavy, the stride long. "Djaga Akoyo?"

Djaga didn't recognize the man's voice. It was deep, resonant. "Who's come?"

The reply came in a thick Malasani accent. "It is Hathahn. I've come to speak to you and your woman."

Nadín frowned, her eyes flitting between the hatch door and Djaga. *What does he want?* she mouthed to Djaga.

Djaga could only shrug. She had no idea. When Djaga raised her eyebrows, asking Nadín for her permission for Hathahn to board her ship, Nadín nodded, though none of her nervousness subsided.

"Come," Djaga said.

In a moment, Hathahn's ample backside appeared as he descended the ladder into the hold. He wore a striped tunic of white and red. He had thick bracelets of beaten steel on his well-muscled arms and a torc of twisted gold around his neck, a thing that accentuated the corded muscles along his shoulders rather than the wide neck of his tunic did.

Nadín's reaction to Hathahn's sudden arrival was anything but pleased, but she still stood and motioned to the stove. "Would you like some soup?"

Hathahn raised his hands, forestalling her. "I cannot stay long, thank you. I've only come to speak to Djaga for a moment, and you as well, if you'd care to hear my tale."

"Very well," Nadín said, and before Djaga could say anything against her, she sat and motioned Hathahn to the nearby bench that doubled as their bed when pulled out and laid flat. Djaga wouldn't have denied her anyway, for she had no doubt this was something Nadín would need a voice in.

"Where do I begin?" Hathahn said, his legs spread wide, his hands on his knees. Gods, the man was huge. He made the galley look tiny by his mere presence. He waved one of his meaty platters-for-hands toward Djaga. "My Afua came to you today. She told you a tale that would appeal to your sense of, shall we say, self-preservation."

"Self-preservation!" Nadín, her soup forgotten, crossed her arms over her chest. "You call fighting a man like you *self-preservation?*"

Hathahn nodded. "We preserve ourselves in this life, and we preserve ourselves for the next, yes? We must think not only of our bodies, but our very *souls*. Unless I'm sadly mistaken"—he fixed his steely gaze on Djaga—"this is a thing that concerns you. Does it not?"

Djaga was beginning to get annoyed with her life being interrupted. "Get on with it."

The smile on Hathahn's broad face was a knowing one. "We worry about many things. Our health. Our livelihood." He turned his gaze on Nadín. "Our ability to provide for our loved ones." He paused and leaning back. The wooden bench creaked beneath his weight. "You know that I'm a slave, yes?"

"I know," Djaga said.

He shrugged. "Your look shows pity, but in truth I've had a fine life. I was raised to fight. I enjoyed it. I grew good at it." He smiled and leaned forward, eyeing Djaga with a jackal grin. "Very good at it." He shrugged again. "But the teeth of all dogs grow blunt. Our bite becomes less sharp. You must know."

Djaga stared, hating this reminder of all she was.

"My master hails from Malasan," Hathahn went on. "I have four wives there. I have twelve children. It's been two years since I've seen them, and I have no illusions that I'll ever see them alive again in this life. I live to fight. Now that I've risen as high as I can, I will fight until I am killed. Why? Because I care only for two things. That my family will prosper and grow, and that I will stand on the shore of the river, celebrated by our gods as my family crosses over to meet me, one by one. My master will not only provide for them, he will see to their welfare, for in me they have a champion of Malasan. A warrior like Shonokh incarnate."

"I grow tired of your tale, Hathahn."

"You do?" He laughed, a deep rumble that filled that confined space. "Then you'll bore yourself to tears when your days in the pits are done. I tell you these things so that you will know my intent. I want this to be—how do they say it in Kundhun?—clear as the spring rains." He eyed her up and down, a feral look in his dark eyes. "I will not lie down for you, Djaga Akoyo. I will not lie down so that Afua can give you this gift, so that you may be released from your foolishness. I would not lie down if your bitch goddess, Sjado, were to stand before me now. Be it you or a Blade Maiden or a King of Sharakhai, I will kill the dog who stands against me in the pits or I will die fighting to my last breath. When I depart these shores, I will go to the farther fields with my sword in hand and my head held high."

"Why are you telling her this?" Nadín asked, her face aghast.

Hathahn didn't look at her. His eyes were only for Djaga. "I tell you this so that you will know. With you and I in the pit? It will be a fight that will summon the eyes of all the gods. Malasan, the Great Shangazi, even the gods of the lazy hills of Kundhun." He stood, hunkered over in the low space, then poked her in the chest, and tried to do so again until Djaga slapped his hand away

and stood herself. "Were you to fight me, your god will listen. And if she doesn't?" He spat wetly onto the floorboards between them. "Then she never will. That is the promise a fight with me will bring."

He swung his gaze to Nadín, then back to Djaga. He looked coiled, ready to spring. Djaga readied herself, but then Hathahn relaxed. He licked his lips and smiled, then turned and strode toward the stairs. "Or fight another sad dog, and see then how your life with your soft tribeswoman turns out."

He was soon gone. The heavy tread of his steps on the pier slowly faded, but the stink of his musk lingered. Djaga found herself breathing hard, her hands shaking. Worst of all, though, was the fact that the hunger in her had exploded like a dawning sun inside her. It took all her effort to sit, to spoon the now-tasteless soup into her mouth.

Nadín said nothing, but she knew everything Djaga was feeling. Djaga could tell by her cold silence.

LATE THAT NIGHT, NADÍN LAY by Djaga's side in the ship's lone bunk. Nadín's skin was warm against hers. The way she and Nadín had made love after, in such a mechanical way, made her feel worse than when Hathahn had left. Afua and her machinations had ruined that as well.

Nadín raked her fingers over Djaga's short hair. Normally, it felt so good. Tonight it grated. She let Nadín do it anyway. She knew it was Hathahn's doing. She'd already felt out of sorts before he'd come to the ship, but it had only been magnified by the strange way he'd spoken to her, as if he could browbeat her into fighting him.

Say what you will, she could hear Afua saying. *He was only telling you the truth.*

Somewhere out in the desert, the grunts of a black laugher were followed by the yip of a jackal. Nadín stilled her movements, then pulled Djaga's jaw toward her until they were eye-to-eye in

the moonlight spilling through the nearby porthole. "Why did you never tell me all of this?"

Djaga shrugged. "How could I?"

Nadín smiled a knowing smile. "One word at a time."

"Each describing my shame more fully."

Nadín shook her head. "There's no shame in the truth. You were only trying to please your goddess. And there's no shame in asking for help, either."

A tear slipped from the corner of Djaga's eye, a tear which Nadín wiped away. "I don't know what to do, my love. I keep asking myself how I can please her. She's insatiable. I feel her, always, gnawing at me from the inside. It's already growing worse. She wants more and more." She went on before Nadín could reply. "I know you think it will pass in time. And part of me hopes it's true, but I worry she will never let me go for what I've done. I worry my debt will never be paid. Not until I pass beyond these shores."

Nadín was quiet for a long while. She licked her lips before speaking. "Could there be truth to it?"

Djaga knew exactly what she meant. "Of course there could."

"But there's no way to know."

"No."

Nadín used her fingers to rub away the tear in Djaga's other eye. "Will Osman find a better fighter than Hathahn?"

Djaga weighed her words carefully before speaking. She thought she knew where Nadín was headed, but she didn't want to influence her. "One never knows. But Hathahn is as vicious a fighter as Sharakhai has seen in decades. Those that have been watching the pit fights for generations all say it is so."

"Then fight him," Nadín said. "If you don't, and Sjado continues to haunt you, you'll always wonder if he might have freed you. In him, you can be freed of your guilt. He *wants* to die, Djaga. It's like the goddess herself set this task before you. I don't wish you to fight,

but you've one last fight ahead, so do this. Fight him. Send him to meet his god. Deliver his pride to his family." She leaned in and kissed Djaga, her lips warm and supple. "Free yourself."

Freedom. The very word felt foreign. She'd been running from her own past, her own goddess, for years, but it had gotten her nowhere. *No,* she thought, *it brought me to Nadín.* And yet it felt like a mirage. She'd been telling herself for years that when she found someone, she could leave the pits behind. Surely the goddess wouldn't keep hold of her forever. But now it seemed she would. Her love for Nadín would not last if the goddess continued to gnaw at her day and night. Or at the very least, Nadín's love for her would not last. It would wither away like a rose cut and left beneath the desert sun.

Afua wouldn't have come all this way to betray Djaga again. She had a debt to pay. High time she started to take responsibility for what had happened.

This time, she was the one to lean in and offer a kiss. When she pulled away, she stared into Nadín's beautiful brown eyes. "I'll do it."

THE CROWD IN THE CENTRAL pit was as large as Djaga had ever seen. Thousands were packed so tightly a man could hardly raise his arms to cheer. But cheer they did. The sound of it was like a wall of sound pressing in on her and Hathahn, who paced across the dirt floor opposite her, staring at the crowd and waving his hand as if he were the savior of Sharakhai.

Osman's pits were not killing pits. Osman had never had a taste for it—*it wastes lives needlessly,* he'd told her more than once—but all knew that this match would be to the death. It had drawn the rich from far and wide. The merchant class. Those born to money. People from a dozen nearby caravanserais had traveled to Sharakhai merely to attend. The highborn of Sharakhai stood in the four boxes set aside for lords and ladies of such means. None of the Kings had been announce by Pelam, but Djaga wouldn't be surprised if one of

them had come in disguise.

Of all the people in the pit, Djaga watched only for two: Nadín and Afua, neither of whom were in attendance. She knew Nadín hadn't come, for Djaga had set aside a seat for her to the right of Osman's box. And though Djaga searched for her in the avalanche of faces around her, she knew Afua was gone as well—she would have felt her presence otherwise.

She had little time to wonder at Afua's absence, however, for Pelam was already introducing her. Even five paces away she could barely hear him as he called, "The Lion of Kundhun!" When he waved, the ground beneath her shook from the stomping and the unified, undignified roar of the crowd. It went on a long while, and Djaga needed every bit of it. As hungry as she'd been for battle in the days leading up to this bout, she was confused now. Worried. She knew she would need Sjado if she was to have any chance of defeating Hathahn.

Like a virtuoso actor who knew how to draw just the right notes of emotion from his audience, Pelam waited until the din had diminished. Only then did he wave to Hathahn and introduce him as the Butcher of Malasan, a title he'd earned time and time again in the pits. Again, the crowd's frenzy built on itself. In all her time in the pits, Djaga had never seen the like, but she was beginning to master her emotions at last.

She paced the pit floor, swinging her arms in circles, flexing her muscles to loosen them. The voice of the crowd deadened in her ears. They became little more than a part of the pit, akin to the walls, akin to the vault of the open sky above them. Her attention was now for Hathahn and Hathahn alone. He was not merely calm. He was like a statue, standing tall, his broad face utterly serene. Only his eyes moved as Djaga paced the pit floor. He hardly seemed to be breathing.

It was likely a way to put her off balance, but if that was so, it

wouldn't work. Djaga could feel the goddess once more. *I ask not for your favor, Sjado. I ask not for your favor. I only give what you require…*

They were words she'd spoken thousands of times. The only way the two-faced god had ever acknowledged them was through the rage that built within Djaga. Sjado might consider that answer enough, and Djaga had never presumed to ask for more, but today was different. She needed more. She deserved it after this long in the service of the two-faced god.

She stopped her pacing and faced Hathahn. "This day," she shouted, her words lost in the terrible din like smoke in a sandstorm, "I would know the truth!"

This was her last hope. She would either die or she would kill Hathahn. If killing him didn't work, she would know that her efforts in the years since that terrible day in her village had been in vain. She would know as well that the curse laid upon her since she'd slain her friends and family in Kundhun was permanent.

The crowd hushed as the weapons were brought out by three pit boys. Hathahn chose a pair of beaten battle axes. Djaga took two khopeshes, the sharply curved swords of the grasslands. Pelam now stood between them, his small brass gong in hand, mallet raised high. In an instant, the noise of the crowd hushed. The moment Pelam struck the gong, Djaga charged forth, releasing a battle cry as she moved to meet Hathahn in battle.

Hathahn met her onslaught with apparent ease. He blocked her swings, the sound of her blades on the metal haft a ringing call to the heavens. Twice in that early flurry he tried to hook a khopesh with the head of an axe and rip it from her grasp, but she was ready for it and used the momentary opening to snap a kick into his stomach.

By Sjado's black breath, he was *solid*. He was also as smooth a fighter as Djaga had ever come across. There were no wasted movements as he blocked and retreated, as he swung his axes in tight arcs before him. He was playing a long game, hoping to let Djaga

wear herself out. But she was well used to such things. The power of Sjado urged her on, to draw blood, but she bottled the desire, used it instead to build her own anger.

Slowly, as sweat glistened upon their skin, as their weapons bit and took small nicks from their armor, her rage built like the glow of forge-kissed steel. She burned from it, red then orange then yellow then white. With each blow, she released a powerful shout. Each shout became more ragged, then slid into a roar as all her frustration from her time since leaving the grasslands for the desert—the shame over what she'd done to her own people, her feelings of abandonment by Afua—came out in one long outpouring, an offering for her god that she might have mercy.

Hathahn was methodical in his defense, axes pinwheeling to block Djaga's swords, helm or greaves or pauldrons taking the blows when Djaga was too quick. But then he did something that showed why he'd won so many matches in the killing pits. He waited for the perfect moment, driving through her defenses like a battering ram. Djaga retreated, scoring a deep cut into the meat of Hathahn's thigh, but he was on the move now, dropping an axe and grabbing her wrist as he came. He bulled forward, sending her crashing into the wall behind her. He drove his helm onto the crown of her head.

Hathahn stood in sharp contrast to Djaga. His eyes were serene. His breath smelled like freshly turned clay. He was a pinnacle of stone rising above the sand dunes, calm in the face of the storm.

"Come, you goat fucker," Djaga said. "It's time to *fight*." She dropped the sword in her free hand and sent two quick uppercuts into his jaw. Again, it felt wrong, as if he were not flesh and bone, but something *else*. "Are you there, Hathahn?"

His only response was to stare with those deadened eyes and to twist her wrist. She immediately pushed away from the wall with all her might. When he tried to press his weight against her, she crouched low, grabbed one tree trunk of a thigh with her free arm,

and lifted with all her might.

She knew immediately something was amiss. She'd lifted men his size before, but Hathahn was much heavier. His skin was *hot*. As she powered him backward, he swiped at her with his axe, she felt the weapon bite, felt the burn spread near the base of her spine, but there was nothing for it now.

She drove him down to the ground, then rolled over him, twisting her arm free in one violent motion. He grabbed for her. She leaned away. He swiped for her ankles with his axe, but she was ready for it. She kicked the weapon's haft, halting it, then grabbed his wrist and dropped, snaking her legs around his arm. She leaned back, applying as much leverage to her lock on his arm as she could, wrenching it over and over until she heard a crack like the snapping of stone.

He'd held onto the axe the entire time, but when his arm broke, he'd released it. She took it up in one hand as she straddled his waist, then lifted it high in the air. She swung it down with all her might, sure Hathahn would try to stop her. But he didn't, and the head of the axe came down onto his helm, sundering it and his skull beneath. Blood leaked from the wound. It smelled acrid, though. Sulfurous. And his eyes. Jonsu's grace, they stared through her as if he were lying on a field of daisies staring at the deep blue sky.

As a long, guttural sigh escaped him, Djaga stood.

Chest heaving, she turned, ignoring the eruption of the crowd as they cheered for her. She looked desperately for Nadín, already knowing she wouldn't find her. A feeling of cold invaded her. Nadín was missing. Afua was gone. And now this—she stared down at the body lying at her feet—this *thing* that was not Hathahn. Had the tales of Malasan not spoken of golems created to mimic those whose blood had been taken? Surely this was one of those, make to look like Hathahn.

The door to the pit's subterranean tunnels slid open. Pelam

walked toward her, ready to raise her hand to the crowd, but she sprinted past him. She ran down the cold tunnel, through the labyrinth, and out the rearmost exit. Breath ragged, she willed her burning legs to keep pumping as she pounded her way toward the western harbor.

WHEN DJAGA REACHED THE QUAYSIDE, old Ibrahim the storyteller was there. For some reason, he was walking toward her. "Best you come with me," he said as she came near.

"What's happened?"

He took her by the arm and led her toward an alley.

"Where are you—" Djaga stopped, for ahead there was a crowd gathered. A body was being lifted onto a cart. Blood coated the broken stones of the street. She rushed forward and saw what she already knew. She'd known from the moment she'd sprinted from the pit.

Those gathered tight around Nadín were from the harbor. The stevedores. The shipwrights. The merchants. The people Nadín had known all her life and whom Djaga had come to know through her. They stared at her, ashen-faced. Djaga moved to the cart's side and, by the grace of the gods, found Nadín breathing shallowly, staring up at the sky not so differently than Hathahn's dead form had done only minutes before. The way her hands were laid tenderly over her stomach—as if she'd simply eaten too much—was so incongruous with the bloody reality laid out on the bed of the cart that Djaga nearly retched.

She brushed the hair from Nadín's eyes. Leaned down and kissed her forehead. "Tell me what happened, my love."

Nadín blinked, her eyes distant. With effort, as if she were pulling her gaze away from the farther fields, she turned to stare into Djaga's eyes. "Hathahn."

The cart lurched into motion, the mule and the driver leading them toward the *medicum.* "What of him?" Djaga asked, moving to

keep pace. Nadín swallowed. Licked her lips. Djaga took her hand and shook it. "Nadín, what of him?"

Nadín lifted one hand and stared at the blood, a deathbed smile distorting her features as if she still couldn't believe what had happened. "I've been stabbed."

A blade of ice slipped into Djaga's heart. "Nadín, quickly now!" She cradled Nadín's neck and shook her gently lest she slip back into unconsciousness. "Tell me what *happened*."

The look of confusion on Nadín's face was profound, as if with the answer to this question she could die in peace. "I was getting ready to leave for the pits when a messenger girl came. She said there was someone I'd be interested in seeing on the *Condor's Wake*. I told her I didn't care." She squeezed Djaga's fingers. "I told her I needed to go see you, but she said you were being fooled, that you were in danger, so of course I went. I saw five men preparing her to sail. I watched them for a time, but saw nothing strange. I was ready to leave when I heard his voice."

"Hathahn's?"

As the cart trundled around a corner and onto a wider thoroughfare, Nadín nodded. On even ground now, they began moving faster. "I dropped to the sand and moved to the rear of the ship. I saw him inside the rear cabin, talking to a man." She rolled her head back and forth. The pinch of her eyes wrung tears from them. "They saw me. They shouted for me to stop, but I ran. I ran across the whole of the harbor and then up to the quay. I was ready to make my way toward the pits, toward you, my love, when something flashed to my right." She lifted one shaking hand, coated in red. "And then this."

"Who?" Djaga asked, somehow already sure of the answer. "Who did this to you?"

Nadín shrugged, but winced immediately and fell still, her breath coming in short gasps filled with soft, pitiful moans. "I remember the pain. I remember falling to the cobbles. I saw the hem of a thawb,

but that was all, and then they were gone."

"Was it Afua?"

Nadín took a long time to respond to this. She looked as though she were debating. "I have no love for your cousin, but I cannot say."

They reached the front steps of the *medicum*, where a stretcher and two attendants were already waiting. As Nadín was being lifted down to the stretcher, Osman and three dirt dogs from the pits came running up from the direction of the harbor. They were all breathless.

"What's happened?" Osman said, his black brows pinched as he stared down at Nadín.

Djaga's fingers flexed. Her lips drew back as her lungs forced hot air through bared teeth. She'd never felt so out of control, not since Sjado had granted Djaga that first, cold kiss. She paced along the amber paving stones, staring at the buildings opposite the *medicum*. She wanted to tear them down. She wanted to tear the whole city down.

Osman took one step closer, reaching a hand out but stopping short of touching her. "Djaga, what's happened, girl?"

She stopped, glared at Osman. "A betrayal."

Osman glanced back at the dirt dogs, fighters from the pits that Djaga knew were very good. "You need help?"

Djaga hardly had to think about it. "Yes." But she couldn't do this alone. "Come," she said, and then they were off, running back toward the harbor.

YERINDE'S NEEDLE, NADÍN'S SLEEK, TWO-MASTED ketch, wasn't much for the eyes, but her skis were true and her sails were full. With the wind to their backs and the dunes tight, she was swift as an amberlark. And she wasn't laden like the *Condor's Wake*. The *Wake* was a dhow: larger, with more men, and likely enough supplies for weeks of sailing. The *Needle's* crew, on the other hand, kept her as light as they could make her.

They'd returned to the western harbor after leaving Nadín at the *medicum*. They'd searched for the ship Nadín had described, and found soon enough that it had left shortly before they'd arrived. They'd readied the ship as quickly as they could, the people of the harbor helping to tow the ship back, to get her moving as fast as they could.

They'd exited the harbor and sailed north, then eastward around the tip of Sharakhai. They spotted the *Condor* shortly after.

Steadily, the *Needle* crept closer, the sand a bare whisper beneath the runners. Nightfall neared, and they came close enough that the crew on the other ship began firing arrows. At first it was merely to warn them away, but when it became clear they wouldn't be deterred, they started targeting Djaga at the wheel and the others about the ship. Osman set up some makeshift shields using the hatch cover and the table from the cabin below decks. It worked, and soon Hathahn's crew abandoned the tactic and, from their hold, brought up clay pots the size of oranges with black wicks sticking out from one end. They lit them and began launching them at the *Needle*.

The first struck the ship's port-side hull. The hull burst into flames, though thankfully most of it splashed downward onto the sand. The second hit the foredeck. Osman ran forward with dousing sand, one of the dirt dogs shielding him with the table to protect him from the renewed onslaught of arrows.

The *Needle* ran alongside the *Condor* now. Djaga called to the other pit fighter, Kaliban. "Take the wheel. Be ready to brake her."

"What are you going to do?" he asked as he stepped over.

Djaga eyed the other ship, where the bulky form of Hathahn had finally come up from the hold. "I'm going to take that rotting ship down."

As the crew of the dhow lit another flame pot, Djaga stepped over to the starboard gunwale. She took her long fighting knife from its sheath along her leg and bit down on it with her teeth. Grabbing the mainsail's halyard tight in her right hand, she crouched, and in

one swift, furious motion, she pulled the belaying pin.

She leapt as the lanyard pulled with enough force to lift her from the deck. The wind in the mainsail, and the weight of the sail and its boom, drew her toward the top of the mainmast. She used her legs to run along it, guiding herself so that she'd be launched in the proper direction.

When she reached the top, the lanyard whipped her up and over the mast. She flew through the air as a fresh fire pot crashed below and spread its fire amidships. As she flew toward the dhow's triangular mainsail, she retrieved her knife from her teeth, gripped it tightly in both hands. The knife's tip met the sail's canvas, puncturing it with a sound like the beat of a drum. Down she went toward the foot of the sail, her knife sizzling as it sliced the thick cloth neatly in two.

Hathahn charged across the deck to meet her, but when she reached the boom, she leapt backward, flipping high over him to land on the deck near the pilot's wheel. Her knife she drove deep into the pilot's neck. After snapping a kick into his chest to knock him aside, she spun the wheel, turning it over and over. It fought her the more the ship turned, but she kept going, muscles straining, until she'd turned it as far as it could go.

The ship heeled toward the starboard side as it turned sharply to port. The rudder, the central, rear ski, was now almost perfectly at odds with the line the ship had been moving in. It dragged, throwing Djaga forward against the wheel so hard she lost her grip on her knife. It went clattering forward across the deck, tossing sunlight as it went. The crew, who'd been rushing toward her, were thrown as well. They grabbed for the rigging to steady themselves, but several fell hard to the deck. They slid scrabbling toward the fore of the ship. Not Hathahn, though. He'd grabbed tight to the rigging. He came pounding forward, sending a powerful jab across Djaga's jaw, an uppercut that glanced across her skull, then a kick

that sent her reeling.

She flailed for purchase, but being so close to the stern there was nothing. The gunwale clipped her thighs as she flew backward over the deck's edge. She crashed onto the sand, and it knocked the breath from her.

She slid and rolled. The sand scraped roughly over her skin. Hathahn dropped from the ship moments before the prow of the *Needle* crashed into it with a sound like thunder. The sails of both ships shuddered as they came to rest at last.

Hathahn approached Djaga, scimitar in one hand, a fighting knife in the other. "Couldn't leave it alone, could you?"

Djaga stood.

"You could have let us leave. Live out your life in peace as the greatest warrior the pits had ever seen."

Djaga ignored him, undoing her leather belt.

This day, Sjado, I do not ask for your favor. I demand it.

She wrapped the belt around her knuckles once, then let the rest hang, the iron buckle weighty.

This day, I do not give. I take what is mine.

With these words, the soul of Sjado filled her as never before. Not since the day she'd slaughtered her loved ones in Kundhun. She wished she'd never listened to Afua and gone to the barrow. But she had. And she'd paid the price. Now, she didn't care if she killed another. She didn't care if Sjado was appeased. She only wanted to feel Hathahn's hot blood coursing over her skin.

Hathahn swiped with his sword. Djaga skipped away. He cut for her legs, then drove in with the fighting knife. Djaga dodged, then swung her belt, going for his eyes.

Hathahn leaned out of range, a smile coming to his lips as he looked her over. "The golem must not have given you much trouble. Or are you truly that good?"

In a blink, she snapped the belt at him. The buckle caught him

across the chin, sending him stumbling backward. Blood collected along a thin line, staining his short brown beard. "Perhaps you are." He took two quick steps forward, flicking the tip of the sword across her line of retreat, scoring a light cut against her thigh. "I wasn't lying, girl. I will fight you until my dying breath."

Beyond Hathahn, swords clashed: Osman and his dirt dogs engaged Hathahn's crew. A newcomer stood at the *Condor's* stern. Afua. She leapt down from the ship but came no closer. She merely watched as Djaga and Hathahn fought.

Djaga felt the anger inside her become something else. She became resolved to what she must do. The furnace in her heart was no longer directionless fury, but a straight-flowing river of purpose.

She slipped the end of the belt through the buckle, and held it like a noose. She baited Hathahn several times. He swiped his sword at her with each one, then charged on the third. She was ready. She ducked beneath his first swing, sidestepped the thrust of his knife. She kicked his knee when he came in too close, then pivoted around a downward thrust. She was a dervish, moving inside his defenses, spinning along his body as he tipped ever so slightly off balance from an awkward, overreaching thrust. Each and every move of her body felt like a prayer to the goddess, prayers that Sjado was answering by granting her grace and foresight and supple movement.

In one simple motion—an act as pure as Djaga had ever felt— she grabbed Hathahn's elbow, lifted it while treading past him in one willowy stride, and slipped the belt over his head. After powering her heel into the back of his knee, sending him staggering, she snapped the belt tight and dropped onto her back. Her foot against the back of his head provided all the leverage she needed. She pulled hard on the leather. Her whole form tightened. Her foot turned Hathahn's head to one side. He swiped at her blindly with his sword. He missed with the first but gave her with a deep gash along her right arm with the second. When his head jerked, there came a loud crunch

like kindling breaking, and his body went utterly still.

Djaga stared at his unmoving form. She heard only the sound of her own breath, the beating of her heart. Warm blood slicked her left arm as she let the belt slip through her fingers. In slow increments, the rasp of her breath and the thump of her heart were replaced by the rhythmic shush of footsteps. She picked up Hathahn's sword and turned.

Ten paces away stood Afua. She held her hands before her, the way a bride might in the moments before her right hand was bound by a grass cord to her groom. Behind her, Osman and Kaliban approached, but they remained a healthy distance away. They were bloodied and bent. Of the other dirt dogs, she could see no sign.

Djaga stepped closer to Afua, sword in hand. The two of them stared at one another, pure opposites, Djaga the essence of battle, of purpose, Afua the embodiment of peace, a woman resolved to her fate.

"Why did you do it?" Djaga asked in Kundhunese.

Afua stared at her, stone-faced. "When you killed our people, I felt Sjado within you. I witnessed the slaughter of three of my cousins. I saw you drive a spear through the neck of my own sister. I watched her die, writhing. I didn't care, Djaga. I didn't care at all. Her death was like the fall of a leaf from an acacia. Meaningless. I knew I should be horrified by it, but I wasn't. The only thing I felt was an itch, a yearning to get back what I had lost. That was why I left, not because I feared what would happen to me, but because I knew that no one there—not you, not my family, not our king— could restore my soul. That could only come from two-faced god."

"You did all of this"—with the tip of the scimitar, Djaga pointed at Hathahn's lifeless form—"to be free?"

Afua laughed, her dark skin reflecting the deep orange of the sunset. "Djaga! Don't you see? I did this to free *you*! All I've done since leaving Kundhun has been in the hopes of finding a way to

force Sjado to release you. You didn't deserve this. *I* did."

Djaga stepped forward. "You *murdered* Nadín."

"And I'm sorry for that." Despite her words, Afua's stone-face expression told Djaga how little she cared. "But Sjado demands sacrifice. You know this as well as I. You've known it from the moment our god took us. You just haven't been able to admit it. But now you can, yes? You can admit it and be *free*."

Afua's smile was mad. It was wrong, and it made Djaga sick to her stomach that she could act so after causing so much pain. Djaga gripped Hathahn's sword. It begged her to use it, as did Nadín's honor. In that moment, all Djaga could think about was how different Afua's toothy grimace was from Nadín's shy smile. How different Djaga's life had been from Afua's since their days in Kundhun. Until now, Djaga had thought Afua cursed in the same way she had been. Of course it hadn't been so. Jonsu, the aspect of peace, had taken Afua as Sjado had taken Djaga.

What would it be like to be cursed with utter tranquility? What would it be like to live and feel no pain, no anger? Those were necessary for laughter and joy. Afua had been made a husk of a woman by Jonsu. But she was no longer. Djaga could feel it in herself, and she could feel it in Afua as well.

Djaga looked over her dirty, bloody hands. She took in the world around her, the desert, Hathahn's dead form, the ships, crashed against one another like two drunks sleeping off their night at the end of an alley, and suddenly wished she'd never come to the desert. If Nadín were going to die—and certainly that was her sentence, a gut wound like hers could lead only to a slow, painful death—she wished she'd stayed to spend as much time with her as she could. Console her. Usher her into the next world with a kiss, their hearts beating as one.

Suddenly, it was very important that Djaga return to Sharakhai.

WITHIN THE *MEDICUM,* DJAGA SAT by Nadín's bedside, holding the lax fingers of her hand. Nadín's eyes had been fluttering closed for the past several minutes. Her face was pale as fresh milk.

Djaga had been telling her the tale, but had stopped when she'd come to the last. The realization had struck her like a hammer blow in the desert, and it was no less impactful now. Wind and grass, how she wished she could sit here forever with Nadín. Tell her stories of the rolling hills of Kundhun. Have Nadín tell her the tales of her life growing up in the desert with her people.

"Go on," Nadín said, her eyes still closed.

"What does it matter?" Djaga replied.

"I would know before I depart for the further fields."

Djaga took a deep breath, then exhaled. "Afua wanted release. I could see it in her, all the emotion that she'd been unable to feel since our ritual coming back to her in a rush."

There had been regret and self-loathing in Afua's eyes as the sun had slipped below the horizon. More than anything else, though, there had been a bottomless well of sorrow. At the same time, all the rage Djaga had felt over the years drained from her like water through a crack in a rain barrel. So much had been kept from her, hidden behind an impossibly high wall. How long she'd wished she could truly bask in Nadín's love. But it had been impossible. Her anger had prevented it.

It's still impossible, Djaga thought, *just for completely different reasons.*

"*Do it,* Afua begged me, pointing to Hathahn's sword. *Kill me.*" She paused, debating on lying to Nadín. Surely, she would learn the truth of it in her next life. "Forgive me, my love, but I could find only pity for Afua in my heart. We'd done wrong, but what our god had done to us was worse. Afua hadn't deserved it."

Nadín opened her eyes and turned to look at Djaga. When she spoke, her voice was a whisper. "Neither did you."

To this, Djaga only shrugged. "Perhaps she deserved death. There's still a part of me that wants to find her and kill her for what she did to you. I denied her. We set her ship aright and sent her on her way to Malasan. She left alone, to find a new life. To find the one she'd lost in whatever way she could."

Nadín squeezed Djaga's fingers. "I care only about one thing."

Djaga knew, but she still asked, "What?"

"Are you *free*?"

Djaga nodded, part of her wishing it wasn't so if only she could have Nadín back. "I am."

Nadín's eyes fluttered closed. A wan smile lit her face. "Then I go with a light heart, Djaga Akoyo, for I have unchained my one true love."

Djaga stood, tears streaming down her cheeks. "You have, my love." As she leaned over and kissed Nadín's forehead, a lone tear fell upon her cheek.

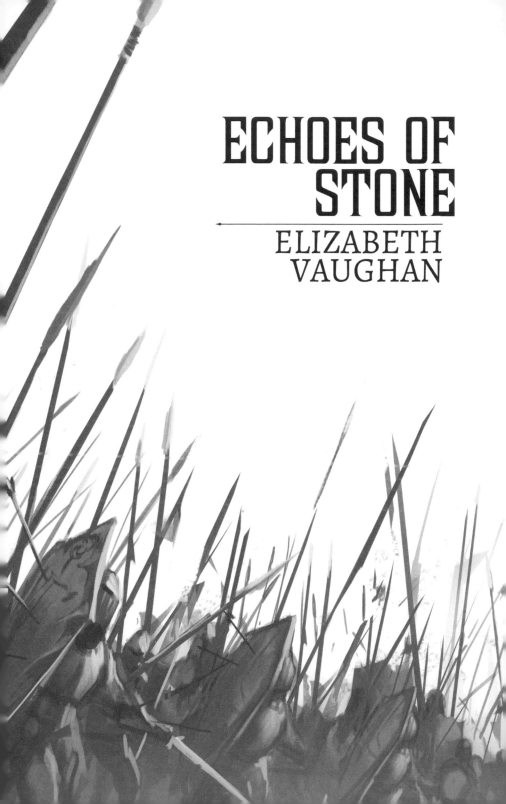

ECHOES OF STONE

ELIZABETH VAUGHAN

I S THERE *ANY CHANCE SHE* will live?"

The moment every healer dreads. Ercula had faced the question before, and she knew she would face it again. She'd decided long ago, against the advice of her teachers, to always meet it with honesty. "No," she answered, direct and simple. "Your babe has passed beyond my skills."

She knelt at the bedside of the mother and child, to be closer to her patients, and so saw the spasm of pain that crossed the thin, almost skeletal face of the mother. Months of illness and lack of food reflected in both mother and child.

"And I not far behind her," the mother whispered.

Ercula reached out and put her hand over the mother's where she clutched the naked babe to her breasts. She let the silence speak, giving only a simple nod. The few remaining bangles in her faded head scarf chimed at her movement, covering the quiet hiss of her snakes.

The dirt floor beneath her knees was hard, the hovel made of not more than dung and wattle. There was a dank smell to the place, rife with despair. The roof was thin bark; their lord would not spare thick thatching for the least of his people. No fire, no food. No hope.

"Damn the Duke and his headman." The mother's voice was

weak but her hate was clear and sharp. "My man gone, his work and sweat poured into the fields. None of his kin left, and all of my blood gone before. No one left to care or grieve. No charity for the sick."

Again, Ercula let her silence speak. Where she could not heal, she could at least bear witness.

Pale, rheumy eyes looked into hers. "I prayed in the Old Ways, and you came, healer, and I thank you. I have no coin to offer."

Ercula quirked her lips and shook her head. The bangles chimed, and her snakes slithered beneath her head scarf in approval.

The babe no longer cried. She lay quiet in her mother's arms, more bone than flesh, her breaths soft and slowing.

"I've a further request," the mother whispered. "I'd ask for release. For both of us."

Ercula nodded, expecting–

"Not your poisons." The woman shook her head weakly. "Your other gift, if it still exists."

Ercula did not expect that. She pulled her hands away, sat back on her heels.

"And not here," the mother said. "I want them to know. Want them to see."

"I–" Ercula stared for a moment, at a loss for words.

"Not what the dying usually ask?" The mother's mouth contorted into a wry smile.

"The Great Mother gave us two gifts to ease the way." Ercula took a deep breath to calm herself. "Few remember us. Fewer still remember that the power was a gift."

"The Gods are gone," the mother said.

Ercula nodded. "But the gifts she gave us remain." She closed her eyes as memories flooded in. "I can still hear her voice when she blessed me so."

The mother's eyes widened with wonder. "Healer, how old are you?"

Ercula almost smiled, for mortal beings were always taken aback at something so normal as her lifetime. "Old enough," she said.

Old enough to have served at the altar. To have offered her body and heart to the snakes of the Great Mother and been accepted into their service.

Old enough to have experienced the Great Silence that descended between the world and its Gods.

The Great Mother's voice had gone silent, but the snakes had remained. Without the Goddess it was hard to interpret, harder still to heal. But they'd learned, oh, they had all learned. Only to see the Order become a hated symbol of evil. To see the Holy Temple torn down and burned, its precious snakes killed.

She'd fled to the shelter of those she had healed in the past, until it grew too dangerous for them to hide her.

So she wandered, using the skills and powers she had left, gaining new ones as she traveled. But only healing at the request of those who still believed. Sometimes she was lead to a place, by a whisper on the wind, or the quiet hiss of her snakes. As she had been drawn here.

If any others of her Order survived, she had no knowledge of them, nor they of her. Better so, to her way of thinking.

"Would it risk you?"

Ercula's thoughts were bought back to the present when the mother clutched her babe with one arm, and reached out with a skeletal hand. "To do this thing?"

Ercula considered, then shook her head. She'd taken care, and used every precaution that she knew. The snakes had whispered to her of a need, and she'd come. She'd leave with no one the wiser.

"Help me," the woman begged, and shifted her child to Ercula's arms.

"Where?" Ercula asked, rising to her feet. The snakes beneath her head scarf shifted in concern.

"The Shrine of Ticena." The mother struggled to her feet.

Ercula hesitated. "But She is Protectress of the Hearth and of Children," she said carefully. "How can they do this and yet—"

"The Duke makes great show of greeting every dawn there with his headmen and workers, paying service with their words and not their deeds—" Her breath caught as she straightened. "He cares more for the flowering plants around the shrine than his people."

Ercula held the child easily, for what should have been fair and plumb was skin and bone, distorted in its frailty. "What you leave behind is only stone," Ercula warned. "It can be moved, broken, destroyed. It is no more permanent than—" She hesitated.

"Our lives?" The mother wheezed as she drew her thin robe around her. "If I control nothing else, healer, let me control this."

That too, was of the Old Ways. "Lean on me," Ercula urged, wanting to save the woman's strength. "Is it far?"

"No." The woman clung to her arm. "Not far."

The village was small, not more than a collection of huts, shadowed by the forest, surrounded on three sides by the fields. The night was silent, but the moon was high enough that they could see.

"This way," the woman's lips brushed Ercula's ear as she whispered.

They walked for a bit in silence, then the woman clamped down on Ercula's arm and tensed, wracked by pain.

Ercula stood, patient, waiting. The babe never stirred.

"O Ferryman, bring forth thy boat, that I may cross to the eastern side of the sky," the woman whispered as she trembled.

Ercula realized she was praying to a God long silent.

"For I am the beloved of my father and my mother, and all of my kin who have gone before, and await our arrival." The woman lifted her hand to stroke the babe's cheek. *"O, Ferryman, stow thy oars and drop thy sail, and await us at the docks."*

The woman slid her foot forward and then another. Ercula moved with her.

"For your price will be paid, and your ship will bring us safely through the stars, to the other side." The woman went silent, needing her every breath.

They walked on.

The shrine was a lovely one, surrounded by thick, healthy blue spider-wort plants, the tiny flowers closed against the night. The shrine doors were open, all finely carved wood and worked stone floor. The rare glass flickered with the lone candle within. The altar lay bare of the offerings to come, of lilies and grain.

The mother staggered to the front and crawled up onto the altar. She took a deep breath, then centered herself there, cross-legged. She put both hands down and braced herself, breathing hard.

Ercula stood close, holding the sleeping babe.

The mother let her robes fall to her waist, her naked breasts hanging empty over her protruding ribs. "Just like this." Her thready voice filled with satisfaction. "They will know. They will see."

She opened her arms. Ercula placed the babe in them.

The child stirred, squirming, its tiny fingers making tight fists. "Quickly," the mother whispered.

Ercula pulled her scarf from her head. Her snakes rose, free and restless, emerging from her skull to writhe. To see.

"Like a crown," the mother whispered, but Ercula focused her gaze on the babe. Those small fists relaxed, fingers reaching out. Her tiny eyes opened wide, staring—

And turned to stone.

The mother grunted at the sudden weight, her tears streaming as she panted. "Just a moment. Let me—"

With great effort, she lifted the stone child in both hands, as if in offering or supplication. Then she sought Ercula's gaze, her eyes pained, and filled with rage.

A common mistake. Ercula shook her head. The snakes twisted and churned.

The mother lifted her eyes higher, to look at them.

Stone claimed her flesh as well.

Ercula rose, swift and quiet, wrapping her head as she sped away. The scuff of her shoes and the chiming of her bangles were the only sound.

At the doorway, she paused, making sure to secure the ends of her scarf. Her snakes lay silent, enclosed in cloth, knowing the need.

She glanced back.

The effect was powerful. The naked woman, raising her child in supplication, her expression grim, her gaze defiant.

Ercula stepped into the night and sought the shadows. She'd be well on her way before dawn, taking the back paths through the fields and woods. She'd be far distant before the Duke and his people found the statute.

They would know. They would see.

She doubted they would learn.

AN ESSAY BY
DIANA M. PHO
ANGER IS A FRIEND TO LOVE

FEW DAYS AFTER THE US election, I was one of millions of Americans feeling absolutely devastated by the results. Many people had their hopes pinned upon Hillary Clinton to be the US's first female elected as President. But, sadly, our world fell into a darker timeline. On the Tuesday night after the election, I lay in my wife's arms and could not stop sobbing at the thought of a President-Elect and administration who vowed to repeal LGBTQ protections once they were in office. For a long time, our country's growing legal protections gave me hope that our lives would become more secure and stable, but now we would never be safe enough. This feeling echoed throughout the United States among many marginalized communities in the coming days: that the struggle was going to be for the long-haul.

Hate crimes in New York City alone increased by 31%, and more than 400 incidents were reported across the nation in the first two weeks after the election. Black students were added to lynch lists. Epithets were scrawled in bathrooms. A Jewish gay senator's home was vandalized by swastikas.

Moreover, when marginalized identities become targeted,

ciswomen, transwomen, and gender-nonconforming people typically face the brunt of the violence. Hate manifests itself in pulling off hijabs and harassing transwomen in the streets. It is ganging up on black women on Twitter for being bold enough to have an opinion. It is threatening to shoot, stab, or kill a woman for rejecting a sexual advance.

For people frightened and outraged by these attacks, they became divided in how to offer support to the most vulnerable in our society. Do we all walk around wearing safety pins? Plaster subway stations in Post-It notes of hope? Donate to charitable causes? Stay mad at fascists for being fascists?

Surprisingly, anger is the reaction most critiqued. "Anger is harmful," we are told. They say it is the opposite of "Love Trumps Hate." But let me tell you this: Anger does not equal hate. Anger is not the opposite of love. Anger is a friend to love, the defense when seeing love torn asunder. Anger can be a logical response to being hated. You can be angry over seeing something you love so much become hurt for no reason other than the illogical, irrational, and inconsiderate emotion that is hatred.

It is time for women to be angry. We must give permission to ourselves to be angry. Anger can be productive. It can be harnessed, focused, and aimed like a laser ready to cut through steel. It is the blood and sweat and fear and courage of many other women, living and dead, who contributed to our place here today. It is empathic, for productive anger is the fire that dies in a vacuum, but it can be stoked by feeling the injustices of the world.

Angry women have always existed; we have always battled and bled and lived and died for causes that are fueled by our passions. As a child, I learned of the Trung sisters, the Vietnamese women of legend who rode into battle upon elephants against Chinese occupation over a thousand years ago. Joan of Arc, fueled by visions and righteous anger, lead troops in France. In the eighteenth century, Mary Wollstonecraft wrote the tract that demanded women have

equal rights to men. Harriet Tubman, armed with a pistol and her wits, led dozens of men and women to freedom through the Underground Railroad. Marsha P. Johnson and Sylvia Rivera threw the bricks and bottles during the Stonewall riots that incited the US gay rights movement.

When I think of angry women from SFF, I think of Leia Organa Solo of *Star Wars*, the princess who fought to save her planet, and when she witnessed it be destroyed, she then gathered and led a Resistance to save her galaxy. I think of the *Hunger Games'* Katniss Everdeen, the soldier whose struggle against her rage and frustration helped overcome the corrupt Capital. I also think of Primrose Everdeen, whose rage manifested in steady determination to become a nurse and help those in need. Most of all, I think of Lauren Olamina, the visionary from Octavia Butler's *Parable of the Sower*, who honed a philosophy of survival based on Change. Living in a world which was slowly succumbing to apocalypse, Lauren wrote:

> God is Power—
> Infinite,
> Irresistible,
> Inexorable,
> Indifferent.
> And, yet, God is Pliable—
> Trickster,
> Theater
> Chaos,
> Clay.
> God exists to be shaped.
> God is Change.

Change is unceasing and will not hesitate to utterly destroy those who passively wait in reaction to seeing its oncoming storm.

These historic and fictional women I named are only a few who have inspired thousands specifically because, in the face of change, they acted and they acted boldly. They continue to inspire because they show the potential that we have in ourselves (cis, trans, and femme). It is fueled by a will to survive. And yes, a fire which drives this can be anger. Anger against the systems of oppression we have been forced to cope with for too long. Anger because our love cannot be contained by inaction, but by furious, unleashed power.

Fury, when concentrated, becomes a blade. We must not let our anger remain sheathed.

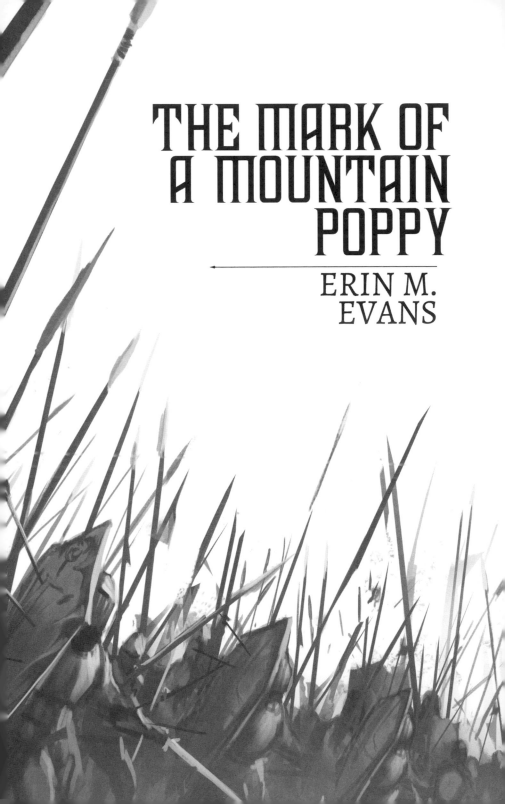

THE MARK OF
A MOUNTAIN
POPPY

ERIN M.
EVANS

PERSONAL PROPHECY FROM THE Heir of Vàorem was a blessing few could claim, but Tarji would have spat in the face of any other man who'd said such words to her.

She'd no more than come into the presence of the heir—Sakavian, he'd insisted, with no regard at all for the awkwardness and informality of using his given name—but he'd studied her boots to brow. His dark eyes grew distant and he smiled. "Tarji Hellonar Kastelleki," he said, pronouncing her full name like a prophecy of its own. "Mother of my children."

Tarji folded her arms. "I'm your guard," she said. "Not your bed warmer."

Sakavian shrugged in a manner so fluid it seemed obscene. "I only tell you what the Bright Ones say."

Maybe it was the words of the *suorinen*, the bright spirits that watched over Vàorem, and maybe it was nonsense—handsome, honey-tongued Sakavian had bastards in every tribe and hold, and it wasn't by wishing on sparks.

"I'll believe it when your mother opens her veins for the *suorinen*," Tarji said, tartly. "Takes away every other possibility"

And *that* had broken Sakavian with a snort and a laugh— she'd found over the years it wasn't difficult to make Sakavian laugh, just

Illustration by NICOLÁS R. GIACONDINO

as he'd discovered it wasn't difficult to make Tarji bristle—bring up that spirit-sucked line about children and she'd be through.

Tarji didn't like children—not her own imaginary ones, not Sakavian's scattered get.

But Tarji Hellonar Kastelleki was of the *vuhenki,* sworn to the Speaker and her heir. Which meant she didn't have a good reason to tell Sakavian she'd rather not deal with his bastards.

In the village of the Aalmeki tribe, a little girl watched Tarji with Sakavian's eyes, black and sharp as threshold flint. Even if someone had reason to doubt she was Sakavian's get, the thickness of the air, like the very belly of summer, and the sense of someone whispering without words, announced the interest of the *suorinen,* the presence of another heir of Vàorem's bastards.

"Your sword's made of wood," the girl said.

"Yes." This one stared, Tarji recalled. She stared every time Sakavian sent the *vuhenki* around with links of silver and iron, support without overt acknowledgment. The *suorninen* were fickle about such things.

"I never saw a wooden sword."

Tarji kept her eyes on the door to the stone hut the old man had ducked through, insisting on bringing her refreshments. *Only a moment,* the old man had said. *Only the best for the* vuhenki. Behind Tarji, near the hold's gates, another *vuhenki*—Jere Hemmel Moreteki—waited, still mounted and holding the reins of Tarji's yak. She wondered if he'd be hauled in, too, before she could get the old man to take the links.

"You didn't have that last time," the girl said.

"No." Last time Tarji came and went in a heavy rain and no one stopped to make her tea or pull conversations and secrets out of her. Last time, the Chalmarais to the south hadn't been clattering their axes, tearing breaches in the threshold, the edge between this world and the *suorninen's.* Last time, she'd ridden alone, and without

a *suori* crouching on her heart, ready to fulfill her oaths and show Chalmar what the spirits of Vàorem were capable of when they were properly honored and heard.

"Doesn't seem like you can cut much with it," the girl said. "Doesn't it break?"

"Sometimes."

"Why do you carry a sword that sometimes breaks?"

Tarji ran her tongue along the chipped edge of an incisor. A moment's thirst—she could have made it to the stream. She could have left the links and been well on her way to the next bastard. She could have told Sakavian she wasn't running this spirit-sucked errand anymore.

No—a *vuhenki* followed orders. A *vuhenki* heard the words of the *suorinen* through their favored Speakers. She blew out a breath and apologized to the spirits, though not to the heir they chose who got her into this.

The girl kicked a flower growing in the gravel, a mountain poppy blooming early. "What's my father like?"

Enough of that, Tarji thought.

"If it breaks, you can replace it in parts." Tarji glanced over at the girl—such a skeptical expression for a six-year-old—and drew the weapon from its sheath. The cold sunlight of mid-autumn glowed on the oiled larch baton, the row of chipped stone embedded along the weapon's edges. Rusty blooms, shimmering with the same strange light of the open gates to the *suorinen's* realm, a world on the edge of this one, marred the deep blackness of the rock.

"Do you know that stone?" The girl shook her head. "Threshold flint," Tarji told her. "The edge it makes is keener than any metal. You can take a man's head off with this. Two strokes. One, if you aim well and he doesn't move much."

The girl's dark eyes widened. "How do you know?"

Tarji slid the blade back into its sheath. "Because I know."

Mercifully, the old man returned then, stemming any further questions from the girl, but three young women followed him, carrying woven platters bearing flatbread, cloudberries, and yak butter, kettles of spruce tea and jars of beer. Tarji stepped back from the encroaching celebration, holding the bag of links out like a shield.

"I need to be on my way," she said. The *suori* Sakavian had guided to her fluttered sulkily, making her heart skip.

The old man frowned, his faded cheekbone tattoos dragging dark lines around his mouth. He looked back at the little girl, who was still staring at Tarji as if she were a mad spirit mount. "Have you finished already, *vuhenki?*" he asked.

Tarji gestured with the sack. "Here."

The old man's brow furrowed, and behind him the girls looked at one another over their heavy platters. "I thought..." The old man glanced back at his charge. "You're not going to test her? I thought they were being tested."

"I just deliver payment," Tarji said.

"Yes, but..." The old man gestured at her loosely, encompassing the threshold flint sword, the raven feather-trimmed cloak of cloud tiger fur, and the silver buckles on her armor.

"Riding south now is dangerous," Tarji said, not lowering the links. "Maybe you haven't heard—the Chalmarais have been hunting, tearing new breaches in the threshold. The Speaker's warnings fall on stopped ears. I ride with a spirit, so I dress as a spirit-warrior."

The old man nodded as if he didn't believe her, but he didn't want to anger her or the *suori*. Still, he didn't take the links. "Seppan Kaukoval Helmiteki—his stepson's also the...he's fatherless." He stumbled, nearly naming what was taboo. The *suori's* edges turned sharp against Tarji's lungs and for a moment, she was sure it would flood her with power and demand retribution.

"He said they came to see . . . that someone was sent to see what he could do, but they left him behind." He gave her a significant

look, carrying all the words he wasn't meant to speak aloud. "You should consider my Yrsa Valausiä. I'm sure she's enough to…make an impression."

The *suori* roiled, torn between fondness for the blood of the Speaker and fury at the old man's repeated near-transgressions, and Tarji's vision swam. The *suorinen* chose the heirs of Vàorem, they chose them when they chose them, and while no one doubted for a moment it would be one of Sakavian's numerous bastards, in the meantime, it didn't do to imply such things were settled.

Especially not when the presence of Chalmarais hunters had the *suorinen* wild as snow monkeys with mouths full of mushrooms.

Tarji held his gaze, drawing one of her daggers from its sheath. She nicked the base of her thumb, letting a bead of blood rise up before scraping it off with the edge of the blade, flicking it to the dirt, an apology to the *suorinen*. The spirit clinging to her went still at the offering, even as the air shifted with the suggestion of more of its ilk, and only then did the man flush.

"I only deliver the payment," she said again, dropping the loops of iron and silver links onto the ground, enough to carry them through the coming freeze even if every other resource the Aalmeki could muster failed. The blood of the Speaker had to be provided for, she thought. At least until the *suorinen* made up their minds. Tarji cast a glance at the girl—Yrsa Valausiä—as she headed back out the gates.

Jere raised an eyebrow, pierced with a silver ring, as Tarji took her yak's reins back and heaved herself onto the snorting beast's saddle.

"Thought you might be settling in," he said. "Any trouble?"

"He had questions."

Jere made a face. "About *what?*"

"Nothing important," Tarji said. "Come on."

They were halfway to the next bastard's tribe when Jere spotted the marks of the breach just before sunset—a muddle of disturbed

snow and churned mud, at the edge of the forest. Tarji eyed the tracks, willing them to be nothing but the mark of predator and prey. Maybe cloud tiger taking down a runaway yak. Maybe—except for the swirling discomfort of the *suori* sharing space with her. Except for the lack of tracks leading to the disturbed spot.

The hairs along her arms stood on end as she spotted the boot prints—beginning in the middle of the disturbed snow and heading into the forest. Beside her, Jere stiffened and the air around grew thick and heavy, as if the spirits in the threshold beyond were gathering, watching, to see what they would do.

Wordlessly, Tarji nudged her yak toward the forest. She tied it to the first larch she found, eyes never leaving the path of boot prints. Six, maybe more—the number seemed to change as they walked, adding and losing men as if they couldn't stop ripping breaches as they passed.

She could hear them now, ahead, beyond the trees. Dimly a part of her thought she ought to be sure of Jere as well, but the spirit in her commanded all her attention, all her strength.

Tarji drew the threshold flint sword, as the *suori* began to bleed into her veins, the powers of its liminal realm softening her steps, drawing her focus. A bent branch of wintergreen here, a broken edge of melting ice there. The sound of a small animal screaming—and Tarji broke into a run.

A clearing. A glen. Lichen peeking through the snow and rust red moss racing up the trees—there. In the center. Three men—pale-skinned, chain-armored. One held an axe out. One held him back. A third held the back half of what looked like a marten, belly-up, limned in amber flames, its head vanished into the ether. A *suori*, forced into the world, into skin.

A fourth, a fifth man stepped out of the amber flames and the *suori* broke free, screaming. The axeman shouted, something in the tongue of the Chalmarais, but his fellow pushed him away, drawing

the crudely made dagger of threshold flint he wore at his belt. A matching blade flashed out of the belt of the hunter holding the *suori,* and before Tarji could reach him, he cut downward, into the beast's belly.

The *suori* in her heart exploded—

*—Tarji's eyes sharpen, hands strengthen. That one becomes a marten but this one—*this one—*this is the eagle that rips grown snow monkeys from their perches, ignores their raking hands, and breaks their necks, rips their bellies open. Her hands grip the blade, but the blade might as well be her claws, it's alive, humming with the same power that fills her to her fingernails. When it hits the hunter's neck, just below his skull, the* suori *screams, too wild, too furious for an eagle alone.*

The others shout, blades up, blades out. Jere slams into the axeman—a bull, a bear, a blur of muscle. Another pair of men come out of the forest, a third, unarmored, limned in amber flames, appears in the breach—the skin of what looks like a hare, pelt the unblemished white of winter, plastered to his chest, peeking out of his shirt, and cradled against it, an amulet to some Chalmarais god, a mountain poppy in glinting gold and crimson enamel—a wound against the dying suori *he's forced into skin and stolen.*

His eyes widen as he spots Tarji. He clutches the pendant, presses a hand to the skin, and more suorinen *surge out of the rift at his call, all of them screaming. They pile together, building into something new, something fearsome, something unwilling.*

The marten spirit whimpers. Tarji feels her lip curl with the suori's *rage, her own rage, as she stalks toward the summoning hunter. Vàorem's spirits will not be taken. All Chalmar deserves is vengeance.*

THE MARTEN SPIRIT WAS STILL whimpering when Tarji came back into herself—blood in her mouth, panting, weeping. Her shoulder screamed with pain and her belly pulsed with a bad wound. All eight Chalmarais hunters were dead, the breach still shivered amber amid them, and the *suori* Sakavian had coaxed into her was

trying to flee her sorry form.

"Jere?" she gasped.

"Down here." He crouched on his knees and knuckles, behind her and to the right, hovering over the dead summoner. Tears streaked his golden cheeks, glinting on his tattoos. "There's four among them. All dead except the one they just pulled. Fucking heathens."

Tarji studied the edge of the hare-skin, peeled back now from where it had gripped the man's chest, showing red, raw flesh. "Fuck. I'm about to lose mine and my shoulder's wrenched. If I nurse the mount, can you reclaim the flint and get me back to the yaks?"

Jere raised his pierced brow. "You got enough blood left?"

"It's coming out one way or the other." Clenching her teeth against the pain and the pull of the *suori* still inside her trying to flee into the breach, Tarji hauled herself over to the little animal, who was still crying and thrashing in the snow. One of the Chalmarais had gotten past her with his flint blade and cut through her padded leather shirt, down to the flesh below. She pulled up the layers of cloth, wool, and leather. A cry escaped her gritted teeth as the cold air hit the wound and blood gushed from it. She cupped her hand under it, collecting a ruby pool as her vision started to crumble. She poured it over the marten's face, splattering its snout.

Numbness spread over the sides of her skull. Tarji held her breath without meaning to, trying to cling to consciousness a little longer, even as she forced more blood out of the wound, more blood onto the trapped *suori,* trying to remind it what it was. Not this form, this mount, but a piece of the liminal world. The *suori* inside her yanked fitfully against Tarji. *Wait,* she pleaded. *Wait. Help this one back.*

She slipped onto the elbow of her injured arm, another cry breaking loose. The *suori* trapped in the shape of the marten stopped thrashing, blinking up at the sky as the blood drip, drip, dripped onto its snout. It licked the blood, calm now. Focused.

It shuddered, then seemed to shift, to coil in ways a marten

never should. The *suori* in Tarji tore itself free, just as the little animal collapsed into ashes and new snow, and Tarji's vision went black.

WHEN TARJI WOKE IN THE Speaker's hold, bandaged and braced, her braids all dislodged, her mind haunted by flashes of the journey home, Sakavian was waiting for her, dressed for an audience in fine velvets, trimmed with more silver and cloud tiger fur.

"So," he said lightly. "How are the children?"

"Chalmarais," she said, flinching as her voice scraped her throat. "Harvesting *suorinen*. A day's ride beyond the...Aalmeki—"

"Yrsa?" he asked. He clucked his tongue and handed her a cup of needle-tea with yak butter from the sideboard. "That *is* far. Jere Hemmel tells me they won't be going home, though."

"They came through a breach." Tarji rubbed her face, the memory of the footprints from nowhere etched on her mind. "Tramping through like the threshold's a Kurushane roadway. Four of them had...skins. We saved a fifth." She shuddered. The Chalmarais, it was well known, had hunted their own spirits in such numbers that their lands were all but dead.

Sakavian nodded, brow tight, jaw tense. "Jere told me. How are the children?"

Tarji peered at him, Arvo Jormano Sakavian Tollatoani— Sakavian to his intimates, the heir to his vassals, and a disappointment to his mother—was rumored to be a lot of things. Wastrel, lecher, libertine, idiot—but Tarii knew better than to call him anything short of dedicated to Vàorem, to the *suorinen* who favored him. His eyes were shadowed with lack of sleep. The lines of black on his chin and cheekbones had been re-inked, the brown skin around them still flushed.

"What happened?" she asked quietly.

Sakavian's lush mouth twisted in a wry smile. "If you ignore our children like you do my question, we're going to have problems.

Drink your tea, and let's try again."

Tarji glowered and took an incautious gulp, swallowing the scalding liquid. She slammed the clay cup on the side table. "They're all alive. They're all irritating. Tell me what's going on or I'll twist your fucking berries off and put an end to all this mother talk once and for all."

Sakavian's dark eyes glittered, and he chuckled. "Well, I'm glad you're feeling better." He hesitated. "There's an echo. Probably an echo."

"An echo of what?"

"I see an army," Sakavian said, his voice slowing, his dark eyes glazing. "Coming up the eastern pass, along the flank of Yroma-Six-Winds, under a falcon-standard. Armored in bronze and wool, carrying swords, bringing horses up the riverside—"

"The Kurushane incursion?"

Sakavian blinked, the distant, dreamy expression suddenly gone. "Exactly. But I can hardly think of anything else."

Vàorem had never been conquered. Let Chalmar unify its swaths of tribes with their murderous magics, their shield-cracking axes. Let Zokarion claim every grain of salt and crumb of iron and bring cities begging for dominion to their gates. Let the distant Vincha ride their wind-swift horses down on every soul that strayed across their grasslands—none could claim what Vàorem could. Only the indomitable Empire of Kurush had ever come near to conquering Vàorem, and even it had failed.

A hundred years ago, an army had marched west, through captive Vinchaland, past the client-kings of Zokarion, over the broken backs of the Chalmarais. All Kurush wanted was *more*, each emperor adding to his empire's reach by force of pride. The army had chosen the eastern pass, no doubt, for its easy entrance, its proximity to the Speaker's hold. They had marched when the snow at Yroma-Six-Winds's feet had melted, not counting on its thickness at the

mountain's crown, not considering the rock loosened by the winter freeze. They climbed on regardless, driven by their emperor's pride, not realizing the *suorinen* had already seen them coming, had already warned the Speaker of every possibility—every chance of Kurush's success, every mistake that spelled failure.

But the Speaker in those days had hesitated, had faltered. The suorinen, they said, had gone wild and fierce at the delay. The Kurushane army had nearly succeeded, but for the fact that the Speaker saw a rockslide, ready to be triggered at mouth of the pass.

"Kurush is *fallen*," Tarji said. "They can't muster an army—they can hardly stop killing their own kings long enough to gather a tithe." She wet her mouth with more tea, recalling the *suori's* quick anger in a different light. "So, it's an echo."

Sakavian's smile grew pinched. "Probably. Except I can think of nothing else. I ask again, how are the children?"

Tarji's breath caught a moment. The *suorinen's* gift of prophecy was Vàorem's greatest shield and weapon, given to the favored scions of their favored bloodline. To the Speakers, and their successors, the *suorinen* would murmur all the possibilities of the future within Vàorem's bounds. The unfolding of the present, the events of the past—to the spirits, everything was immediate. Everything was important. Only a lifetime of listening taught the Speaker to separate out the past from the possibilities, the certain from the unlikely. Heirs were often chosen swiftly, and always by the fickle *suorinen*.

"The seven we saw to were fine," Tarji said. "Hale, well-fed, none of them seemed to be...troubled." She thought back to the little faces, Sakavian's eyes, Sakavian's nose, Sakavian's chin. "Jere Hemmel saw the Moreteki child—"

"Pavo Juhansiö."

"All right. Him and....ah, look I don't know their names, the Helmiteki, the girl one. The baby, the other Aalmeki, I couldn't tell you either. It was quiet but...Do they even choose babes?"

Sakavian chuckled again, but instead of answering, he said. "Mother's called a conclave. She thinks it's just someone downslope—maybe Chalmar, maybe one of the tribes—doing something the Bright Ones don't appreciate too close to the pass, too near to the date. No one likes to be reminded of the Kurushane incursion. She thinks we can settle it without resorting to rituals. Anything you recall might help."

Tarji shut her eyes, trying to recall the downslope villages, to pull up anything that had angered the *suori* that rode her or made Tarji think of foreign soldiers. But she kept returning to the Chalmarais hunters, the spirit trapped in the shape of a marten, dying in the snow.

"I don't remember," Tarji said. "It's not my job to spy for you. That's not what I'm meant for. I'm meant to throw myself in front of danger for you."

"For Vàorem." Sakavian smiled cheekily. "But a *little* for me."

NARAMINTA—HEART OF VÀOREM, SPEAKER of the Unspoken, Blood of the *Suorinen*—tapped a withered finger against the threshold flint of her throne, but said nothing. Pale and delicate as a new-hatched moth, her silver hair hung loose around her shoulders, the black lines of her office curling down her sallow cheeks, bleeding out of the tattoos that had been given to her when she'd been named her father's heir so long ago. Her other children sat at her feet—*vuhenki* and bone witches, all stern as their mother, strong as their *vuhenki* father, blessed by the *suorinen*.

But none so beloved as Sakavian. Some prophecies were blurred and uncertain, they said, but some needed no rituals to hear distinctly, no blood to wash clear. Whatever Naraminta thought of her third son, Sakavian was the only one the spirits wanted, once they couldn't have Naraminta anymore.

If the air around the Aalmeki girl had been thick, near the

Speaker it was as stifling as if Tarji had shoved her face into her yak's sweaty coat. She stood behind Sakavian upon the heir's stool, searching the chieftains arrayed before Naraminta in the great hall for some sign, some secret, some explanation. But there was nothing in the mix of posturing and squabbling voices to reveal what had made the *suorinen* so upset.

"Then it sounds as if we must get a clearer answer," Sakavian said.

Naraminta's tapping finger stilled. "For an echo?" she said.

"For a puzzle, Speaker," Sakavian said with infinite politeness. "I doubt anyone wishes to repeat the mistakes of the Kurushane incursion."

Naraminta's eyes narrowed. "We aren't hearing ten thousand warnings."

"But you cannot deny, the *suorinen* are just as displeased. Just as insistent." He smiled at his mother. "Would you like me to do it?"

Naraminta turned away and beckoned to one of the dark-robed bone witches standing at the edge of the great hall. The man came to her side, carrying a threshold flint bowl in his good hand. In it lay three slices of a moon-pale mushroom cap, its flesh dotted with blood-red sap welling up in tiny pinpricks.

The Heart of the Host, the key to the Threshold, the realm of the *suorinen*. With it the Speaker's gift would be sharpened, turning the cacophony of the spirits' voices into prophecy she could rule by. Naraminta considered the mushroom slices with an expert eye, selecting the center one with a trembling hand. She tucked it into her back teeth and bit down.

One moment Naraminta winced—the mushrooms were bitter, Tarji knew. Most every headstrong young thing had tried the Heart of the Host, to see if they had enough blood to see anything. Tarji got an amber-tinted nightmare and a headache for her efforts.

The next moment, Naraminta's eyes rolled back and she fell slack into the grooves of the Speaker's seat, *vuhenki* springing forward to

keep her positioned. Her breath rasped in her throat.

"Up the mountain—hated Kurush—three across in bronze and wool. Falcon-standards, mountain poppy, Kurush, Chalmar, Vinchaland," she murmured, her voice not her own. "Falls the fortress, down to rubble. Falls the army, doomed to end. Rise the line of Tollatoani. Foes surrounding, needles-stones."

Tarji frowned, trying to sift the answers from the sing-song speech that resulted when the *suorinen* and their Speaker blurred together. Those details and symbols were important. She looked at Sakavian, his eyes locked on his mother. Naraminta began to speak more quickly.

"Up the Eastern Pass, the Inkateki fall before them. Up the Eastern Pass the Inkateki flee before them. Up the Eastern Pass, a soldier trips on a loose stone, falls, a landslide follows. Up the Eastern Pass, and the soldier steps quickly, realizes a landslide would crush the enemies before them."

On and on, Naraminta spoke for the *suorinen*, narrating the possible fall of Vàorem all over again. Tarji kept studying the chieftains, hoping to notice something she'd failed to find before. Tribes from the mountain slopes, tribes from the plateau, tribes from the high passlands—united by their veneration of Vàorem's spirits and little else these days. The downslope tribes eyed Chalmar's luxuries, now denied them by the Speaker's edict, and were thought weak. The passlands sneered at the plateau's softness, the downslope's growing foreignness, and were thought primitive. The plateau considered its flocks and its crops and wondered why it supported its poorer cousins. None of them knew what to do with the *suorinen's* choice of Sakavian.

"In sight of the pass..." Naraminta's voice wavered. "A soldier wipes the blood from his sword, kisses the mark of a mountain poppy. In sight of the pass, a soldier wipes the blood from his sword, thinks of those fallen before him. In sight of the pass..."

Cold horror flooded Tarji. "Mountain poppy."

Sakavian turned at her outburst. "Chalmarais," she said. "The Chalmarais hunter—one wore a mountain poppy like an amulet. Like a god-mark."

"A Kurushane god?" Jere murmured. Tarji shook her head—she didn't know, how could she know?

"No," said Sakavian. "The poppies don't grow on their side of the mountains."

"'Needles-stones,'" Tarji said. "You overlook them because they all look the same."

Naraminta lifted her head suddenly, eyes still glazed. "Sakavian!" she barked. "Beloved!"

Sakavian was at her side. "Here, Bright Ones."

"The Mikateki boy," she said. "The child of the heir, got for us on Mikateki stock. He is here. He is not. He is gone from our sight."

Sakavian turned to the chieftain of the Mikateki, who stood. "We've done nothing!" he said. "The boy is with your men."

"What men?" Sakavian demanded.

The *vuhenki* who had come to test the Helmiteki boy, the ones who had deemed him imperfect, Tarji remembered, the rumor so senseless, she'd dismissed it out of hand. "The Chalmarais took him," she said. "They posed as *vuhenki*, they said they were testing for heirs." She shook her head. "They know."

Naraminta's eyes opened wide, still staring into nothing. "Mountain poppy, hated Chalmar, marching through the precious wheat."

That sealed it: Kurush had been crushed before they reached the plateau, Vàorem's fields and the approach to the Speaker's hold. This wasn't an echo, but a warning. Chalmar had found a crack in Vàorem's armor.

"They gain the plateau and you will die," Naraminta said, her voice a torrent. "They gain the plateau and divide, north and south.

They gain the plateau and sixteen split east, the rest—They gain the plateau, and sixteen vanish from your world into ours, they—they gain the plateau, and they empty their waterskins, melting the snow. They gain the plateau, they melt the snow, seven lie down, seven—eighteen—forty-six—" Naraminta began to shake violently.

"*Listen!*" she roared.

"Their hunters are in the threshold." Sakavian set a hand on Tarji's chest. "To this one, your warrior, I beg you," he said. The warm rush of a spirit—no, two of them—sliding into her chest made Tarji shudder again. He did the same to Jere, to every *vuhenki* in reach, and left the rest to plead for their own *suorinen*. This time, the spirits were already fierce and roiling, ready to burst. Tarji drew her sword, put herself between the chieftains and the heir.

"Ask them how to protect the hold!" Sakavian shouted to the row of bone witches. "Every entrance, every gate. How do we shift the odds?" The rattle of knucklebones on threshold flint mirrors began, filling the spaces between Naraminta's rapidly fracturing prophecy.

Sakavian drew his own flint knife and, pulling up his sleeve, cut a sharp line down his forearm. A curtain of blood flowed down his arm. The air around him shifted so suddenly that Tarji's ears popped. Poison in the plants made the Speaker listen better. Blood made the *suorinen* focus, remember, slow.

"We have failed you," he said. "We have missed the signs. How do we stop them?"

So much blood, so close to Sakavian, and Tarji could have sworn she heard whispery voices, nibbling at her ears. Sakavian flinched, closed his eyes, as the blood splattered against the stone floor. The voices made a cloud of sound, too dense for Tarji to hear much at all.

—*falls to nothing*—

—*Mother-mountain, washed in sunlight, mother-mountain turned to ash*—

—*archer lonely in the glen*—

—and the dead all lay forgotten—

—blood of enemies on our threshold—

—she that speaks for us is silent—

—she that speaks for us in rage—

—lightning-lava comes the storm—

—all our best beloved ended—

—falls to nothing—

—she-bear, night owl, raven queen—

"To save Vàorem," Sakavian said, "the blood must flee." His head bobbed—Tarji looked down. Still bleeding, too deep a cut. "Tarji Hellonar, you'll be the mother of my children." He turned to her, faintly gray. "Tarji Hellonar, you'll die if you don't move."

The *suorinen* surged in her, trying to force their way into her bones and muscles and mind.

"Jere!" she shouted, diving forward to catch the heir as he fell. "We have to get him away." She yanked off Sakavian's fine wool cape and bound it tightly around the bleeding arm, swift as she could. The chieftains were in turmoil, shouting, screaming. The *vuhenki* protecting Naraminta arrayed themselves around her, threshold flint swords ready.

Tarji belted on her own blade and scooped Sakavian up. She'd made it no more than ten steps toward the hallway when the wall came down, crushing half the chieftains and burying the spot where she'd stood.

A creature pulled itself out of an amber rift, higher even that the great hall's roof—not a single *suori*, but a collection of them, merged into something greater, something more monstrous. Merged because the Chalmarais hunter on the beast's neck made it so.

Tarji glimpsed a cloud tiger's curving fangs, the hard scales and flared eyes of a larch viper, the powerful body of a bear, burning through its seams with the core of the mountain, hot and bright. The Chalmarais surveyed his creation's—his *slave's*—havoc dispassionately.

As if what he was doing wasn't abhorrent. The *suorinen* in her raged, their fury rattling her ears with the sense of screaming. She held them back.

More Chalmarais hunters ripped their way into the great hall. With one last look back at Naraminta, still in the grip of the *suorinen*, Tarji ran after Jere, still carrying Sakavian.

"Have to...flee with the blood," he said sluggishly.

"Shush," Tarji told him. "We heard you."

Where could they run? Somewhere near, somewhere hidden. Somewhere where Sakavian could recover enough to coax a better answer from the *suorinen*. Even when Kurush had come, the *suorinen* had known the way to destroy the invaders, to protect Vàorem. They always knew.

"They know," Sakavian said, and it took Tarji a moment to realize he didn't mean the spirits. "They...that's why the boy. They learned how to...how to confuse the *suorinen*."

Tarji bit her tongue, braced for the spirits' anger, but whether the circumstances were too dire, or Sakavian was right to doubt them, they didn't burst free.

"They keep changing," he said, and he meant the Chalmarais now. "They know better than to act predictably."

They'd escaped the hold, making for the stables when another split opened right in front of them, another hunter, another spirit mount that slammed into Tarji and the heir, knocking her off her feet. Sakavian's bulk crushed the wind from her. His face crashed against the stone when she wasn't able to catch him.

This one was smaller—an elk's antlers, a spring-rat's heels, a cloud-tiger's claws. This close, Tarji could see madness in its eyes. A lump rose in her throat.

Jere glanced at her. She nodded once, pulling Sakavian aside as gently as she could. There was nothing for it, the spirit mount might not want to but—

—It startles when the suorinen *in Tarji unfold, the first favoring a yak, a bull in the spring, all ire and vigilance, that seeps into her muscles and twines around her bones. The second expands, tingling over her skin—cold and crystals, a spirit of the ice and snow, the freezing heart of winter, to numb her, make her strong and still. Together, they make Tarji a weapon, and the spirit mount knows it.*

Jere moves swiftly, sharply, aiming for the Chalmarais hunter, but the wizard drives the spirits to shield him first, kill them second. Claws catch Jere's sword arm, toss him aside—he rolls, nimble as a snow monkey.

Tarji draws her own threshold flint sword, the stones that line its edge glinting in the sunlight, and she's angry and she's numb—how dare *the sun shine while the world is ending!—but she knows what must be done.*

The spirit mount isn't whole, isn't airy—when it means to hit Jere, it does, when the Chalmarais darts beyond it, he passes through its flank. A normal weapon cannot harm the suorinen, *even forced into the physical realm like these.*

But threshold flint is something else, and this is the last responsibility of the vuhenki.

The snow spirit cloaks her, closing tight over her heart, over the other spirit as they blend and blur into something new, force and ice, cold and hot muscle. Tarji throws the weight of her body, the weight of her sword into the beast's broad shoulder, knocking it away from Jere, giving him room to attack the hunter. The glossy black blades bite into it like no metal could and the spirit mount screams—

The screaming shocked the *suorinen* riding Tarji, jolting them from her body, taking the cold's numbness and the bull yak's temper. *No,* she thought, feeling the spirit mount buck against her. *No, no, no.*

But there was no space for squeamishness. She sliced the sword across the spirit mount's throat, feeling the fine-edged blades snap off in the wound. They sizzled, as if flint and spirit couldn't touch, but each destroyed the other.

The mount thrashed like no living creature could, its half-severed

head bouncing, everything unnatural about this battle made flesh. The cloud tiger claws raked her, ripped through the leather of her breeches, drawing blood that made no difference to the captured spirits. The spirit mount howled and lashed out again, but as its claws connected, Tarji slammed the broken sword into the back of its neck, hacking the rest of the way through.

Unlike the little marten, the mount hit the stone floor with a heavy, fleshy *thud*, the *suorinen* that formed it snatched away, stripped away from Vàorem forever.

"Jere!" she shouted, her voice too loud. The Chalmarais lay dead beyond the mount, chest torn open, his bearded face bloody. She swung around and saw Jere, crouched beside Sakavian, trying to lift him with his own right arm held close to his chest and bleeding. Tarji limped toward them, pushing the pain out of her thoughts. They could get Sakavian on a yak. They could make for the passlands. The Chalmarais would be fools to try and follow.

But Sakavian could barely lift his head. Blood blackened the cloak wound around his arm—still bleeding. Jere looked up at her, eyes fearful. "Can you lift him?"

The roar of more stones crashing, the pained howl of the giant spirit mount that the calm Chalmarais summoner had ridden. Tarji's heart squeezed as if another *suori* had invited itself in, hiding from the carnage of this world. "We have to leave him."

Jere shook his head. "Are you *mad*? He's the heir. Maybe the Speaker by now."

"I know," Tarji said.

"We swore to protect him!"

"No." Tarji sank to her knees beside Sakavian. "We're sworn to protect *Vàorem*. We're sworn to protect the blood. He's not likely to survive that wound, and if he does, he'll be slow." Her voice caught, she pressed on. "They'll be hunting him. All of us. They brought an army to quash the tribes and they know if they want to take Vàorem

they need to keep the *suorinen* from having a Speaker. We have to make sure that there is *always* a Speaker." She looked down. Sakavian was watching her with those glittering black eyes, as if she'd made a joke. "They might have one bastard," she said, her voice breaking. "They can't have gotten them all."

Sakavian regarded her a moment with such tenderness that Tarji wished she had the luxury of looking away. "Tarji Hellonar," he sighed. "Mother of my children after all."

Without meaning to, she thought of other futures, other possibilities, where his stupid prophecy hadn't pointed to the end of everything. How strange something so contrary to her nature could seem so sweet, given all the wrong alternatives.

"Speaker," she said, taking his hand, "I wish you were wrong." She swallowed. "Should we speed you on your way?"

"No need for that," Sakavian said. "I'll speed you." He grasped for his blade, but it lay on the floor of the great hall. Tarji broke one of the remaining pieces of threshold flint from her sword, cutting her own fingers in the process. He took it in shaking hands and sliced through his other arm, before cutting the bindings loose.

"Give us a gate, my Bright Ones, I beg you," he sighed as Tarji took his hand. "Give my faithful warriors a path to your next best beloved."

All around Tarji and Jere the air grew stiflingly thick and dark, though it shimmered with an amber fire that seemed almost alive. Tarji held Sakavian's hand until it seemed to dissolve in her grasp, until the world slipped away, and she was buoyed unseeing through a frantic river of whispering voices, into a future she had no name for.

TARJI FOUND THE FIRST GIRL—Yrsa Valausiä—buried under a midden in the midst of the still smoking village. She froze, stiff and still as a dead branch when Tarji peeled back the ratty cloak covering her.

"Got her!" Tarji shouted to Jere, lost somewhere in the village. The girl flinched away as Tarji bent down. "Come along," she said more gently. "Your father sent me."

"You're the *vuhenki*," the little girl said, dark eyes wide and staring. "They...they..."

"Burnt your village down," Tarji said. "Good to see the old man had sense enough to hide you. Come along."

Yrsa didn't move. "Are they dead?"

Tarji bit her tongue. The girl meant the Aalmeki, some of whom littered the streets, but most of whom would have fled into the forests at the approach of Chalmar. All Tarji could think about was Naraminta, her fellow *vuhenki*, the court of chieftains and bone witches. Sakavian's hand slipping from her own. The spirit mount dying on her blade.

"Come along," she said again, scooping the little girl up. "Now isn't the time."

"Why?" Yrsa was shaking from cold, from nerves. Tarji realized the cloak in the midden had probably been the girl's, but there was no way she was going back for the muddy, stinking thing.

"What's happening?" Yrsa whispered.

In the threshold, the *suorinen* screamed and stormed and demanded retribution, a return to order. A new heir. But they hadn't chosen.

Too much to explain, too close to breaking taboo and the spirits themselves. What was happening was blasphemy and disorder. Tarji was the last person who knew how to explain it.

But you must, she thought.

"Not now," she told the girl.

Jere met them at the edge of the village, two stolen yaks ready and saddled for a hard ride up to the passlands. He climbed onto his own and gestured for Tarji to hand him Yrsa, but she ignored Jere, climbing onto her own mount and pulling the little girl up

with her. She tucked her cloak around the girl, cloud tiger fur and raven feathers. She couldn't wear it much longer.

"What's happening?" Yrsa said again.

Tarji paused. "Your father is a good man," she said. *Was,* she thought, and wasn't ready for it. "Better than anyone gives him credit for. Loves you very much. Loves all Vàorem very much. That's what he's like."

"Oh." Yrsa snuggled into her and Tarji bore it. "Where are we going?" she asked.

"I'm taking you somewhere safe," Tarji said. "Because we're going to fix this."

Chalmar deserved nothing but vengeance, after all.

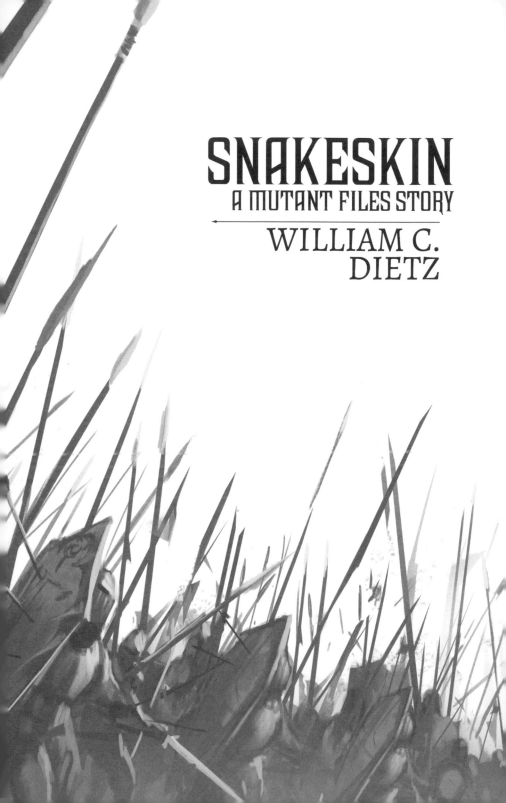

SNAKESKIN
A MUTANT FILES STORY

WILLIAM C. DIETZ

BOUNTY HUNTER MELODY RAINES LOOKED from her outside mirror to the gas gauge as the rat rod raced across the bone-dry desert. The needle was wobbling above the "E" as the men on dirt bikes tried to catch up with her. Their images grew larger with each passing second. All three of the vehicles produced dusty rooster tails and caught air from time-to-time.

Raines swore as the truck slammed down. She'd spent the three weeks, and the better part of 2,000 nu bucks, following a bank robber named Kathy Striker. A search that culminated in a long-range rifle duel with Raines the winner.

She was loading Striker's body onto the roof of her truck when the Mackie brothers appeared. They'd been hunting for Striker too, and weren't above stealing her body to collect the bounty.

Fortunately, Raines had been able to kill one of the triplets and escape. Now his siblings were after revenge *and* the bank robber's body. Raines wanted to consider her options but couldn't come up with any. A sawed-off shotgun lay on the seat next to Raines—and a Glock 32 was ready in the door cubby. Windows were expensive, so Raines pressed a button, and felt a sudden blast of hot air as they disappeared.

The Mackie brothers were firing at the rat rod's tires by then, but

Illustration by OKSANA DMITRIENKO

to no effect, because they could run flat. The one with the mouthful of stainless steel teeth pulled up along the right side of the truck, smiled, and fired a pistol.

Raines heard a snap as the bullet whipped past her nose. She aimed the shotgun at the man on the motorcycle and pulled both triggers. There was a loud boom as the load of double ought buck blew most of his face away. Raines stood on the brake and the dead man disappeared. Dust billowed as the rat rod skidded to a halt.

The last Mackie flashed past. Raines stomped on the gas. Gravel flew as the off-road tires fought for a purchase. Now their roles were reversed. Raines drew the Glock, stuck it out through the window, and fired left handed. The bullets went wide.

The surviving brother heard the shots, looked back over his shoulder, and tried to turn. His motorcycle's front tire hit a rock and popped it up off the ground, which caused the bike to flip.

Raines braked to avoid the wreckage, stopped, and got out. The full weight of the motorcycle was resting on Mackie's legs. "Please!" he begged. "Help me!"

Raines pointed the Glock at him. Brother three had a dog-like snout and a bloody cut on his cheek. She could see one hand, but the other was hidden. "That sounds like a bad idea," Raines observed. "Because later, after you recover, you'll come looking for me. It makes sense to settle this now."

Mackie attempted to bring a pistol up from behind the motorcycle but Raines fired first. A *third* eye appeared in between the others. The bounty hunter's head jerked and his body went limp.

Raines scanned the horizon. It would be just her luck to discover that *more* bounty hunters were closing in. But no, the only scavenger in sight was a turkey vulture riding the thermals above. Dinner was served.

Raines stuck the pistol into the small of her back, and went to get her siphoning kit. It took forty minutes to transfer the gas from

the bikes into a jerry can, and pour the precious liquid into the 4X4. The truck was red. Or had been before years in the hot sun. Now it was pink. Raines called her Ruby.

Once the refueling process was complete the needle on the gas gauge floated a bit higher. Raines estimated that the Mackie brothers had "donated" about two gallons of fuel to her supply. And, since Ruby got a miserable sixteen miles to the gallon, that would provide Raines with thirty-two miles worth of range. Enough to reach a gas station.

It took the rest of the morning to reach the town of San Manuel, Arizona, where the county sheriff would receive Striker's body--and notify the Republic of Texas. The republic was one of five independent countries that rose to replace the United States of America in the wake of the plague spread. The others included Atlantica, the New Confederacy, the Commonwealth, and Pacifica.

The sheriff and his deputies were housed in what amounted to a fort. The eight-foot-high walls were made of steel reinforced concrete, the guard towers were equipped with M61 Gatling guns, and the facility was surrounded by a dry moat. *Why?* Because the Republic of Texas was founded on Libertarian principles, that's why.

"Less government is better." That's what proponents of the philosophy liked to say. And the consequence was fewer schools, less medical care, and sketchy law enforcement. The country's reliance on bounty hunters was a natural extension of that. The people who were running the Republic of Texas figured hell, why pay for federal marshals and state police when bounty hunters are so much cheaper?

It wasn't unusual for the courts to try fugitives in absentia using whatever evidence was handy. And, assuming the defendant was found guilty, to place a price on his or her head. The worse the crimes were, the higher the bounty. At 10,000 nu bucks the reward for bringing Striker in was a respectable though not remarkable sum.

That's what Raines was thinking as she drove Ruby across

the drawbridge. Then she had to clear a checkpoint before passing through the gate and entering the compound.

The complex included an admin building, a jail, and a barracks for the deputies. A sign pointed the way to the so-called "Redemption Center." The name was apt since it could refer to "the payment of an obligation," or "salvation from sin through Jesus's sacrifice," either of which could apply. Since there weren't any other vehicles Raines was free to pull forward and park. A sign said, "Ring for Service," and she did.

Kathy Striker's body was strapped to Ruby's cargo rack so Raines had to climb up and free it. The corpse was covered by a thick layer of white dust—and was starting to draw flies. A portly deputy appeared as Raines freed the last strap. His name was Pib Burns, and they'd done business before. "Hey, Mel," he said cheerfully. "What have you got for me?"

Raines lifted the body up to the point where she could tip it over. Striker landed face down in front of Burns' strangely shaped cowboy boots. The impact produced a puff of dust. "Kathy Striker," Raines said. "Bank Robber extraordinaire. Bounty number 76492."

Burns eyed a data pad. "Yup, that's a match. It looks like Striker robbed two banks *and* killed a guard. You know the drill. The lab will check to see if a DNA sample from the body matches what we have on file. If it does the reward will be deposited in your bank account. If it doesn't a price will be placed on *your* head. Got it?"

"I've got it," Raines agreed, as she jumped to the ground. "You want a hand?"

"That would be right friendly of you," Burns replied. "I'll take her shoulders, you grab her ankles." The so-called "fridge" was large enough to accommodate four bodies on slide-out trays. Two slots were occupied, so they dumped Striker into the third drawer. Then it was time to get a receipt from Burns, climb into Ruby, and head home.

Except Raines had no "home" other than the hotel she was staying in. That was because she traveled a lot, and a home would make her vulnerable to people like the Mackie brothers.

Raines had chosen to stay at the Red Saguaro. It wasn't fancy, but the rooms were clean, and the hot water was hot.

After checking in, and dumping her belongings in room 103, Raines went to dinner. The restaurant was two blocks away. And Raines liked the combination of Tex-Mex food and country western music. Raines's favorite seat was in the back where she could eyeball the front door.

After a chicken burrito and two bottles of Mexican beer, Raines returned to the motel. The night passed peacefully. When she awoke, she made her way into the bathroom for the daily confrontation with herself. Half of her face was human, and more than that, beautiful. Everybody said so.

The other half was covered with light blue scales. They trickled out of her hairline, flowed around her left eye, and down along the side of her nose.

Then the scales cascaded down over her chin and onto her neck. And there was more. The bounty hunter's right eye was gray, while the left was violet, and partially obscured by a reptile-like nictitating membrane.

Snakeskin. That's what people called Raines behind her back. And, even though she lived in a redzone with mutants who had problems of their own, the name hurt. Her condition, *their* conditions, were the result of a terrorist attack perpetrated by a man named Al Mumit (the taker of life).

Back in 2038, Al Mumit had used seven-hundred and eighty-six *Shaheed*, or martyrs, to deliver a bioengineered bacterium called *Bacillus nosilla* to the *Kaffar* (unbelievers) all around the world. The carriers had been chosen because they looked western or were clearly innocent. Like babies.

After entering their target countries, the *Shaheed* sought out sports arenas, music events, and transportation hubs. Any place where *Bacillus nosilla* could spread. The results were everything Al Mumit had hoped for. Thousands fell ill and they communicated the disease to others. People like Tom and Marla Raines. By some miracle they survived even as millions died. But, when Marla gave birth, it was to a *thing*. A snakeskin.

A tear escaped from the human eye and trickled down her cheek. There was reason to hope however. The norms who ran Pacifica had some very skilled doctors. Every mutant knew of someone who had been treated there.

Unfortunately, operations like the ones Raines required would cost at least half a million nu. And she had 152-thousand stashed in the bank. Make that 160-thousand, thanks to the donation from Kathy Striker.

And that was why Melody Raines was a bounty hunter. It was going to take a lot of money to erase her face. Each morning began with the same ritual. After wiping the tears away Raines would brush her teeth and go to work. And someday, when a *new* face appeared in the mirror, the killing would stop.

After checking out of the motel Raines drove Ruby to Jo-Jo's truck stop at the edge of town, where she instructed the manager to check the 4X4's tires. The restaurant was on the other side of the parking lot.

Some of the locals knew Raines and said "Hi," as the bounty hunter made her way to a table in the back. Raines ordered breakfast, and was sipping a cup of coffee, when a stranger approached the table. He had wispy hair and what remained of a horn that protruded from the center of his forehead. "Ms. Raines? My name is Alan Peavey. Jo-Jo said I should talk to you. Can I have a moment of your time?"

Raines eyed him over the rim of her cup. "That depends on what you plan to do with it."

"A man named Thomas Cray took my daughter," Peavey replied. "And I'm trying to get her back. But Cray controls the town of Bliss, and he has bodyguards."

"Sorry," Raines said. "I'm a bounty hunter. What you need is a gunfighter, or a group of gunfighters. Ask around. You'll find them."

"I have," Peavey said. "But I can't afford them. That's why I came to you."

"It's like I said," Raines replied. "I'm a bounty hunter—and I don't do charity work."

Peavey nodded. "I understand. But there's a fifty-thousand nu bounty on Cray's head. So, if you capture him, or kill him, you'll get paid. And I'll get my daughter back."

Raines considered it. Fifty-thousand nu bounties were rare... And fifty-thousand would make a nice addition to the face fund. But why hadn't she heard of Cray? And why hadn't one of her competitors capped the bastard? Still, it wouldn't hurt to listen. "Sure, have a seat."

"Thank you," Peavey said, as he slid onto the seat across from her. When the waitress arrived, Raines saw the way that Peavey was eyeing her breakfast. "Are you hungry?"

Peavey nodded. Raines turned to the waitress. "Mr. Peavey would like to order breakfast. Put it on my tab."

Peavey ordered a modest meal of bacon and eggs with toast. "Okay," Raines said, as the waitress walked away. "Tell me about Cray... Why haven't I heard of him?"

"His *real* name is Joel Wazinski," Peavey replied. "And he's wanted for murder, theft, and rape among other things."

Raines *had* heard of Wazinski. Every bounty hunter had. A lot of her peers called him "the Wizard of Waz," because of the way he'd been able to remain on the run for *what?* Five years? Something like that. The man was like smoke. Here one moment and gone the next. "I've heard of Wazinski," Raines allowed. "But no one knows

where he is. That's why he's alive."

"Except *I* know where he is," Peavey said.

"Oh yeah? How's that?"

"Cray is running a religion," Peavey said. "Except it's more like a cult. The members have to do what Cray tells them if they want to achieve enlightenment. Once they do, their deformities will disappear. That's why I went. To get rid of *this*." Peavey brought a grubby finger up to touch the stubby horn. It had been amputated leaving a stub.

We're two of a kind, Raines thought, as she sipped her coffee. "Okay, you went to some meetings. What happened after that?"

Peavy's food arrived and he hurried to butter a piece of toast. "The meetings were held in secret," Penn told her. "And most of them were led by students called Chelas. They told us that the master would come and he did. We couldn't see him though. He was wearing a mask, air tanks, and a rubber suit."

Raines frowned. *"Air tanks?* What for?"

"Cray was a mutant," Peavey answered. "But after years of study he achieved enlightenment—and his normal body became manifest. But it made him vulnerable to *Bacillus nosilla*. That's what he claims."

"So he came to the meeting," Raines said. "Then what? How does your daughter figure into this?"

"It was *my* fault," Peavey said miserably. "We live out in the desert. I didn't want to leave Lilly home alone. So, I took her along. And everything was fine until Cray arrived. When Cray spotted Lilly, I knew he wanted her. He said she'd been chosen, and took us to the town of Bliss. It had another name before the cult moved in, but that's what *they* call it, and the locals go along. Once we arrived Cray told me that he was going to marry Lilly. But she's only twelve! And Cray has *two* wives already."

Raines felt a rising sense of anger. Somebody needed to bring the bastard in or, failing that, kill him. "I'm sorry," Raines said. "You said that Cray wanted Lilly from the moment he saw her. *Why?*"

"Lilly has an extra kidney," Peavey answered, "but she *looks* normal. And she's pretty. Like her mother was."

Raines nodded. Normal women, and women who *looked* normal, were quite valuable in the redzone. So much so that men would pay high prices for them, or in some cases, *steal* them. "So Cray took you to Bliss. But you're here."

"I ran away," Peavey told her. "And they're looking for me. But I'll take you there," he promised. "I'd walk into hell itself for Lilly."

"Finish your breakfast," Raines said, as she turned to her data pad. "I'm going to check on a few things." It took less than five minutes to verify that Wazinski was still on the loose. And the bounty had risen to *sixty*-thousand nu. The decision made itself. Cray was going down.

Once they finished eating, Raines led Peavey out of the restaurant and across the parking lot. Two dozen big rigs were parked there. It was dangerous out in the boonies, so *all* of the trucks had DYI armor and bolt-on weapons.

Long haul trucking was like bounty hunting in a way. The rewards could be high, but a single mistake would put a driver in the ground.

Ruby's tires had been repaired, and she was ready to roll. The bill totaled 426 nu. That was one of the reasons why most wannabe bounty hunters went out of business in a matter of months. The overhead was high.

After paying the bill, Peavey took Raines to the old airstream trailer where he and Lilly lived prior to meeting Cray. Everything Peavey needed went into the knapsack/bedroll combo that he threw into Ruby's backseat. Then they were off.

Raines was in no mood to talk, but Peavey was, and started to interrogate her. "So," Peavey said, as he pointed to the badge. "What's up with *that?*"

The badge was pinned to the driver's side visor—and a memory

of days gone by. "I was a cop," Raines told him. "In Tucson."

"I guess that makes sense," Peavey replied. "You had to learn somewhere. Why did you quit?"

"To make more money," Raines replied. "So I could fund an orphanage in Prescott."

"That's wonderful," Peavey said enthusiastically. "More people should do that sort of thing."

"Yes, they should," Raines agreed. "Now shut up. I have some thinking to do."

It took the better part of two hours to reach a point where, according to Peavey, they were roughly five miles from Bliss. Raines pulled over onto the shoulder of the road. "Okay," she said, "you'll have to hoof it from here."

Peavey frowned. *"Why?"*

"Because they're looking for you," Raines reminded him.

"Right," Peavey said. "That makes sense."

"I'm glad you agree," Raines said drily. "I might need some help. Take this radio. Turn it on every hour on the hour around the clock."

"I don't have a watch."

Raines sighed. "Okay, leave it on all of the time. The batteries are new, and should last for three or four days. Do not, I repeat do *not*, call me. I will call you. Understood?"

Peavey nodded. "Understood."

"Good. Do you have some food?"

Peavey nodded. "Enough for three days."

"All right. If you haven't heard from me by 6:00 PM on day three, then I tried and failed."

Peavey looked worried. "What should I do then?"

"Find another sucker. Now get going."

Peavey walked away, paused to look back, and disappeared into a ravine. Raines pulled back onto the highway and continued north. According to Peavey the cult had established a checkpoint a mile

from town. And he was correct. An awning was stretched over the road to provide shade. There were two vehicles in front of Raines, so it was necessary to wait before pulling forward.

The cult's security people had shoulder length hair and Celtic facial tattoos. They were dressed in nearly identical pullover shirts with jeans. A woman stepped up to the window. A snake-like tongue flicked in and out as she spoke. "I need to see your invitation if you're here for the wedding."

Wedding? Was the woman referring to Cray's wedding to Lilly? That seemed likely. "My name is Raines, Melody Raines, and I'm a bounty hunter. Have you seen this man?" Raines gave the woman a flyer. "His name is Percy Kraven, but he's probably calling himself something else. I heard he was in Bliss."

That wasn't true of course, but it didn't matter. Kraven could be anywhere. The woman shook her head. "No. I haven't seen him."

"Okay," Raines replied. "But I'd like to look around. Kraven is a dangerous man. He might hurt someone."

The woman nodded. "Go ahead. I'll give your poster to Monitor Hughes. He'll keep an eye out as well."

Raines didn't know what a "monitor" was, but figured Hughes was similar to a marshal. Raines felt a sense of relief as she drove away. The next task was to figure out how to take Craven into custody or kill him.

After passing a doublewide and a row of dilapidated houses, Raines saw the Come-On-Inn motel. It consisted of five cabins and the sign out front read: "Full." Because of the nuptials? Probably.

Ruby passed under a newly constructed archway with the name "BLISS" centered on it shortly thereafter. The town's previous name of Waterville was nowhere to be seen. The old two- and three-story buildings were draped with white and purple bunting, containers of artificial flowers hung from the retro lampposts, and a heart made of intertwined twigs dangled over Main Street.

Raines's thoughts turned to Lilly. She was only twelve years old, and people of Bliss didn't seem to give a shit. *Why?* Did Cray have the town by the balls? Or were the locals that callous? Some of both perhaps. Raines felt sorry for the girl.

When Raines saw a sign for The Antlers Hotel, she pulled over and went in. The lobby was delightfully cool and home to some ancient furniture. The animal heads on the walls included a buffalo, two mountain goats, and enough deer to form a herd.

A cyclops was waiting to greet Raines at the main desk. The retro bowling shirt and short hair suggested that he was a local. His single eye blinked blue. "Good afternoon… How can I help you?"

"I need a room."

"I'm sorry miss, but we're full up."

Raines placed a fifty nu note on the counter and left her hand on it. "This is for you if you find a way to squeeze me in."

The saucer-like eye dipped to the money and came back up. "There's a casita out back. Our manager lived there until she ran off with the cook. It has a toilet and a shower."

"How much?"

"A hundred nu in advance."

"You're kidding."

"Nope."

Raines sighed. "Okay, sign me up." The moment she lifted her hand the fifty disappeared. "Have you seen this man?" Raines inquired, as she placed a flyer in front of the clerk.

The clerk held it up to the big blue orb. "No, I haven't."

"Let me know if you do. I'll pay 200 nu for a confirmed sighting." The man nodded.

After receiving a key and some directions Raines made her way through the hotel's kitchen, across a grubby courtyard, and into the casita. The paint was peeling, but the space was clean. She'd stayed in worse. *Much* worse.

Raines placed her bag on the bed and went back out. The court-yard had a side entrance that led to Main Street. A lot of people were out and about. And, judging from their attire, at least half of them were members of the cult.

Raines had dinner before making her way to a bar called the Green Door Saloon. A wooden bar occupied the right side of the rectangular room. An empty stage was visible in the back—and mismatched tables sat around it.

The man behind the bar had four arms, only two of which were functional. The others stuck straight out from his shoulders and were equipped with flippers. "Howdy," he said. "What'll you have?"

"A beer," Raines replied. "And some information if you have it. I'm looking for *this* man. And I'll pay 200 nu to anyone who can provide me with actionable information."

The bartender eyed the poster. "Percy Kraven, huh? He's an ugly looking bastard. Nope. I haven't seen him. Leave the poster and I'll keep an eye peeled. I could use 200 nu."

"Sure," Raines replied. "I'm staying at the Antlers Hotel."

After taking her beer to a table, Raines knew the parade was about to begin. Because even though half of her face was ugly, the rest of it was beautiful. And she had a good figure. The kind that most men and some women were attracted to.

During the next three hours Raines had conversations with half a dozen people, tried to pump them for information, and came up empty. Either they didn't know anything about Cray's fortress-like house, or they weren't willing to share. By the time she returned to the casita, she was no better off.

Raines slept in, woke up groggy, and showered. After breakfast, she returned to the Green Door Saloon. Men hit on her, but none of the conversations were especially productive, until a man named Pete plopped down. He was already half sloshed. And, according to the story he told, had been working for Cray until the previous

week. That was when Cray fired him for what Pete described as, "No good reason."

Raines suspected that Cray *had* a good reason, since Pete was a drunk, but encouraged the local to spill his guts. It took time. With a rising sense of excitement, Raines learned what she needed to know. Pete was face down on his forearms when she left.

The sun fell like a hammer as Raines left the saloon and walked back to the casita. Once inside she locked the door, removed her clothes, and took a shower. The tepid water felt good. Raines stepped out, toweled off, and slipped into shorts and a tee.

Her first task was to raise Peavey on the radio and give him instructions. Then Raines went to dinner, and took a short walk before returning to the Casita. She tried to sleep but couldn't. Shortly after dawn, Raines packed her things and left the hotel.

Ruby started with a roar, and using the hand drawn map provided by Pete, Raines drove north. The ruins of an ancient gas station marked the spot where she was supposed to turn. A dirt road led her east off the highway, across a timber bridge, and around the south side of a rocky hill. The sun threw shadows to the west—and the air had already begun to warm.

A stand of willow trees and the remains of a burned-out house appeared as the truck entered a small valley. Raines braked. And as Ruby came to a stop, Peavey appeared out of the shadows. He looked none the worse for wear, but had a bad case of B.O., which caused Raines to roll the windows down after Peavey got in.

The mood was somber as Raines followed the road between two hills and turned north. "What's the plan?" Peavey wanted to know. "We need to rescue Lilly *before* they leave for the wedding."

"No," Raines said. "We don't. Cray has at least eight bodyguards, and there's no way for me to get past them."

Peavey frowned. "So, what are you going to do?"

Raines told him and Peavey didn't like it. Not one little bit. But,

as she pointed out, it was either that or nothing. Once they arrived at what Raines judge to be the right spot she pulled over, parked, and opened the back hatch. Her gear was stored in the cage used for prisoners. The next ten minutes were spent getting ready.

"Okay," Raines said, as she handed the ignition key to Peavey. "You know the plan. Don't screw up. Lilly will pay if you do."

"I won't," Peavey promised. "Be careful."

Raines nodded and turned to the west. She was climbing a steep slope as Peavey started the truck and pulled away. Rather than break the skyline Raines elbowed her way to the very top of the hill where she settled into the shadow thrown by a pinnacle of rock.

The ranch was visible below. It consisted of an L-shaped house with a pool, clusters of mature palm trees, an outbuilding large enough to stable horses, and a doublewide for use by Cray's staff. The entire complex was surrounded by an eight-foot high cyclone fence topped with razor wire. Nothing was moving.

Thus began a long morning. As the sun rose higher in the sky and the protective shade drifted away Raines was left to bake. She drank water, she checked her watch, and willed Cray to emerge. Finally, after hours of waiting, he did. And even though Raines knew what to expect, the man's appearance took her by surprise. He was wearing a full facemask, hoses that led back to the oxygen tanks on his back, and a rubber suit which had been modified to look like a tuxedo. It was a scary sight. And it must have been damned hot.

But that was nothing compared to Lilly. The preteen was dressed in a full-on wedding gown complete with a white veil, stockings, and miniature high heels. She was clutching a bouquet, and looked tiny next to the monstrous Cray. Two women wearing identical gowns followed along behind. Cray's existing wives? Probably.

Raines felt the anger rise inside of her and worked to tamp it down. Anger was counterproductive, anger was unprofessional, and anger could get her killed.

Raines bit her lower lip as Lilly climbed up into the SUV closely followed by Cray and his wives. Two pickup trucks, both equipped with machineguns, took up positions ahead of and behind the Hummer.

Raines did the math. There were three vehicles, and two guards in each, so six of Cray's security people were about to depart. What did that leave? *Two* people. Or so it seemed. More staff could be lurking in the house or the doublewide.

Still, things looked good so far. By invading Cray's home and waiting for him to return, Raines hoped to accomplish what would otherwise be impossible. And that was to get the drop on Cray when he was by himself. Yes, Lilly would be married to him by then, but so what? The marriage was illegal. And once Cray was in the slammer, Lilly would be free.

Engines roared, a guard pushed the gate open, and the vehicles left. Shortly thereafter the remaining guards turned and went over to the doublewide. Would Cray approve? That was unlikely. But Raines could imagine how the guards perceived the situation. Their job was to protect Cray, and he was gone, so what the hell?

Raines gave them time to settle in before following a ravine downhill. A short sprint took her to the fence where she went to work with a pair of wire cutters. Once a section of mesh was free Raines pushed it up and out of the way. After crawling through the hole, she turned to pull the flap down. The bounty hunter was confident that nothing other than a close inspection would reveal the vertical cuts.

A quick dash took Raines to the house where she opened a slider and entered the living room. It was full of gilded mirrors, oversized chairs, and ornate tables. Was that the kind of décor Cray thought a rich person should have? Probably.

A voice said, "Howdy partner!" and Raines whirled, pistol at the ready. Then she saw the cage and the parrot sitting within.

Her heart raced. Had someone heard? Would they come to investigate? No. Raines could hear the distant sound of singing. A cook perhaps, working in the kitchen.

Carefully, to avoid detection, Raines explored the back part of the house. A hall led past two bedrooms, one of which was the master. She entered. Was the four-poster bed large enough to accommodate three adults and a child? Yes it was. And the reality of that made her blood run cold. As did the mirror on the ceiling.

Raines heard a noise in the hall and slipped into the walk-in closet. A crack remained after she pulled the door closed. Raines watched a short woman with black hair enter the room and place a vase filled with flowers on the dresser. Then she left.

Raines sat cross-legged on the floor. The waiting began. She knew that the cult's so-called temple was about five miles away. Once the ceremony was over Cray would bring his twelve-year-old bride to the house. Then Cray would head for his bedroom. To change if nothing else… Or to play with his new toy. Would the plan work? Maybe. She hoped so. Time slowed to a crawl.

After creating a hiding place behind Cray's collection of guru style robes Raines fashioned a head-hoop made from a coat hanger and duct tape. She bent the wire so it would fit over her head and rest on her ears, then she made it larger for Cray.

The second part of the project involved marrying the hoop to the shotgun with duct tape, and securing a left-handed glove to the shotgun butt, being careful to leave her trigger finger free.

By the time Raines finished it looked as though her hand was inextricably connected to the 12 gauge—even though she could remove it without difficulty. And that would be important later.

Having completed her preparations, all Raines could do was eat a candy bar, sip water, and wait. After what seemed like an eternity, she heard three clicks on her radio. That meant Cray's motorcade had passed Peavey's hiding place and was ten minutes away.

Raines stood and did some stretches to prepare herself. She was performing a mental run through when muffled voices were heard. Raines peered through the door crack as Lilly entered the bedroom closely followed by Cray.

Raines's heart beat like a trip hammer as she pushed the door open, took one pace forward, and fired the Taser. Cray collapsed as 50,000 volts of electricity surged through his nervous system. His muscles froze and he was helpless.

Lilly just stood there, eyes huge, as Raines went to work. "Don't worry," Raines told her. "Your father sent me, and he's waiting for us. Get rid of the high heels and the dress. The ability to move freely is more important than your modesty."

Lilly seemed to be frozen in place. She was pretty, *very* pretty, and Raines felt a flash of jealousy. "*Move*," Raines said sternly. "Or do you want Cray to rape you?"

That did the trick. Lilly began to strip as Raines pulled Cray's face mask off. The man was Joel Wazinski all right… The misshapen skull and the facial warts made him easy to recognize. The guru thing was a scam.

Wazinski was stronger than she was, and Raines knew that the effects of the tasering would soon wear off. She hurried to slap a piece of tape over Wazinski's mouth before rolling him over and securing his wrists with zip ties.

Wazinski began to struggle as Raines cut the oxygen tanks free. "I know you can hear me," she told him. "I'm a bounty hunter. And you know what that means. Do what I say or I'll kill you, slice an ear off, and cash it in. Got it?"

That wasn't entirely true of course, since Raines wouldn't be able to escape the compound without him. But Wazinski didn't know that. Not yet anyway. He moved his legs as if to get up. "Stop it," Raines said. "Or you'll be sorry."

All Wazinski could do was sit and fume as Raines placed the

metal hoop over his head and slipped her hand into the glove. "Okay, you can stand now. Can you feel the weight? That's a double-barreled shotgun. It's attached to your head, both hammers are on full cock, and I taped my left hand to the butt. If you try to run, or a guard shoots me, it's all over. Lilly, open the door and stay close. Let's go."

Wazinski couldn't bolt, not without killing himself, and took tiny steps. Two guards and both wives were seated in the great room. They stared as a half-naked Lilly appeared followed by Wazinski and Raines. "Don't bother to get up," Raines said. "Not unless you want me to blow your boss's brains out. You, the guy with the radio, call your buddies. Tell them to stand down." The man with the radio made no effort to comply.

Raines was holding the Glock in her right hand. She fired. The bullet shattered the lamp behind the couch. "Do it," Raines growled. "Or I'll put the next bullet in *you.*"

He did it. Raines ordered Lilly to open the front door, nudged Wazinski forward, and followed along behind. And that was when Ruby crashed through the gate backend first. There were three reasons for that. The first was protect the truck's radiator, the second was to make the loading process faster, and the third was to ensure a fast getaway.

After jumping out of the 4x4, Peavey rushed back to open the rear door and the cage inside the truck. "Crawl in," Raines ordered, and the Waz did as he was told.

Raines jerked the hoop off at the very last moment, gave Wazinski a shove, and slammed the door. He made *mmmfff* sounds as the lock snapped closed.

With her back to the guards Raines closed the hatch, dashed forward, and slid behind the wheel. Peavey was in the back by then, with Lilly at his side. Raines shifted and put her foot down. Gravel flew as the rat rod took off. The guards gave chase. But even though the pickup trucks were armed with machine guns the men

couldn't fire them without endangering Cray.

How long would the chase last, Raines wondered? She glanced at the gas gauge. The needle was on full. Could she make it to the Redemption Center in San Manuel without stopping? That would be ideal. But any hope of an uncontested escape flew out the window when a roadblock appeared up ahead. "Uh, oh," Peavey said. "The guards are in contact with Monitor Hughes!"

That made sense. Raines could stop, or attempt to blow through. The second choice was clearly the better of the two, because once stopped, it would be impossible to get going again. "Hang on!" Raines said, as she put her foot down. "We're going through."

The roadblock consisted of a car and a pickup parked nose-to-nose about three feet apart. Cult members scattered as the 4x4 roared towards them, and bullets smashed the windshield as Ruby hit the barricade. There was a crash followed by the screech of rubber when both vehicles were forced to part. Ruby paused, but only for a moment, as the resistance disappeared. Then she was off again. There was no pursuit this time, and Raines was celebrating that fact, when Peavey tapped her shoulder. "We have a problem."

Raines frowned. "What kind of a problem? Is Lilly okay?"

"Yes, she is," Peavey replied. "But a bullet hit Wazinski in the head. He's dead."

Raines looked at him in the rearview mirror. "I thought you said we have a problem."

Peavey grinned. "My mistake. Never mind."

They arrived in San Manuel three hours later. And, after dropping the Peavey's off at their trailer, Raines drove to the Redemption Center. Deputy Burns was on duty. "Hey, Mel… What's it been? A week? We're gonna run out of fugitives at this rate. Who did you nail?"

"Joel Wazinski," Raines said, as she got out.

Burns produced a low whistle. "The Waz! What are you going

to do with all that cash?"

"Fix my truck."

"That's it?"

"Yeah… Boring, huh?"

"Crazy is more like it," Burns replied. "Well, let's get on with it."

It took both of them to carry Wazinski's body to the fridge. Then it was time to say goodbye, climb behind the wheel, and look at herself in the mirror. Snakeskin looked back at her. Their eyes met. Neither one of them flinched.

A SEED PLANTED

CARINA BISSETT

T HE LAST TIME THE PORTAL opened, it did so high above the heads of millions of people going about their ordinary lives in an ordinary world. The media filled the networks with images and suppositions, but Kaliya disconnected the coverage with a decisive click. Despite what some people thought, it had happened before. She had read her father's reports. A ghost ship sailing through the sands of the Sahara Desert. Hanging gardens filled with vividly colored flowers floating down the Amazon River. Towers strung with enormous bells clamoring a strident alarm in the mountains of Nepal. However, unlike the most recent event, those sightings were fairly easy to cover up with cleverly crafted stories.

"Optical illusions," the officials and scientists said, again and again. "Stacked spatial refractions. Atmospheric phenomenon related to thermal inversion. Mirage. Fata Morgana."

Kaliya knew better. The thin places between Earth and the shadow planet Ketu were expanding, stretched to a membrane no thicker than the sheen of a soap bubble rising through the air. Over the course of the latest three minute and thirty-three second event, a drift of golden seeds had rained down from the sky. Before long, the tenuous borders between worlds would fail entirely. Kaliya wasn't about to let that happen. She would make her father's dreams of

sovereignty come true. She would be the one of his daughters to succeed where the others had failed. She would find the key to closing the portal to Ketu forever. And maybe, just maybe, he would forgive her, and love her as he once had, the way he loved Beatrice still.

She tugged at the glove on her right hand, freeing each finger from its silken confines. Once she'd peeled the material away from her pale green skin, Kaliya pressed her hand against the access panel. It flashed purple, acknowledging her as one of Dr. Hawthorn's daughters. The door clicked open and she removed her palm as the panel began to pulse with a red warning light. A mist of antitoxins and sterilizers clouded the panel, obscuring the accusatory warnings. Kaliya scowled at the reminder and sheathed her hand with her glove, effectively creating a barrier between herself and anyone she might come in contact with.

The first time the portal to Ketu opened—for any scientifically measurable length of time, that is—Kaliya's father had been a young man. There hadn't been any seeds drifting from a sky split in two, but the discovery of Ketu had inspired her father to engineer his greatest creations. Dr. Hawthorn had named his seven daughters after the mythical Indian *vishkanya*—damsels so poisonous they could kill with a kiss. He'd named the firstborn Beatrice, a mocking tribute to a dusty story written long ago. Beatrice hadn't turned out as lethal as her literary counterpart. Dr. Hawthorn refined his experiments: Mara, Dakini, Camille, Jovelyn, Iolanthe, and, finally, Kaliya—the deadliest of them all.

Kaliya walked down the corridor leading to the inner sanctum. Unlike the rest of the compound's halls, which were crowded with apprentices rushing to fulfill their masters' whims, the Aconitum was nearly deserted. As usual, the filtered air and laboratory lighting left her feeling anxious and smothered. Sterile shelves of glass and steel lined both sides of the walkway. Relics from Ketu crowded the finely lit cases. Kaliya had spent her developmental years combing

through the catalogs in search of clues on how to access the shadow world, but the relics had proved to be nothing more than fragments of a civilization just out of reach.

She paused for a moment in front of Caliburn, the legendary sword turned to stone. Although most of the stone was weathered to a dull gray, the hilt bore scars from more recent times. Kaliya could barely trace the echoes of the woman's face that had once graced the unearthly object. The memory of her father's hands grasping a chisel and hammer, his forearms flecked with blood, however, was as bright as the metal he'd removed from her ribcage on her twelfth birthday. When Kaliya had recovered enough to return to the hall, she'd wept to discover Caliburn defaced. The shavings and the metal had disappeared, tucked away in one of her father's secret vaults, as though stone and bone had never existed. According to him, they never had.

At the end of the aisle, Kaliya moved through hermetically sealed doors from one ecosystem to another. Once inside, she breathed deep. The loamy smell of turned earth, the delicate scent of poisonous flowers, and the cloying sweetness of death was her heaven on earth. The entire bio-dome served as a greenhouse. Unlike the stale and sterile corridors leading to the heart of the Aconitum, the ceiling and sides of the central structure were constructed from reinforced glass. She sighed in relief and smiled.

In her youth, Kaliya and her sisters had roamed wild among the engineered plants. Up in the canopy of variegated leaves, Dakini's pale pink form could usually be found skipping and spinning along tree limbs that stretched across the artificial sky. But even Dakini's most graceful dances were just shadows when Camille was compelled to move. With her cinnamon skin and innate ability for martial arts, Camille was the first to realize her potential as a *vishkanya*. Jovelyn, with her love of sharp things, cultivated thorns as blue and as large as her hand, which she would whittle into makeshift knives. Their

darker sister, Iolanthe with her dusky violet skin lurked near the wet places, the cunningly contrived springs and streams that wound through the bio-dome. Kaliya had loved them and they had loved her. But that had all changed after the accident. Everything had changed.

Kaliya gravitated to the fountain situated at the center of the dome. The sound of water frolicking among stone naiads always relaxed her. As she walked, she trailed her fingers along the curling vines that reached out to greet her. Near the fountain, her favorite flower bloomed. The air simmered with their deadly sweetness. She hummed a lullaby and the heavy aubergine heads turned to face her. Kaliya bent to smell them, gathering the fragrant blooms in her glove-clad hands.

"Good. You're here." Her father's voice rattled through protective filters.

Kaliya dropped her arms and turned to face him. His vivid blue eyes stared at her through the glass of his hazmat helmet. Kaliya could barely remember a time when she'd actually been able to touch him. One of the last memories she did have was accompanied by tortured screams and blistered flesh.

"Hello Father." She peeled off her gloves and let them slip through her fingers to pool in coiled loops at the fountain's edge. "Is it time?"

He ignored her question and answered with one of his own. "You saw?"

Even though he was completely protected from accidental exposure, Dr. Hawthorn left a few steps untaken between them. Occupied by increasingly frequent appearances of the shadow planet in the sky and the threat it posed to his authority, he was more distant than ever.

That empty space reminded her of Beatrice. Unlike the others, Beatrice had kept to herself, preferring the words of dead poets over the company of her sisters. Their father had protected his eldest

daughter's desire for privacy, something denied to the rest of them. Only Mara, sweet as an overripe apricot and as lethal as the cyanide contained in its seed, was allowed near her. Kaliya had pretended she didn't care, but she had, and she'd tried everything she could think of to gain her father's favor. Kaliya had transformed herself into the perfect weapon, a weapon honed by hate and edged with envy. She just needed to prove she was better than Beatrice, better than all of them.

"Yes." Kaliya leaned back against the stone, alert yet still taking advantage of the heat streaming through the glass dome. "Do you have a sample?"

Her father held out a sealed container. Inside, a scattering of seeds glittered, perfect golden ovals soaking up the sun. Kaliya reached out. She touched his hand, protected against biohazards, and paused. Her pale green skin appeared waxy and alive compared to his sterile white suit. The moment passed and she collected the container. Kayila held it up and peered inside, marveling at the texture and color of the foreign seeds.

"They're beautiful," she said, awed by the potential she sensed in the golden ovoids.

"They're toxic," he snapped, "just like everything else that has come from that cursed planet."

Behind the faceplate, his lined face creased into even deeper furrows and his lips pursued as though he'd sampled an especially bitter fruit. "The Watcher must have gone mad to release such destruction on Earth. Someone has to stop her. Someone *should* have stopped her already."

As far as Kaliya could tell from her father's charts, the way between the two worlds had closed abruptly months before Beatrice had been born. It had remained closed for more than three decades before suddenly appearing in the sky just recently.

Over the course of those long years, Dr. Hawthorn had secured

a seat on the council and had moved up in power through the judicious deployment of his daughters.

"The Watcher?" Kaliya traced the cockatrice etched into the clear lid.

Leave it to her father to take on the sigil of a creature that could kill with a glance. She still wasn't sure if it was his idea of a joke or if he'd actually believed he could engineer daughters as deadly as the mythical beast.

"There's a balance that must be maintained." Dr. Hawthorn looked up as though he could see through the dome, past the city's protective shield, and through the brane that separated Earth from her shadow sister, Ketu.

Kaliya followed his gaze. The only thing she saw was the network of branches crisscrossing the dome like a neural network programmed to feed the fancies of a daredevil dancer. But there was no promise of pink among the green. Daniki had been one of the first of Dr. Hawthorn's daughters to leave the Aconitum on assignment to never return.

Kaliya twisted the lid off the container and lifted a single seed to her lips. She ran her tongue over its smooth surface, feeling the contours, tasting its potential, before swallowing it whole. She repeated the process two more times and then recapped the container, handing it back to her father. "Do you have the coordinates and times pinned down for the next event?"

"I'm a scientist, not a spy." Dr. Hawthorn frowned through the faceplate. "The harp must be silenced. The portal to Ketu must be closed forever or everything I've built will be destroyed. Do you understand?"

"Yes, Father." She looked through the glass, hoping to catch a glimpse of pride in those blue eyes.

His expression remained calm and clinical, as though he was comparing her to someone else—and found her lacking.

"Don't fail me this time."

"Father." Kaliya looked away and gathered her gloves from their resting place on the fountain's edge.

ALTHOUGH SHE KNEW WHERE BEATRICE had taken refuge from the world, she'd never been there. After locating the correct address, it had taken her more than an hour of wandering the winding garden paths before she found her eldest sibling, puttering away in the rose beds as though she were a common gardener.

"Hello, Beatrice."

Her sister froze, pale yellow hands sunk deep in the loamy soil. Of all of Dr. Hawthorn's daughters, Beatrice was the loveliest. She matched the billowy blooms of the hybrid rose she tended. The golden glow of the Alchymist mirrored Beatrice's creamy yellow skin and unbound apricot hair. Her sister's tensed shoulders released, and she returned to her work as though a visit from her deadliest sibling was a welcome event.

Kaliya knew better.

All of Dr. Hawthorn's *vishkanya* had kills to their credit by the time they reached puberty—all of them, except his beloved Beatrice. After the accident, he'd married off his most precious flower to his closest ally, the one man on Earth who'd managed to chart the stars of the dark universe that existed alongside their own.

Kaliya had not been invited to the wedding.

The dark green leaves of the climbing roses stretched up to soak in the sun, but the flowers shifted to follow the face of the poet who tended them. The perfume of Beatrice's fear lay heavy in the air. Kaliya smiled.

"I never understood your fascination with roses," Kaliya said as she moved to kneel next to her sister. "But this strain is lovely in its own way, I suppose."

Kaliya stroked the variegated petals. Her thumb smudged the

colors into a wilted blend as the plant struggled under her touch. Out of the corner of her eye, she saw her sister's peach-colored lips tremble.

"What do you want?"

Kaliya plucked a petal from its stem and lifted it to her mouth. She brushed the creamy velvet against her lips. Its heavy scent made her mouth water with its notes of liquid sunshine and honeyed musk. The damp decay of the turned soil in front of Beatrice tempted the golden seeds lodged in her throat. She suppressed the desire to give them life. Not yet.

"You've been gone a long time, sister." Kaliya placed the rose petal on her tongue and carefully crushed its delicate beauty between her teeth. "You're not his favorite anymore."

Beatrice looked at her then. Her eyes were the same vivid blue as their father's. "I was never his favorite."

"You were his first." Kaliya plucked another petal from the rose and popped it in her mouth. Its softness only sharpened her hunger. "He protected you."

"I might have been the first of us to be born, but you are and always have been his last hope."

Kaliya moved closer. "What do you mean?"

Beatrice appeared to wilt before her. Unlike Kaliya, Beatrice had been created for beauty. Her only claim to being one of Dr. Hawthorn's *vishkanya* was in the subtle effects she had on men's desire. Her poison had a light touch. It thinned the blood, made the heart race. Beatrice had no resistance to her youngest sister's deadly nature. The faded burn scars on her arms proved it.

"There is a story about Father," Beatrice said, appearing calm despite the surge of perfumed fear emanating from her pores. "They say he found a way to Ketu, that he stole riches from the ruler."

"Everyone knows that." Kaliya reached out and trailed a finger across her sister's dirt-covered knuckles. Beatrice flinched, but didn't

scream, not even when her skin began to darken to a dirty gold. "They are evil creatures, those who live in that shadow world," she continued. "They must be stopped."

"There is evil in both worlds." Beatrice took a deep breath as her skin smoldered under the press of Kaliya's fingers. "Iolanthe is dead."

The golden seeds rooted in Kaliya's throat twisted at the sound of her favorite sister's name. Iolanthe had been the last of them to leave the Aconitum before her. She hadn't been gone long enough to know whether or not she'd ever return. The cloying taste of violets flooded her mouth. "You don't know that."

"Yes," Beatrice said. "I do."

Beatrice turned to fully face her sister, knee to knee, nose to nose. "Listen to me, Kaliya. Our father stole more than gold from Ketu." She grasped her sister's hands, creamy yellow enfolding pale green. "He stole us. He stole the golden eggs from which we were born." Kaliya tried to pull away as Beatrice's subtle hues blackened under her deadly touch. "And then he turned us into weapons."

"That's not true," Kaliya said. "He created us to save the world, but you thought you were better than everyone else. You left us there alone even though you knew what he was doing to us."

Beatrice shook her head even as she continued to fade like a photograph left to long in the sun. She almost looked human in her frailty. The resemblance to their aging, blue-eyed father enraged her.

Kaliya's voice rose and her grip tightened. "He cut my ribs out and you didn't stop him. You could have stopped him."

"I'm sorry." Beatrice leaned forward and pressed a peach-colored kiss on Kaliya's dark green lips. "You're the only one strong enough to defeat them both." Her breath stuttered. "That's why he saved you for last."

Her last words whispered their way past a swollen tongue.

"Both? What do you mean?"

Beatrice's lifeless hands fell free and she slumped into the bed

of roses she'd been so lovingly tended. Her apricot-colored hair had turned brittle and her skin had lost its lustrous sheen—a dead rose resting in a thicket of thorns. Kaliya pressed her fingers to her lips where the scent of crushed roses lingered.

KALIYA LEFT BEATRICE LYING IN the dirt and made her way into her brother-in-law's study. She sorted through the classified files, following the trail from one source document to another, until she was finally able to narrow down the most probable location for the next event.

It seemed unlikely that it would occur so close to the last sighting, but the seeds she'd swallowed confirmed the direction she needed to go. She could feel their potential spiraling through her veins. The seeds acknowledged her as one of their own, a safe place to hide until they were needed. They would take her to the ruler in the sky, the king who had once wielded Caliburn in its true form. She had questions only he could answer.

Then, she would kill him with a kiss one hundred times deadlier than any toxin known to man. After all, she'd been created for the sole purpose of assassination. The conqueror living in that floating fairy castle was her first priority. Acquisition of the fabled harp and the destruction of the Watcher was the second.

By the time she reached her destination, the golden seeds had taken root deep in her chest. With each breath, they pumped their toxic mix into her bloodstream. She felt different, alive, and more powerful than ever.

She glanced up, gauging the reach of the coalescing clouds. The towering formation was identical to the one photographed during the last event. Crops stretched out in plowed symmetry around her. Kaliya breathed deep, searching for kinship to the land, but underneath the scent of growth she detected the stench of chemicals designed to kill.

Kaliya bent at the waist and began to cough, a harsh and brutal sound that intruded on the deathly silence surrounding her. The three seeds released their hold on her, working their way back up her throat until she was able to spit them into a cupped palm. The sunlight broke through the clouds' hold on the sky and shone down to illuminate the golden orbs she cradled so gently. She crouched and scooped out a hollow in the fertile soil where she deposited her charges.

And then, she began to sing.

After a few bars, the vines broke through the thin crust. They twined around each other as they thickened and lengthened, climbing towards the clouds. When they had reached a height and breadth sturdy enough to bear her weight, Kaliya embraced the braided ropes and let them lift her skywards. The burnt sugary smell of violets exploded into the air as tiny purple flowers budded and opened along the green length of the vine. *Iolanthe.*

She continued to sing, her voice carrying the notes of a song that reached deep into the material plane, plucking the strings that pulled the worlds together. She sang about the green and the sun and the water. She sang about disease and darkness and death. She sang about hope and despair. She sang a lament for her six dead sisters, flowers bloomed and buried before their time. As the vines broke through the clouds, the portal opened. Through that window, a city from the shadow world came into view.

Kaliya's breath caught in her throat. The notes stumbled and then fell silent as she watched the rip in the sky spread until it came to a halt, just a step away from where she clung to the towering vines. The previous event had lasted just a few minutes, but there was no guarantee that this portal would remain open as long. Kaliya looked down at the fields spread out below and wondered if she'd ever return. She had no reinforcements, no back-up plan, no escape route.

She couldn't go back, not now. She released her hold on the vines and jumped.

Even though she'd hoped she would land on the wedge of visible ground in Ketu, a part of her was surprised that she didn't plummet through the clouds to the fields she'd left behind. Thick mist coiled around her legs. Dark shapes hunched in the shadows. She paused and grounded herself on her heels, preparing for an attack. Nothing moved.

Sunlight broke through a seam in the clouds, revealing the stone precipice she stood on. Directly ahead of her, a watchtower blocked the path to the city beyond. Beneath the retreating wisps of fog, the bleak landscape revealed rocks blackened and scorched by flame. The green part of her shied away from the desolation, but the part of her trained to kill shrugged and moved forward, intent on completing her mission, whatever the cost.

Kaliya approached the watchtower. The silence of the lonely landscape pricked at her exposed skin. A feeling of *wrongness* settled deep in her chest, but there was nothing to fear in this dead land. No birds winged across the open sky. No animals thrived in the barren stretch. Nothing green survived the attack wrought against the watchtower and the land surrounding it. As far as she could tell, not a living thing breathed or moved in this desolate region of the shadow planet.

The sound of harp strings plucked in a violent staccato startled her. As if in response, the sky darkened and the ground shuddered, nearly throwing Kaliya to her knees. She grasped a boulder for support, but as quickly as it had come, the darkness retreated and the ground stilled. Her hand came away from the rock smudged with soot. She lifted her hand and sniffed, catching a hint of perfumed violets beneath the smoke.

"I wouldn't do that, if I were you."

A musical voice startled her from her inspection. Kaliya straight-

ened, briskly rubbing her hands down her thighs as she turned to face the threat.

A woman stepped from a shadowed doorway set in the stone tower. She wore a cloak the color of amethyst. It shaded her face and flowed from her shoulders like a jewel turned liquid. She pushed back the cloak's hood and stared at Kaliya across the blackened waste.

If she hadn't seen her move, Kaliya would have thought the woman to be a cleverly constructed metal sculpture. Her skin held the sheen of polished bronze, her eyes appeared to be plated with gold foil, and her hair hung down in sheets of quicksilver.

Kaliya flexed her fingers. "Who are you?"

The woman sighed through copper lips, a lovely rush of breath that sounded like chimes spinning in the breeze. "Your sisters didn't know me either, but I did hope it would be different with you."

"My sisters?" Kaliya edged closer as she assessed her enemy.

"They were all lovely in their own ways," said the bronze woman. "You father was quite inventive."

"What do you know about my father?"

Up close, she realized the bronze woman's cloak didn't just appear to be moving. It was composed of hundreds of butterflies, which were slowly opening and closing their iridescent wings. When fanned open, the insect's wings revealed shimmery scales painted in every imaginable hue of purple and indigo.

"I know more about Jack Hawthorn than you might expect," she replied with a frown. Her golden eyes flashed in the sun.

Kaliya sorted through memories of Ketu's relics and the catalog of hints she'd gleaned over the years. She didn't like the direction the thoughts were taking her.

"Surely you can see. Your world is diseased and that disease is spreading." The bronze woman cast a glance out across the blackened landscape. "That is not an acceptable option."

"Where is Iolanthe?" Kaliya was close enough to the bronze

woman that she could smell the tang of mineral oil. Other fragrances drifted to her from the wings of the butterflies: the decadence of damask rose, the dripping sweetness of jasmine, the velvety bite of snapdragons, the languid seduction of magnolia, the exotic musk of ylang-ylang, the cloying burn of violet. "Where is my sister?"

"Jack stole many treasures on the occasions he was here, but his last theft was unforgivable." The bronze woman appeared lost in thought: it was difficult to read her emotions through the metallic veneer of her features.

One of the amethyst butterflies disengaged from the cloak of wings and fluttered over to land on Kaliya's arm. With its wings spread wide, the butterfly was as large as an open hand. Its indigo body looked as though its velvety softness would rival the petals of even the most delicate of flowers. Kaliya waited for the insect to shrivel up and die. Instead it tasted her skin with golden feet. The creature's slender purple antenna waved excitedly and it began to make a clicking sound, which was picked up by the other butterflies clinging to the bronze woman's back.

The bronze woman returned her attention to Kaliya. "I have something to show you."

Intrigued by the winged creature's fascination with her, Kaliya acquiesced with a curt nod. After all, her father had never said anything about a woman made from living metal.

Kaliya followed the bronze women into the watchtower.

They climbed a long swirl of stairs that spiraled up along the tower's curving walls. They walked in silence, each step bringing them closer to the top. There were no other doors, no windows. However, ghostly blue flames burned in globes hung from hooks set in the walls at evenly spaced intervals. The illumination from each globe only reached as far as the halo cast by the next burning light. In-between, shadows prowled. There was no guardrail to protect against the deepening hollow in the center of the tower,

nothing to keep someone from falling. Or being pushed. The stone steps encircled the dark emptiness, giving the illusion of a pit that plummeted down forever.

As they climbed, Kaliya thought about her sisters, the poisonous garden curated by their father. She thought about the games they'd played growing up and the more violent competitions as their individual assets developed. They had been fierce and beautiful and deadly. The list of kills confirmed it. *No more*, she reminded herself. She was the last of their kind. If she failed on this mission, if she failed to return, her father would be completely bereft of his beautiful assassins.

What then? Would Dr. Hawthorn make more daughters to discard on the wings of a whim? *Better yet*, she thought, *why hadn't he made them already?*

When it seemed as though they would continue to climb forever, the stairs suddenly stopped in front of a door painted the darkest shade of blue. The bronze woman glanced over her shoulder.

"Try to remember that I'm only offering you the truth." She pushed the door open. "Nothing more."

A golden light illuminated the top floor of the tower. Open windows stretched from floor to ceiling and an aperture cut in the dome above directed a spotlight on a round table situated at the center of the circular room. The table was inlaid with lapis lazuli and trimmed with gold, but the opulent design was overshadowed by the contents of the crystal case it supported.

Inside the case, golden eggs nestled in folds of purple satin. Each egg was the size of a man's fist, and was cradled in a nest of silver vines. Seven of those nests were empty, the silver vines tarnished black, the purple swaddling missing. In the other nests, the purple satin rustled as if in response to their entrance. *Butterflies*, she thought. *Not satin.*

The bronze woman laid a gentle hand on Kaliya's arm. "He

couldn't carry any more than that."

Although made of metal, her hand was as warm and supple as living flesh. The woman did not blacken and die from the exposure to Kaliya's skin. If anything, the metal shone a little brighter. Kaliya looked up from the bronze woman's hand, to stare at those seven empty cradles. Seven eggs stolen. Seven sisters with skin the color of flowers and sweat the sweetest of deadly perfumes. In the space from one second to another, all of the little deceptions and clever clues clicked into place.

"Where is the harp?" The butterfly perched on Kaliya's forearm began to croon and she absentmindedly stroked its velvety wings. "What does he want it for?"

The bronze woman opened the folds of her living cloak to expose her body. The metallic skin ended along the ridge of her collarbone, leaving the woman's rib cage exposed. The bones curved away from a silver spine and strung between those gleaming branches, golden strings quivered.

"I am the harp, my sweet girl." The bronze woman plucked the thinnest string. The clear note reverberated off the stone walls and the ground rumbled in response. "I open the door."

Kaliya dropped her hand. "Who are you?"

The bronze woman laughed, a tinkling of silver bells.

Kaliya stepped away, moving closer to the crystal case and its treasure. "Are all the people in Ketu like you?"

The bronze woman's smile turned sharp. "There is no one like me."

"What do you want?" Kaliya approached the case.

"Don't be such a child," said the bronze woman. "Your father didn't send you here to kill me. I can't be killed. I am eternal."

"You're the one who let him in, aren't you?"

The bronze woman shrugged. The butterflies dropped away in a swirl of velvet wings and perfumed flight.

Kaliya looked out a window cut into the stone wall. Outside the tower, the blackened landscape stretched on for miles and miles before disappearing into the gray softness of clouds blooming with the promise of snow. There were no trees for Dakini to dance in, no warriors for Camille to fight, no springs for Iolanthe to haunt. She had a feeling that there was no one left to sail ships on the seas of Ketu. No flowers bloomed in the hanging gardens. And the bells had been silenced in the empty towers of Ketu's capital.

"You're the Watcher, aren't you?"

The bronze woman pivoted on a heel and waltzed to the table. "I love round things," she said as she ran her finger along the table's gilt edge.

Round things. Kaliya centered her thoughts, keeping her enemy close while she sorted through a dizzying array of images—the woman's face engraved in the stone sword, bronze bones removed and replaced, the cunning glimmer in her father's eyes. She could almost taste the golden seeds that had rained down from a broken sky. "Was it always you?"

The bronze woman smiled again. "Of course."

Dr. Hawthorn's *vishkanya* carried his code in their DNA, some more than others. But the potential she and her sisters carried came from somewhere else. It came from *someone* else.

The clouds rolled closer.

"Is there anything alive left in this place?"

"Ketu has been purified." Those flat golden eyes narrowed. Those copper lips curled. "Earth is next."

Kaliya closed the space between them. The bronze woman watched her, wary.

"Who did this to you, Mother?"

"He lied to me," she said. "He's a deceiver."

"Yes." At this distance, the enormity of her father's manipulations was something to behold. "He lied to all of us."

The bronze woman tilted her head as though she was listening to a tune being played far in the distance. "There's a storm coming," she said, her voice hollow.

Kaliya took three long steps, closing the space between them. "Everything will be fine, Mother. I know what to do."

She reached out to embrace the bronze woman. Kaliya wondered how different her life and the lives of her sisters would have been without their father's machinations. Might Ketu still be a thriving world filled with all of the color and beauty promised in those broken relics gathered to sit on sterile shelves? Had there ever been an alternative timeline where she could have thrived under gentle guidance and a mother's touch? Were the *vishkanya*, living experiments stolen from the shadow planet, destroyers or saviors? Kaliya thought it depended on the point of view.

"Look what he has done to you, my pretty little girl." The bronze woman stroked Kaliya's cheek with fingers so warm they almost burned her with their touch. "He's made you a monster."

"I know, Mother."

Kaliya tightened her embrace, the golden harp pressed hard against her. She spread her legs, rooted her feet, and began to hum. Her body responded. Leafy tendrils sprouted from her skin. Her toes lengthened and stretched deep into the stone, breaking it apart as she settled her weight. Her fingers latched together, elongating and vining into a tangle of branches binding the bronze woman. And then, she lifted the smallest finger on her left hand and concentrated: the nail elongated and sharpened to thin point. Kaliya slipped it beneath the gold foil of her mother's eye and pierced the rotting remains of her brain. The bronze woman struggled for a moment and then went still in her daughter's embrace.

Kaliya's song deepened. The butterflies guarding their golden charges joined in the song. Kaliya thought of her sisters as she sang. She thought of Beatrice and her delicate hothouse beauty. She

thought of Mara's love of sweets and Dakini's desire to dance. She thought of Camille's passion for women and Jovelyn's penchant for knife play. And she thought of Iolanthe trailing the burnt scent of violets as she cut though her opponents with her razor wit.

The loud crash of stone falling away from the sides of the tower competed with the clamor of dozens of golden shells being torn apart by their occupants. Each crack was accompanied by the trill of pure notes slicing through the gilt covering of the eggs. Some butterflies pulled the shards away with their delicate feet. Others flew in a dizzying spiral around Kaliya, but still she continued. Her vines tore away the sides of the stone tower, allowing the light from Ketu to freely shine into the room. She shattered the crystal case, freeing her new siblings from their cages.

Finally, when the last of the tower walls had been torn down and the remnants of the golden shells crumbled to a dust of glittering fragments. Kaliya tossed her hair behind the curving bark spread across her shoulders. *A gift for you too, Father.*

The dark strands of hair shifted into a delicate filigree of stems. At the end of each strand, aubergine flowers sprouted. A breeze lifted the strands to release the deadly perfume of delicate blooms. Under her guidance the flowers turned to seed, which separated and lifted into the sky. The churning clouds that curled around the tower's base would carry the seeds to Earth, where her progeny would flourish.

As the seeds floated free, Kaliya took a moment to marvel at the beauty of her siblings hatched, a new generation charged to bring life back to the shadow planet of Ketu. She would keep them safe. She would stand watch. Their enemies would never be allowed to harm them. All of the humans would be strangled by a kiss one hundred times deadlier than any toxin known to man. And the Earth would thrive in the green places. At her touch, the golden harp strings thrummed.

And the door opened.

THE BOOK OF ROWE

CAROL BERG

ONE THING TO REMEMBER ALWAYS. The men and women of Evanore prized loyalty above life, limb, gold, land, skills, beauty, scholarship, wisdom, logic, cleanliness, or virtue.

An example: Evanori had pledged eternal service to the line of Caedmon, a foreigner two hundred years dead who stole their sovereignty and absorbed their mountain fastness into his kingdom. Why so? Because Caedmon King starved and bled alongside them through a fifty-year siege, loyal to his stolen subjects until the day he died. It mattered naught that the war was of his own making.

Evanori granted such blind devotion not only to Caedmon's heirs, but to their own leaders. If a warlord commanded his house guards to shatter Pinnacle Rock with sticks and feathers, those testy warriors may have argued with him, grumbled, proposed alternative rocks to break, or suggested more practical weapons for assaulting granite prominences. The warriors' wives or husbands may have named the plan codswallop. But such dissent was spoken only within the confines of the lord's house. A householder who expressed doubts, questions, or disagreement outside the boundaries of the lord's demesne reaped punishments that ranged from beating to beheading, from disinheritance to exile.

Some days—most days—I believed the skulls of Evanori war-

lords were themselves granite prominences that should have been shattered, every one. My father's first of all.

"So, Saverian, it appears Prince Osriel will not have you to wife."

Papa positioned his bulk in his favorite chair, as if settling in for a new siege. My father was Cynric, Warlord of Rowe, Rowe being the smallest, driest, poorest, least notable demesne in all of Evanore. He had surely spent all sixteen years of my life with his head in his scabbard.

I stood beside his chair as a dutiful daughter should. Posture and a respectful tone were all I would yield him.

"No, sire. Still and ever no. Osriel and I were playfellows. Never more than that. These days he is interested only in his books and study." And some very dark magic. Yet magic was not a happy subject in our house. Neither was the subject of my future.

"But he gives you books. You speak to him." Papa's thick, hard fingers drummed the tired leather volume on his writing desk.

The Book of Rowe was the single book our house owned. Ancient, yes, but as thin and uninteresting as Rowe itself, which produced naught but goats, pottery clay, and mostly honorable, but unexceptional warriors. From time to time, Papa opened the book and settled into his favorite chair to read, as if expecting that something marvelous might have been written there while he wasn't looking. It never took him long to close it.

I chose my words carefully. "His Grace has kindly given me the freedom of his library, as he knows I relish its variety"—and Prince Osriel knew I had tired of *The Book of Rowe* long ago—"but he never joins me there and no longer receives visitors. The books are loaned, not gifted. I always return them."

His fingers slowed. "Did you offend the prince? I heard you playing games when you were small. You were taunting, impertinent. You still speak so freely. Like *that woman*."

"No, sire. The prince and I simply grew apart. After his mother

died, he changed. Truly, even if Osriel thought of me as other than a childhood friend, I would not—"

My father didn't want to hear my concerns about the prince's dark turn. This was certainly *not* the time to tell him I'd recently met a young man different from any I'd ever known, one I could speak to about books and the ideas they put in my head … about history and the natural world … about *magic.* A young man not born to Evanore. No, I'd best pick that time carefully. Perhaps when we could afford a cask of new mead.

"It's been two years since the prince and I have spoken, sire." And Osriel had left no doubt that my presence was as unwelcome as his own conscience.

Papa's craggy face hardened into a boulder. "But *that woman* is his physician, and you spend your days with her."

Perhaps I should have stood on the far side of his writing table instead of the near. A spread of oak between us was ever a comfort when our conversation took this particular turn.

"Prince Osriel demands privacy. She's forbidden to speak of him even to me." Of late the slightest whisper of the prince's name made her shudder, which was a phenomenon akin to Wulfgar's Mountain taking an afternoon walk. "I accompany her to every patient, save the prince."

"Hah! Exactly so!" The triumphant exclamation and the boom of fist on oak made me jump. "*That's* why the royal whelp won't have you. You view other men's bodies. Touch them. You observe warriors in times of weakness. Scorn them. Pity them. How could any man consider you, knowing that you would forever compare him to other men? *That woman* should know better."

"All Evanori women know how to treat battle wounds, Papa. They take pride in it!"

"But you do the other … diseases, flux, boils, crabs … filthy business. It's indecent. All for *that woman's* spite."

"What else would I do here? I've no talent for military strategy or wielding battle axes. Horses despise me. Your *hounds* won't heed my command to move out of the way. I've a gift for healing, both common and magical. I can stitch a wound, repair a fracture, and sooth night terrors. No Evanori can sit idle as long as Caedmon's heirs need our swords. You taught me that."

"You are *not* Evanori, Saverian, but by the Sky Lord's hand I'll have you wed to one, no matter what *that woman's* wishes."

He stomped out of the room. I kicked his chair, near breaking my foot.

Why did I let him bait me so? Our arguments always ended the same. Because *that woman* was my mother, the source of my father's greatest accomplishments in *The Book of Rowe*, as well as his deepest grievances.

Seventeen years previous, King Eodward, descendant of holy Caedmon, had brought his beloved mistress and infant son to Evanore, knowing that Evanori loyalty would protect them from his enemies. Lirene de Armine-Visori was an Aurellian pureblood, descendant of invaders who had occupied Navronne for two centuries after they discovered their small magics took on immense power in Caedmon's realm. The beautiful, fragile Lirene brought her pureblood physician with her, a high-spirited young sorceress called Nyxia. Nyxia had promptly conceived a child with the virile young warlord of Rowe. That child was me.

By the time I knew enough to notice, my parents had long realized their hasty union was a mistake. My mother never lived at Rowe after I was born, choosing to house her healing practice close to the royal residence at Renna and her own infant alongside the little prince in the royal nursery.

My father had added only two entries to *The Book of Rowe*. He had wed a divinely gifted sorceress with a personal connection to the sainted Caedmon's house. And he had sired a daughter who

shared a nursery with Caedmon's youngest descendent. Whether due to personal incapacity or the shame of a disloyal wife, Papa was never able to record any exceptional *personal* accomplishment in his book, whether deeds of arms, diplomacy, or business. He remained a guard captain at Renna's fortress, bringing a paltry four warriors to his lord's service, all that Rowe could support.

Clearly it mattered nothing that I had been born of his blood, had my fingers properly tied into a fist every day for my first year, and was given my first blade at three. My father would never accept me as a true Evanori. And my mother said that even if her family in Palinur found reason to take her back—a highly unlikely occurrence—they would never accept a halfblood daughter. Halfbloods were an abomination in pureblood eyes. I had no choice but to make my own place in the world. That suited me just fine.

"CHEER UP," I SAID TO the small boy, as I removed stitches from his quivering lip and allowed magic to flow through my fingers to discourage further sepsis. "You have a lovely scar that will terrify your every enemy, yet you'll be able to chew your meat without it falling out of your mouth. Your friends will be hugely jealous."

Brightening considerably, he sniffed away his tears and touched the ragged result of an unfortunate meeting of face and tree stump. "Too bad it didn't run crost my eye."

I rolled my eyes as he bolted from the cold, bright tent where my mother held her commons surgery every morning. Another idiot Evanori male in the making.

A tart, prickling fount of magic poured from my mother as she tightened the screws in a steel frame that constricted an agonized warrior's fractured leg. "A tenday more before you put weight on it," she said, aborting the flow of magic and tossing her screw lever onto a tray. "If your commander balks, send him to me. I'll set his toenails rotting into the bone and see how he 'bucks up' and does his duty."

As the man's comrades carried him out, a shaggy drover sidled into the tent. An ugly scabrous growth the size of an apple bulged from his neck.

"Get out, Vert!" yelled my mother. "I told you, it is not a *demon's wart*. Neither fire nor magic can shrink it. And I might as well slit your throat as cut it out now. Remove your filthy self from my tent, and make your peace with whatever god you favor."

As on every day, Vert slunk off and the tent flap fell into place.

"Stupid clod," she snapped. "I could have helped him, but he spent a year trying to pray it away. Then his wife tried to torch it off."

She rummaged in her satchel and pulled out two small wood boxes. "I've a goatherd with the pox next, and you can diagnose Neyla's knee. Focus carefully on the connecting muscle, not just the joint. Perhaps later we'll have something more interesting to study. Marone said there was a woman with the falling sickness coming from Magora Syne. I've spellwork which can ease the rigors."

I didn't care about my studies. Not today. I'd told her of Papa's latest pronouncement.

"What did you see in Papa?" I blurted. "Even if he was the handsomest fellow in all of Navronne, you had to have recognized his mulish nature. He has not the slightest notion of love or intelligence or companionship."

"Count yourself fortunate, Saverian," she said, as she mixed the powders for dosing pox. "You've no idea how restrictive pureblood society is in the rest of the kingdom. All rules and manners and contracts. You've no choice what to wear of a morning, much less what magic to practice or whom to marry. There I was at two-and-twenty, come to these wild mountains, watching Lirene and her kingly warrior defy the world for love, and knowing I'd never have to go back to that life. Such glorious freedom! Under my mistress's protection, I could have any pleasure I wanted. Cynric was the first man I saw. His body was beautiful and he was very eager. And lively.

I didn't care about his mind. Not then…"

No matter all I'd seen in healing practice, it still churned my belly thinking about her and my father … copulating. Though nearing forty, my mother was beautiful in a way I would never be, lithe and graceful with fine-drawn features, her skin like glowing bronze, her long hair heavy and black like liquid night. She wore shirt, tunic, and trousers of russet and canvas queenlier than Osriel's delicate mother had worn silk gowns.

"…and when the dolt commanded me take up sword and shield like a proper Evanori wife, I refused, naturally. Goddess Mother, I *heal* sword wounds. He asserted his privilege as my lord, threatening to flog me for insolence. So, I asserted my status as a pureblood, and told him that anywhere else in Navronne an ordinary like him would be hanged for touching me. He never touched me again, either, which is all to the good. I've had plenty of good fun with more charming men."

She wiped her hands and stuck her head out of the tent. "Next!"

OF COURSE, MY MOTHER'S WORST offense in my father's eye had been her telling Lirene of their argument. The king's mistress had commanded Papa to let Nyxia do as she pleased. He had never forgiven my mother for such disloyalty.

Despite their everlasting rancor, once I left the royal nursery at seven, my mother had sent me back to Rowe. She said halfblood magic would likely not be valuable enough to keep me fed and clothed, and even Rowe was better than no inheritance at all. Papa's failure to produce sons with other women—which she hinted was a matter of her own magical connivance—meant I was destined to be Warlord of Rowe.

My sex, of course, had been but another blow to my father. Evanori did not dispute the gods' choice of a female heir. According to song and story—and Evanori set great stock in song and

story—most female warlords rose to the task, renowned for their wisdom and ferocity in battle. The rest recognized their duty to wed a strong, honorable warrior and then yield him the right of their house. It was considered a noble sacrifice.

I had no more aspiration to be a proper warlord than my mother had to be a proper wife. I'd told my father that I would gladly yield Rowe when the time came. But first I would ensure a decent future by finding a warrior of compatible spirit to make my husband and lord. My parents had rushed into a marriage without respect. I didn't want to make the same mistake.

Alas, my father's greatest hope for a third accomplishment to enter in his book rested in my marriage to Eodward's bastard son—a bond to the blood of holy Caedmon. That dream was taking a long time to die, which was most annoying, as he would not consider introducing me to other men. Thus, on the day following our conversation, when Papa bade me forego my day's work with *that woman* so that we might sign the betrothal settlement with my future husband, I near choked on my morning apple.

"Papa, you can't mean this. *Fillol?* Your man-at-arms?"

He gazed out of Rowe's finest feature—a window that was not an arrow loop. The small rectangle contained a thick pane of wavy glass that reduced the majestic, ice-streaked cliffs of Dashon Ra to a blue-white blur. "He's a good man. The best fighter I have. Modest and honorable. *Loyal.*"

"I'm sure he is." The words squeezed between my teeth. Outrage constricted my breast so fiercely I could scarce breathe, for I knew Daegle Fillol. "But you would wed your only daughter to a man who brags that he cannot *read* and will never do so. One who has never walked so far as Caedmon's Bridge to look on the rest of Navronne, and never wishes to. Who refuses to join in tale-telling at your fireside because stories, even those of Evanore's greatest glories, are *tedious.* You expect me to yield him the lord's right, making a person

of such…limitations…heir to Rowe? Is this the best warlord you can offer Prince Osriel, the sovereign duc of Evanore?"

I'd never seen my father so cold. "My heir needs to consider her responsibilities before her diversions. The longer we wait, the harder, the more intractable, you'll become. Like *that woman*. Few enough men want a connection to a halfblood Aurellian. You'll end up lone and my line will end. I won't have it. Daegal Fillol is the best of my warriors. He sired healthy children with his first wife. What's more, he's willing."

"I'm not." No man would get a child on me without me wanting it so.

I might have been a gnat in Papa's ear. "The fool would speak with you alone before we sign the settlement. He waits in the well-yard. Be warned: If he turns less willing after this meeting, I will chain your feet to this house, mute your tongue, and set you such drudgery that you forget the ways of human life. I'm finished with your preening, Saverian. You may be only half a sorceress, but your insufferable conceit would outmatch any pureblood in Navronne save *that woman*. Three days from this I will watch you take Daegle to your bed and spread your legs."

I wanted to scream. To smash the ugly glass. To pull his war banners, shields, and spears from the wall and shove them through the ridiculous window along with his history of mediocrity. But horror at his plan, and the fear that this time he meant exactly what he said, bade me behave. For the moment.

I dipped my knee. "As you say, Lord Cynric."

Cheeks afire, I marched down the hall stair and through a buttery and guardroom. Papa's houndsman stared as I shoved through the doors into the heavy stillness of the morning. We'd see a storm by nightfall.

Wit said I should leave Rowe until I could clear my head and make a plan, but fury insisted I make things clear with one man at least.

My prospective husband waited in the cramped inner yard, where an ancient well provided Rowe's salvation in time of siege. A black-bearded, stumpy man of something twice my age, Daegle Fillol carried himself most warrior-like. Strong, confident, but not overbearing.

"Warrior Fillol, with respect, there is no inducement sufficient—"

"Pardon my interruption, mistress, but I must speak first, making two things clear. Though this elevation is none of my aspiration, intent, or conspiring, I will not betray my lord by refusing it. If this union comes to pass, I *will* consort with thee in his presence to breed an heir to Rowe." He raised his hand for pause as my skull threatened to burst. "But I do swear on Caedmon's shield that I'll neither tease nor cozen nor so much as raise my eye ta thee in wishing without thy saying. Before that event, and ever after, I'll sleep only where you allow and keep entirely to my duties, intruding on none of thine."

If there had been a bench nearby, I would have sunk to it, mouth agape. Was the man mad or did he believe me so? I'd grown up around men like him.

Sucking air through my teeth, I said, "I appreciate your plain speaking, sirrah, and will honor you with the same. You know this match is not well considered…that we are such opposite spirits we could never in the world make a decent life together…that I despise the very thought of it. Yet you'd do it anyway, and once we…breed… an heir, you would live celibate forever?"

"Aye. Certain of all that." His black curls quivered with pride. "I've a daughter a few seasons older than you, mistress. Never would I do to her what my lord proposes, but I am a loyal son of Evanore. My lord's word commands me."

I turned tail and ran for the stables.

"KATJE, COULD YOU ANNOUNCE ME to Master de Vallé, the Navron historian? I bring a message. From my father."

My fingers clenched and twisted as the innkeeper's daughter vanished upstairs. I'd never done anything so rash. I was the daughter of a warlord and a pureblood sorceress, and I was the only person in all of Evanore who had ever claimed to be the reclusive Prince Osriel's friend. No one in Evanore would dare assist me, but neither would they interfere. And I felt I already knew more of this stranger than of Osriel or either of my parents. Far more than I knew of the man I was to marry. I was but sixteen and my friends were books. That's how I'd come to meet Merton de Vallé-Cuiron.

A TENDAY SINCE, I'D GONE to fetch new books from Prince Osriel's library. A young man as comely and sleek as a mountain cat had been cooling his heels in the foyer, awaiting audience with the prince. He had journeyed all the way from the city of Montesard, he'd told me, intent on collecting tales of Evanore's history. Carrying impeccable credentials from the university, he'd never imagined it would be so difficult to get Prince Osriel's permission to travel his realm. "I've heard the prince is a scholarly youth."

"He is," I said, hefting my rucksack filled with three small codices and a rolled map, "but of late—"

Just then the servant brought the expected rejection—his fifth. As we exited Osriel's residence, de Vallé asked politely if I might tell him how to reach a good vantage where he could view the whole of Renna, as the day was so fine and he could not yet pursue his investigations.

Well-versed in my mother's disdain of Navron ordinaries—especially scholarly ones—I was surprised at his winsome nature. So instead of just telling him of the view from Howl's Hill, I climbed it with him.

He made notes and sketches in his journal as I pointed out features on the climb. When we rested at the top, he asked what I carried. We sat on the weather-smoothed stones of a ruined wall

and I showed him the map of western Ardra—the central province of the kingdom—and the little codex that told of a wild western tribe called the Aponavi. That led to a discussion of history and its strange windings. When I pulled out the beautifully illuminated little bestiary, we talked of birds and their magical migrations, and whether it was possible that gryphons and dragons might actually exist. Once he recovered from his amazement that I was daughter of a pureblood and an Evanori warlord, a halfblood sorceress who had shared a nursery with the king's bastard son, we spoke of magic.

My mother had warned me never to speak of magic with ordinaries, but Merton was respectful and a historian, knowledgeable about every aspect of the world. No one had ever bothered to ask me what it *felt* like when I raised power or whether I ever succumbed to awe when I willed magic to flow through my fingertips and alter the truth of nature.

"I must add you to my list of interviews," he'd said, as he sketched the view of the ancient fortress called Renna Major, the separate royal residence called Renna Syne, and the scattered village between them. "To explore the rare intersection of two such strong, isolated cultures is a historian's fairest dream."

When I blurted that he did not need Prince Osriel's permission to interview me at any time, we'd both flushed at my boldness and then burst out laughing. He expressed impatience for our next meeting. Every moment since, I'd felt the same. I'd never imagined a man so fair, so intelligent, so well spoken.

"MISTRESS SAVERIAN!" MERTON HURRIED DOWN the inn's rickety stair, still buttoning his doublet of gold-threaded brocade. He was surely a wealthy man; only Osriel's mother had worn fabrics so fine. Though truly his deep-hued skin and graceful form would have looked well in slops. Unlike Evanori men, his well-sculpted jaw was clean-shaven, which made him look younger than my estimate

of five- or six-and-twenty. "Such a marvelous surprise on this chill morning! And a message from the lord of Rowe, as well…"

I could not miss either his particular phrasing or the genuine spark in his dark eyes.

"Might I ask you to walk out with me?" I said, lowering my gaze so that he—or any of the inn's patrons—would not witness how that spark warmed my own heart. I alone would choose what payment to make for his aid. "My lord's message is not for common ears."

"Certainly, mistress. A guardsman told me that tower ruin yonder would give a fine view of the depleted gold works behind the fortress. I've hopes Prince Osriel might allow me to walk there, as such places can give a sense of times past. But until then, might a walk to this ruin suffice?"

"Yes. Good." Any place away from prying ears.

Merton threw his cloak about his shoulders and escorted me out, not speaking until we were away from the street and curious eyes.

"Now," he said, solemnly, as we climbed a steep, rocky track up to the crumbling watchtower. "Is there a message?"

"No. Forgive my rudeness, but I am desperate for friendly advice, and my position in Renna—neither entirely Evanori nor entirely alien—makes it difficult for me to seek it."

"That's not surprising," he said. He did not offer me his arm, which I approved as recognition that this was business, not flirtation.

"Sir, *very* ill consequences could result if any hint of what I say goes beyond this meeting."

My father's threats were not idle. He had the right to do exactly as he said, and I was no warrior mage who could defend herself against armed soldiers.

Prince Osriel could exert his authority on my behalf, of course. The prince and I were not exactly enemies. The last time I'd seen my old playfriend, his attention had been consumed by magic that left my soul cold and sick. We had argued, and I'd sworn not to

return until he forsook whatever he pursued. Quietly stubborn, he had commanded me to leave and not come back. Now, his mere presence shook my unshakeable mother.

"I swear discretion," said Merton, "and I am humbled…and most pleased…that you would trust me with your confidence."

"My mother says—that is, I need to know whether it is true that halfblood sorcerers are despised or maltreated elsewhere in Navronne. If one were to travel there, would that person be allowed to live free? To use magic? It has been almost eighteen years since my mother came to Evanore, where the rules for sorcerers are more relaxed."

My companion nodded soberly, as he picked a careful way up the rocky hillside. "My observations and my studies of history have shown me that pureblood society evolves slowly, if at all. Halfbloods are required to report yearly to the Pureblood Registry and are officially discouraged from using whatever magical talents they possess. They are ignored by the families whose blood they share, and oft forbidden to reside near that family's holdings. *However*, I am personally acquainted with several halfbloods who have found most excellent situations with employers powerful enough to shield them from the Registry's harassment. I've no doubt that others flourish in smaller towns and villages where there is no Registry presence to interfere. Thus, taking up a new life outside of Evanore could certainly be a reasonable, if not risk-free, choice, for a halfblood with sufficient reason to attempt it. Does that answer your questions?"

"Yes." We walked in silence as I churned through possibilities and alternatives.

I appreciated Merton's clarity, and that he spoke to me as an equal, not patronizing me with warnings or suggestions, as if a woman was too dim-witted to see difficulties on her own. Nor did he presume to probe further. Of course, he likely recognized that if I'd brought such a dangerous question to a stranger, I had nowhere else to turn.

"My father is a man of tradition," I said, at last, and with only a smattering of guilt, I told the historian the entirety of my dilemma.

By the time I concluded the sordid tale, I knew what I had to do. "I will not sell my future to conceive an heir for a wretched hold of rocks and goats, but I'd prefer not to spend my life mute, chained, and scrubbing cesspits, either."

"He wouldn't!" Merton's shock outstripped my own.

"He can and he will. Thus, I would ask if it might be possible—it would put you in dreadful danger, and you don't really know me, but I've no one else. To set out on a month-long journey alone into strange country, into cities, when I've never actually crossed Caedmon's Bridge out of Evanore…"

My stammering trailed off, as his back sagged against the rubble foundation of the ancient tower and his well-proportioned eyes stared at me in horror.

"You want me to smuggle a *warlord's daughter* out of Evanore? Mistress, this is a bit more serious than confidential advice!"

My skin heated to an approximation of a midsummer bonfire.

"Stupid. Stupid, yes. How could I have—?"

Goddess Mother, I had lost my wits entire. I wanted to vanish, to mime the legends of the earth's guardian Danae by dissolving into the ground. But all I could do was back away from him, turn, and leave.

"Forgive me, sir. Forget everything I said. I am a presumptuous lack wit."

I had stumbled only twenty paces down the track, when his laughter rolled down the hill behind me. "Certain, I'll escort you into civilization. What an adventure!"

AS THE CHILLY MIDDAY BLUSTERED past, we sat atop the watchtower, careful, for wind and ice had ground the crenellated parapet to rubble. We worked at a plan to get me away cleanly without im-

plicating Merton. I'd only three days until my bedding, but for those three days, no one would care where I was. I could tell my mother I was placating my father with a tour of his demesne. I could tell my father that my mother needed help with an outbreak of the pox at Magora Syne—a remote fortress. Three days was time enough to meet Merton at Caedmon's Bridge, the crossing that linked Evanore to the rest of Navronne, and get a good head start on the northern road. The only problem was Merton's mission.

"If we just had more time," he said, regretfully. "A generous patron has funded this expedition, and to leave with nothing ... without seeing Angor Nav, the fortress heart of the Great Siege, or without walking Dashon Ra, where your father's ancestors stripped out enough gold to build an Aurellian palace..."

A hawk soared above us as Merton's graceful fingers sketched the broken parapet in his book. He said drawing helped him work out complex puzzles. "Where did all the gold go? Why is Dashon Ra deemed haunted? Was it true that the miners refused to sleep there? How did the warlords and King Caedmon hold off Aurellian sorcerers for half a century with such devastating loss that the invaders gave up? So many questions. To write a true history of Evanore is my life's work."

How could I expect a man to risk his life's work for a girl he'd met exactly twice?

"I can help a little," I offered. "I've listened at firesides my whole life. As my father's heir, I sit behind him at the warmoot twice a year, where the history and legends of Evanore are repeated endlessly. My memory is exceptional—part of my healer's gift. Certainly, my information would not be the same as visiting these sites or speaking to elders, but I've visited almost every place of importance. There's likely only one person who could tell you more of the actual battles and the stranger things, like hauntings and Dashon Ra—" My mouth slammed shut.

Merton was beaming. "This is marvelous, mistress! Our first conversation should have told me that you were exactly the resource I needed. I wasn't even sure that warmoots were real. Perhaps a few hours with this other person to cover what you cannot…and then you could be free and I could repay my patron's generosity."

"He won't meet with you." Stupid to think of Osriel. A hundred times in the first year after our break, I had applied to see him. He had refused every time.

"Perhaps if he understood. Other Navrons fear unconquerable Evanore. What makes this place so different? The mountains? The hardship? Demons? Would it not bring our kingdom into better harmony if we learned the truth of our shared past? For me, the future is the truest work of history."

Prince Osriel would never be king. He had always been sickly; his mother and mine had nursed him through illness after illness. And though, on rare royal visits, I had witnessed the love good Eodward held for his youngest, Osriel had two healthy elder half-brothers, both born from legitimate marriages. Yet I believed the prince I'd once known, and King Eodward himself, would relish and approve Merton's vision of history.

"He won't," I said, sighing, "but I'll ask."

HIS GRACE, PRINCE OSRIEL, HAS no hour to spare for visiting historians, however visionary.

I glared at the abrupt response to my application. It wasn't even Osriel's handwriting. And I had worked for an hour on the damnable query, agonizing over whether to include a mention of my marriage dilemma. I'd chosen not. Rather I framed the visit as a matter of state importance to let the true history of Evanore be written. After so many personal refusals, there seemed a better chance he'd admit Merton alone.

"I'm sorry. I thought he might relent if it was just for you and

not me." Of course, I'd counted on Merton to lay out my dilemma for the prince, once they met.

Merton sat on the rim of a cistern halfway between the great battlements of Renna Major and the lesser walls of Renna Syne, the more modern, graceful residence the king had built for Lirene and Osriel. His journal open on his lap, Merton was sketching the sloping road that seemed to drop into an abyss between Renna's plateau and the ridge to the north of us. Evanori knew where to build their fortifications.

"Onward to our plan, then," he said, closing the book with a snap. "You're right we should leave separately. Tomorrow, I'll finish what little business I've done here and arrange for a pack horse and provisions enough to get us as far as Elanus. At dawn the day after, I'll meet you at Caedmon's Bridge and we'll ride north like the summer wind."

He hesitated. "You're sure about this journey? About leaving your home?"

"I detest sleeping out, but I'm capable. I detest the fuss of horses, but I can keep them moving and healthy. I can't stay here." A cold raindrop took that moment to splat on my nose. Nature's mockery. "Are *you* sure?"

"Quite sure." His grin should have made the raindrop turn to steam, but it vanished quickly. He understood his danger. "I value rarities, mistress. My honor is pledged to protect them. I will see you safe to your chosen destination."

"Dawn of the second day from this," I said and we gripped wrists in agreement. My skin warmed at his touch.

Trumpet blasts and barked orders announced the guard change at the fortress gates, so we separated quickly, before anyone could note our meeting. Merton pulled up his hood and vanished into the rain. I headed for the town stables to fetch my mare. Leaving now, I could be at Rowe before nightfall to gather my kit, and head out

before rain turned the road entirely to slop.

Every passing moment made this venture look more foolhardy. If Papa got wind of my leaving before I got to the bridge, he'd have me in irons. If he suspected Merton's aid, he'd gut him. It wasn't fair.

The gates of Osriel's house swallowed the party of fresh guardsmen and spat out those going off duty.

Damnable Osriel. All he had to do was command my father to leave me choose my own path. Papa would obey. He would curse me for betrayal as he had my mother, but I would be free of his odious alternatives.

If I could just speak to the prince face to face. Surely my one-time friend, no matter how morbid his turn of mind since his beloved mother's death, would not abandon me to Daegle Fillol.

But how to reach him? My written petitions were certainly not compelling. The guards at Renna dared not disobey his orders. My mother called Voushanti, Osriel's bodyguard, the Hand of Magrog the Tormentor. My mother …

I abruptly reversed course and sped back to my mother's house, a fine little guesthouse just outside Renna Syne's wall. She wasn't home. *Good.*

My mother's back door opened directly into Osriel's garden, giving her access to her most important patient at any time. But only when she was summoned. The door was locked and spell warded from the garden side. I had once known how to open that door. Osriel and I had sneaked through it many times, back when we were children and knew nothing of consequences.

My fingers touched the latch. Spellwork tickled like feathers, then pricked, so light you almost didn't notice the first drops of blood. The magical feathers had barbs. I whispered the password and fed power into the brass latch-plate, unwinding the spiraling enchantment until the metal grew warm. Exactly as I remembered. The prickling ceased. All I had to do was push the door open and walk through.

My hand hesitated. This would work only once; they'd change the ward when they discovered me. Merton had offered to risk his life's ambition to save my own. How could I do less in return?

I restored the latch ward without opening the door. In case my plan went awry—Osriel would likely throw us out after all—I left Mama a note, telling her of my plan to appease my father's marriage idiocy by touring his demesne. She never argued my plans. Never sent for me. Certainly, she never visited Rowe. She assumed that if I wanted to learn what she could teach, I would come to her. I left the message on her table where she'd be sure to see it. More optimistic than I'd been since Papa had called me into his study the previous morning, I set out to find Merton.

THE INN WAS MOST INVITING. Falling night and rainy gloom made the lantern light sparkle and the smoke tease of soup, hot bread, and mead to warm one's insides. I'd been foolish to show myself there more than once, inquiring after Master de Vallé the historian, so I rounded back to the alley and raced up the outer stair.

The inn had one private room and one that was shared among all comers. I picked Merton for the private, thus the window on the left of the landing. My well-honed latch-lifting spell had the shutters open without a creak.

"Merton," I whispered, as I squinted into the not-quite-dark. "Good sir."

He wasn't there, but I smelled him—an indefinable mingling of soap, skin, smoke, and what my physician's mind had categorized as *clean male*. Goddess knew I'd smelled enough of the other kind.

I climbed in, enjoying the thought of my father's horror at his virgin daughter sneaking into a man's room. Raising pale magelight from my fingers, I searched for paper and pen. I'd leave Merton a message clear enough to lead him to my mother's house, while cryptic enough to prevent anyone else deciphering it. Then, I'd figure out

how to get my mother out of the way.

Merton's journal lay on a scrubbed pine table, alongside a candle-stick clotted with ten years' melted wax and oddments like pens, ink bottle, a small pouch of sand, a stick of wax, an ivory comb, and a silk handkerchief. Thinking to use a page for my message, I ruffled through the book. Every leaf was blank.

This was certainly his journal, scuffed black leather stitched with red. Was it possible...?

My mother had taught me little of magic beyond healing. She believed it a waste of time for a halfblood. But Osriel and I, *both* halfbloods, had learned whatever we could, like door wards and lock magic, fire magic, and how to hide secrets or expose them.

I recalled a little spell we had devised, infused it with my will, and summoned power. Resting my hand on the journal, I swept away the subtle hiding spell that had lurked beyond my perceptions. Half the small book was filled with sketches and notes, scribed in his elegant hand.

Only a sorcerer could lock and unlock such spells.

Merton was a sorcerer! He'd never even hinted at it.

I didn't like that. Yet, he'd not known where my true loyalties lay. If word got out that he was pureblood, no true Evanori would ever have spoken to him, much less told him tales.

The journal's last-written page depicted me, sitting on the cistern rim beside him. No one had ever done a portrait of me. Plain, bony, wind-scoured. Unlovely. I'd have expected nothing else. But determined, too, and looking as if I had a decent mind. I liked that he saw me that way. Behind me he'd sketched in the road from the valley and the fortress battlements, and alongside made notations of heights, and guard positions atop the walls, and the time of the guard change.

Something deep inside my belly shifted. Uneasy.

I paged more carefully through the parchment leaves. His

sketches were more polished than I'd realized: the fortress gates with details of height, materials, and position, estimates of internal fortification, the number and times of guard changes. The view from Howl's Hill was refined to a map of the village, with the fortress, Osriel's residence, stables, barracks, inn, bakery, and shops neatly labeled. The sketch of the watchtower detailed its position and distance from the village. Vacant, he had noted, and unvisited over five-and-thirty days. My five can shelter there. No new or active goldworks evident atop Dashon Ra.

My skin heated. Breath came short.

Another page listed neighboring demesnes and their descriptions. Rowe was noted as meager, unproductive, unthreatening. Four warriors listed, along with a lord who has spent ten years as a minor guard captain. No matter that I'd spoken worse, my jaw clenched in shame. And fury.

A sorcerer. A *spy*. Not three hours since, I had volunteered to tell Merton everything of Evanore's history. I had come here to invite him through a back door, straight into my prince's house.

Stupid. Blind. Naive. Idiot.

Personal humiliation was unimportant beside the dangers, both the one I had just avoided and what remained. Who had sent him here?

One ear on the inner stair, I read from the beginning, details of the routes to Renna from Caedmon's Bridge, conversations he'd overheard at the tavern about Prince Osriel's strange behaviors, rumors of his dead-raising, of demonic rites, and of the odd halfblood girl who had played with him as a child.

When I thought anger had swollen in me beyond bearing, I came upon a sketch of my mother. Naked. Smiling in the way she did when she spoke of her "good fun" with men. I wanted to vomit.

Merton had written notes about her, too:

Nyxia of Rowe, once Nyxia de Soutre-Sala, age 38, estranged wife of Cynric of Rowe, trusted physician of Prince Osriel, as re-

ported. Heals all comers with full use of her pureblood healing. Clever. Willing, as her family told us, but insists on conditions. Fear inhibits usefulness.

Willing to do what, other than take her pleasure with Merton de Vallé? Had she been in contact with her family? She hated Evanore and Osriel terrified her. What might she do to return to her comfortable life as a Navron pureblood? Grace of the Mother, she formulated Osriel's medicines...

A more recent note had been added below the first.

Saverian of Rowe: age 16. Disaffected daughter. Halfblood; strong bent for healing, weakness in other magic (per Nyxia). Self-educated; bright. Possible access. Naive. Malleable.

Malleable! *Goddess Mother, gut the arrogant, conniving beast.*

I was half out of the window, the damning journal in my hand, when I realized that was but another idiot's move. The moment Merton saw it missing, he would run. He must not get out of Evanore.

Back inside, I positioned the journal carefully. Rebuilt its hiding spell. Touched both spell and journal with a spark of magic and breathed on it—another trick Osriel and I had perfected. No sorcerer could detect that Saverian of Rowe had touched either one.

Terrified he would return before I'd set things right, I sought another way to leave him a message. On the tousled bed lay the scrap of parchment with Osriel's refusal. I scraped the parchment with my knife and wrote:

Friend, Find your way to my mother's house at middle night. I know how to unlock a private door to all the answers you crave. Silly of me to forget childhood capers. Freedom awaits us—and glorious history.
Ever in your debt,
S.

I left it on his pillow, as any stupid, besotted girl would.

THE STORM HAD GROWN TO frenzy. Gales howled about Renna Major, as if Aurellian ghosts had arrived to raise the Great Siege yet again. Rain sheeted across the hillside, obscuring all but sparking glimpses of the fortress's wind-crazed watchfires. Renna Syne, though—Osriel's house—sat serenely dark behind its walls, an eerie quiet in the midst of chaos, as if the dead spirits my childhood friend hoped to conjure had laid a pall over it.

I watched from the branches of the apple tree in a corner of my mother's garden as a child rang her bell, summoning her to the woman whose knee I had repaired the previous day. My mother hated visiting commoners' homes, and most times passed the duty to me. Sometimes I thought that was the only reason she had trained me. But my note had reminded her that she'd have to answer calls while I toured my father's demesne, especially for Neyla who could be crippled forever if the healing I'd done was flawed. Healing-wise, my reputation was my mother's reputation. It was all she had here, with Lirene dead and Osriel so distant. Useful.

The child scampered home, my copper in his pocket. A short time later, my mother, cloaked, walked out. Would she go all the way to Neyla's bedside half a quellé south? Perhaps she would suspect the summons a ruse to get her out of her house and stay close.

Either way, I could play my role of the foolish, *malleable* daughter. I hoped the other pieces of my plan were well set. I'd not been idle in the hours since leaving the message on Merton's bed. My father captained the guard at Renna Major this night. For the first time in many years, I had paid him a visit at his post. Now, shivering in the wet, I waited for midnight.

At the second quarter bells from the fortress tower, a small party of guardsmen marched from the fortress across the hillside to Renna Syne, as they did every night at this hour. Orders and bootsteps were drowned by the rain. A small party returned to the fortress. As ever.

This was the critical time. If a rock-headed Evanori guard cap-

tain had believed his fool of a disaffected daughter …

At the third quarter bells, a dark shape—Merton's shape—pushed through the garden gate and slipped behind the lattice work sheltering my mother's herb garden. Time to move.

I dropped outside the garden wall, the thrash of the wind in leafless branches covering my movements. Then, I circled around to the same gate he had entered. My back shivered as I passed his hiding place, forcing myself not to look.

I tapped quietly on the door, calling, "Mama?" Three repetitions with no answer and I pushed open her door and walked in. When Merton's hand fell on my shoulder, it required no playacting to spin in my tracks.

"Good sir! I didn't hear you!"

"I'd no intent you should. Is this what I think? You promised answers, but I never imagined they would come from the prince himself." His beaming face and eager humility near sapped my will.

"Osriel and I used this door a hundred times when we were children," I said. "We called it our door to freedom—from his monkish tutors, from my mother who spent all the day in his house, from studies and practice and sickness. We would climb hills, steal mead, and do all the things ordinary children did. One day when we were out, he fell ill and I had to run for help. I refused to tell them how we'd gotten out. It was not so long after that his mother sickened…and things were never the same."

Merton pushed the outer door shut, but not all the way. A signal? Would my mother join us?

"What will he say when you barge into his house with a Navron ordinary, a stranger?"

I clasped the liar's hand resting on my shoulder, and brought it to my breast. "The reply I got earlier didn't sound at all like Osriel. It wasn't his handwriting. It came to me that perhaps his fearsome bodyguard was purposefully keeping him from reading my inquiries.

So, after I left you this afternoon, I looked up one of his favored guards who was our confederate back in those days. I begged a private midnight audience in memory of our long friendship, at a *door long forbidden*. I said my father had threatened my life."

"And this time, you think—"

"Not half an hour since, I received his answer. The prince said he needed *a diversion from dancing with the dead* and would come alone to meet me. The last time I saw him, I told him I would never go beyond his library again until he needed diversion from dancing with the dead." The last part, at least was true.

"What does he *do* in there? What is *dancing with the dead?*"

The pulse in Merton's hand raced. I had him.

"I'll tell you as we ride north. Tonight is for history and Navronne. You are willing to risk your future for me. I am doing the same."

The fortress bells rang midnight.

As I touched the brass latch of the garden door, Merton's wet cloak rustled behind me. His hand returned to my shoulder, heavier this time. The smell of honed steel was not my imagination.

I pushed the door open. Dark and rain greeted us. They smelled of wet pine bark, of dry rosemary and rue, scents wakened by the moisture. A slender form, gray against the blackness, stood alone across the small courtyard. He'd grown taller. Eighteen now. A man.

I tried not to feel, not to see what my old playmate brought with him. The shadows behind him squirmed and slid across the stone…extended fingers into the deeper darks in the corners of the little garden…twisted despair, sorrow, and magic into shapes that tainted the soul.

"Ah, Saverian, you said we were to be alone."

Osriel's cold anger shrouded mind and limb, crushing me to the ground. Surely my plan had fallen to ruin. He blamed me …

A cloaked figure rushed from behind me, poisonous magic

crackling from sword and hand—Merton. But not alone. Others rushed behind him. Boots stepped on my hair, trampled my hand. Steel crashed on steel.

I threw my arms over my head. This was wrong. My father had said he'd come. Merton should have been captive in moments. Too late, I recalled the journal mention—*my five*, who could shelter in the ruined tower. *Idiot girl.* I'd not imagined he had five comrades with him already.

Thuds, grunts, and clashes broke out on every side. A man screamed. Another moaned.

I wrested my dagger from its sheath and lunged upward. Blazing orange light outlined battling duels and fallen bodies. Red fire gleamed from demonic eyes—Voushanti, Osriel's bodyguard, overpowering an opponent. I planted my dagger in a dark-clad thug who was choking a man in fortress livery.

"Saverian! Look out!" A bolt of magic slammed me to the ground. Then cold, slender hands hauled me across slick paving stones and sodden plants. Osriel's voice and hands.

"Thank—"

A different voice, graveled with murder, interrupted me, bellowing, "Warlord of Rowe! Keep that man alive or your bowels will burn instead of his."

Silence fell as sudden as sunrise. It was over.

Arching my bruised back, I scrambled to my knees. Voushanti plunged his sword into a writhing man. Four guardsmen surrounded my father, who held Merton de Vallé by his hair. Papa's bloody knife pricked de Vallé's throat. A bloody slash crossed each of Merton's cheeks, brow to chin. Another Rowe tradition.

One guardsman and five others lay dead. None of the dead were Osriel, which relieved me.

None were my mother. I wasn't sure how I felt about that.

Man-at-arms Fillol, blood dripping from a gash on his brow,

lifted one of the dead men by his hair and nodded to me, as if serving up the corpse as a betrothal gift. I retched into the crushed herb garden.

MY MOTHER WAS CAPTURED HALFWAY to Caedmon's Bridge. She bore a writ from the Pureblood Registry that she was pardoned of all crimes and indiscretions and forever free to practice magic in all of Navronne. Her family was relieved of all burden of her youthful rebellion and could negotiate her future contracts as they wished. Alas, as she was yet in Evanore when apprehended, the laws of my father's demesne held sway, not to mention the laws of her sovereign, Prince Osriel, whom she had conspired to murder. My father beheaded her at the roadside.

Papa did not tell me this. Our houndsman did, on a morning a few days after the event, as I walked out to clear my head and contemplate the future.

Merton de Vallé—what was left of him after Mardane Voushanti's questioning and his execution, which was not so much—hung from the battlements at Renna Major. I erased all memory of our conversations from my mind. The man I knew had been a lie. Voushanti had sent to me, asking if I had mitigating evidence to present before final sentencing. I'd said no.

ON A SUNNY MORNING, WHEN the air was perfectly clear as only happens after a storm, I was summoned to my father's study for the first time since the incident at Renna Syne.

"*That woman* is dead," he said.

"So I've heard."

"She had promised to tell the spy everything she knew of the prince and Evanore's defenses, once they were safe across the bridge. Then you…I still don't know how you came to know the spy…to know what he planned."

I offered nothing.

He cleared his throat. "You must tell me of your dealings with the man."

"No. I'll tell Prince Osriel if he asks. He can decide what others hear."

"That's fitting," he said, surprised. "But you must tell me if the spy *compromised* your person in any way? Daegle asked me."

"No."

The relief poured out of him, as tangible as Osriel's unhealthy magics. "You showed great loyalty to your prince and to our house that night. In reward, you may set which day of the coming month will see your vows and first coupling. Daegle awaits your word."

"I will not marry Daegle Fillol, Papa."

He rose from his chair, fire blossoming on his visage. "I warned you—"

"I have given you a third entry for *The Book of Rowe*," I said. "You can write that you rescued Prince Osriel on the day an assassin plotted his death. Elaborate your role as you see fit. For myself, I have filed a writ with Prince Osriel's secretary that I intend to remain unmarried and childless until the day of your death, and that upon that day, when I assume the title of Warlord of Rowe, I will yield all right to this demesne to my sovereign prince in thanksgiving for his survival."

"You *what?*"

"*The Book of Rowe* will conclude with me. I will choose my own way in this life, now and forever."

MY FATHER THREW ME OUT of his house. What I had done was unthinkable to any true Evanori. Yet, he had won a victory of a sort.

My mother thought she could buy a new life with secrets she had no right to tell. Her pureblood lover thought he could buy his fortune with a foolish girl's dreams. No matter how granite-headed

he was, my father's aims were clear. He lived by his rules and did not hide them. I liked his way—the Evanori way—better.

On the afternoon of the day I abandoned my father's house, I presented myself at Renna Syne, the little palace King Eodward had built to house his beloved and their son. The ginger-bearded guard knew me well.

"Greetings of the Mother, Philo. I've come to use the prince's library. I bid you deliver him another message. Perhaps today, he'll heed it."

"Aye, mistress."

"Call me Saverian, as I am mistress of nothing and no one. Tell the prince that I understand he is in need of a new physician. I am applying for the position. Though of small experience, I am intelligent, studious, and everlastingly loyal."

The soldier opened the gate, not quite suppressing a shudder. "Guess he knew. His Grace left word that did you come, we should bring you to him straightaway."

I nodded and walked through, ready to serve my dark lord, loyal until my last breath.

CHING SHIH

WHEN WE THINK OF PIRATES, one of the first names that usually pops into people's mind is Blackbeard. Blackbeard was considered one of the most feared and famed pirates. He commanded four ships and some three hundred men in the early 1700s. Compare that, however, with Ching Shih.

Ching Shih started life as a Cantonese prostitute in the late 1700s. When she was 26, Chinese pirate Cheng I married her. Legend has it he pursued her because she had a mind well-suited for business and he admired her ways of manipulating people of high social and political standing. Ching Shih's name means "Cheng's widow," and that's what she would become only six years later.

Most other women would have faded into the background, perhaps going back to prostitution, or falling into an even darker fate, but Ching Shih shrewdly managed to gain control of her late husband's infamous Red Flag Fleet. It couldn't have been easy. While there wasn't the superstition in China that women were unlucky on ships, as there was in the Western world, women were the distinct minority in pirate fleets. Commanding the not hundreds, but *thousands*, of outlaws that made up the Red Flag Fleet would have been

challenging even for the toughest of men. Ching Shih unified her fleet under a strict code. Anyone caught giving their own commands or disobeying a superior was beheaded on the spot.

Qing dynasty officials, the Portuguese navy, and the East India Trading Company (EITC) all tried—and failed—to stop Ching Shih's Red Flag Fleet. Richard Glasspoole of the EITC was captured by Ching Shih in 1809, and upon his release reported that she had 80,000 pirates under her command, with 1,000 large junk ships and 800 smaller ships and boats. Now think about the fearsome Blackbeard's four ships. Most men wouldn't have been able to command a fleet of outlaws that size!

<hr/>

Further Reading:

"The Chinese Female Pirate Who Commanded 80,000 Outlaws" by Urvija Banerji, *Atlas Obscura http://www.atlasobscura.com/articles/the-chinese-female-pirate-who-commanded-80000-outlaws*

SHE KEEPS CRAWLING BACK

DELILAH S. DAWSON

I'M WALKING DOWN THE EMPTY sidewalk when this crazy bitch pops out of a boarded-up bodega and grabs for my suitcase. "Hey, that's—" I start, yanking the handle back.

"If you want to see the inside of a croc's belly or the underside of a giant robot's foot, just keep standing on the sidewalk and yelling," she says, real low. "You've got bad timing."

She doesn't let go of the handle, her dinged-up brown fingers snug against mine. For a moment, we're trapped there, playing tug of war with our eyes and a mostly-empty secondhand Samsonite. I look her up and down. She's in her thirties, not quite pretty but wiry with this honest, determined energy, like she's the kind of person who gets bored in a Jazzercise class. Dark skin, dark hair shaved close, no makeup, tight-fitted tee, cargo pants with stuffed pockets. Her boots are beat to hell and dripping wet, but it's dry as a bone in August. When our eyes meet again, it's like a bolt of heat lightning.

"For serious, girl," she hisses. "Get in here."

I tighten my grip and look up the street. I'm two blocks from the Civilian Conservation Corps barracks, some building they're renting cheap after the Wall Street cats split. Right where it should be, there's an orange cone with a sign stuck in it. CCC SAFE ZONE, it says. The skyscraper is half gone, and it doesn't look particularly safe.

Then I hear it. A rhythmic pumping like a jet engine interspersed with a jackhammer.

I have seconds to choose: government-offered safety or crazy but intriguing girl?

What the hell. Crazy girl wins.

"Fine," I say. "Lead the way."

She rolls her eyes, releases the suitcase handle, and holds open the door. The room inside is dark, but it doesn't look like a bodega. It's a gym—and not the Jazzercise kind. I hurry inside, dodging giant tires and huge weights, and she locks the plywood-covered door behind us.

"This your first time?" she asks, cool as hell.

"My first time for what?"

"In New York since the fights started."

I shake my head. "First time here ever. I hear it was nice, once."

"Once," she agrees. "So, you wanna watch?"

"Watch...?" I look around the room doubtfully.

She snorts and pops out her hip. "The fight."

"How do you know there's going to be one?"

"Because the crocs are creatures of habit and the robots are punctual dicks. Here they come."

I pick up what she means a beat later. The noise outside has gotten louder, and now there's another noise. The machine—that's obviously a robot. And the scraping rasp has got to be what the robot wants.

"Hurry, or you'll miss it." She holds open another door, revealing a dark stairwell. "Just leave your bag. Nobody here wants your pajamas."

I pause too long, and she goes up without me. I guess she knows I'm curious, as I catch the door and follow her up. It must be where she lives. It's spare but tidy, just like I imagined a New York apartment would look like. High ceilings, tall windows, a bathtub serving as the kitchen table with a door laid overtop.

"Over here."

As I walk to the window, I run a gentle palm over the three-legged orange tabby snoozing on an ottoman. It blinks green eyes and stares at me like it's bored to death of megacrocs and giant robots.

"There." The girl points to the left.

Way to the left is a giant croc. It's the size of two elephants taped together and nudging an upside-down Toyota like it's a dog toy.

Way to the right is a... well, robot doesn't seem to cover it. It's three stories tall, looks like an anorexic Transformer. Mostly dull gray metal, although you can see the red and blue designs scraped off by dinosaur teeth.

"Plutonium Commando?" I ask.

"We call him Iron Dick around here."

"He looks different on TV."

"I know, right?" She chuckles and opens the window.

The smell hits me in the face. City in summer, overlaid with swampy sewer monster and hot, oily metal. They haven't seen one another yet, as far as I can tell. I kneel and lean out the window like a little kid watching a parade, and she stands over me, arms crossed like an indulgent babysitter.

"Yeah, it's weird. He scratched off a lot of the paint himself when he went haywire. It was like a suicidal teen cutting. His tech is messed up, and the government can't control him anymore, but he still does the same patrol. Folks used to line the street, waving flags. When he stomped on Mrs. Gunderson's Pekingese, she ran up to his giant foot, crying, and hit him with her cane. When he stepped on Mrs. Gunderson, everyone else started screaming."

"Where were you?"

She scans me, and I figure she's weighing how much she wants to say.

"I was on the street with everybody else, holding up my baby girl so she could see him."

I glance around her apartment. There is no indication of a kid. When I look back, feeling guilty and crappy, her eyes are as hard and gray as the robot marching by outside. She doesn't even flinch. Just keeps talking. She sounds like a war vet who's seen too much and can't shut up about it because then she'd have to feel it, bone deep.

"It's pretty simple. Old Iron Dick really only cares about two things: punching crocs and cracking open Jeeps to guzzle their gas. So, everybody just stays off the street when he's due to pass. Six-fifteen every morning and afternoon. Once he's gone, everything'll creep back to life."

"And the megacroc?"

"Just watch, noob."

Plutonium Commando, or Iron Dick, or whatever, marches patriotically down the yellow line in the middle of the cracked street, his steps even and echoing down the empty block. When I look up, I see shadows behind windows. One little boy has his nose pressed up against the glass like this show never gets old. I used to watch dump trucks and excavators like this, when I was a kid. They were just digging up pipes, but it was still pretty exciting. This, though... it looks like CGI. But it's not.

Iron Dick stops, and a high whine makes me think he must be charging up some weapon. Down the next block, the megacroc stops nuzzling the car and slides into the street. A monstrous shimmy shakes its huge tail back and forth. I see now why there's nothing in the middle of the road—everything gets swept aside as it charges the robot, tail wagging furiously and enormous jaws open to reveal a thousand teeth.

"You never seen a megacroc, either?"

I shake my head and lie. "Just the little guys in zoos. Never one of the..."

"Freaks?"

"Whatever you call it."

"We call this one Mama. She's one of the biggest. See all the scars? No matter how many times she gets punched, she keeps crawling back."

And that's when it happens. The robot's eyes light up green as he charges the croc and lands a fistful of metal in the gray-green armored back. Mama flips over backward to show her white belly, her legs flailing frantically. Then she uses her tail to flip over, spins, and knocks the robot's legs down with a powerful swipe. Iron Dick falls on his square metal ass, his arm raised to show a cannon that could blow up my home town. Explosions of air rattle, but nothing comes out.

"He ran out of ammo on the first day," the girl mutters, smirking.

"But he still tries to shoot."

One eyebrow quirks up. "Just because a guy's shooting blanks doesn't mean he stops shooting."

"Truth," I mutter.

She's right, though. The dude cycles through an arm cannon, a bazooka, and a flamethrower. None of it works. If he were a person, he'd stare at his failed equipment, mouth open, caught between embarrassment and fear. But since he's a robot, he just keeps going. His punches land, but the croc is a hell of a lot bigger than I expected. The news talks about the robots a lot but doesn't say much about the crocs. They used to give death tolls, like it was a contest to see who could kill more civilians, the man-made freaks or the man-made robot monsters. You could go to Vegas and place bets on them. Somebody even managed to lure a weaponized robot and a megacroc to Madison Square Garden for a fight.

And that was the end of Madison Square Garden. By all accounts, now it looks like a bomb went off there.

Watching them now, these two are like toddlers with wiffle bats, bashing while doing no damage. The croc grabs the robot's leg, the robot punches the croc, the croc lets go. Again and again, they

dance around. Chunks of concrete get knocked off buildings. Empty spots on the sidewalks suggest where a bench or mailbox got taken out, once upon a time. There's nothing left to get in their way, now.

"How long do they do this?" I ask.

She shrugs. "Until the croc remembers that she can't eat metal and scampers back down into the sewer."

As if on cue, the alligator lets out a honk of annoyance, knocks the robot over, turns tail, and wiggles down the street and around the corner. By the time the robot is standing again, she's out of sight. The robot stares after her for a moment before letting his arm cannon fall to his side and marching down the yellow line as if he's forgotten the whole encounter.

"The street should be safe now."

"But why—"

She shakes her head. "You ask a lot of questions. I'm not used to talking. If you're headed to the Corps, they'll have answers. Come on."

Holding the door open, she motions me back down the stairs. The gym doesn't feel as creepy now. I stop at the plywood door.

"Can I see you again?" I ask.

"You won't. Good luck out there, kid."

"I'm not a kid. My name's Susan."

She gives me a real smile. "You've got a baby face, Susan. Don't let Iron Dick smash it up, okay?"

"What's your name?"

This smile is private and rueful. "You'll have to ask someone else what they call me these days. Now go on."

All I can say is, "Thanks. I'm glad I met you."

I don't tell her she's only half right about the Corps. I don't tell her I'll find a way to see her again because that's part of my job. I don't tell her I work for the enemy.

I WATCH HER FOR TWO weeks before I show up on her doorstep, shuffling my scuffed-up construction boots. I timed my visit so it's just before the evening patrol. She takes her time answering, only opens the door a crack. Inside, music blares and weights clatter. She gives me a look that says she wants me gone but not necessarily dead.

"Can I come in?" I ask.

She steps outside. "No."

"Uh, so. Like I said, I'm Susan. And you're Rip." My voice is shy and halting, and I do that thing that makes my brown eyes look huge. "That's what the guys say you go by. It's from *Alien*, right?"

She gives a tiny grin. "Not my choice, but it works. What do you want, Susan?"

God, she sounds like a bitch. But that's probably why she's still alive.

"Carlos said you train him. Lots of the guys."

She nods. Her arms are crossed, and I stare at her bulging muscles.

"Would you train me, too?"

"Why?"

I scuff a boot toe. I picked these government-issued pants on purpose because they make me look tinier than I already am. Rip needs to think of me as small and helpless, or this'll never work. "It's harder work than I thought it would be. My arms are killing me by the time we're done. And there aren't a lot of women in the Corps. I could use…"

"Someone to talk to?" Her eyebrow raises. It's a hell of a dance.

"Definitely someone to talk to," I echo, although my eager smile suggests I'd take anything, at this point.

She considers, lips pursed.

"Eight a.m. tomorrow. Be ready to work. I won't go easy on you."

"I wouldn't want you to."

"Fifty bucks a session. Or two sheets of high quality plywood."

My nose wrinkles up. "How would I get plywood?"

"You're in the Corps. Steal it. It's valuable around here."

We stare at one another. Her arms stay crossed. My hands are shoved into my pockets.

"Tomorrow at eight, then," I say.

"Don't be late."

"What happens if I am? Do I get a spanking?"

Her face...shuts down.

"Look, Susan. You're cute. But the flirting won't work. I'm married."

"So where's your...?"

Her eyes go even colder. "I don't know, and it doesn't matter." She holds open the door. "We stick to business, so here's how that works. You get here on time. We train for forty-five minutes. At nine I leave to do something more important than you. You got that?"

The blush that rises to my cheeks is real. "Okay. Sorry. I didn't know. It sounds important."

"Keep busy or go crazy," she says, relaxing a little.

When I don't move, she gently pushes my shoulder toward the CCC.

"If you hurry, Iron Dick won't step on you."

Then she's gone and I'm outside staring at plywood.

A rhythmic thumping tells me the giant robot is on his way. I run.

THEY CALL HER RIP, BUT her real name is Tori Burrell. Born 1985, married Olivia Suarez in 2011, had a daughter with a donor in 2014. Her daughter Bibi died in 2015, when the first crocs showed up and the robots were built to fight them. Sad story. But they all are, in neighborhoods like this. It wasn't that nice even before the fights destroyed it.

It's strange, learning about someone online before meeting them.

I read everything Tori Burrell ever wrote on Facebook, Twitter, and her blog, although she stopped posting everywhere as soon as Bibi died and then Olivia left. I checked out the Yelp reviews for her gym, because even when the city is in rubble, people still have to be rating whatever's left and complaining about service. She gets good reviews, but her clients are united in calling her a hard ass. But not like it's a bad thing.

I'm there five minutes before our appointment. Music thumps the plywood door. I don't know whether to knock or pull it open, so I try both, and neither works. I end up standing there, looking up and down the street like a croc might show up at any moment. At exactly eight, the door opens. Three huge, sweaty guys walk out, casually joking. I get some up-and-downs and a casual up-nod, but I'm not here for them. I catch the door the last one holds open and slip inside.

Rip's waiting for me in a sports bra and shorts, glistening like Southern girls say they do but don't. She doesn't even greet me.

"When's your shift start?"

"I'm on night shift. Down on—"

She stops me with a hand. "Don't care. You ready to work?"

I grin. "I'm always ready."

A cocky scoff. "Yeah, we'll see. Those guys that were just in here won't be able to lift their arms all day."

Although I've seen her plenty and secretly, she's only ever seen me twice, and only in the oversized work clothes they hand out to the Civilian Conservation Corps construction crews. Now, I peel off the huge gray tee with the interlocked three Cs of the Corps logo and step out of the baggy pants. Underneath, I'm wearing a matching magenta sports bra and compression leggings, definitely not government issued. She looks me up and down, her professional observation warring with her interest when she hits my eight-pack.

"You'll probably last ten minutes."

I smile sweetly. "Oh, I can last a lot longer than ten minutes."

"Cut that shit out and start stretching. What do you lift?"

We run through it all as I bend and twist and touch my nose to my knees, and she fills out a form, which I sign. The workout would be exhausting if I hadn't been training for this assignment for months. She's pushing me hard, which is a welcome challenge.

"What do you do in the Corps?" she asks as I pump out chin-ups.

"Arc welding. And hammering up drywall."

She doesn't question the lies because they're good lies.

"You ever think about joining?" I ask.

A snort. Rip snorts a lot. "Hell no. Government couldn't keep me and mine safe, so I don't do what the government says."

A rugged shoulder lifts. "You're gonna pay me with government cash. That's help enough."

Just like that, the flirtiness is gone. She pushes me harder. I meet her demands. The power shifts back and forth deliciously, dares and triumphs, taunts and grunts. It's fun, in its way. Takes me back to training at Quantico. I can see why another girl might fall for her, in the right circumstances. I pretend I'm that girl. I almost believe I'm that girl.

After I finish the final circuit, she gives an approving nod and says, "You know how to cool down."

She leaves to go upstairs. I could go back to the barracks, like she wants me to. But that won't get me what I need.

"Rip?" I call tentatively, my steps shy but quick on the stairs.

I push the cracked door open. I don't know where she went, but she's not here. I hurry to the bathroom like a normal girl who needs to pee and hunt through it silently. No prescriptions. The NSAIDs any athlete would keep on hand. A box of feminine products and old decorating magazines addressed to her wife. Nothing that tells me anything new.

"Susan?"

It's angry, and I flush and hurry out.

"Sorry. I couldn't find you, and I had to go…"

Her mouth twists. "I shouldn't have brought you up here that day. This floor is off-limits. There's a bathroom in the gym, next time."

I give her my perky face and bounce a little. "When's the next time?"

"Pay me fifty dollars, then tell me how many times a week you'd like to pay me fifty more dollars."

I've already worked out how often a Corps worker could reasonably afford her services.

I hold out five tens. "Maybe twice, I guess? Or do you have a group class at a lower rate?"

It's like she's always weighing me with her eyes. "You last a month, and we can work out a trade. I could use some help."

"Doing what?"

"Last a month and I'll tell you."

And just like that, I'm in.

SHE'S TESTING ME, BUT I'M ready for it. I live through four weeks of the hardest training of my life, never complaining. I puke doing sprints once but shake it off, wipe my mouth, and keep going. As I harden, I can feel her soften toward me.

Then one morning, she puts a firm hand on my sweating shoulder and gives me a significant stare. "Tomorrow. Nine a.m.," she says.

I grin as I towel off my forehead and pat a line of sweat slithering down my chest.

"Wear something that can get wet and dirty. Something dark."

I nod like I'm proud, which I am. The fewer words I use, the better. I push out the door and jog down the street. I don't bother with the baggy clothes anymore, and I can feel her watching my butt. Tomorrow, if I'm lucky, she'll finally take me underground.

I SHOW UP IN BLACK cargoes and a black tank top, my hair tightly French braided. The door opens at exactly nine, and she's dressed in cargoes just like mine, plus a long-sleeved black top.

"Are we burgling?" I ask.

I'm rewarded with a rare smile, curling as a cat's. "Not quite."

Rip takes off at an easy lope. I'm on her heels, enjoying the stretch of my muscles. I haven't run like this since I left Maryland, only this time, the forest is broken gray buildings and smashed concrete. There's a gun on one hip, a machete on the other; I watch them dance as she runs. She's ready for trouble and I wonder if we'll find it.

We go up four blocks and dart down an alley. She scans it up and down before kicking up off a dumpster to yank down a fire escape ladder. When she scurries upward, I follow. It's six flights to the roof, where a strange bit of construction stretches between the buildings, crossing the alley. It started as a ladder, long boards placed over the rungs. Metal guardrails and plywood act as walls. It's an open-air hallway.

"You ready for this?" she asks.

I shrug. "I don't know what *this* is yet."

"It's what it looks like. Hope you're not afraid of heights."

Aside from the bridge, it's your average roof, except there are rows and rows of summer vegetables growing in long raised beds and barrels to collect rain. I realize what we're doing the moment I notice that the garden stakes are written in a child's awkward handwriting. Rip's at the door now, the one that leads into the building, and she gives a coded knock. A different knock responds from the other side, and a series of locks clicks before it opens to reveal a dozen or so kids. They're every shade of brown, clean and quieter than I'd expect. But wouldn't a kid learn to be quiet in a world where giant crocs and robots hunt the streets?

As if she can read my thoughts, she says, "You watch the ground.

You see anything remotely big, you let me know. Follow up at the rear."

"What do you do when I'm not here?" I ask as the kids file out onto the roof. They're all elementary age and don't look quite as carefree as I remember being at that age, before the scientists got experimental and everything went to hell.

"Mrs. Gonzalez." She nods at the steel-haired granny standing at the door, broom in hand and mouth grimly set.

I wish the old woman good morning, and she mumbles, "*Usted no esta mirando a la calle...*"

"*Estoy viendo,*" I say, giving her an almost-honest smile.

Over at the makeshift bridge, Rip scans the alley below. She's always scanning, which is probably why she's still alive and there are still kids around here. When she steps on the bridge, she treats it like it's an everyday thing, not a march over a murder-chasm. The wood creaks and sways as the children follow her across like baby ducks, a measured four feet or so between them, like they've been reminded again and again not to cluster together and overweigh the structure. I move closer to the kids on my side and wish I'd brought a bigger weapon. The sky is hot and clear, and the day would be beautiful if not for the near-constant terror.

When the last kid on my side steps onto the bridge, I look up at Rip, and she motions me across like I'm an idiot. It's a good thing they trained me for heights. I wonder what it must've been like for the first person who tested this contraption, and for these kids the first time they saw it. The wood bounces with each step as the metal sways in the wind. I look down at the alley six stories below, imagining what might be hiding down there, mouth open for a juicy tidbit.

Jesus, what these kids will do for an education. I'm amazed that anyone still cares.

I step onto the other roof and look back. Mrs. Gonzalez is gone.

Rip is at the other side of this roof, knocking on another door and leading another dozen kids out onto the roof and toward a ladder down to the next building. She's like the damn Pied Piper, and the kids' eyes follow her with worship and a little awe. They don't even seem scared. This is their new normal, and they trust her.

We gather kids on six different rooftops. There must be at least fifty, and none of them breathe a word the entire time. Next thing I know, Rip's knocking on another door, but this time the children enter the building, quietly thanking Rip as they pass within. She doesn't really see them, though. She's watching the street and the sky.

"Are we going down, too?" I ask.

Rip shakes her head. "We bricked in all the doors and windows down there. Couldn't chance a croc getting in where all the kids are. The orphans live here, too. They don't talk about that on the news, much. They treat it like a war zone, but Amazon still delivers at least once a week."

"Bet those guys get paid well, right?" I ask, trying to lighten the mood.

It doesn't work.

"Look, Susan. When you live around here, it's not about being paid. It's about community. It's all we've got left. The government won't fix our streets, they shut down our schools, they closed the police station. Ambulances don't come here because the roads are blocked off. They gave up on us. If we let these kids grow up without an education, we might as well shove 'em down the subway tunnel. There are still places that are safe. Just not here. Not like they can afford to move to Nebraska."

With another rueful head shake, she hurries back along the bridges, back the way we came. I follow.

"So, why'd you stay here?"

She doesn't answer as she heads back down the fire escapes to our starting point. She doesn't answer as she jogs down the street,

taking so many turns that if I hadn't extensively studied maps of the area, I'd be lost. She doesn't answer as she stops in front of a subway entrance papered in fluttering yellow caution tape and smeared with dark, slimy stains. She turns to look at me. Judging me, as always.

Whatever she sees, she must finally decide it's enough.

"These are the rules. Be quiet. They should mostly be asleep right now, but that mostly means nothing to ancient assholes. If something comes at us, let me face it first. Guns scare them. The noise and the light more than the bullets. I've got a few tricks, but not many. If either one of us gets grabbed, the other one does the merciful thing. You hear me?"

I pause, because that's what a normal person faced with this question would do.

"Uh."

"What's uh?"

"What are we doing, Rip? Why would we go down there?"

Rip's grin is finally a real, feral, fully-made thing.

"To find their nests. And crush all their eggs."

"But isn't that the government's job? If you find a nest, you call 911 to report it, right?"

So slowly, she turns to face me. Her eyes go flat and dark, like those of the creatures she's about to hunt. "The government's job is to make money for the fat cats paying their salaries, and there's a lot of money in constantly rebuilding the city. This is the new Iraq, honey. They don't take out the robots because they keep the crocs in check and make great news headlines, and they don't take out the crocs because it's dangerous and messy and gives the robots nothing to do. Robots vs. megacrocs is better for clicks than the 2016 election. I haven't figured out how to take care of the robots myself, but I know how to kill the crocs before they turn into unstoppable tanks. That's why our neighborhood isn't abandoned. That's why we're not overrun. That's why you were able to walk down my street without

a weapon in the first place."

"Because you smash the eggs."

Another grin. "That's right. You in or you out?"

I pretend to be speechless, but not for long.

"I'm in."

Because I have to be. That's my job. And because I want to be. But that doesn't mean I'm not scared.

Rip pops open an overturned blue mailbox and pulls out a huge flashlight. Her gun appears in her other hand. Her quick glance tells me she still thinks I might run.

"Watch out—the stairs are slippery. Hell, everything from here on out is slippery."

Little does she know that I, too, am slippery.

She starts down the subway stairs like it's totally normal. The ground thunders underfoot, one of the still-running, higher placed lines whooshing by. But no one on two legs has used this station in years. It's weirdly tidy—no trash, no homeless, no junkies—and yet filthy like a swamp, wet and green in the corners. I want to pull my gun, but I settle for fists.

As soon as I'm out of the sun, the temperature drops ten degrees and the air goes moist. It smells like wet metal and moss and predator. The caveman in me recognizes it and the tiny hairs rise on my arms. Rip swings the flashlight back and forth as we go down, illuminating every empty corner. The movies I grew up with have me expecting piles of human bones and tooth-marked briefcases, but there's no evidence of people here. It looks like this place was abandoned hundreds of years ago instead of just three. Moss grows on the walls and floor, and vines reach toward the sunlight. As we hit the next level, I see why: there's a busted pipe leaking everywhere, and no one's bothered to fix it. This place is eating itself, the earth swallowing it into the swamp, long waiting under Manhattan for just such an occasion.

I shake my head. This is not time to get all poetic. There are actual megacrocs down here. *Sarcosuchus.* Fossils told us they could reach forty feet, but in this world, necromanced using DNA, the scientists say they should stay under thirty feet, maybe only twenty if they're still agile enough to crawl up stairs. I saw one up close, once, before I took this job. They wanted me to know what I'd be facing. I asked them what it would taste like battered and fried. I guess that's what they wanted to hear.

"Watch out," Rip mutters, low.

The subway platform is creepy as hell, utterly empty. Weirdly, a few of the lights still work, casting the concrete into a patchwork of shadow and flickering blue. A barricade blocks any contact with the train, cement and steel and razor wire. On the other side, posters remind subway riders that this stop is closed and attempting to stop the train and exit here will end in certain death. *Have a Nice Day!* A few chipped spots in the barricade suggest the crocs have attempted to eat the L train.

"You cool?" Rip asks.

"Hard not to be, down here," I say, letting my voice shake a little. It doesn't require a lot of acting.

"We're going down one more level, and then it gets bad. No more lights."

"Yay."

Her grin is the brightest thing underground. "That's the attitude I like to see."

Damn, she's right. The next steps feel like slowly walking into a swamp to die at midnight. I move closer to her—and her flashlight. Even brave people don't want to be alone in a place like this. My fingers twitch for the guns I've got flat against my back and strapped in my boot. That's my last resort. Better to break cover than die. But we still haven't seen or heard a megacroc, and maybe we won't.

The stairs are interminable and slick with muck. The next plat-

form hovers bare inches over a sea of black water where tracks used to be. One submerged train lists to the side sadly, half full of bog. I shudder involuntarily at the thought of what it would be like to get pulled down, down, down into the darkness.

As if reading my thoughts, Rip murmurs, "At least it wouldn't last long. Megacrocs don't barrel roll. They just snap you right in half at the start." I say nothing and she adds, "I've seen it. Nobody has time to pop off a scream. And then..."

She points with her flashlight, showing me a log on the floor that turns out to be an old croc turd, dry and flecked with chunks of bone.

"This is the weirdest first date ever. You trying to scare me?" I ask, voice shaky.

"Maybe. You should be scared."

"Then why'd you bring me down here?"

"Because I think you've got potential, and this is the best way to find out."

But she doesn't say it's not a date, which makes me grin. They told me she was a hard ass, but they never told me she was funny and kind. It only seems to come out when she's under stress.

"Well, maybe—"

"Shut up." Her arm flies against my chest like she's trying to save groceries during a car crash, and I jolt back as I hear it, too. A scrape and a splash. She steps toward the water and sweeps the flashlight into the darkness of the tunnel beyond the sunken train car. The flash of green eyes makes me shudder, my heart kicking up. My hand goes for the gun and stops before it can ruin everything.

"What do we do?" I whisper.

"We wait to see if it's going to attack or just go on being a stupid dinosaur."

I can hear our breathing in tandem as we watch the eyes blink and keep on swimming. The flashlight reveals a series of spikes in

the water, right down to the wide tail lazily propelling the body down the underground river. Fifteen feet, maybe. Might even be a regular gator somebody flushed down a toilet when it wasn't cute anymore. But it's not, and we both know it. Megacrocs would eat one for supper. That's one reason their growth rate from juvenile to adult is insanely fast. Scientists thought that was marvelous until the first lab-created megacroc escaped through a fence it couldn't have broken through the day before.

When the croc's out of sight, Rip takes a deep breath and flashes her light down the way it came. There's a ledge along the left, just wide enough for a person. Maybe.

"If you're going to give up, now's the time," she dares me. "We're going through a pipe. It's a tight squeeze."

"No biggie. I did some spelunking with my Girl Scout troop," I say, trying to sound nonchalant.

She can't help chuckling. "Yeah, this is just like that. Damn, you've got spunk."

Before I can respond to the compliment, she slides her back against the wall and edges along the ledge, her toes hanging over the water. It's easy and practiced for her, and she's still running her flashlight over the water beyond, but it takes everything I have to stay upright and moving, my shoulder almost touching hers. I want to ask how far it is, if she actually expects me to swim in pitch black water surrounded by crapped-out people, but I say nothing, because I can't remember how good the crocodilian sense of hearing is.

As far as I can guess, it takes a million years and we shuffle along for seventy miles.

In reality, it's maybe twenty feet. Maybe.

I nearly jump out of my skin when Rip's fingers wrap around my wrist, hard and unyielding.

"We're about to duck left," she whispers. "There's a pipe that leads to a shared nesting space I check every month. You're gonna

see what looks like a ton of garbage, but believe me, it's a nest. Just follow my lead. Okay?"

"Okay," I say.

In this moment, I realize that I'm not as tough as I thought I was, and I'm nowhere near as tough as Rip is. I feel her absence as she ducks into the pipe. When my hand hits the rim, her firm fingers grip it for a moment. Then she's crawling, and I crawl, too. Small as I am, it's still a tight fit. It's suffocating in here, and I have to wonder what she was thinking, the first time she squeezed inside. I crawl forever and then nearly fall out. Rip helps me up and gives my shoulders a squeeze more eloquent than words.

She aims the flashlight to show me a room full of overturned desks and chairs. I want to ask why we didn't use whatever person-sized entrance the subway workers used, but I see the water lapping through the crooked door on the far side of the hall and keep my mouth shut. My shoes crunch, and I flinch. I realize that the heap taking up the other side of the room isn't human trash: it's the croc nest.

My skin crawls. It's weirdly warm here, as if the trash—the nest—was just popped out of a microwave, which I recall has to do with how the mother incubates her eggs.

"Take this."

Rip hands me a sledgehammer and places her flashlight on an upturned bucket. After a moment of fiddling with something, light flares. She's got the room strung up with emergency lights, glowing an eerie blue. I can almost see the funky heat radiating off the nest, and I wish I had a flamethrower instead of a giant hammer. Rip picks up her own sledgehammer, the end crusted with glop, and uses it like a pickaxe, pulling off the top layer of the nest to reveal dozens of dirty white eggs, soft and leathery. With another rake of the hammer, eggs tumble down the slope and land at my feet. I don't even have to ask what happens next. I start smashing them,

turning my face away at impact.

We work quickly, silent but for the sound of our tools. Every so often, Rip pauses to hold up her sledgehammer and listens before nodding and returning to destruction. Hundreds of eggs fall under our sledgehammers and boots until we're knee deep in shells and the slimy black corpses of almost-baby crocs. They're so tiny they don't even have toes or eyes yet, and I don't let myself feel any horror or sadness. When I reach up to wipe sweat from my eyes, I see my own blood mixed with the slime, my hands covered in freshly popped blisters.

I don't complain. If this doesn't win her over completely, nothing will. And goddammit, I want Rip to be proud of me, to see how far I'm willing to go for her. Maybe I can lie to my boss and just... stay here. With her.

The eggs seem endless, and I'm about to ask why we don't come back tomorrow, why we don't just burn the whole thing down with a can of gasoline and a cinematically timed match, when I hear the sound I've been dreading.

Splashing water.

Mama's coming home.

I look to Rip. Do we run? Do we fight?

But she just leans against her sledgehammer and stares at me, eyes narrowed.

"Who are you really?" she asks.

I go cold to my toes.

"Susan Marco," I say. "Who else would I be?"

She shakes her head like she's disappointed and kicks the sledgehammer out of my hand. The handle bounces off the concrete, and my fingers twitch to fists at my sides as I consider who'll win if we draw.

"Try again. You with the government or a private investor looking for eggs?"

"I told you. The Civilian Conservation Corps."

"Bull." She chuckles. "If you're an arc welder, I'll kiss a croc. Probably another FBI plant. You're not down here because it's the right thing to do. You're down here because someone's paying you. Because you want to know where your buddies went."

I hold up my hands and shake my head, putting as much pleading and fear as I can into my eyes. I don't have to fake my worried glance toward the water.

"That's not...I mean..." I lick my lips nervously. "That's crazy. You can ask the guys. I sleep in the same barracks as the rest of them."

"Yeah, they told me that. But you don't work the same jobs they do. And your hands aren't as callused as theirs. And you're packing, which I'm pretty sure the CCC doesn't allow. What are the odds that the first pretty, fit, funny girl to show up on my block in three years is really as great as she seems?"

"Pretty good, I guess." The warmth in my voice is real, and so is the loss. Because if this operation is going downhill, then she's the one who's got to go, not me. "Look, I—"

I go to draw, but she's already got her gun, and it's trained on my chest, and the steady splashing is closer now, and I don't understand why we're not running when the two of us together can't take a twenty footer, not in close quarters like this, and not near a nest.

"Tell me the truth, Susan."

"I'm just here to help," I say, which is true.

"Then let me tell you a little story." She reaches behind me and pulls the gun out of my belt holster, then shoves me butt-first into the nest. My back is instantly slick with egg trash, but I just lay there, waiting for her to glance away so I can grab my boot piece.

"We were happy. And then my daughter got taken by one of the crocs, which I guess you already know. My wife left. And then things went even shittier, and I started doing all the dangerous jobs in the neighborhood. Running off the crocs, building the bridges for the kids, carrying old folks to the empty hospital. We

kept waiting for the government to help us, but all the help went uptown. To Park Avenue and Tribeca and the theater district. They built barricades to trap the crocs here and shuttled their help to the rich places. We were living in a war zone, and I liked that, because it was the first thing that made me feel alive again. You got any idea what that's like?"

I take a deep breath. "More than you think. I need you to know—"

"We don't have much longer, so shut up. Now out here, we don't have internet all the time. We barely have cell signal. There's no money. It's the Oregon Goddamn Trail, at least until somebody realizes we've got something they want." She leans close, her gun kissing my belly. "Now by my count, you're the third FBI chump on my turf. So, what is it we have that you want? What is it *I* have that you want?"

"Just you," I say, and it's the truest thing I've told her. "What about—"

"The mama croc? Oh, she won't care about me once she smells you. She never does."

Rip backs into the corner, gun aimed at me. Her eyes almost seem to shine green like a croc's as she watches me, cold and distant now. A giant black snout shoves out of the water and into the room, dripping mouth open a little to test the air, and I go still like thousands of prey animals before me. There's got to be a way out of this.

"What would your daughter think if she saw us now? What would Mrs. Gonzalez and all those children think? That you're some sick freak watching an innocent person about to get eaten?"

She shakes her head sadly.

"Mamas protect their own. I failed once, and I won't fail again. I grew up on this block. Nobody innocent would walk into this neighborhood wearing a smile. If I'm right, I'm doing my people a favor. If I'm wrong..."

I'm an inch away from pulling my gun, just waiting for her to look away.

"If I'm wrong, well I guess that's one less person on my block that Mama's gonna eat."

The megcroc rushes for me, and I pull my gun and fire into her open mouth, emptying the entire clip before dropping it to fumble for my phone. Zero bars. I don't even realize I've been hit until I start coughing blood. I look up at Rip where she crouches on a stack of boxes, gun in hand.

"I just wanted to help," I sputter.

"Yeah, but not us. Not me."

"Definitely you."

"Then you picked the wrong side."

Just like that, she's gone.

The croc's destroyed snout is inches from my foot. I kick it weakly, but she doesn't move. Must've hit her in the brain. When I look down, I see that I'm headed in a similar direction. Even if the FBI bothers to send someone in after me, they have no chance of getting a stretcher through that pipe, and I can't get out on my own.

I didn't lie, though. I did want to help. They sent the first agent here to investigate Rip, a friendly visit to find out how she was able to keep the entire neighborhood operative. The second agent came looking for him and never returned. I'm number three. I wonder who they'll send in to bat clean up and if they, too, will end up in a pile of croc crap.

Funny thing is, I could tell them what they want to know, if I could still speak: because Rip will do whatever it takes.

Damn. I never even got to kiss her. I did admire her. I wasn't faking it. It wasn't a lie.

I reach for an egg and crush it in my hand. Another and another until I can't move my fingers. The last thing I see is my own bloody fingers, crushing an egg.

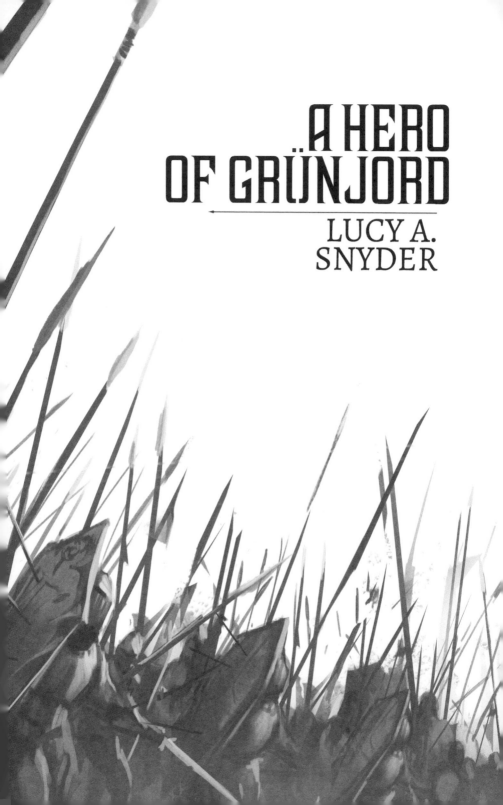

A HERO OF GRÜNJORD

LUCY A. SNYDER

Part 1: Outlanders

VINCA FELT HER STOMACH TWIST as the vast Outlander skyship, black as the night betwixt the stars, rose from the valley Rift. The winter sun shone harshly through wispy clouds and gleamed on the snowy mountains ringing that cursed chasm. But the ship reflected nothing. If it were not for the nauseating hum of its engines shaking her very bones, she would have thought the ship to be a catastrophic *absence* in the sky, like the strange, distant, invisible stars the monks argued over. "Black holes" some called them, but Vinca found that name unsatisfyingly prosaic. A hole was something to be filled, nothing more, and the word did not convey the planet-devouring danger the strange stars held.

Perhaps the Outlanders hailed from a world near one of those dark, hungry stars, and built their ships as homage to those world-eating celestials they worshipped as ravenous gods. Or perhaps the unrelenting darkness was simple camouflage in those cold star-reaches. Either way, if this lone ship made it past the defenses Queen Ahlgrena and her armies had raised, it would wreak terrible destruction across Erd's ten continents.

Illustration by NICOLÁS R. GIACONDINO

A century before Vinca's birth, the Rift first opened after Grün-jord's most powerful wizard botched a spell intended to create a new freshwater spring. One of the Outlanders' ships had burst through and laid waste to kingdoms and nations as far south as the Qiimaha empire. Where the ships landed and the Outlanders spilled forth, those who met their blister-eyed gazes suffered seizures and mad-ness and could not defend themselves. Hundreds of thousands died, mostly humans but dragons, too, and the ship was brought down only when the human kingdoms and dragon tribes pledged to set aside their grievances and work together. The land still bore blackened scars where no plants would grow, and people who stayed too long inside their borders later sickened with malignant tumors. Queen Ahlgrena's great-grandfather took responsibility for his wizard's accident and pledged to the neighboring kingdoms to do whatever he could to keep all their lands safe.

"This one's bigger than Queen Ahlgrena's keep," Bhraxio said as he pumped his leathery wings harder to rise above the Outland invader. His voice sounded profoundly worried inside Vinca's mind.

She could feel the quiver of his wing muscles' strain through her sheepskin saddle. Fire-breathers like Bhraxio were inherently hot-blooded and could fend off the chill far better than humans, but this bright morning was exceptionally bitter. The extreme cold was taking a clear toll on the young dragon. The first breath of outside air had sent her into a coughing fit. If it were not for her magic-imbued flight helmet—which in her wisdom Queen Ahlgrena had commissioned for all the dragoneers—her face would have already frozen as hard as a marble statue's.

"We can bring it down." Vinca leaned forward in the saddle and gave Bhraxio a comforting gauntleted scratch through the woolly fur of his neck. There were thirty dragoneers in the skies today; they'd be able to surround the ship and bombard it with grenades enchanted to home in on and cling to the hot places on the hull

where the strange, tough metal that composed the craft's skin was weakest. It might take two hundred bombs to sunder the ship, but they had plenty of grenades and fliers with hand cannons. "We *will* bring it down."

"Try to bring it down in one piece," Captain Gunther replied through the enchanted helmet. "Sister Lutera told the Queen that the monks need an intact ship for defensive study."

Vinca blinked. Their tried-and-true bombardments couldn't possibly drop the ship whole. "That wasn't the course we plotted this morning."

"New orders from the Queen's captain," Gunther replied simply. "She told me only a moment ago. You're the first to know. I'll tell the others shortly."

"Are we to endanger the towns for the sake of bringing the monks a scientific prize?" Her voice was as sharp as her sword.

Other dragoneers might have feared to speak to Gunther so boldly, but she and he had fought a dozen Outlander invasions together, drunk entire barrels of ale together, and sundered the springs of several beds together. Gunther, often grim and intimidating to his troops, was a surprisingly playful lover. Vinca was reasonably sure that she was only one of perhaps three people who'd ever heard the huge, bearded warrior laugh. If she couldn't speak her mind to him, then she could speak it to no one.

"No." Gunther sounded unruffled. "Endanger none if you can. But a whole ship's better than a burned wreck."

Life was precious in Grünjord; it had not always been so. But the constant Outlander threat had forced the kingdom to change and advance far beyond most other realms. Their King or Queen was no longer simply born to rule but had to be elected by representatives from every district. Grünjorders had become expert at waging war, but they also realized they had to build a country worth battling for. The kingdom was in a renaissance of the arts and sciences, and every

child went to school to learn letters and numbers. Even the plumbing and heating in the average burgher's house was considered rare in the homes of neighboring kingdoms and an unheard-of marvel in more distant lands. Vinca had spent her first seven years in her father's keep in distant Coravia, and she could remember no pipes, only chamber pots and drafty latrines that opened to the polluted castle moat below.

"Our troops wait on the ground," Gunter said. "If you can bring it down within five leagues of the valley, the wizards will be able to slow its fall in the air, and our soldiers are prepared to clear the monsters inside."

"I spy it as being nearly five leagues away now," she replied. "Do you mark it so?"

"Aye," he agreed.

Then they hadn't a moment to waste.

"Rise!" she urged Bhraxio. "Get me well above the skyship! Keep pace!"

With a great press of wings, the dragon did as she asked, and Vinca quickly unbuckled herself, unsheathed her skyship-metal boarding axe, and gathered her legs beneath her to get ready to leap clear of his wings.

Based on the wrecked hunks they'd recovered, there would be a ring of wide, round porthole windows above a room near the center of the ship. The monks believed the monsters steered the craft from that room. From outside the ship, the windows appeared as the same flat black as the rest of the craft, but while the metal of the ship was supernaturally tough and could only be cut with magic, the glasslike material of the portholes would shatter beneath the Outlanders' own metal.

Vinca's stomach churned. Many dragoneers had tried what she was about to attempt, and none so far had succeeded. Half had died, plunging to their deaths, smashed by the hull, or swept into

the furnace blast of the ship's strange engines. The odds that the wind would simply blow her off the top of the craft were extremely high. But if there was even a slight chance of bringing the ship down, she had to try.

"Be ready to catch me," she said. "Pull up on my mark so I can get clear of you, and watch for my fall!"

"Aye!"

Vinca gripped her axe tightly and held her position until they were over the middle of the vast ship; she guessed they were maybe fifty meters above it, but the void of the surface made distances difficult to gauge. "Now!"

Bhraxio swept his wings in reverse, and Vinca used her sudden forward pitch to lengthen her jump. She vaulted over his muscular woolly shoulder and plummeted toward the ship.

She spoke a simple charm to soften her fall. The plunge was quick and disorienting nonetheless, and instead of landing on her feet as she'd hoped, she landed painfully on her hip and began to slide across the ship, nothing but shapeless dark all around her. Her boots hit a metal edge and blackness loomed in front of her: it had to be a porthole.

With both hands, she swung her axe into the mass. The glass-like material shattered inward, huge dark shards falling into a room that at first glimpse was a dazzling constellation of red, blue, and yellow lights. Her second glimpse showed her a gray metal deck three meters below and grotesquely misshapen creatures recoiling from the plummeting shards.

Her mind swam when she saw the monsters below. They were like the bubbling scum that sometimes formed on stagnant ponds. No bones, no permanent limbs or heads that she could see, just roiling, shifting masses of colorless, gelatinous flesh. No—they had a color. It just wasn't one she could name. Eerie green eyes boiled out of their flesh like pustules. There was no rhyme or reason to their forms, and

they made terrible buzzing noises that bored right into her brain like parasitic worms trying to erase her thoughts and will to fight.

Vinca shook her head to clear the vile buzz. She gripped her axe to her left fist, drew her magic-forged skymetal broadsword with her right. Took a deep breath. Leaped down onto the glass-strewn deck. She began to swing at anything and everything, a whirling cyclone of blades. Slashed panels sparked and smoked. The hideous Outlanders emitted fluting shrieks and recoiled from her onslaught.

A tiny part of her was appalled by her indiscriminate brute force. Precise strikes based on careful foreknowledge of a foe's weaknesses were best. But the monks couldn't agree on what the different panels and gadgets controlled. It seemed best to destroy as much of their ability to pilot their ship as she could.

And she couldn't keep this up much longer. Her heart was pounding and her shoulders straining. Worse, the monsters in the room with her were recovering from their surprise, gathering together, melding into a huge, towering mass. She slashed at the looming monstrosity, but its jelly flesh seemed to heal itself the moment her blade passed through it—if these creatures had vitals, she could not reach them. At best she could pop a few of its vile eyes, but three more would blister open in its remains. Quicklime would melt an Outlander. She wished she'd thought to bring a bag of the white powder with her.

"What's happening in there?" Captain Gunther's voice was faint inside her helmet.

"Fighting," she grunted, slashing at the monster.

A light flashed near her, and she whirled and buried her axe in the panel with as much force as she could muster. A solid foot of the broad blade sunk into the metal and wires. Her shoulder and elbow ached sharply at the impact. A moment later, the ship gave a lurch and began to plummet.

"Ah, well done!" Gunther exclaimed.

Suddenly in free-fall, she and the monstrosity both rose off the gray metal floor. Vinca released her axe and kicked off from its stout leather-wrapped handle toward the broken porthole. The Outlander shrieked at her and lashed a gooey pseudopod around her ankle, trying to drag her back down. She slashed the fleshy snare off her boot with her sword and recited a levitation charm to ascend into the blue sky and blinding sunlight.

The bitter wind slammed into her and knocked her breath away as it blasted her clear of the vast, plunging ship. The gale knocked her sword from her numbed fingers. She cartwheeled helplessly, unable to speak a charm to slow her fall, unable to right herself enough to get her bearings. The wind was so loud against her helmet she wasn't sure she'd be able to hear the ship crashing if the wizards weren't able to catch it.

"Do you live? We can't see you," Gunther said.

She couldn't voice a reply in the thin air.

"Bhraxio, please see me!" she thought, praying he could hear her. The mental connections many dragoneers had with their dragons was only as good as their line of sight. If they couldn't see each other, they couldn't hear each other. But Vinca had been able to talk to Bhraxio through castle walls. Now, she had no idea how far the ship had traveled while she'd been inside it, or whether he had been able to keep pace.

"I'm almost there," she heard inside her mind. "Roll yourself into a ball; I don't want to break your limbs."

She hugged her legs to her chest and tucked her helmeted face to her knees.

A moment later, she felt Bhraxio's leathery talons close around her body, then a rough guts-flattening jerk as he winged away.

She felt dizzy from vertigo and relief, and in the sheltering cage of his claws, she could finally take a deep breath.

"I'm alive," she croaked to Gunther. "Bhraxio has me. Have the

wizards got the ship?"

"Yes!" he said. "Our ground troops are clearing it of Outlanders now. You've landed us a real prize! I reckon you won't have to pay for your own drinks for at least a fortnight!"

She smiled and massaged her shoulder. "I think tonight I'd rather have a hot bath and a rubdown."

He gave a sly chuckle. "I'm sure that can be arranged."

VINCA AND BHRAXIO WERE SURROUNDED by ecstatic troops and townspeople the moment he set her down along the main road into the city. She scrambled onto his back, and the next several hours were a blur of cheering people, waving pennants, and proffered goblets of ale and wine as the crowd led them in a parade through the villages outside the city wall, then through the gates and around the town square.

Queen Ahlgrena herself brought Vinca up to her address balcony and gave a rousing speech in honor of the dragoneer and Bhraxio, who'd flown to a sturdy iron perch beside the elevated stage. Vinca, fortunately, wasn't expected to do anything but stand steady and wave to the crowd below; that was enough of a challenge as she was dizzy with drink by then. After three rounds of *huzzah!*, the queen put a golden medal of honor on a red satin ribbon around Vinca's neck. They all went downstairs to a fine banquet for all the dragoneers, wizards, and the men and women who'd slain the last of the Outlanders once the ship was grounded.

In the castle's ceremonial banquet hall, gilded statues of the old heroes of Grünjord gazed down upon them from alcoves ringing the ceiling. Half the alcoves were empty in anticipation of mighty new heroes. Though Vinca drank no more alcohol, her head swam at the realization that this day had earned her a place among them.

After a dessert of intricately frosted cakes that seemed nearly too beautiful to eat, Gunther took her aside and led her through

several gilt-and-marble corridors and staircases to an ornate set of double doors in crown prince Stellan's wing of the palace.

"What are we doing here?" Vinca asked Gunter.

"As I recall, you requested a hot bath," he replied with an enigmatic smile. "Prince Stellan has one of the best soaking pools in the entire kingdom, which likely makes it one of the best in the entire world."

"But not *the* best?" she replied, half teasing.

"Well. It's a matter of opinion, isn't it? The bath is exactly as the prince desired it for himself, so he considers it to be the best. And he is an epicure of considerable taste and knowledge, so it has the best of all the options he prefers."

Prince Stellan was still young, just a few years older than Vinca. His mother likely had many more decades left in her reign, presuming she continued to please the voters of Grünjord, so he hadn't yet had to buckle down and prove himself as a leader and administrator. But unlike most responsibility-free princes who had lived and died in the many kingdoms of Erd, he was neither a rake nor a bully. A hedonist, certainly: he loved fine foods and fine wines, and even finer clothes, which he maintained his figure for through tournament fencing and horsemanship. He advocated beautiful living, and had popularized makeup and fancy hairstyles for men and boys in the kingdom. But the queen had impressed upon him the importance of behaving like a gentleman, and though it was rumored he'd had a prodigious number of lovers, no one had whispered that he'd taken any to bed against their will. Other royals in other kingdoms were rumored to rape for vile, predatory sport, and some openly bragged of it as a mark of twisted manliness. But that evil was abhorred in Grünjord.

So, Vinca knew she would be perfectly safe if Gunter left her to soak alone. Besides, she doubted she'd find a respectful advance from Prince Stellan to be the least bit objectionable. But that had to

be pure fancy; the prince could charm nearly anyone in the kingdom that he desired. He was probably ensconced in his chambers with a lovely bevy of admirers. It was more than enough that he'd offered up his private bath to her.

"Are you staying or leaving?" she asked Gunther, tracing a gilded vine decorating the doors with her index finger.

"That is entirely up to you."

She looked him up and down. He'd washed his face and combed out his long blond hair and beard before the banquet, but he still wore most of his battle armor, and his tunic was white with dried sweat and darkly fuzzed with wind-blown dragon hairs. "You could use a wash."

He arched a bushy eyebrow at her and pursed his lips in disapproval, but the twinkle hadn't left his eyes. "Is that your way of asking me to stay?"

She couldn't keep from grinning impishly at him. "Yes. Stay."

"As you wish." He grasped the golden door handles and pushed them open.

The bathroom beyond the doors was a lavish work of marble and gold. Two round bathing pools were sunk into the floor, both tiled in ocean blue. Arrayed around them were benches and intricately wrought hanging racks for clothes. Two fluffy white bathrobes hung from one of the racks. An assortment of fancy soaps sat in a reed basket by the rightmost pool, and bathing oils by the left.

"The pool on the right is for getting the grime off," Gunther said as he closed the doors behind them. "And the one on the left is for relaxation."

She gave him a look. "I *do* know how bathing works."

"Well, I hear that they only have rags and sticks in Coravia," he teased.

"Our castle had a tub, thank you very much," she replied as they approached the benches. "And my father the king insisted we bathe

once a year whether we needed to or not."

"Ew," he said with a laugh.

"Fortunately, having survived a filthy childhood there, hardly anything here makes me ill."

"You were about seven when our scouts found you, weren't you?"

"Yes." Humans with the ability to bond telepathically with dragons were rare. Queen Ahlgrena had sent her wizards far across the continents of Erd to identify and recruit promising youngsters. "I was the fifth child of eight, and my father never looked so happy with me as the day he sold me to foreign strangers for fat bag of gold."

Gunther looked at her sharply. "People aren't objects. You weren't bought. We don't do that here."

"Well, where I came from, people *are* things. My father most certainly saw the recruitment incentive as my purchase price."

"I'm sorry." Gunther awkwardly gave her a side-hug. "I didn't mean to bring up unpleasant memories."

"It's fine. And it's in the past." She forced herself to smile up at him. "I have a better life as a dragoneer here than I ever would as a princess there. And my father probably got to buy a very nice horse. It worked out for everyone."

"What about your mother?"

Vinca frowned, trying to sort through her hazy memories. "She wasn't happy about selling me off. But she had so many other children, and surely more to come. My absence probably made her life easier."

There came a loud knock from a different set of doors behind them.

"Yes? Who is it?" Vinca called.

The doors opened just a crack.

"May I enter?" Prince Stellan asked.

Her heartbeat quickened. "Yes. Certainly."

The prince stepped into the bathroom and closed the doors

behind him. He was barefoot and wore a white robe that matched the ones hanging on the rack. His curly hair was bound in intricate braids, and he wore golden eye shadow that looked gorgeous against his dark skin. She had certainly admired him from afar, but up close he was even more handsome, and she felt an unaccustomed electricity in her chest.

"To what do we owe the honor of your presence?" She wasn't sure whether she ought to bow.

"Oh, the honor is entirely mine." The prince smiled reassuringly. "You are our hero, and you deserve the finest that our kingdom has to offer. I wanted to personally make sure that everything here is to your satisfaction."

Vinca looked around at the pools and baskets and benches. "All this is wonderful."

"I also wondered," the prince said, "if I might join the two of you? I do want to make sure that you're well satisfied this evening."

It took her a moment to fully realize what he was offering. She felt heat rise in her face, and she looked at Gunther, partly for confirmation of what she was hearing, and partly to see whether he was upset at the prince's advance. Gunther merely smiled at her and gave a little shrug that said, *Why not? I'm game.*

"Yes," she told Prince Stellan. "That would be lovely."

Part 2: Inlanders

VINCA LAY COZILY SANDWICHED BETWEEN Gunther and Stellan in the prince's silken bed. As comfortable as the rest of her was, her bruised leg was starting to ache beneath her. Gunther snoozed like hibernating bear, but Stellan was gently stroking her bare hip.

"I need to shift a bit," she whispered over her shoulder to the prince.

He released her and scooted away on the bed. She rolled over to face him. His amber eyes were bright, and he wore an oddly thoughtful expression.

"Have you slept?" she asked.

"A little. I…would like to discuss something serious, if you don't mind."

Her heart beat faster. What could this be about? "No, I don't mind."

He traced the curve of her face with his forefinger. "Sometimes, ordinary people rise to their occasions and do extraordinary things. I don't think that's what happened yesterday. I think you are an extraordinary woman, and you will do more extraordinary things. My greatest worry about myself is that when you strip away my extraordinary circumstances, I'm not much more than a pretty face. But I hope that if I keep company with genuinely extraordinary people, they will give me occasions to rise to."

"You're asking me to join your court?"

"I'm asking you to be my queen."

Lightning once struck Vinca while she rode Bhraxio in a storm; this felt much the same, and for a moment she couldn't speak.

"Prince Stellan, I am deeply, deeply flattered…" She trailed off, not sure how best to phrase her profound concerns.

He smiled at her. "But we've only just met, and regardless of the intensity of our meeting, we hardly know each other well enough to pledge marriage. You probably believe I am suffering from lust-induced, harebrained infatuation. Am I close?"

She nodded.

He took a deep breath. "I do realize this sounds like madness. But hear me out."

"Of course."

"I *have* been trying to become a man of substance. I frankly lack the talent to become a proper wizard, but I have studied hard, and I do have some natural ability for prognostication. Prophetic dreams. They don't arrive reliably, but when they do arrive, they've been entirely reliable. Does that make sense?"

"I think so?"

"I know you're a woman who appreciates directness and honesty, so I should lay down all my cards, yes? I have dreamed of you. Of *us*. Standing together to lead this country. We're much older in my dreams, so I wasn't sure it was you, not until I saw you send down the Outlander ship. But now I'm certain. I also know that nothing I say will be enough to convince you right now, and that's fine. There's no hurry."

"Why me?" she finally asked.

She wondered if her mother had ever dared ask that question before she found herself bound to a life of royal obligation. Did marrying the King of Coravia seem like a fairy tale escape into luxury, at first? Vinca had witnessed little of her mother's life, yet she knew the gilded edges were cold and hard.

"We're excellent complements for each other," the prince replied. "You've skills I could never attain. You're a genuine hero of Grünjord, and people respect that. You're also a princess of Coravia, and that would satisfy traditionalists. And ..."

"And what?"

"And I think I fancy you a great deal."

She finally gave in to her urge to kiss him. "I fancy you, too. But this is a *lot* to consider."

"I know that. I also know that my proposal might seem like a golden cage. While there will be inescapable responsibilities, your life would be your own as much as possible. I wouldn't stand in the way of your other loves. I know you care for Gunther, and he cares for you. If the time arrived when you wanted to have a child with

him, I would treat the boy as my own."

Vinca felt another lightning shock. "Your dreams told you I'll have a baby with Gunther?"

"My dreams were unclear. But our son seemed very…large. And rather blond."

"Oh." Vinca's whole body felt warm. She hadn't ever considered that Gunther might want to have children with her someday.

"Think upon this as long as you like." He kissed her, and slipped his hands around her hips to draw her closer. Suddenly her flesh was keening for his.

"May I take your mind off things?" he asked.

"Yes, please…"

VINCA GROGGILY AWOKE TO A steady *tap-tap-tap* at the prince's window. Stellan stirred beside her. Gunther snoozed on, oblivious.

"What's that?" the prince whispered blearily.

Vinca's eyes finally focused. "A bird. A crow. It's carrying something."

She and Stellan climbed out of bed and went to the window. The crow was perched uncomfortably on the sill outside, his scraggly feathers fluffed up to protect his scrawny body against the bitter cold. A small scroll was bound to his scaly leg with a leather thong. It eyed them beadily and let out a hoarse caw.

Stellan reached for the latch and opened the window. Vinca shivered at the sudden blast of frigid air as the crow hopped inside, eyeing her and cawing again.

The prince hurriedly shut the window. "Looks like the bird's had a rough time of it!"

The crow gave another caw and awkwardly held out its leg to her. She carefully untied the thong and unfolded the tiny scroll, which was handwritten in the trade language of the Southern continent. A dark lock of hair—Vinca's own, she realized—was sewn to the

bottom of the paper.

Gunther, roused by the bird's noise, had lumbered out of bed. "What's happened?"

"This bird flew all the way from Coravia," she marveled. "No wonder it looks so ragged!"

"That's over two thousand leagues away," the prince replied. "My falconer will want to see this mighty bird."

The crow cawed at him and puffed out its feathers again.

"This is part of a finding spell." Gunther pointed at the lock of hair. "I didn't think the Coravians approved of magic?"

"They don't," Vinca replied. "But like anything else the church forbids, they'll resort to it if the need arises."

"What does it say?" Stellan asked.

"It's been a long time since I've seen this language…I'm still working it out." She tapped a stamp near the lock. "This was penned by a local scribe. But it's from my mother. It says, 'Dearest Daughter, I am dying. I would like to see you again. I wish we had not sold you. Please visit if you can. Bring this letter so the guard will let you in. If you cannot visit, know that I love you.' She's signed it with her mark. I remember it."

"Could this be a trick?" Gunther asked.

Vinca turned the seamed paper over in her hands. "I can't imagine why anyone would try to trick me like this."

"Unfortunately, I *can* imagine reasons for skullduggery here." The prince held out his hand. "May I take that to my wizards for analysis?"

"Certainly." She gave him the letter.

"If it's authentic, do you want to visit her?" Gunther asked.

"I…I don't know." Her mother had given her life. But had not protested very loudly when her father sold her. Did she owe her mother anything, now? And was seeing her one last time a matter of debt? She sometimes wondered how her brothers and sisters

had fared. If she ignored this reason to go back, another was not likely to arise.

"Bhraxio could fly me there in a week," she mused. "Assuming he's willing to take me there. And assuming we're allowed to go."

"You may certainly visit your dying mother," Gunther said. "Of *course* you may."

"But before you settle on a course, let's see what my wizards and agents report," Stellan said. "I don't know enough about that quarter of the world to advise on whether it's safe or not."

THE PRINCE SUMMONED HER TO dine with him that night, and they discussed his experts' findings over tawny port and roasted duck.

"The letter is authentic," the prince said gravely. "I am very sorry for your impending loss."

"Thank you," Vinca replied. "Bhraxio says he will take me to see her."

"Coravia regards dragons as devils. You'll need to travel under cover of an invisibility spell, and he will need to transform into a horse or dog when you arrive."

Vinca nodded. "I'll ask what he prefers."

"And it's such a long way that my wizards recommend he take a potion to increase his airspeed," the prince said. "It might make him feel a bit sick."

"Taking that would also be his choice."

"Another problem is that your father has not been the most… *diplomatic* ruler in the region. He's made threats against the neighboring Xintu kingdom, and our intelligence reports that both sides are amassing forces. Your father has fewer soldiers, and the Xintu leaders know this. War could break out at any time. Coravia is likely to be overrun. If that happens, your duty is to return yourself and Bhraxio safely to Grünjord. Your father made his own political bed a long time ago, and his problems aren't yours to try to fix."

Vinca pursed her lips. She wasn't surprised by any of this news. Coravia was founded by Northern seafaring colonists. They'd treated their indigenous neighbors poorly from the start, and that didn't change as the Coravians abandoned piracy for religious piety. The Xintu royal family still considered the Coravians to be land thieves even though they'd been there for close to a millennium. And, based on the dimly remembered rants she overheard as a child, her father considered their neighbors to be degenerate savages, even though the Xintus had superior art and better literacy and medicine. Despite the ages-old conflict, there was a great deal of surreptitious trade between the two kingdoms. For all she knew, her mother had enlisted a Xintu shaman to enchant the scroll so the crow could find her.

"I couldn't fix my father's problems even if I tried," she said.

"Wear armor and carry a good sword. But not too much armor—tensions are high and you don't want to seem threatening. I'll make sure that Bhraxio's transformation can be reversed at a word."

WHEN THEY ARRIVED IN THE outskirts of Coravia, Bhraxio opted to turn into a large mastiff, reasoning that they would be inevitably separated if he became a horse. It was summer in the southern continents, but even the warmer months in swampy Coravia tended towards a damp chilliness. Vinca wore a knee-length hauberk of light skymetal mail under a light gray chemise and loosely-woven blue kirtle with enough decorative embroidery to look like a proper lady's outfit without seeming ostentatious. She carried a canvas-sheathed longsword strapped beneath her rucksack; at a glance, it wouldn't look like she was armed. None of the flimsy footwear popular with Coravian women was suitable for fighting or riding, so she opted for her regular boots and hoped they wouldn't earn her too many stares.

The hike from Bhraxio's landing spot to her father's keep was muddy and uneventful. They passed a few peasants and soldiers who gave her and Bhraxio curious looks, but none accosted them.

As they approached the outer wall, Vinca realized that the keep was much smaller than she remembered. And it was almost gratuitously ugly, all rough-hewn squared granite angles and spiky wrought iron. Nothing about the structure spoke of grace or enlightenment. Positioned as it was on a steep rocky hill well away from the nearest village, it had never been built to provide protection for the common folk whose taxes paid for its creation. It was a physical assertion of ego and dominance in a sulky, undernourished landscape, the crude architectural equivalent of an armored fist beating against its owner's proud, skinny chest.

Vinca crossed the bamboo log moat bridge, breathing through her mouth to avoid being overwhelmed by the sewer stench of the filthy water below, and approached the guards at the castle gate.

"What is your business here?" one demanded.

"I'm here to see the queen. At her invitation." She handed the guard the scroll.

He looked at it upside-down, clearly not able to read it. "Who are you?"

"I'm her daughter. My name is Vinca."

The guard's eyebrows rose a bit at that, and he gave her and Bhraxio another suspicious once-over. "I'll let my Captain know. Wait here."

THE SUN HUNG LOW IN the sky by the time the gruff captain of the guard arrived to lead them to her mother's chambers in the eastern tower. The castle yard was full of soldiers, all either too young or too old, and most with ill-fitting boiled leather armor and well-worn weapons. To her eye, some of the boys were as young as twelve or thirteen, not even old enough to wield a razor.

"A sad lot, indeed," Bhraxio thought to her.

"Soon they'll have to resort to training women," she thought back darkly. "Or die of pride."

"Is my father here?" she asked the captain.

"He is. He's attending to military matters."

"Does he know I've arrived?"

"He does."

Vinca waited for the man to elaborate, and when he did not, she asked, "Did he say if he was going to see me?"

"The King has much on his mind. If he wishes to see you, I reckon he will."

"Understood."

The captain's tone softened. "It's not safe to travel. If you need a bed for the night, your sisters can give you a place to sleep."

The sour stink of sickness in her mother's room was unmistakable. The Queen of Coravia lay pale and gaunt upon stained sheets and a sheepskin coverlet damp with coughed-up blood. She was attended by two women a few years younger than Vinca.

The captain rapped the butt of his spear upon the stone floor and stood very straight as he announced her: "Lady Vinca of Grünjord is here to see her mother, the Queen."

The two younger women stood, peering at Vinca nervously.

"Is it truly you?" the one with dark brown hair asked.

Vinca was mortified to realize that she wasn't sure of her sisters' names. "Cathara? Camine?"

They both smiled, and Vinca was relieved that she'd guessed correctly. "Yes, it's me."

They rose to give her quick, awkward, but seemingly heartfelt hugs, and Vinca was surprised to discover that she loomed a whole head above them both. She wondered if the household had suffered from famine, or if the girls had been pressured to starve themselves when they were growing teenagers.

"Such a fearsome hound!" Black-haired Camine was staring at Bhraxio, who seemed nearly as large as she was.

"He won't hurt you," Vinca assured her.

"But this is a warlord's dog," Camine persisted. "What master would allow his slave such a beast?"

"Camine!" Cathara's voice was *don't be rude* sharp.

"Master?" Vinca laughed. "I have no master. I'm as free as you or your sister."

Her sisters looked genuinely shocked. Not just shocked, but dismayed.

"By the looks of things, your life has been considerably freer than theirs," Bhraxio remarked.

Vinca wondered if her father had used her as a threat: *Disobey me and I'll sell you to the next peddler!* What must it be like to realize that the sister they'd assumed had suffered a fate worse than death had instead survived and even thrived? By the expressions on their faces, it was a bitter draught, indeed.

"What ails our mother?" she asked them.

"She has the consumption," Cathara replied.

"Tuberculosis?" Vinca blinked. "But that can be treated. Cured."

"Nonsense," Cathara replied.

"Not at all! No one suffers from this in Grünjord."

"Those who allow sorcerers to tamper with their flesh go to hell." Camine's eyes were wide and accusing.

Vinca threw up her hands in exasperation. "It's an extract of bread mold! There's nothing sorcerous about it! You're worried about your mother going to hell? This, right here, looks an awful lot like hell to me!"

"Cathara. Camine." Her mother's voice was a papery rasp, but it still held undeniable authority. "Leave me with Vinca. I wish to speak to her privately."

"But, Mother—" Camine began.

"Leave us!" The queen fell into a violent coughing fit and waved them off.

The two sisters obeyed, eyeing Vinca as if she might be a witch

as they hurried from the chamber.

Vinca took Camine's vacated seat close to the head of the bed. "Mother, truly, this can be cured—"

The Queen raised a shaky hand and made a motion to silence her. "I don't want a cure."

"Why in the name of the heavens not?"

"I'm tired, Vinca. I have done my duty and I just want to rest. Forever. I think I've earned that."

The anguished ache in Vinca's chest told her that her heart was surely breaking. And from frustration as much as anything else. "If you won't let me help you…why did you want me to come home?"

"I wanted to see you one last time." Tears rose in her mother's rheumy eyes. "I wanted to know about your life. I wanted…stories of places far away from here."

So Vinca told her the tale of the Rift and the Outlander invasion. She told her the story of meeting Bhraxio, and of the day they took down the vast dark skyship and were heralded as heroes by the Queen.

She had just started telling her about Prince Stellan when she realized that her mother's jaw had gone slack and she'd seemingly stopped breathing.

"Has she passed on?" Bhraxio asked.

Vinca pressed two fingers against the artery in her mother's fragile neck to check for a pulse. Nothing. "She's gone."

"I'm so sorry."

"Me, too." Vinca wiped at her eyes with the hem of her chemise. "Dammit. It was too late to save her even if she'd agreed to come to Grünjord."

"It was what she wanted," Bhraxio said.

Vinca gestured angrily at the shabby sick room and swore. "This is *never* what anyone wants. People convince themselves that death is a prize when they feel trapped and hopeless."

"Should we call for someone?"

"Not yet." Vinca felt too drained to deal with her sisters and their tears. Especially if the tears were just for show. "We came a long way to see her. I'd like to sit here a while longer."

The old lady's half-open eyes were filming over. Death looked nothing like sleep. Vinca gently closed her mother's lids. Is this what old age inevitably brought? Infirmity and regret after a life broken on the wheel of duty? What might her mother have accomplished if she'd had the knowledge to make good choices, and the power to live as she chose? But none except a few great wizards could scry the future; could anyone but them and those they held in confidence truly exercise free will? Prince Stellan had his prophetic dreams; what did she have besides an uncertain supply of grit and luck?

"I don't fear death," she whispered to Bhraxio. "But I surely fear the hope-lorn decrepitude I see before me."

"This is not your fate," her companion replied. "Your mother may have been strong once, but you are far stronger."

She shook her head. "You can't be sure of that; you didn't know her."

"I know *you*, and I have met thousands of humans. I have yet to meet anyone stronger."

VINCA UTTERED A CURSE WHEN trumpeted alarums blared in the distance and in the courtyard.

"Let's get to the roof and see what's happened," she told Bhraxio.

They ran up the stairs to the top of the tower. Sure enough, legion upon legion of soldiers with siege engines were marching up the castle hill, surrounding it on all sides. Their numbers were hard to gauge in the moonlight, but she guessed that the unready soldiers scrambling to get into their positions below were outmanned perhaps a hundred to one.

"You did promise the prince that we'd go home if this happened," Bhraxio said.

"They're going to be slaughtered. We can't just leave."

"What do you propose?"

"The Xintu wear bamboo armor, correct? That sounds flammable to me."

"I don't like killing humans."

"So let's be terrifying, and hope they have the sense to run off before we have to kill them."

Vinca shucked the canvas cover off her sword, dug her gauntlets and spell ingredients out of her rucksack, cut her dress so she could ride Bhraxio, and spoke the magic word to return him to his dragon size and form.

They screamed down upon the invading troops like a curse from the heavens. Bhraxio breathed great blasts of fire above the invader's heads, while Vinca worked pyrotechnic magic she'd learned in their campaigns against the Outlanders. Blinding midair explosions knocked men flat and toppled their war machines. Some of the Xintu troops responded with volleys of arrows that missed their marks, but after a few blazing passes, the invaders broke ranks and began fleeing for the cover of the forest.

Once the battlefield was cleared, Bhraxio swooped back to the castle and landed gracefully in the courtyard where the Coravian troops cowered.

Vinca didn't necessarily expect a hearty welcome of ale and huzzahs…but she also didn't expect her old, bow-legged father to come storming toward her, his sword drawn and an angry, profane rant about lost honor and sorcery spilling from his bearded lips.

Vinca slid from Bhraxio's woolly back and strode to meet her sire.

"How dare you!" the old king screeched. "This sorcery will bring the wrath of God upon us! You have doomed our souls! DOOMED OUR SOULS!"

He took an unsteady swing at her with his sword. She sidestepped the blade and punched him hard in the face. The King dropped like a sack of manure and lay on the filthy stones cursing her as he clutched his bleeding nose.

"How dare you!" A man a few years older than Vinca drew his sword and rushed at her. She drew her own weapon to parry his blow, and when he inevitably overextended himself, she knocked the blade from his hand and kicked him square in the solar plexus. The air whoofed out of him and he sat down hard on the stones near his father, gasping. He was her eldest brother, surely, but in her rage, she couldn't remember his name. And she didn't feel the least bit badly about that.

"All right," she called to the men around her. "Would anyone else like to be an utter arsehole to me for the unpardonable sin of SAVING ALL YOU FLEA-BITTEN LOUTS FROM CERTAIN DEATH?"

The men fell silent as salamanders.

She stepped forward and addressed the king. "My name is Vinca, and I'm your daughter, gods help me. You sold me for gold when I was just a child. I can't say whether that deed marks you as the worst father I've ever met. But given what I've seen tonight, you are surely the worst ruler still living upon the ten continents. Whatever doom you face is the fruit of your own stupidity and incompetence."

She stepped to the side and addressed her brother, who still hadn't gotten his breath back. "If you're inheriting the throne here, do better than this prideful jackass. Learn to hold onto your sword. For the sake of your people, make better choices. At least take a bath sometime."

She strode back to Bhraxio. "Let's go home."

As they winged away into the night, he asked her, "So, a change of subject. Have you thought more about Prince Stellan's proposal?"

"I think that when we get home, I'm going to learn all about

economics, infrastructure, agriculture, and diplomacy. I'm no wizard. I might never glimpse the future except through Stellan's eyes. But I'm going to be the best damn queen anyone has ever seen."

"I wonder if this is the first time a princess has pledged herself to extreme competence out of spite?"

"It's not spite."

"It isn't?"

"The prince is delicious."

"Ah. So it's thirty percent spite, and seventy percent lust?"

She sighed. "Could we throw some civic-mindedness in there just so I don't sound like an arsehole?"

"Whatever makes you happy, milady…"

THE UNLIKELY TURNCOAT

A GENRENAUTS SHORT STORY

MICHAEL R. UNDERWOOD

COPENHAGEN'S WEATHER WAS UNPREDICTABLE AND quick to change—two things that most spies hated. But Shirin Tehrani was not most spies. She wasn't really a spy at all, but here, in this story world, she played the part as best as she could.

After a day and change on a boat, she was ready to get her feet on dry land again. On the boat, all she'd had to keep her company was a small dossier, her reference texts brought from HQ, and her anger.

Betrayal was the language of the Long Cold War, the story region she was visiting, but there was betrayal, and then there was *betrayal*. A low-level operator with ideological vulnerabilities, a recent divorcee with expensive tastes and a need to feel special again, or a deep-cover agent away from home too long—those were who you'd expected to turn, to flip between the USA's allies and those of the USSR.

But this time, the betrayal had come from the very top. Rupert Amis, head of MI6, the old warhorse himself, turning his coat for the Soviets. In exchange for what?

The sensors back at Genrenauts HQ had registered this as a massive breach, so Shirin hopped to, speed-reading the briefing before making the crossing, securing the ship in their vacant warehouse, and stepping out into the London streets, back in that timeless

world eternally stuck hazily between the sixties and eighties, the height of the Cold War. Her instincts guided her straight toward the nondescript office building which housed Her Majesty's Secret Intelligenciers.

The building was still smoking.

None of that prepared her for the sight itself, for the list of the fatalities she got from Gertrude on her hospital bed. Amis's secretary had been out for lunch, gone early to get pastries for the team. So instead of being inside with the explosives, she'd caught debris from the street.

Copenhagen, she'd said. He'd been there three times in the last two years, developing neutral contacts.

That one thread was enough to get Shirin onto a chartered boat through the North Sea and around to the Danish port city, a half-way point between the warring super-powers. She'd been there with Amis before, years past.

Everything made sense except for Amis's betrayal. The man might as well have been swaddled in the Union Jack. World War II veteran, old money, old guard, connections in the nobility.

And yet, here she was, stepping onto neutral ground, trying to intercept a man who'd helped invent modern spycraft in this region.

Everyone at MI6 was either dead, in traction, or too far away, deployed around the world. So it fell to Shirin, arriving "just in the nick of time" from her extended surveillance mission in Grenada.

She walked past pastel-colored houses, trollies, and dozens of bicycles, mixing and matching different decades from block to block. Here a man with a full beard and bell-bottoms, there a woman with stockings and heels, a dress straight out of 1955. Some regions had more historical consistency, some less. Cold War spy stories spanned decades, so this world was just a patchwork, the vagueness of time only underscoring the sense of eternity, of an unending stalemate

just seconds away from turning hot. Which is just what it would do if she wasn't able to stop Amis from getting to Leningrad.

And luckily, she wouldn't be the only person in town who wanted to keep the Cold War from blowing up.

First, she stopped into a coffee shop to break some bills and top off on coffee. She'd been awake since five or so, the rolling of the boat upsetting her stomach. Then, coffee and change in-hand, she found a phone booth, relishing the regions which still had them, compared to the all-cellular, all-the-time modern story worlds. She flashed back to the Iran of her childhood, of standing on a friend's shoulders to place crank calls to her house.

Holding her dossier open, she dialed a number, waiting three rings. A bored woman's voice greeted her in Danish. Shirin's scant Danish was rusty, but good enough to recognize the passphrase. She spoke the counter-signal, and the woman asked her to hold.

Shirin casually scanned the street, eyes flitting up to open windows and rooftops, checking for tails. No one here should know to expect her, but the KGB might be expecting someone to pick up Amis's trail. An Iranian woman of fifty-something stood out here as much as any foreigner, but age also granted a measure of invisibility, especially when she could wear a heavy coat and scarf, and shield her face from the wind with a hat.

"Hello?" said a new voice, familiar, excited.

"Hello, Axel. Did you miss me?"

A beat. "Shirin? What are you doing in my neck of the woods?"

"Same as ever. Taking in the sights, meeting interesting people. You wouldn't happen to be free to show me around?" she asked, delving into spy canter, phrases with double and triple meanings. She was on the hunt for someone, looking for information.

"I can always spare some time for an old friend. Coffee?"

"The place near the cobbler?" she asked.

"Just what I was thinking. See you soon." And the line clicked off.

She waited another moment, scanning the street once more, then hung up and quit the phone booth.

Every genre had its dangers—some physical, some social. This region was both, often at the same time, and from a direction you never expected. She'd been working the Spy genre beat for a long time now, and coming back was like slipping into a familiar coat and stepping out into the brisk chill of late autumn. The cold bit, and there was the promise of nastier weather around the corner, but it came with a thrill, the exhilaration.

The newspaper boy on the corner. The woman with a baby carriage, child concealed in blankets. The two men smoking in an alley-way, door to a kitchen open behind them. Anyone and everyone could be working for the enemy. Being here helped her feel alive, but it was also exhausting. There was a lot to be said for the straightforward dangers of Heroic Fantasy or the abstract risks of ruin and censure in the Romance world.

Focus on the task at hand, she told herself. She slid through the crowds once more, folding her presence in to disappear, to make herself a non-entity—just another silhouette, no one of note. She'd started early in tradecraft, learning from her parents. The malleability of identity was a refuge for her in her late teens. She'd known who she really was even before she started spy work, even if she hadn't been ready to tell the world. The joy she'd felt the first time she dressed as a woman, not the boy she'd been raised as…it was so intense, she'd nearly forgotten the mission.

Her trainers had seen Shirin's embrace of femininity as just another part of learning the trade, a specialty to exploit. It wasn't. On those missions, she was the most real, the most honest, the most herself she'd ever been. The spying just provided the opportunity. And when the revolution came, and the new regime declared girls like her persona non grata, those skills helped her escape and find a new life as herself.

SHIRIN BEAT AXEL TO THE coffee shop, but only by a minute. She took up a spot in the same back-corner booth—clear sightline to the door as well as a straight shot to the back entrance. Axel was about as likely to give her over to the Soviets as Shirin was to suddenly grow wings and fly to Venus, but the breach here could be spreading, could cause the expected tale types to warp and bend, spiral out of control. Which is why Shirin had to find and take care of Amis as soon as possible. The longer a breach went unresolved, the greater the ripples, both on-world and back on Earth Prime. The last time she'd been deployed to the Spy world, Earth Prime's G-8 talks had devolved into a name-calling match, and a nuclear disarmament agreement twelve months in the making had gone down the drain.

Geopolitics were complicated enough without interference from the multiverse.

Axel stepped in almost without notice, the same softness of step, aura of presence withheld. He spotted her right off, but beat a meandering route, using the restroom and ordering coffee before joining her.

He slid into the booth, setting his saucer and cup down opposite hers. "I didn't figure on seeing you here for another few years, at least. What was it you said?"

Shirin smiled. "'After a hangover like that, if I never see Copenhagen again, it'll be too soon,' I think it was."

"A tad dramatic, wasn't it?"

"I don't know if your missions often involve midnight chases across rooftops and pneumatically launched boot-spokes, but that one was quite memorable for a country girl such as myself," Shirin demurred.

"If you're a country girl, then I'm the King of England." Axel sipped his coffee. "Now, what's brought you back to the humble streets of Denmark?"

"I reckon you already know. And if you don't, we may be sunk."

"We?" Axel raised one eyebrow. The man was so wry, he was only ever a drop of vermouth and some bitters short of a Manhattan.

"We. I'm speaking of Amis."

Usually Axel played it close to the chest, tiny nots and raised eyebrows. Upon hearing Amis's name, he slumped.

"How did you hear?"

His tone was anything but comforting. She adjusted her coat, the feel of the dagger on her thigh a slight reassurance, but only slight.

"He was sloppy. Secretary went off-routine, survived the blast. Is he still here?"

"Maybe he is. It's none of my business, nor Denmark's. Even after what you did last time, my hands are tied."

"There's tied, and then there's tied. What can you give me?"

"He's still here. But that's all I can say."

"Amis goes over, the intel he has off the top of his head will take MI6 completely out of the game. Where does that leave Denmark after the Soviets get their fingers into Western Europe, the subcontinent, and beyond? You and I both know the Americans can't handle it on their own. Brash, flashy, self-important. Balance keeps Denmark safe, keeps civilians from dying. The only way we see the next New Year without open warfare is if Amis never makes it out of Copenhagen."

Axel shifted in his sight, eyes locked on his coffee, like it was an Oracle. The coffee here was uniform, mahogany brown. Tea was better for divination.

"I don't care if he comes back to England," Shirin said. "I'm not doing this for them, I'm doing it for the world. Keep him here for all you want. Her Majesty will come looking, but as long as he doesn't tip the balance, I'm satisfied. Or, you help me bring him in, and England owes you a favor. Not Denmark, but you."

Axel crossed his arms. "I didn't get into this business for the

fame or the power. I want peace. I want a world my children can grow up in without looking over their shoulder like I do every day."

"And you think the Kremlin is going to craft a world like that when they bring down the Brits and the Americans?"

Axel was clearly struggling against his limitations, against orders, against his country's avowed neutrality, the same neutrality that had kept them relatively safe over the years.

She reframed. If pushing wouldn't help, then perhaps pulling. "I just need to know where he is. Now, or where he'll be leaving. I take care of it, you don't have to get your hands dirty."

Axel relented. "Pier 7. Midnight. That's all I know. I don't know how many men he has, what the ship is. There could be a dozen of them, for all I know. And you're going to go there alone?"

"I'll do what has to be done. Any chance of getting me an introduction to your current fixer? As you said, it's been ages since I've been here."

And there was Axel's put-upon look. Far different from the "my hands are tied" look, this was far more amused, the same kind of look she wore when her kids asked for drive-thru for the second time in a week. She could relent and satisfy them, but if she stayed strong, it'd be whining and whinging for hours.

Shirin didn't even have to whinge.

IT COST HER NEARLY HER entire stash of krone, but Shirin walked away from Axel's fixer with a tranquilizer gun, six darts, a pair of binoculars, a balaclava, and some entirely off-the-book homemade explosives plus remote detonator. She had her hold-out pistol for if things got really bad. It would have to be enough. She'd asked for a rifle and some smoke bombs, but Axel put the nix on those. "Be grateful I let her give you the explosive. That I can cover up. A rifle assassination on the docks? A military-style extraction with grenades? Far too much heat."

She grabbed some dinner, then a whiskey to calm her nerves, and then set out for the dock district two hours early. Gun and darts stowed in her coat, she looked like just another traveler with groceries headed back to her rental flat.

First, she scoured the warehouse back alleys, finding doors she could pick. The first was filled with shipping crates, and the second had not actually been abandoned, prompting her to beat a quick retreat before the guard could notice her.

But the third was blissfully empty. She set the charge and checked the wiring on the remote.

"Range of two hundred meters. No more," Axel's fixer, an aging South African woman, had said. "Try not to blow yourself up, okay?" Shirin didn't have Roman's experience with explosives, but she knew her tradecraft. This was her wild card. Best case, she wouldn't need it, and could come back to remove the explosive after with no one would noticing.

Watching from shaded alleys and roofs, Shirin pegged no fewer than three KGB agents on the boat, a forty-foot craft that had seen better days, just like most everything else from the Soviet Union. The Yanks impressed with shiny and new, but it was obvious. The British tried to conceal the best under a modest patina. The Soviets used whatever they could get their hands on.

Four agents she could do. But there'd be another one or two below decks with Amis, plus a pilot if they didn't have one among their number. She bet on the one at the wheel as the pilot, but profiling too hard could get you into trouble.

The minutes ticked toward midnight. She needed to wait long enough for Amis to arrive, but move before the ship disembarked. Timing was everything.

And so, as with a half-dozen missions before, Shirin waited. She moved just enough to keep her blood flowing, thankful for the coat and layered clothes she'd packed and wishing momentarily for

backup. But two operators at the same time were four times as easy to make. The genre called for solo work, maybe with support staff in a nearby building. But she didn't have time to call in help—the Genrenauts didn't have a landing zone in Copenhagen in this region—the London spot she'd used was as close as they got. And besides that, Roman, Mallery, and King were off on another mission, the breaches coming faster than normal this year. And bigger. From the situation with Amis here to the fracas another team had stepped into with Horror-land, it was almost too much to handle all at once.

Focus on the moment, she reminded herself. Just because stakeouts were boring without company didn't mean she could let her mind wander.

And there was Amis. The former head of MI6 stepped out of a car, fedora pulled tight around his silver hair. But she knew that profile, that gait, from half a mile away. And on top of that, his figure was slightly out of focus, the vulgar breach making him pop out to Shirin's finely-tuned sense for stories. It'd taken her years to refine the senses, and some breaches were easier to peg than others. But something this size was obvious.

Her quarry in sight, she triple-checked her gear. Still enough darts, leaving the pistol as backup.

Shirin made her way down to sea level, picking out a water-way that ran under the street. The light was out, so one of the KGB agents stood at the far end of the tunnel, guarding the approach. But his flashlight was weak, barely reaching the mid-point of the tunnel.

She'd start there.

Hustling down, she counted in her mind, pacing out Amis's approach to the boat. Amis would go to great lengths to be absolutely sure he could count on the Soviets to bring him in and not just dump him into the sea, and that would take time, even after months of set-up. He was, after all, old-school. And for men like him, so much came down to relationships, to gut instincts.

She walked into the tunnel, footfalls next to silent. They'd echo in the tunnel, but not that far. The KGB tough didn't know she was coming and definitely wasn't counting on someone with her experience. She took her time lining up the shot, watching the way the flashlight bobbed in the air, wavered back and forth as the Soviet kept his limbs warm on a windy Copenhagen night.

The tough stepped into the tunnel once more, the way he'd done every ten minutes while she watched, and she took her shot, exhaling as she pulled the trigger.

The man grunted in a low voice and slumped to the ground, flashlight landing on his leg instead of clattering on the stone floor.

Shirin reloaded and sped-walked through the tunnel. One hand along the wall, the other holding the dart gun.

Peeking out from the tunnel, she watched Amis disappear below-decks, which meant she had maybe ten minutes before they disembarked. And maybe one minute before the tough at the tunnel was missed. The second tough was too far away for her to be confident of the tranq gun. She'd need to pull him, and quick.

Shirin dropped her voice into her lowest register, the pitches she'd set aside when she found her real voice, and asked for help in Russian. She hoped the echo and distortion from the tunnel and water would let her trick the tough just long enough to get him out of the others' sightline.

Almost time to throw caution into the air. Not quite to the wind. But there was a point in every spy story where you just had to throw yourself bodily at the situation. Adrenaline filled her veins, ready to explode. It didn't get her as far as it used to, when she was still young and more spry, but she'd take what she could get.

The second tough stepped down to check on his compatriot, and Shirin fired as his face came into view. His mouth stretched open to speak, then yawned as he fell to the ground. Shirin reloaded as fast as she could, climbing the steps to cover the distance before

the driver could raise the alarm.

The driver stepped away from the wheel, drawing a gun as he started to shout, but Shirin caught him in the throat with the tranq dart, grateful for the tutoring she'd gotten from her father as the child of a diplomat. She'd been aiming for center of mass, but it worked.

Shirin breathed a prayer for her father's soul as she dashed for the boat. With the guards down, it was time for the endgame. To take Amis alive, she needed to catch him unaware. And that window was narrowing rapidly.

She stepped onto the boat, and checked that the pilot was in fact out. He stirred, moaning toward her, and she put a dart in his back. That did it.

Reloading again, Shirin switched hands and drew the holdout pistol. She wasn't as good with her left, so she took the tranq in her left, holdout pistol in her right. She could afford to miss a vital organ with the tranq, but not with the tiny .22. She checked the remote in her coat, ready for quick activation.

Taking a breath, she headed into the belly of the beast, to bring this rotten story to a quick ending.

SHE FOUND AMIS IN THE captain's cabin, of course. Though barely twelve by ten, it was well-appointed with a bed and a desk, walls covered by a pin-filled map and books on the shelves, interrupted by a porthole.

Amis stood behind the desk, waiting for her with a gun. A modest, very British gun, unassuming but more than deadly enough to match her pair of weapons.

He knew someone was coming for him. But he hadn't expected it would be her.

"Shirin? Now that's a surprise. I was told you'd be in Grenada until the new year."

Amis had a grandfatherly manner about him, two parts patron-

izing to one part indulgent. He gave his people leeway, independence enough to try to impress him, which they never did, but they never stopped trying. Including poor Reginald and sweet Ableworth. Shirin had bled alongside men and women who looked up to Amis. He was supposed to be a fixed point in space, their North Star. Not a traitor skulking aboard a tiny boat waiting to spill his beans to the Kremlin.

Some breaches hurt. This one was personal.

"Ta-da," she said. "The Reds are down, and you're coming home with me."

"From where I'm standing, it looks like I out-gun and out-mass you, my dear. I've taken my share of bullets in the service, from deadlier hands than you."

And so begins the positional jockeying, the conversational combat chess.

"And yet, I'm the one covering the only exit. Plus the men Davidsen has coming to bring you in."

"Poppycock. Davidsen hasn't the spine to make a move like that."

"True. It's as unlikely as the celebrated head of MI6 turning his back on Queen and country. Why, Amis?"

"I don't need to explain myself to you," he said. But he would. Genre demanded it. For him to be the villain, he'd have to deliver a monologue.

And so Amis continued. "I've been playing the game for decades. A game of centimeters, feint and counter-feint. In the war, you could make real moves, take ground and hold it. The spy game is all shadows and proxies, it's not real, not lasting. I grew tired of the game, so I found a way to win it. The general will give me a country estate, a hundred servants, and enough money to retire in peace, comfortable knowing that I'd beaten them all. The self-important lords, the red-tape bureaucrats, the upstarts always looking for the next promotion. I, Rupert Amis, have won the game. Britain and America will burn under a rain of nuclear fire, and I will live out my days in luxury."

"And in doing so, you killed everyone who got you here. Those people looked to you for guidance. Do you think you'll be able to sleep knowing your homeland has become a blasted wasteland? Knocking over the chess board and declaring yourself the winner isn't skill, it's petulance."

Amis's face went cross. This was a man unused to being called out on his crap. And certainly not by a woman, and a Mohammedan at that (as he'd so charmingly called her on their first meeting).

"So what'll it be, Amis? Go out in a blaze, or come back and repent?"

"Nothing but hot air. Make your move or get out of my way. Don't be a coward."

"Coward? I never knew you for a comedian. Give them everything about your Soviet contacts here and in London. You can be remembered as a tragic figure rather than an anathema. But the one thing you can't do is get away. That door is closed."

Amis's eyes hardened. Time slowed. She recognized his resolution to fire, so as she finished saying "closed," she threw one leg out to dive to the side, slapped her wrist on the detonator, and fired the holdout pistol at Amis's throat.

The shockwave of the detonation hit the boat as Amis fired, throwing him off just enough. His bullet shredded through her coat, punching through her arm, but not her ribcage. Shirin's bullet struck true, dropping the Brit onto the desk, staining the polished wood.

She held the gun on him as she regained her feet. The blood continued to flow, but Amis lay still, the once-great spy now slumped over a decades-old shelf, voiding his bowels.

"I'm sorry, Amis. I wish you'd come in."

She patched up her wound, then returned to the KGB agents on the docks. She checked and disarmed each one and left them wrapped up as a present for Axel with a note.

Until next time. —S

The toughs taken care of, she checked the systems on the rickety ship and prepared for the long journey back to England, pulling the boat out into the bay.

She'd held a sliver of hope that Amis would come back. Not for his sake, but for Gertrude's, for the others. MI6 would be in tatters. Operations would have to be scrubbed all over the world, agents recalled to account for their director's treason and to find a way forward.

And so, the Long War went on.

CRAFT

LIAN HEARN

This story is set in a world based on the Coorong in South Australia and I would like to express my gratitude and respect to the traditional owners, the Ngarrindjeri. Nothing in the story represents traditional Ngarrindjeri beliefs or culture. Only the landscape is the same.

THE WAVES BROUGHT IN MANY strange objects which was one of the reasons why men were not allowed on the ocean beach. The ocean and its tides followed the rule of the moon and therefore belonged to the realm of women. The men were confined to the lake the river made behind the sandhills and its quieter waters, to the home strand where they plucked each other's body hair, rubbed their muscles with fish oil to make them shine, danced and gossiped, and prepared the craft we used to navigate that flat world of reeds and inlets, mud flats, and sandbanks where the river spread into a hundred different channels in its quest for the sea.

Some women, and I was one, were lenient and would allow a favorite to accompany us when we went out in the craft, though our grandmothers would never have countenanced it, saying men

Illustration by NICOLÁS R. GIACONDINO

scared the fish away and brought other forms of bad luck. I enjoyed having one or other of my men with me, liked watching the ripple of muscle beneath the oiled skin as they swam my craft home.

Craft had two meanings: the boats we made from reeds and bark, and the knowledge of how to make them and how to live between the ocean and the river. Our mothers taught us craft and we would hand it on to our daughters, for its forms were as many as the branches of the river, and only women had the subtlety and selflessness to master them.

Men were beautiful to look at, their strength was useful, and of course joining with them was highly enjoyable and necessary for children to be born, but their violent emotions and petty rivalries made them unsuitable for leadership. So while we were happy enough when a male child was born—boys were adorable after all—we celebrated the birth of a girl with true gratitude and joy for we knew she would be a new receptacle for craft.

She would know each morning before she opened her eyes what the weather would be, from the feel of the wind on her body and the smell of earth and sea. Her skin would be attuned to the slightest changes in temperature and to the weight in the air that forecast storms. Out on the water she would notice the tiny minnow ripples that broke the surface of a calm summer lake and the loudening of the lapping waves on the farther shore, and be home in shelter long before the changing wind could pin her craft down for days. She would know the cries of birds: the terns, cormorants, ducks and swans of the lake, the doves, nectar eaters, and shrike thrushes of the sandhills. She would follow the gulls' screams to schools of fish, dig for cockles where the oyster catchers strutted, and know how kite and eagle hovered under the midday sun. Every spring she would welcome back the waders in flocks of thousands, and in autumn she would hear their mournful farewells and feel lonely.

Each woman had her own stretch of beach entrusted to her

to tend and harvest. On the lake, everything was shared, but the beach was a series of separate places, maybe a dozen on our stretch of shore. Breaks in the sandhill provided entrance points, all alike: the sea framed as if in a bowl, the blue, green, and gray above, the white surf below, purple flowered plants straggling underfoot, tracks of small creatures in the soft sand. The waves deafened everything. Sight took over from hearing. Motion and vibration sent reptiles slithering away. The sand was almost pure white and dazzling. On those rare times when the surf died down I could hear it squeak beneath my feet.

When I went to the ocean beach it was alone. It was my custom to go after big storms and huge tides to see what the waves had brought in: spars of wood, strange nuts as large as a head, drowned birds, beached fish, unusual shells. I also went then to check and see if my shelter was still standing. We called those high tides *whale tides*. Many years ago, when I was a child, a whale washed up on the beach. I can still remember the smell as it rotted. Its bones remained, half buried in the sand and I had the idea to make a shelter from them. I used driftwood spars and planks, tree branches for the roof, and had my men weave a floor covering, though I did not tell them what it was for.

The other women envied me my luck and it set me apart from them. I was marked as fortunate and received their respect, tinged with fear.

I SAW THE SHAPE FROM the top of the hill. The wind still blew strongly, raking my face and legs with sand. The surf roared, sighed, sucked, and roared again. In a pile of dark seaweed lay a darker lump. I thought it might be a seal, which was exciting. Seal skins made warm coverings for winter and their teeth were pretty. I wore a necklace of them that day, hanging between my breasts, and a skirt woven from the tough slender grass stems that grew at the

lake's edge. On my wrist was a bag, also woven from reeds, in which was the stone blade I used to open shells and gut fish, and a small wooden bowl, to carry berries or drink from.

The seal lay motionless. I kept one eye on it while I checked my shelter. Wet sand had blown through it, piling up against each arched bone. I pulled out the mat and shook it, weighed it down with a rock at each corner, and left it to dry. Then, I went to look at the seal.

Through the clinging kelp I could see, splayed like a pale starfish, the fingers of a hand, and the shape of the cleft legs. I cleared away the slick brown straps and saw the face of a man. Intense curiosity seized me. The wind howled, the waves crashed, the gulls screamed, but I hardly noticed them. I picked off the seaweed piece by piece, brushed away the sand, dug him out with my hands, gazing at my discovery in wonder, almost awe.

He lay half on his side, one leg bent under him, one hand gripping into the sand, the other open at his side. I realized later he had crawled from the waves at some time in the night and they, receding, had washed away all trace. I rolled him onto his back. Not yet stiffened, not yet bloated, though his skin was as cold as a dead fish, and as clammy, his cheeks and eyes encrusted with salt. I thought he was dead and was already wondering where and how to bury him.

His hair was long and black, and had been shaved or plucked out across his forehead. There was a slight stubble on his cheeks and a wisp of beard. His clothes were not like anything I had ever seen: some animal skin, like seal but not seal, cut into strips and laced together to form a carapace around the chest, like a beetle or a shellfish. Attached to one side, the north, was a long rigid case, like the spiny feelers of a crayfish. A handle covered in woven cord protruded from it. Very gently I put my fingers round it and drew it out half way. It looked sharper than my shell blade and it glinted in the sun like the surface of the lake or a snake's eye. I slid it back

and started unlacing the garment. In all my life I had never wanted anything as much as I wanted these things: the garment, the blade, and a second shorter blade I found almost buried beneath him. My heart was pounding in my throat, my hands were trembling, my desire was close to sexual. I couldn't believe my luck. This was a thousand times better than the whale.

Under the animal skin plates was another garment, much softer and more closely woven than my skirt, and a long cloth wound around his buttocks and genitals. His lower limbs were covered in trousers not unlike those we wear in winter. I tugged and pulled at all these layers, putting my spoils in a pile beside me, until he lay on his back, naked.

One of the sweet things about men is the way their knobs swell in death. I stared at the stranger's pale, blue-veined engorged knob, thinking with fondness of my own dear men, sad for him that he would never know pleasure again, and my own sex began to ache in sympathy. I spread my legs and touched myself and when I was wet, straddled him and put him inside me. At once, I felt a huge gush of ecstasy and I shouted, knowing no one would hear me, and at that moment his eyes flew open and salt water burst in a stream from his mouth. He coughed and spluttered and I felt his knob contract and then expand. His eyes met mine, astonishment flooding into them, but his body had taken over, bucking and thrusting in its joy at being alive, and none of my men had ever given me such intense pleasure.

He cried out as loudly as I had as his salty essence spurted into me and I wanted deeply to make a child from it, as I never had done yet with any of my men. I consented with every fiber of my being to the spirit child waiting for a womb, *yes, yes, yes,* throbbing through me.

His eyes rolled back in his head, filling me with terror that I had found him only to lose him. I leant forward and placed my mouth

on his, tasted the crusted salt and sensing the soreness. He moaned and his tongue met mine as if he would suck moisture from me. He needed water.

When I moved away from him, his eyes opened and I saw the plea in them. I patted the air, saying, "Stay here, I am coming back." I made one hand into a bowl and mimed drinking water.

The sun was starting to burn and flies to gather. His pale, naked skin looked vulnerable so I fetched the mat and placed it over him, making a little tent above his face so he could breathe. I gathered up the pile of spoils I'd taken from him and put them in the shelter. Then I went back over the sandhills to the spring.

The sandhills looked dry and the river was tidal and salty, yet there are places where you can dig down into the sand with your hands and, in a few moments, the hole fills with fresh water. There was one of these not far from my ocean entrance.

It was part of craft, knowing where to find hidden water and men are not allowed to approach the springs in case the smell of their sweat turns the water sour. Sweat smells foul: my men shave their armpits with sharp shells and stone blades and rub crushed myrtle leaves into their skin. If I can smell sweat on them I can't bear them near me.

As I dug the hole and waited for it to fill I tried to remember if my seal man had smelled disgusting, but all I could recall was his taste of salt. He had certainly left a faint pollen scent of semen on me and I didn't want my men to notice it. It would only unsettle them and make them jealous. I used the first rise of water, scooped up in my bowl, to wash myself, wondering why I should feel guilty, realizing I was concealing something from my men and would continue to do so.

When I look back, I realized that was the moment when I made the decision that would change my life and my people's. I didn't know it then, I just felt uneasy and excited at the same time.

As I stood with the filled bowl in my hand, I heard a faint hushing noise overhead, the beat of thousands of wings and a thousand faint cries. The water birds were returning, which meant it was the first day of spring.

It was always a thrilling sound. No matter how often I heard it I never got used to it. The Northern people killed and ate birds; they traded ornaments and head dresses made from feathers which they wore at the ceremonial dances that ended each year's meeting. But we never killed birds and if we found a dead one we mourned over it. Our people became birds when we died, and these spirit birds could not be distinguished from real ones. When we walked among flocks of birds we were with our mothers and grandmothers. Sometimes they warned of events, a death or a storm. We could not kill and eat any bird in case we killed one of our ancestors. Consequently, they had no fear of us.

I had no idea where the birds went to in winter, how they reappeared like magic. Sometimes I wondered if they dived into the ocean once they were out of sight over the horizon, changing into the great shoals of fish that turned the sea dark in autumn. I liked to think of them bursting back through the surface when the days began to lengthen and the ocean warmed, their scales drying into feathers, their wings fluttering in joy.

I felt suddenly happy, seized by some spirit that made me want to sing and dance. I thought it might be the child, waiting to know if it was to come to me or not, waiting for me to sing it into being. I didn't want to spill the water so I walked back calmly, singing in a quiet voice, dancing inwardly.

Back on the beach, my new man had pushed away the mat and was staring upwards at the birds. As he listened to their cries, an expression of desolation came over his face and tears sprang into his eyes. He jumped up, gestured at them and then spoke in a way that was completely unknown to me, repeating certain words urgently.

I patted his arm to calm him, made him sit again, and gave him the bowl of water.

I studied him while he drank: his long muscled legs, his flat belly, the tufts of hair in his armpits that both repelled and excited me.

He sipped the water steadily, then spat out the last drops, rinsing his mouth. He spoke again to me and when he saw I did not understand, he smoothed out the sand and with his finger drew something that was not really a picture like the Northern traders used, or like the magic fish we women drew to entice them into our nets. When he pointed at the picture and then pointed upwards and cried like a bird, I saw the bird shape in it. It was a sign that meant *bird* in his speech. It enchanted me. He enchanted me. How strange and clever and delightful he was!

My face showed him I understood; he smiled, smoothed another patch of sand and drew another sign. Looking around, he pointed at my shelter and I saw it in the sign, its roof and walls. He touched his own nose and indicated the shelter and the bird.

I understood perfectly. His home was where the birds came from. They went to him in winter, they came to me in spring. Maybe they had brought him to me.

He patted his stomach and mimed putting food in his mouth. I was a bit shocked that he would indicate so directly that I should serve him. It seemed very bold and unmanly. Again, I felt that heady mixture of disgust and desire.

The tide which had washed him up in the night and then receded, was once more on the turn, which is when the surf clams waken. I went down to the water's edge and began to dig with my hands. I felt the smooth shell under my fingers, hooked it up, saw the little red tongue flicker before the clam snapped shut, and dropped it into my bag. When I had ten or so I took them back to him, opened them with my stone blade and gave them to him one by one, saving the last two for myself. They were meaty, a little gritty,

and quivered as we swallowed them.

I saw his knob had stiffened again, with life, not death as before, so we joined out parts once more with the same extraordinary intensity.

Afterwards, there was something about his behavior that disturbed me. He did not thank me as my men would have done or ask if I needed anything. Well, of course, he could not for he did not know my speech, but there are many ways to show gratitude and affection and he did not use any of them. I waited to see if he would make another drawing, but when he sat up, he looked around, stood, and went through a long movement with his hands, his eyes never leaving my face, his feet gripping the sand.

I could see as clearly as if it were real the invisible blade in his hands. The sun was dancing on the waves, dazzling me. I realized how all the muscles and sinews in his body had been strengthened for this end, to wield his blade.

When he had finished he knelt again and drew in the sand and said, "*Ka ta na.*"

Picking up the mat, I led him to the shelter. I spread the mat down inside, then gestured to him to come in and showed him the pile I had made of the things I had taken from him.

His eyes lit up when he saw the blades and a look of relief crossed his face. He made a sort of bob with his head and in it I finally saw gratitude. He would not thank me for water or food or the joining, but he would thank me for the blade.

I'd been aware for a while of a high keening and now he heard it too. He looked questioningly at me.

"It's my men," I said. "I have to go. Stay here." Then I mimed all this as best I could, and he nodded as if he understood. He gave me a look that was not at all respectful or submissive, but insolent, almost mocking.

MY MEN HAD NOT SEEN me since dawn. The storm in the night had unsettled them and now they feared I had been washed away by a giant wave or eaten by a sea monster. Men jumped to conclusions very quickly and as a result acted impulsively and recklessly.

I had three at that time: my first, and if I were honest, my favorite, was Wing, a boy I had grown up with, from a family who lived two sea entrances down from mine. All girls held in their head the linked system that told us where our men might be taken from. We wove its loops and spirals into decorations or drew them on flat wet sand. Children played together from all families on the lake shore—I could hear their shouts and laughter now—and Wing and I had always been good friends. He was very beautiful, everyone agreed on that, and I forgave him his vanity for he had plenty to be vain about.

My second was an older man on whom I had taken pity after his woman, my cousin, and her child died. Such deaths were considered very bad luck, and many men threw themselves into the river and drowned rather than live on shunned and alone, but my cousin had made me promise I would look after Talon, and because I knew she had truly loved him, I did.

Wing had light brown hair and sea gray eyes, but Talon was dark-eyed and black-haired. My third man, Fin, was also black-haired but had light eyes like Wing. He was younger than me, still very slight, with little facial hair. I was waiting for him to become a little older before I joined with him, though I liked petting him, and the others spoiled him, braiding his hair, plucking the tiny fluff from his armpits, and little by little showing him how to please a woman.

When I appeared over the sandhills, my men cried out like plovers and ran to me, taking my hands, asking me where I had been and if I was all right. Talon had tears in his eyes—he had been abandoned once and knew the reality of a man left without a woman, without craft.

I reassured them and let them carry me to the lake shore where they had grilled the morning fish. It was well past the time when we usually ate the first meal of the day and I was glad to see they had obediently not eaten without me. The fish were the ones we call round bones, for they had tiny patterned bones like pebbles in their heads which we women liked and the men collected and polished for us. I had caught them the previous day, so they were still fresh, and there were still some live ones swimming in the submerged nets.

When we had finished eating, I told Wing to get my craft ready.

"It's already getting late. It will be so hot," he said. "We have plenty of fish. You should rest now."

I made a gesture to indicate he should do as he was told. I knew the wet earth and moist air had produced many insects, that the fish would stay close to the surface and start leaping for me. The tide was flowing back, carrying smaller fish in from the ocean and the larger ones that preyed on them.

Our craft were woven from reeds with frames of branches from the slender tough dune trees, made watertight with seal skin and resin. They were very light and most men were too heavy to ride in them safely, though boys played in them until they began to grow hair, pretending they were women as boys do.

Fin went to the water's edge and began to dig out river clams. They were small and muddy tasting so we didn't usually eat them, but they were good for bait.

Wing asked if he could come with me, but I wanted to be alone and told him to stay and make new fish hooks from the bones and prepare more lines. His face went sulky and I knew he had been hoping for a joining: we often spent the hot afternoons in the shade of the stringybark trees on the island where the pelicans roosted. I would have to make it up to him later.

I took a light catching net and a heavier basket-like one to tow in the water. The lake's surface was smooth and slick. When it was

calm, the waves died down completely, but the ocean's movement still made itself felt and swells appeared and disappeared quite suddenly. You could hear sounds from a long way off, the ripple as the swell hit the shore, the piping of the waterbirds, a pelican scratching its head with one huge webbed foot, and the constant underweaving of the surf's roar. To all this was added, as I'd known it would be, the buzz and drone of insects.

As I crossed the channel where the water was deep and green, I could see right down to the sand below. On the farther side, the fish had stirred the sand up and the ocean had turned white and gray with fragments as blue as the sky, flashing silver as the fish thrashed and leaped.

There were so many fish and they were so dazed by the abundance of insects that it was easy to catch enough for the four of us. I caught some for my seal man and some more just for the thrill of it, and two even leapt into the craft and lay flapping and desperate. I transferred them into the larger net, tied its neck and trailed it behind me as I paddled back before the afternoon breeze pinned me to the shore. The clouds had turned to scales and wisps so I knew it would be windy later.

My men thought it was magic how I know these things, but it was just craft. All women know it. When women give birth, everything comes from them: all life, all knowledge, all craft.

I was almost at the shore when a movement caught my eye on the top of the sandhills. Something flashed in the sun. I heard Fin's voice cry out in surprise. I looked up and saw the dark shape against the cloud-scattered sky. Being low on the water changes the way you see things; they look much larger than they really are. My seal man looked like a giant. He held his blade in both hands, raised it, turned and brought it down faster than a snake strikes or a tern dives. It was like a dance. I watched, fascinated by the subtlety and beauty of the movements, recognizing some deep craft at work.

My men were screaming. To them it must have seemed a terrifying apparition, a figure from a nightmare or one of the ocean monsters about which we spun tales to keep men from the beach and children away from deep dangerous water.

Their screams alerted families from all the other sea entrances, and everyone ran out onto the river shore, women grabbing sticks and firestones, men holding the children behind them, and gazed up at the sandhills.

I beached my craft, pulled the fish nets into the shallow water and told Fin to secure the catch. It was always best in a crisis to give men something to do. It calmed them. I said loudly, "This is my new man, Seal," and, telling Wing and Talon to follow me, ran swiftly up to the crest where he was cutting those exotic shapes in the air with his blade.

As I came closer I could hear the blade sigh, sounding like the sea when it retreats across the sand. I thought it must surely cut through the air and reveal, as lightning does, the spirit world that lies behind. It was craft, equal in every way to my own, just as powerful, just as dangerous, and completely strange to me. I felt like my men must have often felt, awed and uncomprehending.

I stopped a little way from him, and made Wing and Talon stand behind me. I held my hand out to the seal man and beckoned to him. He looked at me, then let his insolent, fearless gaze pass over my men, and the others on the shore behind us. After a long moment, he returned the blade to its casing and made the same bob with his head, like a heron feeding. He walked towards me. I thought he would follow me and turned, but he pushed past me, making a small beckoning gesture as if I should follow him, and headed towards our fire, the nearest one, where he sat down cross-legged, still giving those keen raking glances all around.

I felt he noticed everything: our shelters built from sand pines and thatched with reeds, the craft pulled up on the shore, the dry-

ing fish on poles, the cords and strings Talon had been weaving, the bone fish hooks Wing had made. Again, I saw his smile as though he thought he was superior. His lack of deference and respect irritated and aroused me. I would wipe that look off his face. I would make him join till he could not walk. I would make him appreciate craft in all its forms.

We sat down around him and I told him the men's names. He could pronounce them properly, which made him sound like a child. *Taron* he said and for his own name *Shiru. Ooing,* he said for Wing which reduced Fin to helpless giggles. He didn't like being laughed at. I felt sorry for him for I saw he was proud and vainer even than Wing. He reached out and flicked Fin's cheek. It must have stung for Fin's face reddened and his eyes filled with tears. Talon and Wing immediately drew closer as if they would protect him and there was a moment when the air thrummed with hostility. Seal's hand hovered above his blade's handle. I touched his arm, and made him come with me to the water's edge.

Quite a crowd had gathered around us, watchful, muttering, and they continued to stare as I showed Seal the fish in the basket, took one out, cut its spine with my blade and slit its belly to remove the guts. I threw these into the water and crabs immediately sidled up to eat them. Two large pelicans swam lazily towards the shore to see if I was going to share with them. I tossed a fish to each of them. Seal's eyes flickered as their huge bills opened, as if he had never seen such a bird before.

I indicated that he should help me and he stared at me as if he could not understand what I was asking. His eyes were so black I could not discern his pupils. He seemed offended but I insisted, using the words we use with boys when they are stubborn. He did not understand them, but they have a power of their own. He frowned and as if against his will took his short blade, grasped a fish, and stabbed it.

His first efforts were clumsy and the flesh was spoiled by the spilling guts. I threw the fish to the pelicans and continued patiently instructing him as women have always showed their men how to look after themselves. Eventually, we had all the fish gutted and prepared for cooking.

Talon had built up the fire and Wing grilled the fish on sharpened sticks. They were both very attentive to me, even more than usual. Talon flattered me at every opportunity, Wing made me laugh with his quick wit. He imitated Seal eating, his wary glances, his proud stance, and pretended to flick Fin as the stranger had. It was my right to bring another man into our family—I only had two and a boy—and they were not questioning that. But they feared being supplanted in my affections and wanted to establish their own status.

When the meal was finished the sky was patterned with dark gray clouds, turning the color of fire as the sun set. The glimmer over the sandhills told me the moon was rising, almost full, out of the ocean. When it cleared the crest and cast shadows on the strand, I took Seal back to the beach and joined with him there, many times, for we had an insatiable thirst for each other. Just before dawn I returned to our river hut and found Wing still awake and desperate for me. Afterwards I slept in his arms until after daybreak.

EVERY MONTH THE WOMEN WHO were not carrying a child bled together at the time of the full moon. We celebrated our red stream, painted it on the entrance to our shelters and made intricate designs with it, coloring the sand. It was our strength that we bled and did not die. Our blood's rich smell was the smell of life. It was a time for resting, to replenish and restore. I did not bleed that moon. I already knew my first child was growing within me. I was ecstatic and ripe with love. I had seen other women like this, but I had not known until I felt it myself how all-encompassing, how complete, it would be.

My men knew at once, and their excitement was intense. When

a family was given a child, everyone rejoiced. They could hardly bear to let me out of their sight, and satisfied all my needs and cravings almost before I was aware of them myself. I had never been so happy.

Shiru—we all called him that now—did not seem to notice. He was aware of so much, but he was not aware of the changes that were taking place in me. He was preoccupied and spent most of his time on the beach staring out at the line between sea and sky. He paced the length of sand between the river mouths, gazing at the surf tossed water. He climbed the sandhills at a run, fifty or sixty times, before taking his stand at the top and going through his dance with his blade.

Little by little he learned to speak the way we did, and I learned to understand the word pictures he drew in the sand. Sometimes I let myself dream that he would be with us forever and help raise the child he had made, but I sensed it would not happen. The birds formed strange patterns on the shore, on the water, in the sky, as they prepared to leave. They fed urgently and carelessly. I understood now that they did not disappear into the sea and turn into fish. They flew a great distance, far, far away, to where Shiru lived.

The birds unsettled him as if he would take wing and fly with them. He behaved more like an adolescent boy than a grown man. He and my youngest, Fin, took a liking to each other and often roamed around the river and the lake together, swimming across the channel and basking with the seals on the sandbars in the late summer sun. He was a slow, clumsy swimmer, compared to lithe, fishlike Fin.

One day I smelled smoke and roasting flesh drifting across the river on the off-shore breeze. A little later an eddy of feathers, black and white, floated past, their tips pink with blood.

Even after swimming back, Shiru's and Fin's lips were shiny with grease and their hands stank of meat.

I was angry. Fin cried and confessed they had killed two birds and eaten them. I reprimanded them with harsh words. Shiru's face

went hard and he set off over the sandhills to the whale shelter, without speaking.

I looked at Talon and Wing, saw their expressions of fear and sorrow. We all knew people who had died the previous year. These birds could have been them. Now their souls would never fly free through the clouds to the spirit world. Dread settled in the pit of my stomach.

"You should not have brought him here," Wing said, daring in his shock to criticize me.

"You have to get rid of him," said Talon. Fin cried harder.

I knew they were right, but the decision was too bitter. I said nothing for a while.

"You will have to start making a larger craft for me," I said finally. "One that will carry me and our child. Take this one to the top of the sandhills for me. I will get rid of it in the morning."

For it was our custom to take old craft out into the ocean and sink them there.

It was one of those rare still nights when there was no wind and the sea was still. The silence when the surf stops was huge and astonishing. The sea stretched out like a reed mat and on the line of the sky a low bank of clouds looked like a distant shore.

Shiru was sulking, still furious. He thought I had come to seek his forgiveness but it didn't matter what he thought any more. We didn't have enough words between us to explain things. We let our bodies talk and his anger made him rough. I accepted it as both punishment and justification. What he did to me that night only confirmed what I had to do to him.

I meant to tell him about the baby but then I decided not to. If he could not see what was in front of his eyes he did not deserve to know.

I slept very little, unsettled by the silence, waiting for dawn. The birds started calling while it was still dark. I sat outside the shelter, watching the sea turn gray and the eastern sky pale yellow. There was still no surf and the cloud land looked closer.

Huge flocks of birds flew overhead, towards the northeast, calling, calling.

I woke Shiru.

"I am taking you home," I said.

He came out, looked up at the birds and then at the still surface of the sea. A mad light of hope shone in his eyes. I drew on the sand as he had for me, the signs that meant *bird* and *home.*

He said, "Wait, wait," and began to prepare himself, putting on his clothes and his carapace. He combed his hair with his fingers and twisted it into a tail on top of his head. He took his two blades and fastened them by his side.

I carried my craft down to the water and held it steady while he climbed in, and knelt gingerly on the reed floor. I pushed it into deeper water, sprang in myself and took up my reed paddle.

Craft are made for women who are very light and agile. They are not suitable for men, and Shiru was a large man, made heavier by the plated outer garment that I had thought was like a crayfish shell. But because the sea was so calm we skimmed over the surface. All the while, birds flew overhead, thousands and thousands of them, filling the air with the beat of their wings and their cries. He fixed his eyes upwards as though he would fly home with them.

He did not see me take my blade and cut through the reeds. The water started to seep in. I stood and dived in one movement and swam as far as I could underwater. When I surfaced he was still kneeling, one hand gripping the side of the craft as it sank beneath his weight, the other on his blade as though he would draw it in one last flash.

I cried then. The salt water hurt me in all sorts of places. He had damaged my body more than I had realized. I mourned the loss of the blades and the garments I had coveted, and I cried for men, how pitiful they were, how wrong it was that we treated them so contemptuously and tried to control them so completely.

It took me a long time to swim back. I had gone too far, deceived

by the calm sea.

Maybe he will get home, I told myself as I swam, endlessly.

When I crawled onto the beach, the sea's surface was beginning to crease, the surf had built up and the distant cloud land had dissolved. Wing and Talon found me and carried me home. They should not have been there but I could not rebuke them. They probably saved my life and when I recovered I could not bring myself to punish them.

Every time I went to the beach I looked for Shiru. A pile of seaweed, a seal on the shore made my heart dive like a tern. But the waves did not wash him up again. When spring came, the birds returned and I thought his spirit might be flying with them. My son was three months old then. His eyes sought the birds and their cries made him quiver.

The child was not the only result of the mysterious seal man with his carapace and his two blades. Everything began to change. Wing and Talon often went to the ocean, dug up clams and played in the surf. I had forgotten the reason why they were not supposed to do this and I did not punish them. Other men followed them and no harm came to them.

Fin started meeting one of his childhood playmates in secret and when I confronted him over it, he declared he loved her and could not live without her. Once, I would have mocked him, but I understood such love now. Soon the girl was pregnant, and since she had no sea entrance of her own, came to live with me. This had never happened before, but I no longer knew how to put a stop to things.

I took my son out every day in the new craft Wing made for me. He could swim before he could walk. I whispered to him in a forbidden way: *this is where the round bones dwell. Hear that ripple on the shore? It is the wind changing. See the foam quiver and move away? The tide has turned.*

These are the secrets of craft.

RECONCILING MEMORY

GAIL Z. MARTIN

SLEEP NOW." KESTEL FALKE PATTED the shoulder of the man who lay next to her tangled in the sumptuous satin sheets. He had paid well for her company, presenting her with a diamond bracelet for a weekend's pleasure.

Kestel's companion did not stir. She smiled, assured that the potion she drugged him with had taken effect. He might have slept soundly without the drugs, after demonstrating more amorous vigor than Kestel expected of a man his age. Still, she dared not take a chance he might have awoken and find her gone from his bed.

Duke Leon Hastings lay on his side, with his right arm crooked beneath him. The lantern's glow revealed the tattoo of a falcon in flight, the mark of his noble house. The sight of it goaded Kestel to remember the purpose that brought her to Hastings's bed. She knew he wanted to believe he'd paid for her services, and she allowed him to believe the lie. More powerful men than Hastings had bribed her with exotic and costly gifts far surpassing the gems in the bracelet, all for a few hours of her company.

Kestel retrieved the silver knife from where she concealed it in her discarded skirts, along with a small glass vial. She turned over the sleeping man's right hand, and made a tiny cut on the skin of his wrist, just deep enough for blood to bead. She gathered a few

droplets in the vial, then used Hastings's kerchief to staunch the flow and wipe the cut clean. Moving silently, she replaced the vial in a hidden pocket of her skirts and withdrew a silk pouch.

Kestel smiled as she rose from the bed, gathered a satin robe around her, and slipped the knife into a pocket. Let Hastings believe he pursued her; the falsehood suited her purposes. Her seduction of him had nothing to do with sex except as the lure best suited to draw in her prey. For months she had made certain to be within sight of Hastings but always out of reach, on the arm of one patron or another she knew he envied. Men like Hastings were easy to read, even easier to manipulate. Being seen with those men made Kestel a coveted possession to be pursued and won at any cost, just as she had planned.

She glanced back at the unconscious, naked man. Sleeping with him had been a distasteful means to an end, but she had done far worse things to achieve her goals. After the first rough encounter that took her innocence, Kestel learned to step away inside her mind to a safe distance as her body went through the motions. She had better things to think about, like vengeance.

Kestel stopped to glance in the large mirror that hung on the wall across from the bed. Leon Hastings liked to watch his conquests, voyeur and victimizer wrapped up in one. Kestel moved so that she blocked the sight of him with her body and ran a hand through her dark red hair, assuring the curls fell just so. She bit her bottom lip, making it plump and reddened, then smoothed her hands over the satin that clung to her curves. If she encountered anyone in the hallway, they would see nothing but a courtesan, just another of the elder Hastings's conquests. Men would pay no attention to anything except the rise of her breasts and the slant of her hips, and women would not bother to give her a second glance, merely happy that Hastings found an outlet for his debauchery that did not include them. They would all see what they wanted to see, and Kestel her-

self—the woman who was more than the sum of her beauty and body—would be invisible, as she liked it.

Moving silently, Kestel slipped out of the bedroom. Getting inside the manor house had been the whole purpose of the tryst. She found Hastings no more repulsive than any of her other clients, bored and lecherous rich men who needed to prove to themselves that their youth had not fled. Yet Hastings offered Kestel something far more valuable than the diamond trinket she would break apart and sell for weapons, potions, and spells. He was one of the final pieces in a puzzle Kestel had been working on for nearly a decade, and now that he had granted her safe passage inside the house, Kestel intended to put the opportunity to good use.

The old lech had been more helpful than he knew, vainly showing off his manor as he attempted to impress the courtesan whose affections he had pursued for months. Fate had given Kestel a beautiful face, a sumptuous body, and a mind as sharp as the blade hidden beneath her robe. She'd taken those assets and clawed her way into the Donderath court as the most sought-after courtesan in the kingdom, and she included King Merrill himself among her many lovers. The secrets she'd learned she parlayed into influence or on occasion sold as a spy. One rich man's bed at a time, she gained the information to exact her revenge.

Plied by brandy and Kestel's flattery, Duke Hastings had regaled her with stories of his ancestors' glorious exploits, as well as his own long-faded military honors. Her rapt attention and a hand on his arm had been all it took to loosen the duke's tongue, making it easy for her to turn the conversation to his son, Damian.

Kestel's lip curled as she remembered the duke's obvious pride as he spoke about Damian. She'd hung on the duke's every word as he spilled the details she had gone to his bed to discover. He'd even pointed out the door that led to Damian's chambers, though he was quick to add that his son was in Castle Reach right now, possibly

at Quillarth Castle, busy with important tasks. Papa's pride and joy.

Now Kestel found her way back to Damian's rooms without incident and easily picked the lock. She let herself inside, closed the door behind her, and waited for her eyes to adjust to the darkness. Here in his private rooms, she could pick up his scent, a mixture of sweat, cloves, and brandy. It sickened her. She found a lantern, lit it, and shuttered all but one pane to allow her to see without attracting attention.

An oil portrait hung over the mantel, and Kestel stopped to get a better look at her quarry. Damian Hastings was now a man in his forties, but the portrait showed him much younger, just in his early twenties. *That's what he looked like, when it happened.*

The figure in the portrait looked down on the room with patrician entitlement, a scion of wealth and privilege. Strong jaw, high cheekbones, wheat-blond hair, and grey, cold eyes made him handsome, but no compassion tempered his demeanor. Age and dissolution made it difficult to see the resemblance to his father. The older man's profile was lost in jowls and bags beneath his eyes from overindulgence, and the last time Kestel had spotted Damian, he looked well on his way to the same fate.

Not that he'll live that long.

She tore herself away from the portrait and moved farther into the room, seeking the objects she needed. A comb on Damian's dressing table provided a few strands of hair, which she tucked into a silk pouch. She cut a small corner from the hem of a well-worn shirt, and plucked a few bristles from his shaving brush. Together with his father's blood, these items from the son would be all she needed to draw the younger Hastings to his death. Kestel smiled, the first time she felt truly happy in a long time. Soon, very soon, she would have what she'd desired for so long.

Kestel blew out the lantern, replaced it where she found it, and let herself out of Damian's room. As she rounded the corner into

the next hallway, a servant looked up, startled to encounter anyone at this time of night.

"Can I be of service?" he asked. Kestel noticed that the customary honorific "M'lady" would not be forthcoming for a paid companion of the lord, not even from one of the servants. Kestel ignored the slight, smiling in the secret knowledge of what was to come.

"I didn't want to wake Lord Hastings," she replied, making damn sure her tone reminded the servant that paid or not, she had the ear of his master and shared his bed. "I can't fall asleep. I'd like a brandy."

If the servant thought to question, he thought better of it. She did not have to answer to him.

"Of course," he replied. "Shall I bring it to m'lord's rooms?"

Kestel nodded. "I'll wait just inside the door. Knock softly. He's sleeping well, and I don't want to disturb him." If the witch who sold her the potion told the truth, Hastings would sleep through cannon fire for a few more candlemarks, but the lie made a convenient excuse.

"As you wish."

Kestel watched the servant disappear, then made her way back to Hasting's rooms. She replaced her knife in its sheath and hid the silken pouch in the hidden pocket of her skirt, patting it once in satisfaction. *So close. After all this time, so close.*

When a soft rap came at the door, Kestel was waiting. "Do you require anything else?" the servant asked, extending a silver tray holding a goblet of brandy.

Kestel took the goblet with an enigmatic smile. "No. I have everything I need."

"ARE YOU CERTAIN THIS WILL work?" Kestel eyed the witch appraisingly. For her part, the witch had the good sense to flinch.

"Yes, m'lady. I've warded the room he always takes at the Rooster and Pig when he comes into Castle Reach to drink and gamble." Surana held up a hand to forestall argument. "No one saw me. I

know what I'm doing," she added with a dour look.

"Once he's within the warding, the spell will activate on his blood," Surana went on. "It won't trigger to anyone else. You'll be able to enter the room, but he won't be able to leave. No one will hear what goes on inside until his death breaks the spell."

A slow smile touched Kestel's lips. "You do good work."

"And you keep me alive to do more of it," the witch replied. "We work well together."

With any other witch—and Castle Reach had many—the chance of betrayal would have forced Kestel to cover her tracks. She and Surana had history, old bonds that traced from when neither of them yet wielded the influence they had today. Two young girls, hungry and alone, trying to keep body and soul together in the city's rough neighborhoods. Their shared sins long ago became too numerous and too entangled for either to attempt to leverage that knowledge against the other. And in the years that passed, both Kestel and Surana had gained the skills and hard edge that enabled them to use the talents they possessed to make their mark in the world.

"You're certain he's the one?" The tone in Surana's voice made it clear that she understood the gravity of the situation.

Kestel nodded. "He has the mark. It's him."

Surana withdrew a cloth-wrapped parcel from her bag. She handed the item to Kestel balanced across her palms. "I bathed the blade in spelled water that held the items you brought me," she said as Kestel took the parcel from her and reverently peeled back the coverings to expose the spelled knife. "Don't make a habit of this: dark magic like this is going to take me a while to recover from."

Kestel's brow quirked up and she looked at Surana, worried. Surana shook her head. "You've been after this son of a bitch for a long time. It was worth it. My gift to you—like I promised all those years ago."

I'd give you his head on a pike, if I could, Surana had said. A pledge of undying friendship from one young girl to another, on a night they'd huddled in a cold deserted building too hungry to move and too frightened to venture out.

I'll slit her throat for you, someday, Kestel had returned. Kestel had already made good on her part of the bargain, long ago. Ridding the world of Surana's drunken, abusive mother had been Kestel's first kill.

Surana's sad smile suggested that she knew the turn Kestel's thoughts had taken. "Worth it," she said. "Just make it count." A cold glint came into her eyes. "And enjoy it."

Kestel embraced Surana and watched her friend walk away. The further she was from the Rooster and Pig tonight, the better. Kestel had every intention of surviving the night's work, but had no illusions about the likelihood of the events transpiring without a hitch. Killing a nobleman's son would earn her the noose if she were caught. *Then I just better not get caught.*

Kestel paid her informants well for their tips and their silence. She'd gained a dangerous reputation even in the city's roughest sections. Damian Hastings was a slave to his habits, and tonight he would come into the city to oversee his father's business dealings during the day, then bet and drink all night. Kestel would be waiting.

She paced the small room. Engraham, the owner of the Rooster and Pig, kept a large room for regular lodgers, and a few other discreet rooms for the wastrel nobles who came to gamble in the hidden room beneath the tavern where fortunes were gained and lost. Most people knew the Rooster and Pig for its excellent bitterbeer, but in the upper circles of society, the tavern was most popular for its illicit games of chance and clap-free whores. Damian Hastings was an ardent patron, though luck was against him as often as not.

Tonight, though he did not know it yet, Hastings's luck had turned.

Kestel's heartbeat quickened as she thought about what she was planning to do. *So many years, leading up to this. And if I succeed,*

when it's done and he's dead, what then? What purpose do I have, once
vengeance is satisfied?

She had no answer for that question. Serving as a courtesan to
the rich and powerful meant she no longer went hungry or cold.
Her patrons kept her comfortably ensconced in a private apartment
not far from Quillarth Castle, and their money assured she dressed
and ate every bit as well as her noble clientele. The trifles and gifts
they bestowed paid for protection, or were carefully hidden away
should emergency strike. Being a wealthy man's companion paid
well, a means to an end. Kestel regretted nothing.

When Damian entered the room and closed the door behind
him, Kestel was waiting, just outside the reach of the lantern's light.

"Who's there? Show yourself!" Damian remained sober enough
to realize another presence in the room could mean nothing good.
But when he turned to open the door, the knob remained stubbornly immobile.

"You can't leave," Kestel said, sashaying out of the shadows.

Damian began to pound on the door, shouting for assistance.

"They can't hear you." She waited for him to spend himself, crying out until his voice grew rough, slamming his fist against the door.

When Damian turned to face her, his rum-bleary eyes held fear
and uncertainty. "Who are you? Why are you here?"

"Show me your wrist," she demanded, letting her knife glint
in the lamplight.

Damian raised his arm and turned it so that the falcon tattoo
showed clearly. "My father's a duke. You can rob me, but you'll pay
for it." He gathered his wits and drew himself up, as if reminding
himself not to show weakness to an inferior. Drink gave him courage; privilege made him belligerent.

"I'm here to kill you," Kestel replied. Now that the moment she'd
been waiting for was finally here, Kestel felt nothing. No elation, no
sense of triumph, just a deep, aching cold.

"I'm worth more alive," Damian countered. "My father would pay a ransom."

"You're worth more to me dead." Kestel stopped beyond Hastings's reach, knowing that even weak animals became dangerous when cornered. "Don't you want to know why?"

Damian's eyes narrowed. "Did I bed you and then move on?" His expression grew patronizing. "Darlin', I'm sorry if you expected more, but you really should have known better."

Once, his comments would have made fire surge through Kestel's blood. Now, all that remained was ice. "Fifteen years ago. You raped a woman in the alley behind this tavern, a serving girl. Bring anything to mind?"

Damian licked his lips nervously. "Not really. There've been so many—"

"She bit you, and cut you with a piece of glass."

A nasty glint came into Damian's eyes. "That little wildcat? Oh yes, I remember her. Left me with a scar," he said, moving his right wrist to reveal the faint remainder of a bite mark. "Taught her a lesson real good." He looked Kestel over, his expression torn between appraisal and a leer. "Was she your mama? You look like her. Bet you're a wildcat, too."

"She didn't want your attention. She wasn't yours to take. And she never recovered from the beating you gave her."

Damian shrugged. "She was no one of consequence. Just another slattern. Like mother, like daughter."

Kestel knew Damian intended to bait her into making a rash move. He outweighed her, and his fondness for rough company had no doubt taught him how to fight dirty. Kestel smiled, confident in Surana's magic.

"She was of consequence to me." Kestel lunged forward, slicing down across Damian's chest with the spelled knife, scoring a cut deep enough to slash through his clothing and open a bloody

furrow across his ribs.

"You bloody whore!" Damian roared and started toward her, only to freeze, eyes widening and hands clutching his chest.

"Do you feel it?" Kestel stepped back, well out of his reach, as Damian fell to his knees. His breath hitched and his face paled as the magic coursed through his veins.

"What did you do to me?"

"I wanted you to feel what my mother felt that night." Kestel's calm, quiet voice held the promise of violence. "Fear. Helplessness. Impotent rage."

Damian's body shook as the spell's grip tightened. His breaths came in short, hard pants, and sweat glistened on his forehead.

"You choked her. Held her down and kept your hand on her throat while you forced her. Hit her when she fought you. Cut her. Took what you wanted and strangled her with your own hands, then pulled up your pants and walked away like you'd just taken a piss. I saw you. I saw it all, but I was too young to do anything about it—then."

"You filthy bitch, I'll kill you for this!"

"No, you won't. The spell is fatal. No one can hear us, no one will come to help. Just like no one came to help my mother." Watching Damian suffer fulfilled a long-held goal, but Kestel knew it could never restore what had been taken that night.

"You're going to kill me over a serving wench?" The incredulity in Damian's eyes might have been laughable if the reasoning behind it had not cut so deeply.

"No, I'm putting down a rabid dog who killed the most important person in my world."

The tremors that shook Damian's body grew more violent as the poison progressed. Blood leaked sluggishly from the chest wound, staining his silk shirt and dripping down onto the floor. His skin was flushed and clammy, and the faint blue tinge to his lips told

Kestel vengeance would not be far off.

"We could have struck a bargain. I could have made you rich."

"I didn't want a bargain. Or your money. I saw you kill her. And all I've ever wanted since that night is to see you dead by my hand."

Damian fell forward onto his hands and knees, retching up bile. He fell face down into his vomit, eyes rolling back as the tremors grew worse until convulsions racked his body, arching his back and drawing the muscles of his face into a rictus grin.

Kestel watched, disappointed at the cold emptiness of her victory. She harbored no illusions that her mother would be proud, either of the murder or of who and what Kestel had become to achieve her goal. But as she watched Damian struggle for his last breaths, saw the fear in his eyes as the light in them faded, the small girl who watched her mother's death from the shadows of a stinking alley finally stopped being afraid. Kestel wrapped her arms around herself, reassuring what remained of that young child, promising that she would keep her safe forever. Vengeance wouldn't bring her mother back, but it did mean one fewer monster lived to repeat the crime.

When she was certain Damian was dead, Kestel wiped her knife on his pants and sheathed the blade. She broke the warding and slipped out the back door into the night, shaking off the feeling she was being watched.

KESTEL PACED IN HER APARTMENT, restless and on edge. Killing Damian marked the pinnacle of her life's work, the realization of the dream that had spurred her on night after cold and terrifying night. Wanting him dead, needing revenge, had given her life purpose, and absolved her in her mind's eye of the sacrifices and sins necessary to achieve her goal.

Now that purpose had been fulfilled, and there was nothing to take its place.

Her status as one of the most sought-after courtesans in the court had its perquisites. This apartment, paid for by her patrons, easily supplied the comforts due a lesser noble. Her wardrobe, food, and jewelry, all came from the largesse of her patrons past and present. Kestel knew that few courtesans retained their charms and patrons for long. She made provisions for the time she'd leave the business, by choice or not. Yet she never expected this emptiness. No thrill of victory, no satisfaction of completion. Just a dark void that sapped her energy and turned her thoughts in circles.

A soft rap at the door startled Kestel from her thoughts. She tensed, drawing her knife and keeping the blade behind her back as she moved. She didn't expect any visitors, and could think of no one who would be welcome just then.

A lone woman in a cloak stood in the doorway. "Please, let me in. I mean you no harm."

Wary, Kestel took a few steps back to allow the newcomer to enter. *If I have to kill her, fewer people will see if I do it inside.*

"I know what you did at the Rooster and Pig," the woman said quietly.

Kestel kept her face unreadable. "I have no idea what you're talking about."

The stranger lowered the cowl that had kept her features in shadow. Kestel now recognized her from court, the wife of a minor lord, or perhaps a duke. Someone of enough importance to be in the outer circles of prominence, yet not sufficiently influential to bother remembering. "I know you killed Damian Hastings."

"If you believe that, and you came here to tell me, you're not very smart." Kestel kept her voice low and quiet. She had already considered half a dozen ways the woman could die without anyone being the wiser.

"I'm not going to turn you in."

"You're going to try to blackmail me?" Kestel's smile was cold.

"I don't play that game." She made sure her blade glinted in the candlelight, a warning.

"I want to hire you."

That brought Kestel up short. "Hire me? Look, you're very pretty, and I won't say that I've never taken a woman patron, but it's not really my..."

"I want to hire you to kill someone, like you killed Hastings."

Kestel stared at the woman. "I'm not an assassin."

"You could be."

Kestel gave an incredulous chuckle. "You're crazy."

"Hear me out." The stranger looked serious. "I went to the Rooster and Pig tonight to beg Hastings for his help. One of his guards took advantage of my daughter. Because of him, she hanged herself. I meant to offer Hastings any payment he wanted to punish the man who hurt my baby. I didn't care what it cost me." She paused and took a breath to steady herself.

"Then I saw you go in, and I waited. I thought—well, that doesn't matter now," she said, ducking her head. Kestel knew exactly what her unexpected guest thought, that Kestel and Hastings were meeting for a tryst.

"When you came out, I went in and found him. And then I knew what happened, what you did, and I realized you could help me."

"I'm really not—"

"Please," the woman cut her off. "Do you know how many wronged women would pay handsomely for you to kill the men who hurt them? How many went to the beds of men they didn't love because of arranged marriages, sold off like trollops by their fathers or older brothers? Men who beat them, raped them, abused their children, threatened their sons and daughters if they dared complain?" Tears pooled in the stranger's eyes.

"You are privy to secrets. You have access to the wealthiest and most powerful men in the kingdom. These women would pay you

well, and you'd have no fear of them revealing your secret. Exposing you would expose them. They would lose everything."

Kestel opened her mouth to say, *I'm not an assassin*, and then shut it again. *I sleep with men for money. I betray secrets for money. I've spent a lifetime plotting to murder someone. I've got precious little virtue left to squander, and at least this way, I could do some good for women like mama. Women who might not have to die.*

Purpose. The realization hit Kestel hard enough to make her take a sharp breath. This stranger offered her something more than money, more than vengeance. A chance to do something that mattered, to redeem herself. A reason to live.

Kestel lowered her knife. "Your proposal intrigues me," she said, and gave a genuine smile. "Come in. Let's talk."

MONICA VALENTINELLI

THIS IS NOT ANOTHER "WHY REPRESENTATION IS IMPORTANT" ESSAY

FTER READING THE STORIES AND other essays in *Hath No Fury*, chances are you already know why representation in fiction is important. Maybe you've been part of the discussion for decades, or maybe you've recently joined the growing chorus of writers and readers shouting "We need diverse books!" online through the hashtag #weneeddiversebooks or #ownvoices. You might even possess a deeply personal story why representation matters to you, or you are beginning to understand how poorly written characters hurt the people they represent by reinforcing stereotypes that dehumanize them. Whatever the reason, however you have arrived at the conclusion that representation is important, this is not that kind of essay—because I *agree* with you.

Unfortunately, while many people agree that representation is important, they don't believe it is *necessary*. The distinction is this: if you think it's important, you support the people advocating and actively vying for change, but you personally don't feel obligated or committed to be a part of the movement. For those people, certain adages might even sound perfectly logical. They don't have time or money to get involved. A person of color needs to simply work hard

enough and they'll make it on their own. They don't have any power to effect change. A woman author doesn't get the PR she needs because she hasn't written a quality book. We shouldn't concern ourselves with the portrayal of characters in fiction because it's all made up—so what's the harm? Despite the fact that my simplistic view relates to a complex problem that involves hundreds, if not thousands, of people who edit, write, read, buy, review, sell, and publish books, I can deconstruct this even further to tell you the real reason why it hasn't happened yet. What's more, I can sum it up in a single word: racism.

The call for better representation has yielded frightened, negative reactions that are rooted in deep, cultural biases supported by outmoded methods of decision-making that stretch back decades, if not centuries. Thus, for whatever reason, many people consider the accurate portrayal of various cultures and identities to be risky, progressive, and socially liberal simply because they do not recognize that the default, or most commonly portrayed, identity is that of a white, cisgendered male. These people do not see the harm of their views, because they've internalized that there has been none caused or intended. What's more, when the word "racism" is accurately used to describe actions that support the status quo, they become defensive because they understand intellectually that racism is bad, but can't admit to having acted or spoken in a racist manner.

Racism has existed in the past, does exist now, and, if history holds true, will exist in the future. Though some might believe this either isn't or will not be the case, our remembrance of historic milestones like the Civil Rights Movement of the 1960s doesn't neatly fit the reality. Social progress has never been achieved linearly nor uniformly and, as human rights are not static, representation isn't either. Thus, black characters won't suddenly be well-represented and then *Poof!* the struggle is over. It may be uncomfortable or even frustrating to acknowledge this is the case, but I'm of the mind that

not facing hard truths like this prevents real growth.

Unfortunately, there are a couple of myths that must be overcome in order to embrace change. The first is the myth of personal responsibility that boasts: "You can make it on your own if you just try hard enough." This is so ingrained into the American psyche that many turn a blind eye to the systemic issues underrepresented and marginalized people face *on top of* the harsh realities of being in the publishing industry. The myth of personal responsibility also lends itself to the idea that every individual author's perspective is legitimized by their uniqueness. Unfortunately, internalized biases emerge in the work itself and, if left uncorrected, can hurt readers and perpetuate racist stereotypes that eventually form an industry standard. When that happens, established poor representations prevent better characters from being written, published, and read, because suddenly the truth for some editors becomes unfathomable to read. If, for example, the majority of young adult books portray the majority of Latina teen characters as living in the inner city, then future characters are deemed to be unbelievable if their home is placed in a wealthy suburb. Also, if marketing personnel believe that white characters on the cover of a book sell better than black, the cover art is then whitewashed despite the fact that the protagonist's race is black. Whitewashing is commonplace.

Another myth that negatively impacts representation is rooted in the idea that, because fiction is the product of an author's imagination, it's okay if the details aren't accurate. Or, to put it more bluntly: harm can't possibly be caused by a story because it's all made up—especially with respect to genre fiction. Intellectually, it's true that people understand the difference between fiction and nonfiction but, to riff off of an old adage, any statement that's wrapped in a pretty lie through the art of storytelling becomes a fact that's easier to stomach. Stories have been used to justify genocide and the removal of basic, human rights for indigenous peoples, immigrants,

women, the poor, LGBTQA+ citizens, and so many others. The ideas generated that being poor is virtuous, that racist portrayals such as red face and yellow peril are a thing of the past, that old women are crones to be feared, that being queer is unnatural or can be "fixed" with electroshock therapy, etc. originate from stories. These stories are engineered on a conscious or subconscious level and are used as propaganda to justify harm. Poor representations, then, hurt marginalized people either directly through physical attacks or indirectly through political policies designed to limit, erase, or subjugate their power.

Though opinions and biases are not static, the struggle for better representation is real. Those affected cannot wait decades for a solution to systemic problems, in part because the same issues that fiction publishers face are shared by other media-generating businesses. After all, even well-written indigenous characters who ring true in a novel could be whitewashed or erased completely when the medium shifts to a TV show, film, or comic because some executive decides that the lead has to be white to boost ticket sales. Data, however, also tells a story, and often which story an analyst wants to tell will depend upon their biases. No matter what historic data might be used to support an analyst's conclusion, however, the public's consciousness, trends, and tastes are not guaranteed, nor can they be predicted with any kind of accuracy. If that was the case, then "instant best-sellers" would happen more often than they do. Stories, despite the business mechanisms that produce them, will resonate differently with different people at different times.

Add back in the aforementioned fear of change, fear of being wrong, fear of being hurt, fear of the unknown on top of a pile of reasons and, in many cases, excuses, and it becomes clearer why better, more representative characters of the people who occupy our world today have yet to be the norm. On a fundamental human level, human beings are afraid of change, so representation demands

it. It demands that we examine our own biases, that we read more broadly, that we better utilize our roles in publishing, that we listen to underrepresented voices when mistakes are made, that we examine hiring practices and the books we buy, that we work more closely with teachers, librarians, and educators, etc.

The effort to support better representation may seem impossible, if not improbable, but I believe it can be done and will continue to happen if we work together. After all, if one oft-repeated story can harm an entire culture, then surely a new story can turn the tide in the other direction. Unfortunately, it's impossible to know which story will be the one that resonates. The good news? They are already being told by many authors, editors, and publishers who are leading the discussion online. They include: Courtney Milan, Justina Ireland, Daniel José Older, Michi Trota, Rebecca Roanhorse, Alyssa Wong, K. Tempest Bradford, Debbie Reese, Dominick Evans, Foz Meadows, Victor Raymond, and many, many others on their own accounts and Twitter hashtags such as #ownvoices and #weneeddiversevoices.

Obtaining and sustaining better representation in fiction is not an issue, but a movement that is gaining momentum. Like any movement, there will be setbacks directly tied to a rise in racism and xenophobia. Fighting the latter may seem impossible, but being involved in publishing to ensure that more stories that utilize better characters and plots are not. Now, more than ever, these stories must be written, published, shared, taught, and recommended to bring hope and understanding where none can be found. Without them, we only have our humanity to lose.

TRENCH WITCH

M.L. BRENNAN

THE WOUND ON HIS THIGH was throbbing like the very devil, but John still had his leg, and better yet, he'd taken a quick check when the orderly had changed him, and his rod and tackle were safe and sound, so really, he had everything he needed. He was lying on clean sheets instead of the muddy dirt of the trenches. Instead of making do with his own pack, he had a pillow. Instead of the flea-infested clothing that he'd worn for two weeks, he was wearing freshly laundered cotton pajamas. He could still hear the occasional explosion of shells, but this hospital was five miles back from the front, and he'd been assured by the other men that there was nothing to fear—the shells very rarely came this far. Almost never, in fact. By all standards of measurement, John's fortunes had improved remarkably since that morning.

John Shearer should've been asleep. The sun was down, the canvas sides of the ward tent tied up to keep out any night winds, all around him he could hear snoring from the other men. There had been some screaming earlier, but that man had died just before dinner. He was warm. And clean. And safe.

But the thing from the trenches had followed him there.

He'd caught sight of it perhaps ten minutes before, just when he'd been about to doze off. He knew it was the same one that he'd

seen in the trenches—he'd never seen a thing like this before in his whole life, but he *knew* it. It had been right after that shell exploded and he'd been rolling on the ground, screaming his head off because of the chunks of hot metal in his leg, then screaming even louder because that thing was there. As big as his hand, brown like the worst trench mud mixed with blood and rat corpses and rotted flesh, a dozen limbs that skittered like a spider's legs but were arms as hairy as his grandfather's, each ending with a hand. Its head was human but with a madman's grin that flashed needle-sharp teeth. There were wings, too—lacy like a dragonfly's and a strange beauty beside the terror of the rest of it—but it had dropped its head down to where he was bleeding, and even with the agony of the shrapnel, he'd felt those teeth rip in.

Then Len Haddrill had proven himself to be not quite the ass that John had always thought him to be, and grabbed John by the collar of his jacket and hauled him back and over the lip of their own trench, and the thing had let go with a screech of fury that John had heard even though his ears were still ringing from the explosion of the shell that had nearly sent him to the devil. He'd half convinced himself that he'd imagined it by the time the stretcher bearers were carrying him away, and decided for sure that it was just some mirage dreamed up during the shock by the time he was being given a bed bath by a harried nurse who made him feel like a puppy under a pump.

But now it was back, with each tooth as real as the black trench dirt still caught beneath John's nails, and creeping up to him.

He should scream. John tried, but all that could escape his throat was a strangled whimper. The thing grinned wider. It was over his toes, and he tried to scream again, without success. Past his shins. Onto his knee. This close, he could see it was covered in tiny brown scales, with little glints, like gold powder in mud. Over his knee, and he could feel each of those feet-hands touch down and

move. It was heading for his wrapped wound, and John realized it wanted to finish its interrupted meal. He should push it away, but he couldn't make his hands move at all. John had gone over the top a dozen times like the best of men, no fears of a coward's execution for him, but now he lay utterly frozen, making nothing but those tiny, pitiful whimpers.

It reached the wound and its lips stretched back even farther, showing a second row of those wicked teeth. Its man's eyes narrowed as it drew back to strike, then—

A spoon slammed down onto it, making a loud crunch like a beetle crushed beneath a boot on a cobblestone. It screamed as it rolled off, a hair-raising sound that seemed to scrape across John's bones, and then a boot actually did stomp down, grinding it with a fury.

John blinked up at his savior—the night-duty VAD, who he'd seen earlier that evening distributing bedpans. She was older than most of the VADs buzzing around the ward throughout the day, with a no-nonsense expression that made her seem more like the professional nurses. Now she stood above him, still holding that spoon in her hand and looking thoroughly satisfied.

"And be that a lesson to you," she said, her voice thick with a Cornish accent, stamping down a second time with her boot, to another high shriek of protest from the creature on the ground. "Now"—she fixed her eyes on John for the first time—"let's check that bandage."

IT WAS EASY ENOUGH FOR Tess Nancarrow to dismiss the soldier's questions. By tomorrow morning, this would be nothing more than the wisp of a fever dream for the boy. The fairy muttered evilly to itself as it dragged its way out of the ward. Tess's spoon was made of cold iron, and she'd put all the weight she could into those stamps, leaving her no doubt that she'd made a permanent impression on the

interloper. The malicious of the Small Folk were glutted on death and pain this close to the front, and that had clearly emboldened this one into following its prey rather than staying with its kin and feeding on the easy meals of human blood and misery that scattered No Man's Land.

She could've killed it—she knew how—but this was the better way. Better to let the fairy go back to its kin, tell its tale, and remind all that the hospital was to be left alone. Still, it seemed a small good, when this fairy and much worse would still be free to feed on and terrorize all the poor boys out there, but that was just this war all over. Tess could keep this fairy from making a second meal of this private tonight, but she couldn't stop it from swallowing some man's sanity on the line tomorrow. She could help patch up the private's leg, but once he was healed, there was nothing she could do to keep him from getting shot to pieces by a machine gun after he was sent back to his unit.

"What was all that fuss in the corner, Nancarrow?" Sister Price asked, blinking wearily as she updated the night logs. Not a drop of magic in this one, Tess knew, but a harder worker one couldn't ask for.

"I saw a rat trying to trouble Private Shearer," Tess said. All the wards had rat troubles—all except hers. A small piece of witchery kept rodents out. A small kindness. She wished that she could've offered it to all the wards, but that was well beyond her abilities. Choices—everything here came down to choices.

Just being here had been a hard choice. Tess had a midwife's hands—she'd been at the trade since she was eighteen, and in almost twenty years, she'd never lost a mother, and no baby that fell breathing into her hands had lost that breath. The rest of her gift was good enough that many of her neighbors would ask her to come to call before they resorted to the doctor, but it was mothers and babies that she could perform miracles for. She'd thought to sit at home while Hugh was gone, tending the babies (not babies any-

more, perhaps, their youngest having just turned nine) and minding her own work—but then her cousin Alan had died. The telegram hadn't given details, nor the letter written by his lieutenant, but she'd smelled the gangrene on it—the rot that had taken his life, for his gift was in fishing and the sea, not blood—and had known that if she'd been by his bed, he would've lived.

So, she'd gone and volunteered. Oh, they'd been glad to have her—a relief in the sight of the professional nurses from the delicate girls who dreamed of mopping the brows of officers, had never emptied a bedpan, and nearly fainted at the sight of a man's nethers. And if the war had taught her a few new things about the horrors that could be wreaked on a healthy body, well, she'd seen a few battles in the birthing room and had stood her ground well.

She made her rounds among the ward beds, checking bandages, fetching and emptying bedpans, adjusting blankets tossed aside by sleeping men. As she went, she drew away gangrene, lowered fevers, encouraged flesh to knit together faster. In this ward alone, there were no fleas, no flies, no maggots, no rats scurrying between the rows of camp beds. She'd established her rule early, and the nasty Small Folk (excepting tonight's unwelcome visitor—and she was sure that *it* wouldn't be back anytime soon) knew enough to avoid Ward 12 and the hospital tents as a whole lest she catch them. There were those she'd encouraged—nothing made life easier than a Brownie to tidy used bandages faster, or a water sprite to ward off dysentery—but they were few in number. The benevolent Folk were creatures of habit, preferring to live in old houses and older villages. A hospital that hadn't even existed two years before, made up of hastily cobbled-together huts and tents, occupied by a constantly shifting population of doctors, nurses, orderlies, and patients? She was amazed that she saw any of the kindly Folk at all.

Her shift ended at six a.m. and she headed for the tent that she shared with four other volunteers, all of them rolling out of bed and

heading wearily toward the mess tent. Her head was clogged with exhaustion, but she followed her before-bed habits:

A loud prayer to God, watching with love from above.

A whispered prayer to the older gods, who still watched, and not always kindly, so were best approached rarely and then from the side.

A quick check of the four primrose buds sewn to a sachet pinned to her chemise. One for each of her babies, and blooming still, which meant they continued to thrive under the watch of her Mam and Father. Two prayers of thanks for that.

A longer check of the thistle sewn in its own little silk bag—not a rich bloom, but alive. That meant somewhere along the line, her husband's heart still beat. Two more prayers of thanks as she tucked that one back. Aunt Betts had crafted these for her, and sometimes Tess wished she could spend all day staring at that thistle, as if will and wishes alone could keep Hugh alive.

But that was a silly thing, and Tess Nancarrow was far from a silly woman, so she finished her prayers and went to sleep.

A NEW DOCTOR HAD ARRIVED with the last shipment of supplies, and was apparently handsome enough that two of Tess's tentmates had half fallen in love with him at first sight. The full accounting of this was relayed to her over dinner, at great length, by Lizzie and May, who were nice enough girls but as foolish as a pair of half-grown goats. Finally, Tess appealed to the higher opinion of the three Australian nurses, who were closer enough to her own age that she could trust their assessment.

"Oh, he's fine enough to look at," Sister Jemma Weaver confirmed. "But icy. Even comparing to the rest of your British boys. Margaret Carey told me that when he looked at her, she felt like a mouse in an anatomy class."

"That certainly doesn't sound promising for the girls' romances."

"You never know," Jemma said. "If all they want to do is look

and dream, he's probably a perfect choice. But if they wanted something real rather than a fine marble figure…" The woman gave a confidential grin. Jemma had a fiancé in khaki herself, and Tess had heard a few tales of their engagement on a moonlit tour of the Sphynx down in the Gallipoli theater. "Well, you know my preference would be an Aussie."

"Fine enough figures, I've heard," Tess replied blandly. "Even if they might have feet of clay."

That prompted some good laughter from the Australian sisters, and a bit of pouting from Lizzie and May, who had missed a few of the nuances of the conversation and were only aware that their new god was being somehow maligned.

One woman at the table said absolutely nothing but scowled in a way that reminded Tess rather sharply of Matron Johnson, for all that there was at least thirty years' gap between them and a bitter dislike besides. Vera was another of the VADs, but a whole species apart from Lizzie and May. Morose and beautiful, with all the passionate commitment of a Catholic saint, she'd actually been reading literature at one of the women's colleges before the war broke out. She nursed every boy with a ferocious care, as if that would somehow keep her brother alive somewhere in Ypres. As prickly as a hedgehog, she'd butted heads with all of the other VADs and half the nurses, and Tess knew that even a hint of misbehavior would've been used by the Matron to send her back to England to be someone else's pestilence.

For all that, Tess had an affection for Vera, and sat next to her at meals and listened sympathetically when the girl was in a speaking mood. Matron Laura Johnson had been trying to make the girl quit and pack her way home by giving her the worst and nastiest assignments—currently, Vera had been on duty in the venereal-disease ward for almost two months—which Tess could've told her was absolutely the wrong approach. You never got a donkey out of a

ditch by pulling harder. The more Vera was aware that she was being tested, the more she gritted her teeth and stood her ground. Tess felt a certain vague sympathy for Vera's parents—the girl must've been a trial to toilet-train—but felt an appreciation for her nonetheless. Grit had to be admired, even in its most abrasive forms.

Vera chose that moment to break her silence.

"Three men died yesterday. I laid them out and wrote letters to their parents and wives. There's a man on my ward who will lose his sight because of gonorrhea, which is the most unbelievable foolishness, yet the ward is packed to the brim with men who are invaliding themselves and saving the Germans the trouble. And yet we're sitting here discussing a pretty new doctor?"

Tess sighed and took another drink of tea as VADs and nurses alike fixed Vera with pointed looks of dislike and then shifted away, starting up smaller conversations, leaving Vera and Tess in a small bubble of censure.

"You know I'm right," Vera said to Tess. "You all do. Yet—"

"Vera." Tess put her cup down with regret. The new sugar stores had arrived with the doctor, and she'd been very much enjoying her tea. "I am not your momma or auntie to lecture you about your behavior. But you can be right and wrong at the same time. Everything you just said was right. But half your letters are in Greek proverbs, and you tell me you dearly love a philosophical discussion, so put that good brain to work for a moment and consider why it might also be right to discuss how the new doctor looks."

This speech earned her an outraged glare, a huff of displeasure, and the sight of Vera storming out of the mess tent. So, a rather normal meal.

"Tess, you do absolutely baffle me," Sister Poppy said from down the table. "That is the most ill-tempered and rude creature I've ever encountered, and you have done nothing but be a friend to her, and yet this is how she treats you."

"It's a bit like being a friend with a cat," Tess replied. "If I don't hold my cat at fault when she decides that she's had enough of petting and nips my hand before running off, why should I do any differently to Vera?"

Judging by the expressions of the other women, Tess judged that most of them preferred dogs.

THE APOLOGY CAME ALMOST AT dinner time, with Vera coming up to Tess after their shifts were done, with a carefully studied air of nonchalance, and saying, "I suppose you'll want to try to get a look at the new doctor. I just saw him leave the surgical tent, if you've half a mind to take a stroll."

"Well, I certainly would like to compare my own view to second-hand reports," Tess said, mopping at one rather persistent bloodstain on her cuff. "You must come along and restrain me if his beauty sends me quite off my head."

Some grumbling for the show of it, but Vera fell in step beside Tess quite agreeably, clearly pleased that the afternoon's row had been forgiven, and happy despite herself that she'd been invited. Internally, Tess was wondering about the likelihood of some new doctor being even half attractive enough to make up for all the fuss. And, bless her maddening heart, but when happy, Vera was the kind of beautiful that turned heads, to the point that today, Tess nearly found herself run down by an orderly completely distracted by Vera. Not that Tess was such an affront to the eyes, but a nurse's uniform and cap seemed absolutely designed to hide what she prided herself on as a first-rate bosom, and she certainly knew what her mirror told her, which was that the dewy skin and glossy hair she'd had at eighteen had slunk out the door at some point—probably scared off by the teething screams of her oldest child, she imagined. Tess waved off the apologies of the orderly and pondered whether the hysterics of Lizzie and May in the VAD tent would be worth the

amusement of a handsome doctor falling in love with Vera at first sight. Perhaps the distraction would be an incentive in itself. Playing with infatuation magic (no magic could craft love, but there was quite a bit that could be done with good old-fashioned hormones) was more in Cousin Dorothy's expertise, but Tess wondered if it was worth the effort.

Then she set eyes on Doctor Clive Spall, and all her amusement evaporated.

"Ah, so that's the cause of all of this," she said. She knew how grim her tone was from the wide-eyed look that Vera gave her, but, well, it wasn't as if she had expected to lay eyes on a Summerlord's son in the middle of a hospital ward.

Human mother, of course, and she pitied that girl. Few left the bower of one of the greater of the Folk with all their wits intact. But someone had been prepared for his arrival, because he wore a glamour so old and moth-worn to hide his half-breed traits that Tess knew it had to have been put on him at birth. It made him look human—hiding ears that would do a tomcat proud—but was too threadbare to keep that otherworldly allure from leaking out. He'd never have lacked for girls in his bed or fellows willing to follow him, but glamour always soured. The girls would turn away from him after a night or three, the companionship of friends would always curdle to enmity. Tess read that easily enough in the set of his jaw and shoulders—a lifetime of disappointment in people leading to a preemptive strike, a refusal to allow more hurts. A reliance only on the self.

Not unlike Vera when it came down to it, perhaps, but Tess had no desire to take *this* bird under her wing. The fey were a bloodthirsty lot, and many of their scions inherited the taste.

"I believe you might have the right of it after all, Vera," she said, slanting a glance at the young woman. At least her blasted contrariness was finally doing her some good in life. A Summerlord's son,

however bastard and hybridized, promised no good for anyone. Far better for Vera to give him a wide berth. As for herself—well, who knew how much he was aware of his parentage. But she pressed her finger against the bloodstain on her cuff and traced a quick sign, and his gaze passed over her as if she wasn't even there.

How much of that was from her small magics and how much was from the irritating tendency of a handsome man in his upper twenties to utterly dismiss a woman a decade his senior, who was to say, but in this case, a bit of caution was in order.

TESS'S CHILDREN HAD TAKEN TO sending her a weekly letter where all wrote messages to her. The latest post had brought quite a chronicle, with a squabble between her two middle children. The older had lent the younger money, but at a rate of interest. The younger had not understood what interest was, and had been outraged upon learning the particulars days later. Much back-and-forth followed, complicated by a Sunday sermon that had happened to mention a religious disapproval of usury. Tess's oldest had attempted to keep the letter light, providing odd breaks from the squabbling into a horticultural discussion of the garden, while Tess's youngest gloried in tattling on everyone. The letter was nine pages long, with tensions reaching a fever pitch on page seven, which had apparently been ripped in a sibling disagreement over epistolary honesty and then pasted together later.

Tess's mother had provided a postscript to the incident, lamenting dryly that the Kaiser had seen fit to keep Tess from witnessing (and mediating) the controversy firsthand, and also relating that Tess's father had discovered that his spanking prowess had not dimmed with the passage of years. Solomon's justice had been meted out—the younger forced to pay the interest, the older banned from any future adventures in moneylending, the youngest scolded, and the eldest sternly told to wear a hat while gardening, due to sunburn.

Tess had brought the letter to the ward and read it to the convalescing men, who found it uproariously funny, and she had found herself prevailed upon to reread it several times over the next few days. On the latest performance of the letter, she found her audience increased by one, as Vera had come in to visit her. In the two months since Doctor Spall had arrived, Matron Johnson had transferred her from the venereal-disease ward to a hut filled with injured German POWs. It was awful, thankless work—the language barrier made communication utterly rudimentary, supplies were provided extremely begrudgingly, and Vera had confessed to Tess that she found it profoundly difficult to nurse men who only days before had been doing their best to fill the rest of the hospital.

At the conclusion of the reading, Tess joined Vera by the cart of tea-things, where she was busily filling cups.

"It's very good of you to lend a hand," Tess said. "But you have a day off for a reason. Take a book and go have a picnic. You need some sun. It's July and you look paler than you did back in February."

"I might later," Vera lied unconvincingly. At the other end of the ward, there was a loud shout—the women looked over just in time to see an orderly restrain a private from going for Doctor Spall's throat. Judging that Corporal Brown had the situation well in hand, and that Sister Poppy Sadler was marching over with a glinted eye and a full syringe, Tess continued counting out biscuits.

"Doctor Spall doesn't seem to have made friends with that man," Vera noted, still looking at the fracas. With the doctor safely away, the orderly yanked down the patient's pajama bottoms to give Sister Sadler a good spot to aim her needle, both ignoring the torrent of colorful invective that spewed from the man.

Tess made a noncommittal noise. As she'd expected, most of the hospital staff had gone off Doctor Spall within the first few weeks as the glamour soured. She'd taken care to watch from a distance, but he hadn't seemed affected either by his universal adoration or the

equally shared revulsion that had followed close on its heels—clearly, he'd been used to both. Tess had noticed that while his bedside manner was abysmally poor, he did at least show a pleasing devotion to his duties—checking all of his patients regularly, regardless of the cost to his own sleep or free hours, and seeming genuinely upset whenever his efforts were in vain.

"I really don't care for him that much myself," Vera added.

"Do you see much of him in the prisoners' hut?" Tess asked.

The girl frowned, almost as if she was struggling to remember. Tess looked up, surprised. "Vera?"

Vera blinked and shook her head. "Oh, no. He's never at the hut. Whenever we need a doctor, we're to call in Captain Shealy."

"Heavens," muttered Tess. "Enough to make you pity even a Hun." Doctor Richard Shealy had become infamous around the hospital for his disinclination to follow careful hygiene. Making matters worse, his uncle was rather far up the chain of command, and therefore, great efforts had to be taken to mitigate the worst of his blundering rather than simply returning the man to his unlucky patients back in England.

There was a long pause, and Tess looked up to see Vera still staring at Doctor Spall, her fingers nervously tapping at a teacup. Her brow was pinched, and her lips moved slightly, though no words escaped.

"Vera?" Tess reached over and touched the girl's wrist, surprised at how cold the skin was when she herself was sweating heavily in the summer heat.

Vera started, then looked at her in annoyance. "What?" Then she looked down. "Maybe you're right about taking a break, Tess. An afternoon away from the wards might do me good."

"Maybe more than an afternoon." Tess felt a bit relieved as Vera set down the cup and headed out. The thought of a break turned her own thoughts to happier places. She'd recently had a letter from her

husband, who noted he had some leave coming, suggesting if she could get away at the same time, they could spend a week in Paris. Seeing the sights, sampling the foods, finding something nice for each of the children.

Tess had replied that it sounded like a lovely plan, but that she would be primarily interested in testing out the hotel bed, and a week's leave was barely adequate to do the kind of thorough investigation she had in mind. She could of course elaborate but had no desire to shock the censors.

IT WAS ALMOST A WEEK later, with a nearly full moon lumbering up in the sky, that Tess recalled her conversation with Vera. One of the men was hemorrhaging, and she had been sent out of the ward to warn the surgeons that they needed to get ready for another patient. With most of the hospital in bed, she'd trusted that the eagle eyes of Matron Johnson were probably shut, and had raced pell-mell down the paths of duckboards in complete violation of the rules against running.

Having delivered the message, she'd started to head back to the ward when she caught a flash of movement out of the corner of her eye. Turning, she saw Doctor Spall slipping out of the door to the prisoners' hut—a lonely little building, set as far from the other wards as possible. Instinctively, she stepped back into a shadow and watched as he glanced around him before furtively setting off in the opposite direction from the main hospital. He was dressed in uniform, his shirtsleeves rolled up on this breathlessly hot night, but he had a small medical bag in his hand, and there was something dark rolled up under his arm.

It was just as well that most of the hospital was asleep, and that it was as quiet as it could ever get around there, because as Tess watched him leave, she became aware of a soft hissing on the night wind, a scraping of scales on rough wood. Acting quickly, she

popped her knuckle into her mouth and bit down sharply enough to draw blood. Her eyes automatically filled with tears, but a drop of blood touched her tongue as she whispered the words, and then a film slipped over her eyes to let her see beyond what even a witch's eyes could normally catch.

A creature trotted along in the doctor's shadow, heeling as well as a finely trained hound, but there was nothing canine about it, despite its four feet. The moonlight showed its scales, but there was no shine—instead, they seemed to swallow up the silver glow into a sulky blackness. Tess stayed absolutely still, praying to different gods now that it wouldn't catch sight of her, but luck was on her side, because the creature never took its gaze away from the bundle beneath the doctor's arm. A dog lusting for a bone, Tess thought to herself, and shuddered at the thought of what that creature would consider a treat.

The doctor and his dark companion continued to walk away, off into the direction of a patch of woods that had become a popular picnic spot for the nurses on their days off. Tess hesitated to follow—at home, on Cornish soil, she had a dozen family members, skilled in craft or not, who she could've called up to help her, but here, she was completely alone. Her iron spoon was safely in her pocket, but the creature she'd just seen wasn't one of the Folk, either fair or dark. Cold iron would be of little help to her. Silver, perhaps, if it was blessed by a true-hearted priest.

Tess eyed the sky again. The moon would be truly waxed tomorrow. She was a hedge witch and had no desire to be anything else, but sorcery was tied to the movements of the sky and stars. Whatever the doctor's companion was hoping to sample, it probably wouldn't be able to feast on it tonight. Doctor Spall must be gathering. Once again, she wished that she was home—Aunt Nessa was the one in the family who knew the most about sorcerers, though Tess wondered if even she'd ever heard of a Summerlord's son engaging in that.

Better not to poke further at this particular snake's burrow, Tess thought. Not much that a witch alone could accomplish, and if the doctor was perhaps restricting himself to the prisoners, well—they were a nation at war, after all. Her own husband and all her brothers were on the line right now, doing their best to blow the Huns into the next world, and she didn't think any the worse of them for that.

Even while she was thinking this, Tess's feet were acting on their own, carrying her closer to the prisoners' hut. Staying to the shadows, Tess poked her head inside the door. Not much different from her own ward when viewed with normal eyes—the beds crowded a bit closer, perhaps, the men still in their tattered uniforms rather than tidy hospital pajamas, and the night nurse nodding at her station in a way that Tess doubted was wholly unassisted by Doctor Spall—but the smells of rot and black blood filled her nose and coated her tongue.

One of the German prisoners caught her eye, and bile burned her throat. Barely eighteen, and what was on his cheeks would be more honestly called fuzz than stubble. Something had scared this one badly—the whites of his eyes were showing—and Tess's added sight showed her where Death had already written her sign across his forehead. Tess wondered who was waiting at home for this boy. Bad luck that he looked so much like her own dead cousin—or was it the last little vestiges of her spelled sight, the one that showed the truth that even a witch would rather not see?

TESS CAUGHT VERA THE NEXT morning, in a rare lucky moment when the tent was empty save for the two of them, everyone else either in the mess hall or heeding the call of the necessity. At first, the girl shook her head at Tess's questions, insisting that it was just as she'd said when they'd talked about this before—that Doctor Shealy was the one who tended to the prisoners' needs, and Doctor Spall had never even crossed the threshold. But Tess was paying attention this time, and she could see how the girl's eyes widened with

horror at the sound of the man's name, and the way sweat popped up on her forehead. She'd seen something, all right, and her body remembered what her mind had been forced to forget.

Given more time, Tess could've done it with more finesse, teasing the knowledge out under the veil of forgetfulness before letting it slip down again to cloud the girl's memories forever, but time was a luxury she lacked. So, it was fast and graceless, with a handful of herbs dropped into a basin of water, and then the quick application of that altered liquid to Vera's face, and only sheer good luck keeping her from having to explain to any of the other women why she'd just dumped an entire basin of water over Vera Bloom (though Tess didn't doubt it was something that at least a few of them had dreamed of doing on several occasions).

There was a bit of shrieking when it happened (even on a hot morning, cold water wasn't always welcome), but perhaps there was something to be said in favor of a good women's college after all, because Vera pulled herself together almost immediately and gave a thorough accounting of exactly what Doctor Spall had forced her to forget.

It was the Dark stuff indeed, down below and next to the devil's own furnace, that Spall was meddling with. He was offering the German soldiers' lives as currency—trimming away with the scalpel to keep their wounds from closing, until each would just peter out and die. And with that wretched Richard Shealy in charge, and only German lives at stake, few would question a death rate that was high even for there. Though from the sound of it, *Vera* had certainly questioned it a time or two, resulting in a heavy ensorcellment to keep her quiet.

"So, what are we going to do about this?"

Tess blinked at Vera, who had put both hands on her hips and, despite looking like a half-drowned kitten, had her jaw set at a most alarmingly obstinate angle.

"Really, Vera, you've had a hard time of this, and perhaps you ought to leave it—" Tess knew even as she started that she was going to fail.

"Those are my patients he's been hurting, so don't think for a second you're just going to pat me on the head and leave me out of this."

Tess struggled, then gave up. "Shit," she said flatly. "Well, God knows I could use a second set of hands for this."

WHICH WAS HOW THEY ENDED up crouched in the woods beside a lightly worn path, with Tess armed with a silver chafing dish she'd nicked from the officers' mess, and Vera holding a cricket bat she'd borrowed from one of the orderlies.

"Are you quite certain this is a good plan?" Vera whispered.

"Actually, I'm rather sure that this is a terrible plan, but it's the only one I could come up with in the time," Tess whispered back. "Now, *hush*."

Another twenty minutes ticked by as they crouched down, the fat moon rising lazily in the sky. Then another ten minutes, which felt easily like two hours. Finally came the sound of old leaves rustling beneath boots, and they both tensed.

Clive Spall turned the corner with a bundle under his arm and a demon at his heels, and neither were expecting the cricket bat that whistled out of the darkness and crashed into his fine nose, eliciting a wholly unmasculine yelp of pain.

The little demon jumped to protect the fool who had summoned it, such fools being difficult to locate even in these fraught times, and the easy living that Spall had been providing it must've blunted its instincts, because it went for the white-faced girl wielding the cricket bat and didn't even realize Tess was there until the silver platter was under it and the silver lid smashed from above, and quick as a nip, Tess had sat herself down atop to weigh it all down. She had some

reason to be grateful the years had added somewhat to her rear end when the demon started rattling away. Every little bit helped, and she was trying to ignore the cold sweat running down her back at just the thought of how easily she could've missed with her grab, and just how badly that would've ended.

She'd told Vera to gag Spall as soon as he was down, but the girl hesitated over shoving a rolled-up handkerchief in the mouth of a man with a broken nose. That would've been a deadly mistake with any other sorcerer, but this one burst into tears and the whole sorry story spilled out.

Because Tess had been wrong—he wasn't some Summerland scion eager to bathe in blood. He was a young doctor driven half mad from all the pain and suffering he'd seen, enough that when an opportunistic demon had presented himself with a promise that he, Clive Spall, could end the war with the blood sacrifice of enemy soldiers and the small consideration of his own soul, he'd fallen for it hook, line, and sinker. He was desperate to divulge his important mission, explain his noble sacrifice, receive their gentle understanding and perhaps even blessings before he went forward and gave his immortal soul for the good of all England—

"Bollocks," Tess interrupted him, having tolerated as much as she could stand. Clive blinked at her, a perfect picture of the self-sacrificing knight (provided one ignored the hanky pressed against his gushing nose). Vera also looked taken aback—possibly more susceptible to knights errant than she would have liked to admit.

Tess, however, was having none of it. "Idiot. Do you think you could possibly offer more blood than is soaking France? At best, you could offer a thimbleful more, with your own soul as a chaser, and some dark trickster"—here she banged her heel against the silver lid beneath her rump, and the creature hammered back with quite a bit of pique—"would gladly drink both down and give you nothing in return but the rotting smell of your own lost heart."

And that was rather the end of it. They tied the silver chafing dish closed and threw it and its demon occupant into a pond—not that that would kill it, but Tess hoped it might teach the creature a lesson, and at least gave the rest of them a feeling of accomplishment. They half-carried Clive Spall back to the hospital, where he promptly collapsed, was diagnosed with nervous exhaustion, and was shipped back to England for a long-overdue rest, with everyone in the chain of command apparently looking the other way regarding his broken nose. Thanks to the curdling of his glamour, most everyone apparently felt he must have deserved it, which was rather the truth.

Vera returned to the prisoners' hut with an absolute ferocity and made such a fuss about the treatment of the prisoners, threatening to make a formal complaint every day, that Matron Johnson assigned an extra two nurses to the ward, then retaliated by putting Vera in charge of delousing the enlisted men's uniforms for a month. But the surviving Germans, spared Spall's scalpel and with very good nurses on hand, finally started to recover.

And Tess tended to her ward with small magics—keeping away the flies, fleas, and rats. Holding back the gangrene and urging flesh to mend. She emptied bedpans (that wasn't really magic) and fluffed pillows (that part *was* a little magic—no soldier sleeping on a pillow that Tess had fluffed ever suffered a bad dream), and above all prayed that the war would end soon.

THAT WASN'T THE END OF it, of course.

She was walking to her tent at twilight when the demon appeared again, trotting at her heels as daintily as any lady's spaniel.

"It was a nice little sideline," it said pleasantly. "You really can't blame me for taking what was offered."

"On a platter, you mean?" Tess asked, prompting a low growl as it was reminded of its recent indignity. "I believe I *can* blame you. Quite a bit, really."

The demon pranced. "Don't be like that, Tess Nancarrow. After all, a foolish boy like that didn't know any of the rules at all. Thinking a little imp like me could end this war!" It laughed. "Far beyond me. Though"—and it smiled coyly up at her, and it was an awful sight—"I could watch over *one* life. Just one. Guard against bullets, and trench rot, and shells. I don't suppose that would be of any interest to *you*, Tess Nancarrow? Just one little life, guarded and minded as if I were the gentlest mastiff given watch over a toddler. A man could come safely out of this war indeed, Tess Nancarrow, were I to guard him."

She said nothing, and he laughed again.

"No jokes now, hedge witch, because you know I'm telling the truth."

Nothing. Not a word from her lips, but they were bloodless from how hard she pressed them together.

"Naught to say?" it taunted. "Well, not to fret. If I'm one to judge, this war has quite a bit left to go. Perhaps you'll rethink your position in a few weeks. A few months. A few *years*. I have the time, and I'll be waiting *so* eagerly to hear your voice."

Then it was gone, though its laugh still echoed around her, scattering the birds and making a few ants curl up and die.

She couldn't wait until bedtime but pulled out the sachet as soon as she reached the tent. In went her fingers, out came the thistle. Still wilted and battered, but not dead yet.

"Stay alive, my love," Tess whispered. "Please stay alive."

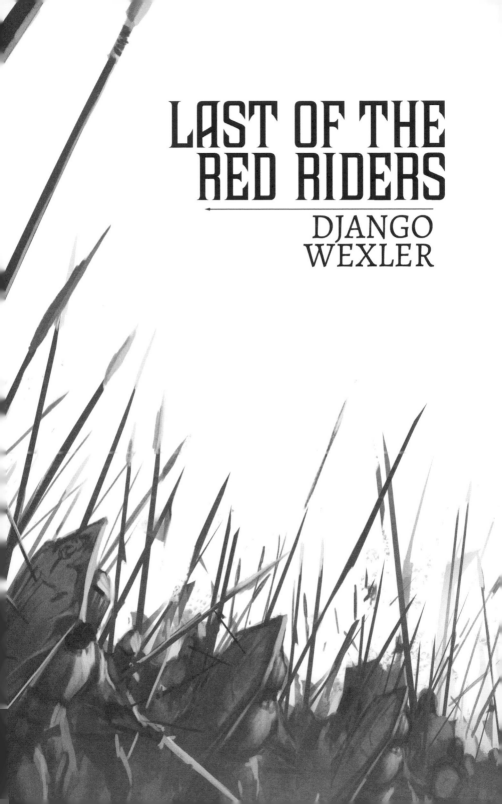

LAST OF THE RED RIDERS

DJANGO
WEXLER

H AWK HILL HAD NEVER BEEN much of a town, just another stop on the Splendid West Line, about halfway up the valley of the Ellial. Fruit country, open fields alternating with neat rows of apple and pear trees, with here and there a sturdy little whitewashed farmhouse. Hawk Hill itself wasn't much more than an inn, which doubled as a train station, plus a church, a general store, and maybe a dozen townhouses. The water tower next to the tracks was painted a cheery blue, and from a distance you couldn't see where it was faded and flaking.

No one's army had marched along the Ellial, but that hadn't kept the war away from Hawk Hill. I'd never been near the place, but I could see the story in the boarded-up windows and dusty, overgrown streets, the ragged double-bar flag that fluttered over the station. Same as a hundred other little towns we'd passed through, this place had just dried up and blown away.

First the men had marched off, when General Wick had thrown down the gauntlet to the Central Counties. More had joined up in those first heady years, sons begging their mothers to let them give their names to the recruiting sergeants before all the victories were won. Then, as the war dragged on, the recruiters had returned, this time with conscription warrants.

Illustration by NICOLÁS R. GIACONDINO

Hawk Hill had it worse than most. The Centrals had cut the Splendid West at Bronco Pass, only fifty miles off, and there was no longer any reason for trains to come so far out. The people who'd lived here had just *gone*, back to their farms to stay with family, or east to Garramond or Featherton or anywhere that would have them. They'd probably boarded up their own windows and told each other they'd be back before too long. One more battle, one more victory, and the war would be over, and everything would be the way it was before.

I remembered thinking like that. War has a way of burning off fantasies awful quick.

The Red Riders came up the valley of the Ellial, the heroes of a dozen songs, scourge of Central quartermasters, celebrated in newspapers all across the Defiant. We were a dozen dusty, mud-splattered shapes, with twice as many dusty, mud-splattered horses and a wagon piled high with crates and stacked gear under a tarpaulin. The long crimson cloaks from which we took our name were piled in the wagon, too. These days, we only wore them when Captain Hays wanted to throw a scare into someone.

I was in my usual spot, out front with Little Barrow, my mare poking her way down a dusty cart-track that was rapidly disappearing into the weeds. Rob was out to the left, Bill to the right, and John Plainsman riding tail. The rest were clustered tight around the wagon, the fruit of a month's sweat and terror. As I came to the edge of Hawk Hill, Captain Hays gave a whistle, and I reined up. The outriders came in, until we were all gathered round.

"We'll stop here for the night," Hays said. No backcountry drawl in *his* voice, unlike most of the rest of us. He had the clipped vowels of an educated man. "Up at the station. Should be plenty of room."

"We got plenty of daylight left," Liz said. She sat uneasily on her big black gelding, the long barrel of her rifle sticking up over her left shoulder. "We could make a few more miles."

"No need to hurry," Hays said. "We're back in friendly country

now. Let's rest up while we have the chance." His eyes went to Gid. "You go back a ways and find somewhere to watch our trail, just in case. I'll send somebody over to spell you at dusk."

"Yes, sir," Gid said. He was a gangly youth, with cornflower eyes in a face cratered by acne. The rest of them laughed at him, sometimes, because he was so keen. I always tried not to join in. Now he turned his horse and rode back the way we had come, without complaint.

Hays led the rest of us up the old street, past the boarded up houses to the train station. It was a two-story brick building, with narrow windows and a peaked roof. We brought the wagon into the old stable, and while the others dismounted and went inside, John Plainsman and I saw to the horses. The regular army might have duty rosters and rotas, but in the Red Riders we just did what we were best at. For me that meant taking care of horses and keeping a lookout. If that meant I stayed up more nights than some, I didn't mind, 'cause I knew I could rely on Dogs to knock someone flat or Liz to put a bullet in them if I ever needed it. We all got our strengths.

John Plainsman didn't talk much, but when he brushed the horses, he talked to them softly in his own language, little clucks and warbles. I never could figure what he was saying, but they seemed to appreciate it. His pale skin was creased and burned until it was old leather, and his long, blond braid swung back and forth as he worked.

I heard the crackle of a fire from inside the main building and smelled bacon frying. Say one thing for the Red Riders—I'd eaten better in the last few months than the whole rest of my life put together, thanks to the generosity of Central supply trains and depots. The Neffies got foul mash I wouldn't feed a dog, but Central officers didn't like to leave their comforts behind.

I must've been drooling, because John Plainsman gave a rare chuckle and waved me away.

"Go eat, Nellie." His accent always sounded somber to my ears. "I'll finish up."

I wasn't going to turn *that* down. I gave Liz's black a last stroke of the brush, patted its side, and went on in.

BACON AND EGGS, SPICY DRIED beef, beans and rice, and bread with real butter, even lobster and crab from funny little tins that hissed when you poked a hole in them. These were a Central invention, Hays said, to keep food from going off. Central people were always tinkering with things, even food.

We'd been feasting every night. There were crates of the stuff in the wagon, alongside the guns, powder, and shot that made up the bulk of our haul. Jude was our cook, and even Liz admitted he was a dab hand over the skillet. I wolfed down everything with my fingers, scorching them a little where I hadn't waited for it to cool, then went back for seconds.

The ground floor of the station was a single room, a big open space with benches around the edges and what had been the ticket counter at one end. Bits of broken furniture made for a tidy fire, and most of the company sat around it on their blankets, passing around a couple of bottles of fancy Central wine.

"Is this the '62, do you think?" said Bill, with an exaggerated parody of a nasal Central accent.

"No, no, it must be the '61," Rob replied, in the same tones. "That year had a particular nutty cheesiness to it."

The others were laughing out loud. Dogs grabbed the bottle in one huge, paw-like hand and took a long swig.

"Yup," he drawled, his accent thick enough to crack rocks. "Tastes like cheesy nuts to me."

More laughter. I saw Ben leaning back on his blanket and I caught his eye. I flicked my gaze upward, then raised an eyebrow. He grinned.

Five minutes later, we were upstairs in one of the old guest rooms, and he was kissing a line of bare skin from my collarbone down toward my breasts while I fumbled with his belt buckle. Funny how things like buckles and knots which normally come so natural get all finicky when you're in a hurry. There was a bed, but was covered in dust and cobweb, so Ben pressed me against the wall and I wrapped my legs around his waist.

I'd been fucking Ben for a couple of months now. After I joined the Red Riders, it wasn't long before I figured out I'd have to pick *somebody* to share my bedroll, else fights were going to start breaking out. I'm no great beauty, but that doesn't mean much to boys who haven't seen a woman for weeks. So I picked Ben. I wasn't in love with him or nothing, but he had a pretty face and a kind manner, and knew enough not to make a fool of himself between the sheets. Once I'd made a choice, the others settled down some, though I still had to crack Big Barrow over the head once and I'd caught Gid making moon-eyes at me now and then.

Liz never had to put up with any of this. It might have been because she would break your arm as soon as look at you if you crossed her. Or it might have been because of the rumor that she and Hays were together, or had been, once. Every man of the Red Riders would rather slit his own throat than cross Captain Hays.

When we were done, Ben pulled the sheets off the bed, and we lay panting on the mattress, which was prickly but cleaner. I liked to watch the way sweat beaded in the hollow under his jaw, and play with the downy hair on his chest. I liked the way he looked at me, too, like a man who'd won the lottery and still can't quite believe it.

"How far east do you think we'll go?" he said. "All the way to Totterhollow?"

That was General Wick's camp, where for the last six months he'd been facing down the main Central army, like two tigers staring at each other across a stream. Everyone said Wick was waiting for his

moment; sooner or later, he'd deliver another of his brilliant strokes and send the Centrals howling back like he had every time before.

"Doubt it," I said. "Probably just as far as the railhead. Captain will have us turned around and headed back for Central territory as soon as he can."

"I guess." There was a reluctance in his tone. "I thought he might join up with the army this time. Paper said Wick needs every man he can get."

"He needs guns and powder more than he needs another dozen mouths to feed," I said.

"I guess," he said again, and sighed. "There ain't much glory in it, though, is there? Bushwacking supply wagons and hiding from every patrol?"

"Glory?" I snorted. "Glory and a shovel will get you a nice grave."

Before he could say anything else, I rolled over and straddled him, which proved plenty distracting for both of us. Ben was a nice boy, but sometimes I thought he wasn't too bright. He'd been at this longer than I had, but it hadn't taken more than a few days for me to figure out there was no such thing as glory in this war.

BEN DROPPED OFF TO SLEEP as soon as we finished, but I found myself with a thirst and it was nearly time for my watch. Another of the guest rooms had its door closed, which I figured meant Bill and Rob were making use of it for the same purpose Ben and I had. Ma wouldn't have approved of them, but the war had showed me there were a lot worse things men could do to each other, and it wasn't any of my business anyhow.

Downstairs, most of the others had fallen asleep around the fire. John Plainsman sat wedged in a corner, as was his custom, hat pulled down over his eyes. Only Liz and Captain Hays were still awake, propped against the old ticket counter with a bottle between them. Big Barrow was nowhere to be seen, which meant he was on

watch. Hays beckoned me over, and I flopped down opposite the two of them.

"Ho there, young Nellie," he said, and I could hear quite a bit of wine sloshing about in his voice. "How's our Ben treating you?"

"Tolerably," I said, with a shrug. When you were twelve riders alone in the woods for days, there was no keeping secrets about who was fucking who. "He wears out quicker than I'd like."

"Ha," Liz said. "Don't they all."

Hays grinned and leaned forward, handing me the bottle. He grew the hair on his left side long, letting it hang down across his face. At the battle of Onsang, back in the first days of the war, a Central bullet had hit him just above the left eye, bursting it and shattering the bones on that side before coming out the top of his head. He'd survived, which nobody expected, and now the left side of his face was a sagging, puckered scar, the broken bone sagging like a butter sculpture beside a fire. It disturbed folks, so he kept the hair covering it unless he wanted 'em disturbed. His other eye practically glowed in the fire, a blue so bright people said he was half Plainsman.

"I'm glad you're here," he said. "I've been meaning to talk to you."

"Am I getting called on the carpet?" I said. I was half smiling, but only half, because you never knew with Hays. He smiled the widest when he was mad at you, and took his time twisting the knife.

"Nothing like that. How long have you been with us?"

I took a pull from the bottle. It was wine, though whether it was '61 or '62 or last Thursday I couldn't have told you. After wiping my mouth on my sleeve, I said, "Three months, or thereabouts."

It had been one hundred and three days. A hundred and four since the Central patrol had come to my farm. But I kept that to myself.

"Three months." He shook his head, the long fringe of hair shuffling. "Three trips over the border, right?"

"Right." I shifted uncomfortably. "Why?"

"This was the last time," he said. "We're done, Nellie. The Red Riders are getting out of this business for good."

"Why?" It was all I could think to say.

"'Cause it's getting too fucking dangerous, that's why," Liz said. She was a short, stout woman, nearly as broad as Big Barrow across the shoulders. Liz was the best shot in the company, and a serious contender for throwing the meanest punch. I once asked Dogs how she got into the Red Riders, and he said she'd just turned up and laid out anyone who tried to stop her.

"None of us signed up for this because we thought it was *safe*," I objected. "It's war."

"There's a difference between war and suicide," Liz said. "Colonel fucking Tzolk and his idiot son nearly had us last time. They're thick as flies over there now."

"But General Wick needs what we bring him," I said, waving in the direction of the stables. "You were the one who told me that, Captain. With the blockade, every rifle's worth its weight in gold."

"I know," Hays said, holding up a hand, but I was on a roll.

"We can't just *stop*," I said. "Without guns, Wick can't keep the Centrals out of Beauport. And if they take Beauport, we'll lose the war."

Hays stared at me with his one eye, but it was Liz who spoke.

"We lost the fucking war a long time ago," she said. "People like Wick are just too damned stupid to realize it. The Defiant's just a chicken with its head chopped off. It might run for a while, but it ain't going to be anything but fucking dinner."

"You believe this?" I said to Hays.

"It's a colorful analogy," he said. "But I don't think she's wrong. The Central fleet's tightened the blockade. They've taken Goff and Veraville from the sea, and Fort Kvir is under close siege now."

"General Wick still has 'em pinned outside Totterhollow!"

"He does," Hays said. "But he needs every man the Defiant can offer to do it. The Centrals have *him* pinned, too, and they've got plenty left over."

"Only because they're got half of Hell on their side," I muttered. "Where'd you hear all this, anyway?"

"He has a good rummage every time we hit a telegraph station," Liz said. "But it's all in the Central papers."

"Their papers lie," I said, with a snorted.

"They don't fucking need to lie," Liz said. "Not anymore."

"So what?" I looked between the two of them. "That's it? You're just going to...what, go home?"

"When we get to the railhead at Novarre, I'm going to tell everyone formally," Hays said. "As far as I'm concerned, you've all filled your obligation to the Defiant ten times over. We've got some money we can split up, Central thalers are better than Defiant scrip these days."

"Some of us don't have anywhere to go back to," I said.

"I know." Hays's expression softened. "But you could go east, to the city. It'd be better than this."

"Ben will just go on to Totterhollow," I said.

"Of course he will," Liz said. "'Cause he's got the brains of a fucking radish."

"I expect a lot of the boys will want to keep fighting," Hays said. "Someone like Dogs has been at this so long, I don't know if he remembers how to do anything else. But I was hoping you, especially, might listen to what I have to say."

"Why?" I said. "Because I'm a girl?"

"'Cause you've only been with us three months," Liz snapped. "You *can* go back. And you might be able to talk sense into Ben and Gid if you do."

"What about you?" I said, looking at Hays. "Where are you gonna go?"

Liz gave a dry chuckle. Hays let out a long breath.

"I'm not going to say," he said. "Wherever it is, I don't want the lot of you following me, out of some misplaced sense of loyalty."

I was about to say that seemed like a shitty way to treat the men and women you rode with, but a noise from outside cut me off. Hoofbeats, loud in the silent town.

"Think about it," Hays said, as we all shot to our feet.

I was more focused on what was happening outside. I heard Big Barrow shout a challenge, and relaxed a little at the sound of Gid's voice. A moment later he was inside, a swirl of dust following him in through the front door.

"Gid," Hays said, all the drunkenness gone from his voice. "What's happened?"

"Neffies," the boy said, gasping for breath. "Coming down the west road."

THE OTHERS WOKE UP, AND there was a general commotion. Hays held up a hand for silence and got it.

"How many?" he said. "And how many riders with them?"

"At least fifty Neffies," Gid said. "Could be more, I didn't stick around to count 'em. And I saw three riders."

"Tzolk," Liz said. "Has to be. He didn't stop at the border."

"But we're in Defiant territory!" Gid said. "He can't just march in after us."

"He can if there's no one to stop him," Hays said. "General Wick's been stripping the backcountry garrisons of able bodies for years and shuffling his worst cases out to replace them. There's probably not a soldier within fifty miles of here who isn't a cripple or a drunk."

"How far out were they?" Liz said.

"Couple of miles," Gid said. "Closer now."

"Too close to ride for it," Hays said. His lip twisted.

It's a little-known fact, in civilian quarters, that over a long haul, a Nephilim can run down a horse. The horse can gallop faster, but not forever, and Neffies don't get tired. With us burdened by a wagon full of supplies, we wouldn't have a chance with such a short head start.

Dogs and Little Barrow came over. The big sergeant's eyes were still heavy with sleep, but Barrow was more alert.

"Somebody coming, captain?" he said.

"Neffies," Hays said.

"It's Tzolk," Liz said. She had her rifle out, busy inspecting the mechanism.

"We don't know it's Tzolk," Hays said.

"Of course it's fucking Tzolk," Liz said. "Who else has such a hard-on for killing you that he'd come this far over the border? He hates you personal after you shot his son at Little Forks."

"Go get your brother," Hays said to Barrow. "Then get everyone on the second floor down here."

"What're we going to do?" Dogs said with a yawn. He scratched his beard with one huge hand. "Hole up here?"

"Don't see that we have much choice," Hays said. He looked at Gid. "You didn't see any artillery, did you?"

"Just the three riders," Gid said.

"If they haven't got any cannons, this place will do for a fort. Narrow windows, thick walls."

"It'll be full dark soon," Liz said.

Hays nodded. "Nellie, take John and Jude up to the roof and get the lamps lit. There's some oil in the wagon."

"Got it," I said. We didn't salute in the Red Riders, but sometimes I wanted to.

I chivvied Jude out of his bedroll and left him tugging on his trousers while John Plainsman and I fetched a cask of lamp oil. We passed the Barrows, Ben, Bill and Rob on their way down to collect their gear. A trapdoor led to the roof, a slope of shingles overlooked

by the looming bulk of the water tower. Lamps hung at regular intervals around the edges. The old station hands had probably lit them from below, using some kind of long pole, but lacking the proper equipment I had to edge out onto the dangerously sloped roof and pull them up. By the time we were done, my heart was pounding hard, and I was glad to get back inside and head down to join the others.

Most of the company was busy with their weapons, checking that the bolts on the carbines moved smoothly and that ammo pouches were full. The Red Riders had the pick of the Central armory, and we each carried at least a pair of revolvers in addition to the bolt-action carbine. Liz had the only long rifle, a monster of a thing longer than she was tall. She had the barrel in her hand, like a strange walking stick, while she talked to Hays.

"It's the best chance we've got," she said quietly. "Fifty is too many. If he gives the order to rush us, they're going to get inside."

"He won't," Hays said. "Mithraim Tzolk cares more about his own skin than anything else, even catching me. If he loses too many here, he'll never make it back to Central territory."

"You don't know that for sure," she said. "If I can put a bullet in him and his cronies, we'll get away clean."

Hays set his jaw. "Where do you want to set up?"

"Water tower," Liz said, without hesitation. "They'll have to come that way, and it's the best vantage. If I get the drop on them, this could all be over by sundown."

There was a moment of silence.

"Do it," Hays said. Then, after a pause, "And don't forget your last shot."

Liz snorted and turned away. I swallowed hard, suddenly understanding. You always saved your last shot, Ben had explained to me not long after I'd joined the Red Riders. If it looked like the Centrals might get you, the last shot was for yourself. They said in

the papers we were irregulars and spies, and thus outside the rules of civilized war. I figured that meant all kinds of rape and torture if they ever caught us, but that wasn't the half of it. In the end, they'd take you back and make you into a Nephilim, like they did with all their prisoners, and that was a fate any of us would rather eat a bullet than face.

Hays didn't think Liz was going to make it back. I glanced at John Plainsman, who was stoically cleaning the action on his carbine, and began checking my own weapons. I saw Liz, towing her long rifle, slip out through a side door before Dogs, at Hays's instruction, barred all the entrances and blocked them with crates from the wagon. The rest of us lined up at the windows and waited.

WE DIDN'T HAVE TO WAIT long.

Figures slipped through the darkening street, two by two, closing in on the station. On the side facing the tracks, the windows overlooked a wide stretch of open ground, but the other side faced the town. That would be where the Neffies would come. They might be demons, but they weren't completely stupid.

Or at least, they weren't completely stupid unless someone had ordered them to be. There was still a whole street between the station and the nearest buildings, and it would become a killing ground if they tried a rush. Human troops might hesitate, but the Neffies would do it, if they were told to. While the two Barrows watched the track side, in case they tried something sneaky, the rest of us lined up next to the narrow windows with carbines raised.

"Stay out of sight," Hays said, peeking out and then ducking back. "Don't fire until they do. I don't want them spooked yet."

"You all right, Nellie?" This was from Ben, pressed against the bricks beside me. I was breathing fast, I realized, and my heart was pounding like it wanted out of my chest.

"I'm fine," I muttered, swallowing again.

In the three months I'd been with the Red Riders, this was the closest I'd come to a stand-up fight. When you're a dozen soldiers in enemy territory, you don't stay put and shoot it out if you can avoid it. I'd thrown up the first time I'd shot a man, a Central quartermaster who'd gone for his pistol rather than surrender, but that had been months ago. It wasn't shooting that bothered me now, but the prospect that they were going to be shooting back.

"Hays knows what he's doing," Ben said. "He'll get us out of here."

Some of us, anyway. I could see what Hays and Liz were up to. Nephilim didn't tire or scare, and they barely needed food and water. But they couldn't think for themselves. They needed human commanders to tell them what to do, or they'd stand around and do nothing. There was a story once about a whole battalion of Neffies whose commander had been down with fever, and when one of our patrols started slaughtering them, they'd just waited like beef cattle for the knife.

We wouldn't get that lucky, I expected. Most Neffies had standing orders to defend themselves. But if Liz could take out the humans—Colonel Tzolk and his officers, if she was right—then it would be a hell of a lot easier to get away. But Tzolk wasn't likely to put himself in the line of fire, which is why she'd hid herself up the water tower. Hays wanted to let the Neffies get as close as possible, to give her as good a chance as she could get.

The water tower was a dark mass against the sky, light already fading as the sun sank toward the horizon. The lanterns made it obvious where we'd holed up, but there was no hiding the trail our horses and wagon had made anyway. I wanted desperately to look out the window, but any motion now would be asking for a shot. I wanted desperately to piss, too. Why hadn't I taken care of that beforehand?

Liz's rifle *cracked*, a sound like a huge stick snapping in two. Someone shouted, and a horse screamed, eerily human-like. There

was another *crack*, and then the deeper growl of Neffie rifles, flashes lighting up the street as shadowy figures turned to the water tower.

"Give it to them!" Hays shouted.

In near-unison, the Red Riders slammed the butts of their weapons against the glass in the windows, letting in a sudden draft of cold air and the smell of burning powder. The noise redoubled, louder than the loudest storm that had ever rocked our old farmhouse. Ben leaned out one window, and I peeked around the other, trying to make out a target in a street turned black-and-white by the flash of rifle fire. One Neffie was running for cover, his gun trained on the water tower, and I tried to follow his movement, looking through the sights as Sergeant Dogs had taught me.

Something went *pok* beside my head, spraying brick dust. It happened again, *pok pok pok*, but it was only when a bullet *thrummed* past through the window that I realized it was gunfire hitting the side of the building. My concentration vanished, and I pulled the trigger blindly, feeling the carbine buck against my shoulder. The sound filled the world, rattling my bones. I ducked out of the window, heart slamming in my chest.

My fingers knew what to do next, which was good, as I seemed to have lost the thread of events. I watched as they yanked back the bolt, ejecting a spent copper cartridge, and thumbed in a fresh round from my ammo pouch. When they slammed the bolt closed again, I crashed back into myself, feeling every shot as a shiver running through my body.

Ben was looking at me as he reloaded his own carbine. He mouthed something I couldn't hear in the noise, but I could see the concern in his eyes. There was enough of me left to think, *the hell with that*. I gave him my best grin and leaned out the window again, sighting on the flash of a Neffie's weapon and pulling the trigger.

Sight, fire, duck, reload, sight again. The world contracted around me. I no longer flinched when shots came close, hitting the wall

of the building or passing through the window to *thunk* into the ceiling. My shoulder ached where the carbine slammed against it, and my fingers were getting scorched where they touched the barrel. I sent round after round chasing fleeting shadows. At least once, I saw a Neffie fall, though whether it was my shot or another I couldn't say. Most of the time, I ducked back before I could tell what had happened.

Jude took a bullet through the throat, in the half-second while he leaned out to fire. He fell backward, kicking, and blood sprayed in a wide arc across the floorboards. Nobody ran to help him; sometimes, one look was enough to tell you when someone ain't getting back up. Bill dropped his carbine and stumbled back from the window, clutching his arm, and Rob pulled him down and propped him against the wall, then kept firing.

I thought I heard Liz's rifle *crack*, twice more. I saw Hays point and shout something, and in the flashes I saw a dozen Neffies rushing the ladder leading up the water tower. The rifle *cracked* again and one of them collapsed. The others kept on, and then something dropped from the tower, a human shape, arms flailing.

"Liz!" Hays's shout cut through the gunfire. "You stupid—"

A new round of shooting drowned out the rest, but I could see Neffies moving over to where Liz had fallen. A few moments later, the shooting from the street died away, and a man's deep voice could be heard.

"Stop!" he said. "Stop firing, all of you."

The Neffies stopped. Most of them were in cover now, crouching behind bushes or the corners of nearby houses. There were a half-dozen bodies in the street, and one man crawling determinedly away from the station, leaving a slick of blood in the dirt behind him. Farther up the road, it was harder to see in the dim light, but I thought there were at least a couple more bodies. Then a knot of figures emerged, the one at the center struggling.

"Shit," Hays said. "Cease fire."

We had mostly stopped in any case, without much to shoot at once the Neffies had hunkered down. Quiet fell over Hawk Hill, broken by the muffled shrieks of an injured horse somewhere out of view. There was a single pistol shot, and the animal went silent.

"What happened?" Dogs said. "Did you see?"

"The idiot fired her last shot at the Neffies," Hays said. His voice was thick. "Then I think she jumped off the tower." He glanced down the line, taking in Jude's still-twitching body and Rob bent over Bill. "He going to be all right?"

"Tore up my arm pretty good," Bill said, sounding a little shaky. "Got it bandaged, but I'm not going to be much help."

"Hays!" said the man outside. He had a strong Central accent. "You in there, Hays?"

"That's Tzolk," Ben muttered. "Damn."

"What if I am?" Hays shouted back.

"Your whore here shot my boy!" Tzolk said. "Blasted his brains all over me."

"Your lot always had few enough of those," Hays said. "Should be easy to clean up."

"You fucking pile of dogshit," Tzolk said. "That's two sons you owe me now."

"Come on out, and I'll give you what I owe you," Hays said.

There was a commotion, and for a moment I thought Tzolk was actually going to give Hays what he wanted. Instead, a pair of Neffies came forward, holding Liz between them. She struggled, but weakly. One of her legs hung limp at an odd angle, obviously broken.

"This your girl?" Tzolk said. "Fuck if I can see what anyone would see in her, but ain't no accounting for taste."

Hays was silent. Tzolk's voice, still thick with anger, took on a mocking tone.

"I wouldn't touch her with a long-handled pole myself, so let

me tell you how this is going to go. I'm gonna let every Neffie in the company have a go at her, and you can watch. You ever seen a Neffie fuck? Sometimes I make 'em do it, just for the laugh. It's like watching a steam piston making love. They don't enjoy it, and she sure as hell won't. And when they're all done, I'm gonna take her back home and watch pers'nally as they carve out her soul and make a Neffie out of her."

"Fuck off, Tzolk," Liz called weakly. "How many sons you got left? I'm running out of bullets."

"I'm tempted to just get started," Tzolk said. "But you know I'm a reasonable man. You come out here, and I'll put a bullet in you both, right here and right now, no fuss. I'll even let the rest of your little thieves skulk back home. Have to drag your body home to get my just reward, of course, but that ain't gonna matter to you at that point."

We all had our eyes on Hays. He lifted his carbine, slowly, and closed the bolt. It was Dogs who figured out what he was up to first.

"Captain, no," he said. "That's too long a shot. And every Neffie out there's watching the windows."

"At least let me do it," Ben said. Several others chimed in.

"Do what?" I said, quietly.

"Last shot," Ben said.

Shit. I pressed myself against the wall. *Shit, shit, shit.*

"Come on, Hays," Tzolk said. "You know you aren't walking away from this. It's the best deal you're likely to get."

"Don't you *fucking* dare," Liz said, her voice cracking. "Kill this bastard and every one of his fucking diseased family—"

Hays let out a breath, raised the carbine to his shoulder, and sighted. It seemed to take an eternity before he pulled the trigger. The report of the weapon was simultaneous with several shots from outside. Liz broke off abruptly, and Hays stumbled away from the window, dropping the gun. Dogs scrambled to his side.

Ben risked a look, just for a moment. "I think he got her," he said, a little bit of awe in his tone. "God Above."

"He's hit," Dogs said. "Shoulder. Rob, bandages, now."

"God *fucking* damn it, Hays," Tzolk said. "You always have to do things the hard way, don't you?"

AFTER THAT, I EXPECTED THE firing to start again, but it stayed quiet. The Barrows kept watch at one set of windows, John Plainsman at the other, while the rest of us pulled back out of view. Dogs carried Jude's body upstairs, leaving a trail of blood drying on the dusty floor, while Rob did what he could for the unconscious captain.

"It didn't shatter the bone," he told Dogs when he came back down. "He'll probably be all right, if we can get a surgeon to dig the bullet out and it doesn't fester." He made a face. "He's finished if it goes bad, though. It's too high up to amputate."

"He'll make it," the sergeant said. "If getting shot through the eye didn't kill him, this sure as hell won't. We just have to make sure we get out of here."

I slipped up the stairs, carbine under my arm, to take care of a need that had abruptly become urgent. When I came back down, the company was circled a few yards away from where the captain lay with his head propped up on a wadded jacket. Dogs sat on his haunches, for all the world like an enormous version of his namesake, and Rob was cross-legged beside Bill, who was hunched shivering under a blanket. I slipped in between Gid and Ben.

"—split up," Gid was saying. "Ride for it."

"There's too many Neffies," Rob said. "They'd run us down."

"Not all of us," Gid said.

"You scared of a few Neffies, boy?" Rob said.

"Four dozen ain't a few," Gid said. "And I ain't scared, I'm just telling it straight."

"The hell you are."

"Rob," Bill said, sounded shaky. "He might be right."

Rob looked at his lover and bit his lip. I could see his thoughts like they were written on his forehead; if we had to ride for bit, hell-for-leather, there was no way that Bill would get away.

"The captain ain't going to be able to ride for it," Dogs rumbled. "Which means I'm staying right here until we can take him with us. An' that means the rest of you are, too, since I'm in charge until he wakes up. That clear?"

He looked from Rob to Gid. Rob nodded, and Gid blushed a furious crimson.

"Right," he said. "I didn't think about that."

"'Course you didn't." Dogs clapped him on the shoulder. "Nobody's mad at ya. We just got to think a little harder."

"It's nearly full dark," Ben said, glancing at the window. "Unless they start shooting or come near the lanterns, there's not much we can do."

"They can't wait around forever, can they?" I said. I don't speak up much, and the others all looked surprised to hear my voice. "Stripped garrisons or no, someone has to know they're here. We're only a half-day from Forganville by train if they've got an engine there, or a day's march for a cavalry company. A hundred troopers would put paid to Tzolk."

"She's right," Ben said. "Tzolk must know it, too."

"Then what's he waiting for?" Dogs said.

"He knows he'd lose half his company if they rush the building. The more Neffies that go down, the slimmer his chances of making it back to claim that bounty." Ben shook his head. "He can't know Hays is hurt, either. He might be afraid we'd try to ride for it."

"So he can't attack," Gid said. "And he can't stick around. Doesn't that mean all we've got to do is wait him out?"

"Don't mean he *can't* attack," Dogs said. "Just means it'd be a risk. And he's already thrown the dice just coming here. I'd wager

that if it comes to it, he'll send the Neffies in to get us and the hell with the odds."

"And once the sun comes up, that'll get harder," Ben said. "So he'll do it before dawn. Maybe with a distraction, try to catch us off guard."

There was a long silence. I looked over at Hays, his good eye closed, his breathing ragged.

"I don't much like the idea of sitting around here until Tzolk decides he's good and ready," Dogs said.

"Neither do I," Ben said. "But what else can we do?"

"Take him out," Rob said, his tone low and dangerous. "Like Liz tried to do."

Ben looked skeptical. "Tzolk himself?"

"Sure." Rob warmed to his subject. "Gid, you said you only saw three riders, right?"

"Right," the boy said. "All together."

"That means we've got Tzolk and two other humans commanding the Neffies," Rob said. "We know Liz killed one, so that leaves two. We get to them, and if they've told the Neffies to wait, they'll keep waiting forever."

"Sure," Dogs said. "But they ain't likely to just walk up the windows and wave hello."

"I saw one of them," John Plainsman said.

Dogs jerked around so fast he lost his balance and fell on his ass. All the rest of us looked at the windows, where John was standing. He had a way of standing so still and quiet you almost forgot he was there.

"Where?" Ben said, while Dogs sorted himself out.

"In the house over there," John said, pointing. "There's several Neffies in there, but there's a human, too."

"Tzolk?" Dogs said.

"Doubt it. Too short."

"How do you know it wasn't another Neffie?" Ben said.

"Neffies don't drink," John said. "I saw him with a bottle in his hand."

"Must be the third man," Rob said. "If we can get to him, that'll leave Tzolk alone."

"I only saw him for a moment," John said. "He won't give us a shot from here."

"Then we go get him," Rob said. "Another half hour and it'll be pitch dark. We can slip out through the stable door, cross the street, and come around behind the building."

"That sounds like a good way to get killed," Bill said.

"It also sounds like about the only idea I've heard that might get us somewhere," Dogs said. "You volunteering, Rob?"

"Yeah," Rob said, not looking at Bill.

"How many you want? Somebody's got to stay with the captain." The big sergeant grinned. "An' I wasn't made for sneaking around in the dark."

"Maybe three more," Rob said, suddenly nervous. "John, will you help?"

John Plainsman nodded. "Bring Little Barrow, if he's willing. He's good in the woods."

"I'll go," I said.

They looked at me again. Ben said, "You sure, Nellie?"

I shrugged. "I'm small, and I know how to move quiet. Better than any of the rest of you, at least."

"Right," Dogs said. "Head out once it's dark. John, keep an eye on the house and say if he leaves."

John Plainsman nodded and turned back to his vigil. Rob got up and went to talk to the Barrows, who were sitting together on the other side of the room, watching the track side of the building. Ben got to his feet.

"You need us for anything until then?" he said.

Dogs looked from him to me, then gave a wicked grin. "Not unless the Neffies come knockin'. I'll give a shout if we see 'em."

"Ben?" I said, but his hand was already on my wrist, tugging me toward the stairs.

BEN FUCKED ME HARDER THAN he ever had before, shoving me down on the dusty bed before I'd even properly gotten my shirt off and pushing into me with a furious intensity. I could see he had something on his mind, so I let him take the lead, and truth be told I can't say I minded it much. I left a couple of nice welts on his neck before we were finished, and a neat semi-circle of tooth marks when I bit down on the meat of his shoulder to keep from screaming.

"Did you have to *bite* me?" he said afterward, probing the tender spot with a finger. I hadn't broken the skin, but he'd have a bruise. "What are you, a wild dog?"

"It was that or shriek loud enough to bring the roof down."

"Go ahead and shriek," he said. "It's not like the rest don't know what we're doing. You hear the noises Bill makes some nights?"

That brought us both back into reality. Bill was downstairs, bandage sodden with blood, wrapped in a blanket and still shivering. Wound like that, it was even odds he'd lose the arm, if we made it to a surgeon. Jude and Liz were dead. And Captain Hays, who'd always been the strongest of us, had looked so frail with his eye closed and his face pale.

"This is it, isn't it?" Ben said. "Even if we get away. It'll be the end of the Red Riders."

I thought about what Liz and Hays had said, that the war was as good as lost. It would be the end of the Red Riders one way or another.

"What if it is?" I said. "You still want to go on to Totterhollow, sign up with General Wick?"

"I would." Ben shifted beside, his hand sliding across my bare chest. "I mean...it depends."

"Depends on what?"

"On what you were doing," he said. "I thought...maybe even if the Riders split up, it doesn't mean we have to. Does it?" He sounded anxious. "What would you do, if—"

"I ain't thought about it," I said. "And I won't until we get out of here."

"But after—"

"Leave after for after. Is that what's been eating you?"

"Nothing's eating me," he protested.

"Liar," I said, wriggling against him. "I can tell by the way you fuck. You're not usually in such a hurry."

"Nellie..." he breathed, then stopped. "Just be careful, all right?"

I snorted. "Like I'd be skipping along singing at the top of my lungs if I didn't have *you* here to tell me."

Leave after for after as all well and good as a thing to tell Ben, but it didn't stop my mind from working as I got dressed, cinching my belt tight and double-checking for anything that might clank or make noise. If we did get away, then what? Back to the army? I had no idea if Wick's army would even take a girl, though if Hays was right about the way things stood I guessed he'd take anyone with two arms and two legs. But if Hays was right, then maybe joining the army was as good as taking my last shot. I hated the Centrals and their Neffies, but that didn't mean I wanted to die in the last ditch for the Defiant.

But what else was there? It wasn't as though I had a trade to speak of. Go off into the country with Ben and bear his children, turn into a fat farmer's wife? The thought made me giggle.

"Nellie?" Rob said, from the stairs. "We're almost ready."

"Coming," I said.

I glanced back at Ben, who looked at me like a puppy in a cage.

I snorted again and went out into the hall. One of the guest-room doors was half-open, and from the blood on the floor I guessed that's where they'd put Jude. I wondered what had happened to Liz, if the Neffies had bothered to take her body away or just left it in the dirt. I wondered what Tzolk would do if he caught me, if he was serious about ordering all the Neffies to have a go. I swallowed, and promised myself I would take my last shot if it came to that.

The others were waiting downstairs. They'd traded their carbines for long knives, which the two Barrows and Sergeant Dogs always carried several of. I accepted one from the sergeant and thrust the sheath through my belt, and checked my revolver in its holster.

"John Plainsman will take the lead," Dogs said. "Stay close to him and stay quiet. Any shooting's going to be like kicking a hornet's nest."

"If we hear a shot, we'll open up," Big Barrow said. "Might confuse 'em."

"Just get back here as quick as you can," Dogs said. "Even if this works, we still got Tzolk to think about."

I looked from the sergeant to the captain, still unconscious under his blanket, and then to John Plainsman. Rob looked a bit pale, and he was staring at Bill. Little Barrow, a short young man with a mop of curly brown hair, had his thumbs in his belt and was pointedly not looking at his brother.

John Plainsman caught my eye. "You remember the hand signs?"

I nodded.

"Good. Let's go, then."

We went out through the door into the stables, a warm, smelly cave full of shadows and the soft sounds of still-spooked horses. There were no lanterns here, and the sky had gone from purple to black in the time that Ben and I had been fucking. The moon was up but still low, visible only in patches between the buildings of Hawk Hill.

John Plainsman led the way out into the street. Once he started

off, I had a hard time keeping my eye on him. He moved slow and smooth, like a stalking cat, watching the patches of moonlight on the dusty ground and keeping his shadow from falling across any of them. Little Barrow followed, not quite as smooth but nearly so. Rob and I were clumsy by comparison, but we could follow in their steps and stay out of the light, and I managed not to trip over myself.

The building we were heading for was a two-story house, painted a soft lavender with white trim, the boarded-over windows and overgrown garden spoiling the neat image. John went to his knees beside the front hedge and pointed for us to follow him along toward the back. The hedge went all the way round, and in the rear was a covered porch, in deep shadow.

John Plainsman stared for a long time, then pointed at the porch and held up one finger. It took me a moment to see what he meant; next to the back door, where the shadow was deepest, there was a tiny gleam of metal, reflected moonlight tracing the edge of a rifle barrel. A Neffie, on guard.

Little Barrow pointed at himself, and John nodded. Barrow crept forward in a crouch, through a gap in the hedge and across the weedy lawn. Somehow he managed not to make a sound, not even a rustle. I realized I was holding my breath, and let it out, slow and regular, so as not to gasp. Little Barrow reached the edge of the porch and gripped it, boosting himself up and slithering forward on his belly. When he was a few feet from the Neffie, he lunged with the speed of a striking snake, knife glittering for just a moment. There was a muffled thump, and then his shadowy form waved us forward.

He *was* good at this. Ben had told me the Barrows had been poachers before the war. The way he used the knife made me wonder if they'd been thieves and killers as well.

We climbed up to the porch, in single file. The Neffie lay on his back, a huddled shape in the coarse gray shirt and trousers the Centrals give them. He'd been a young man, with a wild beard and

mustache, probably untrimmed since he'd given his body to a demon. He stank, too, the sour smell of his body mixing with the metallic tang of blood. Neffies only bathed if someone bothered to order them to. Dead, he might have been a tramp or a beggar, except for the rifle still clutched in his hand.

The door was locked, but John Plainsman did something to it with a knife, and it opened with a soft crunch. It let in to the kitchen, which had been stripped bare, empty racks and shelves and a great wood-burning stove as cold as a corpse. From there a hall led to the front of the house, while a narrow servants' stair led upward. John pointed Little Barrow and Rob to the hall, then gestured for me to follow him up.

The stair was a tight, cramped switchback, and let out into an upstairs hall. A single lantern burned around a corner, its light throwing the shadows of at least two people on the wall. Neffies, I guessed, not people—they both carried rifles.

John Plainsman slipped forward, and I followed. From the shadows, the two were standing on either side of a doorway. He drew his knife, tapped his chest, and pointed left, and I nodded. My own knife came out, a bulky, unfamiliar thing I'd borrowed from Dogs. John held up three fingers, then two, then one.

He moved, twisting around the corner, and I followed. The Neffies were farther away than I'd thought, a few extra steps that threw me off balance. The one John had picked for himself was a tall man, gaunt like all Neffies, his beard matted and filthy. The other was a middle-aged woman, her face wrinkled and sagging, long hair studded with twigs and leaves like a woods-ghost from a fairy story.

It was the eyes that gave her away as Neffie, even without the stench. They were blank—no surprise, no emotion, nothing human. She didn't startle as we came around the corner, only raised her rifle to her shoulder. I barreled into her, slamming my shoulder into the gun to get clear of it. She let it fall with a clatter, hands reaching for

my throat. Her nails were long and cracked at the ends, and they left bloody scratches as she tried to get a hold. I twisted inside her grip, getting a mouthful of the sour smell of her and nearly gagging. As she pulled me close, I jammed the knife in her chest. It was harder than I'd thought, and I felt the blade grate on something tough, but the Neffie stiffened. Her hands tightened for a moment, and I thought she might never let go of me, but then she fell away with a sigh of escaping breath. She blinked, and for the briefest moment I thought I saw something in her eyes, an instant of recognition or humanity. Then she shuddered, and her eyes dulled.

I wondered what she'd done. The Centrals made Neffies out of criminals, debtors, Defiant prisoners—anyone whose body was fit enough to hold a demon and carry a rifle as part of the Central war machine. This woman didn't have the look of a Defiant soldier. She might've been a whore—Central preachers were death on whoring—or just a widow whose debts had gone bad. No way to know, now.

Tearing myself free of her hands, I saw that John Plainsman had opened his opponent's throat with a slash, stepping back to avoid the spray of blood. The body hit the floor with a heavy thump, sprawled over his rifle. Something moved behind the closed door of the room, and I heard a young woman's voice.

"What's going on out there?" She paused, then sighed. Footsteps. "Open the door."

Neffies couldn't talk. The gift of speech was something God had granted only to His favored children, the priests said. It was one of the reasons the demons hated us so much. So whoever was inside was human, and wouldn't be expecting a spoken response. On the other hand, if she was authorized to command these Nephilim, they would obey without hesitation.

I motioned to John Plainsman to flatten himself against the wall, and thumbed the door latch. The woman moved, just a step

or two, but she was wearing boots and the footsteps let me place her inside the room. As the door swung open, I pulled my revolver from its holster. It was the first that she saw as I stepped around the door, and her eyes went wide.

She was in her late teens, I guessed, with pale skin and pretty blonde curls. She was in Central Army uniform, gray trousers, a starched linen shirt, and a dark burgundy jacket, but she'd draped the coat over the back of a chair, and there were a dozen garments of various descriptions spread out on the bed. The closet door was open, and more clothes lay in a pile on the floor.

The revolver and my ragged looks seemed to provide all the explanation necessary. Her belt, with sword and revolver, hung on the chair underneath her coat. I gestured upward, and she raised her hands, lips twisting as John Plainsman slipped into the room behind me.

"If I scream," she said, in a very quiet voice, "there's no way you'll make it out of here."

"The same goes for you," I said, stepping forward. John began to circle around behind her, and I saw her nervous eyes flick between us.

"You're going to kill me anyway," she said. "Why else would you be here?"

"Then why haven't you screamed?"

She clamped her mouth tight, but her eyes said everything. *Because I don't want to die.*

John was behind her, out of her field of view, sliding whisper-quiet over the floor. His knife was out, and I didn't doubt he could take her before she could make a sound. When she made to turn, I shook my head and waggled the gun. A bead of sweat formed on her forehead and rolled down her cheek.

Something was bothering me, but I didn't get it until it was nearly too late. John was only a foot away from her when I said, "What's your name?"

"Why do you care?" she said. Tears glistened at the corners of her eyes.

Those golden curls. I'd seen Tzolk and his son the last time they'd nearly caught up with us. Both blonde as the sun, a rare thing in the Central counties. "You're his daughter, aren't you? Tzolk's."

Her chin rose, just a little. "*Colonel* Tzolk is my father. And he's going to kill every one of you scum—"

"Quiet," I snapped. She halted, swallowed hard. "Tell me your name."

"Ephinia Tzolk," she said, in a barely audible whisper. "They call me Finny."

"Ephinia Tzolk," I said. "You willing to co-operate, if it means you might get out of this?"

John Plainsman raised an eyebrow, knife still poised over her back.

"I..." She stood a little straighter. "I won't hurt my father, no matter what you do to me."

"We won't hurt anything but his pride. If you come with us, we'll trade you to him for a pass out of here."

She licked her lips. "I'm not sure he would take that deal."

"I think he will. He's lost two sons going after Hays. I doubt he wants to add you to the pot." I shrugged. "It's worth a try, anyway. But you have to come along quiet. Otherwise..."

"I'll come," she said.

"You sure about this?" John Plainsman said. Finny startled at the sound of his voice so close.

I wasn't sure when it had become my decision, but I nodded. "It's the best chance we've got of getting everyone out of here."

John stepped forward and tapped the knife, still stained with the Neffies' blood, against Finny's cheek. Her eyes went very wide as he brought it down to the level of her kidneys, then put his other hand on her shoulder. I holstered the revolver and backed up as he

pushed her through the door.

As we reached the top of the stairs, there was a gunshot, loud as a cannon in the silence. All three of us froze.

"Revolver," John said.

"Rob and Barrow," I said. "You get her back to the station, I'll go find them."

"But—"

"Just go!" I shouted, pounding down the main stairs while he headed for the back.

No point in silence now. Everyone in town had heard that shot. From the direction of the station, I heard carbines *crack*, Dogs and the others providing the promised distraction. Answering shots came from the Neffies, the firefight starting up again in an instant, like a blaze sparked in dry tinder. At the bottom of the main stairs was the hall, leading to the open front door. A Neffie was sprawled in the doorway, and I pulled up short as several more shots slammed into the lintel, splintering the wood. A second Neffie ducked out a moment later and fired his rifle down the hall toward the kitchen.

He disappeared a moment later, chased by more revolver fire. Rob and Barrow were in the kitchen, too far to rush the door before the Neffie reloaded, but I was only a few feet away. I sprinted forward, sending up a silent prayer that the pair of them would recognize me before they shot me in the back. My luck held, and I yanked my revolver out and spun halfway out the door to confront the Neffie, who was just closing the bolt on his rifle. I shot him in the chest, the revolver bucking like it wanted to jump out of my hand. Dust puffed off his clothes, and he took a step back against the wall, letting his weapon fall. I shot him again, and he collapsed.

"Nellie?" Little Barrow said.

From the front door, I could see the station, windows blazing with the muzzle flashes of the Red Riders' carbines. Most of the rifle fire was aimed their way, but some of the Neffies had noticed

me, because two bullets blasted chunks out of the house's siding not far from my head. I ran back inside, toward the kitchen, where Rob and Little Barrow were crouched on either side of the doorway.

"Where's John?" I said.

"Out the back," Rob said. "He had a *girl* with him—"

"Come on," I cut him off, "let's get after him. Move!"

We piled out the back door, across the porch, and down the hedgerow, hunched almost double. That left twenty feet of dusty street between us and the stable entrance. Little Barrow started out at a run, then slid to a halt as a bullet raised a shower of dirt only a pace in front of him. He fell on his ass, and Rob and I grabbed his arms and dragged him back to cover just ahead of another couple of shots.

"Shit," he said. "We'll never make it."

"We haven't got a choice," Rob said. "They'll be coming around any minute."

"All at once," I said. "Count of three. Run and keep running, no matter what happens."

"Okay." Little Barrow took a deep breath. "One."

"Two," Rob said, lowering himself into a crouch.

"Three!" I shouted, pushing off.

I don't know that I'd ever run like that in my life. It sure felt like I hadn't, my lungs sawing at the air and my heart going like it was trying to tear itself to pieces. Every step I took I could feel the shot that would get me, slamming into my leg or my belly, doubling me over or spraying my brains across the road. Bullets hit the ground with a sound like *pok pok pok*, raising little fountains of dust. I swear I felt the wind of one of them tug at my coat.

When I got to the stable, I couldn't stop, just kept running until I wrapped one arm around a wooden pillar and brought myself to a halt. My legs felt like jelly, like I'd run twenty miles instead of twenty feet. Little Barrow pulled up beside me, gasping, then turned back and shouted.

"Rob!"

He was down, clutching his hip, blood leaking into a pool that looked black in the dim light. Little Barrow took a step in his direction, and I grabbed his arm before he could go back out. Shots were still raising sprays of dirt all around Rob as he fumbled for his revolver.

"She's right!" he shouted over the racket. "Get inside."

Little Barrow took a step back, hesitated, then turned away. I was about to follow, but Rob locked eyes with me, and I froze in place.

"My last shot," he said, raising the revolver. "Please, Nellie. Don't let them leave Bill behind. One way or the other."

A bullet tore through his coat where it lay on the ground behind him. Rob put the revolver to his temple and pulled the trigger.

INSIDE THE STATION, JOHN PLAINSMAN held his knife at Finny's throat. Ben and Gid were still by the windows, leaning out to deliver the occasional shot at the Neffies, but Dogs and Big Barrow had come over to the stable door.

"I don't remember nothing in the plan about taking prisoners," Dogs said.

"Especially not such nice-looking prisoners," Big Barrow said, his eyes roving over Finny. "Not that I'll complain."

She kept her head up and gave a creditable impression of being unafraid.

"If you're going to rape me," she said, "I'd appreciate it if you'd go ahead and get it over with. I'd say I was surprised, but it's what I'd expected from traitors."

"I'm no fucking traitor," Big Barrow said. "And maybe we ought to, after what Tzolk was going to do to Liz. What are you, his whore?"

"She's his daughter," I said, pushing Little Barrow out of the way. "And I told her we wouldn't hurt her."

"This was *your* idea?" Dogs said, raising a bushy eyebrow.

I nodded. "I figured we could offer her back to Tzolk if he lets us ride out of here."

"Not bad," Dogs said, scratching his chin. "Ben, Gid, get away from the window. If they want to waste ammunition shooting in the dark, let 'em."

"Where's Rob?" Big Barrow said, looking behind us into the stable.

His brother shook his head. Big Barrow stared at him, and Dogs winced.

"Dead?" the sergeant said. "You're sure?"

"Yeah," I said. "He took his last shot."

"Good man." Dogs cocked his head. The fire from outside had dwindled away, leaving the night nearly silent once again. "I gotta think about this. Nellie, the girl's yours to take care of. Make sure she doesn't cause trouble." He turned away, gesturing for the others to follow. Ben lingered behind.

"You're all right?" he said.

I frowned at him. There was a damp patch on his sleeve, the gray fabric soaked through. "I'm fine. Are you bleeding?"

"Only a little. It was just a splinter." He shrugged. "Still lucky."

"Put a bandage on it anyway," I said. He smiled, and I grinned back at him.

"He's your husband?" Finny said, as he walked away.

"Husband?" I snorted. "He's just a man I take to bed sometimes."

She colored and looked away, muttering something. It sounded like, "Savages."

I rolled my eyes. "Come over here, out of the way."

She followed me to the corner, where I sat down against our water barrel. After a moment, she took the seat across from me, back to the wall. I watched her look around the room, taking in the two injured men and the small knot deep in conversation.

"This is it?" she said. "These are the Red Riders?"

I bristled. "This is what's been running you and your damned Neffies in circles."

"You're not even wearing the red capes."

"We only wear those when we want to scare people," I said. "It was Hays's idea. What kind of an idiot would wear a red cape into a fight?"

"Where is the famous Captain Hays, anyway?"

I hesitated, but it wasn't like there was anyone she could tell. "He's hurt. He got hit when he showed himself to shoot Liz."

"That was the woman from the water tower?" When I nodded, she closed her eyes. "She killed my brother."

"She..." My mouth went dry, and I couldn't think of what to say. "I'm sorry. I guess."

"Why?" Finny said. "He was your enemy, you should be happy he's dead. I'm not sorry your friend Rob got killed." She shrugged, and said, a little too quickly, "Besides, Gil was an ass. He used to hit me with his belt when he thought I'd stolen something from him."

There was an awkward silence. I saw Finny look at the others, and followed her gaze to see Dogs staring back at her, his gaze frank and appraising.

"You want some water?" I said.

She looked back to me and nodded. I filled two tin cups from the barrel, passed one to her, and drank deep from mine. Finny took a sip, then a longer swallow.

"What were you doing digging through that closet, anyway?" I said. "Did you think they'd hid the silver in there or something?"

"Of course not." Finny flushed. "The woman who lived there seemed like she was about my age. I was curious."

"You were stealing her *dresses*?" I couldn't keep a note of disbelief out of my voice. I'd done my share of looting with the Red Riders—food, money, ammunition, even shoes—but I couldn't imagine grabbing a fancy dress except to tear it up for bandages.

"I wasn't stealing them," Finny said. "Just looking. I was bored."

"That why you joined the army? To kill people and steal clothes?"

"I joined the army to save the Counties from traitors," Finny snapped. "And *you* ought to talk. Your Red Riders are nothing but a pack of murderous thieves."

"I've never murdered nobody," I said. There *had* been that Central quartermaster, admittedly, but he'd been trying to shoot me, so that wasn't murder.

Finny snorted. "If you're going to lie to me, be a little smarter about it. What about those two guards outside my door? Or did your Plainsman friend do both of them?"

"One of those was mine," I said. "But those were Neffies, not people."

Finny narrowed her eyes. "It's the same thing, surely?"

"Neffies and humans aren't even close to the same. Shooting a Neffie is more like shooting a mad dog."

"But if you kill a Nephilim's host," Finny said, in a slow voice like she was talking to a kid, "the host's soul will have nowhere to return to when the binding is released. It's no different from killing the host outright. Though I suppose the host won't feel any pain, at least."

I didn't want to admit I'd only understood about half of that. "A Neffie is still a Neffie."

"But if you kill the Nephilim," Finny said again, "then it can't go *back* to being the person it was."

Now it was my turn to snort. "You Centrals don't turn Neffies back into humans."

"Thousands of people host Nephilim and return every day," Finny said, eyeing me curiously. "Almost all our factories use Nephilim labor. It's efficient and humane."

"But you make your soldiers out of prisoners," I said. "Defiant soldiers and anybody else who steps out of line. You're never going to let *them* come back."

"There are some of those," Finny said. "But there's hardly enough prisoners to make an army. Most of the Nephilim come from the draft lottery, and they'll be released when their service is over."

"And how long is that?"

A frown crossed her features. "It was supposed to be two years, but Parliament changed the law to make it until the conclusion of the war."

"Of course," I said, feeling like I'd won a point but not certain exactly how.

"Even the prisoners will be released, once the war's over." Finny shook her head. "And what are we supposed to do, fight the war with humans like you do?" She glared at me. "Is that why *you* joined up? To kill Nephilim because some priest told you it would get you into Heaven?"

"I joined up because one of your raiding parties burned my home and killed my family," I said.

There was another one of those awkward silences.

"I'm sorry," Finny said after a while, staring into her cup.

"Why should you be?" I said bitterly. "They were your enemies."

"I..." She broke off and shook her head. "I didn't mean it like that. I just—"

"Nellie!" Ben hurried over, and I got to my feet. He caught my expression and frowned. "Something wrong?"

I shot Finny a glance and shook my head. "Centrals are strange, that's all. What's going on?"

"Hays is awake," he said, the relief obvious in his voice. "I'll watch the girl. He wants to talk to you."

HAYS WAS SITTING UP, PROPPED against a crate, his arm and shoulder immobilized under a tight web of bandages. His face was drawn and pale, with the sapphire blue of his eye bright and feverish amid the bloodless skin. Dogs, Big Barrow, and John Plainsman sat

beside him; Gid and Little Barrow were watching the windows to make sure the Neffies didn't try sneaking up on us.

"Nellie," Hays said, taking a long drink from a canteen. "I hear you've got a plan to get us out of this."

"More an idea than a plan," I said. "But I thought Tzolk's daughter might be more use alive than dead."

"I'm glad to see that the Red Riders were in good hands while I was inconvenienced." Hays grinned, though the expression was strained. "Has Tzolk said anything?"

"Not yet," Dogs said. "He's probably still trying to figure out what the hell happened."

"I still don't like this idea," Big Barrow said. "I don't trust Tzolk, daughter or no daughter."

"We're rapidly running out of options," Hays said. He looked up at me. "You've spoken to the girl?"

"A bit," I said.

"What's she like?"

"A bit scared, but not panicked."

"Will she cooperate?"

"I think so," I said slowly. "Unless she finds out we're planning a double-cross. She's brave enough to shout out if she gets wind of something like that."

"A good thing we intend to be honest, then," Hays said. "Well done, Nellie. You may have saved all our lives."

"Going over there was Rob's idea," I said. "And John Plainsman—"

"I understand," Hays said, holding up a hand. "Tell the girl to get ready. I just need to figure out exactly what to say to Tzolk."

"You sure you're up to this?" Dogs said, as I walked away.

"I'll manage," Hays said dryly. "I have little choice."

"Hays likes the idea," I said to Ben and Finny. "He's going to set up the exchange."

"Thank God," Ben said.

"I don't—" Finny began, then bit her lip.

"Something wrong?" I said, kneeling beside her. "If you know something that'll screw things up, now's the time to say so."

"I just don't know if Pa will go for it," Finny said. "He's never thought much of me. And he hates Captain Hays."

"You're his flesh and blood, aren't you?" Ben said incredulously.

Finny nodded miserably. "But Pa's not...not *sentimental*. You don't know him like I do."

"Let's hope you're wrong," Ben said.

He went back to the front windows, while I settled down beside Finny. She was hunched up, trying to make herself small. I patted her awkwardly on the shoulder.

"It'll be fine," I said. "We'll all walk out of here yet."

"Thanks." She turned her head, resting it on her knees. "You're a strange sort of traitor, you know that?"

For a moment I saw myself through her eyes, a mannish, hayseed of girl, slutty, dirty and stained, a hopeless hick who'd picked up a carbine in a doomed cause. My lips tightened.

"Sorry if I'm not up to snuff," I muttered.

"Just not what I expected. I thought your lot were all fanatics shouting about God. Your General Wick certainly does."

"I've never met General Wick," I said. "All I know is the Red Riders."

"TZOLK!" HAYS SHOUTED. I WAS impressed that he could summon the voice for it, in spite of his injury. "You there, Tzolk?"

"That you, Hays?" Tzolk's voice drifted back. "I was hoping you hadn't gone and died on me. I got *plans* for you."

"I thought you might want to talk," Hays said. "The thing is, we picked something up that belongs to you. Blonde, about five and a half feet high, ring any bells?"

"Say something," I whispered to Finny, prodding her in the back.

"I'm here, Pa!" she shouted. "I'm okay! They haven't hurt me."

I patted her shoulder. "Good enough."

There was a long silence from the town. Finally, Tzolk said, "I suppose you think this gives you the whip hand."

"That was my theory, yes," Hays said. "I'll trade your girl's life for me and my men. That seem equitable?"

Another silence. "You'll get yours," Tzolk said. "One of these days. You God-damned snake."

"I'll take that for a yes," Hays said.

"'Course it's a yes," Tzolk said. "I'm ain't a monster."

I felt Finny stiffen and patted her shoulder again.

"How do you want to do this?" Tzolk went on. "I assume you have it worked out."

"I've given it a little thought," Hays said. "I'll bring the girl out so you can see she's all right. Then you'll order your Nephilim to start marching west. Once they're out of earshot, we'll give you the girl, and take ourselves in the opposite direction."

"Clever," Tzolk said. "All right. Give me a few minutes to get everyone rounded up."

The Red Riders were grinning at each other. Big Barrow hugged Little Barrow around the shoulders, and even John Plainsman's impassable face showed signs of animation. Ben put one arm around me and kissed me in front of everyone, which was enough to make me blush a little, but nobody was paying much attention.

"They are not going to believe this one when we get back," Gid was saying. "Not in a thousand years."

"It's not going to work," Finny said, but nobody was minding her but me. I pulled away from Ben and bent to listen. "Pa's lying."

"About what?"

"I don't know. But he's lying. I can tell." She shook her head. "You should call this off."

"She's trying to spook us," Big Barrow said.

"That better be it," Dogs said. "No offense, young lady, but if you're right, I'm going to make sure you don't get back to your Pa. Always been a man of my word that way."

"No need to scare her," I said.

"It's all right," Finny said, letting out a deep breath. "I'd do the same, in his place."

"Glad we understand each other," Dogs said.

"The Neffies are coming out!" Gid said.

We all looked to the windows. Scarecrow figures in cheap, ragged uniforms were emerging from the doors and alleys of the empty town, lining up in the street opposite the station. I counted, quickly, and came up with thirty-nine.

"May not be all of them," Ben said. "We don't have a good count."

"Even if he keeps a few back," Hays said, "it wouldn't be enough to stop us from getting away." He looked over the group, pursed his lips, and nodded. "Dogs, you're with me. Nellie, you stay on the girl. The rest of you, at the windows, weapons ready in case this goes wrong."

It took Dogs and Big Barrow a few moments to move the junk we'd piled in front of the door so it could be opened. The light from the lanterns outside shone in through several splintery bullet holes. Dogs went through first, revolver in one hand, the other ready to help Hays if he stumbled. I drew my own revolver with an apologetic look at Finny, who shrugged and stepped in front of me. I put the barrel against the back of her head, and we started forward.

There was no sign of Tzolk. Hays looked over the impassive ranks of Neffies, then gave a one-shouldered shrug.

"You'll forgive me if I don't come out in the open," Tzolk's voice came, from one of the nearby buildings. "Wouldn't want one of your men to be tempted."

"I understand," Hays said. "Here's your girl, safe and sound."

"That true, Finny? You all right?"

"I'm fine, Pa," she said, her voice shaky. "They'll keep to the deal."

I shifted the revolver against the back of her head, my breath coming fast. Even Dogs seemed tense, shifting his weight from one foot to the other. Only Hays was unflappable as ever.

"Well," he said. "Give the order, then, and I'll turn her loose."

"It's a damn shame," Tzolk said. "Nephilim, do it."

Dogs understood what was happening before anyone else. He took a long sideways step and lowered his revolver, placing himself between the line of Neffies and Hays. His weapon barked, just once, as thirty-nine Nephilim raised their rifles and took aim.

In that moment, I shoulder have pulled the trigger. I wish I could say I'd thought about it, but the plain fact was I just couldn't. I'm not a murderer, and Finny hadn't done anything to me. Instead I took a step sideways, away from Hays. I only meant to clear my line of fire as I levelled my revolver, but that step probably saved my life.

The Neffies fired all at once, a single volley like old-fashioned musketeers. Dogs jerked as bullets slammed into his huge body, but he stayed on his feet. I saw Hays's knees give way, and Finny falling forward, though I couldn't tell if either was hit. Then I felt pain like I'd never imagined, a stinging, searing pain in my hand like a thousand wasps had stung it at once. I stared at it, like an idiot—my revolver was gone, and something was wrong with my fingers as well.

Once again, my body knew what to do while my mind was still trying to figure things out. I moved quick, reaching out with my other hand to grab Hays's arm before he finished falling. I heard someone scream, and shots flashed from the windows of the station as the Red Riders fired back, but I was stumbling through a dark tunnel with the door at the far end. It was only four steps away, but it felt like a mile, with Hays a dead weight at the end of my arm.

More shots hit the bricks around the doorway as I half-ran,

half-fell through it and rolled to one side, gasping. Someone grabbed Hays and dragged him out of the way, and Ben knelt at my side. I held out my hand to grasp his, and he gasped; it was the hand I'd been holding the revolver in. My index finger was gone, a broken scrap of bone sticking out from the ruined flesh, and my middle finger was dangling by a few scraps of skin and sinew. I rolled over just in time to vomit, nothing in my stomach but water and sour bile.

"Nellie!" Ben's voice sounded distant. "Stay with me!"

"Hays is hit!" someone shouted.

"They're coming!" Gid's voice, high and scared.

No time for being hurt. I got to my feet, ruined hand jammed into the pocket of my coat so I wouldn't have to look at it. Out the window, I could see some of the Neffies running toward the building, while the others loaded and fired mechanically at the windows. At least a half-dozen were down, but of course that didn't bother the rest. Dogs was on his knees in the center of the square, head lolling, at least a dozen holes in him.

Finny was on her belly, blood staining the back of her shirt and her trouser leg, but still crawling away from the station. Even as I watched though, a bullet hit her in the small of the back, though I had no idea if it was one of ours or one of theirs. She gave a little shudder and lay still.

"They're *coming*!" Gid said.

"Then shut the *fucking* door!" Big Barrow screamed, but Gid was down, his gawky frame spread over the floor with a bloody crater in the back of his skull. The first wave of Neffies reached the side of the building, two of them filling the doorway. Ben's revolver fired three times in quick succession, and they both went down, blocking the way for those struggling behind them. More Neffies went to the windows, pushing their rifles through from the outside.

"Upstairs!" John Plainsman shouted. His own revolver slammed out a methodical rhythm, picking the Neffies off as they put their

heads up. "We're sitting ducks down here!"

"Someone get Hays!" Little Barrow said.

"Help me with him," I said, grabbing the captain's arm again with my good hand. Ben took his other arm, and we dragged Hays to the stairs. Another Neffie struggled through the door, but John Plainsman shot him down. Then a rifle bullet hit him in the shoulder and spun him around, and two more found him before he could get back up.

The Barrows came behind us, brothers firing together as Ben and I carried Hays up the stairs. They remained at the top of the stairs, reloading as we stumbled through the closest open door. It was Bill's sickroom; the wounded man lay on the bed, sweating and feverish, eyes closed.

Hays groaned as we propped him against the foot of the bed.

"Captain?" I said.

"I'm here," he said, one hand pressed against his stomach. Bright blood leaked between his fingers. "Unfortunately."

"We've got to hold them on the stairs," Ben said. He feverishly loaded bullets into his still-smoking revolver as more firing came from that direction. "Stay with him, Nellie."

"Ben—" I started to say, but he was gone. For a long time, I could only stare.

"Nellie." Hays's croaking voice broke through to me. "Nellie, please. Listen."

I blinked and looked down. He was holding his revolver, awkwardly, holding it out to me.

"Bill," he said. "He can't take his last shot. You have to do it."

"Oh."

I walked to the bed and raised the weapon, left-handed. Bill barely jerked as I put two bullets into his chest, only seemed to relax with a little sigh. It was probably for the best, I figured. He never had to hear that Rob was dead.

"Good," Hays said. "Go next door. Jude's body. Bring it."

"But—"

"Now!" he said, then started coughing, blood spraying from his lips.

I went. Manhandling a cold, stiffening corpse with one hand meant I didn't have much time to spare for the gunfight at the end of the hall, but I could see that Big Barrow was hurt but still shooting, braced against the wall. Ben and his brother were on their bellies at the top of the stairs, firing down at the Neffies.

"Put him on the bed," Hays said.

"But—"

"Get some blood on your chest and lie down between them," he said. "Breathe shallow."

I finally realized what he wanted. "Don't be stupid," I said. "I'll fight."

"I told you I wanted to get you out of this," he said. "This is the only way. Once he has me, Tzolk isn't going to hang around here."

"But—"

"Don't *argue*, Nellie. Just do it." He jerked his head toward the bed. "Keep the revolver under the bodies. Last shot. In case it doesn't work."

"What about yours?"

He gave a bloody chuckle. "I'm not going to last long enough for them to hurt me much. And Tzolk's more likely to leave if he finally gets what he's wanted all this time."

"But..." I shook my head, the pain in my mangled hand getting worse. "Why *me*?"

"Because you can go on, after this," Hays said, gasping for breath. "Any of the others...would only keep fighting. Going to die anyway, might as well die here. But you...aren't drowned in blood. Not yet. Just...walk away. No more war." He closed his eyes. "They're coming."

I crawled into the bed, in between two dead men. Jude's hand

was chilly where it brushed my skin, and Bill's was still fever-warm. I wet my fingers with Bill's blood and smeared it liberally across my shirt, though honestly there was more than enough blood on me as it was. Then I heard the firing stop, and booted feet coming down the hall. I knew that Ben was dead.

I'd arranged myself so Bill's limp body half-covered me, but with one eyelid barely cracked I could still see the doorway. Two Neffies appeared, a man and a woman, both skeletally thin and dressed in rags. They looked over the room and raised their rifles to aim at Hays. Before they could fire, Tzolk said, "Don't. Not that one."

I saw the peak of his officer's cap, behind the pair of him. He gave the room a long look, then said, "Gather the others and wait downstairs until I come get you."

The Neffies turned and went. Tzolk stepped through the door and looked down at Hays. He was a short man, with a bald spot his cap didn't quite cover, dressed in a Central officer's burgundy jacket with gold braid. He had a pearl-handled revolver in one hand.

"Hays," he said. "You've looked better."

"I had something clever to say," Hays gasped. "But it hurts too much." He sucked in a breath, then coughed wetly. "Better kill me quick, Colonel, or you'll miss your chance."

"Fair enough." Tzolk cocked the hammer on his weapon. "I'd say something about you being a worthy opponent, but in the end you're just a thief and coward."

"And you're a double-crossing bastard who shot his own daughter."

"I've got others." Tzolk shrugged. "I'll tell her mother you raped her and slit her throat. She'll be proud of me for bringing in your head."

Hays gave another wet laugh. "You...really are...a son-of-a-bitch."

"I never claimed otherwise." Tzolk raised his revolver.

I clutched mine, under Bill's body. The last shot. One last shot. Never let them take you alive, not ever, or else you'll end up as a Neffie and shoot at the people you used to love.

Everyone I loved was dead.

Ten paces. Left-handed. One shot. Not good odds.

My hand was moving before I finished the thought.

Tzolk noticed, looked up, but not fast enough. I got the revolver level and pulled the trigger. The recoil was enough to jolt it out of my numb fingers, but the shot was on target, catching the colonel high in the chest. His gun fell from his fingers, and he staggered back through the doorway, sagging against the opposite wall.

I climbed off the bed of corpses and got to my feet, unsteadily. Tzolk was pawing at himself, eyes wide and uncomprehending. I picked his gun up off the floor and took careful aim.

"Finny deserved better than you," I said, and shot him in the head.

Hays was dead, his blue eye staring into nothing, an enigmatic smile on his lips. Out in the corridor, Big Barrow was on top of Little Barrow, shielding his brother's body with his own, both of them riddled with bullet holes. Ben lay on his face, a neat hole in the front of his skull and a nastier one at the back. It looked like it had at least been quick.

A dozen Neffies lay on the stairs, and more on the floor below. There were twenty-one left standing, some of them wounded. They waited in a tight bunch, eyes moving to watch me as I picked my way down, but making no other move.

"Wait until I come get you," Tzolk had said. Not "stand guard" or "keep watch". An experienced commander like him really ought to have known better. I killed all twenty-one of them with John Plainsman's long knife, slitting their throats like they were cattle while they stood watching silently. If Finny was right, I was a murderer many times over, now. But Neffies were Neffies.

"Just go," Hays had told me. He'd said that the war was as good as over. No point in dying for a lost cause.

When I'd finished them all, I went to the stables. A few of the horses were dead, caught in the crossfire, but most had escaped, kicking their way out of their stalls as the battle got close. That was all right. They wouldn't go far, and I could catch one once they calmed down.

Our wagon was still there, full of supplies. I bound up my hand as best I could, though it needed a proper surgeon's attention. I filled a spare pack with food and water, a Central-issue revolver and a pouch of bullets. Last of all, I took one of the bundled cloaks, brilliantly crimson in the slowly rising light of dawn, and tied it around my shoulders.

Then I went to look for a horse that would take me to Totter-hollow and General Wick. The last of the Red Riders.

CHRISTINE JORGENSEN

O N DECEMBER 1, 1952, THE front page of the *New York Daily News* shouted this headline for the world to see:

"Ex-GI Becomes Blonde Beauty: Operations Transform Bronx Youth."

Christine Jorgensen had been named George Jorgensen at birth in 1926. She grew up in the Bronx, NY, and since she had been born with a male anatomy, was eligible to be drafted in World War II. After the war, she went to school, where she became increasingly aware and concerned that her body didn't reflect the person she truly felt she was. She traveled to Europe, which was the only place gender reassignment surgeries were legal at the time, and privately underwent therapies and surgeries that helped her become the person she knew she was, both inside and out. In a letter to friends, Christine said:

"As you can see by the enclosed photos, taken just before the operation, I have changed a great deal. But it is the other changes that are so much more important. Remember the shy, miserable person who left America? Well, that person is no more and, as you can see, I'm in marvelous spirits."

Christine never meant to be famous. She only wanted to find happiness. But when the *New York Daily News* came across a letter she wrote to her parents, they published the story. One line that stands out from the letter, that attracted the newspaper's attention, was:

"I am still the same old 'Brud,' but Nature made a mistake, which I have had corrected, and I am now your daughter."

Once the story ran, Christine had two choices: to go into hiding and try to reclaim her privacy, or…to not. She chose the latter, and became a voice for people who faced the same issues she had. Her courage paved the way for many others to seize their identities and live their lives as they felt they should, rather than struggling to live with "Nature's mistakes." She traveled to college campuses, where she answered students' questions and raised awareness, and helped medical professionals refine their practices in order to help people have healthy transitions. She helped create awareness of the gender spectrum, and while she made her living as an entertainer, also spoke with dignity and eloquence at lectures, talk shows, and other appearances, giving the transgender community a voice at a time when it had none.

Further Reading:

www.christinejorgensen.org
Christine Jorgensen: A Personal Autobiography
by Christine Jorgensen

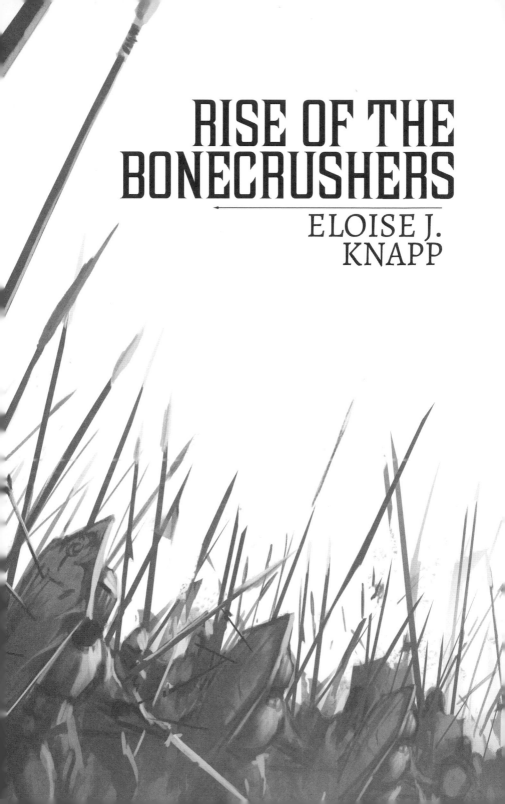

RISE OF THE BONECRUSHERS

ELOISE J. KNAPP

T HE VALKYRIE7 TRANSPORT SHIP SHUDDERED and groaned. I decided the only thing holding it together was a hope and a prayer. That or a fuck ton of duct tape and maybe a bit of chewing gum.

"We're good! Just a little turbulence," Jimmy shouted from the cockpit. "Puke bags under the seat if you need 'em!"

Why the hell did he always shout? I had a mic and an earpiece. He didn't need to shout. I was a moderately healthy thirty-five-year old woman, not a decrepit senior with hearing loss. Plus, in the golden age of genetic modification, you'd have to go out of your way to be deaf. *And* I'd never lost my lunch a single time flying with him.

The bodyguard Boss issued, however, looked like he was going to puke. If he hadn't been strapped into his seat, he'd have keeled over. MegaCorp owned the company he came from, and my own news station for that matter, and since I'm not the biggest fan of MegaCorp, I felt a faint obligation to hope he *did* puke all over his perfectly tailored suit.

I'd been an investigative journalist for nearly a decade. I'd been

shot at, stabbed, and kidnapped once. Got through those messes alone then, I sure as fuck could do it now. But Boss insisted the bodyguard come with me since I was on a high-profile story.

You don't bite the hand that feeds. Well, unless you have a good contingency plan in case you get bit back.

"How about you? You okay over there, Suit?"

He didn't look at me. His gaze remained firmly on the ground between his feet. I felt a little bad for teasing him so much and made a mental note to go easier on him. It wasn't his fault he was from MegaCorp, riding a rust bucket with me.

The Valkyrie7 couldn't fly above cloud level so, staring out the window at ancient abandoned cities as far as the eye can see, I did see why Boss paid for a bodyguard. This far away from the safety of a Haven city, there was nothing but Infected. Wild, sick humans who'd dominated the land for nearly two hundred years. They looked like us, but they weren't us. They reproduced like rabbits so their numbers never dwindled.

They'd tear a person to pieces the second they saw them.

No, I wouldn't fly out of my giant, safe city on an old transport ship over millions of Infected for any old thing. In a world where one percent of the population was interested in hearing something other than bullshit about celebrities and trends, being a journalist was an unfulfilling job.

I was out risking my life to cover my last story. My early retirement piece. The big one that would give me enough credits for a lifetime and then some. The futile slog of trying to get through to the ninety-nine percent was over. I'd still keep up on my totally unprofitable articles on the Web, but no more fluff for the news station.

This particularly fluffy piece on an infamous retired Bonecrusher. That's all. What she was up to, what clothes she wore and food she ate. I suppose the one sweet tidbit was that I was the only person Boss trusted to cover it. Lucky me.

"How much longer?" I yelled because it gave good old Jimmy a taste of his own medicine.

He didn't care. Or notice. Probably the latter.

"Not much longer, MC. How about another relaxy? Koku, give them relaxys on the house."

The Valkyrie7 was small. It seated six. There were three seats on the walls of the aircraft that faced each other. Jimmy's ancient model android, Koku, was by the cockpit. She stood up and clunked over to Suit. Her kimono was busted. I saw wires and a sharp piece of metal protruding from her synthetic, pale skin. I had no doubt she was a sex bot when she was created at least seventy years ago.

Jimmy had the bot set to extra stereotypical. Her accent was thick, exaggerated really, her outfit unreasonably short.

"You want?" she cooed in a singsong voice. She held out a relaxy. The drug was in a tiny aerosol can the size of my pinky.

Suit waved her away, then his hand snapped right back to his knee. Koku staggered over to me.

I didn't *need* it, but Jimmy was offering. I took it and put it to my nose. My eyes rolled back into my head as the drug took hold. I barely heard Koku go back to her charging dock or Suit start to retch. A sweet blissful calm overtook me and suddenly I didn't mind Jimmy's flying anymore.

THE DRUG WORE OFF BY the time we landed in a podunk little settlement called Mercy. The settlement was located in a place known as "Texas" before the United States of America was dissolved in favor of the Havens. Boss already paid Jimmy for the flight, so I grabbed my bag and walked down the ramp in the back of the airship. The ramp had lost most of its traction, the yellow metal rungs worn down smooth and silver. I slipped more than walked.

Suit glided down it without fumbling, his head turning slightly as he scanned our surroundings. Now on steady ground, he had his

cool back, and I was reminded he was a professional. He pressed his sleeve against his mouth and muttered something I couldn't hear.

"*Arigato!*" Koku said enthusiastically as we left. She bowed and one of her oversized breasts slipped from the kimono. When she stood, I reached out and fixed her outfit. I pulled off the loose obi then wrapped it around her waist and double knotted it in front for good measure.

The Mercy airship landing zone was small and enclosed only by a chain link fence. The sky was a brilliant scorching orange where the sun was on the verge of disappearing below the horizon. Without towering buildings and electrified walls enveloping me, I felt incredibly vulnerable. A handful of Infected would tear those fences down as though they were paper.

For the first time since we boarded the transport ship, Suit spoke to me, breaking me from my thoughts. "Fuck me, it's hot."

Despite almost being night, it *was* hot. Too fucking hot for someone from a rainy, cool Haven up in the Pacific Northwest. I smelled hot asphalt, smoke, and behind that hundreds of miles of grasslands. There wasn't even a breeze to give some respite.

"Astute observation." I wiped my forehead and the back of my hand came away slick with perspiration. "Bet you didn't know what you were getting into coming here."

"Actually, I did. If I didn't, I wouldn't be doing my job right. Fun fact, Mercy was formed by a radical anti-tech group who abandoned the Southern Haven fifty years ago."

I bit my lip and raised a brow. "That's a fact. Not a fun fact. Why do you think a top tier Bonecrusher would retire in a place like this?"

He shrugged. "Hell if I know. I've never understood it myself, what they do."

The Valkyrie7's engine rumbled to life and ended our conversation. We started walking across the tarmac and headed towards the more substantial wall separating the landing zone from the city.

The sliding gate was open, not a care in the world, and behind it I saw the motel.

Now in speaking range, I slowed my pace, curious by what Suit said.

"What's there to not understand? When you were a kid, didn't you want to be a Bonecrusher? Insane fighting skills, sick guns and blades, millions of adoring fans, and a badass costume?"

"No."

"No...?"

"Fighting in the Arena, risking my life for people's entertainment doesn't get me off. I'd rather watch." Suit slapped a mosquito on his neck. A tiny smear of his own blood threatened to stain the edge of his stiff white collar. "And look, they obviously go crazy once they retire. Why else would someone live outside of a Haven?"

That was the question, wasn't it? What if the infamous Darla Dreadful was a washed up drunk who was just looking to make a quick buck? All I needed was enough info to write a decent piece, so as long as she was coherent enough to answer the questions I'd prepared, I suppose it didn't matter if she was a total loser.

Suit stepped in front of me and opened the door to the motel reception office.

The corner of the door tapped a bell mounted to the wall and it chimed, the sound clear and delicate. There was one woman leaning back in her chair behind a waist-high counter. She was reading a genuine *book*. A book made out of dead trees.

"Hello." The wrinkles in her tanned skin deepened as she smiled. "You're the only guests we've got so I've been expecting you. Flight okay?"

"Flying over Infected isn't any good for my blood pressure. Other than that, it was fine," I answered. "Definitely need some rest."

I noticed two incredibly high-tech Beretta laser rifles mounted on the wall. It took me a moment to recognize the model. It wasn't

a lethal force weapon. It was a tranquilizer.

Weird. And slightly creepy.

She slid a metal key across the counter. Room 10. "Locks aren't electronic and I lost the master key a couple years ago so don't lose this. Vending machine out front if you're hungry."

Paper books, metal keys. I was transported through time into the dawn of the 2000s. "Great. Thanks."

Suit had Room 1, so we stopped at his place first. The motel was shaped like a U, and his room was directly across from mine.

"Don't leave your room. Tomorrow, bright and early, we interview Darla Dreadful and head home. Got it?"

I smiled real wide. "You got it."

The motel was much nicer than I expected. Sure, there were water stains on the wall—one looked a lot like Boss—and the yellowed tile in the bathtub had grout stained a suspicious shade of reddish brown. But the sheets were clean and the place smelled like nothing much in particular. Better than most places you'd find in a Haven. I had a nice view of an overgrown lot with the skeleton of a burned down building protruding from the dead grass.

Not a second had passed since I did my preliminary motel room checks that my phone chimed. I grabbed the earpiece from my bag and popped it in. I already knew who it was.

"What's shakin', Boss?"

"Your bodyguard informed me you'd both arrived and were settled in for the night." His voice was all gravel. "I'd like to stress that last part about being *settled in for the night*."

I masked my laugh with a cough. "Right. I know. There's a lot of money in this story. Don't fuck it up."

"MC," he sighed. I imagined him leaning back in his rickety desk chair, sweat trailing down his forehead no matter the temperature around him. "It isn't just the money. MegaCorp has their fist so far up my ass I can taste yesterday's breakfast."

That was news to me. I knew a story on Darla Dreadful would get us a lot of hits, thus a lot of ad revenue, but…

"Why's MegaCorp so interested? You didn't tell me that when I came down here."

"Shit. I shouldn't have said anything at all."

"It's five o'clock over there, isn't it?"

"Get off my back, MC," he grumbled. Five o'clock meant Boss had no less than three scotches in his belly. "When they found out she contacted us—which isn't a scandal, they own our damn station—they asked for updates. So, as soon as you interview her, I expect all your raw interview files sent straight away. With the Arena so soon, I think they want to keep close tabs on what the media is posting. You know how it goes."

I did, all too well. I could tell the Boss wasn't going to give me anything else so I promised I'd be good and bid him farewell. After that, I climbed out the back window and took a breath of fresh air.

I'D BEEN TO TOWNS SMALLER than Mercy and a thousand times bigger and they always had one thing the same. A seedy bar. A hub of life, the oasis in the desert all animals flocked to.

The bar was situated between a boarded up, unmarked building and a pawn shop that offered repairs on laser rifles. The front windows were blacked out. There were posters tacked onto the ancient wood exterior, most of them faded beyond recognition.

When I walked in, the piss scent of homemade beer hit me hard. The place seated thirty comfortably but only a dozen scattered around the tables, single pool table, and beat up bar that extended from one end of the building almost to the other.

I received some interested glances. I didn't think it was my spiky red hair or shiny neon blue pants, currently popular in the Havens, thank you very much. It was because I was an outsider.

Without missing a beat, I crossed the grimy wooden floor to

the bar and plopped myself down in a seat that offered me a good view of the place. I scanned for Darla Dreadful just in case. There were a couple women, but it was mostly men. No Dreadful.

There was a bar over the TV. It was bulky and ancient by modern standards, but there it was. A recap of last year's top kills from the Arena played. A tight shot of Dandy Randy flashed on the screen. His perfectly styled white hair was slicked back from his head, his curly mustache bleached to match his 'do. Sometimes he wore a bowler hat but that year at the Arena he opted to go without. He stood on the back of an Infected and literally ripped off its head with his bare hands. Blood spurted across the sandy arena and onto his old-timey suit. The camera zoomed out and followed him while he used the head as a bludgeoning device on an oncoming Infected.

I'd seen the clip dozens of times. He was one of my personal favorites. His Gimmick was unique and he was gorgeous. I wrote a piece on how that year's blood-splattered suit was auctioned for two million credits to a mega-fan.

The bartender wandered over to me. His nose was a tad big and crooked—a fistfight, I'd guess—but his jawline was sharp, covered in more than a few days growth. Not bad, but no Dandy Randy.

"I'd ask you what I can get you, but we've only got two options."

"Yeah?" I leaned in. "What are they?"

"I've got Strong Stuff and Really Strong Stuff. Thinking you want the Really Strong Stuff."

"I guess you've got me pegged. I'll take the Really Strong Stuff."

He smiled and poured amber liquid from an unmarked bottle into a short glass. I took a sip. It tasted like liquid fire going down my throat and once my mouth stopped stinging I felt warmth wash over my body. I shuddered and licked my lips.

"Decent."

"Big fan of the Arena?" he asked, catching me watching the TV.

I shrugged. "Of course. Infected are scary as fuck. Makes you

feel a little better seeing the Bonecrushers take them out like they're nothing."

He chuckled but there was no humor in it and the smile certainly didn't reach his eyes. If anything, there was some reluctance to it. I hit a nerve, which was odd because I'd never met someone who was squeamish about the Arena.

"What's your name?" I asked, changing the subject before I lost him. I lifted my glass, signaling I wanted another.

At the same time I asked him for his name, his gaze shifted behind me. His body tensed and he set down the bottle beside my empty cup.

"Get out of here."

I turned and saw a woman leaning against a pool table. She was drunk or on some kind of drugs. Her body swayed. She could barely keep herself up.

"Ffffffuck you, Wolf. And fuck this chick."

The drunk staggered over to the bar. She was close enough to me that I smelled the Really Strong Stuff wafting off her. Both of her eyes were genetically augmented. Behind the collar of her oversized jacket, there was a tattoo creeping up her neck of an ornate cross. Her hair was ratted and pulled back, but I recognized the flaming red color. It was almost the same as my own.

"Sister Slaughter?"

She sneered. "Haven't heard that name for a long time."

Sister Slaughter was a household name about six years ago. Her Gimmick was a nun getup—with a dangerously short hemline of course—and her red hair braided into pigtails. I remembered kids buying plastic toy versions of the pearl handled revolvers she used. They had the same cross as on her neck etched into each handle.

I dressed up as her for a costume party.

She'd been a rising star. Then, one day, she dropped off the face of the media world.

"People think you went off outside of the Haven and killed yourself."

"You get too old they take you out back, know what I mean? I left on my own instead. Tell me something…" Wolf started to speak but Sister Slaughter continued. "Do you like it when you see us get torn apart by the Infected? How's that part of the gladiator bullshit? Good?"

"No, I don't," I stammered, losing my cool. "That rarely happens, though."

"Right, a few here and there doesn't mean anything to you. You watch us on screens. We aren't real to you."

"Miranda, don't do this," Wolf begged. "Just go."

Sister Slaughter plopped onto the stool next to me. "I tell you what, give me one drink and one more question for MC here and then I'll leave. I swear. Now, MC, what makes you think you can save everyone when you don't even care about a couple Bonecrushers?"

I stiffened. I never told her my name.

"I don't know what you're talking about." I paused. "How do you know me?"

Miranda guzzled her drink in a single gulp. She peered at me from behind hooded eyes. "You watching this bullshit on the TV, you're just like the rest of them. If you can't see us as people you won't see Them as people either. You can't do a damn thing…"

She swayed. One hand snapped to the edge of the bar with lightning speed to stop herself from falling.

I tried to keep my voice even. "What are you talking about, Miranda?"

"Make us…kill them, make us…" There were tears in her eyes. Miranda pulled out a tiny vial from her pocket. I recognized it. It was a relaxy. Before I could stop her, she put it to her nose and inhaled. She slumped down, head resting on the bar at an angle she was going to regret when she woke up.

"What the fuck was that?" I didn't break eye contact with Wolf as I asked.

"I didn't want anything escalating."

Throughout the years, I had a lot of luck as a journalist. Some would credit it to my tenaciousness, to my commitment to the story. These things were all true. But really, it was good intuition. My gut was telling me there was something more to Sister Slaughter. This wasn't just a drunk rambling. There was a story here, one a hell of a lot better than an interview with Darla Dreadful. But I wasn't going to find out until morning. With the amount of booze that must've been running in her system, plus the relaxy, she'd be out until dawn.

I sighed and gestured to my glass, pretending everything was okay and I believed Wolf. "Give me another."

WHEN I WOKE UP, MY body was sore from the hard, unfamiliar mattress. The Really Strong Stuff hadn't sat well with me and I spent the better half of the night puking. Not the best start to my interview with Dreadful.

I stretched and groaned, then flung off the sweat-dampened sheets.

There was complimentary caffeine powder on the dresser. I filled the electric kettle with water from the bathroom and tore open two packets. It fizzed as it dissolved into the liquid.

I paced around the room and stretched the tired out of my muscles. When the coffee was done, I poured myself a cup and took a sip. It was hot and acrid; tasted like it was scraped from the bottom of a barrel. Perfect.

My tablet was ready and waiting on the desk. I went over my interview questions for Dreadful, simultaneously jotting down notes in case I managed to follow up with Sister Slaughter.

My stomach started grumbling and I remembered I should eat.

I shoved my feet into my boots and wandered out into the crisp,

misty morning. Beams of sunlight carved through the mist, all hard geometric shapes as it made its way around the squat buildings of Mercy. You'd think you were living in a different era. No screen billboards, no four hundred story buildings or airships flying every which way.

I found the vending machine the motel lady mentioned. The model was new, a sleek black thing a little taller than my five-foot-ten height, and my wingspan across. It dealt in soy products. Not my favorite, but I could see why the little town had it. Feed it a bag of soybeans and sixteen chemical tubes, additives, and some kind of magic, and it would spit out a variety of different "foods." All made of soybeans. I got one and chomped away as I returned to my room.

By the time I realized there was someone already in there, I had one boot kicked off and a mouthful of flavorless soybean rolling around in my trap.

She was small statured. Even sitting, I could tell she was shorter than me. But her presence made up for her size. She commanded the room, sitting straight yet at ease, as though with the wave of her hand her will would be done. Maybe it would.

I didn't normally feel intimidated or afraid. Didn't have time for that bullshit. But looking at the woman in front of me, head shaved, scars across her cheek and neck, sitting there like a predator ready to strike, all I wanted to do was turn around and run. But there was that asshole part of me that said, *No.*

I swallowed my breakfast.

"Darla Dreadful, I take it?" I asked.

The slightest smile tugged at her lips. Her scars crinkled.

"The one and only."

I positioned myself at a better angle to the door in case I had to run. Her showing up could be weird behavior or crazy. I puffed my chest up a bit. "What are you doing in my room?"

She went to my coffee pot and poured herself some. I noticed

her hands. Two fingers on the right were unskinned machine. All exposed metal and wiring. It clinked against the mug as she lifted it to her lips. She sighed after she swallowed and sat down.

"Listen, I flew all the way from Haven to this place. Just for you. Don't play games with me."

Dreadful took another gulp of coffee. "What do you know about the Infected?"

"Fuck me, what is it with people these days? No offense. I mean, I just want to get this show on the road."

Her eyebrow raised. "Please, proceed."

I sighed and topped off my coffee, then brought up my recording software on the tablet.

The morning sunlight was muted through gauzy white curtains. Close, I could tell her head had been shaved recently. There was only a fuzzy layer of stubble. Her eyes were gray, but then I noted the subtle pattern of neon blue and silver. Both augments. I jotted that down.

"So, where's your costume? And your hair?"

"I'm retired. I choose what I wear, how I look."

"Huh." It made sense. Slaughter hadn't had a trace of her getup on, either. That answer eliminated at least a dozen follow-up questions. The Boss wasn't going to be pleased there were no fashion plugs. I regrouped. "So, nearly a thousand kills in the Arena. How does it feel knowing you have the highest, unbeaten kill count in history?"

"It makes me sick."

That surprised me. I set down my coffee and studied her face. "Why?"

"How would you feel if you knew you killed 973 people?"

"They aren't people. I don't have to imagine anything."

Dreadful grunted. "MC, I'm not going to waste any more of your time or mine. I didn't contact your news station for an interview for credits. There's something about the Infected that you—that *no one*—knows."

This town. Sister Slaughter. I knew something was going on and, finally, someone was going to level with me. Darla Dreadful suddenly became a lot more interesting. "Tell me, then. I'm waiting."

Her mouth opened at the same time sirens started wailing outside.

"Fuck, what's happening?" I asked. My heart thundered in my chest and my fingers started to tingle as adrenaline flooded my system.

Darla Dreadful stood. Her long jacket fell aside. Two sleek guns were holstered on both hips. At least a dozen knives were strapped against her ribcage. A sash of magazines ran around her hips just above the guns. She was carrying tranquilizers. She pulled out a little vial, some kind of combat nano aug I guessed, and inhaled it.

"There's something you need to see," she said. Her pupils dilated as the augment took hold. "Something that will change everything."

THE SIRENS WERE MUCH LOUDER outside. I didn't want to follow her, but my gut knew there was a huge story to be had. Whatever was happening, I needed to know.

Mercy seemed quiet, borderline dead when I first arrived. Now it was bursting with action. Townspeople rushed outside with guns. No, tranquilizers.

Mingled with them were more Bonecrushers. I recognized them from the way they moved, even without their Gimmicks. They shouted orders to the townspeople as they led the charge towards the gate. The gate that was wide open.

Dreadful pulled out her guns.

"You'll be fine. This happens all the time."

All towns, even Mercy, had walls to keep out the Infected. In Haven, they were twenty feet thick, electrified, and heavily guarded by dudes who had *real fucking* bullets. Mercy's were ten feet tall and

made of chain link, welded metal, and rusty patches of vehicles from a hundred years ago.

The gates were open and we were headed straight for them. A story wasn't worth it if I wasn't going to survive to write it.

When I spun around to run back, Dreadful grabbed my wrist. "Don't."

I glanced at the motel. Suit. I needed to get to my bodyguard. This town was full of insane people. Who knew what they were going to do with the Infected once they tranquilized them. Yeah, I was curious. Not enough to let my throat get torn out by the snapping jaws of an Infected.

She handed me one of her knives. It was heavier than it looked. "This will make you feel better, but you won't need it. Just stay here and watch, got it?"

The first Infected barreled around the corner of the gate and my body stiffened. My grip on the knife was so hard it became a part of me. The crowd rushed past, fearless. The first Infected I locked onto was a woman. She looked the same as they all did. Wild hair, dirty face, tattered clothing. If I were closer I'd see how her iris and pupils were jagged.

I spotted Dreadful. Her jacket fluttered as she moved. She raised her arms and squeezed the triggers on her dual wielded tranquilizers…

And suddenly someone was bear-hugging me from behind, dragging me back. Their grip around my chest was so tight I couldn't even take a breath to scream.

Everyone was focused on the Infected. They didn't notice me vanish into a narrow alley. I was on my own.

I dropped my bodyweight and took a low squat position, then thrusted my butt towards the attacker. It knocked them off-balance. They grunted and tried to haul me up off my feet. I let my body go dead, making it harder for them to lift me.

My hands were free. I was so busy struggling with the rest of my body I didn't realize my best tools were in front of me. Dreadful's little knife was still in one hand. I focused on their hands—which were huge and knobby, definitely male—and made sure I was going to slash him and not me.

The first cut sliced deep, right through his glove and across the top of his hand. His grip on me weakened and I used that chance, stomping hard on his instep. When I felt him start to release, I spun to face him and go straight for his face with my knife.

"MC, stop!"

"Suit?!"

Bloods gushed out of his hand. His face was red and sweaty. "Jesus, I was just trying to get you out of there!"

My second of hesitation and confusion were all he needed. He rushed me, grabbed my knife hand and twisted it so hard I dropped the weapon.

His other hand came around the back of my neck. Suit yanked me forward and tripped me. My hands broke some of the fall, but I was sure my wrist was broken.

I went to roll onto my back to get into a defensible position, then felt his knee digging into my lower spine. His hand was on my head again, pushing the side of my face into the cement.

"This is Jackson in Mercy," Suit said. He was on his com. "Connect me."

He had me pinned and I couldn't move. He was banking on me staying still and cooperating. Or being too afraid to fight back. He expected me to make it easy for him.

I took a deep breath and screamed as loud as I could. When Suit pushed my face harder, I felt my teeth digging hard into my cheek. Tasted blood. I could barely get a breath, but I kept trying. Wriggling despite the pain.

"Sir, Mercy is a hotbed of insurgent activity, just like you

thought." Suit said. "We need to get a sweep team in here immediately. The reporter needs to be debriefed immediately. I think she met with Darla—"

The weight on my body lifted and Suit was gone. I rolled onto my back and scrambled up against the alleyway wall. Suit was on the ground on his side, getting to his feet. Darla Dreadful walked towards him purposefully. Her guns were gone and she was out of knives.

Suit tried to take the offensive and threw a punch. Dreadful shifted and dodged it effortlessly. Suit's momentum caused him to stumble forward. She spun and grabbed the back of his neck with one hand, his hurt hand in her other. She pulled his arm so far back I heard something snap.

His free hand slipped into his suit jacket. There was a flash of silver and I saw a knife. Dreadful saw what he was doing and evaded his wild slashes. She took advantage of his unsteady position and dropped to her knee, taking him to the ground with her.

She raised his head and beat it against the ground. Once, twice, three times. Suit's face was nothing more than raw meat when she was finished.

Dreadful pried the knife out of his hand and jammed it into his throat. Not missing a beat, she turned her face to the edge of her jacket where I guessed there was a mic. "Our position is known. Evacuate the town."

"Holy fuck," I choked. "*Holy fuck!*"

"Are you hurt?" she asked.

I got to my feet and put a few extra feet of distance between me and Dreadful. "Answers. Now."

"Your bodyguard just tried to kill you. I saved you. The town is being attacked by a small wave of Infected. The attack is almost over."

"Okay, great. That answers the here and now. I'm talking big picture. *Why* did my bodyguard try to kill me? *Why* did you save me and *what* do you want from me?"

"MC, I will explain everything to you, but we need to evacuate the town. MegaCorp knows we're here. In ten minutes this place will be flooded with people a lot stronger than your bodyguard and with a lot more firepower." She took a step towards me. "If you stay here, you will die. I don't want that."

I looked at her and swallowed the lump in my throat. The coppery taste of blood was still strong in my mouth. My wrist and face stung.

I flashed a smile. "Lucky for you, neither do I."

MY VISION OF A THRILLING escape from Mercy included fast, sleek motorcycles speeding away as the town exploded. It was a bit of a surprise when Dreadful led me and a handful of Bonecrushers back to the empty lot behind the motel to the charred building I spotted the night before.

She crouched down and pulled a matted swath of dead grass aside, revealing a closed metal hatch. It was rusty, ancient, and I suddenly thought of how much I disliked small spaces.

Dreadful tilted her head. Someone must've be talking to her on com. When I looked at the Bonecrushers around me, they all had the distant gaze.

"Splicer, Baron—you're with me," she said after a moment. "MC, stay behind us. Wolf says there might be some Infected in the tunnels."

The two Bonecrushers she called on stepped forward. Even without their Gimmicks their names fit them. Splicer's skin was augmented to look reptilian. The scales provided a small amount of defense against punches and light slashes. He had yellow eyes to match and a pair of sleek katanas on his back.

Baron had a jaw like a shovel and a black beard. He had a rifle slung across his back. Another tranquilizer. I noted he still wore his trademark spiked knuckles. He squatted down and turned the

wheel on the hatch. Veins bulged in his neck as he lifted open the heavy door. There was nothing but blackness below.

Splicer shot me a wicked grin and a waggle of his thin eyebrows before he stepped into the hatch and disappeared. Chuckling, Baron followed.

"Take the ladder," Dreadful told me as she started climbing down. "They just like to show off."

I squashed down my fear and followed her. The shaft smelled damp and earthy, the rungs of the ladder slippery under my hands. My wrists and face still throbbed and it made getting a good grip tricky.

A loud squeak overhead grabbed my attention. The lid to the shaft slammed shut and we were thrown into darkness. A second later there was a cracking noise and then a warm orange glow illuminated the shaft. I continued down, counting the rungs as I went. We must've been at least forty feet below the surface.

When my feet hit the ground, I took a deep breath and scanned my surroundings. We were in a round brick tunnel. A thin trail of water ran down the center of the floor where it sloped inward. The tunnel went forward about fifty feet before turning into a Y.

There was a metal case to the side of the shaft. It had a hand scanner on top that shone a soft blue, cutting through the orange of the glow stick. Dreadful put her hand against it. The panel beeped and the lid opened. Inside were gleaming guns and knives. She grabbed a canister and tossed it to me.

"For your wrist and face."

It was a spray made of nanobots that self-destructed as soon as they had assessed and healed whatever they were sprayed on. Expensive as fuck and generally only used in the military and emergency medical services. They were only good for superficial wounds and wouldn't mend broken bones.

I sprayed it liberally onto my face and wrists. There was a tingly sensation and the pain started fading as the bots got to work.

"I'm not taking another step until you give me something," I said. I was feeling more like myself already.

Dreadful refilled her tranq dart sash and started sliding knives into her girdle. She looked at Splicer and nodded towards the Y ahead of us. "Scout left. Baron, guard right."

The two Bonecrushers moved forward, feet splashing in the water. They must have had high-end eye augs because neither had a light with them and soon disappeared into the ominous abyss.

"You're here because out of the millions of other hacks in the Havens who work for news stations, you seem smart. I've followed your work. Not the shit you write for your news station. The underground stories."

Now *that*, I didn't expect.

That whole being shot at, stabbed, and kidnapped thing? That didn't happen in the name of the news station. That all happened on my own time, writing my own stories that my buddy Techno Joe posted online from untraceable origins.

I wrote about the kind of corporate and social corruption you'd get threatened and hurt over. It was the journalism I cared about that no one else did.

"How did you link me to those stories?"

"Techno Joe. When I told him I was looking for the writer who wanted to take MegaCorp down a notch, he named you."

Techno Joe and his Hacker Harem were the only people I trusted with my conspiracy theories and exposés. It appeared that might've been a huge mistake.

"Enough bullshit. I get you've been tracking me and something big is going down. Tell me exactly what you want from me."

She secured one more knife into her girdle and looked me straight in the eyes. "Human existence is owned by MegaCorp. You live in Havens, you're fed by Havens, and you exist by the grace of the Havens."

So far, none of this was new to me. She was rehashing theories I'd been spewing for years. MegaCorp had monopolized human existence. They were too powerful. The problem was, there was no way to destroy a force that was, for all intents and purposes, God.

I sighed. "If you want to take down MegaCorp, forget it. They're too strong. I've been trying to get people to listen for years. They don't care. All that gear you're wearing and toting about? They fucking made that, Darla Dreadful. Jesus, they own *you*. Bonecrushers are patented by MegaCorp. If you've read my work, you know the revenue generated by anything relating to Bonecrushers counts for billions of credits every year."

"You're right, of course." A sly grin tugged at her lips. "What's the one thing critical to MegaCorp's success? What's the one factor that *must* be present in order for them to own us?"

I glanced upward, imagining the wave of Infected that tried to take out Mercy. "The Infected."

Suddenly Splicer was beside me. I hadn't even heard him approach.

"Seems clear," he said.

Dreadful grabbed a tranq gun from the trunk and handed it to me. "What if I told you I can end the Infection. What if I told you I have the proof you need to make people care?"

"I'd say lead the way." I took the tranq gun and inspected it. "And that you'd better not be fucking around."

WE MOVED IN A SQUARE formation with Splicer and Baron in the lead. No matter how lightly I tried to step, my footsteps echoed much louder than my Bonecrusher companions'.

The glow stick didn't illuminate the tunnel very far. We were a little blip of orange light amongst darkness that was trying to swallow us whole. There was a sheen of sweat across my body that caught the light when I moved.

I swore I heard a faint howl somewhere ahead of us and was about to chalk it up to adrenaline and overworked nerves, when I heard it again.

Closer. Louder.

Splicer stepped ahead and centered his katana low in front of him. Baron stood adjacent to him, his legs slightly apart, knees bent. Why did they have the killing weapons and all I had was a tranquilizer?

An Infected burst from the darkness. He was naked and pale with scratches across his chest. His mouth was wide open, eyes glittering, howling as he lunged for Splicer with his bare hands. I'd never seen one like this before. This one barely seemed human.

"Reapers!" Splicer yelled. "Lethal force!"

Splicer stepped aside and the Infected fell into Baron. Baron punched him in the temple so hard his frail body slammed with a *crack* against the tunnel wall. With one stomp from Baron's massive boot, the Infected was down. Dark, shining blood and brain matter seeped from the jagged mess that was once his head.

It happened in a split second, then there were more of them clamoring into the light of the glow stick. Splicer moved into the horde, slashing and jabbing with his wicked blade. Soon he disappeared.

Baron threw punches. The Infected were so thick every strike met a head. I wanted to use my tranquilizer but I couldn't get a good shot.

It didn't matter. One last Infected came running down the hallway, unaware and indifferent to the fact that he was outnumbered. Instead of cutting it in half, Splicer dodged it and the Infected ran straight into Baron's arms. Baron spun him around and dropped him to the ground, placing his knee on the Infected's back.

The thing struggled wildly to get free from the weight of the huge man.

"Not a Reaper. He can be saved."

"What the hell? Kill that thing and let's get out of here!" I shouted.

Dreadful shook her head. "We need him. This is your proof, MC."

Baron hogtied the Infected. He lifted the skinny thing with one hand and carried it down the hallway.

AT THE END OF THE tunnel was an old hatch, similar to the one we entered up top. Baron set the Infected aside and spun the wheel. The door swung open on well-oiled hinges, revealing a gigantic room buzzing with activity.

There were at least a dozen tables set up with monitors and computers. Some tables were in plastic enclosures, their inhabitants wearing face masks and goggles, handling vials of a bright orange liquid.

In the center of the room was a ten by ten foot clear box with a small touch screen panel by its door. The box was empty. Baron hauled the Infected over to it and pushed him inside. He untied his feet and briskly stepped back out, locking the Infected in. The Infected was up and on its feet in a heartbeat, throwing itself against the door as it howled. All I heard was a soft thud every time it hit the shatter and soundproof glass.

The people in the room stopped working and wandered over to the box. Dreadful stepped forward.

"It's happening and it's happening real fucking fast. Lucas, what's the status of Mercy?"

A blond man next to me cleared his throat and shook his head. "We've lost almost everyone. MegaCorp made sure no building was left standing."

"We knew this could happen. We'll save our tears for after we've won," Darla said. "Baron, show MC what we're fighting for."

Baron tapped a few commands into the panel on the box. Vents in the floor opened up and a fine orange mist escaped them. The Infected tilted its head and looked at the vents curiously, ceasing its attempt to escape.

He morphed right before my eyes. First, his posture relaxed. His shoulders dropped and his chest stopped heaving. The frantic, wild eyes stopped scanning.

When he wrapped his arms around his naked body and looked at the group outside, not with bloodlust, but with confusion, I realized what happened. Baron immediately opened the door and a team of people entered with a blanket and water. They started talking to him and taking his vitals. He had the demeanor of a scared toddler.

"Holy shit," I gasped. "You have a cure."

Dreadful gestured for me to step away from the crowd with her, most of whom were already going back to work. She led me to a workstation set aside from the rest.

"We can't save all of them. We don't know exactly how it's affecting their brain, but we do know people experience it differently. Some of them are too far gone to come back. Usually the older ones." She tapped at the screen, pulling up video footage. "You'd probably be surprised to know a cure has existed for nearly a century."

Dreadful showed me a video of a low-tech lab. In it, an Infected was strapped to a chair. The tendons and veins budged in her neck as she strained against the strap secured against her forehead. A figure clad in biohazard gear injected something into the Infected's neck. I watched another transformation take place, startled by how quickly the feral look in her eyes gave way to fear and confusion.

There was a watermark on the footage. That same logo was on the biohazard suit.

"I've known about MegaCorp's corruption since I started writing. I knew it went deep, but withholding a cure?" I glanced at the man in the box. My mind was putting the puzzle together and

everything fit. "They wouldn't release it. They own the infrastructure of the Havens. They own the media, our economy. They own you. There's more profit and control in allowing the Infected to live and reproduce than to eliminate them entirely."

Then I realized what piece didn't fit. "If you have a cure, why aren't you releasing it?"

"Because, curing the world isn't enough. The world can't truly change unless people understand why it's fucked to begin with." Dreadful opened up schematics of a building on the screen. I recognized them immediately. It was the Arena. "We need to make sure MegaCorp is obliterated and that they will never have power again."

Screw retirement. This was it; the story of all stories. The one that would make a difference. No more conspiracy, no more pointing figures from the safety of the Web. This was the truth and every person deserved to hear it.

PACIFIC NORTHWEST HAVEN, 2459 A.D.

H EAVY RAIN POUNDED THE CEMENT of the airship landing pad. The news station building was the second tallest in my Haven. From my vantage point I could see the blur of hundreds of billboards and neon signs glowing in the night, the ones farthest away nothing more than a smudge of blinking color as ships passed them by.

I waited until Jimmy's ship floated off into the night sky, then popped in my earpiece while I took the elevator to ground level. I'd given up on settling my nerves and accepted the nervous electricity pumping through my veins. Minutes later, I hit the bottom floor and walked onto the street.

I'd never seen the streets so empty because every year prior to

this, I was at the Arena. The spectacle of Bonecrushers obliterating hordes of Infected was the highlight of everyone's year. No one missed it. Including me.

All the street food vendors and shops were shuttered. There was something lonely about the billboard screens advertising to no one, the lingering smell of noodles and airship exhaust. Yet I knew I wasn't alone. Not really. I felt the mechanical eyes of hundreds of security cameras on me—me, the only person walking the streets on the annual night of the Arena.

Three deep breaths. Slow in, slow out. I made the call.

"Holy shit, MC! What happened? Are you okay? I thought you were dead!"

I heard the roar of the crowd in the background and knew Boss was at the Arena. While in the back of my mind I assumed people thought I died in Mercy, it was still unsettling to hear him say it out loud.

"I'm fine. Still alive and kicking."

"What the hell happened?"

"I was attacked by that damn bodyguard you sent. Darla Dreadful saved me. Boss, you won't believe what I found out. I'm going somewhere safe right now. I'm sure MegaCorp is gonna be after me once they find out I'm back in the city."

My blood turned to ice as all sound went dead in my earpiece. I stopped walking and stood, looking around, waiting. This was part of the plan. That didn't make it any less terrifying.

"Boss?"

"An airship will pick you up in approximately twenty seconds," a cool, calm female voice answered. "You will be scanned for augments, nanotech, and weapons by a MegaCorp representative prior to entering the ship. Thank you for your cooperation."

Just as she finished her spiel, the promised airship landed ten yards in front of me. It was a sleek, vaguely insectoid looking model

that was almost silent as it touched down. A lone man in a dark suit stepped out of the ship.

"WOULD YOU LIKE A BEVERAGE? Perhaps a relaxy?"

Despite the fake plants and landscape paintings on the wall, the giant waiting room was sterile and a few degrees too cold to be comfortable. The walls were white, the black floor so polished it was a dark mirror. The receptionist was so augmented and modified I wasn't sure if he was human or bot. It didn't matter, but I found myself looking for seams in his skin.

I was in the Arena itself, though you'd never know it. The walls in the lobby were soundproofed so well I couldn't hear even the slightest hint of the half million people in the arena around me. When we touched down on the executive roof landing pad, I heard the full force of them. I could almost feel the presence of the nearly two billion people across the world watching the live Arena broadcast.

Behind me were the elevator doors where I entered, and on the opposite side behind the receptionist, were what I guessed were the doors leading to the private skybox of the Directors of MegaCorp. I'd seen their skybox before, jutting out atop the Area. Of course, then I was a patron of the gory display.

"No," I answered, finding my voice. "How long is it going to be?"

The receptionist turned and glided back to his desk. He had to be a bot. A nice one. Humans couldn't move with that much grace.

"They're here now, actually. Just arrived from their mid-ceremony speech down below."

The elevators opened with a soft *swoosh* on cue. Four suited guards stepped out, followed by two men and a woman. These last three were dressed in varying shades of gray, their faces neutral.

"Well, well. If it isn't our favorite journalist, risen from the dead," the woman cooed.

"Bartholomew. Drinks." The order came from the eldest of the

men. He was tall and impossibly thin, his skin stretched taut over his skull.

Without missing a beat, the trio crossed the glossy black floor to the other doors, which slid open as they approached.

"Go right on in," the receptionist said and gestured with an open palm to the doors. "Let me know if you change your mind on that relaxy."

Glass windows floor to ceiling were the first thing my gaze snapped to, because beyond it was the sprawling, bloody arena where a battle between Bonecrushers and Infected raged. Nearly three hundred yards long, I only saw a fraction of the display.

One wall of the skybox was covered in monitors showing close-ups from the drones flying about the entire Arena. I spotted Randy Dandy using a flamethrower on an oncoming horde of Infected. Betty Butch and Princess Chainsaw were at his back, shooting down dozens of Infected charging them. They were dangerously close to a Feeder—one of a hundred gated tunnels that released Infected every twenty minutes. But the lights around the Feeder were a cold shade of blue, indicating the waves had stopped for the mandatory mid-ceremony break. The Bonecrushers were mopping up the stragglers. Still, it was no time to relax. The Infected could still overtake them, and if they did, thousands of gallons of fatal gas would be pumped into the arena, killing everything in it.

Bonecrusher or Infected.

My stomach churned. Out of everything I stood for, how could I have participated in this?

"My dear," the third, portly member of the trio said. He collapsed into an oversized leather chair facing the window. "Look at that hair. That skin. So pale. Come sit by me?"

Bartholomew pranced in with a tray of drinks and distributed them to the Directors.

"God, Richard. Introductions first. You're so crass." The woman

took a sip of her drink and flashed me a shark-like grin. "Of course, I'd imagine you know who we are. But still. I'm Constance Mallen."

Portly Man raised his hand in a flourish. "Richard Carlyle."

"August Von Berg," the thin man finished. "Windows, dim."

The windows darkened to a solid black. I shifted my attention to the room. The carpet was a rich redwood. I figured it had to be real. Three oversized chairs were placed in the center of the room on a platform that looked like it could spin if the Directors wanted to face the monitors. On one wall was a bar where Bartholomew was already mixing another round of drinks.

All seated, the Directors watched me from behind the rims of their glasses. Von Berg set his glass aside and steepled his fingers together. I sensed he was the true powerholder among them.

"So. An uprising? Tell me more."

"I don't think I will," I said.

"Don't be foolish. Whatever your Bonecrusher friends have planned, it will fail."

"I doubt that."

Von Berg snapped his fingers. "Bring him in. I'm already tired of arguing with this woman and we've barely begun. MC, I don't like wasting time. Let me show you how serious I am."

A moment passed, then the guards dragged someone in. Not just any someone.

"You let him go, you bastards," I shouted.

Boss was gagged, his face red and sweaty. From the time that I called him till now, they'd beaten him. His right eye was swollen and one of his legs wasn't quite at the right angle.

This wasn't supposed to happen. Darla Dreadful promised me she and her team would grab the Boss after I made the call. That they'd protect him.

Either Dreadful lied to me, or something had gone wrong.

Von Berg took long strides to Boss and reached out for the

handgun one of the guards offered him. He pressed it against Boss's temple, his eyes never leaving mine.

"You're in over your head, darling," he said simply, then pulled the trigger.

Blood and brain splattered across the floor. Boss's body hit the ground. More red bloomed around his head. Von Berg handed the gun back and returned to his seat, unfazed by what he'd done. Bartholomew brought him a steaming, pristine white washcloth with which the thin man wiped his hands. He dismissed the guards, leaving us all alone.

"Enough. Let's put all our cards on the table and get this over with. The Arena is resuming shortly." He finished off his drink. "We know those pitiful, rogue Bonecrushers are up to something. When Darla Dreadful contacted your Boss and requested you specifically, we knew it was a fine opportunity to find out exactly what.

"Why did she choose you? That was the question. We dug deep and quickly learned of your ridiculous, unsuccessful, *and* slanderous articles and figured she wanted to use you to spread a message. We were right, weren't we?"

I opened my mouth to rebut. Von Berg didn't give me a chance.

"Of course we were. So, you go to Mercy and meet up with Dreadful. You kill one of our own and then show up here claiming an uprising. Know this, my dear. Your life is meaningless to us, but everything to you. So tell me, what does Dreadful have planned?"

Holy fuck. He was insane. That knot in my stomach twisted tighter, now in rage. My body began to tingle. I needed to gain the upper hand and fast. Boss wasn't my favorite person in the world, but he wasn't evil and he sure as hell didn't deserve to get shot in the head to make a point.

I cast my eyes down and played defeat. The trick in telling a convincing lie was to put a dash of truth in it. I took a breath. "They can cure the Infected. They know you came up with the cure and

they're going to show the world you've been hiding it. Darla Dreadful was going to prove it tonight at the end of the Arena."

The directors were silent as they exchanged glances and communicated solely in expressions. Finally, Constance laughed.

"Releasing the cure now wasn't part of the three-century plan our forefathers set in place, but…" A wicked grin crossed her lips. "Oh well. We'll make it work."

Richard snapped his fingers for another drink. "Certainly, it will be more manageable than the accidental release of the virus in the first place. God, now *there* was a mess. My great grandfather said the collapse of society was quite hard to deal with until the Havens were built. The cure getting out prematurely isn't so bad. August, I'd imagine we should let Dreadful carry out her display? Then martyr her somehow and claim credit for it all?"

Stay cool. Stay cool. I repeated it in my head despite the excitement building inside me. Darla didn't know this. *This* wasn't part of the plan but it sure as fuck worked for us.

Then Von Berg was up again, his long limbs graceful as he strode towards me. This close, I could smell the fumes of alcohol on his breath, see the topography of his face.

His eyebrows softened. He set his hand on my shoulder and spoke softly. "You're a victim, MC. How little you know."

"What does he mean?" I asked, loud enough that the whole room could hear. "Accidental release of the virus?"

Again, that fucking hyena laugh from Constance. "If he tells you, he'll have to kill you."

"Tell me. I know too much. I know I'm not making it out of this alive."

Von Berg tapped my nose and smiled. "Smart girl. If you insist on knowing, we made the cure right after the virus escaped. The virus escaped before MegaCorp finished it due to an accident involving improper lab procedures. It forced MegaCorp's grand plan into action

eight years too early, but we recuperated over the course of a decade."

This was bad. Horrifying. Tragic. But at the same time, this turn of events was better than what I expected to get out of him. If he was going to go all Evil Villain Reveals the Big Plan on me, he was more than welcome to.

He had no fucking clue what was coming.

"Why?" I clenched my fists and stayed firmly planted. "Why would you want to release a virus like that? You killed *billions* of people."

"Darling, you have no idea what it was like back then. Our forefathers saw the polarization. The corruption. The imminent doom of mankind. The virus wasn't finished yet. They were still tailoring who it would target when it escaped and caught the world on fire." Constance pouted. "Many were lost who didn't deserve to die."

Von Berg leaned against the bar, running his finger up and down the polished wood surface. "We saved the world. Unified it. The next generation was meant to release the cure, further proving MegaCorp's greatness and allow us to reclaim the rest of the world from the Infected. Humanity is still too ignorant and idealistic to see the grand scope of it all. Richard, let's not let the cure out quite yet. If anything happens, gas the arena. In fact, gas the stadium, too. Population control, anyway. We'll play it off as a huge, awful accident. What do you—"

The tint on the windows disappeared. Light from the Arena flooded the skybox.

The Bonecrushers in the arena were gone. Instead, there were thousands of Infected. Some idled about, others fought out of boredom or rage. Every screen in the Arena showed crystal clear footage of the interior of the skybox. The shot came from behind the bar, where Bartholomew stood. It came *from* him. I knew Techno Joe had cameras planted somewhere. I hadn't anticipated he hacked a high security bot.

Bartholomew was standing still in that way only bots could. His eyes were wide open, watching the scene. For the first time since I stepped into the room, I moved, making my way behind the bar.

The wall of screens adjacent to the windows all went to the same feed. The volume was deafening.

"In fact, gas the stadium, too. Population control…in fact, gas the stadium, too…"

It replayed Von Berg's last statement over and over.

No one moved. Richard and Constance were frozen, their faces slack in horror.

Darla Dreadful's face suddenly appeared on all the screens.

"You are not a means to an end. You are people. You are *all* people."

A thin orange mist pumped into the arena. Slowly, the Infected stopped moving. They stilled as the cure took hold. The mist began to spread upward, but didn't flood the entire arena. Techno Joe had come through, hacking the gas system. Dreadful had the toxic gas replaced with the cure mere hours before the Arena commenced.

The world knew everything. They knew who MegaCorp was and what they'd done. They had proof of it all right in front of them.

Von Berg made a struggled, choked sound. He spun on his heel and ran for the door, futilely trying to open it. Too bad Techno Joe had it locked down.

I found the nicest bottle of whiskey the bar had to offer, poured a glass and savored the burn as it went down. Richard and Constance were openly weeping in each other's arms.

"It's over! Christ, they all know!" she sobbed. "August, get us out of here!"

Von Berg returned to the window where he leaned his forehead against it. His arms hung limply at his side. His face was ashen.

The doors slid open. Dreadful and her Bonecrushers flooded the room.

I finished off my drink and patted Von Berg on the shoulder as they surrounded him. "You're in over your head, darling. Let's put all the cards on the table. You're fucked."

I'd been shot at, stabbed, and kidnapped.

Tonight was the first time I'd ever helped bring down a corporation that owned and ran human existence.

I sure as fuck hoped it would be the last.

FOLLOW THE
AUTHORS

In order of appearance:

ROBIN HOBB

robinhobb.com

MARGARET WEIS

margaretweis.com

SEANAN MCGUIRE

seananmcguire.com

NISI SHAWL

nisishawl.com

S.R. CAMBRIDGE

twitter.com/SRCambridge

MELANIE R. MEADORS

melaniermeadors.com

PHILIPPA BALLANTINE

pjballantine.com

SHANNA GERMAIN

shannagermain.com

ANTON STROUT

antonstrout.com

ELAINE CUNNINGHAM

elainecunningham.com

SARAH KUHN

heroinecomplex.com

MARC TURNER

marcturner.net

DANA CAMERON

danacameron.com

BRADLEY P. BEAULIEU

quillings.com

ELIZABETH VAUGHAN

writeandrepeat.com

DIANA M. PHO

beyondvictoriana.com

ERIN M. EVANS

slushlush.com

WILLIAM C. DIETZ

williamcdietz.com

CARINA BISSETT

carinabissett.com

CAROL BERG

carolberg.com

DELILAH S. DAWSON

whimsydark.com

LUCY A. SNYDER

lucysnyder.com

MICHAEL R. UNDERWOOD

michaelrunderwood.com

LIAN HEARN

lianhearn.com

GAIL Z. MARTIN

ascendantkingdoms.com

MONICA VALENTINELLI

booksofm.com

M.L. BRENNAN

mlbrennan.com

DJANGO WEXLER

djangowexler.com

ELOISE J. KNAPP

eloisejknapp.com

BACKER
ACKNOWLEDGMENTS

Thank you for your pledges! This book wouldn't have been possible without your support.

`David Ting • 1Zachman • Aaron Christensen • Aaron Karper
Aaron Slusher • Adam T Alexander • Adora Hoose
Adrian Collins • Adrian Shotbolt • Adrian Tatro
Ainsley Pincombe • Alejandro Suárez Mascareño
Alek Dembowski • Alex Demille • Alex Eizenhart
Alex Herriott • Alex Nine • Alex T.
Alex Tigwell • Alex von der Linden • Alexa Shelton
Alexandra Brandt • Alexandra Pitones
Alexandria & Elizabeth Quigley • Alix Malorie
Alma Vilić • Alysia Murphy • Amanda Nixon
Amanda Stein • Amber Fallon • Amelia
Amy Sarfinchan • ANA BARBARIAN • Andan
Anders M. Ytterdahl • Andrew Alvis • Andrew Brereton
Andrew Murray • Andrew Taylor • Andrew Tudor
Andrew Tudor • Andrew Z. Sieminski • Andy
Andy Cook • Andy Holzer • Anestis Kozakis

Angel Fiszlewicz • Angie Booth • Angie Flunker
Anna Davidson • Annclaire Livoti • Annie Sauer
Anniella Klang Fält • Anonymous
Anthony "HachiSnax" Giordano • Anthony Haevermaet
Anton Strout • Antonio Vincentelli • April Boutelle
Ashley Long • Ashley Melanson • Ashley Morton
Auroch Digital • Austin C. • Aynjel Kaye
Barb Moermond • Ben Fried-Lee • Ben King
Benjamin C. Kinney • Benjamin Hausman
Benjamin Juang • Berni • Bill and Zoe Carter
Bill Emerson • Bill Seymour • Blake Muxo • Bobby Hitt
Bonnie Warford • Boyd Stephenson • Brad Goupil
Bradley Russo • Brandon Collins • Brandon Petersen
Breanna M • Brenda Carre • Brenda K. Beard
Brian D Lambert • Brian Doob • Brian Mooney
Brian Zuber • Bridget McKinney • Bruce Shavas Bevens
Bufón • C E Hinton • C. Corbin Talley
C. Marry Hultman • C. Roberts • Callum Barber
Carina Bissett • Carmen Brack • Carmen Maria Marin
Carol J. Guess • Carole-Ann Warburton
Carolina Edwards • Caroline Duvezin • Carolyn Reid
Cathi Scheid Perez • Cathy Green • Cathy Mullican
Cathy Schwartz • Celine Courtois
Chad "Doomedpaladin" Middleton • Chad Bowden
Chad McMann • Chall T. Dow • ChanieB
Charles "Lukkychukky" Ulveling • Charles Kronaizl
Charlotte Passingham • Cheyenne Cody • Chinami Wirth
Chris Allen • Chris Arnold • Chris Brant • Chris Clogston
Chris DuMelle • Chris Eleveld & Amanda Green • Chris Janes
Chris Matosky • Chris McLaren • Chris Sasaki
Chris Vian • Chris Vincent • Chrisie Bentley
Christian Brunschen • Christin Miller • Christina D

Christina Payton • Christina Sauper Stratton • Christine Bell
Cindy Womack • Clare Lunawolf • Claus Luetke
Cory Miller • Courtney Getty • Craig & Lillian Irvine
Craig Hackl • Craig Johnson • Craig Wright
Cristina Macia • Crystal Sarakas • D-Rock • D. L. Ward
D. Moonfire • Dalan Tran • Dale Russell • Dan Brewer
Dana Cameron • Daniel Clasen • Daniel D Magnan
Daniel Gregory • Daniel L. Reese • Daniel Lin
Daniel Ortiz • Daniel Provencio • Daniel Traylor
Daniela Alexandra • Darrell Z. Grizzle • Dave Brown
Dave Gross • Dave Medley • David "thricebedamned" Brideau
David and Stephanie Jones • David Annandale
David Churn • David Cole • David Holden
David Jarrett • David Mortman • David Quist
David S. Robinson • David Schneider • David Stanley
David Torres • David Zurek • Dean F. Wilson • Dean Whirley
Deb Blakley Rasmussen • Dedren Snead • Denis Gagnon
Denise Davis • Denise Murray • Derek & Dena
Derek Devereaux Smith • Derek Feddon • Derek Roy
Derek Siddoway • Devan Barlow • Devon Apple
Devon F • Devon Tabris • Dominic Franchetti
Dominic Quach • Don P • Doug "Kosh" Williamson
Drea Shumate • DS Mandeville • Dylan Dunne
E. J. Hones • Eddie Patton • Edea Baldwin • Edmond Hyland
Edward Greaves • Edwin & Eli Hunt • Ehud Kaminer
Elaine Cunningham • Elaine Tindill-Rohr • Elendilmirana
Elizabeth Kite • Elizabeth Willse • Ellen Sandberg
Elyse M Grasso • Emily Beamon • Emily June Street
Emma Lord • Emory Knott • Epper Marshall
Eppu Jensen • Eric Feay • Eric Landreneau • eric priehs
Eric Wegner • Erica "Vulpinfox" Schmitt • Erik Jarvi
Erik Skorpen • Erin Kowalski • Ernesto "Montalve" Ramirez

Erynn Lehtonen • Essie Bee • Evan Miller
Felicia Kosegi • Ferran Selles • Festus Ghent
For Debbie, Eloise & Olivia x • Fran Friel
Francesco Martinati • Francine Ting Yu Qing • Fred Bailey
Gabriel Eggers • Gabrielle Kitaro • Gail Z. Martin
Galena Ostipow • Gareth Bradshaw • Gary Nye
Gary Phillips • Gavran • Gerald P. McDaniel
Gerry Noij • Gertjan • GMarkC • Goran Lowkrantz
Grace Gorski • Graham Hall • Gray Detrick • Greg Jayson
Greg Rappaport • Gregory "Happy" Rappaport • Gregory Duch
Gregory McCausland • Gwenaël F. • H Alexander Perez
Hannah Bloczynski • Hannah Richardson-Lewis
Hannah Wallenbrock • Heather K. Wertz Leasor (elvenmageus)
Heather Parra • Hebah Amin-Headley • Hcidi Cykana
Henry Lopez • Hina Ansari • Holland Dougherty
Hoose Family • HRvdBerg • Ian Chung • ildiko
Inuminas • Isis • Ivan Donati • J. V. Ackermann
J.T. Evans • Jacob Jardel • Jacob Magnusson • Jacob Weiss
Jaime O. Mayer • Jakub Narębski • James Arnold
James Downe • James Goodwin • James Lucas
James Morrison • Jamie Jeans • Jamie Manley • Janelle Young
Janet H Stewart • Janito Vaqueiro Ferreira Filho
Jason Peters • Jason Plowman • Jason Templeton
JasperB • Jean Duteau • Jeff and Michele and Tori
Jeff Dowd • Jeff Hotchkiss • Jeff Jensen • Jeff Scifert
Jeffery Mace • Jen Woods • Jen1701D • Jenna E. Miller
Jennifer Berk • Jennifer Brozek • Jennifer Davidson
Jennifer K. Koons • Jennifer Lynch • Jennifer Shew
Jenny Langley • Jeremy Brett • Jeremy Hochhalter • Jeremy Kear
Jeremy Mohler • Jeremy Rowland • Jessa Michalek
Jessica A. Rasmussen • Jessica K. Meade • Jessica Rasmussen
Jill Chinchar • Jill M. Randazzo • Jim "The Destroyer" Bellmore

Jim Burzelic • Jim Marengo • JJ Ashton
JKLM Eggleston • JNM • Jo Robson • Joanne Burrows
Joe Murphy • Joe Slucher • Joe Thibedeau • Joe Urbaniak
Joel vonD • Joel vonDickersohn • Johan Rapp
John Green • John Heine • John Iadanza • John Idlor
John Prichard • Jon (WEKM) Krupp • Jon Woods
Jonathan Cruz • Jonathan D. Beer • Jonathan Palm
Josalynne B • Joseph Hoopman • Joseph Huddleston
Joseph S. Fleischman • Joseph Urbaniak • Joshua Hislop
Joshua McGinnis • Joshua Takashi • Judy Kashman
Julia McKinney • Julie E Stein • Julio Capa
Justin Farquhar • Justin Hebert • Justin Mansfield
Justin Terlisner • K. Nelson • K. Nisenshal • K.G. Anderson
K.L. Webber • Kai MillsKai Schrimpf
Kaitlin A. Schaal • Kaitlin Thorsen • Karen Shaw
Kari Blackmoore • Karl Markovich • Kas Severson
Kate Mergener • Katherine • Katherine Malloy
Katherine Socha • Katie Bruce • Katie Cord • Katie Riley
Katrina bresnick • Katrina Smith • Katy Hill
Keith "Hurley" Frampton
Keith West, Future Potentate of the Solar System
Kelly Bell • Kelly Jensen • Ken McLennan • Kendra
Keri Hayes • Kerri Regan • Kerry aka Trouble
Kevin Henderson • Kfrill • Kimberly Ann Long • Kris Wirick
Kristin Evenson Hirst • Kristina P. • KT Wagner
Kurt Phillips • Kyle 'the bald avenger' Spencer • Kyle B.
Kyle Baker • L "King" Williams • L Evans • L Stump
L.E. Harrison • Lambert/Muenchow Family
Larissa Haluszka-Smith • Larry Couch • Laura B.
Laura J. Kelly • Laura Lavelle
Laura M. Hughes • Laura S Johnson • Laurel Hedge
Lauren Hoffman • le4ne • Leah Webber • Lee Nixon

Lee Sims • Leila Gabasova • Lenore Jean Jones
Leron Culbreath • Leslie Y. Rieger • Líadan Monroe
Lidiya R Williams • Lilly L. • Lily Connors • Linda J. Lee
Lisa Herrick • Lisa Taylor • Liz • Logan "Jebal" Smith
Loki Carbis • Lori & Maurice Forrester • Lorna Bain
Lorri-Lynne Brown • Louise Wren • Luc Ricciardi
Luca Andrea M • Luke Wilson • LuQ • Lyn Murnane
M. Goetz • Macktion • Marc Collins • Marc Rasp
Marcia Franklin • Marco Nahrgang • Margaret St. John
Maria Galloway • Maria Lima • Marie Blanchet • Marion E
Marissa Andrews • Marjorie-Ann Garza • Mark Boettcher
Mark Carter • Mark Walker • Marti Wulfow Garner
Martin Helsdon • Marzie Kaifer • Matt "Jebus" Jones
Matt Converse • Matt Gasper • Matthew Carpenter
Matthew J. Rogers • Matthew L Wilbur • Matthew Pham
Matthew X. Gomez • Max Kaehn • Max Pfeffer
Meg Ward • Megan Krantz • MeLissa Bennett
Melissa Harkness • Melissa Shumake • Melissa Tabon
Michael Ball • Michael Brassell • Michael Everly
Michael F Voss • Michael Hicks • Michael L Miller
Michael Mair • Michael Skolnik • Michael T Bradley
Michael Taylor • Michael Williams • Michaelle "Isis" Forbus
Michelle Carlson • Miguel Angel Devesa Fillol • Mihir W.
Mike Ball • Mike Leaich • Misha Dainiak • Misty Massey
Mo Foley • Mollie Bowers • Molly Reed • Monika W. Holabird
Nacho • Nancy B Rugen • Nancy M. Tice • Naoland
Natalija Fucadzi • Nicholas George • Nicholas Outterside
Nicholaus Chatelain • Nick Colombo • Nick Watkins
Nicola Urbinati • Nicole Lavigne • Nicole Sijnja
Nigs Phillips • Nirven • Nobilis and Dee Reed
Olaf Heijnen • Olga Kochergina • Oliver Ockenden
Olivia Jane Sieminski • Olivia Newsom

Olivier "Eivoril" Raquin • Olivier Menard
Osye E. Pritchett III • Otter Libris • Pat Hayes • Patrick
Patrick & Sarah Pilgrim • Patrick Banfield
Patrick E Johnson • Patrick King • Patti Short • Paul Bulmer
Paul Genesse • Paul Sheppard • Paul y cod asyn Jarman
Peggy J. • Penny Ferguson • Peter Bradley • Peter L Larson
Peter Mancuso • Peter Mazzeo • peter peretti
Peter T • Philip Overby • Philip R. "Pib" Burns
Philippe Boujon • Piper J. Drake • Pop Connelly
Preston Thomas • puzzle23 • Quentin Lancelot Fagan
R J Theodore • R Kirkpatrick • R Richards
Rachel "Ku" Woolley • Rachel Sasseen • Randi Rainbow
Randy P. Belanger • Raven Oak • Rayhne
Rebecca Sims • Rekka Jay • Revek • Rhiannon Raphael
Rhiannon Rippke-Koch • Rich Riddle • Richard Eyres
Richard L. Skinner III • Richard Smeeton • Richie Finn
Rob Matheny • Robbie C. • Robert Avritt Jr • Robert Biegler
Robert C Flipse • Robert Elrod • Robert Rhodes
Robert Slaughter • Robin Anne Reid • Robin Brail
Roger O'Dell • Roland the Great • RolleRocker
Roman Yeremenko • Rose Beetem • Ross Clegg • Rowan
Rowan D'Ausilio • rowanlobos • Rowie McDonald-Moss
Rowland Gwynne • Russell Ventimeglia • Ryan H
S Nowakowski • S. Kay Nash • S. L. Horn • S.A. Moffett
Sadir S Samir • Sally Qwill Janin • Sallyann Devlin • sam baskin
• Sam D • Sam Sussman • Samantha Enright • SAMK
Sandra Stauffer • Sandra Ulbrich Almazan • Sara Cox
Sarah Celiann • Sarah Fuentez • Sarah Jump • Sarah LeBlanc
Sariah Hafen • Saz • SC Malarky • Scizor_g45 • Scott Austin
Scott Drummond • Scott Early • Scott Macauley
Scott Maynard • Sean Anderson • SeanMike Whipkey
Sebastian Nielsen • Sebastian Zivota

Selvis Morales • ShadowTiger • Shane Charleson
Shawn T. King • Shelly Mccann • Sheryl R. Hayes
Sidsel Pedersen • Simo Muinonen • Simon Dick
Simon Kingaby • Simon Vindevåg • Simone Heller
Skylar Rosewood • Solistia • SometimesKate • Sophie Lagacé
Ste Chandler • Stef Maruch • Stephen Abel • Stephen Warren
Stephenie Sheung • Strella • Stuart Chaplin • Sue DeNies
Sune Kristensen • Susan Frank • Susanne Schörner
Suzanne Holczer • Suzanne Pearce • Swany • SwordFire
Sydney Shafer • Szél Anaya • T. E. Stacy • T.O.Munro • Tanbiere
Tara Ashley • Tara McInteer • Tara Zuber • Tasha Turner
Tehani Croft • Tessa Teunissen - Hastjarjanto
The Great and Mighty Poo • The Hetman • The Justice Family
The Portner Family • thelibrarycat • Theo Johnson • Theresa Y
Thile • Thomas • Thomas Dorf Nielsen • Thomas Grayfson
Thord D. Hedengren • Tibicina • Tiffany Reynolds
Tim Dhanens • Tina M Noe Good • Tobi Hill-Meyer
Todd L Ross • Todd Whitesel • Tom Champion • Tom Clews
Tom Kruijsen • Tom Smith • Tomas Burgos-Caez • Tony Anjo
Tracy Kaplan • TrashMan aka Seth Lee Straughan
Trip Space-Parasite • Trystan Starlight • Ty Wilda • Tyler Rhea
Tyson J Mauermann • Ulrik ConDoin • Victoria Sandbrook
W M • Walt Bryan • Warr Byrd • Wendelyn A. Reischl
Wendy Clements • Wendy Scodeller • Wes Rist • Wil A
Will Donovan • Will Hodgkinson • Willhameena Power
William A. DeMarco • William Munn • William Seaton
Winton Davies • WolfDC • Y. H. Lee • Yve Budden
Zach Chapman • Zé Manel Cunha • Zion Russell
Zoe and Bill Carter • Zoe Pitt

Aunt P claimed she shouldn't have got the record for that—*I was far up and they was stupid from hunger, not in no condition to fight*—but Mam and Aunt C and I insisted that it counted.

Like Nana, Aunt P died in the wild. I was the one who found her: her chest ripped up with buckshot, her skin pecked by seagulls, her hand still curled around her rifle.

I had one picture of Aunt P. When I was fourteen and Kaja was thirteen, a convoy of traders visited New Creemore. Most traders skipped us and headed straight to Georgian City, but these one set up aboveground for a few days. While I was trading for bullets, Kaja snuck away from me and swapped three jars of her good preserves for a broken camera.

I told Kaja she was stupid to do it. She was forever trading for unnecessary things: an old sewing machine, the kind you powered with your foot; a necklace of blue beads; a red hair bow. The silliest was a magazine from before that was filled with pictures of clean-looking, white-teethed, once-famous boys.

But Kaja was always a whiz at fiddling with things. She took that camera apart and had it working in no time. There wasn't a way to print the pictures or even put them on a computer to look at proper like people used to do, but you could squint at them on the camera's small screen.

Kaja and I ran around for days with that camera. I can't remember if it was me or her who snapped the one of Aunt P. But after Aunt P died, I would sneak to the school to plug in the camera, since Mam would've given me an earful for using power for something unnecessary, to look that one picture. To me, Aunt P was beautiful and always in motion, like a hummingbird, a creature you can't catch in a quiet moment. In that picture, she was static and sour and her face looked worn out and *over*, though she was thirty when it was taken.

Anyway, Nana's words. They were the closest thing I had to a personal creed. *The women in our family die young.* When I got shot or